I0641000

First Published 2011.

Copyright © Fuzz Enterprizes Pty Ltd (ACN 127 510 169)

ISBN: 978-0-9874188-0-7

Cover designed by Brendan Sanders.

www.sevenstonesofpower.com

THE RUBY STONE

ANDY STONE

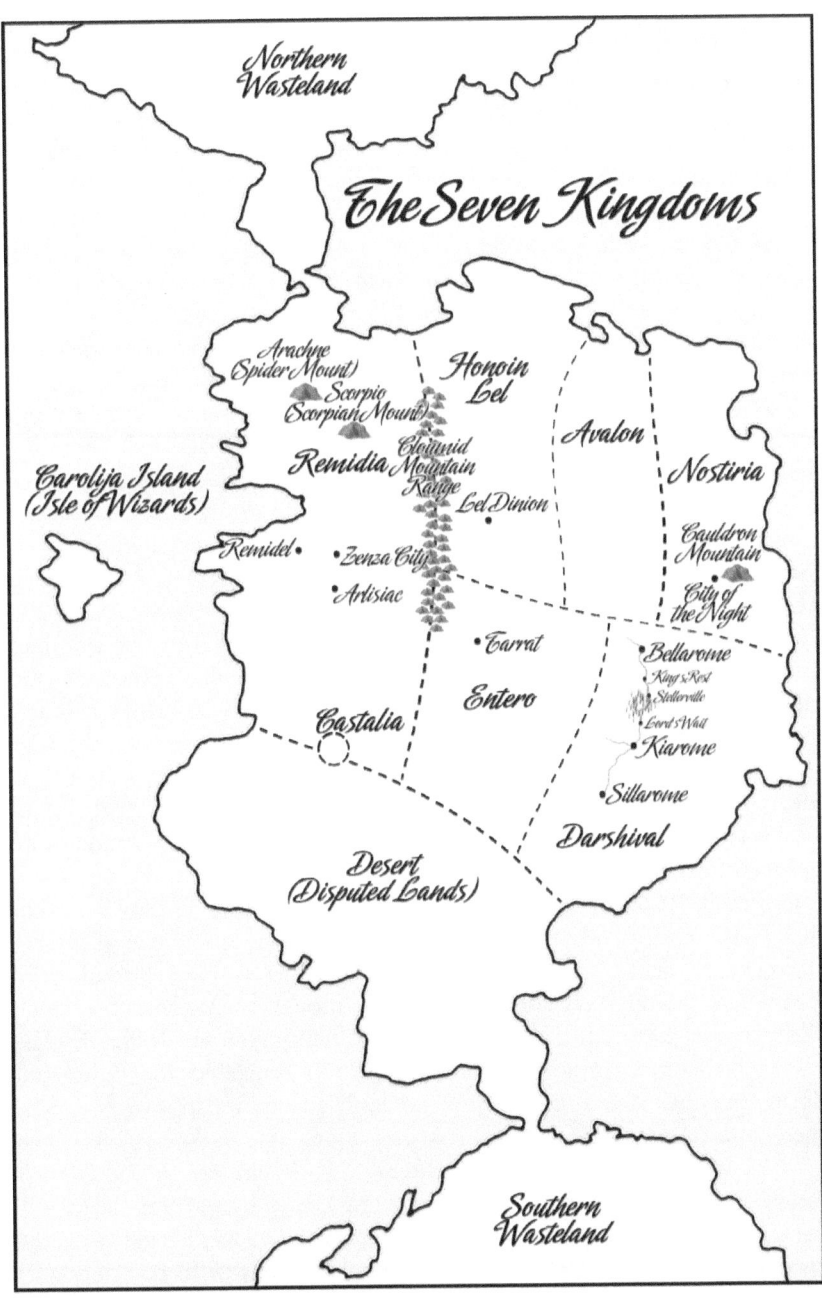

Chapter 1: A Meeting

The sun shone down on Arsiliac, a small village nestled deep in the farming country in the Kingdom of Remidia, owned by the Duchy of Zenza, a village of around three hundred people. Nothing out of the ordinary ever happened. In fact, if the village hadn't been on the Duke's tax list then it could have been forgotten altogether.

That was true, at least, until the arrival of an orphan child. The twelve-month old baby boy was left on the doorstep in the middle of the night of a couple who had lost both their children in war. They had lived in Zenza City and moved to Arsiliac to forget their previous life. The child, whom the couple named Alaric, enabled them to regain their lust for life.

Alaric's father, Wirt, was a young merchant from Zenza City and his mother, Allyson, was a minor noble heiress from Darshival. They had met when Wirt was trading in Darshival and married quickly, despite objections from her parents. Wirt brought his bride back to Zenza City and they settled down to raise a family. They had a good life, but when their two sons died in a skirmish they knew that it was time to move on. There was no real reason why they decided to move to Arsiliac, but it was as if they were drawn there. The villagers were not happy, no one had moved to Arsiliac from the outside since it was founded. Instantly the villagers kept their distance from the newcomers. Wirt and Allyson didn't mind. They felt much better being left on their own to grieve and felt as though it was where they belonged. It was time for them to start a new life.

The village was positioned two leagues east of the major trade route between Castalia and Zenza City, yet most of the merchants did not know it existed. Wirt and Allyson changed that by opening a trading house in the village centre. Their trade was in money, unheard of outside of the big cities, yet it made perfect sense. The merchants coming to and from Zenza City could leave the bulk of their money in Arsiliac at a much cheaper rate than that in the city, helping them avoid costly duties. The village blossomed in wealth. The population remained the same, but during the peak season the town could easily accommodate twice as many merchants.

With the town's new found wealth, it should have raised Alaric's family's status in the eyes of the community, but instead the village still ostracized them and poor Alaric bore the brunt of it. He was excluded entirely at the learning classes, so much so that he was forced to stay at home. The townspeople were civil to his parents, even if they weren't grateful they were not stupid. They knew if they were too rude they risked everything they had gained, and after a few years, had accumulated a lot.

This did not hinder Alaric and his family. He thrived at home and helped his parents run the business. In time, one family befriended them. They too had one son, a boy named Bern. Bern's family lived on a farm outside the town and didn't have much to do with the rest of the townspeople either. The two families got on famously and Bern and Alaric soon became the best of friends spending all their spare time together. They would play pranks on the other children in the village whenever they were left alone. This only added to them being left out, but it strengthened their relationship.

As Alaric grew it became more apparent that he was not from the village. The differences were so apparent that most of the village people did not believe that he was even from Remidia. Then rumours began of Alaric's true origin. If anything this caused the rift to increase and by the age of twelve Alaric was as tall as the average man, his skin retained more of the colour from the sun making it darker than most and coupled with his blonde hair and green eyes he couldn't have looked more different if he came from another world.

Before Alaric reached the age of twenty, the age of manhood in Remidia, Wilt and Allyson were tragically killed. They were travelling back from a business venture in Zenza City when they were ambushed by bandits. When the bandits realized that there was nothing of value to steal so they murdered them. Alaric was supposed to be with them to help oversee the transaction, but had been struck down sick and had insisted that they left without him.

As the sole benefactor of his parents' estate, Alaric became the wealthiest person in Arsiliac. Again this set him apart from the rest of the village, but his grieving period was very short and although he blamed himself for his parent's death, he was not going to let their business fail. Still being considered a child did not make this an easy task. Respect was nearly impossible for him to gain; the merchants, however, had been dealing with Alaric for years and knew he was a smart boy and could more than accommodate their needs. Alaric knew that he could not sit and wait for the townspeople to accept him, so he diversified his investments and started trading in commodities as well as other smaller investments.

He didn't see it at the time, but it was luck that Alaric was sick when his parents were murdered. More and more of these lucky events fell into Alaric's lap, although not quite as large as saving his life. Unless you were actually looking you would never notice them, as Alaric himself did not. They were subtle, like a business deal working out cheaper than expected. There was one time when he was waiting on a large shipment of grain to arrive in Zenza City and the sky was black for the entire day. It wasn't until mid-afternoon, when the grain was safely in the storehouse, did the skies open and the rain come down. There were storms for the next week and if the grain hadn't been under cover then the entire shipment would have been lost. That much grain would have set Alaric's turnover back over twelve months. Another time there was a labor strike in Zenza City. The strike however did not start until after Alaric had all his cargo loaded and the caravans had left the city. This was just the tip of the iceberg. All of Alaric's good fortune made him more successful than he could ever have imagined.

Shortly after his twenty first birthday Alaric received a strange visitor. In the middle of the night a man came and claimed to be his uncle. His parents had never spoken about having any brothers or sisters and he looked nothing like them. The man made a rather loud and compelling argument to come inside, so much so that Alaric's neighbours started to come out of their houses to see what all the noise was about. Finally, Alaric let him in.

"Thank you Alaric. I know things have not been easy for you over the last two years. My name is Eldred and as I'm sure you already know I am not really your uncle." Eldred had a soothing voice, it made Alaric feel relaxed, even though he had just been lied to.

"What is it you want, coming in the middle of the night?" Alaric had a feeling something wasn't right.

"Is there somewhere more comfortable where we can sit?"

Without thinking Alaric led Eldred into his sitting room. The room was small and homely. The only furniture in the room was a sturdy oak table and four matching chairs. On top of the table was a single, leather bound ledger that Alaric pushed to one side before offering Eldred a seat. "That's much better," commented Eldred when he had made himself comfortable. "I have ridden a long way to be here. Ever since I heard that your parents were murdered I feared the worse. To see you alive and well brings joy to my heart." Alaric was taken aback by Eldred's candour.

"Who are you and what are you doing here and how do you know about my parents?" All the questions came out of Alaric's mouth at once and there was nothing he could do about it. Taking a deep breath, he steeled himself for his next question. "My parents didn't have many friends; so how would you know they are dead?"

Looking up Alaric really saw Eldred properly for the first time. The man looked aged, but not old. Soft grey hair flowed down to his shoulders and although he had obviously been travelling throughout the night it looked perfectly brushed. His face was covered with a bushy grey beard and deep blue eyes looked as though they held a world of knowledge. He wore a dusty brown robe that looked well worn. There was something very familiar about him, like Alaric had met him before.

A sudden crack of thunder made Alaric jump. The sky had been clear all day, and there had been no sign of a storm.

"That is a very good question, but one for another time. Right now that is something that I don't have a lot of. Time!" Eldred looked towards the only window as a flash of lightning illuminated the room. The inevitable rumble to follow snapped Eldred back to attention.

"I have been away too long, but in my line of work days can turn into years without a second thought." Eldred looked as though he was speaking to himself.

"Enough with the double talk, tell me why you are here?" Although Alaric wanted to get angry, he just could not bring himself to yell.

"Yes of course. As I said earlier my name is Eldred. I should have come to see you earlier. We have a lot to do in such a short time. The purpose of my visit is just to introduce myself. Things are starting to change in the world and you will understand in time. You won't remember this meeting once I leave, but next time I visit you will remember who I am." Eldred's voice was calm, as if what he was saying was just matter of fact.

"What are you talking about? I can see you. I can hear you. Of course I will remember in the morning," Alaric was really starting to get agitated. "Give me a straight answer."

Eldred started to laugh quietly. It was a deep rumble coming from somewhere within his beard. This was something that should have made Alaric furious, but instead he found it rather comforting. Without another word Eldred stood and made his way to the front door.

A moment after Eldred had left Alaric opened the door slowly and looked outside. The night was calm and dark. There was not a breath of wind or a cloud in the sky. Things seemed odd, for some reason Alaric thought there should be thunder and lightning, at least some clouds. It was at this point that Alaric realised he was standing outside for no clear reason. Shrugging his shoulders, he returned to his sitting room.

The ledger, which usually lived on the centre of the table, was pushed off to one side. Alaric could not remember moving it. There was something very strange happening. Standing in silence he listened carefully to hear if there was someone else in the house. After a minute or two he decided he was being silly and retired to his bedroom. It had been an ordinary night, yet it seemed so strange.

Waking the next morning Alaric had no memory of the previous evening. The strange feeling that plagued him throughout the night was lost and gone forever. The sun was shining and Alaric thought it was going to be a good day.

It was the start of the working week, a day which Alaric liked the most. There were so many new opportunities. He had no appointments planned for the day, but he never knew what was going to happen. His office was in the heart of the village, which was a thirty-minute walk from his house. Alaric liked to walk, he hated horses and had only ever tried riding once, carriages were acceptable, but they were too much effort for day to day life. He only hired one whenever he travelled out of town.

In the office were the two staff members that Alaric employed. They worked five days a week, whereas Alaric always worked at least six. Idina worked as his secretary. She was a couple of years younger than Alaric, so the usual prejudices where not as strong, although her parents had warned her against him. She had worked for him for the past year, but would leave as soon as she was old enough to marry. Most of her time was filled with taking messages for Alaric, both sending and receiving.

"Good morning Idina, are there any messages for me?" it was Alaric's standard greeting. He knew that there were no messages, as none would come in over the weekend.

"Nothing yet, sir." Idina giggled as she replied. She did that often, but Alaric couldn't figure out why.

She could be quite attractive when she tried and she always tried to look her best when she was working. Alaric was amazed with how many different outfits she wore. Her long brown hair often hung half way down her back either free or in a single tie. Occasionally she would wear it up, exposing her neck completely. Her deep blue eyes had an innocence about them that Alaric couldn't explain. He was going to miss her when she finished working for him.

"Rylan is waiting for you in his office." Idina smiled as she spoke.

"Thank you."

Alaric wished that Rylan was as easy to deal with as Idina. Rylan helped to manage the day to day running of the business. He was very important to Alaric and he knew it well. Without him there would be no expansion and Rylan used that to his advantage. He was not openly rude, but he was short and to the point. There was never any small talk, like there was with Idina. He received more than adequate pay, in fact twice as much as anyone else would be paid in his position. Alaric knew he was getting ripped off, but he had no choice. Rylan did a good job and that's all that mattered.

The office was a small room, yet more than enough for one. A small writing desk stood at one end with two chairs, one on either side. Along the walls were many books and accounting ledgers. Sitting on the far side of the desk was Rylan, a short man, even when sitting he looked short. A few years older than Alaric, he still had a young looking face, about his only comforting feature.

"Good morning Rylan. Idina said that you wanted to speak to me." Alaric had learned not to try to be pleasant, that only aggravated their already tense relationship.

Rylan only looked up from his work when Alaric spoke, not when he entered the room. "We are expecting a shipment of silks in from Castalia today. It should be arriving by noon. You need to check over its contents before it goes on to Zenza City. There have been reports of green beetles coming out of Castalia, even the sight of one in the silks will cause the entire shipment to be burned when it reaches the city." Rylan explained slowly.

Alaric already knew all of this and Rylan liked to act as though Alaric couldn't survive without him. Alaric humoured him, even though it annoyed him greatly. If nothing else, it kept the peace. "Very good, I will make sure I check everything thoroughly," he said.

Checking shipments before they reached the custom houses was the job of about ten of Alaric's store men. Not only did he check his own shipments, but he also provided this service for other merchants. It was a lot cheaper for cargo to be checked in Arsiliac than in Zenza City. It had taken him a long time, but now his paperwork was accepted in the city. He owned a warehouse about three leagues from town where he conducted this work. The incoming shipment he would check himself. As much as he trusted his staff, the load of silks was too valuable to him to leave to others. Losing the load wouldn't break him, but it would be a major setback. An infestation of green beetles could cost Alaric half his annual turnover.

After discussing a couple of medial issues with Rylan, Alaric made his way back to his office. There was nothing really pressing for him to do, his mind was solely focused on the incoming shipment. There was a lot riding on its safe arrival to Zenza City. All Alaric accomplished that morning was shuffling paper around on his desk… waiting. As soon as Idina came in with the news that the shipment had arrived, Alaric left. A carriage was waiting for him outside and he could feel his heart pounding as he rode out to the warehouse. He usually prided himself on staying calm under extreme duress, but there was nothing he could do to ease his nerves. He wished the carriage would move faster; he'd have to be patient.

Soon enough the carriage arrived and Alaric ran inside. The ten wagons were being unloaded, each loaded with five crates, lined up neatly at the far end of the warehouse. Alaric's staff were working feverishly. Normally Alaric used a shipping company to help, but to save money he bartered a deal where they only loaded at Castalia and unloaded at Zenza City. Now he wished he had spent the extra money. It would be at least another two hours before the crates where unloaded and ready   for checking. At least at the warehouse Alaric could be more productive. Without a second thought he rolled up his sleeves and started to work. Each crate weighed approximately two hundred pounds and had to be moved from the back of the wagons to the quarantine shed about one hundred paces away. When all the crates were in quarantine, only then would it be safe to check the silks, otherwise he could risk infecting all the other cargo in his warehouse.

Even with the use of the push-pull carts, moving the crates was slow and arduous. Each cart could only carry one crate at a time and required four men to push, pull and steer it to the shed. The work was slow and hard and to make matters worse, they were half way through when one of the carts broke an axle. By midafternoon, Alaric resigned himself to the fact that they were not going to be able to check the shipment that day. It would take another two days to clear the silks and then an additional day to load them back onto the wagons. The price of silks was at an all-time high in Zenza City, but that could change in a matter of days. If someone else brought in a shipment of silks of similar size to Alaric's, then the price could plummet before half his cargo was sold. It was the first time in a long time that Alaric regretted a decision that he had made. The sun was low on the horizon when the last of the crates was secure inside the quarantine shed.

That night Alaric went to bed early with a mixture of tiredness from the day's labour and the anticipation of the following day. Yet he slept well and in the morning he was out of bed before the sun was up. After a quick breakfast, he made his way to the warehouse where there was a good two hours before anyone else was due to arrive. This was what he wanted. He could have two crates checked and resealed before his staff were due in. It wouldn't save him a lot of money, but it would give him a chance to see what they were up against.

The silks were packed in fifty pound rolls, four to a crate. Transporting the silks in rolls instead of flats was the only saving grace. The green beetles could crawl around the crates, but not inside the silks. If they were packed in flats, then the beetles could roam around freely making the job of checking almost impossible and definitely not financially viable.

Using a crowbar to jimmy open the lid of the first crate, Alaric slowly peered inside. To his relief there was no apparent sign of any beetles. He lifted out the silk rolls and inspected each one thoroughly. With all the rolls out of the crate it was easier to check inside. The green beetles, fully grown, were about an inch long and half an inch wide and as their name suggested a shiny green colour which made them easy to see against the light brown of the crates. The adult beetles could survive on eating the silk, whereas the infant beetles need green plant life to survive. Their eggs take four months to hatch and the dying of the silks would kill them off. As it was impossible to thoroughly check the silks for eggs, anyone purchasing raw silks during a green beetle warning knew to have them dyed within two months of purchase.

Carefully replacing the silks Alaric sealed the crate and then stamped it clear of infestation. His heart was racing as he lifted the lid of the second crate. As with the first there were no beetles in sight. After removing the silks though, it was a different story. At the bottom of the crate, dead, crushed by the weight of the silks was one solitary green beetle. Alaric's heart sank. Where there was one there was inevitably dozens more. He knew that it was going to be a long day, he just hoped he didn't lose too much of his stock.

Doing a final check of the silks before replacing them, Alaric sealed and stamped the crate just as the first of his staff arrived, a man by the name of Morley. He was the foreman of the warehouse and, like the other men, he was civil, but never pleasant.

"How goes it, Boss?" the greeting would have sounded friendly if it wasn't given in a monotone voice. Alaric knew well enough by now not to get offended by his staff and Morley was considered one of the better ones. Without him, Alaric would have to deal with the rest by himself and that would probably have broken him.

"It looks like news is not going to be good. One of the crates was clean, but the other had a green beetle squashed on the bottom. That's never a good sign," Alaric explained.

Nodding his head in agreement was the only response Morley gave. As he finished, the rest of the staff slowly started to arrive. They were never quick off the mark in the morning, but they were always on time and quite efficient. The morning continued along well with twenty crates opened and not a single green beetle. His breakeven figure was thirty and if the trend continued then they would be finished by the end of the day and Alaric would get a good night's sleep. Alaric would supervise the loading to make sure all the crates had been stamped. He would leave nothing to chance.

Opening the first crate after lunch was a different story. The lid wasn't even off before the first of the green beetles came scurrying over the edge. Alaric managed to crush it before it was able to escape and wreak havoc. Unfortunately, that was not the only beetle in the crate and as soon as the lid was off the beetles started teeming out.

"Shut the door!" Alaric screamed as he saw them make their way towards the door. They had all become complacent having not seen a single live beetle all morning. The men who wheeled out the last crate had left the door to the quarantine shed open and now there was a risk of the entire warehouse becoming infested. Luckily Morley was just entering as Alaric yelled out and he promptly slammed the door shut.

Once the door was safely closed and beetles trapped inside, Alaric returned the lid to the crate sealing in the remaining beetles. That crate would have to be burned and even without looking inside Alaric knew the silks would be ruined. His main concern now was catching and killing all the beetles that had escaped.

There was only Alaric, Morley and two others in the shed. At a rough guess, Alaric estimated there were probably about twenty to thirty beetles and it would not be easy to locate and kill them all.

"What's the plan, Boss?" asked Morley, though he knew but preferred to hear it from Alaric.

"Since we don't have any spray, I guess we'll have to catch and crush them." That was one of the main problems with exterminating green beetles; the spray to eliminate them was expensive and had a very short shelf life, making it all but impossible to keep handy. It was only used to stop further outbreaks of an already known infestation. It would take at least a month for Alaric to obtain the insecticide. The only advantage was there was nowhere for the beetles to escape.

It was a long and tedious affair, but after an hour and a half they had killed the last of them. It was only after another five minutes of searching and not finding anything did Alaric allow the door to be opened.

"Okay let's learn from this little mishap. The first sign of a live beetle and we seal the box and sort it out later."

Of the next five crates opened, two of them contained beetles. No matter how hard they tried, it was impossible to stop some from escaping. The lower the number, the longer it took to find and kill each one. All in all, Alaric was fairly happy with their progress. There were only three damaged crates out of the first twenty-six and even if things got twice as bad then he would still be very happy.

Again, it was another quiet night at home for Alaric. If all went well, in two days he would be riding with his cargo towards Zenza City. There was no relaxing until the silks were sold and he was on his way back from the city. It was dark when Alaric woke the next day and after a quick breakfast he was on his way to the warehouse.

To no great surprise, Alaric found himself alone in the quarantine room. He was thinking about making another head start, but if he opened an infested crate then it could set them all back by up to half a day. Instead he spent his time looking over the log books and checking the inventory. At any one time, he could hold about one million Remidian gold coins worth of cargo, most of which were owned by merchants. Normally Rylan checked the logs daily and gave a brief weekly report to Alaric who checked everything once a month, but since he was already in the warehouse there was no harm in checking.

The morning passed with only one more crate being added to the infestation pile. Fifteen more were clean. The progress was promising and Alaric could feel the stress melting away. By the time the sun was setting, all the crates were stacked in the warehouse and ready to be loaded. There were forty-three in total. Four were only good to be burned, whereas the remaining three could be salvaged if sprayed in time.

Shortly before lunch the following day, the wagons were all loaded and ready to leave. The horses were well rested and chomping at the bit to get moving. Alaric was also restless to leave and was pacing up and down in front of the horses when the men from the shipping company arrived.

"I don't like this at all," started Jett, the lead man from the shipping company, when he heard that Alaric planned on leaving that afternoon.

"I've already lost two days. I can't afford to lose another!" Alaric would not be dissuaded.

"Taking this load to Zenza City in the dark is not a good idea. You of all people should know the number of bandits there are between here and the city. You're just asking for trouble." The normally strong set face of Jett was now riddled with concern, not only for the cargo, but for his life and the lives of his men.

"I understand the risks. If we push the horses, we can be in Quinaliac a couple of hours after nightfall. We'll be safe enough." Alaric could only think of getting his shipment to Zenza City, nothing else mattered.

Shaking his head, Jett checked the horses one last time before they started out. Alaric rode in a carriage at the head of the group. Apart from the driver, he was alone at the front of the procession. Alaric always carried a sword with him whenever he travelled to the Zenza City; it was there as a deterrent as he had no idea how to use it. If it ever came down to a sword fight, Alaric would always back down, but luckily it had never come to that.

The road was empty apart from their caravan. This was never a good sign. Bandits would be restless and more inclined to attack if there was no one else around. Alaric had not taken things lightly though. He had hired two guards for each wagon and since the wagons had been reduced by one he was able to send out two scouts. Alaric was confident that they would make it to Quinaliac without incident.

As soon as the sun disappeared, the attitude of the men became very sombre. It had been over an hour since the rolling hills of outer Arsiliac turned into the dense forest of Zenza. They were about another three hours before they would reach the safety of Quinaliac. The lantern lights not only lit the road, but they also acted as a beacon to anyone watching. All the men knew that and they also knew they had been riding the horses hard to make up time. If they were attacked, there would be no chance for a quick escape. The horses would last for half a mile at a gallop, at a stretch with their loads attached.

The night was still and quiet. There was not a breath of wind and the moon was almost completely covered by clouds. There was an air of mischief and everyone was on edge and rode with their eyes searching through the darkness around them. The horses picked up on the men's moods and started to get jittery and hard to control.

About half an hour out of Quinaliac the trouble started. A rustling in the roadside shrubbery was all the notice they received. Before any of the guards could move the caravan was surrounded, including Alaric's carriage. The bandits were more than just a mere rabble. They were organised and knew exactly what they were after. Before any of the guards could draw their swords, two of the wagons had been commandeered, the drivers knocked to the ground and wagons steered into the darkness of the woods. The lanterns were instantly extinguished to avoid detection.

The attack was quick and organised. At first no one could believe what had happened. The bandits had managed to steal two wagons without killing anyone. A few bruises on the drivers were the only injuries. Two guards, on horseback, were the first to react. Without thinking they charged into the woods.

"Wait! Stop! Don't go into the woods," cried Jett as he saw the guards kick their horses into action. The order was enough to stop anyone else following, but not for the unfortunate guards.

After they disappeared everyone was quiet. The night itself seemed to stop and the only sound was the horses' hooves on the forest floor. The twang of four bowstrings followed by two thuds and two horses' cries made everyone's heart sink. It was obvious that they were not returning. Alaric could not believe what had happened. Leaving the safety of the Duke's highway was their first mistake.

"Move it on boys. Nothing else we can do here," his voice was cold, but everyone knew Jett was feeling the deaths deep inside. The cold glare he gave Alaric was proof enough. It was a life and death job and everyone knew the risks of transporting high profile cargo.

Alaric told himself this as he lay in bed at the inn of the Horse's Head, but he couldn't help thinking that it was all his fault. Two men were dead for the sake of an extra day. He could see them in his mind. The cold dead eyes looking up through pale white skin, two arrows piercing each man's heart. Even with his eyes open Alaric could see them. This would be a night that he would never forget. It was the worst decision he had ever made.

The night passed slowly. Alaric tossed and turned, the dead guards haunting his dreams, not allowing him to get any rest. He was glad to see the rays of sunlight sneaking through the shutters. The morning helped to wash away the disaster of the previous night. He would never forget the faces of those men who gave up their life for his cargo.

"I hope you had a good night's sleep." Fayne, the inn owner, greeted Alaric as he walked into the dining hall.

The Horse's Head was one of a dozen inns in the town of Quinaliac. That was the main trade of the small town. Cut out of the woods, the town was completely bordered by the trees. It was built as a stopover along the Duke's highway on the way to Zenza City, it had grown, but not by much. Alaric always stayed at the Horse's Head, becoming good friends with the owner, his wife, Dilys, and son, Kayne. He was not looking forward to talking to anyone.

"Not the best, but for reasons other than the rooms." Alaric yawned after he spoke.

"Anything I can help you with?" offered Fayne.

"No, thank you. Just something I would rather forget about. Not my finest hour."

"Well, I'll have Tanjela bring out some breakfast. The men are harnessing the horses as we speak, so I'd say that they are keen to get moving." Fayne smiled as Alaric sat down.

Hearing the news that the men would soon be ready to leave was comforting. He didn't want to sit under their gazes. Their accusing looks wouldn't be pleasant. At least on the road, he could hide himself in his carriage. He would be a lot happier once they reached the custom houses of Zenza City. Originally he had planned to stop at four of the customs houses, but with his reduced stock he was now only going to three.

Breakfast was fried bacon and eggs with toasted bread, a standard for Alaric when he stayed at the Horse's Head. The livestock was bred locally from small farms, so the food was always fresh. Tall timber fences kept the livestock safe from the predators that resided inside the forest, although there were regular cases of animals being taken by wolves and other predators.

Alaric had hardly put his cutlery down when Jett came in. "We're ready to go. I think we should head out now. Idleness gives time for reflection," He spoke with the same cold voice as the night before.

"Thank you. I will be out soon." Alaric kept his reply brief. He knew exactly what Jett was saying. Given enough time they would leave without worrying about finishing the job. Alaric couldn't allow it all to be for nothing.

After saying goodbye to Fayne and paying the bill, Alaric joined the others outside the stables. The men were standing around waiting and readied themselves when they saw Alaric coming. They did so without looking directly at him. No one wanted to make eye contact in case they had to make small talk.

The journey to Zenza City was made in silence. Alaric was surprised the men were taking it so badly. It was fairly standard business for trade caravans to be attacked and for men to be killed, it was part of the job. The sombre mood only reinforced his opinion that it was his fault.

The sights of the approaching city made Alaric's heart lift. It was getting late and the day had passed without a hitch. Unfortunately, there was not enough time left to make his deliveries. With an early start and a brisk pace the trip could be done by midday, but the mood of the men was reflected in the pace they kept.

The city was the second largest in Remidia, second only to the capital Remidel. A large stone wall circled the city with four main gates, North, South, East, and West. Small and large farms were scattered for miles around the city. The soil being unsuitable for grains or grapes meant they were mostly sheep and cattle, but there was also a good variety of other animals bred for food and clothing.

The highway became a lot busier as they came closer to the city gates, mainly farmers taking their stock to and from the city. With the extra traffic, the security of their load was sealed. No bandits, no matter how desperate, would try and highjack a caravan in broad daylight with so many people around. Alaric knew they would make it safely to their destination. Once inside the city, they would make their way to a holding warehouse, similar to the one in Arsiliac, where it would stay overnight. In the morning, he would make his three stops, cash in and then return to his home where he could hopefully forget about the entire ordeal.

The guards at the Southern Gate stopped Alaric. It was standard for the guards to check any outside cargo coming in. Alaric was good friends with the head guard and one thing Alaric learned was to look after those people who could make his life difficult. A gold coin here and there went a long way to getting his way in the city with the least amount of discomfort.

"Hi Alaric. What are you bringing in today?" greeted Maks, the head guard.

Leaving the carriage, Alaric followed Maks to the first wagon. "I've got a shipment of silks from Castalia." Alaric spoke casually, it was a conversation they had had many times before.

"I've heard rumours coming out of Castalia that there is a green beetle plague. Have those crates been checked?" Maks knew that Alaric would have cleared them, but it was his duty to ask.

"I've checked and cleared every crate personally. I've lost a couple, but all those are ready for sale," replied Alaric cheerfully.

"Very good then. Will you be bringing anything out with when you leave?"

"No Maks, I'll be going back empty." Alaric shook his hand before he left, leaving behind a gold coin.

Inside the walls the streets were even more crowded than the highway. People moved out of the way for Alaric's carriage and wagons, but they took their time about it. Things were always the same travelling through the Southern Quarter. It was the poorest quarter of the city, filled with beggars and petty thieves. Even with the streets full there was still a chance of having your throat cut. Alaric always rode nervously through the streets even though he was safe enough inside his carriage and the guards would keep anyone from upsetting the caravan.

Even with all the protection he had, Alaric would not be happy until they had entered the Eastern Quarter. That was where most of trading was done in the city. It was more commonly known as the Merchant's Quarter. The change was obvious. The run down, single story buildings changed to larger two storey stone houses. The streets became wider and less congested. The stone houses skirted the many warehouses and offices that made up the majority of the Quarter. The holding warehouse was very close to the Southern Quarter, one of the reasons why Alaric used it. The other was the very reasonable price and exceptional service.

The sun was very low when they finally arrived. A large sign depicting three wine barrels indicated they had arrived at the Three Barrel Warehouse. The wagons pulled straight in and Alaric went into the office to arrange the storage.

"Hello Sharee, is Jory around?" Alaric greeted as he walked in.

"Oh hi Alaric," Sharee, the receptionist, replied as she looked up from the book she was reading. "What are you doing here? You're not on the books, was Jory expecting you?"

"No. Things haven't gone quite to plan, so I need to leave some things here overnight."

"I don't think that will be a problem. I'll just get Jory to make sure that's okay."

A few minutes later Jory came through the back door. He was a large man with strong features. Many years working in the shipping industry made for a strong physique. He had a friendly face, even a small scar over his left eye. He was getting on in years, but could still hold his own.

"I saw your men out in the warehouse. They said you had a few problems on the way over. I'm sorry to hear that. They're unloading your silks as we speak." Jory paused before he spoke again. "Have you been to see the city guard?"

"I spoke to the local watch in Quinaliac, but I don't expect much to come of it. The forests have always been too large to patrol. The thieves are smart too. They only stole two wagons. If they had taken the entire shipment, then they would have no chance of selling them without being caught. Once the silks I've brought hit the market it will be impossible to tell which are the legitimate silks and which are the stolen ones. It's a chance of damned if I do and damned if I don't." Alaric sounded defeated.

"I suppose you are right. There's not much you can do about it. Are you going to the Singing Swan tonight?" Jory thought it was better to change the subject.

"I don't think so. I'd like to, but I'll need to get an early start in the morning."

"Harela is singing tonight. I'm sure she would like to see you." Jory winked. Harela was a regular singer at the Singing Swan, the tavern where Alaric usually drank when he was in the city. It was a well-known fact amongst the locals that Harela had a crush on Alaric. She had a pleasant face, nothing you would call beautiful, but nothing ugly either. She was also nearly twice his age, which was the deciding factor for Alaric to stay away from her. Her feelings for him had been inflamed one night when Alaric had one too many ales and spent the night in her bed. It took him almost six months before he could return to the tavern. Harela made that all the worse by flirting with him all night.

"I think that is a very good reason not to go. I have absolutely no desire to be pawed at all night." Even though he talked it down, he really did like the attention. It was a welcome change to the usual disregard he received in Arsiliac.

"I'll make sure to send her your regards and apologies." Jory ignored the acid look Alaric gave him.

Breaking the light tension Jett walked into the office. "We've got the wagons unhitched and the horses stabled for the night. The cargo has been warehoused. The wagons are nice and close so we can get a running start in the morning. I'll try and keep the men out of the taverns tonight, but I don't like my chances. I think a few of them will write themselves off." Alaric nodded his head as Jett shrugged his shoulders. There was no need for Alaric to reply and Jett simply walked away.

"See, someone has to be on the ball tomorrow. I'll see you in the morning." Alaric sighed as he started to follow.

"I'll see you then. Have a good night." Jory laughed as Alaric left. It was not a malicious laugh, but there was something about it that irritated him. He shrugged it off as anything at that moment would irritate him.

Alaric stayed at the Sleeping Watchman when he was in the city. He had word sent ahead as soon as the silks had arrived that he would be spending the night. The inn was neither fancy nor dingy. It was a two storied grey stone building with a similar grey slate roof. The inn had a common room as well as a small bar area, both for patrons only. The owner was a local man, by the name of Elsdon. He had owned and run the inn for the past forty years when his father had left it to him. His son and daughter and their respected partners also helped. It was the family atmosphere that drew Alaric.

Elsdon met him at the front desk with a warm smile and a handshake. "Good evening Alaric, I hope everything went well."

"I'm here in one piece, so that's a bonus." He tried not to let his morose mood show, but was not doing a very good job.

"I see." Elsdon tried to size up Alaric's frame of mind with his ambiguous statement. "Your room is ready for you. Would you like something to eat in the common room? Sanna is spit roasting two pigs. We have a full house, so she decided to prepare something a little special." Elsdon was very proud of his daughter's cooking abilities. "It should be ready in about half an hour." Alaric looked exhausted. "You look like you could use a bath. Do you want me to get Pollard to run you one?"

"Thank you, that is just want I need and if it's not too much trouble I'll take dinner in my room." The thought of a bath and hot food lifted his spirits.

"And will you be going to the Singing Swan tonight? I hear that Harela is singing a little later." An even broader smile showed on his face.

"No. I'll be having a quite night in." Alaric ignored the jibe completely.

"Very good. I'll have some food brought up to your room as soon as it's ready." The smile remained on his face until Alaric disappeared up the stairs.

His room was the largest of the one bedroom rooms in the inn. Elsdon always gave Alaric the best room available, another reason why he stayed at the Sleeping Watchman. After dropping his bags, changing into his underclothes and the bath gown they had left for him, Alaric made his way to the bathing rooms. Another reason he liked the Sleeping Watchman was the fact that the baths were all individual. Most of the larger inns had communal baths, one for men and one for women.

A sign on the door indicated which room was his. The bathing room was small and apart from the tub in the middle there was a chair, basin and mirror. Steam rose and Alaric didn't wait long before he was soaking himself. The water poured over his body as he lowered himself into the water releasing a lot of the tension he had been carrying all day.

The water was becoming cold when Alaric finally lifted himself out. His stomach rumbled for the second time. He had not felt like eating all day, the tension had taken his appetite, but now it was back with a vengeance. Alaric quickly toweled himself dry and returned to his room.

True to his word Elsdon had a large plate of food waiting for him, a steaming plate of roasted pork and vegetables. The aroma filled his nose and promptly made his stomach rumble again. Without delay Alaric made short work of his dinner. The events of the previous night seemed so far away, but as soon as he closed his eyes the images of the dead men returned. He knew it was going to be another long and restless night.

The morning came around all too soon. For the second night Alaric woke feeling as though he had not slept at all. There was no avoiding his conscience.

After dressing he stumbled downstairs. The grey light of dawn crept into the otherwise dark room. The downstairs of the inn was entirely empty, even the kitchen was vacant. Breakfast was the farthest thing from his mind. He would regret that decision by mid-morning, but all he wanted to do was get the silks to his potential buyers. The deals were all but done, although nothing was final until the gold had changed hands. He knew that Jory would have the warehouse opened early for him.

Waiting out the front was Jett looking worried and a little blurry eyed. He looked somewhat relieved to see Alaric. Alaric on the other hand did not look pleased to see Jett standing by himself.

"I trust the rest of the men are inside preparing the horses." Alaric's tone was less than friendly.

The look was all the answer he needed, but Jett spoke anyway. "I don't think anyone is going to show today and I think for your benefit that's a good thing. I don't think any of them would be too careful with your cargo today." Alaric was close enough to smell the alcohol on Jett's breath. He could only imagine what was going through his head.

"Well how do you suppose we're going to get the crates on the wagons then?" Alaric did his best to keep his anger in check.

The reply did not come from in front of him, as he expected, instead it came from behind. The voice was familiar and comforting.

"I took the liberty of organising some labourers. They have been working since daybreak and should be ready to go in a few minutes." Jory sounded pleased with himself, the look of relief on Jett's face showed that he had not been privy to the information.

"How did you know?" the surprise was clear in Alaric's voice.

"I've worked long enough to recognise disgruntled labourers in my time and know the result. My guess would be that it would only have taken a couple of ales before they decided they wouldn't show up this morning."

The only reason Jett had shown was to make sure he collected the rest of the fees. Of course Alaric was going to deduct Jory's extra charges from the remaining account.

"Well it looks like you are no longer required." Alaric turned to Jett as he started to speak. "You can be sure that when I settle the account it will be short a few fees."

"You can't do that. I demand you pay the rest of the account now. I need to pay the men their wages." Jett fingered the hilt of his sword as he spoke, Alaric was unarmed.

"I think you will leave now and be thankful if you get paid at all." Jory interjected. When he finished speaking he put two fingers in his mouth and blew a high pitched whistle. Immediately two heavy set men appeared from the large warehouse entrance, each brandished a menacing looking cudgel. Maybe sober he could have beaten the two men, he was not too bad with the sword, but in his current state it would be a short lived battle.

"I will make sure you never have any dealings with any shipping companies anywhere ever again." Jett spat on the ground at Alaric's feet before he turned and slunk away.

"Thank you," Alaric sighed at Jory, he was truly grateful.

"Not a worry. I know the circumstances and it is not your fault. Those men shouldn't have left the safety of the road at that time of day. It was your choice to risk your cargo, but it was theirs to risk their lives. Don't blame yourself." The words were very reassuring and made Alaric feel better. "Come in for a coffee. Afterwards you'll be ready to get going."

The coffee was of poor standard, but Alaric didn't care. As he sat and drank he could feel the butterflies in his stomach. Although the deals were almost complete he knew that nothing was final until the papers were signed and the gold exchanged.

True to his words Jory had the wagons waiting for him out the front, he had also organised a carriage. Jory had already said his goodbyes, so there was nothing left for Alaric to do but to keep going.

His first stop was only a half hour ride. It was a dressmaker's shop and the owner was a regular. It was where he was hoping to make most of his coin back. Not only did the dressmaker supply the wealthiest shop stalls, they also made to order. The owner was very wealthy and normally paid whatever price he asked.

Wendy was a portly lady with a pleasant face. She always wore a smile whenever she saw Alaric. She had a motherly feel about her that made him feel comfortable. Wendy knew she had that effect on people and used it to her advantage. She was a ruthless business woman, although always fair.

"Hi Alaric, how are you today?" She greeted Alaric as he walked through the front door. He had instructed the wagon drivers to take the cargo to the rear of the shop where she did her sewing and stored her materials.

"Tired!" Alaric gave a weak smile as he spoke. He knew he was giving away the advantage, but he did not have the energy to keep up pretenses. "But still alive."

"So you have some silks from Castalia?" She paused, but not waiting for an answer. "I heard rumours that there have been infestations coming from Castalia?" Again the unasked question would remain unanswered. Hearing those words Alaric knew he was not going to get the price he had hoped.

"I can assure you that there are no green beetles in any of my crates. I have seen to that personally. These are the very best quality of silks." Alaric's voice was rock hard. Once business had started he would show no weakness.

"Well here in lies the problem. When you were late with your delivery I could only assume the worst. Yesterday a shipment of silks came in from the Zenza City. They were selling at a reasonable price so I had to buy," it was not the final word, but Wendy was now holding all the cards.

The outcome could not have been worse for Alaric. The shipment of silks from Remidel would lower the price of his silks considerably. Although Castalian silks were unsurpassed for colour and quality, a flooded marketplace would do him no good.

"You know the quality of my product. I only deal in the best, that's why I came to you first. I always give you the first pick." Sympathy would do him no good, but he had to give it a shot. He knew he would be able to sell some of his silks; it would only be a matter of how many and at what price.

"Well I guess I could use some more. Quality for my more discerning clients, but I can only pay you half of our agreed price." Wendy did not blink as she put in her offer. "That price is still better than what you would have got six months ago."

"But that won't even come close to covering my costs." Alaric thought for a moment before he continued. He had known she was going to be a tough customer, but things were becoming disastrous. "I can sell you the remainder of my silks at three quarters of our original price."

Hearing the offer Wendy laughed out loudly. "You know well enough that I don't need that much silk, even if I didn't just make a large purchase. I will take five crates at three quarters and that's the end of it."

Alaric was just about to speak when he recognized the look on Wendy's face. The deal was either done or over. If he tried to barter any further, then she would not buy anything. The amount was not even close to the original order and he was hoping to off load half the crates to Wendy.

It took the rest of the day for Alaric to sell all the silks, having to travel to a dozen different shops. With each sale the price got lower and lower, and he knew that whatever he didn't sell he would have to throw away. The entire deal had gone sour.

Chapter 2: Creation

It was five years to the day before Eldred returned to Arsiliac. It was a long five years for Alaric who was rebuilding what it had only taken him three days to lose. On his return to Arsiliac, Alaric had to let go most of his staff, including Rylan and Idina. It was heartbreaking for him. All that his parents had left him and all that he had built up was gone in one fell swoop.

Again it was late in the evening when Alaric was disturbed from his reading by a knock on the door. Putting the ledger down Alaric yawned before getting out of his seat. If he hadn't been half asleep then he would have been suspicious of a caller so late.

As soon as he opened the door, Alaric saw the old man and the memory of their first meeting came flooding back. The memory seemed so clear, it was as though it had only happened the day before. Alaric knew that something was strange, but could not figure out what.

"Good evening Alaric. I see by the look on your face you remember who I am." Eldred greeted Alaric as he walked into the house, not waiting for an invitation.

Alaric followed Eldred into his study without saying a word. There was an overpowering presence about Eldred that kept Alaric from speaking. There were so many questions he had to ask, but he knew he would not get a chance to ask them unless Eldred allowed it.

"Would you like something to eat or drink?" It was a stupid question, but the only one he could voice.

"Thank you Alaric, but I am fine for the moment." Eldred smiled as he sat. "Please have a seat. We have a lot to discuss this evening and not a lot of time to do it." Eldred pointed to an empty chair.

Doing as he was told Alaric sat on the opposite side of the table from Eldred. He felt a strange sense of déjà vu as he looked across at the older man sitting before him. "How's your history Alaric?" The question was so abrupt that it took Alaric a moment to respond.

"My trade and economic history is pretty good; the rest is fairly none existent." Alaric answered as honestly as possible. Even if he had wanted to lie to hide his ignorance he couldn't.

"It was more the history of the world's creation I was talking about."

The questioning look on Alaric's face was the all the answer he needed.

"Very good, I'll start from the beginning then." Eldred paused briefly and cleared his throat.

"In the beginning the seven God Kings roamed a bare and desolate rock. There was no other life, just rock and dust. Each of the God Kings were gifted with the power to create and they all yearned for something more than the naked land before them.

The seven God Kings went to sleep for the first time and what they dreamt became reality. They each had separate powers of creation and separate dreams of what the world should contain.

On the first day Sapphire had a dream. His dream was of the seas, oceans, rivers and all things related to water. The fish and all other water life became alive. When Sapphire woke this is what he had created, yet there was no consistency to his work. Nothing seemed to flow together, yet he was happy with what he had created and didn't want the world to change.

On the second day Emerald had a dream. His dream was of the trees and the forests, the grass and the flowers. He also dreamt of animals and birds. These were the things that made his heart sing with joy. When Emerald woke this is what he had created, yet there was still no harmony. Great trees grew from the middle of the deepest oceans. Dogs roamed the air and the eagles the water. Emerald was happy with his work and did not care if it contradicted what Sapphire had made.

On the third day Onyx had a dream. He had a dream to make the land fertile, to rid the world of the desolation that remained amongst his brothers' creations, a dream to see the land come alive. He fed the land and gave it sustenance. Then he formed the rocks into great mountains and gave them purpose. When Onyx woke this is what he had created. The earth was rich and alive.

On the fourth day Topaz had a dream. Now he had seen what the others had created he knew something was missing. He knew that there should be a creature that was superior to all the others. His dream was of Elves, created in his own perceived image. When Topaz woke he had created the life he wanted, yet there was still something missing. Although he had created a superior life form, they were still no better than the other beasts that roamed the land.

On the fifth day Opal had a dream. Opal saw what Topaz had created and knew what was missing. Opal dreamed and gave Topaz's creation awareness. He gave them what all other creatures were missing. He gave them a soul. He gave them the ability to speak and communicate with one another. He also gave them the ability to communicate with the other creatures of the land, sky and water. When Topaz woke it was done, yet with awareness came the fear that the world was still not right.

On the sixth day Jade had a dream. Jade liked what he saw from his brothers. The forests were beautiful and peaceful. The land was rich and full. The Elves were intelligent and lived in peace with all other creatures. Jade saw that all these things were glorious, but there was no coherence. Jade dreamed that everything should have a place. Jade brought all his brothers' creations together and gave them a purpose and when Jade woke the world truly came into existence. The sun rose and set, the tides ebbed and flowed and the wind blew.

On the seventh day Ruby had a dream. He saw the world for what it was, both beautiful and harmonious. He felt contempt for what his brothers had created. His passion was for chaos. The completeness of what his brothers had created made him sick. Ruby dreamt the first and worst nightmare. He created disease, pain and mistrust. He twisted the creatures that the others had made into evil beings, at least as many as he could find. He created thunder, lightning, storms, hurricanes and earthquakes. When he woke the world was born. Both terrible and beautiful in its finality." Eldred paused, sat back and looked around the room. "Could I get something to drink? Hot tea would be nice."

The question caught Alaric off guard. He had been so enthralled with Eldred's story he had to think before he answered. "Err, well, yes, that's fine. I'll boil the kettle."

Alaric left the room stunned. The break had given him time to think about what he had just been told. There was one burning question that he needed to ask. "What does this lesson in theology have to do with me?" he said as he placed a tray on the table.

"Ah, a very pertinent question," Eldred explained. "This is not, however, a lesson in theology. Much of the history of the world has been lost in myths and legends, but what I have just told you is fact. At least as close to fact as time will allow." Eldred smiled at Alaric's reaction. There was a glimmer of comprehension in his eyes, but he did not believe the story. Eldred knew in time Alaric would believe.

"The world was complete and the God Kings were satisfied with what they had created. For a millennia or two the world moved in peace and harmony, but eventually the seeds that Ruby had planted started to grow. Change crept into the world. Man came into being, believed to have been Elves born with defects, although that has never been proven. One thing was certain though; man was inferior to the original creation. Men were more susceptible to disease and lived shorter lives. Their only advantage was their ability to breed. Soon their mass of numbers made them the dominant species and the Elves retreated into the wilderness to live in isolation and mystery. Dwarves came into being although their evolution is completely unknown." Eldred paused and sipped his tea. Alaric was again mesmerised. "As the years continued man grew with his knowledge. They would not live within the confines of what the Gods had set, which the Elves had abided by since the creation of the world. They started to believe and worship other gods. They started to war with each other, and the Elves. They sought power and domination. Sickness and disease was rank throughout the world. Plague and pestilence filled the land and the first Dark Age began.

The God Kings found that their very existence was being threatened. Every day less and less men were acknowledging them and this made them weak. The Elves had forsaken the old life, believing the God Kings favoured man above them. The world sank deeper and deeper into despair.

There was only one option left to bring the world back into the light, not to mention restore their power. To do this they needed to work together again. They created seven stones imbued with their own powers. Each stone was named for the God King whose power it contained. They then found seven men and possessed them with special powers. Each was given a power from one of the God Kings and the knowledge they required to control them, thus creating the first Wizards.

The seven Wizards used the stones to bring the world back towards the teachings of the God Kings. The chaos quietened and peace returned to the world, but it did not last long. Nyrra, the Wizard in control of the Ruby stone, became twisted with the power it contained. The God King of Chaos was again having his effect on the world. Nyrra sowed the seeds of revolution amongst the other six Wizards and soon enough they all longed to be free of their cruel oppressors.

Leading his brothers, Nyrra made his way to the Cauldron Mountain. Through his years of study of the forbidden texts, Nyrra had found a way to banish the God Kings from the world. With the aid of the stones the Wizards could devise their freedom, but the plan had to be timed perfectly to succeed.

The night was dark and the full moon completely covered by storm clouds. The highest peak in the world was steaming with the threat of erupting fire. The Wizards chanted, in unison, the black spell that would exile the God Kings. With the aid of the stones the spell grew in potency. Lightning crackled around them, the very air itself was electric. Before the God Kings could realise what was happening, the spell was complete. With a thunderous bang, heard throughout the world, it was all over. A hush fell and for a second the world was completely quiet. Then the horror of what had happened was realised. Nyrra had succeeded. It was now too late for the other six to reverse the spell."

"What happened?" Alaric asked excitedly.

"That is something that has been lost in history." Eldred looked uncomfortable with the question. He paused for a moment before continuing.

"All was silent now, except for the laughter from Nyrra. Only then did the others realise what Nyrra had planned all along. Before they could react he disappeared.

Knowing what they had done, the six remaining wizards went into isolation, unable to face the rest of the world. Little did they know that this was just the beginning for Nyrra. For years before that night on the mountain, Nyrra was building an army. He found creatures from deep within the bowels of the world, creatures that were never supposed to see the light of day. He built an army of men on the surface, leaving the rest of his army underground. He built his fortress at the base of the Cauldron Mountain and from there he made his attack.

He used his army of men first, considering them weak and expendable, without regard. He managed to take the ancient Kingdom of Da'eeshinal, you know now as Darshival, without much resistance. Ravaging the land, he was bent on annihilation, taking no prisoners. Before Nyrra had taken Da'eeshinal, word had reached the other Kingdoms. More importantly, word had reached the six wizards in hiding.

With a great amount of convincing, the Wizards united the five remaining Kingdoms to bring the war to Nyrra. Not knowing the horror that awaited them under the ground, the Wizards led the united army against Nyrra in Da'eeshinal. When victory was in sight, Nyrra revealed his evil plan. The ground trembled with a mass movement. All across the world streams of evil poured from the depths.

Goblins, trolls, ogres and many other evil creatures stormed the world of men. Nyrra's own creation, the Orglin, a cross between goblins and ogres, were the most vicious. With most of their armies fighting in Da'eeshinal, the other Kingdoms were vulnerable and unready for attack. Yet again the Wizards knew they had been manipulated by their brother." A yawn by Alaric caused Eldred to stop. "I know it's getting late. I will try and speed things up."

Alaric had not even realised what he had done. He had been so enthralled in the story he felt as though he was living it.

"The Wizards knew they could not win the war. They split up and visited the many clans of Dwarves and the secret societies of the Elves. After over a year of delegation the Wizards had managed to unite the six Kingdoms of Men, the nine Clans of Dwarves and the three Societies of Elves making the Alliance of the Light. The numbers were now overwhelmingly in their favour and not a day too soon. The Kingdoms of men had suffered massive losses on all fronts.

War raged on for the next fifty years, the Alliance of the Light slowly pushed the Army of Darkness back towards Outer Da'eeshinal and the Cauldron Mountains. Again Nyrra had foreseen the Wizards' strategy and had sown the seeds of despair amongst the alliance. His greatest espionage was the dissention he created between the Elves and Dwarves.

There had always been a fractured relationship between the two races and Nyrra knew it. His spies sent rumours through the camps.

With each passing day the tension grew within the alliance. The final battle was looming. Both armies were stationed on the plains of Outer Da'eeshinal. Nyrra's final plan did not come to fruition in time to save him.

The final battle raged on for two days, the longest lasting single battle in the history of the world. In the end, Nyrra and the remainder of his army was defeated and he was forced to retreat back to his fortress under Cauldron Mountain.

As the alliance advanced, trouble started between the Elves and the Dwarves. No one could remember what started the fight, but the war continued for many years. The battle was the only thing that saved Nyrra from being destroyed completely. Both the Dwarves and the Elves left the battlefield before things got out of control. The six wizards could not complete their task, to separate Nyrra from his stone. Even with their combined powers, they could not risk an attack on his fortress.

Not realising the threat that Nyrra still held, the Kings took their armies home to sort out their own nations. The war had left the world ravaged. Nyrra went out of everyone's mind as he was safely tucked away in a desolate land without a decent army. The next hundred years was spent rebuilding what had been destroyed. It was also a time of war between the Kingdoms of Men. At one point it seemed the entire world, except that of Nyrra, was at war with one other. Nations rose and fell, borders were written and rewritten. Until finally there came a time of peace and the world entered a golden age of prosperity.

Nyrra, however, was not sitting idly by. He watched the ways of the world from his fortress. He knew what he had not taken into consideration on his last attempt for domination and that was his six brothers. Their ability to lead and rally the nations had brought him down. Nyrra had spent that hundred years planning their demise. Nothing else mattered to him.

Slowly Nyrra started to venture out in the world again, further and further each day until he finally realised he was free again. The world had forgotten him, even his brothers did not seem to care. One by one Nyrra tracked down his brothers and murdered them, all but one, Alpheus, the Onyx wizard was able to avoid attack.

Knowing he could not match Nyrra in power, Alpheus could not challenge Nyrra into open combat. He spent his time studying the ancient texts in hiding, trying desperately to find a way to destroy his brother. In his final hour, Alpheus found his way to salvation. Leaving his place of study only minutes before Nyrra came down upon it, Alpheus now had a new mission.

It was written that every millennium a child is born. A normal child to the unseeing eye, but to those who knew better could see the power the child possessed. Known as the gatekeeper, he was the only way out for Alpheus. Leaving on a quest, Alpheus searched the world for the gatekeeper, all the while Nyrra kept searching for him.

Alpheus found the child wandering through the forest. Only six years old and able to survive, living in equilibrium with the forest and the animals. There was an aura around the forest, which led Alpheus straight to the child. The gatekeeper had been born with the knowledge of what he must do.

To create the wall was an easy spell for Alpheus. To hold the wall in place, that was the job of the gatekeeper. The only problem was how to get Nyrra to the Northern Wasteland. This however was simpler that Alpheus thought. All he had to do was send a challenge to Nyrra to meet him there.

Mad with rage Nyrra did not even consider the thought of a trap. Bringing the remainder of his army to the Northern Wasteland, Nyrra prepared to end it. Knowing his power was greater, all he had worked for was about to become reality.

Coming through the peninsula, separating the mainland from the wasteland, Nyrra found Alpheus standing alone on ridge. Not realising his impending doom, Nyrra sent his army to climb the ridge and destroy the last of his brothers.

What happened next is hearsay, but from what I can gather when Nyrra was separating from his army is when Alpheus started his spell. It is said that when Alpheus finished his spell his body collapsed, completely drained of energy. Other tales tell of Nyrra's army overriding him as he finished the wall. Whichever of the many stories is true, one thing is certain. Alpheus has never been seen again." Eldred finished with a deep breath.

"That's all well and good Eldred, but what has any of this got to do with me?" Alaric had a confused expression on his face. He had followed the story well enough, but he could not see the relevance.

"All in good time," Eldred remained mysterious. "Now with Nyrra safely trapped in the North, the Kingdoms rounded up all of his followers and had them executed. With the threat gone and years passing the world forgot the tragedy that had been. The Seven Stones, which had been lost with the wizards, were now fading into myth and legend." Eldred paused and looked around the room. He looked as though he was trying to listen hard to something far in the distance. "I must go now." The comment was so sudden that it made Alaric jump. "I had hoped to have explained more, but my time is up." Eldred stood as he spoke and made his way t o the door. Alaric quickly came to his feet before Eldred disappeared around the corner.

"I will return by the end of the week and finish my story." Eldred spoke as he walked out into the night.

There was nothing Alaric could do except stand in the doorway and watch Eldred disappear into the darkness. There was something very familiar about the evening. It had not been the first time Eldred had left leaving him confused only now he remembered the encounter.

Alaric shook his head as he shut the door. He couldn't place why things seemed so odd. He knew there was something missing from Eldred's story. He could not, however, figure out what it had to do with him. It played on his mind as he lay in bed, but eventually he fell asleep.

In the morning the events of the previous night did not seem so strange. The nagging question that had been in the back of his mind was now gone. He was glad to be up with sunlight streaming through his bedroom window. It was going to be a very exciting day. His first port of call was his friend, Bern's house.

Chapter 3: A Deal to be Done

The farmhouse was about three leagues from town. Normally Alaric would walk to his friend's house, but he was in a hurry that morning and had ordered a carriage. He wanted to make it by breakfast and on foot it would have been closer to lunch. The information he had to give Bern was far too important to wait.

The morning was fresh, but not as cold as it had been in previous months. Spring had well and truly started. The flowers were blooming in the gardens and on the sides of the road. The sun was shining in a cloudless sky signaling a warm and pleasant day.

Alaric made regular visits to Bern's house, for work and pleasure. Ever since Bern had taken over the farm from his parents when they had passed away, Alaric had helped him manage his finances. It was more an excuse to spend time together than a necessity.

The sweeping fields of wheat, barley and rye indicated the start of Bern's farm. Of all the farms surrounding Arsiliac, Bern's was one of the most successful. The small river which provided Arsiliac's water supply ran through the top end which made irrigation easy and fed nutrients into the soil.

The farmhouse was a short walk off the main road. Alaric allowed the carriage to turn around at the main gate and walked up the small path the house. It was a modest two storey building, pleasant to look at, but no special trimmings.

The smell of freshly baked bread welcomed Alaric as he let himself in through the front door. There was always the smell of food cooking. It gave Alaric a sense of home whenever he arrived. Bern's wife, Mary, was the best cook he knew.

Mary met Alaric in the front hallway. She was a very typical mother. Over the last few years patches of softness appeared where there had been none before, the after effects of childbirth. Her mid-length blonde hair had yet to be brushed and two spots of flour were on her cheeks. The sight of Alaric brought a warm smile to her face, a smile that was returned just as warmly. She leapt into his arms and kissed him on the cheek. It was a standard greeting for the two. They said a cheerful hello and then she called out to Bern.

"Bern! We have a visitor. Come down and say hello," she called out before speaking to Alaric again. "Bern slept in this morning. He's been working hard over the last couple of weeks. This is the first day off he's had in a long time."

Suddenly Bern appeared at the top of the stairs, still in his nightclothes. "Good morning Alaric. I'll be down shortly."

Before Alaric had a chance to move two loud screams came from the kitchen. "Uncle Alaric! Uncle Alaric!" came the voices of Bern's two children. Johnathon, aged six and Holly, his daughter aged four, came running towards him. Alaric braced himself as the two children jumped into his open arms. He held them close before returning them to the floor.

"That's enough you two. Let Alaric go, you can play with him later." Mary smiled. "You go through to the study and I'll start on breakfast." Alaric made his own way to the study, as Mary ushered the children into the kitchen. A few minutes later Bern joined him, even with the extra sleep he looked tired. His strong form slumped as he walked and he sighed loudly as he collapsed into his chair.

"It's been a long month. Sometimes I wonder why I do it." It was same thing Bern said every year.

"Because you wouldn't have it any other way," was Alaric's common response.

"I know. I just can't wait for Johnathon to grow up and take over the farm." Bern had a glazed look on his face as though he was picturing what he was saying.

"You know you would miss it too much." Alaric wasn't sure if Bern was serious or not.

"Anyway, enough about my problems. What is that you wanted to speak to me about?" Bern came back to reality with the change of subject.

"I caught a rumour two days ago about a mill that's coming up for sale on the outskirts of Zenza City. I heard that it was having financial trouble and the Grain and Millers Guild want nothing to do with it. All being well, it will go for rock bottom price. As far as I know everything is still in perfect working order." Alaric rubbed his hands as he spoke, obviously excited with what he was saying.

"Why would I want to invest in a mill that's going broke, especially one that isn't receiving any help from the guild? Normally the guild will help out anyone, unless it's a lost cause. It doesn't make a lot of sense." Bern knew that Alaric would have done his research and that there would be a very good reason why he should invest.

Alaric knew that Bern was not in the frame of mind for investments. The time of year was especially hard. Work was long and hard and there was not much money around. Alaric could not make the deal on his own and the mill would not be on the market for long. If it didn't sell soon, it would be knocked down.

Alaric took a deep breath before he started to speak. "That's exactly why it's a good idea. The owners didn't pay their membership to the guild, so they are not receiving any help. Without help from the guild the owners will be desperate to sell. We'll get it at rock bottom price." Alaric tried to contain his excitement.

"That still doesn't change the fact that the mill has gone broke. What is the point of purchasing a mill that isn't making any money?" Bern sounded exhausted. He tried to act interested in what Alaric was saying, but only because they were friends.

"With our connections we can't fail. Everyone knows the local miller is a rip off. No local should have to pay those prices. I can offer them discounted transportation rates and then we can charge them for the milling." Alaric was excited. "You have a good enough reputation with the local farmers to get the business. I can get my clients to use us. Within twelve months we'll have our money back and then some. An investment opportunity like this comes along once in a lifetime. You'll be able live out your life in luxury." Alaric was sitting on the edge of his seat in anticipation.

"That's all well and good, but who's going to run it. I don't have time with the farm and my family and I can't see you having the time." Alaric had Bern's attention now and there was a possibility the idea wasn't as stupid as he had originally thought.

"I know someone in Zenza City who could run it for us. The labour side of it should be easy. There are always people looking for work in the city." He seemed to have thought of everything. He knew Bern would not go in on face value; he had done his research and knew it was a winning idea.

"I guess you've thought things over. Okay then, how much money would you need from me?"

"One hundred… gold marks," Alaric said the amount slowly. "That would give you a fifty percent share. I don't know exactly how much we can buy it for, but that will be the absolute highest price."

Bern took a deep breath, one hundred gold marks was more money than he would make in a year of farming, but Alaric knew that he had the money saved.

"That's a big risk. You know that I don't make that kind of money. If things were to go south, then what would I do?" Bern was on the verge of agreeing, but wanted to make sure he had covered all his bases.

Suddenly the door was pushed open. The smell of cooked food filled the room. As soon as the scent hit Alaric's nose his mouth started to water. Any excuse was a good excuse for Mary's cooking.

"Enough business talk boys, breakfast is ready, so go clean up," Mary's voice was firm, but caring, as if she was talking to her children.

"How can you argue with that?" laughed Alaric.

"We will be there in a couple of minutes," Bern smiled at his wife as he spoke.

He waited for Mary to shut the door before he started to speak. "Well it seems on the level. As long as the figures match up and the wife gives us the okay then we are good to go."

"Excellent. We can go over the current and my projected figures after breakfast." Alaric smiled as he stood. He knew that Bern didn't have a very good grasp of economics.

Bern led the way into the bathroom where the two of them washed their hands before walking into the dining room. It was probably the nicest room in the house. It was where Bern did most of his entertaining and he wanted it to look nice. A large glass chandelier hung from the ceiling, the candles had been recently replaced and the wax removed from the holders. Although the chandelier would comfortably provide enough light there were still many other candles scattered throughout the room. The chandelier was only used for special occasions.

Paintings of Bern's family were strategically placed along the walls, dating back to his great great grandfather. The dining room table had been extended after his parents had died. It had been originally made to seat sixteen. Now it could seat over twenty, but it was unlikely Bern would ever entertain that many people.

The table looked a little ridiculous with just the two of them sitting, normally the family ate in one of the other rooms, but Mary insisted whenever there were guests they had to eat in the dining room. A couple of moments later, the two children came racing in. Johnathon jumped into Alaric's lap whilst Holly climbed onto the chair next to him.

"Tell us a story Uncle Alaric, tell us a story," the two cried in unison.

"Leave Alaric alone," Mary called out as she brought in their breakfast. She swatted Johnathon playfully on the back of his head on her way back to the kitchen.

Breakfast consisted of scrambled eggs, bacon, sausages and freshly toasted bread. Alaric licked his lips as Mary placed the food in front of him. It was the best looking breakfast he had seen in a long time. Normally Alaric just ate toast or cereal. It was a treat for him to eat so lavishly.

They only made small talk over breakfast. Alaric knew not to bring up the subject of the mill before Bern had spoken to Mary. The conversation stayed mainly on the comings and goings of the town and the activities of the children. Normally Alaric didn't hear or care about the town gossip, but he did enjoy Mary's account of what she had heard. There was one conversation, however, that really caught his attention.

"I hear there is an army gathering in the forest to the east. Rumour has it something bad is going to happen, maybe an attack on the town.

That's what I've heard anyway." Mary could feel the eyes of the others staring at her.

"Don't be silly dear. It's common knowledge that the Duke's army always trains in the woods. They come down once or twice a year," retorted Bern.

"If it was the Duke's men, then why haven't they come into town? When they train they come in to drink at the tavern and flirt with the local girls." Mary didn't like the tone in her husband's voice. "I've heard that they are not part of the Duke's army."

"You know full well that sometimes they can train without coming into town. That's all that it is. Now enough of this silly talk, let's talk about something else."

Sensing the tension starting to rise Alaric changed the subject to some of the deals he had been making over the last month. It was a boring topic, but it made everyone forget about the rumours. Alaric had heard them, but dismissed them as idle chatter.

"That was the best breakfast I have had in a long time. I don't think I could eat another thing," complimented Alaric as he finished eating.

Mary blushed slightly as she started to remove the plates from the table. As soon as she disappeared into the kitchen, the children leapt down and ran outside to play. Alaric was glad to have Bern to himself again. He wanted to make arrangements so he would be ready to travel to Zenza City the next day.

"Shall we look through the finances now?" asked Alaric as he rose from the table.

They returned to the study where Alaric produced the documents from the mill. He knew that Bern wouldn't understand what he was showing him, but he tried his best to explain it. When he had finished, Bern was convinced he had to have a go.

"I hope you know what you are doing, but I trust your judgement. When do you need the money?" Bern wasn't completely sure, but he trusted his best friend.

"I'm going to Zenza City tomorrow to try and seal the deal. If all goes well, I'll be back by the end of the week and I'll need the money then." Alaric was relieved. He couldn't make the deal without his friend's help.

"Do you want to stay for lunch?" Mary asked Alaric as they left the study.

"I would love to, but I have some business I have to take care of this afternoon. My carriage should be here any minute," and as if on cue a call came from outside.

"Good luck." Bern shook his hand and Alaric embraced Mary warmly.

Bern watched his friend walk down the path towards his carriage before returning inside. Mary met him inside the front door and wrapped her arms around him.

"What was it that Alaric was offering?" Mary asked softly.

"I'll tell you over lunch," replied Bern

Giving her a quick kiss on the cheek before removing her hands he went and sat down in the dining room, as Mary went to prepare sandwiches for lunch. If Alaric had stayed she would have prepared something a little more extravagant.

Bern was glad to have some time to contemplate what he had just agreed to. He knew that she would not be completely happy with his decision, but it was his decision to make. He had known Alaric all his life and had faith in his friend.

"So what was it that Alaric wanted?" asked Mary as she served lunch and sat next to her husband.

Bern quickly stuffed a triangle of sandwich into his mouth, chewed and swallowed before he answered. "Alaric wanted me to join him in an investment opportunity in the city."

"And you turned him down I take it?" Mary's tone had lost a lot of its sweetness.

Shaking his head Bern looked down at his half eaten lunch. He knew that this was not going to be easy, but it had to be said. "This is a chance for us to make some real money. If all goes well we will be able hire some help, or even sell the farm. We could travel and see the world." As Bern continued to talk he started speaking faster and faster until he finally controlled himself and stopped.

"What are you talking about?" There was genuine surprise in Mary's voice. "Sell the farm? Our life is here. We're settled here." Mary was in shock from her husband's speech.

"I know sweetheart. It's just sometimes I wonder if there is something else out there for us." Bern looked resigned. "It's in the lap of the Gods now anyway."

That was clearly the end of the conversation and they sat in silence while they finished their lunch.

***

Smiling as he walked down the path to the carriage Alaric was pleased with what he had achieved. He knew this venture was going to make him and Bern a lot of money. All being well he would be able to retire on what he had, not that he would. He would like to travel one day and the thoughts raced through his mind as he sat in the carriage on the way back to the house.

The sun was high in the sky when the carriage dropped Alaric back home. Still full from breakfast, Alaric went straight to his study. He wanted to check and recheck his figures on the mill. He had not taken a risk since his silks disaster five years prior; this deal had the potential to be just as disastrous, but twice as profitable. One thing he had neglected to tell Bern was that he had already spent half their money on a deposit. Now all he had to do was travel to Zenza City to pay the remaining amount before the mill was shut down. It was late in the evening when he finally closed the ledgers and went to bed.

Morning came around and although the deal was done he was still nervous. The carriage came for him as soon as he had finished breakfast. Alaric always packed his travel bags two days before leaving, just in case he ran out of time. Before leaving for the city, Alaric went to the office as he had just recently employed a new manager. He was nervous about leaving town without refreshing his memory on any upcoming work.

"Good morning Alaric." Myria welcomed him when he arrived. "I thought you would have been on your way to the city by now. What are you doing here?" Myria knew Alaric was checking up on him. It frustrated him, but he understood Alaric's position.

"I just wanted to go through the schedules with you whilst I'm away," said Alaric.

"Not a problem," Myria smiled as he replied. He was well aware Alaric would want to quiz him on the weekly jobs. He had already laid out all the documents on his desk, ready for Alaric's inspection.

Alaric had faith in his new right hand man. Within two weeks he had already surpassed his predecessor. Myria actually showed an interest in his job and gave Alaric respect. There was something, though, that wasn't quite right. He had told Alaric when he arrived in Arsiliac that he was from the capital looking to settle down in the country. His dark skin and light brown hair was like no one he had ever seen from Remidia. Myria's features reminded him of a trader he had seen from Castalia, the desert sun bronzing the skin and lightening the hair. His accent was also unfamiliar. Most of the time he had Remidian tones, though it sounded rehearsed and forced. Occasionally Alaric notice a slur on certain words when he least expected it. There was something in the man's past the he didn't want Alaric to know, but Alaric respected Myria's privacy and didn't push the issue.

"We have a shipment coming in the afternoon from Lel Dinion, furs and pelts, I believe. They'll want storage and quarantine overnight before moving on to Zenza City." Myria paused when he finished. He knew Alaric would want to question him on the deal. It was the first deal Myria had made without Alaric's assistance.

"I remember you mentioning briefly about a shipment of furs coming in, but you didn't say they were coming from Lel Dinion," Alaric looked puzzled.

"I didn't think it mattered where they came from." Myria watched Alaric closely for a reaction.

"We are not on the main trade route between Zenza City and Lel Dinion. In fact, we are at least a two-day journey off the main highway with no towns in-between. There is no reason at all why a caravan would come here before going to the city. Make sure the shipment is thoroughly checked before it leaves the warehouse. We don't want anything suspicious passing through our quarantine." Alaric knew there was something wrong with the deal.

"I'll check every crate myself, nothing will get past," Myria reassured him.

Smiling, Alaric was a little more confident after hearing Myria's words. There was still something that didn't add up, but there was nothing he could do about it. He wasn't going to call off his trip for one suspicious shipment that would no doubt turn out to be safe. All the other deals in process were all straight forward. It took only a half hour for Alaric to make sure Myria knew what to do in his absence. Myria knew the week's work back to front, but he humoured him all the same.

Since that night five years ago, Alaric had only made the journey to Zenza City two or three times a year. He only went when it was absolutely necessary. Each time he reached the forest between Arsiliac and Quinaliac, he became very nervous.

As usual the journey to Quinaliac was eventless. There was one small caravan travelling towards Arsiliac, but besides that there was no one else on the road. Even though this was a common occurrence, he still had two guards up front with Erhard his driver. Truth be known, they would not be much use against an organised attack, but it reassured him.

Alaric could not relax until he reached Quinaliac and seeing the town, he let out a deep sigh. The relief of arriving alive was clear in his demeanour. He was glad that no one was in the carriage with him; the open emotion would have embarrassed him a great deal.

It was close to dusk when Alaric arrived at the inn. A fog had crept in from the forest making the evening quite eerie and he was relieved that they were settled before nightfall.

"I have everything ready for you," greeted Fayne as Alaric entered the inn.

Three days ago Alaric had sent word that he would be arriving. He had requested three things: a room, a meal in his room, and a lockable box for his documents. No one knew the reason for his visit, but Alaric had to be safe. If his papers landed in the wrong hands, then he could forget all about the deal. He had no plans to socialize; a good meal and a good night's sleep were all that he was after.

The sun was just over the horizon when Alaric was on the road again. Skipping breakfast, he wanted to be in Zenza City as soon as he could. The road was empty at that hour of the day giving them free range.

The mist was still thick on the ground, but by mid-morning it had vanished. The hot sun beating down on them gave away any advantage of the empty road. The horses were thick with sweat by midday and had   to be rested and watered at regular intervals.

By early afternoon they were approaching the Southern Gate. The sight of the large grey walls allowed Alaric to relax again. He had been through the Southern Gates many times, but now there was something different about them. Alaric couldn't place it when suddenly it struck him. The gates were closed and there was a long queue of wagons and travelers waiting to gain entry. The line trailed back through the outer city for almost a league.

"Nearly there, Sir," called Erhard, as he joined at the end of the line. The line itself was not an uncommon sight at the time of day, although it had never been so long. The problem was the gate. Never had Alaric seen the gate shut before nightfall. The only reason why the gate would be closed was if the city was under attack, or there was one looming.

"Erhard!" called Alaric as he climbed out of the carriage.

"Yes sir."

"All the times you've been to the city, have you ever seen a line this long?"

"No sir. Not by half." Erhard had not yet thought that there might be something wrong. It was his job to drive the carriage. Beyond that, he didn't like to think too much.

"That's what I thought. I'm going down the line to see what I can find out." It would take over two hours for him to reach the gate and back again. If the news wasn't favourable, there wouldn't be enough time to make it back to Quinaliac before nightfall. Alaric hoped he would get an answer before making it all the way to the front.

"Very good sir." Erhard nodded.

Walking for about fifteen minutes, Alaric decided to try his luck in getting some information. He found a friendly looking caravan and spoke to the head driver.

"What's the holdup friend?" Alaric asked, trying to hide his concern.

"No one's being let in today. Don't really know why." The portly driver didn't seem interested in Alaric's question. If he knew anything, he wasn't divulging any information.

With his curiosity unsatisfied, Alaric walked on. He knew there was something up; they wouldn't close the Southern Gate on a mere whim.

Continuing on for another fifteen minutes, Alaric came across a small group talking around a large wagon. They didn't seem to all be from the same caravan and Alaric hoped that they might be more useful.

"Excuse me." The men with their backs to Alaric spun around, whilst the others looked up at him. With the movement he could see three dice on the ground. Alaric realised that some of the traders had resorted to gambling to pass the time.

"Don't do that," a heavyset man with red hair and an even redder moustache said after he had a good look at Alaric. "We thought you were the local guard. They've been patrolling since midday and they don't like unauthorized gambling, not that there is anything else to do."

"Do you know what the holdup is?" Alaric thought there was no point in small talk. He didn't have any interest in joining a game of dice.

"I see it is information you seek," the man standing opposite the red headed man spoke with an unfamiliar accent. His body looked well-toned, even when wearing loose fitting clothes. There was an awe about him that Alaric couldn't explain. "It is coin that we seek and I think that we can do business." When he finished the man looked at Alaric's coin purse hanging on his belt.

The look in his eye showed that he would not be persuaded any other way and Alaric thought about moving on, but these men looked as though they would have all the information he needed. He didn't want to waste any more time walking up and down the line and money almost assured he would get the most accurate information.

"Okay then, how much do you want?" Alaric tried not to sound desperate.

"Oh no friend. You get me all wrong. A simple game of dice. Your coin against my information." The smile on the man's face made Alaric nervous.

The game of dice was one of pure luck and Alaric had heard stories of people playing with loaded dice, but using the same dice in the same game made the chances even. Alaric wasn't sure what the catch was, but he knew it was going to be easier said than done. He would have preferred to just pay for the information and move on, but it seemed that wasn't an option.

Dice was a relatively simple game to learn. Each six-sided dice had four pictures roughly cut into them. Two sides had pictures of a dagger, two had pictures of a rose, one of a cup and one of a crown. Six dice were rolled at one time and then a second roll with as many dice as required. Each picture was worth a certain amount of points, daggers being lowest and crowns being highest. Extra points were award for doubles, triples, fours, fives and sixes whilst the six of crowns being the highest hand and unbeatable. Generally, the highest scores came from triples, doubles or fours.

"Okay." Alaric said after a moment of contemplation. He had seen the game being played in the taverns in the city, but had never played himself. "How much do we play for?"

"One silver half mark for one piece of information." The smile on the man's face disappeared. Alaric knew his type well. When business started all frivolities disappeared. "Standard rules. Best of five rounds. Six crowns wins all." The man waited for Alaric's response.

"I guess I don't have any other option, do I?" Alaric responded without emotion.

"Good then," the smile returned "Udi is my name and this is the Midway Tavern, haven for the tired and weary. First ale is on the house for you my friend." Only then did Alaric realise that everyone had mugs in their hands. Udi was obviously a very shrewd business man, seeing the best in any situation. If it wasn't apparent before then it definitely was now, Alaric had to be careful.

Accepting the mug gratefully Alaric introduced himself to the group. Although the ale was warm and bitter it was still refreshing. After a deep draught Alaric accepted the dice from Udi and suddenly he felt a strange buzz in the air. His heart started to pound and his vision became blurry. Without even realizing it, Alaric had rolled the dice.

A quiet hush came over the otherwise rowdy group. Alaric looked down in the dust at the dice he had thrown. What he saw in front of him left him speechless. Lined up in a perfect row, head to tail, were six crowns. Even Udi's expression was that of pure surprise.

"How did you do that?" He said when he finally regained his senses. "That's an impossible roll."

"I don't know. Lucky I guess." The look of surprise on Alaric's face was enough to prove to Udi that he was not lying.

Udi knew the odds of rolling six crowns. In all the years he had been gambling, he had only ever seen two people roll six crowns. Never had he seen them so neatly lined up on a single roll. "Okay, information is what you want. Ask a question and I'll answer. Then we roll again."

"Why is the gate closed?" That was the burning question on Alaric's mind.

"What I have heard is that there is trouble brewing around the city, skirmishes between the Duke's army and some unknown army. Now if you ask me, I think it is all rumours and innuendo. For the last twenty years I have been travelling these highways and not once have I ever seen or heard of an invading army. I think there's another reason, but the guards are not indulged to tell us." That was all Udi was going to say.

"So why is everyone lined up?" Alaric asked as soon as Udi finished speaking.

"Quid pro quo Alaric. Roll to dice and winner takes all. One question for one silver half mark. The rules remain the same. Loser rolls first."

Udi swept up the dice in one hand with a moderate amount of dust. His routine never changed. After he collected the dice in one hand, he let three dice fall into the other. Cupping his hands together he shook the dice five times before releasing them onto the ground. His first roll scored him a pair of daggers and a pair of roses with a cup and a crown. It was the worst roll possible. Udi kicked the dust before snatching up all six off the dice again. His next roll was exactly the same.

Eyeing Alaric suspiciously Udi collected the dice and passed them over. There was no logic behind his train of thought, but he was sure Alaric was somehow cheating. It didn't make sense but Alaric's next roll only added to his suspicion. The buzzing and the nausea returned as soon as Alaric touched the dice. After his roll, the dice were again perfectly lined up this time all cups, the second best roll.

The look Udi gave Alaric was enough to make he him fear for his safety. He was sure nothing would happen out in the open with so many people around, but he couldn't be certain. The worst thing was that Alaric had no idea how he was spinning the dice.

Four more rolls for Udi was as unnecessary as if Alaric had rolled crowns. The best Udi could manage was three daggers and three roses, quite low in the scheme of scoring.

"Well I don't know how you're doing it, but you win again. I will answer your question. We are all lined up because there is still a chance to get into the city." And that was all he said. "Roll again?" said Udi when Alaric tried to speak.

"But I need more answers," Alaric shrugged his shoulders as he spoke, praying that his next roll would be as suspicious.

The next game lasted right to the finish. Alaric's wish to roll poorly came true. His first three rolls were well under those of Udi, but his last roll was high enough to win another answer.

"How do people gain access to the city?" If he could still get into the city, then all would not be lost.

"Quite simple really. All you need are the correct rite-of-passage papers." Again Udi stopped short in his answering.

"Let's go again." Alaric was starting to get impatient. It would be nightfall before he even got anything answered and Udi would divulge any further information.

Before Udi rolled again he insisted that Alaric purchase an ale at his inflated price. Even if Udi didn't win at dice, he would make it on ale. The next game went the same way as the last. Udi started off looking like he was going to win, but Alaric saved the day on his last roll.

"If we can get in with rite-of-passage papers, why are we lined up like sheep?" Alaric hoped that the question would give him the answers he needed.

"That my friend is simple. Everyone has papers." Udi remained mysterious, even though it was quite clear that Alaric was about to lose his temper.

Another game went by and again there was very little response from Udi. He would give Alaric just enough information to cover his side of the bargain. Udi's luck did not change as the game wore on and with every limp answer given, another game of dice was lost. The day wore on and Alaric felt as though he was not getting any closer to a final answer.

"Enough of this," barked Alaric. "One more roll of the dice. Winner takes all. My money bag against all the information I require."

The offer instantly brought a hush over the rest of the group. All the other games stopped suddenly as they waited for Udi's response. The large grin on the man's face made Alaric believe that he had not made the best decision. He didn't know how, with a game of luck, but he knew Udi was about to roll some good dice.

"All or nothing?" Udi paused as if he was contemplating the offer, even though it was obvious now that it was what he waiting for. "I think I can play those odds," the smile was even broader on his face when he accepted. "One roll and I get to go first."

Udi scooped up the dice just like he did every other time, yet there was something different. Something that Alaric only glanced out of the corner of his eye. So subtle he couldn't even be sure what it was, but he knew that Udi was going to have some extraordinary luck.

Very deliberately Udi followed the same routine as he did in every game. When the dice finally settled there were six cups scattered in the dust. Alaric stared at the dice, half in disbelief and half knowing.

"Six cups? What are the odds of rolling them in a shootout? The Goddess of Luck must be shining on me today." Udi seemed to forget that Alaric's first roll had been six crowns. "You would have to be the luckiest man in the world the beat that." Udi spoke like he didn't possibly believe that Alaric could roll better.

As soon as the dice had been witnessed and verified that they were indeed six cups Udi snatched them up and offered them to Alaric. It had been the same in the other games, but again this time there was something different. Even the dice felt different in his hands. Again it was all subtle enough that it could just be his paranoia. It didn't take long for the nausea to return and the dice flew out of his hand without his control. As the dice moved through the air everyone held their breath. Most of them knew what the result was going to be. It was a regular scam of Udi's, wait until an opponent became complaisant and then hit them in the hip pocket with loaded dice.

The result should have been six roses, a close but honourable loss and one that would not be too suspicious. However, to the dismay of everyone watching, including the two players, the dice did not fall as they were destined. The dice landed exactly how the first roll landed. Six crowns, top to tail in a perfect roll, an impossible roll.

"That's impossible. You cheated!" Udi cried out in surprise, pointing an accusing finger at Alaric., ironic considering it was he who was in fact cheating.

"How can I cheat? I rolled the exact same roll the first time." Alaric feigned innocence. He had no idea how he had done it.

Drawing a small dagger, Udi cried out in anger. He moved towards Alaric, but before he could get within stabbing distance three other men stepped in. They were regulars and had seen Udi cheat many people out of their money, and had been cheated themselves. They took great pleasure in Udi being beaten for once. Their only regret was that it didn't cost him any coin.

"Pay up Udi. You've been beaten fair and square," The man with the red hair spoke with a certain amount of aggression.

"Arrr!" Udi spat at Alaric's feet before returning the blade. "I will tell you what you need to know. But first have another ale." If Alaric was going to get the answers he required, then he was happy to buy another. "Good." Udi said when Alaric had a fresh mug in his hand. "Now the reason why we are all in this line is because the guards are checking everyone's credentials and their loads. They believe that these so called insurgents are trying to sneak their way into the city to cause havoc. I think that they are just doing it to be a pain."

"But if they are checking and sending people into the city than why haven't we moved all afternoon?" It didn't make sense.

"Unfortunately, I don't know the answer. The line was moving this morning and shortly after noon it suddenly stopped. The only report that I've heard is that there was someone with suspicious cargo and they were not letting anyone through until it's been cleared. My guess is that the line

won't start moving again until the morning. Either way, I'm happy."
Finally, Alaric received the answers he needed.

"Thank you Udi, maybe we can play again sometime?" Alaric
finished his ale in one long drink and then started back towards the
carriage.

The news was not good. He had wasted the whole afternoon
playing a silly game only to find out that he would not be admitted before
nightfall. It was now too late to attempt riding back to Quinaliac. If Udi
had been there since morning when the line was moving, he doubted if he
would make it to the city gate by the following night.

"How goes things sir?" asked Erhard when Alaric arrived back at
the carriage.

"Not well. Not well at all." Alaric looked around before speaking
again. "Where are the two guards?"

"Henrad and Signe have found themselves a makeshift tavern
down the line. They arrived about half an hour after we did," explained
Erhard before stifling a yawn.

It seemed that Udi was not the only entrepreneur. Alaric was
amazed that even in the confusion, people could still make the best of the
situation and could make a profit. The makeshift taverns were not the
only temporary shops. Many goods and services were available, from food
and drink to clothing and jewelry.

"I see. I suppose we are not in any danger whilst the sun is shining.
I hope they decide to come back when the sun starts to set. The Gods
only know what's going to happen when it gets dark."

"Yes sir. I'm sure they will come back." Sometimes Erhard's
indifference annoyed Alaric.

Alaric spent the remaining hours in the back of the carriage going
through his documents. He knew them all back to front by now, but there
was nothing else for him to do. It was dusk when he put the papers away
and even though the guards had not returned, Alaric wasn't too
concerned. He had no cargo and not a lot of coin on him. There would be
no reason for anyone to attack.

Leaving the carriage to stretch his legs, Alaric found a lot of people
milling past towards the city. "What's going on out there?" Alaric asked
Erhard who was still sitting in the driver's seat.

"There seems to be some meeting happening ahead." Erhard
seemed not to notice the people walking around him.

Shaking his head, Alaric ignored Erhard's detachment. He was,
however, curious to see what all the commotion was about. Waiting for a
place in the moving line, Alaric started to follow the crowd. It was only a
short walk before the crowd stopped. A sentry dressed in the livery of the

Duchy stood atop a large wagon. He was the centre of everyone's attention.

"Listen up!" the sentry's commanding voice quietened the crowd. "As you now know, the city has been closed for the moment. Developments have occurred that prevent us letting anyone else in today. Guards are moving into position up and down the line. They have been instructed to arrest anyone who is making trouble and there will be no exceptions. By midnight, everyone is expected back at their own caravans. Anyone out after midnight, will be arrested. The temporary taverns will be allowed to remain open, but will be watched carefully. This is an unpleasant situation for everyone and we don't want anyone to make it more difficult."

Alaric felt relieved knowing the highway was now secure. There would be some brawling and other mischief, but it would now be few and far between. Alaric thought about going to drink at one of the taverns, but then thought better of it. Only trouble could come of being away from the carriage.

The two guards had returned and were speaking quietly to Erhard when Alaric arrived back at the carriage. He was a little angry at them for leaving, but thought better of scolding them. He would need them around later in the evening and didn't want to risk them leaving again.

"Why don't the three of you go enjoy yourselves? You may as well try and make the best of this situation," Alaric tried to sound friendly.

Erhard had already laid out the three bedrolls, which he always carried underneath the carriage. Alaric would sleep inside the carriage, giving some protection to himself and his cargo. It would not be perfect, but it would be better than sleeping outside.

After the three men had walked away Alaric checked to make sure the chest containing his documents was secure before he reclined back on the seat and closed his eyes. With the light gone, there was nothing more for Alaric to do. He knew that the possibility of trouble was high and wanted to avoid it. The carriage would give him all the security he needed.

Without even realising he had fallen asleep, Alaric was awoken by a sharp wrap on the carriage's left hand door. The sound was so sudden that it woke Alaric with a shudder. Before he knew what he was doing, he opened the door and leaned out to see who it was.

To his surprise he found a rather dirty, if not attractive, female face looking back him. Shaking the remainder of the sleep out of his head, Alaric spoke. "Can I help you?"

"Are you looking for some fun tonight?" The voice was very seductive, yet there was something amiss.

With a shock Alaric realised who the woman was. He should have known the Ladies of the Night guild would be working the night. There was a long train of mainly male merchants and traders with nowhere to go. "Ah, no thank you!" Alaric was so surprised with the question that he didn't notice the movement on the other side of the carriage. Sensing more than feeling the movement, Alaric moved his head to look back into the carriage and to his horror he realised what had happened.

With Alaric's attention diverted a second woman had opened the other carriage door and removed the chest. With his head now turned he was open for attack. Without delay she slammed the door shut, knocking Alaric square in the back of his head. The blow was not enough to knock him unconscious, but was enough to make him see stars.

When he recovered cv Alaric was quick to move. Snatching the sword, which he kept hidden under his seat, he ran. Normally his first reaction would have been to call out for help and wait for assistance. The document, however, was more important to him than his normal cargo.

"Stop!" He called out as he chased the two women who had almost disappeared into the night.

Carrying the chest had slowed them down, but they were moving slower than they should have. This should have a set off warning bells for Alaric, but his only thought was recovering his chest.

Alaric chased them towards a small group of trees. He knew that if they got inside then it would be hard for him to find them. The trees would give them ample cover from the dim light of the moon. To his surprise the two women stopped only feet from the safety of the trees. Alaric held his sword by its sheath tightly in his left hand as he reached them. He slowed to a stop just outside striking distance. Although he had a sword and the two women seemed unarmed he knew better than to take it for granted.

"Please. I just want my chest back," Alaric puffed as he spoke. "There is nothing in there worth stealing."

"I don't think you would have chased us all this way if there was nothing worth stealing inside," the first woman spoke. This time her voice was strong and steady. He knew the seductive voice had just been an act. Movement from the trees behind the women made Alaric nervous. He knew now why they had not continued. Two armed men walked out slowly. The chase had just been an ambush. Quickly looking over his shoulder for a means of escape Alaric saw that a further two men had appeared from the dark. There was no room for escape and he was now too far from the road to call out for help.

Without thinking Alaric drew his sword. The sound of sliding steal rang out into the night. It was the first time he had ever drawn it.

Although he had never used the sword before it felt natural in his hand, but this did not give him confidence. He knew that the sword was just for show. He had no idea how to fight and if attacked it would soon be over. He would not, however, give up.

"There are just papers in the chest. Nothing worth selling." Alaric hoped to talk them out of slitting his throat. Even in the darkness Alaric could see the expressions on the two women's faces, they did not take him seriously. "Open it and see." Desperation crept into his voice.

The first woman raised her arm. As she did the four men stopped their advance. Drawing a small stiletto, she slid the blade in between the lock, a sharp twist of the blade was all it took to snap. It was obviously not the first lock she had broken. Opening the lid she saw that Alaric was telling the truth. After rifling through the entire chest to make sure there was no gold hidden underneath she slammed the lid shut and knocked the chest onto the ground.

"Well that's just a shame," the first woman now had disgust in her voice. "I hate to kill someone without getting something in return."

Hearing this made Alaric's heart sink. There was no way he could beat four armed men. The woman made the signal for the men to attack and slowly they started their advance again. Alaric took a stance that he had seen his guards take when it looked like there might be trouble. Besides that, he had no idea what to do.

"What's going on down here?" a voice boomed from somewhere behind him.

Hearing the voices, the two women and four men suddenly bolted into the trees. Alaric let out a deep sigh of relief when he turned around to see a group of six soldiers standing in front of him.

"Are you okay?" The tone did not lose any of its volume or command.

"Yes, thank you," Alaric's voice wavered with the stress of his near death experience.

The soldiers escorted Alaric back to his carriage and the commanding officer spoke as they walked. "You were very lucky; we were just passing your way on our patrol when we heard you cry out." Alaric was still too shaken to make conversation. "It seems that this group has been causing trouble all night. They have already hit two other caravans. Just make sure you stay in your carriage and don't open the door for anyone."

Alaric nodded. He had no intention to open the carriage doors again. Alaric thanked the guards before they left. He found his own two guards and Erhard asleep. Alaric shook his head at his luck. If they had returned only minutes before then he wouldn't have been attacked.

Entering the carriage Alaric made sure he securely locked both doors. He thought about waking one of his guards to stand sentry, but figured his attackers wouldn't be back. They knew that there was nothing worth stealing and didn't think they were in the business of killing needlessly.

The morning came around without incident. Alaric was keen to be on the move again and woke his three companions who were still sleeping like babies. By the look of them they had drunk too much the night before.

The early start did not seem be much use. The line moved at a snail's pace. No more than fifty paces every fifteen minutes at best, sometimes not moving for over half an hour. The tension was starting to get to Alaric. At this rate they would not make it to the gate for another week.

By noon they had not even travelled a quarter of a mile. Alaric had started leaving the carriage and pacing up and down the highway. The more the day wore on the more Alaric knew his plan was becoming a lost cause. Little did he know the approaching soldiers would seal the deal.

As the day before, Alaric joined the crowd huddled around a commanding officer standing on the back of a nearby wagon.

"Listen up everyone!" the officer's voice brought a sudden hush over the crowd. "The city will now remain closed for the rest of the day. There is no guarantee that the city will open in the morning. I suggest if your business isn't urgent, you turn around and leave." Without another word the officer jumped from the wagon and started to walk away. Instantly, he was flooded with questions from the nearby merchants. The other soldiers cleared a path in the crowd and made it quite clear that there would be no further answers.

Alaric swore an oath under his breath as he returned to the carriage. He knew that there was no chance of making the city in time to purchase the mill. The owners would be bankrupt by the time he arrived and the mill demolished.

"What's the news?" asked Erhard as Alaric returned.

"Turn the carriage around." Alaric yelled, letting his disappointment get the better of him. "We're heading home. I want to make it out of here before everyone else gets the same idea."

It took Erhard only a couple of minutes to have the carriage turned around and heading back down the highway towards Quinaliac. The journey back to Arsiliac was not going to be enjoyable and the conversation with Bern even less.

Chapter 4: More Questions than Answers

It was late in the day when the carriage reined in outside Alaric's house. Rain clouds had formed overnight and had broken early in morning. The weather seemed to reflect his mood… dismal. Not wanting to ride out in the rain, Alaric had waited until the last minute to finish the trip. The rain, however, did not subside and only worsened as they left Quinaliac. The journey home was utterly miserable. All the time Alaric was thinking how he would explain to Bern about their deal.

The sun had almost set when Alaric opened his front door and walked inside. Even though his mind had been elsewhere, as soon as he entered the house he knew that something wasn't right. Dropping his bags Alaric looked for his sword before he realised that he had left it in the carriage. It was a common thing for him to do as he rarely used it.

His tension subsided when he saw a familiar face waiting for him, his initial reaction would be anger at the intrusion, but he only felt relieved.

"Good evening Alaric. I see that you have been out of town. I don't think that was the best of ideas. We have a lot to do and not much time to do it." Eldred greeted him with a warm smile. Even though his words were chastising there was no animosity.

Not really knowing why Alaric recounted the events of the past few days. He told of the dice and the attack in the night. When he had finished he felt as though a great weight had been lifted from his shoulders.

"It seems that your trip was more fortuitous than I thought. Things have started to move very quickly, both good and evil. More quickly than I would have liked though. It seems I am less prepared than I thought," Eldred continued with his mysterious speech.

"I still have no idea what you are talking about," this time Alaric felt more comfortable speaking.

"I believe that the reason you were not allowed into the city is that Nyrra has agents inside causing dissention. As far as the rumours go with an army building that is not true. Nyrra and the bulk of his army are still trapped in the Northern Wasteland and I believe his followers are building an army not so far away from any capital city. They are obviously trying to cause panic through deception. The fact that he is controlling the Duke is not a good sign. His power is reaching further than I would have hoped. Only the Gods know where else he is sowing the seeds of mistrust," Eldred looked past Alaric in thought when he finished.

Alaric waited, watching Eldred in his apparent state of trance. He wanted answers, but didn't want to disturb his reverie.

"Sorry," Eldred apologised as he snapped out of his daydream. "There is much to explain and much more that will remain unanswered."

"You said there was also good from the last couple of days. What did you mean?"

"In good time… firstly, when your parents died they left you some effects. Do you still have them?"

"I left the sword in the carriage this evening. I'm going to see Bern tomorrow so I will get it back then. The rest of it I have stored in the back room. My parents left me a note before they died. They told me to hide the chest and don't tell anyone about, don't even look inside. I did as they asked."

"Will you get the box? There is something you need to see."

Alaric hurried to where it was safely hidden. It was a small ornately carved mahogany chest. The light weight indicated there was not much inside. He had not thought about the chest since his parents had died and he had concealed it. Now, he wondered what it contained.

Eldred quickly took the chest from Alaric when he returned. He gently placed it on the coffee table between them. He took a good look at it before returning his attention to Alaric.

"Would you please open the chest and put the contents on the table?" Eldred asked. He seemed somewhat excited at the prospect.

Wondering why Eldred didn't just empty the contents himself Alaric slowly ran his finger over the smoothly cut design on the lid. He didn't know why he did so, but it seemed important. Slowly he flipped the small latch and surprisingly a soft click was heard, even though there was nothing in sight to make the sound. Eldred smiled at the querying look on Alaric's face.

Slowly as he lifted the lid Alaric peered inside the chest. The timber was polished to a smooth shine. Inside there were only two items. A golden ring with a small dark stone set in it and a small leather pouch with a pull string tied in a tight knot. "These were left to you by your parents," Eldred spoke, closely watching Alaric's reaction carefully.

"Yes, before they died."

"No. I mean your real parents. This ring belonged to your Father."

Before Eldred could continue Alaric interrupted him. "You knew my real parents? Why haven't you told me about them before? Tell me about them," desperation and urgency filled his voice.

"I'm sorry, but now is not the time. I shouldn't have said anything."

"What do you mean?" Alaric was becoming flustered. "Tell me about them. I need to know."

"In time you will learn about your parentage. We have so much to discuss and no time to spare," as Eldred spoke he raised his left hand and placed it in the air between his face and Alaric's. As the words came out of his mouth Alaric thought he saw a small shimmer in the air. When

Eldred finished speaking Alaric had forgotten what they were arguing about.

"Please open the pouch and drop the contents on the table."

Alaric was excited to see what was inside and quickly untied the knot and poured the contents out. Inside was a ruby stone encased in crystal. As he opened the pouch Alaric could have sworn he heard someone whispering behind him. He couldn't make out the words, but he knew someone was talking. Alaric felt a cold shiver run down his spine.

"This is what I need to speak to you about," Eldred pointed at the ruby stone, making a point not to touch it. "As I told you last time I was here, there were seven stones created by the God Kings." Alaric's eyes widened. "This is the Ruby Stone, the stone Nyrra used to destroy the God King Ruby."

Hearing the words, Alaric backed away from the stone in terror. At the same time, he was enthralled by its majesty. Alaric couldn't take his eyes from it and they glazed over as he peered into its centre.

"Be careful," the words quickly switched his attention back to Eldred. "The stone has enchantments that will ensnare you if you are not careful. The stone will try and take control of your mind. It will try and use you as its conduit to this world," the words sounded ridiculous, but Eldred's tone indicated that he was not joking.

"Is it alive?"

"That is a very good question and unfortunately one that I cannot answer. It has been debated many times whether or not the stones are in fact living creatures or just very powerful talismans. Some say yes, others say no, but no one can be certain for sure. The secret was lost with the seven Wizards. Only Nyrra can tell us now and I don't think he would be too keen for that conversation."

The most important question still remained unasked. The thought only just entered Alaric's head. "Why do I have the Ruby Stone?"

"Another good question," there was much Alaric needed to know and much he was not ready to hear. Eldred knew he had to step very carefully if he was going to lead Alaric in the right direction. "Unfortunately, it is one that will have to remain unanswered for now. What you need to know of is the prophecy."

Alaric snorted trying to suppress his laughter. He had heard religious fanatics in the city crying out about the prophecy and the end of the world. Alaric felt sorry for them, believing so fervently in something that was so ridiculous.

"I have seen the men and women on the street and listened to their rambling enough times to know that there is not one all-powerful prophecy commanding my life," Eldred sat patiently waiting for Alaric to finish before he started to explain.

"The problem is not with the Prophecy itself. The problem is over the years, with it being copied over and over again, the ideas have been changed. Some versions have even been tampered with to suit the needs of the writers. The fourth High Chancellor had the Prophecy rewritten to make him look like the saviour of the world. Unfortunately, for him, his crusade ended with his bloody death within a month of leaving Castalia. His followers soon realised that he was not the man they had thought he was. The entire army fled the battlefield in disgrace, with a nice amount of embarrassment. The army's Generals were promptly beheaded before they arrived back to Castalia." Eldred watched the expression on Alaric's face very closely. "So you see there are many different versions out there, but I can guarantee that there is only one true Prophecy."

"Well, that still doesn't explain anything."

"Needless to say, when studying the Prophecy is it very hard to decipher the truth from the knowledge. A lifetime could be spent studying and not figure out half of it. Anyway, to get to the point, here is what I've gathered." Eldred paused for a moment as he tried to recall the passage of the Prophecy he needed to recite. "The return of evil shall bring about the birth of good. The family shall be torn asunder. The Father of Evil shall battle the Son of Good. On a mountain of fire shall the fate of the world be decided. For good or for evil, one shall live and one shall die." Eldred waited for the words to sink in. "This is the main passage that I need to discuss. The return of evil is the first part and easy to decipher. Nyrra is the Father of Evil and his return marks the first part of this stage of the Prophecy. The wheels are now in motion and cannot be stopped."

Alaric gasped as he realised what Eldred was saying. The words did not seem true, but there was something that made sense. Even though he knew what Eldred was about to say, he wanted to hear it.

"We believe that you are the 'Son of Good', The Chosen One, who will lead us into the light, to quote another verse. I have dedicated my life to following the Prophecy and ever since we got word that Nyrra was breaking free, I've been looking for the Chosen One." Eldred twisted the truth a little, but only because he knew Alaric wouldn't be able to accept the whole story.

His ability to accept what Eldred was saying surprised both of them. Normally Alaric would have taken the tall tale with a grain of salt and then dismissed it, but this time something was different. As the words came out of Eldred's mouth he knew they were true. It was almost like his life was finally starting to make sense. There had always been something missing.

"Okay. I don't know why, but I believe what you are saying. What happens now?" It was Eldred's turn to be shocked with Alaric's words.

"In five days, we leave for the east. You mustn't tell anyone you are leaving. We believe that there is at least one person in town who is an agent of Evil. Nyrra also knows the Prophecy and knows that you are reaching your potential. Obviously, he doesn't yet know that you are the Chosen One or else he would have made an attempt on your life."

"Why do you think there will be an attempt on my life? Nyrra doesn't know who I am?"

"We believe that Nyrra also knows the truth behind the prophecy. One of the earlier passages gives a vague reference to where the Chosen One would be found. The land that was mentioned is over a thousand years gone. Its general area is central Remidia. That is how I found you." Eldred knew he had to be careful. If he explained too many inconsequential facts, then he would have to explain things Alaric was not yet prepared to hear.

"You keep saying "we". Who are We?" Alaric brushed off the idea that someone was out to kill him. He had a million questions and knew he would only have time to have a few of them answered.

"We are a small group who follow the Prophecy and try a make sure that Good wins over Evil. There are fundamental flaws, however; it doesn't tell the whole story, just parts of it. If the Prophecy is not fulfilled, then there will be universal chaos. This works on both sides, good and evil. The only problem is that Nyrra wants chaos, so it would make his job easier if the Prophecy isn't fulfilled. Already the odds are stacked against us, but we have two major advantages," Eldred paused again. "The first one is the fact that he doesn't know where you are and the second is that you possess the Ruby Stone, the main source of his power."

"But if the stone is the source of his power, then why don't we just destroy it?"

"We don't know if the Seven Stones can be destroyed. Some say the fires of the Cauldron Mountain would melt them. Another belief is that the breath of the Dragon Lords could destroy the stones. In time you will learn to use the stone as well as other abilities," Eldred bit his tongue, knowing he had already said too much.

"What abilities? How can I learn to use the stone?"

"I'm sorry. I should not have said anything," Eldred raised his hand as he spoke. Alaric thought he saw the air shimmer again. It was only there for a second before everything returned to normal. When it did, Alaric wasn't sure what he had been thinking about or why things seemed so odd.

"Now where was I?" It was a testing question.

"Possibly destroying the Ruby stone in the Cauldron Mountain." Alaric was sure that was last thing Eldred had said.

"Ah yes. And some say that the Dragon Lords could destroy the stones with their fiery breath." Eldred paused to examine the expression on Alaric's face. It was obvious that he had not remembered that Eldred had only told him about the Dragons just moments before.

"Dragons? They are just stories for children!"

"Well that's not true, although no one has seen a dragon in over a thousand years. They did exist at one point in time, but that's not relevant at the moment. We have a race against time now to get you to the temple deep within the Cauldron Mountain before Nyrra does."

Alaric knew that there was something very important that Eldred was leaving out. Something about his past that he desperately needed to know.

Sensing Alaric's reverie Eldred started to speak again. "In five days' time, I will come for you. We will travel to a small community within the Darkened Woods. From there we will decide our best course of action. I fear that we will have more to do than just get you safely to the mountain." Eldred's words had their desired effects. Alaric had forgotten his line of thinking. "You cannot tell anyone that you are leaving. You must continue your duties as normal. This is vital to your immediate safety."

There was nothing Alaric could say. He knew what Eldred said was the truth. He had always known his life was leading to this moment. It was as if Eldred's words had unlocked something that had been safely hidden away.

Seeing the look on his face, Eldred knew the words had sunk in. Alaric now knew his destiny was far from the small town of Arsiliac. In five days, they would start on the quest of a lifetime. The fate of the Seven Kingdoms would hinge on their success, which also depended upon Eldred's accurate deciphering of the Prophecy.

Happy with what he had accomplished, Eldred stood and let himself out. Alaric remained in his chair and watched the old man leave. Even though the words made sense, they had not yet fully registered. Although he knew it was his destiny, it meant the life he had created would be completely left behind. He could not even tell anyone to look after his business whilst he was away. That was not the worst thing. He would miss his childhood friend. He wished he could say goodbye to Bern before he left. The last conversation he was going to have was the bad news that their business deal had failed. That was his last thought before he went to bed.

***

Bern had sat with his mouth open for the last half an hour. He had listened without being able to speak. His life had been so simple before the old man had walked into his house that afternoon. He had claimed to be a friend of Alaric's, yet Bern knew he didn't have any friends in town. He seemed harmless enough and before he had a chance to react, Eldred had already pushed his way into the house.

Previously his life revolved around his farm and family. If the weather was true and his family well then all was good in his life. He prayed to the Goddess of earth and nature, as did all the farmers in the district. Beyond that, he did not believe in greater powers within the world. In one short conversation, that had all changed.

Unlike with Alaric, Eldred had to use a slight amount of magic to help Bern believe his words. He wished he could have saved himself the time, but he could not bend Bern's will with magic alone. The prophecy had to play itself out and all the players had to make their own decisions.

"So you see that you have a pivotal role to play in the prophecy. The fate of the world rests as much on you as it does on Alaric." Without his friend, Alaric would not make it to the Cauldron Mountain. This was one of the easiest passages in the prophecy for Eldred to decipher. If Alaric had just one more friend, then it would have taken far longer to ascertain the person in question.

"I see," it was the first words Bern had spoken since Eldred had entered his house. "There is much for me to think about. Obviously I have my family and I can't just up and leave them."

"And you cannot take them with you."

"Yes, I see," was all Bern could say, still lost in thought.

"Someone will come for you in five days. Don't say anything to anyone outside your family and make sure they don't say anything, not even to Alaric," as he said the words Eldred carefully wove another spell making it impossible for Bern to retell the story.

Without saying goodbye, Eldred stood and left the farmhouse. He knew there was no point in pleasantries. Bern was now so engrossed in the information that he didn't even notice him leave. What would he say to his wife?

Like Alaric, Bern had known this day was coming. He had felt a strange pull over the last few months. Something dragging him away from his mundane life, which had previously been all he had wanted.

Chapter 5: A Short Goodbye

The next day Alaric woke with his head swimming with ideas. He had hoped the night before had just been a dream, but he knew it wasn't. The images were too vivid for it to be anything but the truth. Continuing his normal life for the next five days would be difficult. It surprised him to realise that he would miss more people than just Bern and his family. Myria, for one, was someone he had come to depend on. He had been a huge asset ever since he had started working for him.

When Alaric left his house for work he knew that he could not tell anyone he was leaving. There was so much he had to do before he left. All the loose ends would have to be tied up. It was going to be a hard task without telling Myria.

Three days passed slowly. Alaric's mood decreased considerably as his leaving date became closer. Through politeness, Myria did not push Alaric for the reason why he was so distracted. He knew the deal had fallen through in Zenza City and figured that was the reason for his despair. On the fourth day, however, he had had enough of Alaric's sulking.

"What's wrong with you this week?" Myria failed to hide his annoyance. "I know about the deal in Zenza City. We've had deals go bad before and you've never been like this."

"Nothing." Alaric didn't even look up from his paperwork as he replied. He was just about finished with all the loose ends.

"Don't treat me like a fool, I've known you long enough to realise when something's wrong."

Hearing the words snapped Alaric out of his reverie. He felt a sudden compulsion to tell Myria the truth. The stress of having to leave and not tell anyone became apparent.

Without thinking of the consequences Alaric started to explain why he was upset. In the back of his mind he could hear the words Eldred had told him, but he knew Myria and trusted him. It wasn't until he finished speaking that he realised what he had said. The look of shock on Myria's face was to be expected.

"You can't tell anyone. There may be someone in town looking to kill me." Alaric's heart started to beat faster, waiting desperately for Myria to respond.

"Of course not, I understand completely the risk you're taking," Myria seemed lost in thought as he spoke. After a moment of reflection Myria spoke again. "Why don't you go home? There's not much point in you staying here. There's nothing that I can't handle."

He still had a lot to organize at home before he left and Myria would be able to carry on without him. He was glad he had someone like Myria, it would definitely make his life easier.

"I think you're right. I'm sure you'll be alright to keep the place going without me." Alaric stood up abruptly when he finished speaking.

The sudden movement took Myria by surprise. They said a quick goodbye and since that the idea was in his head, Alaric just wanted to go home and finish packing. Myria was just as glad when he saw Alaric leave. He smiled to himself when the office was empty. His fortunes had finally turned around. He had always had reservations when he arrived in Arsiliac. He thought that he was going to be left behind in life, but now he knew that he would be living a life of luxury soon enough. The smile broadened on his face as he put his feet up on the desk and leaned back in his chair, but his moment of glory was short lived. He knew he had a lot to do in a short period of time if he was going to succeed. Luckily he had been preparing for this day, even though he believed it was never going to come.

The smile broadened on his face as he raced out of the office.

If Alaric had of been aware of his surroundings he would have noticed Myria leaving the office in a hurry, however his current thoughts were so deep he didn't even notice the people walking past him.

Even though he left work early, it was still late in the day when he arrived home. It was the last time he would walk into his house. It had been his home his entire life. He could not imagine living anywhere else. His fondest memories of his parents revolved around the house. He could remember playing in the sitting room with Bern as a child whilst their parents discussed matters in the kitchen. There had been a lot of good times and that was all about to end. When he left the next day he had a bad feeling he would not be returning. The feeling sat in his stomach as he continued to pack his bags.

He didn't know exactly what he needed to take. One thing Eldred had omitted was what he needed to bring and what was going to be supplied. His plan was to try and take as many of his possessions as possible. Once he had left, and it was known throughout the town, someone would appropriate his house and whatever was left inside. Of course, he would have claim if he ever returned, but that was not the point. When he had finally finished, the moon was high was in the sky and he had filled all the bags he had. He had packed one bag of essentials and then filled the rest with everything he could think of. The last thing he packed was his sword and the chest that his parents had left him. Just as he placed them down he heard the sound of movement coming from somewhere in the house.

Panic was his initial reaction. Eldred's warning of an assassin in town rushed back to him. Slowly he reached down and lifted the sword by the scabbard. Pausing to listen he could no longer hear any noise. Waiting in silence Alaric couldn't breathe, afraid the sound would give him away.

Only when he was about to faint did he let the air fill his lungs. After taking two deep breaths, he concluded that he must have been imagining things. It had been a long day and was just tired. Replacing his sword Alaric started to make his way towards the bedroom, walking into the hallway when his heart jumped.

"What are you doing here?" Alaric's voice relaxed when he saw who it was. "You made me jump."

"There was something I needed to speak to you about before you left," Myria's voice was very soothing.

A sudden bolt of lightning lit the hallway, as it did Alaric thought he saw a shadow through the doorway. The inevitable clap of thunder was followed by a gust of wind. It seemed that there was a storm on the way. It seemed odd as the weather had been fine all day.

Again Alaric had a strange feeling of dread. Something deep inside told him not to trust Myria. The entire situation seemed wrong.

"Where is it Alaric?" his voice remained calm and soothing.

"Where is what?"

Myria took a step forward and as he did Alaric took a step back. There was nothing threatening about the gesture, but Alaric was starting to believe that Myria could not be trusted. It was as if he could sense the evil coming from within. "You know what I want. We can do this the easy way or we can do it the hard way." Myria's tone was starting to change.

For the first time Alaric truly saw Myria towards the other end of the hallway. His usual soft features had turned hard. His hair was now a darker shade of brown hanging loosely above his shoulders. His dark skin was now paler than it had been before. The man before him looked a lot different to the man he had come to trust.

"What are you talking about?" Alaric knew he hadn't mentioned the Ruby stone when they had spoken earlier in the day.

With that thought, it finally dawned on him who Myria really was. It could only be by pure chance that Myria was working for him, or was it? Alaric knew he should have listened to Eldred. There had been no reason for him to tell Myria he was leaving. The more he thought about it the more he realised there were many occasions when he revealed more to Myria than he had originally intended. Fear suddenly rushed through his body.

Slowly Alaric started to walk backwards. He knew there was no chance of escaping forward. Even if managed he knew there was at least one more man waiting for him. The only chance he had would be out the back.

"Stop moving," Myria called, drawing his sword.

Chancing a glance, Alaric found his sword and the chest were sitting amongst the rest of his bags. If nothing else, he needed to get those two items before leaving. If Myria truly was an agent of evil, then he would only want the stone.

Taking a deep breath Alaric dashed into the room. As he moved Myria let out a sharp whistle. Quickly collecting his sword in his right hand and the chest under his arm he started for the door. Before he could get half way across the room a heavy set man blocked his path. The man stood a foot taller than him and brandished a large cudgel.

There was no way for Alaric to draw his sword without dropping the chest and he was not about to relinquish it. Even with the sword in its scabbard, it still made a reasonable weapon, although he had no delusions about being his ability to best the hired thug.

Myria had moved and there was a third man standing behind him. There was no escape. Even if he was able to beat one of his attackers, the other two would easily overcome him.

The many bags on the floor gave him his one advantage. As much as it hindered Alaric, it also didn't allow enough room for all his attackers to advance at once. If he was lucky, he might survive with his life intact.

The large man standing behind Myria moved to get past. With a slight flick of his wrist, Myria indicated for him to remain behind. Drawing a small blade, he started to advance towards Alaric, the other two men safely guarding any chance of escape. If he was going to get out alive, then he would need to overcome Myria. He was sure that it wasn't going to be as easy as it sounded. Myria deliberately moved towards him. Holding the chest tightly Alaric raised his sword, ready to strike out.

Just as Myria came within striking distance a high pitched whistle came from the back of the hallway. The man standing in the doorway sunk to the ground, his eyes rolled up into his head and his limp body made a deep thud as it hit the floor.

Alaric was the first to recover from the initial shock. He had no idea why the man had fallen, but now he thought he might have a good chance of escaping. Taking the advantage Alaric swung his sword as hard as he could towards Myria's unprotected head. Myria's attention was not as diverted as Alaric had expected. Ducking out of the way, he made his own counter move. Slashing with his dagger he caught Alaric, making a deep cut on his arm. Dark red blood appeared quickly on his white, silk shirt. Alaric cried out in pain, but did not lessen his grip. If Myria was able to counter his attack so easily then Alaric doubted he was going to stand a chance.

Standing in the doorway was someone Alaric had never seen before. He had the shape and form of a man, but there was something different. Only a quick glance was enough for Alaric to realise the stories he had heard where in fact true. His saviour was tall and lean with golden hair and blue eyes. His ears were slightly pointed on the tips, which was the giveaway trait. There was no doubt that this was an Elf, a race which Alaric had previously thought was only myth.

The Elf had aimed a blow dart towards Myria, it was clear now what had made the sharp whistle. As he fired the dart there was another whistle. Myria, unlike his cohort, was prepared for the attack and was able to back away as it flew through the air towards his throat. Even though the dart didn't hit its mark it had a good effect. The quick backwards movement caused Myria to trip on one of Alaric's bags causing him to fall.

Not wanting to test the remaining strength in his arm Alaric jumped over his bags and made his way towards the elf. A cold sweat had appeared on his brow as the pain from the gash finally started to take effect. The blood was still flowing freely, but there was no time to bind the wound.

As Alaric reached the doorway Myria was back on his feet. The remaining assailant was now half way across the room and ready to take matters into his own hands. The elf ushered Alaric past him before sending another dart into the room. Not waiting to see if it hit its mark the elf followed quickly after him.

Outside, the cool night breeze was very refreshing against Alaric's face which was now drenched in sweat. He was breathing heavily as he raced away from his home, his right arm hanging limply at his side. The vice like grip he had on his sword was the only feeling left in his arm that wasn't in excruciating pain. He doubted he would be able to make it very far before he lost consciousness. He was already feeling light headed.

There was only one way he could see himself staying alive throughout the night and that was to outrun his attackers to the northern edge of town. The small forest to the north had enough hiding places for them to lose their followers. There would be no safety in the streets of Arsiliac.

The elf continued to run on ahead, every now and then stopping to send a dart or two back towards Myria. The stop-start attacks were enough to allow the injured Alaric to keep ahead of the other two. The darts were shot quickly and easily missed their marks, but they were enough to make their pursuers falter.

Just before they reached the edge of the forest the elf struck home. The shot was rushed and not even aimed properly, but blind luck was on their side. Myria's partner sunk to the ground as soon as he was struck. The poison tipped darts were not enough to kill a man, but were enough to knock him out instantly for a good five to six hours.

Myria cursed loudly as they disappeared into the forest. He knew there was no point in following them past the tree line. It would not take long for the elf to disappear from view. He cursed again. From the story Alaric had told him earlier he thought the man would be alone. He had clearly miscalculated. He should have known there would have been someone watching the house. There was one thing that stayed his anger. He knew that they would be traveling to the east and that meant they would have to exit the forest at some point. Myria would regroup and wait for them in the morning. As much as he didn't want to take the risk, he made a calculated guess that they would spend the night in the safety of the forest. He didn't know if the two with him where dead or alive and for that matter he didn't care. He had many men left secreted around the town. He would not take anything for granted. Every inch of the tree line would be covered by the time the sun rose.

Stopping about twenty paces from the forest, Myria swore for one final time. There was nothing he could do now. Panting to regain his breath, he watched the darkness fall before him. One good thing would come out of the night. The Cursed One was finally revealed and it was he who had found him. The night's failure would not come to bare when he had the Cursed One dead at his feet and the Master's stone in his possession. Then he would sit on the Great Lords right hand side for eternity. That would be his reward.

All would be revealed in the morning. If Alaric had made his way to the Eastern Woods, then he would be long gone by now. Soon enough it would all be over. Myria was rather disappointed that the Cursed One didn't put up much more of a fight, he had expected more. A broad smile crossed his face as he walked away from the forest.

***

"Hello Alaric, I'm Palentonal," the elf introduced himself when they stopped.

They walked for about half an hour before Palentonal was sure they were not being followed. There was not much light in the woods making the going slow. Palentonal found them a nice sheltered hollow for the night. He was sure Myria wouldn't follow, but didn't want to second guess the stupidity of the men.

A cool breeze blew through the forest, but didn't reach them in the hollow. It was small, only a half a dozen paces wide. As soon as they stopped moving Alaric collapsed, the sword dropped from his hand. His arm was drenched in blood whilst the rest of his body was drenched in sweat. He tried to focus on the elf, but all he could see was blackness.

"Are you feeling okay?' Palentonal asked as he concentrated on the darkness around him. The night was usually still.

Alaric tried to reply, but the words would not come, the best he could manage was a stifled moan as his head went limp. There was no energy left in his body and if it wasn't for the tree trunk he was leaning against he would have been flat on the ground.

Palentonal would have liked to check for any sign of pursuit, but he knew now that he needed the start a fire. He would need light to check Alaric's wound and possibly the heat to cauterise it. There was no point hiding from murderers if the person you are protecting dies anyway.

There was plenty of dry timber on the forest floor and it was not long before Palentonal had a small fire burning in the middle of the hollow. For the first time since they had left the house, Palentonal could see Alaric. The sight made his heart sink. Alaric's skin was deathly pale and covered in a cold sweat. The sleeve of his shirt was completely soaked in blood. His eyes remained only half open, an extreme effort in itself. They stared blankly towards the fire and Palentonal couldn't tell if he still conscious. The only sign that he was still alive was the slow laboured breathing and the weak movement of his chest.

Quickly Palentonal cut the sleeve away from Alaric's arm with a small knife he kept attached to his belt. Palentonal cleaned away the coagulated blood as best he could with water from his pouch; he saved as much as he could for drinking. Alaric would need to replace all the fluids he had lost.

With the wound as clean as Palentonal could get it he used Alaric's remaining sleeve to make a bandage. He decided not to cauterise, but to make a quick poultice instead. With the small pouch of herbs he carried, he was able to make a mixture that would help the healing of Alaric's wound and keep out infection.

Alaric cried out in pain as Palentonal attached the bandage. The herbs in the poultice caused a pain to shoot through his entire body. With that outcry, Alaric finally lost consciousness.

The sudden noise sent Palentonal's nerves on edge. If they were being followed, then there was no doubt they would be found now. The scream was a locator and the fire a nice little beacon. Quickly rising to his feet Palentonal left Alaric in the hollow.

The forest was dark and still, as if expecting his presence. His elvish eyes didn't take long to accustom to the darkness after leaving the light of the fire. It was less than a year ago since Palentonal had left his home in the Northern Woods, as it was commonly known. Lynethlas was its ancient name, but few outside of the elves remembered it. His life had been so much easier then. He was young, as far as elves were concerned, not even one hundred years old. Although he had only spent a year in the Hunters, he had enjoyed his new lifestyle. He had previously been part of the Gatherers, where all children began helping the tribe.

Palentonal's parents had been part of the ruling council. Eventually, Palentonal would join them on the council and it was important that he be trained in all the duties of his fellow elves. His life was all set out in front of him until one day, a strange traveller came. By design or pure chance, it was Palentonal's day to sit on the council and listen to what was being discussed. Even while the man was speaking, Palentonal knew that it would be his duty to leave, to lead his tribe into battle. He knew that this was the right thing to do. He had always known that one day he would leave his home, although it wasn't until that day he knew the reason why.

The ruling council did not agree with what the man was saying. Although Palentonal knew every word he spoke was the truth, the council refused to believe. They refused to let Palentonal speak during the meeting and, afterwards when he requested to leave, they refused him again.

The man pleaded his case to the council for over a week before he left without any success. Palentonal was the only one who watched him leave the forest. There was sadness in his heart that he could not explain. That feeling festered over the next month until he could deny it no longer. He knew the council would not change their minds, so, in the middle of the night, he packed a small bag, took his blow dart, sword, knife and bow and arrows. He knew that he would need all his weapons for the journey and left, not knowing if he'd ever return to his home again.

Not surprisingly he found the man waiting patiently for him. There was a look of sorrow on his face as he watched Palentonal leave his home. He had hoped the council would have helped, but he knew deep down it wasn't going to happen and Palentonal would have to bear the burden alone.

Palentonal spent the next ten months travelling with the man, gaining more companions along the way. He learned the ways of the outside world and that there was more to life than what he had been taught. At first the world outside seemed cruel and scary but eventually Palentonal found beauty. He had learned to fear for the first time in his life, the sanctity of his previous existence was now closed to him. He would not be able to return until his mission was complete.

The woods gave Palentonal a sense of calm. Even though the trees were foreign, they still reassured him. The fear that he had initially felt had completely disappeared; it had been that long since he had been this close to trees that he had forgotten about their protective nature. He relaxed considerably when he realised they would not let their attackers sneak up on them.

His faith in the trees was not absolute. Returning to the hollow, Palentonal made himself comfortable, but did not sleep. If there was an attack he wanted as much warning as possible. He watched Alaric in the dim light of the fire; his flesh was still pale and covered in sweat. Palentonal wondered if he was asleep or in a coma. He hoped the dream world would keep Alaric safe during the night.

Chapter 6: A Strange Night

Waking suddenly, Alaric opened his mouth to scream, but nothing came out. The small fire had long burned itself out and not even a hint of smoke remained. The night was still dark, although the light of the moon gave off an eerie glow. With a sudden shock, Alaric realised that Palentonal was no longer in the hollow. He was completely alone and looked down at the bandage covering his right arm. The pain had completely gone and most of his strength had returned. Alaric wondered at the medicine the elf had applied; it should have taken over a week for his arm to recover. Any ill effects from the knife wound were now completely gone. His skin had returned to its original pigment and was free of sweat. He stood up to test the strength in his body. There was nothing inhibiting him, which seemed a little strange; he thought there should have been some side-effects from his injury.

Suddenly he heard the sound of a voice calling his name. "Alarrriiicc!" It was very distant and he could only just make out the words as they drifted towards him. It was not a voice that he recognised. He was sure it was that of a woman and it sounded like she was in trouble. The voice came again, more desperate than before, but just as softly. It seemed to echo around him, making it impossible to get an accurate direction of its origin.

Alaric strained his ears and moved around the hollow trying to pinpoint the desperate pleas. As he did his left ankle lodged itself in a tree root causing him to trip and fall. As he fell he did not stop, instead he kept rolling and rolling down the side of a hill.

The fall didn't hurt, yet it made his head groggy, he had no memory of the hollow being on the side of hill, yet there was a lot he couldn't recall from that night. The light from the moon clearly showed him that he was wrong.

The voice called to him again. This time it was a lot closer, though the pitch and tone remained the same. The cries for help haunted his soul and he strained to listened, he still did not recognise the voice… he was mesmerised by it. Slowly he started to walk.

Each time he heard the voice it seemed to be getting nearer. The voice still whispered on the wind. It was as if the closer he came the further away it sounded; that thought didn't make any sense. Alaric paused and tried to concentrate. He started to reflect the panic in her voice in his inability to find her. The sound bounced off every tree and surrounded him.

As he stared into the darkness a small ball of yellow light appeared in the distance. He could only just make it out through the trees, which seemed to part to make a pathway for him. As the light appeared he   was finally able to pinpoint where the sound was coming from. It was coming from the light.

"Hello! Are you there?" Alaric called.

As the words disappeared into the night, the light started to shimmer. It looked as though it was starting to move. As he watched, waiting for a reply, the light started to grow in intensity. Just before it was too late, Alaric dove out of the way as a ball of yellow flame came spinning towards him. The flame exploded against a tree a dozen paces behind him and within seconds the tree was completely engulfed. The fire did not move onto any one of the other trees; it simply turned the tree to ash.

When Alaric picked himself up from the ground, he found that there was enough light for him to see. The sight in front of him was terrifying. The creature standing before him, now not more than twenty paces away, was the largest he had ever seen. The giant scaled reptilian body had two large leathery wings on its back. Alaric estimated the length of the body to be at least thirty feet starting with a head resembling that of a giant horned serpent and ending in a large pointy tail. Its legs were short and stumpy, not accustomed to quick ground movement. The creature was obviously designed for flight. There was no doubt in his mind that this was a dragon. He had heard stories of them before, but didn't really believe that they existed, but now there could be no doubt. The dragon studied Alaric. Ever since its arrival, the woman had stopped calling for help; he hoped that in his rush to find her, he hadn't caused her death. It was that thought that stopped him running for his life.

As if the thought came to life, the woman's voice came again. This time he was able to see where it was coming from. He could clearly see a woman hiding in a small cave to the left of the dragon. Then he realised that she had not been calling for help, but calling to warn him. Now she was hurrying him to join her in the cave, although he could not see her face he knew that she was beautiful.

Before Alaric knew what he was doing, he had his sword drawn and took a defensive stance as the dragon slowly waddled towards him. There was something extremely odd about what he was doing. He knew he should be running for cover, but for some reason, staying and attacking seemed to be the right thing to do.

"So you think you can defeat me?" the low guttural voice came from the dragon.

"I do not want to kill you, but I will if I must." Alaric's voice didn't have an ounce of fear in it, although he was scared to death.

A noise came from deep within the dragon. Alaric could only assume that it was laughter as what seemed to be a smile appeared on its face.

"You are very brave, although I should have expected nothing less. I almost feel sorry for having to kill you," the dragon paused, "but what sort of dragon would I be if I let you go?"

"You can win Alaric, have faith in your power," the voice came to him again.

Alaric realised he was standing no more than ten feet away from the giant beast. He could feel the heat coming from its breath. There was now nowhere for him to run. His only escape was to defeat the dragon. Although the idea should have seemed to be a stupid one, be began to laugh when he realised that it wasn't.

There was a sudden sense of understanding between the dragon and Alaric. The dragon knew that there was no escape for its prey, yet there was something different. He knew the scent of fear, the scent of death. There was nothing, only calm. It was a feeling new to the dragon. Sure there had been brave men come to slay the dragon before, but they all had the scent of fear. There was never anyone like this before. There had been fear at the start. He could sense it before he could sense the prey. Now there was nothing. The dragon was curious at his new feeling. In over a thousand years, he had never hunted something that had not felt utter fear on his approach.

Alaric was now the one to be surprised. He had expected the dragon to attack without remorse; he would if the situation had been reversed. Now he was also faced with a strange situation, one that he had not been prepared to encounter. There was something rewarding about the fact that the dragon had not attacked and now seemed confused. For an instant, Alaric believed that he was not going to die.

That moment of hesitation was enough for dragon to react. As much as he was unsure about the creature in front of him, he knew that its slight indecision could have been his downfall. A small rumble, which could have been called a laugh, came from somewhere within the dragon. If only the creature knew how close it had come to defeating him. Now all that was left was the killing blow. Fire would be a suitable death.

A sudden thought came to Alaric and a smile appeared on his face. He now had an idea how to defeat the dragon; all he needed was a little time. He hoped that it would follow his lead. Without waiting for another idea, Alaric started to run towards the cave where the woman was waiting. He knew that he wouldn't make it; in fact, he was banking on the fact that he would not.

The dragon smiled as a scent of fear wafted into his nose. So the creature was not as brave as he thought. Now he would have some fun. This would be a good night. The taste of death would be all the sweeter due to the extra effort.

Flicking its tail, the dragon knocked Alaric off his feet. Prepared for the attack, Alaric rolled as he hit the ground, avoiding any major damage. The blow was enough to wind him, Alaric stayed down knowing that it would buy him enough time to complete his task.

Disappointed in the creature for remaining on the ground, the dragon decided to do something about it. Gripping the limp body in his front talon, he lifted the creature up onto its feet, resting it against a tree to keep it from falling back to ground. He had expected more of a fight from this one, but a death was a death and it had been a long time between meals.

The jaws of the giant creature slowly opened, its teeth dripping with an oily liquid. A forked tongue slithered out of it mouth and moved towards Alaric. It stopped inches short and flicked in front of his face, slopping him with saliva. The extra fuel would cook him a lot quicker and this was the dragon's preferred method of preparing its food.

A deep hiss came from the dragon's mouth, and with it came a heat that almost ignited the saliva covering Alaric's face. Alaric opened his eyes for the first time since he was knocked to the ground. The first sight he saw, although it was the one that he expected, almost scared him out of his plan. All he could see was the mouth of the great beast. Past the razor sharp teeth and the forked tongue, a small flame danced at the back of its throat. The flame grew in its intensity before it was suddenly snuffed out. The smile that appeared of Alaric's face was outdone by the screech that came from the great dragon.

At that instant Alaric knew he had won. Two tremendous wings spread from the dragon's back. A great gust of wind knocked Alaric to the ground as the dragon lifted itself into the air. The dragon's scales glistened multicoloured in the moonlight.

As soon as the dragon was high in the sky, a great line of flame blew out of its mouth. The sudden light forced Alaric into motion. His legs wobbled as his tried to run towards the cave. He was still groggy and just before he reached its safety and the mysterious woman, the dragon landed heavily on the ground. The dragon had completely blocked his path. There was no way for him to reach the cave without disposing of the dragon and he didn't think that same trick was going to work twice.

"You will pay for what you have done," the low guttural tone indicating that the dragon was not used to speaking.

As if in slow motion, a ball of flame shot towards him. With each moment, Alaric could feel the heat intensifying. Only one thought ran through his head: it had all been for nothing!

Suddenly Alaric sat bolt upright. The mid-morning sun was shining through the trees. The small hollow was disserted except for a small fire which had nearly completely burnt out. The sudden movement caused a fierce pain to shoot up his arm and into his head. The pain made his head swim and made him sink back to the ground. He knew that if he had tried to stay upright then he would have lost whatever was remaining in his stomach. Sweat still covered his entire body.

"It looks as though you've had a difficult night. The poultice I gave you can have that effect." Palentonal appeared and it took all of Alaric's energy to lift his head to see. "Let's have a look and see if it has had the desired effect."

As Palentonal checked the wound, Alaric realised that the dragon had just been a dream. He had never had a dream feel so real. Even now that he knew it had been a dream, yet it still seemed as though it had really happened. He let out a small cry of pain when Palentonal removed the bandage.

"Excellent. See, it's almost healed." Palentonal rolled his arm over so Alaric could see the result of his poultice. The wound, which should have taken over two weeks to heal and need stitching, was now almost completely healed, but Alaric was still suffering the effects.

"What was that?" Alaric speech was slow and slurred.

"The herb can have a hallucinogenic effect. It should have worn off during the night, but it still seems to be having an effect on you." Palentonal watched Alaric carefully as he spoke. "It shouldn't be too long before you're back to normal." Alaric wasn't sure whether he said it for his benefit or the elf's.

Although Palentonal truly believed that it would take Alaric no more than an hour or two to recover from the effects of the herbs, that was not going to be the case. Shortly after the sun had reached its pinnacle and started its decline, Alaric was still flat out on the ground. The sweat had continued to emit from his body without relenting. Palentonal had still had to feed him water as he was too weak to drink himself.

"Something isn't right," Palentonal commented after he had eaten his lunch.

"You're telling me." Alaric's voice was so hoarse that Palentonal had to strain his ears to hear.

"I'm going to have to find a stream or a river. I'm out of water and it doesn't look like you are going anywhere any time soon."

Alaric strained to watch Palentonal leave the hollow. He was glad to be alone. He never liked people around him when he was sick. He let his eyelids droop and tried to make himself as comfortable as possible on the hard ground. His breathing was heavy and laboured. His lungs struggled to fill with each breath and he wished the effects of the herbs would wear off.

It didn't take long for Palentonal to return. He had found a small brook not fifteen minutes away from where they were camped. When he returned he found Alaric barely conscious. Even after he poured some water down Alaric's throat, there was still no improvement. Palentonal was starting to get worried. The herbs shouldn't have had this much effect on him. There had to be something else.

"Let me have another look at the wound," Palentonal spoke quickly, now realising that he might have made a fatal mistake.

Alaric could only manage a grunt. It was all he could do to keep breathing. Palentonal didn't really expect a reply. He slowly peeled back the bandage. The wound was almost completely healed and Alaric should have recovered. This time Palentonal took a closer look, and found what he had previously glazed over. There was a small green tinge on the inside of the scar. The poultice had covered the tell-tale marks that Myria's blade had been poisoned.

"Damn it," Palentonal swore loudly.

The sudden curse made Alaric stir. His eyes slowly opened to look at the elf. His eyes were so bloodshot that there was no longer any white. Although Alaric was looking at him, he know he could not see anything.

If the wound had not been treated, then the effects of the poison would have been easier to identify. Now it could be any one of a hundred poisons. There was no way for Palentonal to treat him from their current position. All he could do was attempt to counter the symptoms.

"Chew this," said Palentonal as he produced a piece of root.

Palentonal placed the root inside Alaric's mouth. Slowly Alaric started to chew. The expression on his face showed the extreme effort that it was taking. He managed to swallow just before his throat almost completely closed over. Alaric's body went completely still. Although he could not move he still remained conscious.

Alaric's condition seemed to be worsen. All Palentonal could see was a limp, lifeless body in front of him. He had been too late and the Chosen One was now dead. He slumped to the ground and let his head rest against his hands.

"Why look so sad," the transition from complete immobility to complete functionality happened in the blink of an eye.

Slowly lifting his head, Palentonal was startled and relieved to see Alaric sitting upright. The sweat was almost completely gone and the colour had returned to his skin. His eyes were no longer bloodshot and his breathing had returned to normal. There seemed to be no side effects from the remaining poison.

"Thank the Gods that you are still alive. I thought for a moment that you had died."

"I feel fine. Whatever it was that you fed me, did the trick," and to prove his point Alaric jumped up onto his feet.

"No you're not, the jongra plant root will mask the effect of the poison and slow the reaction for a while. The poison will still be eating away at your body. If we don't get you cured by the time the effect of the jongra root wears off, then it will be too late. I had hoped to use the cover of night to escape the forest, but it seems as though have no choice. We need to reach the others."

Alaric's senses suddenly came alive. He could feel the forest growing around him. The cool air blew through the trees from the east. Small leaves rustled on the forest floor and an old buck could be heard in the distance. Alaric had never noticed the majesty of the forest before. Previously his experience of forest had just been the hiding places for bandits. Now he saw the trees in a totally new light.

"The root also heightens your senses," Palentonal noticed Alaric's reaction to his surroundings. "You need to concentrate if we are going to reach the others safely."

Although Alaric heard the words, they seemed to pass over his head without sinking in, as if the words were caught in kind of fog. Alaric looked around the forest in awe. The trees seemed to come alive, the entire forest seemed to come alive. There was nowhere else he would rather be. He could remain where he was for the rest of his life. The new sensations were magical.

"Snap out of it Alaric. We have to get going now." Palentonal barked. Hearing the sharp words brought Alaric back to reality. The root was definitely taking effect. He shook his head once and tried to focus on the elf. It took all his effort not to drift off into fantasy again. He knew that his life hung by the balance, but at the moment, he just didn't care.

"Let's move!" Palentonal collected the small chest and Alaric's sword as they started back towards the town.

As if he was still in a dream, Alaric followed him, but kept staring at the trees around him. He could have walked straight into a group of bandits and not even realise it. Palentonal moved on ahead to scout for any attackers. He knew that there was not going to be any stealth coming from Alaric. The only way he was going to stop Alaric from being captured was to find their assailants first.

The forest itself was completely void of human life, which was what Palentonal had expected. He knew that the men they faced were no idiots and would not attempt to follow them into the woods. The day passed slowly as they made their way through the forest. Their progress was slow as Alaric kept stopping to enjoy the beauty of the trees.

By mid-afternoon they reached the outskirts of the town and it could be seen clearly through the trees. The effects of the jongra root was starting to dull, though Alaric's senses were still clearly affected. Without a thought for what might be waiting for them, Alaric stepped out into the open. Quick as a flash Palentonal grabbed him by his shirt and dragged him back into the safety of the trees.

"Take care. This is not the same safe place where you grew up." Palentonal had crouched behind a tree and pulled Alaric in beside him. As he spoke, he pointed out into the open. Alaric tried to concentrate through the haze, but the fuzziness still remained in his mind making it hard for him to focus on one spot. Slowly the figure that Palentonal was pointing to came into view. A large man was riding a dirty old mare. He was not someone that Alaric recognised; the man had the look of a foreigner. It sent a warning bell off in his mind and on closer inspection it became clear that the man was searching for something. He was peering into the trees, intent on finding something that he couldn't see. It wasn't hard to figure out who he was looking for. For the first time, Alaric's heart started to race as the reality of the situation came streaming back to him. The sudden rush of adrenalin through his body counteracted the effect of the jongra root.

They both held their breath as the man rode past, within a hundred feet of where they were hiding. Up close the man looked as dirty as his horse. He was obviously a hired goon, loyal only whilst the money was being paid. There was no telling how many other men Myria had paid to watch the forest. This was going to be harder than what Palentonal had originally thought and there was no way for him to get word to the others to send reinforcements.

Once the man had ridden out of sight, the two of them started to move. Before they left the woods, Palentonal donned a hooded robe to hide his appearance. Once they reached the town, they would be discovered easily if anyone noticed an elf walking with Alaric. The rumours would spread within moments and it would not take long for them to be found.

The clearing between the woods and the edge of the town was about two hundred paces wide. There was no telling how long it would take for the man to return or if there was someone else watching the woods. There was no way they could race towards the town. The last thing they wanted to do was to draw attention. All they could do was walk out into the open and hope for the best. The walk seemed to take forever, their tensions growing with each step and thankfully they made the outskirts without incident.

After the initial calming effect of the adrenalin, the effects of the jongra root returned. The streets of Arsiliac were strangely quiet that day, which didn't help to ease the tension. As they continued, Alaric again became lost in his fantasy world. Palentonal looked around nervously, now not being able to scout ahead all he could do was to stop danger when it happened. The truth was if they were found now, there would be nowhere for them to hide.

Luck was on their side as they walked towards the eastern end of the town. The few people who did see them didn't seem to take any notice. The townsfolk seemed to be deliberately ignoring them. Normally the townsfolk ignored his presence, but did acknowledge that he was there. Alaric, of course, didn't notice that Palentonal found this to be odd.

It wasn't until they rounded a corner that they found out why. Again Palentonal had to stop Alaric from walking out into plain sight of their assailants. Grabbing Alaric sharply by the arm, he pulled him behind a small hedgerow. Their vantage point was close enough for Palentonal to hear what was being said.

Myria and one of his goons were talking to one of the townsfolk. Palentonal couldn't see them. He was only able to catch up after a few words, but he knew by the tone in Myria's voice that they weren't having a friendly conversation.

"So if you see Alaric and his elven friend, then you come and see us. If anyone tries to help him, then we will burn this little town to the ground." Myria's words were harsh and left no room for doubt.

"Yes, I will tell you straight away," the man's voice was shaking with fear.

"Good, now get out of here and tell everyone you see."

The sound of running footsteps came right past the hedge where they were hiding, but the man was in too much of a hurry to bother looking down.

"Let's keep looking," Myria barked to his cohort.

The sound of footsteps walking away brought relief to Palentonal. Alaric had started to become restless and it would only be a matter of time before he did something stupid. The relief only lasted a moment. Now he knew why the townsfolk had made a point not to look at them. It would only be a matter of time before someone told Myria and then the chase would be on.

"Come on Alaric. We have to hurry now." There was no point in trying to remain anonymous.

Pulling Alaric up by the arm, Palentonal started to rush towards the eastern edge, speed was their only ally and he kept their pace at a quick walk, he still didn't want to risk running. Caution was still a requirement for their safety.

As he reached the edge of the town Palentonal looked over his shoulder to make sure Alaric was still with him. In his haste to make sure their advance was safe, he had neglected their rear. To his horror he saw that Alaric wasn't there. In his drugged state, he became distracted and wandered off. The streets were completely empty. The only sound was the wind blowing in the trees.

Palentonal started to run. Caution was completely gone as he raced back frantically searching. He had almost reached the hedge where they had been hiding when he heard voices from behind a building. He recognised the voice immediately as Myria. He was talking with a man who sounded very nervous.

"Yes, I…I…I saw him."

"Tell me where, tell me where!" Myria's excitement was uncontrollable.

Palentonal didn't wait to hear the response. He knew that they had been revealed. His only hope now was to find Alaric and make a dash for safety.

As he ran back the way he had come Palentonal saw Alaric stroll out of a small building. The expression on his face showed no concern for his safety. Palentonal slowed only enough to grab Alaric's arm and pull him along the street. Alaric stumbled after him in what could only be described as a drunken run.

"What are you doing?" Alaric's voice was weak.

The sweat which had plagued him the night before had returned. The jongra root was starting to wear off and the fatigue had returned. His time now was short. It would not take long before the poison took its toll. Time was running out and Palentonal knew if he didn't get Alaric to the others within the hour than it would all be over.

"Keep moving Alaric. We have to get to the forest," Palentonal's voice didn't sound puffed or strained, even though he had been running for the last fifteen minutes.

Alaric stumbled and fell as Palentonal pulled him, desperately trying to get to safety. He fell to his knees and his head drooped down again onto his chest. The sweat dripped onto the ground. His body remained limp as Palentonal tried in vain to lift him to his feet.

The small amount of jongra root that Palentonal had saved in reserve had as much chance of killing Alaric as it had to revive him. The effects should have lasted at least another two hours. Taking another dose was very risky. For an elf, it would have been fine, but for a man it was a different story. The decision was already made, if they remained stationary they would be dead.

The root took effect almost instantly. There was not enough for them to be as potent as before or last as long, but Palentonal could only hope there was enough to get them to the forest. Thankfully Alaric was not as dazed as before and was able to follow Palentonal's lead without getting waylaid.

It wasn't until they reached the edge of the town did they hear a voice call out from behind them. Myria and his goons had finally caught up with them. The distance to the edge of the forest was only a quarter of a mile. With the extra exertion, the medicinal effects of the jongra root was already starting to wear off and Alaric was starting to fall behind.

If Palentonal had bothered to look around he would have seen that their pursuers were not far and on horseback. He would also have seen that Alaric was slowing down by the second. It was not until he made it to the safety of the tree line did he dare look back.

Alaric was only fifty paces from the trees, but he had now slowed to a half-walk, half-hobble. Palentonal started back towards him, but something held him back. Half a dozen men on horseback were nearing Alaric and would be upon him in a matter of seconds.

Hearing the pounding hooves Alaric glanced over his shoulder. The diversion of his attention was all it took for him to misjudge his step and trip over his own feet. His vision was blurred and his body was again drenched with sweat.

All that was left of Alaric was his consciousness. He could barely see in front of him. What he could see made his heart sink even further. No more than half a dozen paces in front of him was the start of the Eastern Forest and his sanctuary. Although it was so close it was still too far away for him to reach.

Just before Alaric blacked out he thought he heard a whistle over his head and the cry of both man and horse. He thought that it must have been a dream, because the next thing he felt were a pair of strong hands lifting him into the air. He knew that his time was up. His entire body was limp. He couldn't have struggled with his captor even if he tried. Slowly his eyes rolled back into his head and he faded out of reality.

Chapter 7: With Friends

"Please don't go." Mary pleaded with her husband as the inevitable knock on the door came.

She had known this day was coming. Bern had told her from the start that he had to leave. At first she didn't believe him; the entire story seemed so farcical. When he had finally managed to convince her she felt shattered. It took over two hours for her tears to subside.

It took them two days to tell the children. They didn't really seem to understand the situation and would not until Bern had actually left. That would be another heartbreaking task for Mary. She didn't know how she was going to be able cope without her husband. Since they had not been able to tell anyone that he was leaving, she couldn't employ anyone to take his place.

As the days passed she had started to believe that his story had been a dream. The idea was so ridiculous it couldn't be true. Bern didn't want to discuss leaving any more than Mary did. His heart grew heavy over the week as he watched his family go through their normal day to day routines. Although he had seen them almost every day since the children had been born, it was as if he was seeing them for the first time. Every little thing brought great joy and great sorrow to his heart.

On the morning of the fifth day he started to pack his bags. Even as he did so, Mary refused believe that he was leaving. It wasn't until the knock on the door that she truly believed it. Now, more than ever, she desperately wanted him to stay. Standing between him and the doorway she begged. "Bern please, don't go, I love you." She knew there was no way for her to physically stop him, but she wasn't going to allow him to just leave.

A second knock came before Bern replied. "You know that I must. I didn't believe Eldred when he told me the story, but over the past few days I've been feeling this pull. Something is calling to me from the outside. I think that it would be only a matter of a few days before this feeling becomes uncontrollable." Bern moved toward the door, but Mary stood firm.

"What about the children. What are they going to do without their father?" Mary was trying to remain strong, but her voice was starting to waiver.

"I will miss them like crazy, as I will you." Bern was also feeling emotional, but was hiding it better than Mary. "There is nothing that I can do. What is the point of staying here if in twelve months, Nyrra marches an army through and wipes us out?" There was a lot of sense in his words. "Now please, get the children so I can say goodbye.'

Mary knew that she couldn't argue with his words. If what Eldred said was true, then he was pivotal to the prophecy and saving the world from destruction. The only problem was if Eldred was lying then her husband was leaving her for no reason. It was that thought she couldn't shake.

A third and more vigorous knock came on the front door. Bern was not going to let whoever it was on the other side wait any longer. Very gently he picked up his wife and moved her off to the side. She had forgotten how strong her husband really was. He didn't even strain as he lifted her off the ground. As much as she didn't want to get the children (maybe he would stay if he didn't get to say good bye), she knew she had to. It wouldn't be fair on either of them if they didn't get to say their last farewells.

Bern opened the door and Mary went to find the children. Bern looked around, but could not see anyone. All he could see was a horse and cart parked at the front of the house. He was about to shut when he heard a gruff voice.

"One of the many problems about being short," Bern looked down to see where the voice had come from.

Standing before him was one of the strangest men he had ever seen. He knew he was in fact a dwarf, not a man. Alaric had told him stories of dwarves he had seen in the capital. He had long brown hair and a bushy brown beard, both grew halfway down his torso. The dwarf stood no more than four and a half feet tall. Although he was small, he looked strong enough to challenge Bern in a test of strength. Besides a small knife strapped to his belt, the dwarf also carried a long handled war axe. A large scar across his left cheek showed that he had occasion to use it.

"Hello Bern, my name is Hulkan; I'm here to take you to join the others." Hulkan's voice was very deep and resonant.

"Come in and I'll be with you in a moment." Bern led Hulkan inside and then went to fetch his bags.

He knew that whatever he had packed wouldn't be enough, but he didn't want to take everything he owned. Eventually he decided that two full bags were sufficient. Mary stood, teary eyed, with the two children. Hulkan was quick to realise the situation.

"I'll take your bags out. Meet me at the cart when you're done." Hulkan was about to leave but then added, "don't be too long we need to get moving."

Bern waited for him to leave before embracing Johnathon and Holly. Tears welled in his eyes. He knew the children didn't fully understand what was happening. They would think that he would be returning by nightfall. That was always going to be the hardest part.

"I will see you all again soon." Bern tried to regain his composure. "And remember what I told you. If there are a lot of strangers around the town, leave immediately for Quinaliac.

Bern gave his wife a deep passionate kiss that should have never ended, but too soon it was time to go.

Mary held her children close to her body as they all watched Bern climb up into the wagon with the dwarf. The tears flowed freely from her eyes although she did not openly weep, that she would save for the privacy of her bedroom.

***

It was dark when Alaric finally opened his eyes. His head was ringing and his mouth was dry. There was a dim light flickering somewhere. His sight took a long time to get accustomed to the darkness. There was nothing around him that he could see to figure out where he was. His first sensation was that he realised he wasn't bound. Both his hands and feet were free. That either meant that his captors didn't think he was going to regain consciousness in any hurry or he had not been captured. If it was the latter, then he had no idea how he had managed to survive.

Slowly he tried to raise his head. He managed to lift it a couple ofinches before the strain became too much. Only when he let his head rest did he realise he was laying on a soft down pillow. That was enough to convince him that he was with friends and not enemies. The dust was starting to clear in his head and the events from the previous day were starting to come back. The sweat that had covered his entire body earlier in the day was completely gone. Although he felt terrible, he was in less pain than before. He had been cured, or at least he hoped he had.

All he could do at the moment was lie on his back and stare up at the sky. It wasn't long before he realised that he couldn't see the sky. All he could see was the canopy of the dense trees in the Eastern Woods. He was at his destination, his heart raced as he was now positive that he was with friends. He only wished that he could move to let the others know that he was awake… and very thirsty. He tried to move again, but he was still too weak. As he relaxed he could now hear voices around him. There were only murmured sounds; he could not make out any words. One of the voices he thought was Eldred's, although without knowing the words he could not be certain, and there was another voice that sounded familiar, but he couldn't place it either.

"I think he's awake now." Alaric's heart pounded at the sudden voice coming from somewhere close by. He recognized the voice immediately; it was Palentonal. "Are you okay?"

"A little worse for wear, but besides that I'm fine," Alaric's voice was hoarse. The dryness in his mouth and throat made it difficult to speak. "Is there anything to drink?"

"Of course, what was I thinking?" Palentonal produced a water pouch and handed it to Alaric. "The after-effects of the jongra root can be quite severe sore head and dry throat. Add the effects of the antidote for the poison you were given, weakness and dizziness, it will be a while before you'll be up again." Alaric drank a long draught as Palentonal spoke. He didn't stop until he had completely drained the pouch.

"You need to rest now. It will take a while for your strength to return and we need to be moving by first light."

Alaric tried to focus on Palentonal as he walked away. The more he tried the greater the pounding in his head. The effort made him pant for breath; the aching in his head was almost unbearable. He let his eyes close and tried to relax. The voices started up again somewhere… again he couldn't make out any words, as if Eldred and Palentonal were deliberately keeping their words from him. He wanted nothing more than to be able to hear what they were saying. He also had questions for Eldred, but until he was able to move again there was nothing that he could do.

The night was cool. There was no wind blowing through the trees and the forest was very still. Other than the movement within the camp, there was nothing else stirring. The night was unusually quiet. It was as if it knew what had transpired earlier in the day and was waiting for an attack.

Slowly Alaric drifted off to sleep and sleep he did. Even though he was lying on a thin bedroll on the forest floor with a light blanket for warmth, he slept as if he hadn't slept for over a month. The tiring effects of the antidote were taking full effect. Not even dreams worried his sleep that night and in the morning he woke refreshed. As he rose he notice the scar on his arm was healed; it was as though nothing had ever happened.

"Good to see you up and about," greeted Eldred when he saw Alaric. "How are you feeling this morning?"

"All better now." Alaric paused as his head started to swim. It seemed as though all the effects had not passed during the night. It only took a moment for Alaric to settle himself and then he realised that he was ravenous. "Is there anything to eat?" he asked.

"There are some bacon and eggs being cooked as we speak. It should be ready shortly." And as if on cue Palentonal appeared with the results of breakfast.

At that moment Alaric realised that he should have been able to smell the aromas of the cooked food. He looked down at the plate. The expression on his face made it clear to everyone that something was wrong.

"What is it Alaric, don't you eat bacon and eggs?" The plate had been loaded with food in anticipation for Alaric's added hunger. Palentonal was now worried that he wouldn't eat it.

Alaric looked up from the plate as he heard Palentonal speak. "No, of course I do. It's just that I can't smell anything, and my nose isn't blocked." worry filled Alaric's voice.

"That's just another side-effect of the jongra root. It should wear off soon," Palentonal's smile indicated that it was of no concern, although that did very little to reassure Alaric.

Hunger was starting to take control. Whether or not he could smell or taste the food, he needed to eat it. Sitting down on a nearby stool Alaric started to stuff the food into his mouth. Even if he had been able to smell, he was eating far too quickly to be able to taste anything. Normally he wouldn't have eaten half of what was on the plate, but now he finished within a matter of minutes.

When he had finished, he placed the plate on the ground next to his stool and looked around the campsite for the first time. There seemed to be no set order, except where the cook fire had been set up. The camp was set up amongst a grove of pine trees with the fire in a small clearing. Bedrolls, similar to the one that Alaric had slept on, were scattered amongst the trees in no apparent order. He could see Eldred and Palentonal speaking by the fire. They seemed to be within earshot, but again Alaric could only make out mumbled noises. Finally, Eldred nodded and Palentonal left him alone. When he realised that Alaric was watching, Eldred motioned for him to join them.

"I see that nothing is wrong with your appetite," Eldred joked as he started the conversation.

Alaric couldn't help but smile at the jest. "Yes, I think I could have eaten twice as much."

"Good to hear." Eldred stared into the fire as he listened to Alaric's response. "Now we need to get going. We are already a day behind before we have even started. The others should be returning from the forest line any time now. They have been scouting to see if your assailants are following us."

Alaric suddenly started looking around frantically. Eldred read the expression on Alaric's face as if he was reading his mind. When Alaric's façade changed, Eldred pointed to a spot just behind where Alaric was seating.

"Your things are there. We will be leaving shortly. You will need to take them over to where the pack horses are picketed."

Alaric was relieved to see amongst the two bags, which had been taken from his house, were his sword and the small chest containing the Ruby Stone. With all the commotion of the past day, Alaric had forgotten all about the stone. The thought of losing it made him shiver. Ignoring the other items, Alaric snatched up the chest and then returned to where he had been sitting. Letting the chest rest against his knees, Alaric stared at the intricate patterns inlaid on the timber box. Eldred watched him quietly.

Holding his breath, Alaric slowly opened the latch and lifted the lid. As he did he could have sworn he felt a gust of wind blew past his ears. The forest around him seemed strangely quiet. There was no movement that suggested there was any wind blowing. Suddenly a number of voices seemed to be whispering from somewhere behind him. He could not make out the words and when he spun around quickly there was no one there. The light seemed to shrink away from the forest now. There seemed to be a perpetual twilight.

"I think you should close that now." The sudden words of Eldred made Alaric jump.

The words made sense, but all Alaric could do was stare at the perfect red stone sitting somewhat sadly in its box. It seemed to be calling to him. The whispering voices wanted him to pick it up. He still could not understand any of the words, but he knew what they wanted. Eldred's words came again, a little more forcefully this time. The words had their desired effect and Alaric snapped out of his reverie. Without thinking he slammed the lid shut and replaced the latch. As soon as he did the voices disappeared and the forest returned to its normal state.

Alaric stared up at Eldred. He knew the question that he wanted to ask, but couldn't find the words. It was as if he didn't want to know the answer, or that he already knew it and didn't want it confirmed. Whatever the reasons it made no difference. Eldred knew exactly what he was thinking and the answer to his unasked question.

"The stone is a magical artifact like none other you will ever find. Very little is known about it. All we know is what we've read and what we've assumed. From what we can gather, the Ruby Stone will try and use you as much as you try to use it. It will tempt and deceive. How this will happen we don't exactly know. The look on Alaric's face showed that he might have only comprehended one sentence, maybe! "A story for another time. What you need to know is that without training the stone is not going to be easy to control. The chest acts as a barrier between us and it. When the lid is shut, the stone can have no effect on you or anyone around you." Eldred knew that he wasn't helping. There was so much that Alaric needed to know, and no time to tell him. The information would have to be drip fed to him or else he could lose his mind. His reality was about to be turned upside down.

"Eldred!" A gruff voice called to them from behind the camp fire.

"Hulkan, come over," Eldred's voice relaxed.

The dwarf walked over the where Eldred was standing. Although there was no apparent danger, his hand remained poised above the handle of his war axe. His eyes darted around the clearing until he spoke. "We are almost ready to go. The last of the bags are being loaded. The elf is back from the edge of the forest. He says that no one has entered. Everything being well, we should be gone before they get the sense to follow us."

"Very good. I think we are done here." Eldred returned his gaze to Alaric. "Would you follow Hulkan to the pack animals and take your bags with you?" the question was rhetorical and Eldred did not wait for a reply.

"Come on then, no time for standing around staring." A strong hand slapped him on the shoulder and then clamped down firmly. The sudden shock did not, however, knock Alaric out of his reverie. Eldred's words echoed inside his head. The story didn't seem to make any sense. The whole idea went against everything he had known and now he wasn't sure what to believe.

"Snap out of it Alaric, we need to get moving." Hulkan shook him briefly and he came around.

"Sorry." Alaric turned around and looked up. To his surprise the dwarf stood only as high as he was seated. This was another shock to his system.

"Not a worry, I know that this has all been very stressful for you. It will get easier in time, trust me. I don't think anyone, except for Eldred, truly understands why we are here. Sometimes I don't even think that he knows. Anyway, even though we don't truly understand, we know that it's what we are meant to do." Hulkan could see him losing Alaric back into thought. "As I was saying, it will get easier with time. Who knows? You might even get to understand it all. As for now, we need to get moving. None of us will get any answers sitting around here." Those final words seemed to have their desired effect.

It was his face that was the first to regain itself, quickly changing from deep thought to awareness. The change was so sudden it took Hulkan by surprise and he removed his hand from Alaric's shoulder. Alaric's entire body stiffened for a moment and then he stood. There was a sudden glint in his eye and then it was gone.

"You're dead right. Sitting here isn't going to get me any answers." Alaric collected his possessions as he spoke. "Now, if you would show me to the pack animals, we can be on our way."

It was now Hulkan's turn to be surprised. The complete turnaround in Alaric's attitude had him dumbfounded. His recovery didn't take so long. Shaking his head he led Alaric towards the animals. The real journey was about to begin and the dwarf knew that things were going to get interesting. He didn't have much faith in their new companion; he thought the saviour of the world should be a little more intrepid. Even if he had no faith in Alaric, he did have faith in Eldred. He was heading down a dangerous path when Eldred found him. Ever since he joined Eldred, his life seemed to have meaning and he wasn't going to start doubting him now.

The horses were picketed in a large clearing not far away from where they had been seated. The pack horses were lined up and loaded to bursting. The only bags left to be packed were Alaric's. He looked nervously at the animals. They looked edgy. He had only ridden a horse once and that was not an enjoyable experience.

Hulkan took the bags when they reached the final horse. He tied the bags with a skill that showed Alaric that he had done it many times before. Alaric tried to watch the intricate knots, but couldn't follow them. There was going to be a lot of things he would need to learn if he was going to survive.

"Don't worry. You'll pick things up pretty quickly. Before I met Eldred, I couldn't even ride a horse." Hulkan saw the expression on Alaric's face.

"Thank you." Alaric's mind was racing.

"We won't be riding for a while, but you should strap the chest to your own horse. Hopefully you won't need it, but it would be a good idea to keep your sword on you." Hulkan smiled as he spoke. Even the thought of danger sent a shiver down his spine, yet the dwarf spoke about it like it was yesterday's news.

Alaric nodded, not really knowing which horse was his or knowing how to strap the chest to it. He took a couple of nervous steps towards the horses, looking up and down, not really expecting to see anything; he found the horse he was looking for. A grey mare picketed in the middle of the group had a special saddle. In front of the pommel the saddle had been altered to make a neat resting place for his chest, two clips allowed for extra anchorage and Alaric secured it easily.

"Good, now let's go and meet the rest of the group. I think you will find them quite the motley crew; though I believe there might be one member whom you'll recognize," Hulkan winked as he said the last part.

"What are you talking about?" his words fell on deaf ears.

Hulkan had already started back towards the other clearing. The slight movement of his shoulders showed that he was chuckling to himself. There was too much secrecy for his liking. He was supposed to be the major player in the game, yet he seemed to be the only one who didn't know the rules.

Now the small clearing was filled with people, not that there were many. Standing next to Eldred was Palentonal. Next to him was another elf, similar in appearance to Palentonal, only that this elf had jet black hair. Standing on the other side of the clearing from Eldred and the two elves was another dwarf. The four of them were enough to almost completely fill the clearing. With the inclusion of Hulkan and Alaric, there was no standing room left.

"Welcome back, are we all ready to go now?" Eldred greeted the two. The nod from Hulkan was all the response he needed. "Very good then. I shall introduce you to the rest of our little group. The elf next to Palentonal is Craven and the dwarf next to you is Dorn." Eldred paused as they all shook and hands and greeted each other. Eldred turned to walk away, stopped and then turned to face Alaric again. "Oh, I nearly forgot. There is one more to make the group complete.'

Suddenly Alaric felt a hand touch him on the shoulder. The sudden feeling made him jump in surprise. Spinning around quickly, the shock only increased when he saw who it was. The look on his face increased the amusement on Bern's.

"When Eldred told me this was how he wanted to introduce me into the group, I couldn't help myself. The look on your face is priceless." Bern knew what his friend must be going through, but he couldn't help but laugh. "I am sorry," He spoke as his laughter died down.

"W-what are you doing here?" Alaric still couldn't believe his friend was standing before him.

"I'm not really sure myself. All I know is that there has been something drawing me away for the last year or so. Until Eldred knocked on the door, I didn't know why," Bern tried to explain it as best he could. Although he knew that he didn't make any sense he knew that Alaric would realise exactly what he was talking about.

"Well, whatever reason you have I'm glad that you are here." Alaric had gained his composure and gave his friend a hearty handshake. "But what about your family?" Alaric realised the implications of Bern's decision. "What about your farm?"

"It's better for my family if I leave than if I stay. If you are what he says you are, then you are going to need me with you. Staying behind would be worse for my family, and everyone else's."

"Enough of the chit-chat. If we don't leave now it won't matter who is left and who is not, there won't be any families left for you to worry about," Eldred spoke firmly.

There were no arguments. When Eldred spoke a command, the entire group would react. He was the one who had brought them all together and although they had never discussed who was their leader, it was clear to all that he was their general. It was not known if he had all the answers or whether he was drawn into the prophecy like the rest of them, but for now he was all they had.

The forest was wild and untamed, the oak, ash and birch were packed in together with no apparent order. Wild flowers, in a multitude of colours, fought for room amongst the many brambles and thorns. The ground under foot was undulating and although it was not rocky, the many roots protruding from the ground made riding all but impossible, even walking was treacherous.

Palentonal led the pack horses whilst Dorn led the others. Eldred led the group with Hulkan guarding the rear. Craven scouted ahead and around the group as they walked, leaving Alaric and Bern time by themselves to talk. This again was a decision that Eldred had made. He thought that it would help Alaric come to terms with his situation if he could spend some time alone with his friend.

"Do you know much about the others in the group?" Alaric finally asked when they were out of earshot.

Bern had spent two days with the group while they had been waiting for Alaric to return. He had spent most of that time with the two dwarves. They seemed to have taken a shine to him. Craven and Eldred had spent the time scouting for Alaric and Palentonal.

"Hulkan was the former leader of the Western Federation of Dwarves."

The Western Federation of Dwarves was the largest and most respected Dwarven guild in the Seven Kingdoms. Its headquarters were based rightfully in Castalia. Its main operation was the mining of sand and the production of glass. The guild also dabbled in other mining interests, but none as profitable as glass.

"He didn't lead into too much detail of how he was ousted from the guild. Dorn made mention that he was betrayed by his brother who now runs it. It was about this time that he felt the tug towards the prophecy. He told me that he roamed the streets of many cities, mostly in a drunken haze, not really knowing what he was looking for. It was then that Eldred found and recruited him to the prophecy. Hulkan was the first one to be recruited. His first task was to find Dorn and recruit him." Bern paused as the information settled in. "This was not as easy as it sounded. Without a name or description of the fifth member, all he could go on was a gentle psychic pull that he was feeling deep inside him." The words didn't seem like those that Bern would normally use. Alaric could tell by the look on his face that he was repeating word for word something that he had been told. This was closer to the truth than Alaric realised. Eldred had cast a small spell allowing Bern to repeat everything he had been told. He had figured that it would be better for some information to come from a familiar face and it was important it didn't get misinterpreted.

"Dorn was part of the Mining Guild and worked in the mines of the Cloumid Mountains. The mountain range stretches for almost one hundred leagues in length and at some stages over ten leagues wide. The depth of the mountain from peak to depth is completely unknown. The dwarven mine structure might take up only one tenth of the range, but that is still over a thousand leagues of shafts and corridors and over five hundred halls and underground villages. The task itself should have been completely impossible; even if he knew the name of the dwarf it could take over a decade to locate him. The journey was long and hard and took almost twenty years until Hulkan finally came upon Dorn deep within the mountains."

The approaching footsteps brought a sudden stop to Bern's story. The dwarf was not used to stealth in a forest. The elves could sneak up on anyone without them knowing they were there. The dense undergrowth didn't make concealment too easy for the others.

"Coming up is a small trail. We should reach it in about five minutes. When we do, we'll be able to ride for a short while." Dorn spoke with a gruff voice very similar to Hulkan. Alaric had seen many dwarves before in Zenza City, and found it very hard to differentiate between them. Dorn didn't wait for a reply, but just left them by themselves.

True to his word they all stopped five minutes later. The ground leveled out for the first time and a large clearing appeared. It was obvious that the area had been cleared by man. The trees surrounding the clearing were in an unnaturally perfect circle.

"This is where the Ancient Kings of Remidia would meet the elves, back in a time when elves and men were at war." Eldred pointed out two small trails leading away from the clearing, one to the north and one to the east. "The Old King started the peace talks in this very place. This is a place of magic and even though no one has been here for over a thousand years no trees will over grow the clearing. A great peace deal was signed here and the entire forest respects it," Eldred smiled as he spoke.

There was a sense of awe amongst the group. Even Alaric had read about the famous meeting between King Rohne and the Elf King. Over the years the details of the meeting had changed, but the mysterious site of the meeting remained the same and remained a secret. People had journeyed into the forest to try and find the sacred site. Those who had returned said they had no luck, many did not return at all.

A tingling sensation filled Alaric's body. He looked around the group to try and get an indication if anyone else was feeling it. There seemed to be no change in anyone, at least he thought Bern would show some reaction. No matter where he moved there was nothing he could do stop the sensation.

"We shall not linger. The magic is still as strong today as it was those many years ago. If we stay, we risk becoming entrapped. We shall follow the eastern trail until it ends at the Jurindi River. From there we shall continue on until we reach Elhjem and Orric."

The mention of Orric's name sent whispers throughout the group. Besides Eldred, the only two who didn't say anything were Bern and Alaric. The two elves looked as though they were either excited or concerned. This was opposite to the two dwarves who looked either worried or outright scared. Both creatures twitched so much Alaric couldn't decide what they were feeling.

"Who's Orric?" asked Alaric as the muttering became too much for him.

"All in good time. We should now saddle and ride out. We want to try and make the river by nightfall. A short ride and the track widens to two abreast. They were designed that way to allow only one at a time into the clearing and only limited numbers. That way if one side had a stronger force there would still be no real advantage." Cutting his history lesson off abruptly Eldred moved towards his horse.

A pure white stallion was the leader and Eldred's horse, Hel'rion, stamped his foot in anticipation. Whenever Eldred was in civilized company many lords and ladies would plead with him to allow Hel'rion to sire a foal with one, or more, of their mares. His answer was always no, no matter how much gold they would throw at him. Although they all thought it was Eldred being secretive, it was always Hel'rion who made the final decision.

Once in the saddle Eldred wasted no time in leaving the clearing along the eastern trail. In turn the others mounted their horses and followed Eldred. Alaric had a mild tempered, grey mare. Although she was very sedate, she could sense Alaric's unease which in turn made her nervous. The grey started to jerk in her movements as Alaric bobbed around in the saddle. He kept his head low, close to the mane, entirely uncomfortable. He wished that he hadn't given up his riding lessons when he was younger.

None of the others seemed to be having any problems with their horses. Even the dwarves, who as a race normally travelled by foot and steered clear of riding, seem adept at what they were doing. The journey was going to be long and painful if he could not learn how to ride.

The trail itself was similar to the clearing. Although it had not been used in many years it still remained clear of any undergrowth. The roots and brambles that plagued the rest of the forest did not touch the trail. They did however make it all but impossible for anyone to leave the path.

As Eldred had explained, about half an hour later, the trail widened to allow them to ride two abreast. It was not long before Eldred called for Alaric to join him at the front of the line. Luckily for Alaric his horse understood the call and quickened her pace to reach him.

"Now Alaric, you cannot ride all the way slumped over the saddle. Not only will you damage your back, you're more than likely to fall off at any given time, especially if we need to go at a gallop." Eldred's words were kind, although they sounded condescending.

For the next fifteen minutes, Eldred gave Alaric a brief riding lesson and by the end Alaric with sitting high in the saddle. Even if he didn't feel all that confident he now looked the part. His new posture gave the mare a little more assurance and was able to relax a little as she carried her load. "Now, you wanted to know about Orric?" The question was rhetorical. "Orric is a descendant of the great Elven Kings. His great-grandfather was the one who signed the peace treaty with King Rohne."

Alaric scoffed at hearing that last comment. "How can his great-grandfather be the one who signed the treaty? That was over a thousand years ago, the entire idea is completely ridiculous."

Eldred's face turned stern. He knew that there would be revelations hard for Alaric to understand, but this was one he thought he would already know. "Elves do not live the same life span as men. They leave for many more years. The oldest age recorded by an elf was five hundred and thirty-two years. Again Alaric you need to open your mind to ideas that you had never thought possible."

Alaric felt a sense of shame come over him. He knew that he had disappointed Eldred, his ignorance was showing once again. He made a silent vow to himself that he would never doubt anything Eldred told him and he would open his mind to new ideas.

"Never mind though, I know it is hard on you. Not all the elves agreed with Olrohn's decision to make peace with men. They believed that they were superior to man and should not share anything with them. What the elves didn't understand was that the peace treaty allowed them to have their own territory, separate to the rule of Remidia. All they could see was that they were surrendering to a stronger opponent and subjugating themselves. That was just not true. The elves had to abide by the peace treaty, but they did not have to remain under Olrohn's rule. This is one part that you won't read in your history books. The rift created by the peace treaty was never made apparent to men. It remained, and still does to this day, a secret shame. The location of Elhjem is now unknown to most and is protected by some strong magic. Even those who used to live there have no idea how to return. From that day on, Olrohn and his followers lived a life of solitude.

It wasn't until Orric became their leader that those from the outside were allowed entrance. The prophecy takes a hold of us all. The pull of the prophecy led me to Orric and together we have been formulating a plan for many years. Between the two of us, we've tried to filter out the lies and learn the truth. Without his, I would have been lost." This time as Eldred spoke Alaric tried his best to soak up the information, rather than poke holes in it. "We have both been living our lives for these times. All our hard work is finally coming to fruition. In a matter of months, we'll see if it has all been worthwhile." Eldred seemed to drift off into melancholy. For the first time, he didn't seem completely confident in what he was saying. "I for one will be a lot happier once we reach his village."

That last comment gave great concern to Alaric. If Eldred was worried, then there was cause for concern. When Alaric asked what there was to fear, Eldred gave no response. The look on his face was all the answer he needed to conclude that they were in some sort of danger. Realising that there were going to be no more answers, Alaric decided to return back down the line until he reached Palentonal who was riding by himself.

"Eldred seems worried; do you know what about?" the question took Palentonal by surprise. The elf had been lost in thought before Alaric rode back beside him.

"It's hard to say. These forests have been uncharted for so long, who knows what creatures reside here? Since the peace treaty and the mutiny, the elves no longer come to this part of the forest. Although this land is still owned by Remidia, they still don't enter it either. There is a fear that the old hostilities may reignite and that is something that neither side wants. Everything has grown wild; even the thorns and brambles have grown out of control. If I was to take a guess, I would say that nothing good lives here anymore," Palentonal's words were ominous.

Now Alaric was taking notice of his surroundings. For the first time, he noticed that there were no animals, not even birds in the trees. The trees seemed to loom over him and in every shadow lurked some new unforeseen evil. There was a reason why he never entered the forest when he was younger. Now he knew the tales his mother used to tell where not all lies.

Alaric did not relax for the rest of the day, even when they stopped for lunch by a small creek. It was late when they reached the edge of the Jurindi River. The river stretched for over half a mile. By the bank, the water looked calm and inviting. Towards the middle, the current took control and thrashed the water against the many jagged rocks.

It wasn't until Alaric dismounted before he realised how sore and tired he was. It took a great effort to stay on his feet, trying to hide his pain from the others.

"Tonight we camp here," started Eldred when they had all dismounted. "Tomorrow we make for the Jurindi Bridge."

The mention of the bridge started the murmuring amongst the group again. Even Alaric had heard tales of the Jurindi Bridge. He had always assumed that the bridge was a myth; now that he had heard Eldred say the name he was not so sure. There was now a true sense of fear within the group. All but Eldred looked afraid.

"I know the rumors you have heard about the bridge and I can assure you that *we* have nothing to fear," Eldred's voice was very reassuring. "The Jurindi River used to be the disputed border between Remidia and the Elvish Territories. King Rohne of Remidia believed the forest west of the river fell under the borders of his country, and therefore the elves should pay taxes. Although the elves very seldom traveled west of the river they believed the forest was under no one's rule and they lived in harmony with their surroundings. Olrohn would not submit to Rohne's demands and although they did not claim lordship over the forest they would not accept foreign rule." Eldred's words sparked something between the two elves. They both seemed somewhat irritable. "At the end of the war there were many bridges spanning the river. When the peace treaty was signed and King Rohne gave the forest land east of the river to the elves, Olrohn wanted assurance that there would be no sneak attacks across the Jurindi. All the bridges were destroyed except for one. A spell was cast on the bridge allowing no one to cross without the permission of the elves. The integrity of the spell has been compromised over the years, as with all set spells without someone to renew them every now and again. The chances now of someone falling afoul of its magic would be a million to one," his words were comforting, but they did not alleviate everyone's anxieties.

There was not much conversation during dinner, which consisted of a hearty lamb stew and dried bread. The meal was more than what Alaric had expected. He thought that they would be on meager rations until they reached Elhjem. He was pleasantly surprised to have a full stomach.

No one complained when Eldred suggested that they all had an early night. Palentonal was on first watch. Everyone else was quick to unpack their bedrolls and lay down to sleep. Alaric slept with his precious chest resting under his left hand. Although Eldred would have suggested he keep the chest closed, he needed no encouragement. Even with the stone in the chest, he didn't feel quite right unless he was close to it.

The night passed without incident. The only stir was when Palentonal changed his shift with Craven at midnight. Eldred had everyone up minutes before the sun was starting to rise. By the time they had eaten breakfast, the sun had risen and they were ready to move.

The sleep did nothing to ease the pain Alaric was feeling from the previous day. Walking was bad enough, but when he mounted the pain shot through his entire body, though he kept up his brave front.

They followed the trail along the river to the south until it stopped abruptly. Along the edge of the river, the ground started to rise and become rocky and they were forced to dismount and continue on foot.

"Are you alright?" asked Bern as he caught up to where Alaric was walking.

"Yes, sure I'm fine," Alaric spoke through clenched teeth as the pain became almost unbearable.

The look on his face easily gave away his lie. "I think I've known you too long. It's clear that you're suffering. Anyone who is not used to riding would be feeling comfortable."

"Now that you mention it, I am a little sore." As he let out his confession his body physically slumped and a grimace crossed his face. "No, that's still a lie. It's all I can do to keep myself upright." The strain was evident on his face.

Bern laughed loudly. "You stubborn fool." A confused look came over Alaric's face. "I haven't been on the back of a horse for over a year. Do you think that I could hold up to a full day of riding, even at a walk?"

"What are you talking about? You look fine to me," the strain entered into his voice.

"Of course I do. I spoke to Eldred this morning before we left and he gave me a tonic to drink. Within a few minutes I was feeling fine." Bern was still chuckling to himself as Alaric hurried along the line to Eldred.

Bern had not been lying. Eldred also started to laugh when Alaric asked the question. "I was wondering when you were going to say something. I would have offered, but I didn't want to push."

The small glass vial of light green elixir did the trick. No sooner had the liquid past his lips and down his throat, did he start to feel better. The pain didn't leave all at once, slowly but surely the aches and pains disappeared.

"Wow! This stuff is great. I should take this every morning," although the comment was offhand, it did hold some truth.

"That is the very reason why I do not offer it to anyone. The elixir will cure you, for a while. It is not without its side effects. Prolonged use can cause great damage to your entire body. More than two or three days of use and you will start to see the negative effects. Not only that, but I do not have very much left." Eldred realised that he was lecturing Alaric and took a deep breath. "Sorry Alaric. I have seen too many people become addicted to the elixir. The results are not pretty."

Alaric started to shrink back away from Eldred. This was the first time he had seen Eldred become animated and it wasn't pleasant. Just as Eldred was about to start again, they crested a small ridge and the Jurindi Bridge was upon them.

The rope bridge spanned the length of the river for the total of one hundred feet. Although the rope itself looked old and worn the construction of the bridge itself looked very secure. Despite the apparent safety, no one wanted to get close to it. They formed a semi-circle around the entrance with Eldred standing in the middle.

"Don't be afraid. This is a natural reaction to the bridge. An *apprehension spell* has been cast on the entrance. Anyone who comes along the bridge thinks twice before they cross. Most people, if they were ever to stumble upon the bridge, would keep walking without thinking about crossing." Eldred's words did little to ease their concerns.

As Eldred casually walked out onto the bridge, he looked unsettled. Even though he was trying to keep a calm façade, it was clear to all that he was nervous. That did nothing for the confidence of the group. No one started after him for a long moment.

To the surprise of everyone, it was Alaric who was the first to follow Eldred. The anxiety that had come over him, suddenly disappeared once he had stepped onto the bridge. Once gone, there seemed no good reason for him not to cross. His casual movement caused the rest of the group to start to follow.

Everyone went through the same process. When they approached the bridge, the feeling to run away was almost overwhelming. It was only the sight of the Eldred and Alaric further ahead that kept them going. Once they had stepped onto the bridge, the feeling of dread passed. With everyone following after Alaric, Eldred's posture changed. His shoulders started to bounce as he tried to suppress a laugh. His confidence had fully returned.

The added weight made the ropes of the bridge strain. The timbers groaned under the added pressure of the group and their horses. As they all walked the bridge, it slowly started to sway. Gently at first, but as they continued the arc became wider.

"Everyone stop moving and make sure the horses don't move!" the worry in Eldred's voice was genuine.

They were all quick to obey, but even though they had stopped moving the bridge continued to sway. The only difference was that the arc remained the same. It was now clear to all that the swaying was not natural. A wave of fear now crossed over them. This made the horses very nervous and they started to stamp and snort. It was all Craven could do to keep them from breaking their line and bolting.

"What's going on?" called Palentonal from the middle of the group.

"It seems that the protective spell is still active. This is something that I hadn't counted on." Eldred looked all around him as he spoke. "If we continue along, the bridge will keep swaying until it tosses us into the ravine."

Hearing those words made them all look down towards the river. Sharp jagged rocks waited for them at the bottom of the three-hundred-foot drop. Although the arc didn't change on the bridge they all felt as though it had increased. "What are we going to do?" the fear in Hulkan's gruff voice seemed out of place.

"Just everyone relax and I'll think of something." As much as he tried, there was no confidence in voice.

The swaying of the bridge started to make Alaric feel nauseous. His eyes started to glaze over and he felt as though he was going to vomit. He did not realise, but he had started mumbling under his breath. No one else could hear what he was saying.

"I think I have it!" called Eldred with some excitement.

After a moment had passed, Eldred muttered a few words. No one heard what he had said, but as he spoke, he spread his arms out in front. Alaric felt a tingle in the back of his mind. He took a staggered step forward as if something had compelled him. His head started to ache, although there was no reason why it should. It did not take long for the bridge to reduce its amount of swaying and finally come to a halt.

Once on the other side, a sense of relief washed over him and his head no longer ached. Alaric didn't like the time spent on the bridge, realizing something strange and unknown had happened, but he didn't know what it was.

The forest on the other side of the river was not as dense, the undergrowth was not as thick and the ground was smoother. Riding was not going to be a problem.

The group rode for the rest of the afternoon in silence. The bridge had left them all feeling as if something had happened that none of them understood. Eldred was the only one who didn't feel that way. He acted as though nothing special had happened at all. Strange that Eldred, who was always the first to notice peculiarities, had no idea what the others had felt.

By dusk, Eldred reigned the group to a stop by a small grove of elm trees. A cool breeze had blown in about half an hour before they stopped. The wind brought an unnatural chill as though it was somehow out of place and there was a feeling of unrest in the air.

The small fire that Eldred lit did very little to take the chill. There was little conversation around the fire as they ate dinner. Everyone was reflecting on the events of the day. The experience on the bridge had taken something out of them. It was the first time when their lives had been in danger. Shortly after dinner, they all retired for the night except for Dorn who was due to take the first watch.

Despite his exhaustion, Alaric didn't fall asleep straight away. He lay on his back on his bedroll staring through the forest canopy, up at the sky. Something had happened to him on the bridge and he really wanted to work it out. He was deep in thought, not getting any closer to the answer he was looking for, when he finally drifted off to sleep.

Chapter 8: The Well of Wisdom

"I haven't smelt anything like it in a long time," the words didn't seem to fit the low guttural tone.

A long period of sniffing was followed by two pairs of nostrils. There was a feeling of excitement amongst the two brothers. Something was in the forest that they had not come across in a long time, too long as far as they were concerned.

"Mother could smell it from the cave. I didn't believe her at first, but now that I can smell it for myself, I'm glad I came out," the second voice was just as strange as the first one.

"Quiet now. We are getting close. We don't want to alert them to our presence."

The two trolls did their best to sneak through the forest. They did surprisingly well, considering their mass. Trolls were not well known for their stealth abilities, yet the two managed to avoid any major obstacles. They crept through the forest making only the slightest of noises.

"Mother said they would have someone on watch. We need to make sure we get it first. Make sure it doesn't make any noises and wake the others," the sound was strange as the troll tried to whisper.

The first troll was a good foot taller than his brother. He stood just less than ten feet and his body matched his height. Two great tusks protruded from his mouth making his already grotesque features even more horrible. Mismatched hair patched the troll's body which was completely naked except for a loin cloth. His brother looked very similar except for the difference in height and the absence of tusks. His dark hair seemed to be in the right places. They both looked ugly and ferocious in their own rights and it would take a brave man not to run away crying if they met the two in the middle of the night.

A small fire lit the way for them. They could see a small one sitting by the fire. That must have been the guard. There were six others lying around. It would not be easy catching the small one without him making a noise.

"It looks alert. How are we going to capture it without him warning the others?" the second brother tried to keep his voice as quiet as possible.

"Leave it to me," the first brother said.

Slowly, as they crept towards the camp, he produced a small slingshot from a pouch in his loin cloth. It didn't take him long to find a suitable rock to use as ammunition. They moved a little closer to the fire before he signaled for them to stop. It only took a moment for him to take aim and fire. A small snap of the slingshot was the only warning it got before it was struck on the back of the head. There was no time for a warning cry before its limp body sunk to the ground.

Before long the trolls each had a body each safely tucked away in separate bags. They took the bodies outside of earshot of the others in case they made any noise. Things were looking good for them. Within another five minutes they had another two bagged up and safely away from the others.

"I'm hungry. Can we eat one of them now?" the second brother asked.

"No! Mother wants us to bring them back to her and you know how Mother gets if we don't do what she says."

"Well what about the four legs. She didn't say anything about them," the second brother was whining.

"Yes, I think that would be acceptable. Mother didn't mention anything about the four legs. We have some dinner, then grab the rest of them and head home." The first brother seemed excited with the idea.

The horses were picketed about twenty paces from where the others rested. The trolls came down wind of the animals, not giving them a chance to smell their arrival. The trolls hunted with a grace that was uncommon to their kind. The horses didn't have a clue until the trolls were upon them. They systematically slaughtered all the animals before they started to feed. Their patience and organization was far superior to any other troll.

The feeding frenzy didn't stop until all the animals had been devoured. There was a distinct lack of food in the forest and when they had the chance to eat, they didn't stop until all the food was gone. Blood stained their bodies and they reveled in the carnage they had created. Besides the blood stained ground, only a few bones and hooves were the only sign that the horses had ever been there.

"I want to eat the others now." Blood filled drool seeped from the second brother's mouth.

"Calm down, we have to get these back to Mother," the first brother panted.

The feeding frenzy was euphoric for the trolls. Once started, it was very hard for them to stop. It took all of the first brother's will power to control himself let alone his brother. There was one thing that made it easier for them and that was the fear of reprisal from their mother.

"Quiet." the first brother hissed as they approached the camp. The fire had burnt out, but his troll eyes were more than able to see in the dark. "I think one of them is starting to stir. We should get out of here. We don't want to risk losing them."

The second brother growled lowly. "What are you afraid of? There are only three two legs left. If they wake up, we can kill them," it took a great effort for him to keep his voice down.

"I know, but Mother prefers them alive. It is better if we take four back alive than seven back dead."

There was no arguing with his logic. The second brother was not happy, but knew that he couldn't overpower his brother. Even if he could, he probably wouldn't; he would never be able to explain it to his mother.

Without waiting to see if his brother was following, the first brother made for where the other two legs were safely stored in their bags. Four of them would make a nice meal for their mother and she would be pleased with him.

They grabbed their prey and made their way back towards the cave. No one from the campsite came to stop them. They had succeeded in more ways than one.

***

Alaric slowly woke. Their fire had burned out and all that remained was tendrils of smoke. If he had been completely awake, he would have found it strange. Whoever was on guard always made sure the fire was kept burning. In his half asleep state, this didn't seem strange at all.

He could have sworn it was a deep growl that had woken him. As he sat up and stared around, the forest remained quiet. It must have been part of a dream he couldn't remember. The moon was covered by some low clouds keeping the forest floor all but pitch black.

Something was not right; there was a scent in the air that reminded him of death. The feeling would not leave him no matter how many times he told himself he was being silly. He couldn't help but feel that something terrible had just happened.

Alaric sat stock still for five minutes concentrating all his senses on the forest around him. He could not sense any movement and with a deep sigh, Alaric lay back down. He decided there was nothing wrong and he had to get back to sleep. The feeling must have been caused by some bad dream, he tried to reassure himself.

It didn't take long for Alaric to fall asleep again. Even when he did, he could not shake the feeling of dread. His dreams were filled with the screams and cries of those in great pain. He tossed and turned until finally he was woken by a firm shake on the shoulder.

"Wake up Alaric!" Eldred's voice was filled with concern.

"What's happening?"

The night was still dark and the fire had been relit to give them enough light to see. Alaric could only see Eldred and Palentonal, the other bedrolls were empty. The look on Eldred's face proved that something was wrong.

"Get up, quickly. We need to keep moving."

"Where is everyone?" he asked as he rose from his bedroll. "And what is that smell?" A putrid odour hung on the breeze that made Alaric gag.

Eldred looked back at Palentonal who in turn nodded. Something unspoken passed between the two. When Eldred returned his gaze, Alaric's face was riddled with concern.

"It seems we have had some visitors during the night. By the looks of the tracks, they were trolls."

A flicker of fear crossed Alaric's face. "Where are the others?" desperation filled his voice.

"You need to remain calm. It seems as though the others have been taken prisoner. Palentonal has found their trail. It looks as though they left about two hours ago. They've destroyed the horses, so we are going to have to follow them on foot."

"What do you mean destroyed the horses? How are we going to carry our things?" Alaric was starting to panic.

"We only take the bare essentials. If we weigh ourselves down too much, we will never be able to catch them. We all take a bag of food and all our weapons. The rest will have to stay here."

They started off at a jog with Palentonal leading. He kept his head down following the trail of the trolls. Alaric was next in line with Eldred following at the rear. Eldred and Alaric both carried torches, while Palentonal found it easier to follow the trail in the dark.

Alaric was amazed at the grace of the elf in front of him. His movements seemed so effortless. Alaric struggled to keep pace. He had never really enjoyed running and avoided it as much as possible. Now he wished he had taken the opportunity to stay in shape many years prior.

It was not long before Alaric had to stop for a rest. Sweat poured down his face, whilst the other two looked as fresh as if they had just woken. He was amazed that someone as old as Eldred could keep pace. The only reason why he had been able to keep running for the last mile was the thought of Bern being eaten by trolls. That could only take him so far, he was now out of energy.

"You scout on ahead," commented Eldred. "I'll stay here with Alaric while he catches his breath."

Palentonal quickly disappeared into the night. Alaric wanted to question Eldred about the trolls, but all he could do was pant. He wanted nothing more than to ask Eldred for some more of the elixir, but he thought   he should wait for Eldred to offer. A blind man could see that he was suffering.

"Now there is something you need to know before we reach the troll's cave." He watched Alaric closely to make sure he was paying attention. "These are not any ordinary trolls."

"What do you mean?" puffed Alaric.

"I've have experience with trolls. The first thing that strikes me as strange is that trolls are solitary creatures, unless they are mating." Eldred shuddered as he mentioned that. "By the tracks there were two trolls working together tonight. The second thing is the control. Trolls are never tactical. They slaughtered the horses before they ate them, hence why we didn't hear any noise. Normally trolls will kill and eat as they go. Thirdly, when a troll is in a feeding frenzy they never stop until all the food has been eaten. They showed great restraint not to eat us after they had finished with the horses. It also means that they must have subdued Dorn before they attacked the horses. These are not attributes of typical trolls."

"So what does that mean? We are facing unusually smart trolls? Why should that make any difference?" Alaric's breathing was becoming more settled.

Eldred shook his head slowly, more upset with himself than with Alaric. He wished he had more time to train Alaric in the ways of the world. Things were going to turn ugly if they became separated. "One troll can take down fifty armed men. There's no telling what damage two trolls working together could do, especially ones as seemingly intelligent as the two we are facing. One thing that has me perplexed is why they carried off our friends. It makes no sense at all."

"Why would they not take supplies back to their home? They would have been full from eating the horses," this appeared logical enough for Alaric.

"That would make sense, but you need to know something about troll physiology. They can live for over a year without eating. The more they eat at any one given time the longer they can survive without eating and they can eat a lot more than what they did tonight. This is why their entire attack doesn't make any sense."

Before Alaric had a chance to ask another question they heard Palentonal returning. The sky was starting to turn grey as dawn was approaching.

"What did you see?" asked Eldred, excited for news.

"The cave is not very far away; I would estimate about an hour's walk. I didn't hazard a look inside. I thought it was better to come back and get you first." Palentonal still didn't look flustered.

"We better keep moving. If they are still alive, we have no idea how long they will stay that way." Eldred had already returned to his feet.

They started off again. The rest and the news that Palentonal had found the cave gave him renewed energy. He wanted to run, but the other two did not think it was a good idea. He would need his energy once they reached the cave. Even at the slow pace it did not take Alaric long to tire again.

"I'm sorry Eldred." Alaric panted as he stopped again. "I'm not used to this." He struggled to say more than two words per breath.

"That's alright. You better have some more of the elixir. We need you fighting fit when we reach the cave." Eldred handed Alaric another small vial. "Only take half this time. If you take any more and you risk suffering some side effects."

Alaric heeded his warning and only drank a small amount, the liquid warming his body and instantly his breathing returned to normal. The pain quickly left his body, he felt as though he could run a hundred leagues. Along with his physical self, his spirits were also lifted. He felt as though he could take the trolls on singlehanded.

"Okay, what are we waiting for?" Alaric's voice was uplifted.

"In a minute," Eldred had not finished his warning. "You must promise to wait once we reach the cave. The elixir is giving you a false sense of yourself. You have to listen to my judgement."

With a quick nod from Alaric, they were on the move again. This time he did not feel tired. He had no problem keeping pace with Palentonal who, even at a walk, had increased the speed.

The sun had broken over the horizon and was a good hour in the sky when Palentonal stopped them. They had reached the foot of a small ridge. The face was sheer and would have been impossible to climb. The cave they were looking for was half a mile along the ridge to the north. The forest had changed considerably with everything completely dead within a two-mile radius of the cave. The ground under foot was rocky and dusty. Greys and dull browns were the only colours to be seen.

"The death of the forest is not natural. There is something very wrong here," Palentonal sounded sad as he spoke. "The cave is not far from here; we should be careful. I know that trolls aren't renowned for coming outside during the day, but we don't know what to expect."

"More to the point we don't if there are only two. I would love to have a sneak preview of what's in the cave. I have a bad feeling we might be walking into a trap." If Eldred was unsure, it was not a good sign.

They walked along the foot of the ridge. They were all vigilant of their surroundings. It would be hard for anyone, or anything, to sneak up on them. The forest was open and bare, leaving no place to hide. Even so, they did not want to leave anything up to chance.

Within half an hour of stalking along the edge of the ridge, they came to the mouth of the cave. The smell coming from the opening reminded Alaric of the smell at their campsite, only much worse.

"You must steal yourself." Eldred spoke when he saw the look of revulsion on Alaric's face. "There is going to be much worse once we get inside."

Alaric swallowed down the urge to vomit and took a deep breath. He would be strong to save his friend. It was his fault that Bern was with them, no matter what the others said, and he was not going to let him die.

"Do you want me to go in and scout?" offered Palentonal.

"That's okay. I have a feeling that scouting is going to work more against us than for us."

Before they made their way into the cave, they left their bags, and the others' weapons under a large bush. Eldred slowly made his way to the mouth of the cave. This was not the first time he had crept into a troll's cave. Even so he still felt uncomfortable; the smell of rotting flesh slapped him across the face as soon as he entered. It took an extreme effort to keep his stomach down. He hoped that Alaric would be able to do the same. There was something strange about the cave, but not even Eldred could work it out.

Palentonal followed closely behind Eldred with Alaric behind him. Once inside the mouth of the cave, the smell didn't seem to bother Alaric anymore. It was if he was able to shut off his sense of smell.

Inside there was a large tunnel leading into the ravine wall. The three of them could have easily walked side by side, with plenty of room between them. They chose, however, to walk in single file hugging the wall. There was no light in the cave after they had rounded the first corner. The wall helped them guide their way through the cave and as they moved further into the tunnel, the air became musty and humid. The temperature gradually increased as they continued deeper.

They didn't have to walk far before they could see the flicker of a fire light against the wall ahead. There was no doubt that around the next corner they would see the trolls. As soon as he saw the light, Eldred motioned for them to stop.

"I have to warn you both of what to expect when you get around the corner. What you are going to see will be one of the most terrifying things you will ever witness. Not just the trolls themselves, but their living area will be scary enough." Eldred paused as the thought sunk into their heads. "We need to assess the situation once we reach the corner. There will be the urge to charge in, fear will do that, but you must suppress it and wait for my command.

All three of them drew their swords, as quietly as possible, before Eldred started to move again. Slowly they crept towards the light. Alaric's heart pounded. The noise echoed in his head. His palms were sweating, making his sword slip in his hand, he quickly grabbed it before it came crashing down onto the tunnel floor.

As they neared the corner they could hear the grunts and laughter coming from the trolls. Soon they could make out what the trolls were saying. The guttural voices made them hard to understand. The words did not seem as though they should be coming from the voices speaking them.

"This will be a great meal; you boys have done well." The voice, as rough as it was, could only be called female.

Satisfied grunts came from the mouths of two different trolls. The two of them seemed happy with the approval of the female.

As soon as he heard the words, Eldred waved the others to a stop. He wanted to scout ahead by himself. Although no one could see him in the light, they knew that he had become deeply concerned. Step, by slow step, Eldred inched his way closer to the corner. A quick movement was all that he needed to peer around the corner and into the troll's cave. Once he was back to the others he spoke very quietly.

"We need to go back to entrance." He turned the other two around and pushed them back the way they came.

Once they were out of the cave, they could clearly see the concern on Eldred's face. Alaric's heart sank suddenly. The fact that Eldred made them come out of the cave and the look on his face could only mean one thing. He had to breathe deeply to keep from collapsing at the thought of his best friend being eaten.

"What did you see?' asked Palentonal, not making the same connection that Alaric did.

"It's much worse than I originally thought." Eldred paused as he looked for the words to explain what he had seen. "There are three trolls in the cave, two brothers and a Mothertroll."

"But have they eaten the others?" Palentonal interrupted, not able to wait to find out the others' fate.

"No, they are still alive." The words brought Alaric to attention. "But I don't know for how long. These are not ordinary trolls. Something has made these trolls intelligent. I didn't have enough time to look around to see if there was anything in the cave that had affected them."

"How do you know that they are any different than other trolls?" Alaric had renewed faith that their friends would be alright.

"They can communicate with each other for starters. Normally trolls can just grunt and gesture, but these can talk. The three of them also seem to be co-existing with some sort of organisation. The how and why at this point in time is inconsequential. What we need to be concerning ourselves with is how we are going to get them.

Eldred explained, with great detail considering he only saw the layout of the cave for a split second. In the centre there was a small stone well. A small fire burnt to the left of the well close to the wall of the cave. Sitting just above the fire was a large cauldron, the water was not yet bubbling. Standing around the cauldron was the Mothertroll and the two brothers. Towards the back of the cave, almost in the dark, were four neat little bags.

"What do you suggest we do?" asked Palentonal when Eldred had finished.

"I don't think an all-out attack is going to be successful. One troll, on its own, with the element of surprise we might succeed. Three trolls, working together, there is no hope. I think the only way we can rescue our friends is to try and draw the trolls out of the cave. If Palentonal and I draw the trolls out, then Alaric can rescue the others," there was very little confidence in his voice.

Eldred was about to return inside when Palentonal grabbed him by the shoulder. "I think we have one more option we need to think about." Palentonal looked back at Alaric before he spoke. "We need to keep him alive, the others are expendable. Maybe we should think about leaving them and making for Elhjem."

"That is not an option. I am not leaving Bern in there to be eaten by trolls," Alaric burst out, almost yelling.

"Calm down, we need to keep our heads. You are right though; we cannot leave them here to die. For the prophecy to play out, we need all the players," Eldred tried to explain without giving anything away.

"So what happens to the prophecy if we fail here today?" Palentonal asked accusingly.

That doesn't bare thinking about, so let's concentrate on what we have to do to get everyone out alive," Eldred's words were ominous.

There was going to be no more discussion on the matter. Palentonal knew that Eldred would not risk their lives needlessly; at least he would not waste Alaric's life. Eldred gently brushed Palentonal's arm from his shoulder and made for the cave. Palentonal followed quickly behind, but Alaric hesitated. There had been something nagging him. He knew that Eldred had told him not to use the stone, but he thought that it might come in handy if the plan didn't work.

Alaric hurried to where the last of their possessions were hidden and quickly found the stone's small chest. His fingers ran over the runes and then paused on its latch. His heart was racing again. Closing his eyes, he reached inside and let his fingers clasp around the small stone. A sudden burst of heat raced through his body that nearly knocked him off his feet, but as soon as the heat arrived it was gone again. When he regained his composure, he stuffed the stone into his shirt pocket and hurried after the other two.

The smell in the cave seemed more potent now. Even though the stench was stronger it didn't have any effect on him. There   had been no change in the light in the tunnel, but now he could make out small markings on the wall. After a closer inspection, he could see that they were not marking but scratches. Some, which were clearly made by the trolls, were large scratchings. The others were a lot smaller. Alaric almost gagged as he thought who or what had made them.

Eldred and the elf were almost at the corner leading into the cave. He could clearly see them staring back at him, waiting for him to catch up. He could also see the fear across their faces. It was not going to be an easy plan to execute.

"They know you're here," the sudden voice, even at a whisper, almost made Alaric cry out in shock. He spun around to see where the voice had come from, but there was no one there. He thought it was the tension that had caused him to hear things. Shaking his head, he continued along the tunnel.

As he approached, he could hear something very quiet in the distance. It was like a deep whisper. The noise did not make any sense, but what he did know was that their plan, now, had no chance of succeeding. Before he had a chance to reach the others, there was the sound of a deep rumbling voice.

"You can come out now. Your miserable attempt of sneaking around is becoming boring," the female voice of the Mothertroll did not sound right.

Eldred motioned for Alaric to stay behind. He hoped that the trolls had only managed to sense the two of them. If all of them had been found then they were all dead. Once he was sure that Alaric wasn't going to follow them into the cave, he led Palentonal in.

Palentonal was physically sick when he saw the state of the cave. The sight was more repulsive than the smell it was omitting. The smooth rock walls and the floor of the cave were stained almost black with years of dried blood. A multitude of bones covered the floor, from many different animals as well as many bones from men and elves. A small pile of entrails remained from their last meal, although Palentonal couldn't tell what manner of beast they came from. Besides small patches of clean stone, the only thing that remained untouched by the trolls was the well in the centre of the cave.

"You're not safe here. Run away while you still have the chance. The others are all dead now." The voice came to Alaric again. This time it sounded as if it came from right behind him.

Again there was no one there when he turned around. He knew that it wasn't a hallucination this time. He had definitely heard someone whispering to him. Nothing was really making sense, why should this be any different.

"You may as well tell your friend to join us as well. There is no point in him remaining by himself in the dark," the guttural voice brought Alaric's attention back to the trolls.

His heart sank as he walked into the cave. The sight should have horrified him, but all he could think of was the strange voice that couldn't possibly have been there. That was his only hope now. If only the mysterious spirit could save them.

"Good. Now that you're all here, we can start our dinner." The water had started to bubble and the Mothertroll had what could only be described as a smile on her face.

The two brothers moved around to face the trio. They both brandished large cudgels, the club end as large as a man's head. Drool dipped from their mouths in anticipation of the kill.

Eldred did something that surprised the other two. He raised his staff in his left hand and lowered his sword in the other. Taking a deep breath, he boomed out the words "Azüré ët Illonüe!" in an ancient tongue that Alaric didn't recognise.

Everyone in the cave paused in an eerie silence. Even the trolls seemed confused at Eldred's outburst. The next sound was the fearful laughter of the Mothertroll. It was enough to set the three on edge and truly fear for their lives.

"A wizard no less," the Mothertroll almost growled. "I don't know if that's a good thing or a bad thing. You might be all old and gristly. Then again, if I eat you, I may gain all your powers; now isn't that an interesting theory?" the Mothertroll seemed to be enjoying herself. "I must admit though, I would have thought a wizard would have more sense than to come in here."

"What are you talking about?" Eldred was just as confused as everyone else. The Mothertroll seemed as though she wanted to talk. The more time he could stall the two other trolls from attacking, the more time he had to think of a plan to get them out.

"This is the cave of knowledge." Eldred instantly knew where they were and why his spell didn't work, but the look of confusion on his face kept the Mothertroll talking. "Very disappointing. If nothing else, I will teach you something before you die. That," she pointed at the well in centre of the cave "is the *Well of Everlasting Knowledge*, one of the seven magic wells. This cave is protected from magical attacks from the likes of you." She paused as she watched Eldred's face intently. He feigned interest as he desperately tried to devise a new plan. "I came to this cave many years ago when I was pregnant with my two sons. Back then, I was a mindless monster, but now I'm a sophisticated creature of the world. The knowledge from the well flooded into our heads. Within months, we were smarter than the average animals. Now we are the smartest creatures in the world. I never realised before how stupid and mindless trolls were; I guess that's why we were all but annihilated." All three trolls started laughing at her last comment. When they had finished she continued to speak. "Now I think that is all you need to know and don't think that I don't realise that you are trying to devise a plan." Eldred looked shocked, but knew that it would not have its desired effect. "The only reason why I carried on was to give you a false sense of hope. You see I like to play with my victims before I eat them. Now I must say that I was satisfied with your four friends, but since you decided to join the party it would be untroll-like of me to let you leave."

"You have to let me help you." The voice whispered into Alaric's ear as the two trolls advanced on them.

Eldred and Palentonal stood in front of Alaric in a protective manner. There was only one thing they could do now and that was to try and get Alaric out alive. They both knew that no one else was going to make it.

"You must get out of here," Eldred spoke urgently over his shoulder at Alaric.

Alaric didn't hear a word Eldred said. The voice that seemed to be inside his head now, was all he could hear. It just repeated the same words over and over again. "You have to let me help you." He had no idea who it was that was speaking to him, but he knew he had no choice but to agree.

"What do you want me to do?" Alaric didn't care who heard. The sudden outburst caused the trolls to hesitate which in turn gave Eldred and Palentonal a chance to attack.

The offensive was as useless, as they thought it would be. The sword strokes, as adeptly as they were given, simply slid off the trolls' thick skin. This allowed for the trolls to swing their cudgels in a counter attack. Both Eldred and Palentonal were lucky to escape with their heads still on their shoulders.

"Let yourself go." The voice coaxed him.

"What do you mean?" No one was listening to him now as they were in the heat of battle. Only the Mothertroll seemed to notice that he was there at all.

Alaric could have sworn he heard the voice scoff at him, but with the raucous going on in the background it was hard to hear. "You need to submit yourself to my control." The voice was dripping with anticipation.

Something didn't seem right to Alaric, but he knew he had no choice. If he stood there much longer, they all would end up dead. If he ran, there would be no way for him to find his way out of the forest. His only choice was to obey the voice in his head.

Suddenly Alaric felt a heat fill his body. The feeling made him light headed and he wobbled on his feet and he fought to stay upright. Sweat poured down his body, but he refused to collapse. If the trolls had been paying any attention to him, then he would have been dead.

"Release yourself. Stop fighting me." There was strain in the voice that shouldn't have been there. The voice was hard to hear as ears were filled with the rushing of blood.

"Okay!" cried Alaric at the top of his voice.

His outburst brought silence to the cave. It was not the fact that he had spoken, but the tone in his voice. All eyes were on him now. Even Eldred couldn't take advantage of the trolls' distraction.

Alaric's body had gone completely rigid. His eyes had rolled back into his head. Nothing moved. The sudden transformation shocked everyone in the cave. It was the Mothertroll who regained her composure first.

"What do you think you're going to do? Did you think when your friends trick didn't work, that yours would? Boys, kill him!" the order was sent with love and the purest confidence that it would be completed.

"I think that you might want to reassess your situation." The voice came out of Alaric's mouth, but it was clear to all that it was not his.

The trolls kept up their advance, not foreseeing the imminent danger to their lives. The light in the cave seemed to waver, even though the fire did not die down. Palentonal was about to advance on the trolls, but Eldred held him back.

"This is your last chance," although the words spoke of a treaty, there was never going to be one.

Just before the two trolls were within striking distance their feet froze to the ground. No matter how hard they tried, they could not move a step closer to their prey. They looked around at their mother, hoping that she would be able to give them an answer.

"What are you doing?" the Mothertroll obviously had no idea what was happening.

"I thought you were the smartest creature in the world?" his words were dripping with contempt.

The two brothers were starting to whimper where they stood, stuck to the floor. The Mothertroll knew that she was starting to lose control of the situation. What should have been an easy kill was quickly starting to look like their downfall. She had to think quickly if she was going to get out alive.

"I'll give you this offer once and be sure that I will not offer it again. You can leave. Walk away now and leave the others. Do this and I will let you live," there was no confidence in her voice. This only increased the whimpering of her sons.

Hearing the words brought a tirade of laughter from Alaric's mouth. The sound sent a chill down Palentonal's spine. As he started laughing, the two trolls were released. Both fell head first onto the floor, not expecting the sudden freedom.

With Alaric's apparent attention diverted, the Mothertroll decided to make her attack. With agility uncanny of her structure, she charged toward him. To her folly, she did not prepare herself for Alaric to regain his composure.

One moment Alaric was mindlessly laughing and the next in a stance that would make a hardened sword master blush. The edges of his sword started to softly glow red. Palentonal thought it just a reflection of the fire light, Eldred knew better.

Just as the Mothertroll was about to strike, Alaric deftly ducked and stepped to his left. The Mothertroll had committed too much to her charge and could not change her course. With one swift movement, Alaric thrust his blade straight through her middle. She slid backwards whilst her legs made another two stumbled steps before crashing to the ground. As he pulled the sword free, the wound suddenly burst into flame. Within a matter of seconds, the Mothertroll was turned to ash.

Seeing the death of their mother sent the two brothers into a further state of fear. Without a thought for their surroundings, they jumped to their feet and starting running towards the exit. With their mother dead, they knew they had no chance.

Turning around slowly Alaric waited until the trolls were just about to round the corner and leave. Just when they were about to reach freedom, Alaric outstretched his arm and levelled his sword until it was pointed at the farthest troll. The tip of his sword glowed a gentle red, flared for a second and as it did the troll burst into flames. When the tip of his sword returned to its gentle glow, the troll had disintegrated into a pile of ash.

The final troll froze in pure terror, a feeling not normal to trolls. Alaric's face remained cold as ice as he prepared the troll's fate. The eyeless gaze of Alaric held the troll captive. The monster was unable to move.

Alaric moved his sword until it pointed at the last troll. This time a bolt of red light shot forth from the blade. Within seconds, the light had consumed the troll and left nothing but a wisp of smoke.

Once he was done with the trolls, he turned on Eldred and Palentonal. Palentonal had relaxed considerably, once the trolls had been dealt with. Eldred, on the other hand, was aware of the eminent danger. No emotion showed on Alaric's face. There was no sign of stress.

"You need to fight it Alaric," his voice was thick with concern.

A slight twitch above his left eye was the only indication that he had heard Eldred's words. Slowly, he raised his sword and pointed it towards the wizard. The tip started to glow more fiercely. With the power Alaric was wielding there, was nowhere for Eldred to hide.

"Aùritaël!" Eldred boomed at the top of his voice.

It was like someone had poured a bucket of freezing water over his head. The intense warmth that had filled him was suddenly extinguished. With the heat, also went all of Alaric's energy. His body crumbled to the ground as if he was made out of jelly. Sweat covered his entire body and his breathing became laboured.

Eldred quickly rushed to his side. "Get the others!" Eldred called over his shoulder when he realised that Palentonal still hadn't moved. "Can you hear me?" Eldred spoke gently to Alaric.

"Where am I?" Alaric's voice was weak.

"Just relax. There will be time for explanations later." Eldred was relieved to hear him speak.

Lifting Alaric over his shoulder, Eldred left Palentonal to free the rest of the group and headed out of the cave. The fresh air hit them immediately; the stench remained on them, but it was dampened by the cool forest air.

After making sure Alaric was comfortable, Eldred checked his pockets for what he knew must be there. Finding the stone, Eldred took a deep breath. He was not looking forward to what he had to do. Closing his eyes, he snatched it up and stuffed the Ruby Stone into its chest. With a great effort, he closed the lid and locked the clasp. Once done, he dropped the chest and slumped to the ground, resting against a thick oak tree. He took another deep breath, glad to be outside the cave with everyone still alive. They would leave with a valuable experience.

Shortly after the two had left the cave, Palentonal led a rather embarrassed group out into the fresh air. The two dwarves seemed to be the most uncomfortable. Bern was the only one who looked truly horrified, which changed shortly after with a look of total relief.

"I think I could die a happy man if I never experience anything like that again," his voice cracked as he tried to make light of his fearful encounter.

"I'll drink to that," barked Hulkan, breaking into a fit of laugher.

"We'll rest here for a while." If it wasn't for Alaric being Unconscious, Eldred would have pushed the group to their feet. "Palentonal, why don't you go hunting while the others are resting?"

Eldred quickly dismissed the questioning look on Palentonal's face. He didn't want to answer any questions on what had happened in the cave until he had a chance to speak to Alaric.

"So what happened in there?" asked Dorn.

"Rest for now. There will be time for answers later," Eldred returned to his feet and walked away from the group. He had a lot of thinking to do before he could give anyone any answers.

The rest of the group ate a light meal. There was not a lot of food left in the packs they had taken with them. There was only enough for another two or three meals before their supplies were completely exhausted. Palentonal had little chance of finding any food for them. No one had seen any animals since the trolls had taken them.

It was just after midday when Palentonal returned with a small deer draped over his shoulders. There was not a great amount of meat of the animal, but it was better than nothing.

Alaric had just regained consciousness moments before Palentonal returned. Eldred had given him another dose of the elixir when he was able to sit up. He was loathed to give Alaric any more of the drug, but it would take him too long to recover enough to walk. There was not enough for the others. They would have to fight through their pain.

There was no way for them to preserve the meat Palentonal had brought back, but nobody was too disappointed they had to eat the deer before they left. Alaric, especially, was starving. Even after eating his share, he was still ravenous. Knowing they had little food left, he refrained from speaking.

Eldred started the group moving again. Those who had been captured could not keep a fast pace. Although no one was seriously hurt, they did sustain some injuries. The slow pace frustrated Eldred. The rescue had led them off course. If all had gone to pla,n they would have been resting comfortably in Elhjem that night. Now it would be at least another day, if not two, before they reached their destination.

They walked constantly for the rest of the day and didn't stop until the sun was all but set. Eldred had to push the group to keep them going. Palentonal was the only one who didn't complain. Besides the occasional gripe, the rest of the walk was done in complete silence. The kidnapping had taken more out of them then Eldred had hoped.

There was complete silence around the campfire as they ate that night. Not just from pure exhaustion, but also from a lack of anyone wanting to talk. It was clear that the two dwarves had lost a lot of pride by being captured. The whole experience was demoralising for the group and Eldred not giving any answers, did not help. In fact, Eldred had very few answers to give.

Once they had settled in for the night, Eldred motioned for Alaric to take a walk with him. The effects of the elixir were still in full force and he wasn't feeling as tired as the others.

"What did you want to talk about?" asked Alaric when they were out of earshot.

"What happened in the cave?" Eldred came straight to the point.

"I..." Alaric paused as he tried to remember exactly what had happened. "I don't remember. The last thing I remember is taking the stone and entering the cave. Everything after that is a blur."

"You must remember something. Even the most inane detail might be important." Eldred was starting to get frustrated.

Alaric tried to remember what had happened. There was something in the back of his mind. Whenever he tried to recall the memory, his mind diverted to another thought. It was as if something was blocking his memory. He was sure it was what he needed to remember.

"There is something there, but I can't recall it." Alaric was starting to worry.

"Good, very good!" Eldred's response confused him. "Stand still for a moment and close your eyes."

Alaric did as he was commanded. Once he was in position, Eldred placed his hands on Alaric's head. A sudden shot of power passed through his body making Alaric feel a little shaky.

"How do you feel now?" Eldred asked as he stepped away.

Alaric thought for a moment. Suddenly the memory that he was lacking returned. "There was a voice. At first it seemed to be behind me, but as I moved into the troll's cave, it seemed to be coming from inside my head."

"What did it say to you?" Eldred sounded excited.

"It's hard to remember." The memory was still very hazy. "I think it said something like relax or relent."

"Release yourself?" The question didn't need answering.

It was as Eldred had feared. The stone had taken control of Alaric and used his body as a receptacle to destroy the trolls and all of them if Eldred had not been able to bring him back. This time they had managed to remain unscathed. There was no telling what would happen next time.

"Yes, but what does it all mean? I still can't remember what happened after that. The next thing that I can remember, I was lying on the grass outside the cave." Alaric knew that something had happened, something that involved him and the stone.

"When you relinquished your will to the stone, it possessed your body," Eldred continued to tell Alaric what had happened in the cave.

"So the stone just gave up control once it had killed the trolls?" Alaric knew that the story was lacking some vital information.

Eldred failed to mention that he had attempted to kill them. He figured that little piece of information should be left out. "Whilst the stone is encased in the crystal, we had a certain amount of control. There is a magic phrase that causes the stone to go dormant. This is also something that we need to talk about." Alaric knew that there was a lecture coming.

He also knew that there was going to be valuable information that he needed to know. "The stone will work both ways and you will need to know how and when to use it. The first and least dangerous is for you to take control of the stone's power. With the power of the stone, you will be able to do things that you only dreamed possible. The second and extremely dangerous way is to let the stone take control of you." Eldred watched Alaric carefully as his words sunk in.

"But isn't that what just happened?" Alaric didn't think what Eldred said made any sense.

"There are things that you won't be able to do on your own. You will need the stone's direction. With the proper training, you will be able to learn to control yourself while the stone possesses you. I know that it's not making much sense at the moment, but it will in time. Once we reach Elhjem, we will start your training. Until then, you need to make sure that you leave the stone in its chest."

"But if you can nullify the stone with a simple phrase, then what's the problem?" Alaric wished he had not asked the question as soon as the words left his mouth.

"Because once the crystal has been removed, the vocal commands will no longer work. Once you remove the crystal, you will need to overpower the stone with your will alone."

All the information seemed to make sense. There were still ideas that he didn't fully understand, but Eldred said he would explain further in due course and that was enough for him. He had received enough information for the moment. He needed a good night sleep to let everything sink in.

When they returned to the campsite everyone, except for Palentonal, had gone to sleep. He quickly came to his feet when he saw the two approach. Eldred shook his head. He waited until Alaric had gone to sleep before he spoke to Palentonal.

The two spoke long into the night. Palentonal had a lot of questions, but Eldred had few answers. By the time Palentonal went to sleep, he was comfortable with what he had been told.

No one had a comfortable sleep that night. A cold wind blew in taking all the heat out of the fire. They had not managed to take any of the blankets or bedrolls. They had only taken packs containing food. The ground was rough and uncomfortable. There were a lot of bleary eyes when Eldred woke them at dawn.

They ate a light breakfast, as their food stores were dwindling away and they didn't have time to go on a hunting expedition. The morale of the group had not increased from the previous day. Eldred was still being cryptic about what had happened in the trolls' cave. He had sworn Palentonal to secrecy and he would not break his promise. Eldred did give them a little comfort by saying he would speak to them all one by one during the day. He had to be careful who was told what. There were pieces of information he didn't want Alaric to find out, at least not until the time was right.

"We're going to have to keep a brisk pace today. Hopefully we should be able to reach the edge of the village by nightfall,' on that note Eldred started them on their way.

"Are you sure you know where you're leading us?" asked Palentonal as the sun neared its pinnacle.

"We're heading in the right direction. That is the best I can tell you. The path to Elhjem is very specific. Our little sidetrack has put me completely off course. I just need to find one of the landmarks."

By nightfall, he had not found any of the landmarks he had been looking for. They had walked a long way, stopping only briefly at midday for another small meal. Once they had eaten their evening meal, their rations would be low and there would only be enough food left for one more meal. This fact brought the morale of the group even lower. Even though Palentonal was the only one who knew they were off course, they all knew that something wasn't right.

Sensing the ever growing depression amongst the others, Eldred made a decision to share his concerns. "As you might have noticed, we haven't exactly been heading straight for Elhjem."

"Why is that? I thought that you knew where you were leading us," barked Hulkan.

"It's not quite that simple." Eldred was again getting into lecture mode, this time slightly defensive. "The village is protected by some powerful magic. We were following a fairly specific course when we got waylaid. In the morning, I'll send the elves out to scout for a couple of landmarks that should be around here. If we keep walking, I fear that we are going to go straight past the village." Eldred looked towards their food supply as he spoke.

His words didn't bring a lot of hope to the group, but they did accept that he was doing all that he could. Again everyone was keen for an early night. Only the elves and Eldred didn't seem to be struggling from the long day's walk.

In the morning, Eldred gave the elves instructions on what the landmarks were. They left the campsite without eating, being able to find some nut and berries whilst they were scouting. The rest of the food would be divided up amongst the others for breakfast.

Craven was the first to return. The broad smile on his face showed that he had found what he was looking for. He had found a small oak tree with a cleft trunk. If he had not known what he was looking for, he would have assumed that it was a normal tree. The description Eldred had given had shown him otherwise.

"We should keep moving," Eldred's tone was more promising now. "By midday we should be at the edge of the village."

"What about Palentonal?" Alaric asked.

"He will catch up to us." Craven had no problem leaving. He knew his fellow elf would be able to follow their tracks.

Eldred nodded before Alaric could ask the question. They left quickly with a new spring in their step. The thought of being stuck in the forest without food was not pleasing. Now that they would soon be somewhere with a roof over their head and a soft bed underneath them, their spirits were renewed.

Palentonal caught up with them shortly after they left the campsite. Although it was clear that he had been running, there was no sign of fatigue. Alaric wondered at the elf's ability to continually run.

"I assume that you have found a sign?" Palentonal asked when he returned to the group.

"We should be at Elhjem in a couple of hours," Eldred replied quickly, his attention was still diverted on his surroundings.

In just over two hours, Eldred realised that the others had stopped behind him. He had been so concerned by what was around him that he had not noticed what was straight in front of him. What he did see gave him a sigh of relief.

A deep fog had settled in the forest before them. The fog was thicker than anything Alaric had ever seen before and it didn't seem to move with the wind. It was clear to all of them it was not a natural fog.

"I'm not going in there," Dorn looked at Eldred when he spoke. "I'm not real smart when it comes to this sort of thing, but I know an evil fog when I see it."

The others nodded and grunted their agreement. The large smile on Eldred's face didn't reassure anyone. He couldn't blame them really. He would have steered clear if he didn't know any better, there was going to have to be a very good excuse to get anyone to step into the fog.

Chapter 9: Elhjem

"You were all right to avoid the fog. It is good that you can recognise danger. That is one of the keys to our survival. The enemy will come at us in many forms, some harder than others to decipher. If you kept going into the fog, there would be little chance of being seen again." Eldred had stopped them for lunch and explained what was ahead of them.

The remainder of their stores was not enough for a decent meal. The fact that they were on the border of Elhjem was not reassuring. They did not feel comfortable with their surrounding and, even though Eldred was explaining the limited danger, he was having a hard time getting them to understand.

"What do you mean? Why would we not come out if we entered the fog?" Hulkan sounded confused.

"The fog is a magical barrier protecting Elhjem." Eldred continued. "It's a powerful spell that will keep out anyone who should not know the location of the village. Once inside the fog, the spell will keep anyone from finding the village and will also keep anyone from finding their way out."

"So if we go in, there is a chance that we might not ever come out?" Palentonal was getting his head around the situation.

"But you didn't say we could *never* leave the fog; isn't there still be a chance to escape?" Craven looked hopeful.

"Please, give me a chance to explain." Eldred didn't like having questions thrown at him without having a chance to answer. "Although the village itself isn't very large, the ground area needed to make the fog effective is. A spell cast over such a vast area cannot be perfect, even with a number of spellbinders constantly updating it. There is a slight chance that if someone wanders into the fog they will find their way to the village or their way out, but the odds are not great."

"So we're just going to take a chance in the fog?" Hulkan sounded confused.

"Of course not! I have been to see Orric many, many times. I know how to get in and how to get out again. What you all must do is keep the person in front of you in view. We need to keep very close. The thickness of the fog doesn't allow for a great depth of vision. Everyone must be able to either see me or see someone who can see me or someone who can see someone who can see me and so on. This is not something that is negotiable. If you lose sight of the person you are supposed to be watching, then you will be lost in the fog and so will everyone in the line behind you. If anyone feels like they're starting to fall behind, call out for us to stop. Then we move from back to front until we are all together again."

Everyone nodded. His explanation didn't ease anyone's nerves. There was something very eerie about the fog. The fact it hadn't moved an inch since they had sat down was probably the most disturbing fact. Eldred didn't seem to notice their fears.

As soon as they had all finished their meals, Eldred was quick to get them on their feet. He would not be able to relax until he had them all safe in the village. He walked to the edge of the fog and then disappeared inside without waiting for anyone to follow. A moment later the fog opened up around him. He looked back towards the others, but it was clear he was not going to give them any answers.

"I told you to keep close. Next time you won't have a second chance," Eldred's voice was full of concern.

As soon as everyone was lined up behind Eldred he started to lead them deeper into the fog. Once they started moving, the thick fog closed in around them. It seemed strange enough from the outside, but on the inside it was even freakier. It stayed completely still except for the small amount which moved around them as they walked. The fog also kept out all sounds from the forest; the only noise that could be heard was that being made by the group. There was a strong feeling that at any minute, something was going to jump out and attack them.

The tension was thick. Everyone was well aware that they could not see a thing except the person directly in front and directly behind. Alaric was the only one who could see Eldred and therefore the only one who knew that they were still on the right track.

Without warning or explanation, Eldred suddenly called out for them to stop. Alaric could see the Eldred was talking to someone, but could not see who it was. He could only hear muffled voices. It was as though Eldred was deliberately trying to keep his voice low.

"What are you doing here?" asked a tall, attractive, well-built elf.

"I am Eldred and I am here to see Orric. I have with me the Chosen One. We are expected," Eldred kept his voice low so no one behind him could hear.

"I do not recognise that name. We are on high alert at the moment. That means no one gets through unless we know about it. The only party we are expecting today has already arrived." The elf lazily brushed aside a lock of blonde hair with the tip of his bow. Although he had not drawn an arrow, Eldred knew that he could have one nocked within a second.

"We were due in two days ago. I'm sure there will still be a record of our pending arrival. We have travelled a long way and are short of supplies." Eldred tried to plead to the elf's sense of compassion, although he knew that he was not going to have much luck.

"Now that does ring a bell. I haven't been on duty for a few days. I'm sorry though, I can't let you in without the proper clearance. All I can say is go back to the edge of the fog and I'll send someone out to see you. It probably won't be until tomorrow, but that is the best I can do." The elf was not going to budge.

"Send a message to Orric and tell him that Eldred is here." Eldred was starting to become impatient. He could easily overpower the elf, but there was a very good chance that everyone in the group had an arrow aimed at their heads and he also didn't want to upset Orric by knocking out one of his sentries.

"That sounds all well and good, but it wouldn't be until the morning before someone will be back with a message from Orric."

Eldred had to think. There had to be a way he could get them all inside. They could survive another night out in the open, but they were already two days late.

"What about Darziel? He's still head of the guard, isn't he?" It had been a long time, but Eldred hoped that Darziel was in command.

"Well I give you one thing; you definitely seem to know what you're talking about." A quick flick of his head was the only indication that the elf was doing anything. "Lucky for you, Darziel is working today. I'll go and get him for you." The elf flicked his head again, but made no move to leave.

"The fog seems to be losing some of its potency," Eldred tried some small talk as the elf didn't seem to be in any hurry.

"Every year the price of anonymity has to be paid. Each time one of us dies, there is not necessarily someone to replace them. As you may know, elves who possess the power for this kind of magic are few and far between. Our numbers dwindle with each year." The elf didn't seem to mind passing on information.

"Who was in the party that arrived this morning?" He thought he might try his luck on some more information.

"I don't think I know you that well, but if you are who you say you are, then you will find out in good time. Wait here." That was clearly all the elf was going to say before he walked into the dense fog.

Eldred returned his attention to the others. They had all moved up behind Alaric and were clearly trying to listen to the conversation. He realised that they couldn't hear or see who he had been talking to. The anticipation was clear on their faces.

"It will be fine." Eldred's voice left no room for doubt. "We just need to wait here for a moment."

They stood in an uncomfortable silence as they waited for Eldred's mysterious friend to return. It was clear they were all exhausted and wanted nothing more than to be in a safe comfortable place. With every moment that passed, their hopes started to fade.

Just when they were all about to give up hope, the elf returned. This time there was a second elf with him. They both made themselves clear to the entire group and Darziel nodded to the first elf who in turn saluted and left.

"It is good to see you at long last." Darziel shook his hand fiercely. "What took you so long?"

"We were held up by a group of nasty trolls," Eldred spoke to Darziel as they walked. "I hope you don't mind, but it has been a long few days and I think we could all do with a bath and somewhere comfortable to sit down," Eldred's voice held nothing but relief.

"Of course." Darziel patted him on the back with his right hand. With his left hand, he signaled to the elves watching them from within the fog.

Slowly the fog started to dissipate as they followed Darziel towards the village. The forest, to their relief, was now returning to normal. The normal sounds, smells and scenes were flooding back into their surroundings. In less than a minute, there was no longer any sign of the fog.

The forest had suddenly sprung to life. The oak, elm and willow trees spread a sparse canopy. The forest floor was alive with both flora and faunae. Many small animals scurried around without a care. A curious rabbit hopped its way along until it was keeping pace with Alaric. He thought it very strange that the rabbit seemed to be taking a great deal of interest in him.

Small buildings started to appear not only on the forest floor, but in the trees too. Alaric stared at the intricacies in the trees above him. The small, dark coloured houses were joined by a network of rope bridges. As he walked, the light changed in the shadows and Alaric could swear the buildings and the bridges disappeared. Trying to focus on them was starting to make Alaric feel nauseous. Although the feeling to stare at the beauty around him was overwhelming, Alaric forced himself to look at the ground in front; he was glad to see Hulkan and Bern doing the same.

The further they walked, the larger the village grew and the trees became sparser. The village was like nothing Alaric had ever seen before. Trees still dominated the bulk of the scenery and the forest canopy kept most of the village in a virtual twilight. Even at the peak of the day, most of the forest remained in shadow. It gave the village an aura of mysticism.

In the distance, Alaric saw a group of horses. Even Alaric, whose distaste for horses had only increased, since he had been forced to start riding them, was in awe of the creatures' beauty. He had only seen a horse like them once before. As he looked over at Eldred, he thought that he saw a tear in the old wizard's eye. The horse that Eldred had been riding was clearly from the same stock.

Although they had not seen another elf since they had passed through the fog, they knew that they were not alone. Alaric could feel the many eyes watching them as they walked. He peered into the trees and around them, but could not see anyone watching.

"Has there been any word from the North?" Eldred spoke casually to Darziel.

"I have only heard rumours." Eldred knew that Darziel didn't sit on the village council and was not privy to the information that he was after. All he wanted to do was get a general feel of what was happening. "What I have heard isn't good. I think that Orric might want to tell you himself though."

"I suppose you're right. What's been happening, since I've been gone?" Eldred was still keen on some information. He always liked to be up to date whenever he was meeting Orric.

"Besides the ever growing nervousness that any day we will hear word that Nyrra and his army have broken free, things have been carrying on as normal. There is one thing that I have noticed over the last month or so," he paused, considering whether or not he should tell Eldred. "What you must understand is that I am not one hundred per cent sure that this is true. Also Orric does not agree with my findings." it was quite clear that Darziel was not comfortable speaking.

"I understand, but you wouldn't have brought it up if you didn't think I should know." Eldred placed a warm hand on Darziel's shoulder; he obviously needed to tell him something.

"I know. I just need to find the right words. It's more of a feeling than anything else." Darziel paused again. "I've been head of the guard for over a century and as much as I've never helped with the maintenance of the cover, I feel as though it's a part of me. None of the spellbinders have said anything, but I can see it in their eyes. They have a connection with the spell that I will never have. If I can feel it then I know that they can, I just think that they are too proud to say anything."

"What are you talking about? You're not making any sense," Eldred snapped in his impatience, wishing instantly that he hadn't. "It has been well known for a long time that the fog is starting to waiver. It only makes sense since there are not as many spellbinders as there used to be."

"No, it's not that. Everyone accepts a small amount of waning due to the lack of numbers, but this is something completely different, something much more terrifying." There was another slight pause as Darziel looked at the others. For the first time, he realised that they had all stopped their conversations and were listening intently on what he was saying. "It's as if there is something working against the fabric of the spell. It's like someone is trying to unthread the weaves that have been so carefully sewn. I don't think it is just one person out their either. This feels like a carefully orchestrated attack." The more he continued the bolder he became.

"I see," Eldred's comment was very noncommittal. He had his own suspicions about what was happening to the concealment spell, but he didn't want to share them until he had spoken to Orric. "The elf who met us today said there were other visitors. Who's here?" Eldred thought it best to change the conversation.

A broad grin spread across the elf's face. "You have been away for a long time. There have been some interesting developments recently, but again I think that Orric will want to tell you," Darziel chuckled to himself.

Eldred only grunted in reply. He didn't like all the secrecy, but he knew Darziel wouldn't tell him anything that Orric didn't want him to know. His curiosity was at its peak with the new arrivals. With Darziel's reaction, he had a feeling that something very good had happened. That thought lifted his spirits.

The further they walked, the closer the buildings became to each other. The forest floor became busy with elves walking around going about their own business. Although it was clear that they had a purpose, they didn't seem to be in any hurry.

"When you live as many years as elves do, there is no need to rush," Eldred explained to Alaric as they walked.

"We'll be at the guest rooms shortly. Would you like some food brought in for you?" Darziel jumped in before Alaric could ask a question.

"Thank you. That would be nice. The others can rest, but I will be going straight to see Orric," Eldred replied.

"I thought as much. I have had word sent on to Orric that you will be joining him shortly." The grin remained on Darziel's face.

"It is good to see you again." Eldred smiled and slapped Darziel across the shoulder in a sign of friendship.

"As you, my old friend."

Their accommodation comprised of three small buildings, each containing two bedrooms and one common room. The buildings were of a small simple wooden design. On the inside, there was a multitude of pictures and runes carved into the walls and floors giving an aura of mystery.

"I want you all to rest up well tonight. Hopefully, we will have some time here, but we must also be prepared to leave at any moment." Eldred was about to leave when Alaric motioned him over. "What is it Alaric? If you hadn't noticed, I'm in a hurry to see Orric."

"Something's not right," Alaric kept his voice low. He didn't want the others to hear him.

"What are you talking about?" Eldred didn't seem interested and kept walking towards the door.

"I can't say exactly what it is. For about the last hour or so I've had this really bad feeling." There was a serious look of concern on his face.

Eldred paused for a moment and seemed to be lost in thought. He had been so worried about being delayed, that he had missed something that should have been completely obvious. Now, he really did have to get to Orric.

"Don't worry about that. Everything is fine." The look on his face showed that he really didn't believe what he was saying.

Alaric was about to question him when Eldred turned on his heels and hurried out of the door. Darziel shrugged his shoulders and followed him out.

"What was that all about?" asked Bern.

"I don't know." Alaric had no idea what he had said to cause Eldred's reaction. He knew that something was very wrong, but without Eldred to confirm anything, he was not going to worry the others.

"Do you think that there is somewhere for us to bathe. I would love to wash and a fresh set of clothes.

"I don't know, but I'm sure there will be somewhere." Alaric could not concentrate on the conversation. He could not help thinking about what he had not been told.

As if on cue the door opened and a blonde haired elf stood in the doorway. In his arms was a large tray, laden with food. All everyone could think of was eating.

"Once you are done with your meals, you can all go to the bathing stream to wash. There will be some fresh clothes coming shortly."

Darziel had to hurry. Alaric had said something to Eldred that had got him all flustered. Darziel really wanted to know what it was and knew that there was no point in asking, he wouldn't get a satisfactory answer.

***

Orric's house was in the centre of the village. It was built around a large oak tree. Not just a large oak tree, but the largest oak tree in the forest. The house was built on three levels, one on the ground and two leading up the tree. It was definitely the focus point of the village

A stairway wrapped around the tree leading to each level. The ground level was his main residence and was not directly connected to the other two levels. From the outside it looked like it could house half a battalion.

The second level was used for entertaining, something that did not happen much anymore. The feasting hall was built to entertain visiting foreign dignitaries and for the festival of life. Dignitaries rarely visited and it was mainly used just for the festival.

Finally, the top level was used as a meeting room. Being high in the canopy meant it could not be as large as the lower two. The arduous climb up the stairs made the view even more spectacular.

Darziel left Eldred at the base. He knew that he was not invited to their meeting and he was not traipsing up the stairs only to have to come back down again.

"I must get back to my post. I hope to see you again before you leave," Darziel spoke sincerely.

"As do I. I thank you for all your help." Eldred quickly made his way up the stairs as soon as he had finished his pleasantries.

Eldred had never enjoyed the climb. It was not so much the stress, he had climbed much higher and much steeper passages in his time; he just felt the height of the meeting room was completely unnecessary.

At the top of the stairs there was a small landing leading to a set of double doors. Standing on either side of the doors were two elves. Each wore dark green breast plates and steel helmets. The helmets had small intricate green leaves embedded on them, whilst the breast plates had the same leaves in silver. Both of the sentries held a menacing looking pike in their right hands.

The sight of the two guards brought a small flutter inside Eldred's chest. There had not been guards set at Orric's door in over one hundred years. There was something seriously wrong. There was no danger for Orric, or any of the other elves for that matter, inside the village, the fog kept all enemies from his door.

Taking a step closer to the entrance, both the guards lowered their pikes, blocking the doors. The deep eyes under the helmets showed no sign of emotion. Eldred didn't recognise either of them. He hoped that he had not made the trip up the stairs for nothing. That would really set him in his current mood.

"I am here to see Orric!" Eldred spoke in his most commanding voice. Any sign of uncertainty would deny his entry. "My name is Eldred. I'm a few days late but…"

Eldred didn't get to finish what he was saying. As soon as the guards heard his name, they instantly retracted their pikes and stepped aside. The sudden movement caught Eldred by surprise. As much as he hoped, he had not thought it was going to be that easy to gain entry. He knew Orric's guards by reputation only, as they had not been needed for many years. Once they were set a task, they would die to defend it. The only way they would fail would be if they were dead and to his knowledge only a handful had ever been killed.

The sentries didn't blink an eye as Eldred walked past them and opened the door. He could sense the tension, even though it had been a good fifteen minutes since anyone had been in the room with Orric. He was the eldest elf in Elhjem, although there was nothing in his looks that showed it. His face didn't show his advanced age, but for the little wrinkles. His hair held its soft blondness of youth. He kept his hair cut short, unlike most his fellow elves. There was strength and surety in his body. Eldred was happy to see his old friend. He gained comfort every time he was in Orric's presence.

Orric didn't look up when Eldred entered. He remained seated at the head of a large table with his head in his hands.

"Thank the Gods you are here." Orric didn't need to look up to know who had entered. "When you didn't arrive two days ago, I thought things must have turned sour."

"Things did go astray for a little while, but nothing that I couldn't handle,' Eldred didn't want to share with Orric what had transpired in the cave. "Now, I haven't been here more than five minutes and I've already heard enough disturbing news to last a year."

"Well I have another little piece of bad news." Orric slowly lifted his head to look Eldred in the eyes. "It seems that another crack has appeared in the barrier. As far as we know, it doesn't seem that Nyrra knows about it. The reports have been sketchy, but it looks as though that if he does find out, it will only be a matter of days, not months, until he breaks through," Orric spoke without a hint of emotion on his voice. He watched Eldred intently looking for a sign of what he was thinking.

"It was only going to be a matter of time." Eldred knew that there was no point in getting upset. "Is there any way to repair it?"

"We don't know yet. We have people working on it, but it doesn't look good."

"Well, since there is nothing that we can do, is there any other good news?"

"Yes, actually," Orric's expression changed slightly. "Faxon and his son Hawthorne arrived with a small battalion of soldiers yesterday."

Eldred couldn't hide the surprise on his face. It had been a long time since a King of Remidia had entered Elhjem. Ever since the wheels of the prophecy started to turn, they had been trying to arrange a meeting with King Faxon. Each time their emissaries returned empty handed. He also thought it was odd that Orric would allow a foreign army inside his village.

"So you let Faxon bring his army into the village?" Eldred asked.

"Of course I didn't," Orric sounded somewhat offended with the question. "His soldiers are camped outside the fog. Only he and his son, plus a small amount of his personal guard and servants have been allowed in."

Eldred relaxed a little, unknowingly tensing up until he heard Orric's reply. A foreign army would have no doubt caused problems. Although there was no official bad blood between the two races, the old stigmas would not completely die. Soldiers with nothing better to do than relax and drink, always got up to no good. At least outside the village, they couldn't offend anyone but themselves.

"Well I'm assuming that you have met with them. What did they have to say?" Eldred was a little upset of having to force every answer out of him.

"Sorry, Eldred, I am still processing a lot of information. I'm not deliberately trying to be obtuse." Orric recognised the hint of annoyance in Eldred's tone. "I think that Faxon is ready to barter a deal. We are due for another meeting tomorrow morning. I wanted to wait until you arrived, but Faxon was keen to get to business. It was all I could do to put him off until tomorrow, and then you arrived." Orric paused. "I only spoke briefly with the pair, but it seems that they have been having some troubles with regional bandits and believed that Nyrra is somehow involved. If this is the case, then we have indeed been blind."

Eldred thought on Orric's words. He had suspected that Nyrra had agents scattered around the Kingdoms. What he had not suspected is that they would have enough numbers to cause a noticeable effect. If what Orric says was true, then things were indeed dire. Nyrra would only start making his move if he was prepared to leave the wasteland. If that was the case, then they had less time then he thought.

"This is very disturbing." Eldred spoke purely to break the silence.

"I know. We shall cross that bridge tomorrow. What I need to know is how the Chosen One is fairing?" Orric quickly changed the subject.

Now it was Eldred's turn to consider the question carefully. He had been prepared for it, but now that it had been asked, he wasn't entirely sure what to say. Orric and he had shared council for longer than he could remember, never hiding any information no matter how inane. Since the prophecy had burst into motion, Eldred had found himself hiding little pieces and was sure that Orric was doing the same. It was not that they were deliberately trying to be devious; they just wanted to be sure of the facts before they spoke.

"There is no doubt he is the one we have been looking for," Eldred started.

"And does he have the stone?" Orric was almost on the edge of his seat with anticipation when Eldred had told him he had found the Chosen One, but he had his suspicions. Even when he had said the Chosen One had the Ruby Stone, he was not completely satisfied.

"Yes he does, there can be no doubt about it now. He and the stone have a connection." Eldred waited for the information to sink in.

"So he has used the stone?" Orric sounded appeased.

"Not as such." A questioning look crossed Orric's face. "When we were in the trolls cave, the stone took control of him." Eldred continued to explain what had transpired.

"It is as we feared; he is not yet strong enough for the trials before him. We need to have him trained before he leaves," Orric spoke when Eldred had finished his story.

"He is strong in both body and spirit, even if he doesn't know it yet. With the right training, he will become more powerful than we ever could have hoped." Eldred was exaggerating slightly.

"But does he have the patience and the willingness to learn? As you know, it takes more than talent to be great."

"He will learn. We don't have any other choice, he must!" Eldred's words were ominous.

"I suppose you're right."

"On a different subject, I heard some disturbing news from Darziel on the way here." Eldred could see a melancholy pass over Orric and wanted to change the subject before it set in, not that his choice of topic was much better.

"I wouldn't take anything Darziel has told you too seriously. He sees doom and gloom around every corner," Orric scoffed.

Eldred had to pause and think carefully. Being a wizard, he could sense magic a lot easier than Orric, but he could not openly say that. That fact that Darziel could sense the attack and Orric could not, would not please him. Being the leader of the elves, Orric was supposed to be the most powerful. Although it didn't really mean anything, as Darziel was more accustomed to the defence of the village, he didn't think Orric would see it that way.

"I sensed something on the way in." He paused again to consider what he should say next. "There is someone out there trying to bring down your defences." He couldn't think of any more soothing words.

Orric dropped his head into his hands, much the same way as he looked when Eldred had walked in. Eldred was preparing for a tirade, but was astonished by his response.

"I know, I know," Orric sounded dejected. "I think that I know my own land better than anyone else, even if I don't have the strongest gift anymore." Eldred looked even more astounded. "Don't look so surprise, I'm not that arrogant that I don't know my own mortality. I know that my strength is waning, but it will be a cold day in the depths of despair before I don't know when someone is attempting to attack my own village."

"I'm sorry. I didn't mean to offend you; it's just that Darziel said that you didn't believe him." Eldred was completely confused now.

"That is correct. If everyone knew that we were under attack and could do nothing about it, then there would be panic. It's the only way I can keep Darziel from spreading the word. If I don't agree with him, then there is enough doubt in his mind to think that maybe he is wrong."

"Okay then, do you know who is trying to attack you?" as soon as Eldred asked the question, he realised how stupid it was.

"Of course we don't," Orric snapped, but when he saw the expression on Eldred's face he softened his tone. "I don't even know how many there are. All I know is with each day, the fog becomes weaker and weaker. Soon there will be patches that someone could walk through."

"Wouldn't it be better to tell everyone? That way you can prepare for the inevitable."

"I will tell the rest when the time is right." Orric was now starting to get upset with Eldred's lecturing.

Eldred was quick to apologise. "I could always have a scout around and see if I can find them."

"Thank you for the offer, but I wouldn't want you to waste your time. I have a small group of my most trusted guards out every day combing the forest for them. They've never seen a single sign. Even if we do find them, I don't think it will be long before Nyrra sends someone to replace them. I knew that the fog would not protect us forever. This war is coming to all of us and sooner or later we're going to have to fight," Orric's words made perfect sense.

"Okay, I suppose that makes sense. Well I might leave it at that then. It's been a long time since I have had a good night sleep in a warm bed." All of a sudden the fatigue caught up with him.

"Of course, we'll have a better perspective when we know what Faxon has to say. Your apartment is ready for you. I will have someone bring up some food," Orric gave a weak smile.

Eldred motioned for Orric to remain seated as he rose and left the room. It was clear now that Nyrra knew the location of the village. He had known that Nyrra would find the village eventually, but was hoping that it was not going to happen for a long time. Things were starting to progress a lot faster than he had hoped.

Eldred was allowed to wander around the village by himself; Palentonal and Craven were also extended the same curtsy. The others, whether they knew it or not, would always have an escort. Most of the elves who lived in town knew Eldred, if by no more than face and name. He had stayed many times, sometimes for longer than a year.

The one thing that plagued his mind was the arrival of King Faxon and his son. It was either a very good sign or a very bad one, nothing in-between. He only hoped that the situation hadn't gone beyond his control.

The apartment was on the first level of the canopy. It was one of the more lavish buildings in the village. There were three rooms, one for sleeping, one for entertaining and one for bathing. The bathing room was what set it apart from the houses of the other elves. Orric was the only other elf who had a private bathroom. All the others bathed in communal bathing pools.

Once inside, Eldred relaxed on one of the large couches in his meeting room. His body ached as all his muscles tried to soften at the same time. A wave of exhaustion past over him and his eyelids started to flicker. The only thing stopping him from sleeping was the thought of food and the large tome sitting on the coffee table in front of him.

The *Prophecy of the Stone*. It had been an age since he had read it. The attack from the trolls had jogged something in his memory, something that he believed he had read before. He had originally believed that the *Prophecy of the Stone* was one of the more poorly written prophecies. It contained very little information that the other prophecies did. Now the problem was it was the only prophecy that mentioned anything about the trolls.

It was going to be late in the night before he would be able to roll into bed. It would also be early in the morning when he would need to rise again. He would need to scan the tome for any new information that would help them in their quest. With the new development, he wondered if he was following the right prophecy or if he really did know what he was doing.

A light rap on the door brought him out of his reverie. The door slowly opened after Eldred granted entry. The smell of hot food wafted through the door as soon as it was opened. A small female elf carried a tray and placed it on the small dining table and curtsied gracefully before leaving.

Although Eldred knew the she-elf, he did not speak to her. All he could think about was the food. He moved his eyes from the tome and moved to the table. It would not take him long to eat, but he would love every minute of it. The prophecy would have to wait until his stomach was full.

Chapter 10: A New Friend

The meal was the best Alaric had ever eaten. He was so hungry that any food would have been the best. He was completely satisfied and let out a loud burp.

"I know how you feel," Bern laughed his agreement.

The two of them were sharing the one guest house. The two elves and the dwarves also had a house each. The situation was amicable for all.

"I think I might wander down to the bathing pond. I need to wipe the filth off my body," Alaric said, as he rose from his chair.

"I will join you down there later, when I've finished my meal," Bern said between mouthfuls.

"I'm sorry. I'll wait until you have finished."

"No, no, you go on ahead. I will join you there shortly." Bern ushered him away with his hand.

The thought of sitting around waiting for Bern to finish eating didn't appeal to him; the filth that clung to his body made it impossible to get comfortable. All he wanted to do was soak in some warm water and wash away his weariness.

"Okay, I'll see you shortly," Alaric stood and left the guest house. Outside the refreshing cool breeze blew against his face. It was mid-afternoon and the sun shone gently through the trees. The reflection on the leaves made the forest radiate, if he wasn't feeling so tired he would actually consider himself content.

There was no one else around as he walked to one of the bathing pools. The only movement came from the gentle sway of the trees and a multitude of birds chirping in harmony.

The bathing pond was exactly where Darziel had explained, but it was not what Alaric had expected. He was not prude enough to believe that it was going to be completely private, but he did expect it to be covered. It was, however, exactly as its name suggested. A small round pond sat out in the open, fed by a small stream.

Alaric suddenly felt very conspicuous. It felt as though hundreds of eyes were on him. When he looked around, he couldn't see anyone. The thought of becoming naked in the open was not very appealing, but he had no choice.

Taking a deep breath, Alaric quickly peeled off his clothes, took a quick look around to see if anyone was watching and plunged into the water. To his surprise the water was warm, almost hot. Feeling the warmth soak over his body, he was able to relax, he closed his eyes and let his head rest against the embankment.

The water had a rejuvenating effect that made Alaric wish he could spend the rest of his life there. He felt as comfortable as he had been in a long time. The last thing he wanted to do was get up.

Suddenly there was a gentle splash over the other side of the pool. Alaric didn't look up. "I wondered what was taking you so long. I thought you must have gone back for seconds."

"I beg your pardon." The voice was not who he was expecting. Instead it was soft and feminine. It had a hint of mirth as she knew she had taken him by surprise.

His eyes shot up, he was about to jump straight out of the water when he realised he was stark naked. His face turned crimson when he noticed that he was not the only one bereft of clothes. To his relief, and somewhat disappointment, she had already submerged herself up to her shoulders. From across the other side of the pond it was impossible to see under the water.

"I'm sorry. I was expecting someone else," his voice cracked with his embarrassment.

Alaric felt a flutter in his chest, for the first time he noticed the she-elf gently lazing in the pool. Alaric had never seen anyone so enchanting in his life. Her long, soft blonde hair floated casually around her creamy white shoulders.

"You must be Alaric." She spoke with the sweetest voice he had ever heard. "My name is Alena, welcome to Elhjem."

Alaric remained silent. He didn't know what to say.

Alena giggled softly, the sound sent Alaric's face on fire. "That is the name of where we live."

"I'm sorry, I... err... I know that."

"Not many from the outside know its name," Alena explained slowly.

"I must get back to my room now," said Alaric wishing that he had kept his mouth shut.

Alena was surprised to see him remain where he was. The thought did not occur to her to look away. Alaric, on the other hand, couldn't understand why she kept staring at him. Suddenly Alena realised and she felt slightly embarrassed, also a little confused at his modesty. The naked body was something that elves did not find taboo and she had forgotten that men were a lot more particular.

With Alena's back to him, Alaric didn't waste any time leaving the bathing pond. Then he realised he had left the guest house in such a hurry that he had forgotten to bring a towel. He was forced to put his dirty clothes back on.

Back at the guest house he quickly pulled off his clothes and threw them on the floor. Bern had already left to take his bath and Alaric secretly hoped that Alena had left the pool before he arrived.

On his bed was a clean towel and some fresh clothes; they looked as though they had been recently made. He had no intention to dress himself again; the fatigue was truly taking hold. It was all he could do to sweep the clothes off his bed and crawl in. As soon as his head hit the pillow, he fell asleep.

It was dark when Alaric woke. He could hear the heavy breathing of Bern in the bed next to him. The room seemed surreal; the haze of sleep still clouded his judgement. He stretched, but his body still seemed weak; he felt like he needed another day's worth of sleep to recover.

Suddenly his heart started to race as the door to his room was slowly pushed open; someone was sneaking in. A feeling of dread passed over him and he remained still, unable to move, as the intruder moved around slowly. With a shock, he realised that they must be after the Ruby Stone.

Alaric sat bolt upright. A cold sweat had broken out on his forehead. The dim light of the moon shone over Bern's bed, but it was not enough to see anything clearly. Letting out a deep breath Alaric realised that there was no one else in the room. The intruder must have been a dream, his heart began to slow down and the sweat instantly started to dry.

To be safe he wanted to find the chest. As he stood, he realised that he couldn't remember where he had left it, so he sat back down on the bed and tried to retrace his steps. The thought suddenly came to him that he had left the chest on the table in the other room. It had been sitting there before he left to have his bath. It was there before someone had come to give him his new clothes.

Slowly Alaric made his way through the dark. He tried his best not to wake Bern. He ran his hands over the top of the table and found no sign of the chest. Panic filled his body.

He collapsed on a nearby chair doubting if the intruder had been a dream, or maybe he had not placed the chest on the table at all. He tried to find a light, but couldn't. The only thing he could do was go back to bed and hope he could find it in the morning.

Lying back down on his bed, it took him a while to return to sleep. The thought of the stone being stolen, especially in the apparent sanctuary of Elhjem, was very disturbing. He remained restless all night and didn't wake until noon.

The smell of bacon and eggs was strong throughout the bedroom. The thought of food put the events of the night far from his mind. Alaric felt as though he hadn't eaten for days. Bern was already sitting at the table and half way through his breakfast when Alaric joined him. His friend looked as though the night's sleep had done him a world of good.

"You're looking well this morning," Alaric greeted him with a smile.

"I think this place is starting to grow on me. Yesterday, when we arrived I felt like death. This morning, after a decent meal and a good night sleep, I feel like a new man. What about you?"

"I do feel better then yesterday, but I don't think I feel as good as you. I think maybe another day or two and I'll be back to normal."

Bern just nodded as he continued to eat his breakfast. Alaric didn't wait for an invitation. A plate of food was sitting on the table waiting for him. He did wonder, however, where it had come from. He had not seen a single pig or chicken since entering the village. There had been no sign that any land had been cleared for farming. The thought quickly left him when he tasted the food. It was the best breakfast he had ever eaten. He thought he could get used to the lifestyle.

"How long do you think we will be staying here?" Bern asked.

"I don't know, but I hope a long time. I wouldn't mind staying here the rest of my life."

"Somehow I don't think the party will last forever. I think they're only treating us this way because we're guests." Bern always made a lot of sense.

"I know. I'd just like to take it easy for a while. The last few days have been rough," Alaric stuffed the last of his breakfast into his mouth and leaned back. No sooner had Alaric placed his knife and fork back on his plate then a knock came at the door. Without waiting for an answer, the door was slowly pushed open. The thought of the possible intruder of the night before came rushing back to Alaric as Eldred walked in.

"What's wrong?" asked Eldred when he saw Alaric frantically looking around the room.

When he could not see the chest, he thought he better explain. He hoped that he would be able to explain things without sounding crazy. The idea sounded crazy even to him.

"Have you checked the wardrobe in the bedroom?" Alaric was surprised that Eldred was so relaxed.

"No, no I haven't." Alaric felt a little embarrassed. If he hadn't been distracted by his breakfast then that would have been one of the first places he would have looked. "How did you know it would be there?" Alaric returned to the front room with the small chest in his hand. He had also found his sword stored neatly in the wardrobe.

"I figured in your state you would have left the chest out in the open. The elf who is assigned to look after you would have stored everything away nice and neat." Eldred spoke so matter of fact, as if the information was unimportant.

"So what can we do for you this morning?" asked Bern, who had otherwise been ignored.

"I just wanted to tell you that you will have the rest of the day to relax and recuperate."

"Does that mean that we are on the road again tomorrow?"

"No, tomorrow your training begins."

"What are we training for?" Bern sounded interested in the idea; he was getting bored sitting around.

"You will both be trained in the art of war. All facets, from hand to hand combat to firing a catapult. As the days pass our journey is going to become more dangerous. You will need the skills to be able to defend yourselves."

Alaric looked a little dejected. His body was still aching from the events since leaving Arsiliac. He felt as though he could use a week's worth of sleep and still need more.

"I would give you more time to rest, but there is no telling when we should have to leave. It is of vital importance that you have the skills you need to complete the journey," Eldred let the information sink in before he continued. "I must go now. You are free to wander around the village, but be careful. It has been a long time since outsiders were allowed free movement. Try not to do anything to upset the elves."

When Eldred had left the room, Alaric looked at Bern. Suddenly they both burst into a fit of laughter.

"What do you think?" Alaric asked. "Should we go and upset some elves?" His comment brought another round of laughter.

"I don't know about that, but I would like to have a look around the village," Bern replied when the laughter had died down. "Come on…"

When they left the guest house and started to explore the village, they were both in awe of the beauty around them. The buildings interacted with the forest in complete unison. Nothing conflicted with anything else and the architecture was beautiful in its simplicity.

Shortly on their walk, they came across Hulkan and Dorn standing around the base of a large oak tree. Although they couldn't hear what was being said, they had the look as though they were up to no good.

"Let's go see what those two are up to." Bern had a devious look on his face. It was as if he was a young child again, out for the first time by himself.

Alaric couldn't say why, but there was something telling him not to join the dwarves. Something was tugging at him to go in another direction. He knew there had been bad blood between dwarves and elves for a long time. He didn't know what had happened but he knew something dreadful had caused a rift between the two races. Hulkan and Dorn both had the look of mischief about them and Alaric didn't want to get involved in any tomfoolery.

"I don't think that we should. I'm sure they are up to no good," Alaric warned.

"What harm can they do? Two dwarves up against a full village of elves? They couldn't be that stupid."

Bern's mind was just as set on joining the dwarves as much as Alaric's was on leaving them. Although Bern had not recognised the feeling there was something drawing him towards the dwarves and he admitted to himself he found them fascinating. They both greeted him warmly when he walked over and instantly started talking to him. Their voices were too low for Alaric to hear, which frustrated him no end.

As soon as Alaric was sure that Bern was staying with the dwarves, he turned and walked away. The light forest breeze invigorated him; the scent of a thousand flowers filled his senses. He thought for a moment that he could be truly content living in the village, there was something very familiar about the place, almost as if he was coming home for the first time.

"Halt!" a gruff voice commanded from behind him. "Who do you think you are to wander around unattended."

Alaric stopped and spun around to see two armed elves standing before him. One had a long, slender sword, much the same as his, already drawn. The other had a pike resting casually in his right hand. Neither wore armour, but both were dressed in dark green with a silver oak tree emblazoned on the chest. The one holding the pike looked as though he was ready to spear Alaric if he didn't like the reply.

"I was told I could walk around freely." It wasn't much, but it was the truth.

"No outsiders are allowed to move around the village unattended." The elf sounded almost arrogant in his statement.

Alaric didn't know what else to say. He only had Eldred's word to go on; every second that passed without an answer the lead elf just got angrier. Alaric shrugged his shoulders to try and change the awkward standoff. That was probably the silliest thing he could have done. The apparent lack of respect made the lead elf even more irritated.

"It has been too long since someone has been in the hole. I think that we have a candidate." The elf had an evil grin on his face and he lowered his pike menacingly.

"Kiere, lower your weapon," the female voice was firm yet beautiful.

"But he is…" Kiere tried to explain, but his confidence had gone.

"Take my advice. I would leave now before anyone else finds out and take the time to read the new amendment. I think you'll find it most interesting."

"Yes, of course." Kiere glared at Alaric, sending a shiver down his spine, before turning on his heels and marching away.

"Thank you for..." Alaric trailed off as he spun around and saw who had rescued him.

It may have been a trick of the morning sun, but the she-elf seemed to glow. Her long blonde hair was tied back in a neat braid. The simple white silk gown clung to her body. Alaric's face turned a light shade of red when he realised who it was.

"Hello, Alaric. I'm sorry for that. It seems that there had been some confusion. I'm sure it will all be sorted soon," Alena spoke with a voice that had Alaric spellbound.

He stood with his mouth open for longer than he should before he regained his senses. "Thank you." It was not much of a recovery.

"Would you walk with me for a while?"

"That would be nice." Alaric scolded himself when her back was turned. He had never lost his composure in front of a woman before.

Alena led Alaric around the village, pointing out landmarks as they passed. Alaric was fascinated with his surroundings and Alena, on the other hand, pressed Alaric for news from the outside world. Very little news came to the village and what did arrive was always of an important nature. There was never any gossip.

Alaric had never considered himself a gossip, but when he answered question after question he had to change his opinion. The expression on Alena's face made it worthwhile. She listened, captivated, by every answer, even if he had to make up some of the information. Their time together helped Alaric forget about his dire situation. When he returned to the guest house, he couldn't wipe the smile from his face.

***

Eldred walked away from the guest house without a second thought of what Alaric and Bern would do for the rest of the day. He was on his way to see Orric. The meeting with Faxon and Hawthorne was about to start and he was running late. He scurried up to the top level and rushed past the guards. They quickly stepped aside when they saw him coming. Since yesterday, they knew not to bar his entrance.

Inside he found that he was in fact not late for his meeting and Faxon and Hawthorne were yet to arrive. Orric sat at the head of the table. To his right sat his son Valen, Darziel and the head of his guard, Towen.

"Good morning all." Eldred gave them all a token hello.

No one returned his greeting. They had been sitting in silence when he arrived and it seemed they wanted to remain that way. Eldred didn't care; his mind was racing with reasons why Faxon had been called to the meeting.

It was not long before an attractive young man in the livery of the Remidian Royal Servitude entered. He was visibly shaking and his forehead was wet with sweat.

"Presenting! King Faxon. Liege Lord of the Western Realm, and Prince Hawthorne, heir apparent."

King Faxon, dressed in his regal finery, was the first to enter. Behind him, and dressed just as formally, was his son, Hawthorne. All at the table stood for their entry. The formalities would continue until the situation relaxed. No one spoke until they were all seated.

Orric introduced everyone in turn before the meeting started. Throughout the introduction, it was clear to Eldred the hostility coming from Hawthorne. It was obviously wholly his father's decision to have the meeting.

"We greet you King Faxon, with a warm welcome. It has been too long since our two nations have met." Hawthorne couldn't, and didn't try too hard, to suppress a scoff at the mention of Elhjem being a nation.

"Please excuse my son. He is still young in the ways of the world." Hawthorne was about to protest, but Faxon silenced him with a scowl and a wave of his hand. "We have all feared for many a year the escape of Nyrra from the north. No more than me with my Kingdom bordering his prison."

"Yes we do appreciate your position," Orric spoke in the gap Faxon had left for agreement.

"We have noticed more and more that our lands are becoming infested with bandits," Faxon paused and thought. "More than that though, I think Nyrra has agents in my major cities."

"That is terrible news, but not surprising. I don't really understand what we can do to help."

"Well it's more of what we can do for each other. I understand that you have been building an army." Faxon's gaze held firm.

"That is correct. We have sent many emissaries to you and you have rejected every single one."

"Unfortunately, I do not get to see every emissary. I have a large council that filters through the information and tells me what they think I need to know. It's not a perfect system, but when you have a nation as large as mine you need to delegate. It was only by chance that this information came to me." He glared at his son when he finished speaking.

"All well and good, but that still doesn't explain why you are here," Valen jumped in, picking up on the tension.

"Calm down son." Orric waved his hand.

"No, that's fine. I am beating around the bush. I suppose the crux of why we are here is to ask for mutual support." Faxon continued.

"I don't see how we can possibly help you. You may not know that we have committed the bulk of our force to the army heading east." Orric didn't want to admit they too were under attack.

"I know, but I think you will find my proposal more than fair. I will commit a battalion of my royal guard as well as another ten thousand soldiers from my regional armies… In return I only ask for a handful of your elves to clear our forest of bandits." Faxon rubbed his hands in anticipation.

"I still don't understand. Why can't you send your own army into the forest to capture the bandits?" Orric was confused.

"That is simple. My army is not suited to fight in the forest. The denseness of the trees gives the bandits a great advantage. Truth be told, we could capture all the bandits, but it would take too long and use up too many of our resources. It makes more sense to pledge those soldiers to the alliance. It's no secret the elven affinity to forests. Your elves could clear our forests in half the time."

"Hmm," Orric sighed. "What do you think Eldred?"

"I think that it is an idea that needs considering. On the surface, it seems like a good plan." Eldred was not happy with Orric putting him on the spot; he knew he was just buying time to think.

"That is sound advice. I think that I will need some time to take council before I make a decision," Orric was grateful for Eldred's comment.

"Of course, I understand. As I'm sure you appreciate that time is of the essence. I need to leave tomorrow. My army is marshalling outside Remidel. It will take a good two weeks for my message to get back."

The meeting was short and sweet. Neither side was interested in small talk. Once Faxon had finished speaking, he motioned for his son to join him in leaving. Hawthorne was reluctant to go, but could not openly disobey his father.

"Well I must admit that I was not expecting that!" Orric wasted no time in speaking his mind once they were alone.

"What do they say? There's always good news in the bad or bad news in the good," Eldred spoke mysteriously.

"This is no joking matter, what in the name of the Gods are you talking about?" Valen rose in his chair in defiance to Eldred's comment.

"Sit down Valen," Orric snapped at his son. "What do you mean, Eldred?"

Valen remained standing despite his father's harsh words.

"The news that Faxon is willing to join the alliance, and at such a small cost, is very good news..."

"Small cost!" Valen almost spat. The look on Darziel's face showed that he agreed. "You come and you go, but you know nothing of our world," Orric tried to silence his son with a wave of his hand, but Valen was not going to stop until he had finished his rant. "Do you know what happens if an elf is found in Remidia? He is dragged through the streets of the nearest town at the back of a horse. Then he is hung up in the main street where the town folk throw rotten food, and the less civilized town, excrement. Then they are tied up outside of the town to die of either starvation or by an attack by wild animals. We have been persecuted for many years, so much so that no elf would dare set foot in that land. We have been forced to remain here in exile for fear of our lives."

Eldred tried his best to remain calm. "For someone who has remained safely ignorant, you speak as though you know the outside world, a world which you have never experienced. Now what you say has some truth, but not much. A long time ago, some small communities did catch and kill elves. When the Kings of Remidia heard about theses atrocities, the guilty parties themselves where hung and displayed as examples. Ignorance works both ways. Only the truly wise know that they only know half the truth."

Valen was not appeased by Eldred's words. It would take more to convince Valen to change his beliefs.

"I'm sorry Eldred." Orric turned to face his son. "My son does not appreciate the intricacies of modern politics. He also listens to too many wives' tales." He returned his attention to Eldred. "Now please continue, I really need your council on this one."

"It would take more than a few extra bandits for Faxon to come here to make a deal. There is something very wrong in Remidia. Being on the front line, it is possible Nyrra is starting trouble to try and divert our attention from his real plan. Something doesn't completely ring true with his offer."

"I know what you mean. There is no apparent reasoning for it. He has more than enough men to clear his forest of rogue bandits."

"Exactly! Secondly, if he is expecting an attack from Nyrra, then I can't see him readily emptying his lands of soldiers."

"So what do you think I should do?" Orric was no closer to making a decision then when they started.

"I don't think you have a choice. Our army cannot be even close to half that of Nyrra's. We need all the soldiers we can get. The only way we will know what Faxon is planning is to make the deal." Eldred words did not reassure anyone.

"I think that we should reconvene with Faxon in the morning. A good night's sleep might do us all some good and give us a better perspective. Darziel, would you get word to Faxon to meet us back here in the morning." With that he dismissed the council. "Eldred, stay a while."

Eldred was half way up in his seat before he sat back down again. He was keen to get back to his house and back to his reading. There were passages in the tome that he wanted to re-read.

"I understand you have been reading the *Prophecy of the Stone*. I thought that we had already discounted it as fallacy. What has rekindled your fascination?"

"I haven't found the passage that I have been looking for. Not only is one of the more tedious of prophecies, it is also one of the longest and nothing is in chronological order," Eldred explained, trying to dance around the question. He didn't want to give anything away until he had the answers.

"I know that Eldred. That is the main reason why we discounted it. Why has it piqued your interest?"

"The incident at the trolls cave jogged my memory. There is a passage in the prophecy that I believe refers to that incident," Eldred spoke slowly.

"I don't recall any mention of trolls, the cave, the well or the abduction, when I read it," Orric kept pushing.

"You should know better than that," Eldred actually laughed. "When have any of the prophecies been that open. You know as well as any of us that the prophecies need to be decoded. It would be too easy if they were just written out in plain language. I am sure there is a passage that explains what happened. If that is the case, then who knows what else is in there that we have overlooked as nonsense." Eldred had already said too much, he might as well say everything.

"You do know what you are saying?"

"I know exactly what I'm saying," Eldred paused. "If I am right, then it is quite possible that we have no idea what we are doing."

There were no words that could follow a statement like that. If Eldred was right, then there was no telling what sort of repercussions it could have. Orric had as much to do with deciphering the many prophecies as Eldred had. He had read the *Prophecy of the Stone* and dismissed it as jargon.

"But we know that not one prophecy tells the entire truth. There are passages in all of them that have not come true. We were careful when we picked which passages were fact and which were fiction."

"We don't know anything," it was almost as if Eldred had already resigned himself to the fact that they had failed. "Who's to say that there isn't one prophecy that is the truth?"

"There is only one way to find out," Orric was not as willing to give up hope.

Eldred only nodded.

***

It was late in the night and the candle had almost burned out. Eldred's heart started to pound as he started to read the passage that he had been searching for; the passage that he had wished had not been there.

In the days of dark when the light will shine
A day will come when the beast who walks
Will steal the time and make his mark
A test of skill, a test of fate
The waters will fail the task that set
And treat the bad a taste so fine
A dullard changed a mind unmatched
And normal task impossible fetched
The light will come and fade away
To meet his fate and sell his soul
When all is lost and gone away
The test will tell whose heart is true
The winds will fail to blow its tune
A piece of night will wake from sleep
To bring to life the little sheep
There is no way to tell the truth
For past is past and nothing new
To beat the day a pact be made
For dark and light to work as two

From there the passage faded into obscurity, but Eldred had no doubt that it was what he had been looking for. All he could do was stare at the passage over and over again. No matter how many times he looked there could be no doubt.

The candle suddenly burnt itself out, shaking Eldred from his deep reverie. The room was only lit by the greyness of dawn creeping through the window. Eldred had no idea that he had spent so much time flipping through the prophecy. He would now get very little sleep before his meeting with Orric and Faxon. His mind was racing with the repercussions of his new revelation. The one thought kept coming to his mind. Was he right about the location of the final fight?

Chapter 11: A Decision Made

The room was thick with tension. Eldred had hoped to catch Orric before the others joined them. Unfortunately, Orric arrived with Darziel and Valen. Eldred had been waiting for over two hours and was bursting to reveal his information, but would not divulge anything in front of the others.

When Faxon and Hawthorne arrived, announced by their page, breakfast was served. Eldred almost throttled Orric when he suggested it. They would not discuss business while they were eating and he was almost jumping out of his seat. Faxon accepted the offer out of politeness although it was clear that both he and his son were keen to get down to business.

When the room was cleared of the china and cutlery, the air was abuzz with anticipation. Both sides had no idea what the others were thinking. A lot was riding on the meeting, for both sides.

"Have you made a decision?" Faxon forwent the normal pleasantries and got straight to business.

"We have," said Orric, not surprised by Faxon's abruptness. "We agree to your terms. We will give you ten of our trackers and one hundred archers. This should be enough to clear your forests. In return, your army shall join the Alliance under our lead."

Hawthorne was about to snap, but Faxon silenced him with a stern look. "That seems reasonable enough, all except for being under your lead. General Jarwe shall lead the army." Faxon raised his hands to stop anyone from interrupting. "I think you will all agree that he is the most qualified. I have done my research; of course, he will listen to the others involved in the leadership of your army."

His last statement seemed to appease everyone in the room. The meeting was going too smoothly. Eldred knew that there had to be more behind Faxon's offer, but couldn't put his finger on it.

"I don't see anything wrong with that." Orric spoke slowly, looking at Eldred who in turn simply shrugged his shoulders.

"Very good then, we have the contracts ready for your signature." Faxon smiled as he produced three contracts from a small case.

A small smile crossed Eldred's face. There had to be something in the contract that would void the deal. Faxon wouldn't give up a sizable portion of his army without an ulterior motive. He was quick to snatch up one of the contacts, which was rather small, all things being considered.

It didn't take long for Eldred and Orric to peruse the paperwork. To their surprise there was nothing untoward. One of the stipulations made them suddenly look up at each other. The contract stated that Hawthorne would ride with Eldred until they reached the army.

Eldred mouthed the words "The prince of a land that's lost shall join the fateful lot," before he returned to the contract to Faxon.

"Why does Hawthorne need to ride with Eldred, and not with the rest of your army?" Orric didn't looked convinced.

Faxon looked at his son before he answered. "Let's just say it's a feeling that neither one of us can deny."

That was enough to convince the elf. Once Orric had read over the contract a second time, he quickly signed all three copies while Eldred witnessed his signature. Faxon had already signed them in anticipation of success.

"Very good then." A broad grin appeared and Faxon's face. He did not care who saw his happiness. "So when should I tell my border guards that you will be moving the army into Remidia."

Faxon's words brought confused looks on everyone's faces, except for Hawthorne. Eldred was the first to realise what had happened. He thought for a moment over the wording in the contract and then smiled.

"What are you talking about?" asked Orric, who still didn't understand.

"You will need to bring your army into Remidia, if it is to make its way north to fight Nyrra," Faxon seemed very smug.

"The army is not travelling north. It is currently on its way east to Avalon. It is there we will fight Nyrra's army." Orric still didn't realise Faxon's motives.

"That's insane. All the information that we have been gathering suggests that Nyrra will attack us in Remidia. It makes perfect sense. Why would he take his army so far around to the east?" Faxon was shocked.

"We have every reason to believe that Nyrra will move his army towards his home land. He will want to recapture his city and once there, he will strike out at us. He will have the position of power. We must move our army to the fields of Avalon; there we will have the power. We will crush his army before he reaches his home land," Orric spoke casually, knowing that he had the upper hand.

"Why? Because of this prophecy of yours?" Faxon literally spat the word. "You put too much faith in those incoherent scrawls. Our finest scholars have studied these so-called prophecies. All they concluded was that they are a bunch of dribble. I will not allow you to take my army to the east when it is clear the fight will come from the north."

"It is not for you to decide. You have signed the contract. Those men are now ours to command. Jarwe will lead once he joins the rest of the army in Avalon." Eldred stood from his chair as his voice boomed. As much as he was now unsure of their plans, he could show no uncertainty.

"A contract with a fool is no contract at all. I will not honour our deal." Faxon was becoming flustered. He was searching for any insult he could muster.

"I don't think that would be a wise choice," it was Eldred who spoke, calmly now, before anyone else could retort. "If word got out to the other Kings that you have reneged on a contract, how soon do you think it would take for them to shut down your trade routes. No one will trust you again. You will always be on the wrong side of every deal."

Faxon knew that he had been defeated. There was no way he could come out on top. The deal he had thought would gain extra forces had indeed back fired on him. "Very well then. I see that there is no reasoning with you. You will have your army." He then stood and turned to his son. "Come Hawthorne, we shall leave these ravens to their feast. We shall leave immediately."

"I don't think so!" Eldred continued. Faxon gave him a confused look. "The contract states that Prince Hawthorne shall travel with us until we reach the army, and as it happens, we will be travelling to Avalon." Eldred could not suppress his smile.

"Yes, of course." Faxon waved a dismissive hand at Eldred as he turned and faced the door. "But I shall not stay a moment longer than I n have to. I would appreciate it if you would send someone to my quarters in half an hour to lead me out of this god forsaken place. It would be good if the elves you are sending with me would be ready as well. I need to head back to Remidia to make new plans for the inevitable war that shall be on my doorstep soon enough."

"It will be so." Faxon didn't wait for Orric's answer as he made his way to the door.

"Come, my son. I would have words with you before I leave."

"As you wish father," Hawthorne replied as he stood up from the table. "You will all live to regret this day, that I swear to you." The words sounded ominous coming from the young prince.

As the two left the room, Eldred indicated to Orric that he wanted to speak to him alone so Orric dismissed Darziel and Valen. He knew that once they got started, they would be talking about Faxon for the rest of the morning and there was no time for idle chatter.

As soon as the two elves had left the room, Eldred spoke slowly. "I found the passage that I was looking for. There can be no doubt that it refers to our meeting with the trolls." Eldred continued to recite the passage. He had stared at it for so long that it was etched in his memory.

"You should know better than to jump to conclusions," Orric visually relaxed when Eldred had finished. "That passage could mean a hundred different things. There is no way to be sure that it refers to the trolls." After he had spoken, Orric knew he was wrong.

"You cannot be serious. It is as clear as if it was spelt out word for word. 'The beast who walks', 'the waters will fail', 'to meet his fate and sell his soul', 'for dark and light to work as one.' There can be no doubt what it is referring to." Eldred knew it would be harder for Orric to understand. Eldred had been there in the cave; he could see what the prophecy was alluding to.

"So what does that mean? Are we leading the army in the wrong direction? Is Faxon right? Is the attack going to come from the north and strike down through Remidia? Most importantly, are we leading the Chosen One in the right direction or are we leading him to his demise?" The questions kept pouring out, and there were more that Orric wanted answered.

"I don't know. All that I know at the moment is that we have found out something very important. We have made a mistake that we can ill afford to make again." Eldred spoke slowly, not really sure if he could appease Orric's concerns.

"So what do we do now?" Orric sounded defeated.

"The only thing we can do. We stick to the original plan. We only tell Alaric what he needs to know. He mustn't know the truth yet, especially now that we are unsure what the truth is. I will take the *Prophecy of the Stone* with me and try and decipher its clues. I'm sure I'll be able to find something." Eldred didn't sound as convincing as he normally did. "I think the prospect of Hawthorne joining us is a good sign that not all of the other prophecies are completely wrong."

"But do we fully trust Hawthorne not to betray us the first chance he gets. His words did not fill me with confidence."

"He will come around. With a little time, he will come to see that the world is not always black and white."

"I wish I shared your confidence, but I don't trust him. He is more unpredictable than his father. He could ruin everything. Now that we are unsure of the prophecy, I don't think that he should be allowed to join your group. There is too much at stake."

"I don't think that this meeting was a coincidence. It was the prophecy that drove Faxon and his son to meet with us. There is no other explanation. Faxon would have known that we were not planning on bringing the army into Remidia… No, Hawthorne shall join us. We have no other choice." Eldred would not be dissuaded.

"Oh, I suppose you're right. This meeting did come out of the blue and seemed rather odd. I guess we better get down to other matters. I think it is about time that I meet our saviour." Orric rang a small bell and a young looking elf appeared in the doorway.

"Send for Alaric will you," Orric commanded.

"Yes my Lord. I believe that he is walking with Alena in the village." The extra information seemed unnecessary, but with it, Eldred gave Orric a sharp glare.

Once the elf had left again Eldred spoke sternly. "Have you been playing a hand in the prophecy?"

"Of course not." Orric looked completely innocent. "You know that I'm smarter than that. To force the prophecy is almost as dangerous as ignoring it."

***

Alaric woke with a start and looked around suddenly. The room was empty. He thought that he must have dreamt the knock on the door when it suddenly came again.

He looked around the room for any sign of his friend. Bern had apparently already left. When a third knock came, Alaric lifted himself out of bed. He had slept well that night and was almost feeling back to normal. He thought that another good night would be all that he needed.

"Good morning Alaric, how are you feeling this morning?" Alena asked brightly.

"Feeling much better, thank you," he smiled as he spoke, something about Alena that made his heart flutter.

"Would you like some breakfast?"

"Thank you," was all he could say as a droplet of saliva appeared on the corner of his mouth. He looked at the plates she was holding and felt as though he could eat both.

Alena almost had to push her way past Alaric who was just standing there. Her scent overpowered the smell of the food as she brushed past, and for an instant, Alaric forgot all thoughts of his stomach.

"You don't mind if I join you, do you?" Alena asked cheekily.

"Be my guest. Since you brought the food, it is the least I can do." He couldn't believe his luck.

Over breakfast they continued speaking as they had the day before. Alaric answered Alena's questions on life outside the village and Alena answered Alaric's questions on life inside the village. The only silent moments were when they were eating. The two of them had an instant rapport.

After breakfast they left the guest house and Alaric had lost all thought on whether Bern was safe. He had forgotten that there was anything else in the world as they walked through the village. Alaric wondered at the peaceful nature, nothing seemed in conflict with anything else. Even the animals that scurried about seemed at perfect ease.

The morning sun was high in the sky when a dark-haired elf came upon them. He looked as though he had important news.

"What is it Reigher?" Alena asked before he had a chance to speak.

"Orric has asked for me to bring Alaric to him."

This made Alaric nervous. The look on his face was clear to both of them. "Don't worry Alaric; there is nothing to worry about." Alena's words did little to reassure him.

"He also wants you to bring the chest. He said you would know what I was talking about," Reigher said.

Alaric looked back at Alena, searching for an answer. "It's okay. I will come and see you when you've finished. You have nothing to worry about. Orric won't do anything to harm you."

He nodded his agreement and followed Reigher. There was something in her tone that made him feel safe. As soon as she was out of sight, his insecurities returned. His heart pounded. He had no idea why Orric wanted the stone, but he was sure it was for no good.

On their way to Orric's house, Alaric's nerves increased. Reigher had nothing to say as he led the way. If Alaric had spoken, then the elf would still not have said anything. He had been instructed not to give any information away.

To Alaric's relief, he found Eldred sitting with an elf, he presumed to be Orric. The two of them were deep in discussion when he entered. Their voices were low and he couldn't hear what they were saying. Alaric stood in the doorway, not wanting to move further without an invitation.

"Come in and sit down," the voice was warm and welcoming. "I am Orric and I have been waiting quite a while to meet you," Orric stood for the introduction.

Alaric sat in a chair next to Eldred and opposite Orric. His hands shook visibly as he pulled the chair out from under the table. His nerves were starting to get the better of him. He slowly, carefully placed the chest down on the table making sure it was out of Orric's reach. He felt uncomfortable having the chest in view.

"You can relax Alaric. There is nothing here that will hurt you. There will be things that will scare and disturb you, but nothing that will harm you." Eldred tried his best to reassure him.

"Let's see it." Orric sounded ardent.

"See what?" Alaric was taken aback by the sudden demand.

"The Ruby Stone, Alaric." Eldred sounded somewhat perturbed.

Slowly Alaric placed his right hand on the lid of the chest. There was something inside his head telling him not to open it. The only thing compelling him was Eldred's smile. The wizard had looked after him ever since they had met so taking a deep breath he flicked the latch and slowly opened the lid.

Inside the stone glowed a soft red. Alaric couldn't help thinking how beautiful it was. The last thing he wanted to do was to lift the stone out and show the others. They didn't deserve to share its beauty.

"Come Alaric, you need to overpower the feeling." Orric's words washed over him. They sounded as though they were being passed through water.

"They will take the stone, that's what they want." The voice seemed to come from behind him. He didn't flinch as he recognised it. "Close the lid and leave the room."

Alaric's fingers passed over the rim of the chest. There was nothing more in the world that he wanted to do than to close the lid, but something was preventing the urge. There was something, deep in the back of his mind, that was stopping him from obeying the voice.

Orric looked at Eldred. There was concern on his face. Eldred, on the other hand, seemed as relaxed as he ever had. Alaric, in the middle of it all, was starting to break out in a sweat. All he could do was stare at the stone and try to control his urges.

"You must overpower the stone, Alaric. It is trying to get a hold over you. It wants to possess and control you. The only way is with will power," Eldred soothed.

The sweat on his forehead started to drip on the table around the base of the chest. Eldred's words seemed to make sense to him, but he couldn't remember what he was trying to do. The room around him looked blurred; the only thing that he could comprehend clearly was the voice, which was now inside his head. The voice had changed its tune, now it was telling Alaric to take the stone and use it to destroy Eldred and Orric.

"You have the power. You don't need to take orders from them. What do they know that you don't? Finish them and we can move on."

Suddenly the voice was snuffed out of his head and the room returned to normal. The change had been so sudden that Alaric nearly vomited. His entire perception had been altered. He looked around slowly to see what had caused the change… Eldred had closed the lid.

"What happened?" Alaric still felt a little dazed.

"The stone is trying to dupe you. It is trying to take control of your body and mind. What we are here for is to try and teach you to block that voice. Once the crystal is removed there is nothing that I can do to help you."

"You must try again Alaric. It is an important part of your training." Orric tried to sound helpful.

Alaric returned his attention to the small chest; he knew that if he was going to succeed, he would have to do it quickly. If he gave the stone any chance, then he would fall under its spell. While he was thinking, he didn't realise that once again he was stroking the chest. He didn't know why but he was reluctant to show the others the stone.

Taking a deep breath, Alaric closed his eyes. He thought if he couldn't see the stone, it might make it easier. Suddenly he flicked the lid open and snatched it. He wanted to drop it on table but his arm and hand would not co-operate. His arm automatically retracted until his clenched fist was packed tightly against his chest.

"What do you think that you are doing? They just want the stone for themselves. If you put it on the table, then they will take it and leave you with nothing. They fear your power. They know what you are capable of and they fear it." The voice came again.

"That's a lie." Alaric strained, closing his eyes. "They are here to help, not hurt me. They don't want the stone. If they wanted it, I would have given it to them a long time ago." The comment made more sense to Alaric than anything else.

"Trust me! I know what they want. They will use you until they no longer need you. Then they will take the stone and they will kill you. They are not doing any of this for you. They are only doing it for themselves," the voice persisted.

"You can say whatever you like, but I'm not going to believe you."

Both Eldred and Orric watched as Alaric sat, frozen, with his knuckles turning white. His eyes would flicker every now and then, the only sign of life. Suddenly his eyes opened as wide as they could go, a look of great pain crossed his face then his eyes rolled back. His body collapsed onto the table, his arm stretched out in front with his hand still clenched in a fist. A great pain ripped through his body, but he couldn't cry out. He tried to open his mouth, but it wouldn't budge. He knew the stone was trying to take control of him. He had to fight if he was going to retain his sanity. Finger by finger his hand opened and the ruby stone noiselessly rolled onto the table. Once the stone had been released, his body went completely limp.

"Well I'll be damned. I didn't think he had it in him." Orric was the first to break the silence.

"He has great strength and we are yet to scratch the surface of his potential," Eldred added.

"I am beginning to agree with you, though I can sense something troubling inside him. There is a great fear in his heart. If the stone can manipulate that fear, then we are in great danger. If the stone can control him now in its docile state, then what will happen when the crystal is removed?" Orric's words were troublesome.

"That is why we need to train him now and quickly. With the right teaching, he will be able to control the power within. He has the will; he just doesn't know it yet. In time, he will come to realise it." Eldred sounded confident.

"Yes, my old friend. I have dearly missed your counsel."

Slowly life returned to Alaric. At first it was a subtle twitch of his left hand but soon enough he was again sitting upright. His face looked pale, completely drained of colour. It was clear that the test had taken a lot of energy from him. He looked like he would collapse at any minute.

The Ruby Stone sat on the meeting table. There was a gentle pulsating light at its centre. It was almost as if it was preparing for something. The glowing intensified as Alaric regained consciousness.

"How are you feeling?" asked Eldred.

"Drained! I feel as though I have been running all day."

"Good, I would be surprised if you had said otherwise." Eldred seemed satisfied with his answer.

"Now pick up the stone again," Orric's voice was harsher than he meant.

"What?" Alaric seemed shocked. "I couldn't. I don't have the energy to go through that again." Alaric's hand started to shake as it involuntarily moved towards the stone.

"This is what your training is all about. When it comes the time to do this for real, you won't have time to wait until you feel better," Eldred's voice was calming.

As soon as his hand clasped the stone, a rush of heat filled his body. With the heat came a feeling of relief. The complete tiredness was washed away. It was the best he had ever felt in his life. A great joy filled his body, it was euphoric. He felt he could do anything and then the voice came again.

"What are you doing? They are using you. They want to destroy you. I am the only one you can trust. I am the only one who is looking after you."

The room became blurred again and the sounds became muffled. It was as if he was in a dream. The only thing that was clear was the voice inside his head. He knew that the words were false, but he wanted nothing else in the world than to believe them.

"Destroy them both so we can leave. I know how to get out of here. I can find a way through the fog."

"No!" Alaric screamed out.

"Calm down Alaric, you need to focus." He could only just hear Eldred's words.

The voice seemed to be roaring now. Alaric couldn't hear anything else. He could see both Eldred and Orric moving their lips, but there was no sound. He threw his hand up to his ears in a vain attempt to block the noise.

"Be quiet!" Alaric shouted so loudly and suddenly that Eldred jumped in his chair. "I will not listen to you anymore." Alaric closed his eyes and tried to focus on something in the room. There had to be some background noise.

"Do not try to ignore me. I have been nice up until now. If you want, I will become nasty." The voice now grew malevolent.

As much as he didn't want to believe the words, a touch of fear entered his body. The voice didn't sound like it was bluffing. Alaric shook his head, trying to think straight. The voice was so loud that he couldn't think.

"You have to be strong." The reassurance fell on deaf ears; neither of them knew how loud the voice was for Alaric. If he was going to survive, he would have to do it on his own.

The room was so hazy that Alaric felt as though he was going to pass out. Things started to spin and his body started to sway. Reality was starting to slip away from him. With a last effort to regain his composure, Alaric took a deep breath through his nose and slowly let it out through his mouth. As he did the volume of the voice lessened slightly and the room became clearer. With another deep breath, things became clearer still. A smile crossed his face as he realised how he could control the stone.

"Stop, I beg you. I will do whatever you want," pleaded the voice.

Alaric was not listening; he had finally worked out what he needed to do to block it. After another half a dozen breaths, the voice was now outside his head. It was floating somewhere behind him. His confidence was now rushing back.

With one final breath Alaric closed his eyes and the voice was gone. When he opened them, the room had returned to normal. Eldred and Orric were watching him intently. Both of them had stopped speaking when they realised that Alaric couldn't hear them. Casually Alaric opened the palm of his hand and looked at the stone. It had stopped glowing and now it just looked like an ordinary ruby encased in crystal.

"The voice has stopped!" Alaric was relieved and somewhat proud of himself.

"Very good, but that is only the first part of the test." Orric kept any sign of praise out of his voice. "Now you need to bend the stone to your will."

"What are you talking about?"

"The stone has a great wealth of power, more so when the crystal has been removed. You need to be able to tap into that power," Eldred explained.

"And how exactly do I do that?" As Alaric spoke the stone started to glow again, so faintly that no one noticed it.

"First you need to know what you want the stone to do. For now, a simple test. I would like you to raise the table a foot off the ground and hold it for three minutes before lowering it again. Then you must concentrate on the heart of the stone. It is from there you must draw the power." Eldred tried to explain things as simply as possible.

"That doesn't sound too hard." Alaric still felt on top of the world.

Alaric looked deeply into the centre of the stone. As he did the glowing started to intensify. The voice also returned. "What do you think that you are doing? You can't do this, you're not strong enough." Alaric simply ignored it; he was doing too well to fail. The voice tried one more time to deter Alaric and then fell silent of its own accord.

The warmth that had come with collecting the stone slowly started to increase and with it a stronger feeling of wellbeing. Alaric was starting to enjoy what he was doing. A broad smile came across his face as the table slowly started to lift into the air. He felt a moment of clarity and it was easy for him to count out exactly three minutes. When the time was up, however, he did not lower the table. He wondered to himself what else he was capable of. Slowly the table started to spin in the air, faster and faster the table spun until finally it burst into a thousand pieces. As it did, the feeling of wellbeing and the heat suddenly rushed out of his body. The rush was so intense that Alaric had to gasp for breath and struggle to remain conscious.

The stone now glowed more intensely than it had all day. Alaric could feel something grasping at the back of his mind. The voice was now laughing insanely and his body suddenly seized.

"Aùritaël!" Eldred cried out as he could see Alaric slipping away.

As the word took effect, the stone went suddenly dormant. Alaric's body went completely limp and he collapsed onto the floor. The stone rolled out of his hand and came to rest amongst the rubble of the table. Before Eldred did anything else, he scooped up the stone and returned it to the chest.

"Well, was that a success or failure?" asked Orric.

"I think it might have been a little of both. It is hard to say. We still don't know the true effects of the stone. It seemed as though he had some control, which is a promising sign. When Alaric wakes, he will appreciate why he should never do more than he intended."

"Will he wake up soon?" Orric looked at Alaric's limp body with concern.

"Hard to say, he's been through a lot today. I wouldn't be surprised if he remains unconscious for the rest of the day. Either way, I think we have done all that we can. I'll take him back to his room. We shall reconvene in the morning, if he wakes by then."

"Very good. What will you do for the rest of the day?" Orric wanted to make sure he knew what Eldred was up to.

"I will continue to read the *Prophecy of the Stone*. If I am right, then there will be more information in there that I need to know." Eldred didn't sound very enthusiastic.

Before Eldred could rise, the door was opened and Darziel burst into the room. He didn't even seem to notice the complete mess that the room was in or Alaric lying on the floor. The look on his face showed that his news was not good.

"What is it Darziel?" Orric was a little perturbed at being interrupted.

"Faxon's soldiers have been murdered. It's seems as though they were ambushed late last night. They were slaughtered down to the last man. I haven't seen the campsite, but from what I heard, it wasn't pretty." Darziel spoke quickly trying to get his words out a fast as possible.

"Well, I guess that puts my reading out of the question." Eldred gave a weak smile.

"Darziel, have someone come and take Alaric back to his room. I don't think he will be able to walk for a while," Orric commanded.

Darziel left, a little surprised by the response he received. He had expected both of them to be a little more concerned.

"You can't say this is a big surprise," Eldred said, completely unperturbed.

"I can say that this is very disturbing. The forests have been clear for so many years. For an outright attack, this is an outrage." Orric was fuming.

"You knew there were forces out there attacking your shield. It would only make sense that they would attack a friendly army camped outside the fog."

Darziel returned with two strong looking elves who promptly removed Alaric from the floor. Neither of them commented and Darziel motioned for them to leave quickly.

"Faxon is on his way up here. I think he's quite upset."

As Darziel spoke, the door burst open and Faxon marched in. Orric was becoming annoyed with people just barging into his office. The situation was starting to get out of control and Faxon was just going to make matters worse.

"I cannot believe you would let my soldiers be slaughtered. Have you lost complete control over your land?" Faxon was fuming and cared nothing for protocol.

Eldred silenced Orric with a wave of his hand. It was clear that Orric was about to lose control. This was not the time for rash words. Eldred knew that Faxon could construe the attack as an act of war. If he declared war on Orric, then the contract would be void. The last thing they needed was to give Faxon a reason to break it.

"We have had no reports of any hostile parties in the area." Eldred spoke calmly, hoping that Darziel would keep his mouth shut.

"That's all well and good, wizard, but I would prefer to hear from the ruler."

"What Eldred says is true. We have had no reports of anyone in the forest surrounding the village." In fact, that was the truth; there were suspicions, but nothing concrete.

"You are either the worst or the dumbest ruler. For you not to know that your village is surrounded by hostile forces is ridiculous," a thought occurred to Faxon. "Unless it was your elves who attacked my men. I can see no other explanation." Eldred cursed silently at Faxon's accusation.

"That is an absolutely ridiculous accusation." Orric was again silenced by Eldred. "This is not going to get us anywhere. Tell me what happened and I might be able to work out who did this."

"It was like nothing I have ever seen before," said Darziel. Faxon and Orric were glaring at each other like children, each looking for a reaction on the others face. "The men were not only killed, they were slaughtered. The strangest thing is that these were battle hardened soldiers and there was not a single enemy found."

"What about the way they were killed?" Eldred asked.

"Like nothing I have ever seen before." Darziel seemed almost afraid to speak of what he had seen. "The men, they were…"

"Come on Darziel, this is important." Eldred was getting frustrated.

"I'm sorry; it's just what I saw…" Darziel suppressed the urge to vomit as he remembered what he had seen. "The men, they were torn to pieces, mauled, as if by wild animals. The ground was stained with blood and not one dead body remained. This makes no sense." Darziel breathed a sigh of relief.

"This is very disturbing news." Eldred tried to hide the look of horror on his face.

"What is it?" asked Faxon abruptly. "Who was it that killed my men?"

"I don't know." Eldred hoped the lie would be convincing. He didn't want to reveal his suspicions until he had spoken to Orric. The look on Orric's face showed that he had his own suspicions. "I will have to think about it for a while. You should return to your rooms. It will not be safe to leave until we know what we are up against."

Faxon actually snorted as he stood to leave "I will get to the bottom of this and there will be retribution," he snarled.

Once Faxon had left room Orric turned to Darziel. "Take a group of your best trackers and comb the forest. I want these animals found, and I want them found today!"

"I think that we have a serious problem," Eldred spoke candidly when they were alone again. "If my suspicions are correct, then there are a group of orglin in the forest."

Orglin were one of Nyrra's most evil creations. A mix of ogre and goblin, there were bred for Nyrra's army. The creatures were pure malevolence, with only one desire. To do their master's bidding, which was generally to cause murder and mayhem. A job they did with extreme efficiency.

"That's impossible. They were either trapped with Nyrra or completely annihilated." Orric didn't want to believe it.

"I know I led the team that hunted them down. We may have missed a nest."

"Not a sighting in over a hundred years. I don't think so. We would have seen some sign of them feeding."

"No, you're right. It's much worse than that. It seems that we have been less vigilant than we thought. If Nyrra has managed to sneak a nest of orglin this far south, then the Gods only know how many more of his legions are roaming the country side," Eldred cringed.

"That makes no sense. If there were that many orglin in the forest, then we would have noticed them a long time ago." Orric shook his head.

"That brings us to our next problem, if what I think is correct then we are in even greater danger than I first thought."

"That's very ambiguous. Would you care to elaborate on that statement?" Orric's attention was piqued.

"Not at the moment. Let's wait to see what Darziel finds. If he tells us what I think he will, then we're in a whole lot of trouble."

This did nothing to increase Orric's mood and the two of them sat in virtual silence waiting for Darziel to return.

It was late in the afternoon when Darziel returned, his face a picture of frustration and dismay. That was all the answer Eldred needed. He knew exactly what Darziel was going to say.

"Well, don't just stand there. What did you find?" Orric had waited long enough.

"That's the thing," again Darziel seemed afraid to speak. "There was nothing. No tracks, no skin, no blood, no hair, no fur, no... anything. A battle like that should have had some signs of the opposition. It's almost like Faxon's soldiers went crazy and did this to themselves." Once Darziel started explaining, he didn't want to stop. "We searched and searched, but there was not one single sign. There was plenty of evidence of the soldiers, but nothing of anyone else."

"Okay Darziel. That will be enough." Eldred dismissed Darziel before he could continue his ramble. He had already received more than enough information to make his decision.

Darziel threw a questioning look at Orric. The old elf, didn't know what to say. "Make sure that you keep this to yourself until we know exactly what we're dealing with, I don't want a panic spread throughout the village." Darziel nodded and slunk away.

"Okay, spit it out man. What is it that Darziel said that has given you so much clarity?" said Orric.

"Without actually seeing the site, I would say that it was definitely orglin."

"I know, but that makes no sense. As we all know, orglin are not the most stealthful of creatures. They are not well known for covering their tracks after an attack. That's why we were so successful in wiping them out in the first place." Orric was getting tired of hearing things that he either knew or did not make sense.

"Exactly, but I do think that it was orglin. In fact, I would bet my life on it."

"Well, I would love to hear your theory."

"There is someone, or something helping them." Eldred silenced Orric as he was about to speak. "I think this attack and the attack on your defences are related. There is at least one out there with a good knowledge of the black arts. It would make sense why your trackers couldn't find anyone. If they were not cloaked, they would have been found within a matter of minutes."

"You would know if there was someone that strong out there." Orric was keen on playing devil's advocate.

"That's another disturbing thought, and yet promising as well. When we arrived, Alaric made a comment that he felt as though something was amiss. I believed that he felt the magic that was being used to hide the attack on Faxon's soldiers, or the attack on your shield. The fact that I couldn't sense the magic means that whoever is doing it is very powerful."

"Powerful indeed if they can hide an attack of this nature. This is very disturbing; do you think that you can find them?" Orric was more hopeful than anything else.

"Unfortunately, I don't think that I am going to have the time. The situation has become much worse. We can only stay as long as it takes me to make sure we don't leave here and walk into an ambush. If the forest is swarming with orglin, then leaving is not going to be easy."

Orric sighed and let his head rest in his hands. "I knew that we would not be safe here, that the war would eventually come. I just didn't think it would come so soon."

"I know. Neither did I, but there is nothing we can do about it for the moment. Unfortunately, you are just going to have to sit and wait and be prepared for an attack any day now." Eldred's words were ominous.

"Is there any chance that we can win an attack like that?"

"There is always a chance. Your elves are stalwart. They will not roll over without a fight." Eldred tried his best to reassure his old friend. "With a little luck, whoever it is out there will follow up once they realise we have left. Let's just hope we have a good head start."

"What are we going to do with the Chosen One? We had planned that his training take at least a month, now it looks as though we'll have less than a week." Orric had to change the subject.

"We will start his physical training tomorrow. Have him sent to the training house as soon as he wakes. Hopefully he is as quick a learner as I think he'll be. If so, it might not all be a waste of time."

Orric was unsure if Eldred was talking about the training or the entire quest. If he asked the question, Eldred wouldn't have known the answer.

***

Palentonal took a deep breath. Elhjem felt like home. There were, as to be expected, subtle differences between Elhjem and the Nordligträ. He could feel the magic and beauty of the forest around him. It was a feeling that he had not felt since he had left his home. For the moment, he was at peace, although that was going to be short lived.

"Hello Palentonal," a voice came from behind him.

Palentonal's shoulders stiffened as he recognized Craven. He had been deliberately avoiding his old friend and counselor. He knew the reason why Craven had joined the group and it was not something he was happy about. He had managed to avoid the inevitable conversation so far, but now it seemed inevitable.

"I was wondering how long it would take for you to speak to me." Palentonal didn't turn around.

Craven turned and faced Palentonal; he knew that was the only way he was going to get a direct conversation. He had been dreading the moment; they had once been good friends, but now the situation was different. He had been given a job to do and he had to complete it. It had taken him so long to build up the courage to speak with Palentonal. Now he had to finish what he started.

"How are my parents?" Palentonal spoke before Craven had a chance.

"They are well."

"That is not what I was asking."

Craven paused, he need time to think. "Their feelings have not changed. They have sent me to bring you back."

Palentonal wanted to strike his old friend, but that would not prove anything. It was not his fault. He should have known that his parents would use one who was close to him. They didn't have the courage to come after him themselves; that was a stupid fantasy. He had to admit, if they had come themselves, he would have been tempted to return. Seeing Craven brought back fond memories, but it was not enough to change his mind.

"You know the reason why they sent me. You know the reason why they want you to return," Craven's voice was grave.

"I know. I know all too well but that doesn't change the fact that I have a part to play. It is my responsibility to see it out."

Craven didn't know what to say. Both sides had good points. Now that he had time to see the Chosen One, he was not so sure that Palentonal's parents were making the right decision. There was a very good reason why he should bring his old friend home. That was something that he didn't want to think about; it was also something he could not get out of his mind.

"What do you want me to do?" Craven finally asked.

Palentonal didn't know the answer to the question, but he knew what he was going to say. "You have to leave. Tell my parents that I will not be coming home."

The two stood in silence as his words settled on them both. It was one thing to know something, but another to say it out loud. For a moment Palentonal's resolve started to waver. If Craven had spoken, he thought he would break. Luckily neither of them wanted to. Eventually Craven was the one who broke the silence.

"I am going with you."

They were not the words Palentonal wanted to hear. He didn't want to drag his old friend into such danger. That was not the reason why he left. He had left to make sure that those he loved would be safe. He wanted to send him away, but he didn't have the heart. He could also feel the hypocrisy. He had no right to send Craven home.

"I am glad that you're coming. I think I will need a friend before this is all over." Palentonal resigned himself to the fact. For right or wrong, that was the way it was going to play out and there was nothing he could do about it.

Chapter 12: Training

The day started much the same as the previous. Alaric was woken by a knock on the door. He woke with a start and then realised that he was alone again. Bern had already left the guest house; the early morning was not by his choice. Although Bern was used to early mornings working on the farm, this was completely different. There was much to be done and little time to do it. Bern was already being trained in the art of war.

Remembering what had happened the day before sent a shiver down Alaric's spine. Another knock came and he jumped out of bed, quickly dressed and then opened the door. The smile dropped from his face when it wasn't who he was expecting. A tall elf, with shoulder length blonde hair was standing in front of him. The friendly expression on his face did little to lift Alaric's spirits and he yawned.

"Good morning Alaric, my name is Kellan. I am here to take you for your sword lesson."

"Can I have something to eat first?" The last thing Alaric wanted to do was hard work.

"No, we have already lost good hours as I was instructed to let you rest. Now we need to make up for the time we have lost." Kellan's tone left no room for debate.

Alaric turned his back to get his sword; he only managed to take one step before Kellan spoke. "You will not need your sword today. You have a long way to go before you are ready to use a real sword."

Hearing those words made Alaric's shoulders slump. This was going to be more than a day's work. By the sound of it, this was going to be a long task.

Alaric followed Kellan to the sparring building. Along the walls were portraits of all the former blademasters. Alaric was amazed at the detail on the paintings. He could almost swear they were alive.

"To be a sword master you must have a body of steel. What you do now, you must do every morning before I come to give you your lessons." Kellan spoke like a true teacher.

For the first hour Kellan put Alaric through his paces. Between running, sit ups, pushups and weights, Alaric was thoroughly exhausted. Kellan didn't give him a moment to rest. When Alaric was done with his last lap of the room Kellan handed him a wooden training sword.

"Give me a moment to rest," Alaric gasped as he used the sword to prop himself up.

"Will your enemy give you a moment to rest?" to accentuate his point, he slapped Alaric sharply across his thigh causing him to drop to his knees. "He will push you to the limit and when he passes that, he will kill you. Once you leave here, you will have no time to rest, so you have no time to rest whilst you're here."

Regaining his feet, Alaric took what he assumed was a defensive stance. This time Kellan nearly took his head off with a sharp swing of his blade. Alaric ducked and fell backwards as the blade brushed past his hair. It took too long for Alaric to return to his feet and Kellan had already planned his second attack. With a deft flick of his wrist, Kellan disarmed Alaric. Now without a weapon Alaric was open to Kellan's stabbing attack. Kellan rammed the tip of his blade into Alaric's midsection and instantly he doubled over in pain, gasping for breath.

As Alaric rolled around on the floor, Kellan watched, smugly standing over him. The last thing that Alaric wanted to do was stand up. He wasn't being taught anything. All Kellan was doing was beating up an inferior opponent.

"On your feet and I will tell you your problem." Alaric stumbled. "Now you know that you know nothing. I shall build you from the ground up. As you can see, without the proper training, you are no better than a newborn child. I will teach you how to be a sword master, but you will have to listen to my every word and do exactly as I say, otherwise we may as well stop now."

Alaric only nodded his head. He didn't have the energy to speak. Luckily for him Kellan was happy with his response. He spent a moment studying Alaric's stance. This would be the beginning of his training.

Kellan started his next lesson a lot slower than the first. Now that he was starting with a fresh ball of clay, he didn't want to make any mistakes. Once he had Alaric's stance right, he continued to some basic moves. To his surprise, Alaric picked them up instantly. Very rarely did he have to explain something twice. Alaric was starting to become excited and forgot that he was bone tired. He even forgot that he was hungry.

It was Kellan who finally called their training to end when the sun was low. Alaric was still keen to keep going, but Kellan was tired. He had trained many elves in his time as blademaster and none had come even close to learning at the pace of Alaric. He had a feeling of hope.

"Remember you have an hour of training to do before I arrive in the morning and I will be coming at daybreak."

With the training finished, his weariness returned. After Kellan had left him, Alaric slowly walked back to the guest house. Inside he found Bern eating dinner by himself. A plate had been left out for him.

"Have you been out training today?" There was a great deal of tiredness in Bern's voice.

The two of them spoke briefly as they ate their evening meal. Alaric was glad to see Bern was also tired. Bern was no stranger to physical labour and there was no doubt that he was a lot stronger and physically fitter than Alaric.

Neither of them wanted to stay awake once they had finished eating. The sun had only just disappeared over the horizon when they lay down to sleep.

Alaric slept like the dead. Although he had spent a lot of time sleeping the last few days, it had not been relaxing. In the morning, he woke with the darkness of night still heavy. He could hear the gentle breathing of Bern, but as he was unsure if he was on the same training regime, he decided to let him sleep.

The sun crept over the horizon just as Alaric returned from his morning exercise. Kellan was waiting for him and the look on his face showed that he was not impressed.

"When I told you I wanted you ready by daybreak I wasn't joking. Timing is of the essence. Seconds can decide who lives and who dies." Kellan's words were solemn.

There was no talking on the way to the sparring house. Alaric walked a full step behind; this was a deliberate ploy on Kellan's behalf. Whilst he was the master and Alaric the apprentice, he would not do anything as his equal.

At the sparring house, Kellan wasted no time in continuing the training. He started with the same drills as the previous day and it was obvious that Alaric didn't need any refreshing. He had remembered all the basic skills that he had learnt and Kellan was amazed at his progression.

The new techniques started slowly, with Alaric making many mistakes. Kellan was beginning to wonder if he had made the right decision. Alaric didn't seem to be learning the difficult patterns as well as he had learnt the easier ones, but just as he was about to give up, Alaric suddenly clicked. What had previously been impossible for him was now coming naturally.

The techniques that had taken Kellan years to perfect were taking Alaric a matter of minutes. By mid-afternoon Kellan decided it was time to put his training into practice. His pride had been wounded, as Alaric's teacher he could take little solace, and was hoping in combat Alaric would not be so quick.

To his relief, Kellan defeated Alaric quite quickly and easily in the first bout. All Alaric could do ,was to try and defend the vicious attacks that Kellan beat down on him. Kellan was not going to give him an inch of leniency.

"What you must remember is that sword fighting is like dancing," Alaric didn't understand the analogy at first. "Your forms must flow together both when attacking and defending. You must also learn which forms flow smoothly together. When you're defending, you can plan your defence and counter attacks ahead of your opponent."

Alaric nodded. With the new advice, he was confident he could now beat Kellan. He was a little angry that Kellan had waited before explaining it to him. He didn't need another whack around the head.

The next bout started as Alaric had expected. Kellan moved about with his standard attacks, flowing one technique into another. Alaric waited patiently for his opportunity to make his final blow. A broad smile crossed his face when he recognised the start of a routine pattern.

Alaric waited for a change to make his move. He had been defending all along so he figured that Kellan would not be expecting an attack. Just as he was preparing for a lunge, which should have taken Kellan across the chest, Kellan suddenly changed his move. For all of his trouble, Alaric took a blow across the back of his head that made his teeth rattle.

Of the next three bouts, Alaric made good progress, but could not get Kellan into a position to finish him off. In the end, it was always Alaric trying to push the boundaries and Kellan waiting for the inevitable mistake that would give him the win. Each time Alaric lost, some less painful than others, he would stand up and take his position for the next fight. He was not going to stop until he had beaten Kellan at least once.

Every muscle in his body ached. All the energy had left his body; he was now running on pure adrenaline. There was nothing that was going to stop him from winning one bout, at least that's what he thought.

"Okay, that is enough for today." Kellan was also physically exhausted, although he looked better than Alaric.

"I don't think so, or are you that tired that you can't keep going?" Alaric puffed as he spoke, giving away any sign of advantage.

"You are exhausted and you can hardly stand up. I don't think Orric will be too happy if I work you to the grave."

"I'm not the one who is ready to quit." Alaric was trying to goad him into a fight. "If you leave now, you'll never know how badly I'm going to beat you."

"Fine then. Let's finish it and go home."

Kellan wanted the fight to be over quickly for two reasons. The first was to wipe the smirk of Alaric's face and the second to go to bed. This was his first cardinal mistake. Alaric had deliberately tried to get him riled. With the fatigue and his angst working against him, Kellan was already in trouble.

The trap was set and Alaric played for it. Kellan started quickly making some aggressive moves. Alaric did his best to play tired, saving himself only at the last minute and only in the most desperate manner. Kellan could feel that he was going to finish the bout soon and that's when Alaric turned the tables. After defending another killing blow, Alaric went on the attack with more aggression that Kellan thought he could muster. It was Kellan's turn to be on the back foot. He struggled with each attack to keep Alaric's sword away from his body. The longer the fight continued the more Kellan came to realise that he had been beaten at his own game. He had underestimated his opponent and now he was going to lose. It didn't take long for Alaric to batter Kellan down. There was no more finesse in his sword play. It was now just pure aggression.

"Very well done," Kellan puffed after he had finally been beaten. "I think that you will be ready to train with a real sword tomorrow."

Alaric almost fell over at the prospect. Since the fight was over he was exhausted. His sword dropped from his limp hand and he swayed as his stood. A grave look of concern crossed Kellan's face.

"Let's get you back to your room before you fall over."

All Alaric could do was nod his head. He didn't think that he would be able to make it back to his room. The last fight had taken all the energy he had left. He did not, however, want to show Kellan. He would make it back to his room if it was the last thing that he did, and for that day it likely was.

Alaric collapsed on his bed. There was a plate of food waiting for him that had already gone cold. Even if he had been hungry, it would have been less than appetizing. He was relieved to find that Bern was still out; the last thing that he wanted to do was to make conversation with anyone and within a minute he was asleep.

In the morning, it took all of Alaric's will power to drag himself out of bed to do his exercise. When he had finished, he waited out the front for Kellan. It was just before dawn when he arrived back at the guest house. He knew that Kellan would be arriving as soon as the sun peeked over the horizon, but when the sun had risen there was no sign of him. Alaric hoped that nothing had happened to him.

Another hour had passed and Alaric was starting to become concerned. Kellan had made him more than aware that if he was late he would be dead. Then again, this could be another test. Maybe it was to do with his awareness or maybe it something else. Alaric looked around nervously. He did not want to be caught out again. Today was going to be his day. Kellan wouldn't know what hit him when they started sparring.

It was not, however, Kellan who came to collect Alaric that morning. Just as he was letting his eyes droop from boredom, he heard footsteps approaching. Quickly he scolded himself for his lack of concentration before looking up. Instead of the hard-faced sword-master he had been expecting, he was met by a gentle smiling face.

Alena casually strolled over the where Alaric was seating. Quickly remembering himself Alaric stood as she approached. It had been two days since he had seen her and he realised that he'd missed her. The feeling was strange, as he had only known her a short period of time. He was not used to people taking an interest in his life. Alena had instantly shown him compassion and friendship.

"I see that you're ready for your training," Alena greeted him. "Unfortunately, Kellan won't be coming today." Alaric was surprised that he was disappointed. "Your time here is running short and there are other forms of combat you need to be trained in."

"What do you mean?" Alaric had assumed that once he was proficient with the sword, then he would be ready to leave. "I was only just beginning to get the hang of the sword."

"There is more than just sword fighting you need to learn before you leave, and according to Kellan you are dangerous enough with the sword." Alaric wasn't sure if she was being complementary or sarcastic.

"Okay, so what am I to learn today?"

"That we can discuss over breakfast. I do believe it's that time of day." Alena smiled

Alaric only then realised how famished he was. He had been working hard and not eating much. The thought of a large breakfast overtook all thoughts of his training.

They ate together in the guest house; Bern had already left and Alaric was glad that his old friend was not there. It gave him another chance to speak with Alena alone.

"Today I will teach you to use the bow. It will be imperative for you to learn how to shoot."

Once they had both finished their breakfast, Alena led Alaric to a small open field. At one end there was a hut and inside contained a variety of bows, from the compact cross bow to the powerful long bow and amongst them, there were a multitude of bolts and arrows.

Stretching out across the field at different distances was a number of large and small targets. There were also two moving targets. Alaric stared; he had never lifted a bow in his life and was unsure how he was going to be any good.

To begin, Alena showed Alaric what the different bows could do. She was capable of using them all and Alaric was surprised to see her pull back the long bow. As much as he had never drawn one himself, he had watched the Duke of Zenza's archery contests. Only the strongest of men could accurately draw and fire a long bow. Alaric doubted he could draw it himself, yet Alena did so and hit the target just to the left of centre.

The day continued much the same as the previous days. Alaric was slow, initially, but just when it seemed he was getting nowhere something suddenly clicked. Not only did he start hitting the targets, he was only ever half a hand span away from the bullseye.

By the end of the day not even the moving target at top speed could hinder him. It was if he had been shooting his entire life. Alena had to hide a hint of envy behind her praise. Like Kellan, it had taken Alena many years to perfect the bow. Alaric had not only mastered it, but had also surpassed her in a single day. As much as she was glad with his success, she was somewhat perturbed.

Instead of leaving Alaric at the guest house, as Kellan had done the past two nights, Alena invited him back to her house for dinner. This would be the first time, besides his brief visits to Orric's house, that he had been inside one of the other houses. He was surprised at the invitation. The two of them had been getting on well together, but Alaric figured it was only out of politeness. No one who looked like Alena had ever invited him back to their house. At that moment Alaric realised that he had not replied to her offer and she was staring at him with a confused look on her face.

"I'm sorry. I was just thinking…" Alaric stumbled. "Thinking about how wonderful this place is and how sad I'm going to be when we have to leave," Alaric stared around the village to accentuate his lie.

"You will come back one day," a broad smile crossed her face, oblivious that his lie had worked; she linked her arm in his and led him towards her house.

Although he knew that it was stupid, his heart started to race. From the moment he saw Alena, he thought that she was beautiful, but since that moment the thought of any relationship between the two went out of his head. He wasn't even sure if it was right for humans and elves to mix. Again, he realised that he had been lost in thought when they had stopped in front of small, but magnificently beautiful house. Alena again looked at him with a concerned look on her face. It was obvious that she had asked a question.

"I'm sorry; I was lost in thought again." Alaric went red in the face.

"If you don't wish to eat with me, I understand. I know that this is a strange place for you," even though she kept her voice level, Alaric could tell that he had offender her.

"I'm sorry," he apologised again. "There is no other place I would prefer to be." Alaric smiled warmly to try and prove his point.

Alena was unsure, but accepted his answer. Alaric made sure to give her his undivided attention for the rest of the evening. He didn't want to make her feel uncomfortable again and he did his best throughout the meal. They had plenty to talk about the day's training. The discussion didn't much change and Alaric wasn't going to try to. It was clear that she wanted nothing more than friendship. Alaric chided himself for thinking that there could be anything else.

The night ended much as it started, with Alaric lost in thought and Alena staring at him. Again, Alaric apologised, Alena accepted and made the decision that it was time for bed. Alaric shook his head as he walked away. He had been an idiot. He only hoped that he hadn't hurt her feelings.

When he returned to the guest house, it was empty. As much as Alaric wanted to speak to his old friend, he was glad to have the place to himself. There was nothing more that he wanted to do then rest his head and go to sleep. He knew he had another long day ahead of him.

Alaric didn't have long to wait until he was fast asleep. If nothing else, he had become an excellent sleeper.

***

Bern had not been enjoying his training. He was nowhere near as efficient in his leaning as Alaric had been. Where the sword was an extension of Alaric's arm, it was like a dead weight to him. He wished that he had his friend to discuss matters, but Alaric was busy. Instead Bern turned to the two dwarves for solace. He felt akin to the two little creatures.

"Welcome Bern!" Hulkan greeted. "How was your day?"

The expression on Bern's face should have been all the answer he needed, but he asked the question anyway. Bern sighed and let himself drop into the spare chair before he spoke.

"Much the same. I don't think I will ever get the hang of the sword."

"Then I think it's time you let us train you in a much more ferocious weapon," Dorn suggested. Bern didn't like the sound of more training. "The axe is the weapon of choice for a dwarf and I think it would suit your build better than a sword."

Dorn dropped his war axe on the table to accentuate his point. Bern stared at the weapon. There was a blade on one side and a gruesome looking spike on the other. He wasn't sure he wanted to pick up the weapon, but the look on Dorn's face told him he should. Instantly he felt more comfortable with the axe. The extra weight felt better in his hands and the balance seemed to suit. Tentatively he swung the blade through the air. He had to admit that he was more comfortable.

"Don't worry about the elves. You can keep up your training with them during the day. Once you are done, we will teach you true meaning of battle," Hulkan added.

The thought of extra training didn't appeal to him, but the thought of being able to use the axe efficiently did. He wanted to start straight away, but the rumble in his stomach had different ideas. It was time to eat. His training would have to wait until after dinner.

***

Alaric woke fresh and ready for his daily exercise. Even though he knew that Kellan was not going to be coming for him, he still wanted to be ready at dawn. He wasn't sure if it was going to be Alena who came, but he hoped that it was.

As soon as the sun had crept over the horizon, an elf appeared. This elf was very similar to Kellan in looks and posture. He had an expression on his face that meant business; his look was a lot rougher than Kellan.

"My name is Devin. Come with me." There were no pleasantries from this elf. He spoke his command and expected to be obeyed. He didn't even look back to see if Alaric was following.

Devin led Alaric, always a pace ahead, to the training house. Alaric wanted to know what he was going to be learning, but didn't want to disturb Devin. He knew if he asked the question, there would be no reply.

"This will be the most important part of your training. This is where you will learn how to defend yourself when all else has failed you. This is where you must learn to trust flesh over steel. This is where you will learn to let yourself go." Devin left no doubt in his convictions. He believed every word he spoke and left no room for questions. "First you must sit," he commanded and Alaric obeyed, even though he had no idea what was happening. "Now close your eyes and breathe. Empty your mind of any thoughts. Concentrate on the room around you. Focus on the sounds and the smells. Know your surroundings without using your eyes."

Alaric did as he was told, but the whole situation seemed a little ridiculous. There was a sense of awe radiating from the elf and Alaric had the distinct impression that if he questioned Devin at all, then there would be trouble. As much as he thought that the elf might be slightly unhinged, he knew that he contained a great amount of power.

After a few moments, Alaric started to notice things that he had never noticed when he had been in the room with Kellan. As he breathed slowly, he could smell the soft scent of lavender coming from the far end of the room. The lavender was easily overpowered by the smell of timber oil from the newly varnished floorboards.

The only sound he could hear inside was his own gentle breathing. Outside, however, he could hear the quiet chirping of the multitude of birds hopping around the trees. He thought he heard the footsteps of someone passing by, but he couldn't be positive. Just as he tried to concentrate harder on the footsteps, he felt a hard fist strike him on side of his head. The blow was strong enough to knock him over.

When he opened his eyes, he saw Devin standing over him, a broad grin on his face. Alaric rubbed the side of his head as he attempted to stand. Before he could rise to his feet, Devin pushed him over with the heel of his left foot. Alaric's head hit the floor, hard.

"Your first lesson. Be aware of your surroundings. Know your place. Anyone can sneak up on you when you're not paying attention. You must learn to focus all your senses at all times or else you are as good as dead. Now sit and resume your breathing," again Devin left no room for questioning.

Being aware there was going to be an attack, Alaric concentrated on the room surrounding him. He would be able to hear Devin's first movements. He was concentrating so hard that when the blow came across the other side of his face it came as a complete shock.

"Feel, don't think. You're trying to force it. When you are out in the world, you will not know when an attack is coming or where it's coming from. Your instincts must come naturally or they will not come at all." Devin paused as Alaric came to his feet, thinking about knocking him down again, but resisting the urge. "We will go back to that later. Now I will teach you how to fight."

Hand-to-hand combat was, like the other two events, completely new to Alaric. Devin started with some basic punching and blocking. Devin did not go easy on him for a second. Whenever Alaric dropped his guard, Devin went in for the kill. More than once Alaric ended up lying on his back. Devin didn't do any lasting damage, but did enough to hurt.

By midday Alaric felt bruised and battered. Not only did he feel it, he also looked it. He had managed to pick up a few simple techniques, but had yet to land any blows. This was by far the most arduous aspect of his training.

"You need to be able sense what your opponent is doing. It's not like sword fighting where you can judge the patterns of your opponent. Hand-to-hand combat is much different, but no less deadly. To kill an opponent without a weapon, you must use your entire body." Devin was reciting the words he had spoken many times before. "You have the skill and the frame to be a great fighter."

"But I'm not strong enough. You beat me every time," Alaric puffed out his complaints.

"Strength has nothing to do with it," Devin paused. "Although it does help, it is more to do with technique and speed. In fact, having a slighter frame than your enemy can be a great advantage. If your opponent thinks you're an easy target, then they won't be expecting your attack."

Devin didn't give Alaric much of a chance to rest. He soon had him back on his feet and deflecting a flurry of attacks. As with sword fighting, Alaric was learning that even in defending there was a chance for attack. Again, Alaric learned that whenever he thought he was winning, he was just playing into Devin's hands.

By nightfall Alaric had learned a lot, although he was not as proficient in hand-to-hand combat as he was with the sword and the bow. He had learned enough to make Devin smile when he finally called an end.

"You have learned well today. Remember what I have taught you and keep practicing your moves." Devin had a serious look on his face.

"Won't we continue tomorrow?" Alaric's voice was weak with exhaustion.

"Unfortunately not. I would have liked to have given you another week of training, but I have only been allocated one day. As I understand it, you are having a rest day tomorrow, before leaving the day after."

'We're leaving in two days?" the surprise brought life back into Alaric's voice.

"I'm not really privy to those stories, but that is what I have heard. Now let's get you back to your room."

Devin escorted Alaric back to the guest house before saying a cheerful goodbye. It was all Alaric could do to keep himself from falling over. He only took a brief glance at the plate of food sitting on the table before he stumbled into the bedroom and collapsed.

Chapter 13: Leaving With Friends

Eldred looked up at the half-burnt candle and rubbed his eyes. He had not left his room in the past four days. The only person he had seen was the elf who brought him his meals, which he barely touched. His full attention was on the great tome in front of him.

All he could do was sigh when he looked back down and realised that he was not even half way through. It was not just the fact he had to read the book, he also had to try and decipher every passage. Some pages would take more than an hour to read and even then, there was no guarantee that he had read it correctly.

So far he thought he had managed to find two passages, besides the one referring to the trolls, which were applicable to their quest. There was also a passage which he thought referred to something they were about to do, and it was not promising. If he was correct, then there would be hardship sooner than he thought.

Slowly his eyes drooped with the strain of trying to stay awake. It was only an hour past midnight, but Eldred had only taken two hours sleep over the last four days. He had gone almost a week without sleep before and was well used to it, but the strain of deciphering the prophecy was exhausting.

He knew it would be the last chance he had to read the prophecy before they had to leave again. They would be setting off in two days. The next day would be taken up with discussions with Orric and one final test with Alaric and the stone.

Eldred was sure, more than ever, that it was the true prophecy. If it was true, then their entire thinking had been incorrect. He had been sure for many years that the true prophecy consisted of excerpts from all the many prophecies. Now his reading led him to believe that all the other prophecies merely copied passages from the *Prophecy of the Stone* and then filled the rest with plausible lies.

Early in the evening he had found another passage he had been looking for, the passage that explained the next leg of their journey. He had read many passages that referred to the Cloumid Mountains, but none had been as foreboding. The passage was as vague as the one that he had found on the troll's cave, but he was sure he recognised its meaning. Nevertheless, he wanted to run it past Orric before he made any hard and fast decisions.

The thought of meeting with Orric shook him back to reality. The last thing he wanted to do was to go into the meeting without sleep. It was a good three hours before dawn and that would be enough to recharge. He would need to sleep for at least eight hours the following night before they left, but for the moment he was grateful that he had not read throughout the entire night.

As he expected, a young looking elf came for him at dawn. He was already dressed and was waiting for him by the door.

"Good morning Loman, how are you this morning?"

"I am well, thank you Eldred. Orric is waiting for you." Loman kept his greeting brief.

The two walked in silence towards Orric's house. Although Eldred knew the way Orric had insisted on an escort. Loman had to quicken his footsteps to keep pace. The quick pace concerned Loman, something wasn't adding up.

They arrived at Orric's house before the sun was up. Eldred wiped away the sweat from his forehead as he said goodbye to Loman and entered the room.

Orric was seated at the head of the table, the rest of the seats were empty. He looked up when he heard Eldred enter. The expression did not change on his face; something was worrying him and the presence of Eldred did not comfort him.

"You look like you've had as much sleep as me over the past few days," a small grimace, which could only be called as an attempted smile, crossed his face.

"Indeed."

"Things are not exactly going to plan."

"I only wish that it was so. I think that things are going exactly to plan and that's the problem."

Orric raised an eyebrow "I should now be used to your cryptic ways, but please, time is very short."

"I believe now more than ever that the *Prophecy of the Stone* is the true prophecy. I found another passage; one that I believe explains the next leg of the journey."

"But many of the other prophecies explain the next stage. In fact, that is the only reason we know that the well is in the Cloumid Mountains. This is nothing new." Orric was not convinced.

"But none of them are anything like this." Eldred did not need the passage in front of him to be able to recite it word for word. He had read the passage over and over again, making sure he hadn't missed anything.

The day will come when those will leave
The haven that will fall in course
The path will lead to doom's
doorstep
A chance for fame or total loss
Deep in earth, up on high
The choice will come to live or die

An old friend or enemy true
Will show his face and lead the tune
The trap is set and good to go
There is no chance to void the play
But do not fear for all is clear
And trap will play a friendly part
Though chance will fade with every step
And choice to make must be made
The waters will bubble and fade away
When all is done then choice be done
For good or bad the day be gone
A friend be found to join the hunt
May just be lost as was before
The mount will toll a final tone
When sun will set will see will see

"Another sketchy description of something we already know is going to happen." Orric shifted his posture.

"All the other passages have only ever given us one solution. They have never once mentioned anything about a choice or the fact that there could be anything other than a simple stroll through the mountain. There's a mention of a 'friend be found'. Normally lines like that indicate that there is someone else to join the group. We were always under the impression that once we left here then the group would be complete. There are so many new and disturbing…"

"I just had a thought," Orric interjected. "I have read the *Prophecy of the Stone* albeit many decades ago." Eldred was about to interrupt, but was silenced by a sharp look from Orric. "One of the reasons we discounted the *Prophecy of the Stone* was because there was no mention of the Cloumid Mountains or the well. That was the key passage that we looked for when we were deciphering the prophecies."

"What's your point?"

"Even I could see the relevance of the passage. There is no way that we all could have missed it." Orric smiled as he could see acknowledgement cross Eldred's face.

"That's not possible," a look of horror came over Eldred. "There is nothing like that in the world. There is no way. The *Prophecy of the Stone* was always the most obscure of the prophecies and by far the hardest to read. It is quite possible that we all skipped over the passage without noticing it. We almost discounted it from the start."

"You know as well as I do that we all didn't just skip over the passage. The passage wasn't there before and you know it as well as I do."

"What does it mean?" Eldred's voice dropped as he knew that Orric was right and silently scolded himself for not seeing what was now blatantly obvious.

Orric took a deep breath, his face changing to that of deep concern. "If you are right and this is the one and only prophecy, then things have just gotten a whole lot worse." Orric paused, trying to think and speak at the same time, but the enormity of the situation was getting to him. "We have always based our moves on what we thought was written in the prophecies. Now it seems as though the prophecy is changing; it seems as though the prophecy is not as definitive as we thought. If the prophecy can change at will, then we'll have to go back to the drawing board. We can believe nothing we would have once backed our lives on." Orric's shock grew.

"But it cannot be all false. I remembered the piece about the trolls from before it happened. Some of the prophecy must still be correct."

"Yes, of course," again Orric paused. "We have no option, but to continue what we have started." His words held no confidence.

"There is more than just the words of the prophecy that we listen to. We have all felt the pull, drawing us to where we need to be. It has helped us where words have failed. I still have no doubt that we're heading in the right direction. The fact that the prophecy can change at will can only mean any situation can have more than one outcome. We can no longer rely on the final battle as the only ending." His words made complete sense. "Now I think that's enough worrying over something we cannot change. What was the reason that you wanted me here before everyone else?"

The sudden statement put the thought of prophecy towards the back of Orric's mind. There had been a very good reason why he had asked Eldred to meet with him and it had nothing to do with prophecy. "Whilst you've been pouring over your precious prophecy," the snide remark was taken with the good humour it was delivered, "I've been dealing with the politics of our good King Faxon." Eldred had forgotten all about Faxon and the threat to the village. "I believe that he gives us a good way to get you and the others on the road to the Cloumid Mountains."

"I don't think that Faxon will go for your plan,' Eldred knew exactly what he was talking about. "I don't think that he will like to be bait for our escape."

"Well, not if you put it like that. However, he has been on my back every day to get him on his way. I had been stalling him because I wasn't sure how I was going to get him safely out. Today, I will be able to give him the good news that he will be leaving at dusk."

"Are you sure that's wise. If there are any others besides Nyrra's petty thugs out there, and I strongly believe that there are, then travelling at night will only increase the risk. This would be a suicide mission." Eldred was in shock with what Orric was suggesting.

"I know what I'm planning," to Eldred's surprise Orric shouted the words as he rose in his seat. "I'm sorry." Orric composed himself. "This was not an easy decision to make. The cover of darkness will disguise the members of each group. If they are specifically looking for Alaric, then they'll not be able tell which group he's in. I will send two other groups out, in total there will be four groups leaving the compound, all at various times. One will go south, one north, one east and one west. Only the two groups acting as decoys will know that they are decoys. In truth Faxon is not a true decoy."

"If they are looking for us then they'll know that we will be heading east."

Orric had to pause before he answered to keep his irritation in check. "This is something that I was well aware of when I came up with the plan. Your group will ride to the south shortly after the sun sets. There is a clear path that you'll be able to follow by moonlight. If you follow it until dawn before turning east, then you should be far enough away from the village to be safe."

"And what if Nyrra's men decide to go after our group and not the decoys?" Now he was playing devil's advocate. He knew that Orric's plan was their best chance of making it out of the village.

"Then I'm sure you'll be able to overpower them." Orric gave Eldred a wry grin.

A sharp rap on the door made them both jump. They had been so engrossed in their conversation that they had forgotten about the others.

The first to arrive was King Faxon and Prince Hawthorne. They were followed shortly after by Darziel, Valen and Alena. Everyone who walked into the room could feel the tension and looked around nervously.

"Please come in and sit down," Orric broke the silence with a friendly greeting.

That was all it took for Faxon to regain his composure and strike out. "I have been here for too long. Do not tell me that I'll have to wait here any longer."

"Indeed, I have some good news for you. You will be leaving slightly before dusk," Orric replied, ignoring his harsh words.

"Good, then what more do we need to discuss." Faxon now seemed somewhat confused.

"There is nothing more that I need to say. Darziel can run through the preparations for your departure. That is all." Orric quickly dismissed the King.

"Then I thank you for your hospitality."

"I must ask that you leave your son behind. We need to speak to him about his own journey," Eldred spoke this time, trying to stem the need for a fresh argument.

Faxon was already on his way to the door. "Do what you wish, but I do want to speak to Hawthorne before I leave."

No one spoke again until Faxon and Darziel had left the room. Darziel knew that one of their main purposes was to divert attention away from Alaric and not to mention anything to Faxon. He also knew that it was a priority to get Faxon back to his Kingdom, only there could he verify the deal that they had agreed upon.

"What is it you want from me?" Hawthorne snapped, even more stubborn than his father.

"We will also be leaving later today. You will need to be ready to leave by nightfall." Eldred ignored Hawthorne's rudeness.

Hawthorne's brow furrowed and his expression turned to anger. Standing ,abruptly, he slammed his hands down on the table. "I know what you're planning. How could you possibly think that I would agree to you using my father as bait for you to escape? You must all be insane to think that I will simply go along with your plan." Small droplets of spittle flew from the corners of his mouth as he spoke with such a rage.

"Sit down and listen." Standing from his chair Eldred used a simple spell to make his body loom over the table. At the same time, he drew a shadow over the room creating an ominous appearance.

Hawthorn could do nothing but obey and returned to his seat. A look of horror replaced the anger on his face. He almost shook as he sat.

"It is true that your father's group is in part a decoy for ours, but there are also two other groups of elves which are the real decoys. It is important that you don't say anything to your father. It is imperative that he leaves today." Eldred kept his façade until he finished his speech. When he was done, he returned to his seat and the room returned to normal.

"And give me one good reason why I should keep this secret from my father?" Hawthorne did his best to keep his voice level.

"You have been feeling a strange pull to this place for the last month." Eldred spoke slowly now, watching Hawthorne's reaction. "Deep down, you know where your place is."

Hawthorne looked down at his hands, contemplating what Eldred had just told him. "That's ridiculous," he said finally. "I have no idea what you are talking about. There has been nothing drawing me here. Now if this is all you have to say, I will be leaving." Hawthorne waited for an answer. When it was clear that none would be forthcoming, he stood up and left.

"Why did you tell him that?" Orric barked. "He will be sure to tell Faxon everything. There is no way Faxon will agree to leave now when he finds out what we have planned." Orric did nothing to hide his anger.

"How long have you known me? I think you will be surprised with Hawthorne's reaction. He knows exactly what I was talking about. The prophecy has been tugging at him all his life. Now that he knows why, he will not betray it. He is as bound as we all are." A wry smile appeared on his face.

"Even so, I don't want bad news to sneak up on me." Orric's mood only lightened slightly as he turned to speak to his son. "Valen, would you follow Hawthorne and make sure that he doesn't give anything away to his father."

Valen did as his father asked without question. He wasn't entirely sure that he agreed with Eldred, but he would do whatever he could to make sure nothing went wrong.

"Now would you be so kind as to get Alaric and bring him here," Eldred's voice softened completely as he spoke to Orric's daughter.

Like Valen, Alena did what her father told her without question. Truth be told, she was excited of the thought of seeing Alaric again. They had not seen each other since the disastrous dinner and she was concerned that she had hurt his feelings.

As quickly as they had been joined by the others, Eldred and Orric were again left alone. The tension in the room when they were joined had only increased. Simultaneously they both took a deep breath and then slowly exhaled.

"All in all I think that went rather well." Eldred smiled at his old friend.

"I agree. I don't think that anyone has any idea what's going on, least of all you and I." Orric laughed as the tension melted away.

"Now the next big question, how much do we tell our Chosen One?"

"As little as possible. I don't think he needs to know any more than we are leaving tonight. I think that we should also forgo the training that we had planned. If we have to leave tonight, than I think it would be best if we let him rest."

"He doesn't have the skill that he requires. He needs more training before he reaches the well or else he will have no chance," Orric argued.

"Then I will have to train him as we travel to the mountains."

"You know as well as I do that would be suicidal. Once outside the protective barrier of this village, the stone will be like a beacon to Nyrra's agents."

"Then there is nothing we can do. The journey tonight will be dangerous as it is. If things don't go well here, then there will be no telling what condition he will be in. There is no guarantee he will be conscious and that could be fatal."

Before they could come up with a solution, the door opened and Alaric appeared, both of them jumped with surprise at the speed of his arrival, sweat dripping from his face.

"I didn't expect you so quickly." Eldred was the first to recover.

"I was running past the house when Alena found me," Alaric panted.

"It is good to see that you have started working out. Your journey is going to be hard and you will need to be fit if you are going to survive." Orric's tone returned to that of a strict teacher. "However, I think that you should take it easy for the rest of the day. At dusk, you will be leaving and it will be a hard ride throughout the night."

Hearing about the ride made Alaric feel suddenly very tired. That was one thing that he had not practiced was his horse riding. No one had thought that had been important.

When Alaric didn't respond, Eldred decided that he would explain the situation. Alaric listened intently, but showed no emotion. There was something that disturbed the other two in his apparent lack of regard.

"I think that it might be worse than you think," the comment took them both by surprise. The confidence in his voice seemed so out of place. "I have been having these feelings ever since we arrived. Sometimes they were strong and other times they were like a tickle in the back of my mind. I don't know what they are or what they mean, but if Nyrra's agents are out there trying to break in, then they're definitely getting closer to their goal."

"What do you mean?" Orric asked, aghast by the statement.

"As I said, I'm not really sure. All that I do know is that whatever is happening is going to come to an end very soon." Alaric didn't show any concern over his revelation, which was more disturbing than his words.

"We should bring our plans forward then and have Faxon move out as soon as possible." Orric spoke directly to Eldred, ignoring Alaric completely.

Alaric spoke as though he did not realise that he had been ignored. "I don't think that will be necessary. I think that your plan is sound enough."

Now neither of them knew what to say. Alaric waited for a response, but when none was coming he continued to speak. "I have to assume that since we are leaving tonight that there will be no training today." Eldred could only nod his response. "Then I think that I will ready myself for tonight, by your leave."

Again, neither of them could speak. Orric nodded towards the door giving Alaric his leave. They were both silent for a long time after Alaric had left the room. Their meeting had not at all gone to plan.

"What just happened?" Orric was the first to speak.

"I think we have just seen a change in Alaric. It seems that the training over the past few days has done wonders for his confidence."

"I hope that is all that has given him confidence," replied Orric ominously.

"Do you think there's an outside source interfering with him, or are you worried that the prophecy is playing out too quickly?" Eldred raised an eyebrow.

"I don't think that part of the prophecy has been proven yet. No, I think that the latter is the case."

"That can't be possible. The stone can't have any effect on Alaric whilst it is in its chest."

"What do we really know about the stone? We only assume that it can't affect Alaric because it has not done so yet. What if the stone is only playing dormant to hide suspicion? You must admit that for someone who didn't really know what he was feeling, he seemed very confident in its meaning. I think that you will need to be extremely careful from now on." Orric had no problems in expressing his opinion.

"You are right. There is something going on that does not seem right. I guess all we can do now is hope that the decoys do their jobs," all Eldred could do was smile. There were so many things that were left unexplained.

***

The first of the decoy groups left on time. They left in a group of nine and were dressed and sized to match the other group. Up close no one would be fooled by their ruse, but at a distance they would pass, at least for a while. The group headed due east towards the mountain range, the obvious direction Alaric would have to take.

Whilst they did so Darziel prepared the group with King Faxon. Besides the King and Darziel, there was an entourage of one hundred elves. That was all that Orric could spare. With all the decoy groups and the extra men to follow, there were not many elves left in the village. If Nyrra's agents decided to attack the village and not follow the decoys, then it would struggle to stand.

As much as Orric wanted to keep the village fully manned, the mission was much far more important. If the death of his village meant the Chosen One escaped, then that is what he must do. He had seen the first group off in a great show of farewell. From there he returned to his house where he remained for the rest of the evening, contemplating.

King Faxon paced around whilst Darziel checked the last of the supply wagons. Once they had left the village, it would be close to a month before they reached the next town and it was Darziel's responsibility to make sure they all arrived safely.

As much as he hoped the first decoy group was safe, he secretly hoped they were currently being tracked by whoever was in the forest. The last thing that he wanted was to be attacked. Most of the village's experienced warriors, including Colin, were with them. Orric was not taking any chances. He wanted Faxon back in his palace as soon as possible. They needed his soldiers to be moved to Avalon immediately.

As the sun was starting to set, Darziel was finally satisfied that they were ready to leave. He had to suppress a tear as he led the column out of the eastern gate. He had been out of the village on hunting expeditions, but had never been away more than a day or two. Now there was no telling if he would even return.

"Are you alright, sir?" asked a young faced elf riding to his left and a pace or two behind.

"Yes, thank you." Darziel strengthened his shoulders and corrected his posture. He could only imagine what the rest of his small army was thinking. As their leader, he had to show a confident façade.

The forest canopy clouded the fading light leaving them in almost complete darkness. The gloominess did nothing to brighten Darziel's sombre mood. Every shadow, and there were many, contained possible assassins. Every rustle of the leaves on the forest floor brought nervous looks throughout the convoy.

Shortly after they left the village, Faxon rode up to speak with Darziel. He had an agitated look on his face, which Darziel could only just make out in the fading light. There was something that disturbed Darziel about Faxon.

"How long are we going to ride before we stop?" The question seemed innocent enough.

Even though Darziel thought that Faxon already knew the answer, he answered it anyway. "We shall have to ride all night if our ruse is going to work."

"I see. Do you think that is a wise decision? There are many roots and snags on the forest floor. It would be too easy for the horses to sprain an ankle in the dark."

"Don't you worry about the horses," there was a hint of superiority in his voice. "Elven horses can see quite well in the forests, even at night, now I think you should go back to the middle of the column."

"I don't think so. It's not right that I ride back with the others. I am the King and should be riding at the front of the line," now Faxon revealed his true reason for approaching Darziel.

"That's all well and good, but you hardly look like an elf and riding at the front makes you very conspicuous. They know that you have been in the village and will be watching for you to leave. At least if you're in the middle of the line, they will not be able to see you. That can only work in our favour. Now, please, if you would go back I would appreciate it." Darziel had a low opinion of men and Faxon was only reinforcing his feelings.

With a loud snort, Faxon did as he was told. He was not used to hiding in a crowd. He was the King of Remidia and should be leading the group, not following like a brainless cow. As much as he hated it, he had to admit that Darziel was right. They would be watching for him and if he was at the front he would be an easy target.

Darziel relaxed as soon as Faxon disappeared back behind the other elves. The distraction caused by Faxon was enough to make Darziel lose his concentration. With Faxon gone and his heightened senses back on the job, he sensed something and heart skipped a beat.

There was something waiting for them not far away. The feeling was strange. It was not the terror that he had thought he would feel when they were confronted. Instead, he had a feeling of curiosity. There was something up ahead and he wasn't entirely sure if it was the enemy they were all fearful of. As he rode on, he could hear the murmurs of his comrades from behind him as they sensed to same thing, his palms started to sweat with anticipation.

Darziel stopped his horse and barked the order for everyone else to do the same. There was a single figure in the middle of the trail in front of them. It made no movement. There was no sense of malice from the figure.

Slowly Darziel started to ride forward motioning for the rest of the column to stay where they were. For better or worse he knew that he had to do this by himself. As he came closer he could make out small characteristics of the creature and his heart started to race. The closer he came the more he didn't think things were going to end well.

Chapter 14: The Road to the Mountain

Night had fallen and the group had finally gathered at the southern entrance to the village. Alaric sat astride his horse staring into the fog. He had not spoken to anyone as they began to join him and Eldred. Not even the arrival of the two new members of the group brought him out of his reverie.

"Okay, I will keep this brief as time is of the essence. Hopefully by now the decoy groups have successfully led Nyrra's agents far enough away to give you safe passage. Nevertheless, be careful. Nyrra is not the only evil presence in this world and they will all be drawn to you. If you fail in your quest, then all will fail with you. Good luck and farewell." Orric spoke his solemn words before turning to Alena. "Keep safe my daughter and remember this, no matter what the prophecy says, there is nothing that you *have* to do." His words, although meant only for Alena, were heard by all. They made no sense to anyone except for Eldred, who in turn gave Orric a look that could melt ice. Orric, in return, shrugged his shoulders and walked away.

The second conversation brought Alaric back to attention. He was the only one who caught the silent dialogue between the two. He knew what words had brought the look from Eldred and could only wonder at their meaning. Something had happened since they had arrived that had made Eldred nervous. He did not sit on his horse as confidently as Alaric had remembered. There was something else that disturbed him, only he could not work out what.

The nine of them all sat on pure white horses. The creatures were magnificent to look at and just as pleasurable to ride. Alaric felt more self-assured on the back of his stallion than he had previously. It was almost as if he had an affinity with him.

"His name is Adelanta, which is the elvish word for swift." Alena whispered to Alaric as she moved her own horse next to his. "These two are twins. Her name is Rázidio." She nodded at her own mare.

Alaric looked at her briefly. They had only spoken for a moment before Alaric was summoned to meet Orric. She had seemed nervous, which confused him. Alaric, himself, was a little worried that she was still upset with him for ignoring her over dinner. Alena had tried to start a conversation, but as soon as she mentioned the proposed meeting with Eldred and Orric, his attention disappeared. She had realised there was nothing she could do to regain his attention and had left him to walk alone. Now he seemed as cold as ever. He gently patted the chest which was secured to his horse; no one else noticed him.

"He should keep you safe while you are on his back." Alena would not be perturbed.

"I do hope so, I hate riding." Alaric spoke to the space in front of him, not a hint of emotion in his voice.

"Let's ride out." Eldred had ridden to the front of the group. "We have a long way to go before the sun rises and it already has an hour's head start. We will need to make it to the Longcastle highway by daybreak. From there it is a two-day ride to the town of Longcastle where we will be able to rest for a couple of days before continuing on towards the mountains."

Eldred slowly led them through the southern gate into the fog. Besides the nine horses and riders, there were also two horse drawn wagons. The horses were of the same stock and needed no waggoneer to control them; they would follow quietly behind the group.

The fog reflected the moonlight creating an eerie grey radiance. The white horses of the elves knew their own way through the fog so it wasn't imperative that they remain within sight of each other, although no one wanted to be riding alone in it; no one felt truly safe.

The only noise they could hear was the gentle clip, clop of the horse's hooves. No one wanted to speak in case there was someone listening. Their fear, however irrational, was warranted. There was something outside the fog that was hunting them and if the decoys didn't work, they would be waiting.

There was a group of fifty elves scouting around them. If there was anyone outside, then hopefully the scouts would find them first. If not, then they were sure to fail. Eldred was the only one who was truly confident that they were going to make it to the Cloumid Mountains unharmed. If nothing else, he believed that the prophecy guaranteed it. He did not, however, share his theory with the rest of the group.

The ride through the fog seemed to take forever. The horses carefully picked their way through without a care for their surroundings. They felt the anxiety of their riders, but that didn't seem to bother them.

As soon as they reached the edge of the fog the horses became jittery. The night was dark with the forest canopy blanketing them from the moonlight. The contrast from the dull grey of the fog to the pitch black of the forest was so startling that it took a moment to regain control. The night was alive with fear. As they continued onward, the trees seemed to whisper in their ears as if they were working for the enemy.

"Things are not right in the forest," commented Palentonal

"What are you talking about?" Hawthorne barked, fear making his words harsher than he intended.

"The trees," added Alena in a whisper that could only just be heard.

"There is something not right about the trees," Palentonal continued. "Something has happened, something has made them angry."

The three elves were well in tune with the forest around them and could easily sense the change. There was a viciousness about them that made everyone nervous.

"They are angry because of the evil that has been infecting the forest. Slowly that evil is twisting their otherwise placid nature. We would do well to be cautious around them now," Eldred explained solemnly, a hint of regret in his voice.

The two dwarves looked around nervously. Out of all of them, they were finding the ride the hardest. It was not the darkness, as they were used to working in the mines for days at a time; it was the trees that upset them the most. It was the way that they loomed over the top of them. There was something very eerie about the forest.

A halt was called at even the slightest of noises. They would only start again when they were completely sure there was no one around. Every time they had to stop, Eldred slowly cursed under his breath. The plan to make it to the Longcastle highway was slipping further and further away. The longer they had to stay in the forest, the more chance they had of running into Nyrra's agents.

The night passed slowly, they continued to stop at the slightest of sounds even when someone only thought they had heard something. When the sun finally peeked over the horizon, they were nowhere near the Longcastle highway.

Light, which should have brought comfort, only brought a new terror. It was one thing to sense the animosity of the trees, but another thing to see it. The trees loomed menacingly over the top of them. From the corner of their eyes, it looked as though they were snarling, their branches reaching out to grab them. Their exhaustion was setting in and all of them, besides Eldred, were all but asleep in the saddles.

As much as Eldred wanted to keep going, he knew that he had to let the others rest. They were still deep in the forest and the threat was still upon them. If they were attacked, there would be no way they could defend themselves.

"Okay, we will stop for a rest." Eldred reined in his horse. "Three hours sleep before we have to get going again. I will keep guard."

No one complained at the thought of sleep, no matter how short it was. They all quickly unpacked their sleeping gear and within a matter of moments were sleeping soundly. It was a testament to their exhaustion that they could sleep with the trees looming over them.

Eldred shivered at the thought of their impending doom and then busied himself starting a small fire. The last thing he wanted to do was upset the trees any further, but since they had stopped riding, he could feel the morning chill. The small fire did little to heat the air, but it was better than nothing.

Eldred had a small meal ready for them to eat as soon as they were awake. Eldred had eaten before he woke the others and spent his time packing their bedrolls. He wanted to make sure they were back in the saddle as soon as possible. He had received word from one of the scouting parties that the forest was clear and they were returning to the village as instructed.

"How are you?" Bern asked Alaric as he rode up next to him. Alaric had spent the entire night riding by himself and he jumped at the sudden voice next to him. He had been lost in thought again. Once he came around, he couldn't remember exactly what it was he was thinking about; he only knew that it had been important. "As well as can be expected," in truth he was doing well. The training he had received, albeit short, had strengthened both his body and spirit.

"You seem different, somehow." Bern looked at his old friend and could hardly recognise him.

"As do you, my friend. I guess a week with the elves can do strange things to a man."

"Yes, they do. They have been trying to train me to fight, but I wasn't very good at it. Hulkan and Dorn showed me how to use a battle axe. I started to pick that up fairly easily and then Orric even gave me an old axe that he had lying around." Bern spoke quickly as he was excited to finally be able to speak about his experiences. "What about you Alaric? Did you learn much?"

Alaric didn't want to belittle his friend by bragging about the progress he had made. "A little bit. They tried to teach me a few different things, but I really didn't have enough time on anything to learn properly."

"Hopefully, if we're not riding nonstop, we can get a chance to practise." Bern seemed excited with the prospect.

"That would be good." Alaric showed very little enthusiasm.

"Bern!" Hulkan called from somewhere behind them. "Come back here, we want to teach you some more about the axe," the two dwarves had clearly befriended him.

Alaric waved Bern's question away and watched him ride back to the dwarves. He had no great need for conversation as he still had plenty on his mind, but he was given no time to sink back into his thoughts. As soon as Bern had left him, Alena approached.

"I'm sorry if I have done something to upset you," the words were genuine, but seemed strange coming from her.

"You have nothing to apologise for. It is me who should be apologising. I haven't been myself for the last few days, or maybe I have and it is the last twenty-five years that has been a lie." Alaric spoke as softly as he could.

"Nothing has been a lie. You are who you are and you adapt with every new circumstance."

"Thank you." Alaric smiled warmly at her. "If you don't mind, I would like to ride alone now," there was something about Alena that made him uncomfortable. He wasn't sure if it was her stunning beauty, even after riding all night and only having three hours sleep, or the way that she spoke to him. It was as if he made her nervous and tha,t in itself, was enough to make him uncomfortable.

Alena returned his smile and the rode up to Prince Hawthorne. Immediately they struck up a friendly conversation, which irritated Alaric even more. They seemed to be speaking so effortlessly when every word seemed to stumble out of his mouth. He silently cursed himself for being a fool before returning to his trance-like state.

They stopped in a small clearing for a mid-afternoon meal. It was the first time since they had left the village that they had been in open sunlight. The warmth felt good against their faces and there was a relaxed atmosphere amongst the group; they were all grateful to be out from under the trees, even the elves were happier to be in the open.

The constant riding continued to tire everyone. Only the horses didn't seem to tire from the constant travelling. Any normal horse would have collapsed under the strain, but the elven horses were stronger. They took the opportunity to rest and graze, to ensure they would be ready to ride out that afternoon. There was a small stream nearby where they went to drink. They didn't need to be picketed; no matter where they roamed, they would always return when needed.

"Something doesn't feel right. The forest feels very unnatural, more so than any time since we left the village." Alaric tried to keep his voice low so only Eldred could hear, but in the confines of the clearing it was impossible.

"What are you talking about?" Dorn was the first one to speak.

"I'm sure that it's nothing." Eldred spoke casually, doing well to hide his concern. "The forest is alive with anger, but I don't think that there is anything for us to worry about."

There was something else out there, Alaric was sure of it. He had felt the trees' anger ever since they had left the fog. It had been very disturbing at first, but he had grown used to it; this new feeling was different. There was an inherent evil somewhere in the forest and it was getting closer.

"I think that we should keep moving," Alaric blurted out the words.

"Please Alaric." Eldred seemed a little annoyed. "We shall be leaving shortly. We need to give the horses as much of a rest as we can."

"The horses are ready and I really think that we should be leaving now," the desperation in his voice was making everyone else agitated.

"Okay Alaric, we will leave now." Eldred suppressed a sigh and came to his feet.

Within a matter of minutes, they were all in the saddle again. Eldred remained at the head of the group. Alaric had made an attempt to speak with him, but Eldred had waved him away. Eldred was trying to sense what it was that had upset Alaric and didn't want anyone to distract him.

After fifteen minutes, as the feeling of dread grew even stronger, Alaric rode forward and demanded Eldred's attention. This time he received it instantly.

"You're right. There is something out there emitting a great amount of evil," Eldred sounded exhausted.

"Do you know what it is?" Alaric asked slowly.

"Not exactly, but I have to assume that it's some of Nyrra's agents. It seems that our ruse didn't work after all." Eldred was unsure if what he said made sense, but it was the only logical answer.

"So we should ride hard then," suggested Alaric only a slight amount of panic in his voice.

"That's not a good idea. The terrain is too uneven for the horses to travel any quicker than a walk. Only very skilled riders could manage a gallop. If we push them too hard, there is a very good chance that one of them will break a leg. Once we get to the Longcastle highway, we will be able to ride a little faster. From there we should only be another day's ride to Longcastle where we should be able to rest for a couple of days. Even on the highway though, we will only be able to ride as fast as the wagons can travel." Eldred wanted to ride hard as much as Alaric, but knew it would be no good. If they were able to make it to the highway, they might just be able to avoid Nyrra's agents.

Eldred asked Alaric to find Craven. He wanted to speak to the elf. Alaric did as he was told without question. He knew that he was not going to receive any more information from Eldred.

"I believe that we are being followed. I want you to ride back and see if you can find out who it is," Eldred commanded.

"I will go by foot. It'll be easier to stay hidden without the horse," Craven replied.

Eldred simply nodded his head and took the reins of Cravens horse as he leapt from the animal's back. Within moments, Craven had disappeared amongst the trees. Eldred had every faith that the elf would be able to find who it was that was following them and remain hidden.

"We must rest soon," Hawthorne rode up to meet Eldred as the sun started to fade. "Everyone is exhausted."

Eldred too was starting to feel the strain. He didn't want to stop until Craven returned, but at the same time if they stopped, Craven would return all the quicker. Again, he had little option. If they were attacked before they were able to rest, then they would have no chance to survive.

"We should be at the highway soon. We'll rest once there," it was the only excuse Eldred could use to keep them going.

"We should have been to the highway by now." Hawthorne barked back, exhaustion getting the better of him.

Before the words came out of Hawthorne's mouth, Eldred knew it to be true. He had been too concerned about what was following them to worry that they had not yet reached the highway. It was as if something was deliberately leading them away. That thought was even more disturbing.

"You're right. We'll rest here for a while whilst I find our bearings," Eldred said before he called the others to a halt.

Alaric was the only one who didn't fall asleep immediately, although he was deathly tired, there was something important on his mind.

"There's been something troubling me," Alaric started as Eldred finally sat down to rest.

"I know, you've told me already. Now please I need to concentrate." Eldred dismissed Alaric quickly.

"No, it's not someone following us. There's something else out there, something more subtle. It's almost like nothing at all. Just when I think it has disappeared, it creeps back." Alaric tried his best to explain what he had felt.

"I haven't felt anything," this fact worried Eldred more than the fact that there was someone else tracking them. "Do you know who or what it is?"

"No. I was hoping that you might be able to help me." Alaric didn't lose any of his edge.

"Well I ask you two more questions. Is there anything you can do about it and is it an immediate threat?" Eldred asked.

"No, I don't think so."

"Then there is no point in worrying about now. Now please, get some rest so I can concentrate on who is following us." Eldred left no opportunity for Alaric to continue the conversation. What he spoke of was disturbing, but he had to focus his attention on the job at hand. He was extremely tired himself and could only focus on one thing at a time.

It was well into the night when Craven finally returned. The heat of the day was quickly lost, but Eldred was loathed to light a fire. If they were being followed, then the fire would be as good as a fifty foot beacon. He was able to shut out the cold and no one had stirred from their sleep.

Eldred had decided to wait until Craven's return before waking the others. He wanted to know what was behind them before he decided on their best course of action.

"I could not find anyone," Craven finally said once everyone had woken. "The only sign of travel through this part of the forest was us. There were not even signs of any animals."

"So what does that mean?" barked Hawthorne.

"That means that we are not being followed," replied Palentonal, defending his fellow elf.

"Hopefully yes," replied Eldred who had been pondering Craven's words. "But more likely that whoever it is who is following us have covered their tracks extremely well."

"That's impossible. No one can evade an elf in the forest," Palentonal almost spat the words.

"No, I think that Eldred is correct. Something just wasn't right. I can't believe that there have been no animals in this part of the forest. Something has hidden itself from me and that in itself is very disturbing." As much as Craven didn't want to, he had to agree with Eldred.

"So what are we going to do?" Hawthorne repeated the question.

"The only thing we can do." Alaric voice was cold and flat. Everyone turned to the direction the voice came from, since no one could see him in the dark. "We continue to ride towards the highway and hope that we don't meet with whoever or whatever it is."

"So we ride blindly into the night again?" Hawthorne lost his temper.

"Alaric is right. It's either that or we wait here to be attacked," Alena added.

Once Eldred had agreed with Alaric, there was no need for further discussion. The dwarves seemed to take little interest in the conversation, they didn't care either way. Dwarves were aggressive by nature and would prefer an open fight, but also knew that the dark would do them no favours.

They rode through the night without a word of complaint. A new tension had fallen over the group. There was a fear of the darkness that kept them all on edge. Every moment that passed could have been their last.

The morning came around without incident. They had ridden as hard as they could, making sure the wagons didn't lag too far behind. When the sun rose above the tree line, they were all exhausted and there was still no sign of the highway.

Again, Eldred let them all rest. All he could do now was keep an eye on their surroundings. If he tried to use his powers to sense the surrounding forest, then he would surely faint. The journey from the village was now starting to take its toll. He had been relying on the fact that they would have been in Longcastle and he would be able to rest, he knew that he had to rest sometime in the next couple of days.

Eldred let them sleep until noon. With every second that passed, his nerves grew. He was now confident that they would be attacked soon and he wanted to make sure that everyone was well rested and prepared. The one disadvantage that could cause them all to die would be fatigue. As much as he was confident that they would make it safely to the Cloumid Mountains, he didn't want to take any chances.

The day continued without sign of their would-be attackers or the highway. Eldred still led, although he could hardly stay upright in the saddle. At first he hid his exhaustion well, but eventually it was obvious to everyone that he was struggling.

"You haven't slept in days. You need rest," Alena spoke softly to him at the front of the line.

"I will be fine," Eldred's words were only just audible.

"What good will it be if we get attacked with you in this position?"

"We need to keep going until dusk. Once it becomes dark it will be harder for them to find us." Eldred was unyielding.

"Please."

"It doesn't matter now anyway." Alena jumped in her saddle as Alaric spoke from behind them. Not only because she had not heard him ride up, but also the coldness in his voice. "We stop here."

"But I have felt nothing, are you sure," Eldred spoke softly as he reined his horse to a complete halt.

Before Alaric could answer, he felt a tickling sensation down the back of his neck. Before he could act, a bolt of lightning shot from the sky and struck the spot where Eldred would have been if Alaric had not stopped him. The explosion caused the three at the front to be knocked from their horses. The others twisted and turned in their saddles trying to see where the attack had come from.

Alaric was the first to recover from his blow. He was quickly on his feet. He had expected to see his horse bolting into the forest, but instead he saw Adelanta standing calmly in front of him. Alaric snatched his sword and remounted.

With the sword in his hand, Alaric was able to concentrate on his surroundings. They were out there somewhere, but as of yet he could not locate them. To his relief the tingling sensation had gone.

"What was that?" asked Palentonal when the confusion died down.

"That was a lightning strike, a powerful incantation, even more powerful to have that sort of accuracy. I believe whoever cast it will not have enough energy to cause us any more problems." Eldred seemed to have regained most of his vitality; he too was now standing with his sword drawn. "The only downfall is that I don't think I can cast any spells either."

"Then it looks like this will be an old fashion sword fight," Hawthorne almost sounded excited.

"Where are they," boomed Hulkan, brandishing his axe as he jumped from his horse. The two dwarves and Bern would not fight from horseback. The axe did not lend itself to that type of combat.

"That bolt could have come from over a league away, if its creator is as good as I think he is. There is no telling if there is anyone else with him." Eldred explained.

"Oh there are more and we should be seeing them at any moment." There was still no emotion in Alaric's voice.

Eldred didn't know what was more concerning: the fact that there were more and they were close or the fact that Alaric didn't seem to care. He had expected Alaric to be more confident since his training, but his current attitude was something completely unexpected.

"How do you know where they are coming from?" a sight amount of strain entered Hawthorne's voice.

There was no time for Alaric to answer, suddenly the silhouette of a man appeared through the trees no more than half a dozen paces from them. There would be no chance for either side to create a formation. There would be no advantage in numbers. No more than three or four had room to fight any one battle. Soon there were more than twenty figures encircling them. The numbers were more than two to one, yet the terrain made the odds even. The better fighters would win the battle.

As one the twenty men moved in, it was clear that, in the failing light, they did not know which one was Alaric. They stalked amongst the trees to allow them the best vantage point.

By pure chance, Alaric was the closest to the advancing men and was soon engaged with one of the assailants. Although he had never fought on horseback Adelanta had been trained as a warhorse and knew exactly what to do. He moved into the best position for Alaric to attack. At the same time, he made sure that none of the other attackers could circle around him. His position amongst the trees made it almost impossible for Alaric to be attacked by more than one man at a time.

The swordsman attacking Alaric was proficient enough to cause some trouble, but being on horseback caused as many problems for Alaric as it had advantages. Without the freedom of movement, Alaric could only hack at his opponent. In the confined space Adelanta had created, there was not enough room to create any great forms. Even though Alaric didn't know it, he had the clear advantage.

Both Alena and Palentonal had drawn bows when Alaric had confirmed the imminent attack. Each had managed only one shot before they had to discard their bows and draw their swords. Palentonal's shot hit an approaching man in the arm, although not fatal, it would deeply hinder his attack. Alena's shot hit another man straight through the left eye and instantly he fell dead to the ground.

Soon enough they were all engaged in battle. The two dwarves were the only ones working together. Their short stature worked in their favour in the tight confines. There was just enough room for them to swing their axes without colliding with the trees or each other. They also tried to keep Bern out of harm's way, they knew that he had never been in battle before and wanted to keep him safe.

Hawthorne was the first to face more than one opponent. This only seemed to lift his spirits and he laughed loudly as the second man joined the fight. He moved his sword with the grace it was made for. As Prince of Remidia, he had received many years of training. Fighting on horseback was as natural to him as fighting on the ground. Within moments he had slashed each of his opponents numerous times across the body and arms.

Alena was having no problems with her assailant. She deftly swept away the attacks without worrying about countering. Her form of attacking was waiting for the perfect moment to make her killing blow. Her tactics would not be adequate against a swordmaster, but against lesser adversaries they would almost always work. True enough it did not take long before Alena saw her opening. With one great thrust, she drew the tip of her blade deep into the man's skull.

Her second opponent was suffering from the arrowshot in his arm. He did not retreat as Alena thought that he would. Whatever it was that was driving him to attack must have been worse than death. As he neared her, she could see a thick layer of sweat of his forehead. The man could hardly stand up under the pain and as soon as he was within striking distance, he made one desperate attempt at an attack. All he managed to do was fall directly on Alena's sword. His dying eyes stared up at her, as if in gratitude.

Although the two dwarves were trying to keep Bern away from the fray, there were simply too many attackers for him to remain passive. He was the last to engage in battle, but was just as fervent. He moved the axe through the air like he had been using it all his life. The strength he had gained by a lifetime of farming added to the weight of the blade, his opponent stood little chance. Bern quickly buried the full weight of the axe into the back of the man's skull.

The two male elves fought closely together, yet too far away to be any help to each other. Between the two of them, they had three assailants with the fourth dying by arrow. Palentonal fought one, whilst Craven contended with the other two. There was a definite disadvantage to the ground that Craven was fighting on. He had managed to find himself at the bottom of a dried-out stream bed. The two attackers were able to attack from the same height on the embankment. There was not enough room in the stream bed for Craven to move out of reach. With a desperate lunge, Craven managed to skewer one of the men. As the man fell, Craven's sword became trapped and dragged him from his saddle.

With Craven on the ground, he was an easy target for the second attacker. Before he could pull his sword free, Craven received a boot to his face. The blow left him disorientated and he was given no time to recover before he felt the sweet pain of cold steel slice through his chest.

Palentonal didn't witness the death blow, but saw Craven on the ground out of the corner of his eyes. The sight of his fellow elf dying sent a wave of anger coursing through his body. Within seconds Palentonal, had slashed the neck of his opponent before turning on the man who had killed Craven.

Seeing Palentonal through his hazy vision Craven made one final move. With the last of his strength Craven took hold of the hilt of the sword protruding from his chest and drove it deeper. The man was so surprised, he could do nothing to stop him. This was all he needed to do to allow Palentonal's victory. There was no time for the man to snatch up another weapon before Palentonal ran him through.

Once it was clear that the man had died, Palentonal returned his attention to Craven. If there had been any chance for Craven to survive, it was now completely gone. The sword had pierced his heart and Palentonal had only enough time to witness Craven's last breath.

The fatigue that had plagued Eldred for most of the afternoon had simply vanished in the heat of battle. He fought no less fiercely than the others. The two men who attacked him were having a hard time to keep up with the pace that Eldred was setting. His blade whizzed past his opponents who could only just defend themselves. Adrenaline coursed through his veins as he forced the attacks. The result of the fight was known from the start and soon enough Eldred managed to get his sword past their defences and cause the fatal blows.

Alaric had managed to kill the first of his opponents and was battling his second. He had completely given up on trying to use his superior sword fighting skills to win and relied upon his fortuitous advantage. With each blow, there was a clear strain on his opponent; in the end the only thing he could do was hold his sword above his head until Alaric hacked it out of his hand. Even when he was unarmed, he would not retreat. Alaric easily finished him off.

Soon enough all the attackers lay dead on the forest floor. After all the fear and sneaking around, there was really nothing for them to worry about. They had tracked them all the way from the village and then not had the skill to affect an attack.

Alaric sat high in his saddle with his sword still in his hand. He stared into the forest and could swear he could see a man sitting on a horse on top of a small hill. Although the man was clearly out of sight, he seemed to be staring straight at him. He thought the man looked familiar, but could not place from where or when. The man snorted and then turned his horse and rode down the far side of the hill.

There was something very disturbing about him, although Alaric had no idea who it was, or how he could see him, but knew that this was the man who had created the lightning strike. He was also the man who had hidden their tracks. There was no way that the twenty men who had attacked them had the skill to remain hidden.

He thought about telling Eldred, but when he looked at the wizard he thought better of it. The old man looked completely wiped out from his ordeal.

Besides the death of Craven, there were few injuries from the fighting. Dorn had a small cut on the side of the face and Hawthorne had a gash down his right arm. Both injuries had been through lucky blows more than good swordsmanship. Neither of the wounds were life threatening, although Hawthorne's arm was bleeding profusely.

"We should ride on for a short way and then rest for the night. There will be no more attacks tonight." Alaric spoke as he finally cleaned and sheathed his sword.

Eldred was about to speak, but then thought better of it. The scent of death would bring a whole number of predators and scavengers to the battle ground. If they stayed near the dead, then there was a chance that they too would be attacked.

Palentonal was still grieving by Craven's side. He had removed the sword from his chest and thrown it onto the bank. The blood from his chest spilled onto the ground. Palentonal said a quiet prayer before returning to his feet.

"We must take him with us. We can't leave him to rot with the others," Palentonal spoke with deep emotion in his voice.

"Of course," Eldred's voice was hoarse with the strain. "Load his body onto one of the wagons and then catch up with us."

Surprisingly, it was Hulkan who stayed behind to help Palentonal with Craven's body. The two of them didn't speak as they wrapped him and placed him in the back of one of the wagons. There was a silent understanding between the two.

The sun had almost completely set before they stopped to rest, and Eldred literally fell out of his saddle and collapsed to the ground. Once he had known that there was no further need to travel, his body shut down.

The sight was somewhat disturbing to the others. Eldred had always been stalwart. To see him frail and in pain was troubling.

With the immediate danger gone, they were all happy to stay the night where they were. They had managed to find a small clearing where they could all fit. They all busied themselves with the tasks that needed to be completed, everyone except for Alaric and Eldred.

The two dwarves and Bern collected fire wood for the night. Palentonal made sure that they left their axes behind, the trees could become dangerous if they felt threatened. Palentonal busied himself preparing a pyre for Craven and he had managed to find another clearing not too far away from their campsite. He collected all the fire wood he could find and started to build.

Palentonal brought Craven's body to rest on top and spoke the sacred prayers before lighting a fire at the pyre's base. Soon the flames burst up through the wood and engulfed Craven's body. The entire forest seemed to cry out in sorrow over the elf's death.

Alena busied herself cleaning and dressing Hawthorne's wound. The cut to his arm was far worse than they had originally expected. It took a lot of effort for Alena to stop the bleeding and clean it. As she stitched and dressed the wound Hawthorne sat completely still. It was obvious that this was not the first wound he had received.

Alaric sat next to the sleeping Eldred and stared into the darkness. There had been something very disturbing about the man who had sat on his horse in the distance. Once they had left the battlefield, the thought had been plaguing him. He knew who it was. Somehow he knew exactly who it was. The only problem was he couldn't remember.

Once the fire started burning everyone relaxed. It was the first time they could rest since they had left the village without the threat of attack. They ate a large meal and chatted around the campfire like they were on vacation.

"We should not stay up much later. We have a long day's ride tomorrow and there are more threats out there than the one we have just defeated." It was first time Alaric had spoken since they had all sat down. "I will take the first watch tonight."

Alaric's tone left no room for argument. His words brought a sombre mood amongst the rest of the group. Not only because it put a halt to their merriment, but because it was true. For a while they had all been able to forget the direness of their mission.

Chapter 15: A Trap Set

In the morning, they all woke refreshed. The night had passed without incident despite Alaric's warning. During his watch, Alaric had time to concentrate on his surroundings. There was still someone out there, someone watching them, someone who wasn't the man on the horse, someone who could be much more dangerous than the day's attack. He was almost certain that it was the person who was leading them off course.

They were in the saddle as the sun crept over the trees. There was no talk of what had happened the day before, at least not until they were well on their way. There was something about the attack that had been bothering Alaric and he could wait no longer to discuss it with Eldred.

"There was something not right about the attack yesterday." Alaric started as he rode up next to Eldred.

"What do you mean?"

"It was a little too easy and…" Alaric started to explain before Eldred interrupted him.

"I don't think that it was all that easy. Don't forget that we lost an important member of our group yesterday." The death of Craven had worried Eldred no end. There had been no mention of a death in the prophecy. "Hawthorne was also deeply wounded and he is very proficient with the blade."

"The death of Craven was unfortunate, true," Alaric kept his voice low, he didn't think that Palentonal would appreciate him speaking of Craven's death so flippantly. "But I think that was more luck on their behalf than skill. Either way that is regardless of the point. The point is these men managed to wipe out Faxon's army without a trace of their attack and yet were not able to defeat a small group of nine, why?"

Eldred considered his statement carefully. He had realised that the attack was all too easy to defend, but had not thought about their previous campaign. "Maybe our decoys worked and they sent the bulk of their forces elsewhere."

"I don't think so. I don't think these were the same men who were attacking the village or Faxon's soldiers."

"That is interesting, but who do you think they are? Mere bandits looking for some quick score?" Eldred didn't like the theory.

"No, the leader, the one who brought the lightning bolt down on us was no mere bandit." Eldred had to agree. He had almost forgotten the lightning bolt that had nearly killed them. "I think that whoever was leading them wanted to test us. They wanted to see how we would handle an attack. I don't think that it was really designed to cause us any great harm. In fact, I don't think he was expecting to kill any ofus."

"What gives you that impression?"

"I really don't know." That was all Alaric had to say. It was clear he was going to get no more answers from Eldred and did not want to reveal too much of what he thought.

Alaric's words disturbed Eldred greatly; something was happening to him that Eldred could not explain. It was clear that he was no longer confiding in him. He would only share his thoughts if he thought he could get answers. The more they continued the more Eldred was starting to believe that the chest had no effect on the stone at all.

By midday the peaks of the mountain range could be seen. Alaric estimated that they could be no more than a day's ride away. He thought that this should lift their spirits, but was surprised to see a worried look on Eldred's face when they stopped for lunch.

"What is the problem Eldred?" It was Bern who finally asked the question in-between mouthfuls. "By the looks of those peaks, we can be no more than a day's ride from the mountains."

"That is exactly what the problem is. We should be at least another three days away from seeing the mountain peaks. Not to mention the fact that we should have reached the Longcastle highway over two days ago." Eldred spoke gravely.

"What does that all mean?" asked Dorn.

"It means that someone has been altering our path," Palentonal added. "Not only that but it seems that they have also sped our journey along."

"What can we do about it?" asked Dorn, he had no love of magic and this reeked of it.

"I've been trying to sense who's doing this, but I have yet been able to find the source. Until I know who it is and what exactly they are doing, I don't think that we have any choice. We have to continue as we have been and hope for the best." The words didn't seem right as they came out of his mouth, yet there seemed no other way. They had to continue as they were as there was no other option.

No one was pleased with his answer, but they too knew that there was no other option. The worst part was that whoever was casting the spell was at least as powerful as Eldred, if not more so. If they were walking into a trap, then there would be nothing they could do about it.

They continued until nightfall without diverting from their course. Eldred knew no matter which direction they took they would still end up in the same position.

The frivolities of the previous night had been completely forgotten. The freedom they had felt with the threat behind them had disappeared. There was now a new threat, one that none of them was able to fight. They ate their evening meal in silence and then went quickly to sleep.

Morning came around all too quickly. Eldred had to rally everyone out of their bedrolls. No one wanted to continue their journey. A feeling of dread had settled over the group during the night. The morning sky reflected their emotions, dark grey clouds loomed in the sky, completely blocking out the sun and casting the forest into a virtual twilight.

Their spirits lifted slightly once they were on the move again, but that stopped as soon as the rain started to fall. At first it was only a drizzle, which was little more than an annoyance, but as noon approached it increased in its ferocity. No one complained when Eldred suggested that they ride through lunch to reach the mountains and get out of the rain.

It was early afternoon when they came to the edge of the forest. On the other side of the trees was a clearing about half a mile in diameter between them and the foot of the mountain range. A small stream dissected the clearing in almost perfect halves. There was something disconcerting about the open expanse in front of them. What was more concerning, although no one seemed to notice, was that the rain had completely stopped over the clearing whilst they were still getting drenched in the forest.

Alaric sat on his horse right on the edge of the trees and stared in wonder towards the mountain peaks. He had never seen anything so massive. The mountains seemed to loom over the top of him. The peaks were capped with a layer of snow, even though it was still summer. The trees started again at the base of the mountain on the other side of the clearing and grew almost half way up.

Without thinking he pushed Adelanta forward. The elven stallion remained motionless. When Alaric tried to force him forward, he took a step backwards and shook his head violently. Alaric raised his hand to slap him across the back of his head when Eldred called out to him.

"Stay your hand Alaric," there was a sense of power in his voice. "There is no need for violence. We should take note of the horse's reactions. It is not just Adelanta who will not pass the tree line. None of the animals will cross."

"But there is nothing to fear. Look! It is calm and peaceful," Hulkan put forward his protest.

"Yes, you're right. There's nothing wrong with the clearing. It's the easiest route to the mountain." Even as the words came out of his mouth he knew that they made no sense. "We were going to have to leave the horses sooner or later. They wouldn't be able to transport us in the mountain. They will be able to make their own way from here." No matter what Eldred wanted to do, he could not stop speaking. It was if someone was speaking for him.

The entire situation seemed suspicious, but no one cared to notice. Eldred was telling them what they wanted to hear. They all wanted to walk out into the sunshine and safety of the clearing, it was all they could do to stay where they were and listen.

"We need to take the supplies," Eldred had to force the words out of his mouth.

Begrudgingly, they all did as Eldred had suggested. Only Palentonal seemed uneasy about the clearing. He wanted to voice his opinion, but knew that it would do no good. If Eldred said it was safe, then he had to trust the wizard's judgement.

Once they had emptied the wagons of all they could carry, they returned their attention to the clearing. As much as they wanted to rush out into the sunshine, there was something holding them back. They all stared at Eldred, waiting for him to make the first move.

"What are you waiting for?" Eldred snapped the words, uncomfortable with the way they were all looking at him.

Eldred shook his head in disgust and took the first step into the clearing. The sun felt good on his face. Standing in the clearing he wondered what he had ever been worried about. He now felt as if a huge weight had been lifted. Whatever he had been concerned with had gone.

Seeing that Eldred had stepped into the clearing and survived gave everyone else the confidence to follow. Once they were all in the clearing, there was an overwhelming feeling of joy and safety, all they could think about now was crossing the stream to the grass on the other side, which looked greener and softer and more appealing than the field they were standing in.

No one seemed to notice that the grass had just been freshly cut. They were all ecstatic at being over the other side of the stream. None of them could see the trap closing in around them. As the spell ensnared them the euphoric feeling slowly dissipated.

It was pure horror that replaced their joy. Whether it was the fact they knew they were trapped or whether the change in the spell caught them off guard, the feeling was mutual. Bern and Hawthorne both sank to the ground in shock. Only Palentonal wasn't a complete mess.

Alaric felt like bolting back to the forest, but he knew it would be of no use. Whatever the trap was, they were securely caught in it. Running was out of the question. All they could do now was to try and figure their way out.

Suddenly the smell of roasting meat filled the clearing. A small campfire had been lit near the base of the mountain and a side of beef was hanging on a makeshift spit. No one knew where it had come from, but their horror was replaced by extreme hunger.

They moved as one towards the food, which was mysteriously ready for eating. No one seemed to notice that it had cooked itself in a matter of moments. No one seemed to care how or why the food had appeared. All they cared about was their ravenous hunger.

Sitting by the fire, eating the meat provided for them, they forgot their terror. The sun was starting to set over the forest and they were all getting ready to spend the night. No one remembered that they were caught in a trap. As far as they were all concerned, they had decided to stop for the night.

"Wait," cried Palentonal. "What are we doing here?"

His words fell on deaf ears. Alaric was the only one who seemed to notice what he was saying. All the others continued to eat their food and talk about more joyous events.

"This entire place is a trap. What are we doing sitting and eating? We should be trying to find our way out of here. At least we should be trying to work out who it is who has trapped us," Palentonal pleaded with the others, even as he took a bite of meat.

"He is right." Alaric had to force the words from his mouth. "Something is seriously wrong here." Even as the words came out, he didn't stop eating. "Eldred, you have to do something. This is obviously a spell."

The words struck Eldred like a bucket of cold water. He shook his head and blinked once. There was magic in play and they were all falling for it. With each breath, Eldred could feel himself sinking back into the spell and had to use all his will power to fight it.

The sun had completely disappeared below the horizon. No one seemed to notice that time seemed to be moving at a phenomenal rate. The only light that remained was that of the fire. There was no moon and not a single star in the sky, but under the shroud of mysticism no one noticed.

"I will see what I can do," was all Eldred could say.

The others were happy to relax and allow the spell to take them back into their fantasyland. It required too much effort for them to fight the magic. Palentonal and Alaric were the only two who didn't suffer the full effects of the spell. The magic was like a warm blanket on a cold night. It allowed them to escape from their impossible situation.

Once aware of the spell, Eldred didn't have any problems in ignoring the effects. He became fully aware of his surroundings and it was clear they had been created. He was yet to figure out what the trap exactly was, but it was obvious that it was made by a powerful wizard.

"What do you think?" Alaric asked quietly after they had been sitting for over an hour.

Palentonal had finally succumbed to the spell and had drifted off into delusion. This only strengthened Alaric's resolve. He knew that if he faded as well then they would be out of hope. He had faith that Eldred would eventually find a solution

"I know for one thing, whoever created this trap knew what they were doing."

"Are they more powerful than you?" Alaric didn't want to ask the question, but felt compelled.

The question brought Eldred to full attention. "What did you say?"

"Are they more powerful than you?" Alaric felt uncomfortable with the question.

"No, I don't think that they are. They are proficient and know how to mask a spell, but I don't think that they are as powerful as they think they are." A wry grin appeared on Eldred's face.

"They were powerful enough to capture you." There was a slight amount of annoyance in his voice.

"That is true, but there is one important thing that they have forgotten." Eldred left the comment tantalizingly unfinished.

"And what might that be?"

"I think that I might go to sleep now. I doubt very much that anything exciting is going to happen tonight." Eldred seemed pleased with the conversation.

Alaric spat loudly when Eldred stood and left to prepare his bedding. The others didn't seem too worried about sleep. Alaric tried to talk to them, or at least try and get some sense from them, but when he did, they suddenly all claimed to be dead tired. This annoyed him, but he too was suddenly very tired. Now there was nothing in the world he wanted to do more than sleep, and feel asleep immediately as soon as he lay down.

Eldred was the first to wake. He wanted to make sure of a few things before the others woke. If he was going to figure out exactly what was going on, then he would have to tread carefully. He already knew that he was not going to be able to break the spell magically. Whoever made it had been sure to protect it from attack.

The sun seemed somewhat faded. The light was dim and dull leaving a strange aura around them. It was as if there was something blocking the sunlight. It was something that Eldred had been expecting, although dreading at the same time.

"Good morning Eldred, I hope that you slept well." Alaric's greeting was less than friendly. It was exactly what Eldred had expected. "Have you had any further luck in figuring out what is going on?"

"Why yes I have," replied Eldred with a happy tone in his voice.

"Tell me, what have you discovered?"

"I have discovered more than you have wanted me to know"

"What are you talking about?" Alaric quickly changed his tone to a defensive one.

"I know that it is not my friend I am speaking to. I know that you have briefly taken over his voice. I will tell you one thing. You have messed with the wrong people this time. You would do well to let us loose and forget you saw us."

Eldred was not going to wait for a reply. He had been working on a spell all the time he had been speaking to Alaric. Before anyone knew what was happening, a gentle glow appeared encircling Alaric. Somewhere in the distance there was a faint cry of anguish. When the glow disappeared ,Alaric had a confused look on his face.

"What's happening?" he looked around the clearing as if seeing it for the first time.

"Yes, I think we would all like to know what is happening," added Hawthorne who had just woken.

Before Eldred could reply the ground started to shake and slope. Everyone was knocked off their feet and they were slammed to the ground. It was clear that it was unnatural.

It didn't take long before everything settled down and returned to normal. At least they thought that it had returned to normal. Once they had picked themselves off the ground they realised that things were far from normal.

The clearing had completely gone. Where there had been lush soft grass was now a hard, cold stone floor. The mountains and the forest had disappeared. Now they were surrounded by a large purple dome. Light shone in from above the dome covering the group in a sickly purple haze.

"Hello my small friends," a voice boomed down from above them. "Eldred, it is nice to see you again. I have been waiting for you for a long time. I must admit I had my doubts if my trap was going to work, but obviously, your skills are not as good as they used to be." The voice had more than a hint of superiority in it.

"Damn it!" Eldred yelled towards the roof of the dome. "You don't know what you're doing."

"On the contrary, I know exactly what I'm doing. Now I think that I will leave you there for a while. I will get back to you shortly."

"What is going on Eldred?" Hawthorne re-asked the question, his voice filled with venom.

"An old friend of mine." Eldred shook his head as he spoke. "Well, that's not exactly true. I was his teacher and he was my apprentice. It was the last time I ever trained anyone." Eldred had a blank look on his face, as if he was reliving the memory.

"Who is it?" Hulkan barked, frustrated with Eldred's obtuseness.

"His name is Fahd; at least it used to be when he was my apprentice. Later he changed his name to Dhlark after he became a wizard."

"So why is he so keen on catching you? What happened to ruin your relationship?"

"If you will be patient, I will explain it all to you. It's a long story, but I guess that we aren't going anywhere anytime soon." Eldred took a deep breath before he started. "A long time ago, before I was drafted into the prophecy, I trained wizards and magicians. I met Fahd when he was a young boy. It was clear when his parents brought him to the magic school, that he was going to be a powerful wizard. It was around the time we were lucky if we were taking on one novice a year with any potential. I think that is why we all turned a blind eye to his inherent nature. There was always something about him that didn't add up, but he learnt everything so quickly that we were all blinded. He was more adept than anyone I had trained in years.

The months passed and he soaked up years of information. There was nothing that he couldn't do. It was also coming more apparent that there was something wrong with him. When he thought no one was looking, he would be cruel to the school cats. In spite of his great progress and the other teachers pressing me for results, I decided to slow down his training. Until I could figure out exactly what I could do with him, I decided that I would only train him enough to keep him interested. I made up excuses every time he questioned me, but they were starting to wear thin and one day the complaining simply stopped. No matter how slow I trained him, he did not question me.

This made me more concerned than the original problem. It was not in his personality to let a conflict rest, yet he was able to continue as if nothing had happened. He never complained, even when I gave him the most medial of tasks to complete.

One night I went to his room to confront him. The council had voiced their concerns to me and finally I knew I had to speak to him. I found his room empty, which was profoundly peculiar. The only night time activity that was allowed for apprentices was meditation, which was always done in one's room. I cast a small searching spell to find him, but that failed. As I was searching, I sensed some unusually magical activity."

"Please get to the point," Hulkan interrupted.

Eldred thought for a moment before continuing. "When I found him I was shocked and disgusted. He had found a small cave not far from the city. He had started to worship Nyrra and the black arts. I walked in on him in the middle of sacrificing a goat. He had spilled the blood and covered his naked body in it." Most of them cringed at his graphic description of the ceremony. "When I looked upon his face, I knew that he had changed. All the time I thought his mild manner was a resignation to my teaching, but instead he was just placating me. He didn't even look ashamed that I had found him. The look on his face was of sheer contempt." Eldred looked up towards the roof of the dome in deep thought. It was a good minute before he spoke again, no one wanted to interrupt. "I took him before the council where he was quickly found guilty of the charges. A block was put on his abilities to perform magic and he was thrown out. Little did we know the extent of the training he had received. He had already become powerful enough to be considered a wizard, even though he had not passed his final exam. The block only partially worked and he was still able to cast certain spells. On leaving, he vowed vengeance against me and the rest of the council. Whilst the block remained, we knew that he was no threat and until today I hadn't thought about him for many, many years," Eldred had a resigned look on his face. "It seems that we should have done more than just block his powers."

"That's all well and good, but I think we should be concentrating on the present not the past. The important question is what are we up against and how do we get out of it." Hawthorne tried his best to hide his impatience.

Eldred lowered his head and shrugged his shoulders before returning his gaze to Hawthorne. "I'm afraid I don't know. I have never seen anything like this before. Whatever this is, he has learnt it from the black arts. We are aware of the black arts, but it is dangerous for any wizard to practise them. The dark magic can twist your mind and menace your soul. I can't even see the magic fabric that made the spell. Whatever Dhlark has done, it is beyond my knowledge.

Alaric slumped against the purple barrier. It felt cold against the back of his neck. A shiver shot down his spine and he knew that it was not from the coldness. He could feel the magic that made it and subsequently the evil within.

Seeing Alaric gave the others the same idea. None of them, not even Eldred, could sense the same thing that Alaric had. He knew that somehow he could use the information to their advantage. He just didn't know how.

"Hello down there! I do hope that you're enjoying your stay in my dome. Please don't try to think too hard about its construction. I think that you'll find it's absolutely impossible for you to escape," the voice coming from the room of doom was smug.

"You have me. Let the others go," Eldred called back to the roof, confidence returning to his voice.

"Ah, that would be assuming that I only wanted you. Now I will leave you to think about your short comings," loud, booming laughter trailed off into the distance like a peel of thunder.

When the laughter subsided Eldred spoke. "Something is not right here."

"Well that is an understatement," Hawthorne scoffed.

"What do you mean?" Alena asked.

"I don't really know. I thought that Dhlark was just after me!"

Alaric didn't hear the exchange. The feeling of pulsating energy consumed his body and mind. He could understand now how evil could corrupt the soul. He wanted nothing more than to scream out, but another thought had entered his mind.

If Eldred couldn't break the spell then there was no other option. He did not know why, but he knew that using the Ruby Stone was his only hope.

Standing slowly Alaric ran his fingers over the chest. The others continued their conversation without noticing Alaric's movements. It was as if he was in another world.

He wanted to flick the lid open, but something inside him knew that it was wrong. The evil pulsated even stronger, threatening to engulf him. Now he knew the only thing he could do was open the chest. If he didn't, then they would all die. They would all be consumed by the spell. Without thinking, he opened the chest and clasped the stone. As he did the world around him changed, so suddenly that it nearly knocked him off his feet. What had once been a purple dome was now an intricate weave of coloured light. Small shocks of lightning rippled along the weaves.

Instantly Alaric knew what it was. He could see the weaves of the spell. The pattern was magnificent. All thoughts of the evil that it contained were forgotten. He had never experienced such a joy in his heart before. It was as if he had found the missing piece of his life that he never knew he had been looking for.

At the same time a voice screamed inside his head. "Noooooo!"

The moment the stone was out of its chest, everyone's attention turned to Alaric. There was a clear shift in the dome's structure. Eldred saw the stone in his hand and knew what had not made sense. He also knew that it was all too late.

Alaric could feel a great power welling inside him. The feeling was both glorious and terrifying at the same time. For a moment, he lost himself in the feeling, but then reality rushed back to him. He now knew that if they were going to escape, then it would be up to him.

"Kill them all, that we set you free." The voice came again.

"No, it is time that you did something to help." Alaric spoke with his mind voice. "Break the spell around us!"

There was a moment of silence in his head. No one else could hear the conversation. All they could do is watch Alaric and hope that he had the answer.

"You will do what I ask!" Alaric commanded.

His head started to turn red as he strained to command the Ruby Stone. He had no real idea what he was doing, but it seemed to make sense. He needed to use the stone if he was going to break the prison.

"NOW!"

The weave around him suddenly collapsed in a sprinkling of sparkling coloured light. Alaric was the only one who saw it. The others only saw a brilliant flash of blinding white light. Alaric saw none of their reactions. He was transfixed as the sparkles slowly fell towards him.

As the weave collapsed, a feeling of wrongness came over him. Alaric realised that it was not the stone that had caused the spell to break. He turned to tell the others when his vision became blurred. A deep heat filled his head and his legs started to wobble. Before he could say anything, he collapsed the ground. The last thing he heard before losing consciousness was the deep rumble of faraway laughter.

Chapter 16: Cloumid Mountains

Alaric suddenly regained consciousness. He was confused at his surroundings. He was not lying on the grass at the foot of the Cloumid Mountains as he expected; instead he was in what he could only describe as a prison cell. The walls were a deep grey stone as was the roof and floor. He was lying on a less than soft bed of hay and by the smell it had not been changed in a long time. There were no windows and the door was solid oak with iron straps for reinforcement. The only light came from a small lantern on the floor.

Standing up Alaric felt faint. It was as if he had been drugged; maybe he had. He tried to recall what had happened and suddenly it all came back. The dome, the trap, the stone and Dhlark! Moving groggily to the door he pounded it with his fist and yelled for help. He called out for nearly five minutes, although it seemed like hours. Only when it was clear that there was going to be no response, Alaric slumped to the floor. It was only then that he saw the large chest.

Slowly he returned to his feet, transfixed on what was in front of him. The chest was made out of mahogany with strange symbols carved into the sides and to his surprise the binding straps where made of pure gold and the finish of the timber was exquisite. He stood over the chest, impulsively running his hands over the many intricate carvings.

Alaric pulled his hand away from the chest when he realised what he was doing, there was something very compelling about it. What was such a magnificent chest doing in a prison cell? Then he realised it had no lock. Whatever was in it was not important enough to keep locked. He tried the cell door one more time, but it was clear it wasn't going to budge. His only hope now rested on the mysterious chest. There was something quite disturbing about it and Alaric didn't feel right about opening it. For some comfort, he drew his sword. He strained to lift the lid with one hand; it was heavier than he expected which forced him to drop his sword. With a great effort, he heaved the lid open and let it crash to the floor. There was a soft whooshing noise as Alaric took a quick step backwards and then all was quiet.

A dark, oily patch appeared above the chest. The dim light seemed to shrink away from the darkness. Alaric knew that it was no good. It was so obvious. Why would there be a chest in a prison cell?

The oily patch changed into a dark rain cloud in front of his eyes and started to rise. The light retreated as the cloud rose casting shadows throughout the cell. Alaric didn't know what it was, but he was fearful of it. He could feel the evil emanating from it.

It hovered over him before there was a short, sharp piercing sound. The cloud started to spread across the ceiling until it completely overshadowed the cell, then it descended to the floor.

Alaric fell to the ground; he didn't know why but the cloud struck such terror into his heart, he was sure it was going to engulf him and swallow him whole. Just before the first wisp of cloud touched him it stopped. It paused, as if considering him. Once it was satisfied it started to coalesce.

Covering his head with his arms, Alaric was afraid to watch. Something very bad was happening and there was nothing he could do about it and his sword was now out of reach and...

The Ruby Stone and its chest were missing. A new panic surfaced, without the stone his entire mission would be in jeopardy. Even if he did manage to survive the new ordeal, there was a chance he would not be able to find the stone.

"I wasn't sure that it was you and I am not sure I want to believe it," the voice came. "Come on, it's alright. I'm not going to do anything to you."

The feeling of horror had completely left him. Now he only felt foolish for cowering on the floor. The voice sounded friendly, even if it was slightly condescending. Alaric carefully raised himself to a sitting position, but kept his gaze on the floor.

Taking a deep breath, he looked up.

He wasn't sure what he was expecting to see, but the little man hovering no more than three feet in front of him was definitely not it. He was hovering with his legs crossed and Alaric guessed that he was about five feet tall. He was dressed in a funny green suit with a yellow shirt. His short brown curly hair looked almost comical. It was all Alaric could do to stop himself from laughing.

"Who are you?" Alaric managed to speak after a minute of silence.

The little man lowered himself to the ground and strolled over to the chest. He quite easily replaced the lid and promptly sat on it. He turned to face Alaric, a cheeky grin on his face.

"My name is Heryion. I've been waiting for you for a long time. I must admit though, I was expecting someone a little more heroic." Heryion spoke as though he was having a boring conversation over morning tea.

There was something not right about the little man. His confidence astounded Alaric. The words that came out of his mouth worried him.

"What are you talking about? How did you know that I was going to be here and why were you hiding in that chest?"

"I have been here for longer than I can remember, waiting for you. I must admit though, that for the last few years I was beginning to wonder if I had made the wrong decision, but here you are and now I think that it might be time to be getting out of here."

"Fine then, well where are we and how *are* we going to get out of here? I've already tried the door and it won't budge." Alaric tried to suppress his annoyance.

"We are deep within the Cloumid Mountains. About a two day ride from where you were trapped, so in a way you have been done a favour by being transported here." It was clear that his last comment was an afterthought. "We are not very far from the *Well of Cleansing Power*; the only problem is that is where Dhlark has made his home. It will not be easy for you."

Alaric was concerned at how well Heryion knew his situation. "That is not the only problem. I don't have the stone anymore." Alaric bit his tongue as he spoke. As much as Heryion seemed to know about his situation, he had yet to mention the Ruby Stone.

"I had thought as much. I was sure that if you still possessed the ruby stone, then you would have used it to escape from this cell." Heryion only sounded a little worried and even less surprised.

"That would be true if I knew how to use it," again Alaric scolded himself for revealing too much.

"Then I see that Eldred has been very amiss with his training. I would have thought you would have been most proficient by now. Oh well, I suppose that it will be up to me then." Heryion seemed somewhat disgusted.

Alaric watched Heryion carefully and was surprised when he heard a loud click come from the large wooden door. There had been no indication that Heryion had done anything, not that he was hundred per cent sure that Heryion had used a spell, but he could think of no other solution.

Heryion motioned for Alaric to exit first. He took one step towards the door before he stopped. He had only just met the man and seemed to trust him completely. There was something very wrong and Alaric had to become more suspicious. The last thing that he wanted to do was to walk straight into another trap.

"I think that you can lead the way." Alaric gestured with his hand.

"As you wish. I'm here to help you, but it is good to see that you are not too trusting." Heryion smiled warmly as he walked past him and out of the cell.

Alaric smiled to himself as he followed Heryion. He knew he had made the right decision. If he was going to survive the ordeal, then he would have to start relying on his own decisions. He couldn't rely on Eldred being there for him. It was going to be a valuable learning experience, especially if he made it out alive.

There was a musty, damp smell in the air which reminded Alaric of the entrance to the troll's cave. Heryion carried the small lantern from the prison room, which gave them only just enough light to see where they were walking. Alaric obediently followed behind.

They had been walking through the mountain passageway for an hour, up and down, left and right. Nothing changed much in their scenery, an old stone out of place here or there and an occasional bump in the floor. Alaric had thought it all so normal. He followed the little man without a thought about where he was leading him. And then the thought hit him. Why was Heryion in the cell? Was he working with Dhlark? Was he leading him to his death?

With those thoughts Alaric stopped suddenly. The halt was so sudden that he was left in complete darkness before Heryion realised. He had a questioning look on his face when he returned.

"Why have you stopped? Are you feeling alright?" he sounded so matter of fact that Alaric almost dismissed his concerns as mere foolishness.

Shaking his head, to clear away his doubts, Alaric answered. "Where are we going?"

"We're going to find your friends, the stone and get out of here." Heryion now seemed confused.

"How do I know that you're not working for Dhlark, trying to trap me?" Alaric sounded concerned.

"I did help you escape from the cell. Isn't that enough to prove to you that I'm your friend?"

The answer seemed legitimate enough and Alaric was about to except it and move on, but a voice inside his head told him to wait.

"Maybe you are leading me to an even worse trap, maybe even to my death."

The words changed Heryion's demeanour. "As I see it, you don't have any choice. You can either trust me or you can wander through the mines of the Cloumid Mountains for the rest of your life." The words were short and sharp. Heryion didn't wait for a reply before moving down the passageway.

Although he did not want to believe it, he knew that Heryion spoke the truth. Without help he could wander through the mines without ever seeing daylight again. His legs started moving even as he made up his mind.

The passage sloped gently upwards before it started down. The downward slope was dangerously steep. Heryion strolled along with little concern. Alaric, on the other hand, was struggling to keep his footing. Standing on something slimy was all it took for him to hit the ground hard and start tumbling down the floor. Heryion was all but bowled over when he slid past.

The journey was short and swift and Alaric came to rest in a large square room. The walls were polished stones and each held a lit torch in a sconce. In the middle of the room sat a large table laden with steaming hot food. Alarm bells should have sounded, but all Alaric could think of was his stomach.

Without a second thought, he walked to the table. There was a slight tingling in the back of his neck, but he simply ignored it. The food all looked so appetising. He was about to pick up a loaf of bread when Heryion shouted.

"Don't eat that!"

Alaric paused for a moment before continuing towards the food.

"Alaric, I know that you don't trust me, but if you give me a moment I will prove it."

The words seemed to make sense, but there was something drawing him closer. He knew that it was not just his hunger, there was something else making him want to eat. That was enough to make him believe Heryion. Slowly he retreated.

Heryion raised his arm and a small, clear ball appeared in the palm of his hand. Alaric wasn't sure if it was magic or sleight of hand. There seemed no point in parlour tricks so Alaric assumed it was magic. That was another reason for Alaric to be suspicious of him. Heryion threw the ball towards the food, the ball struck and huge ball of flame engulfed the table. Alaric could only look on in shock. When the flames died down, the table had completely disappeared. Alaric knew that if it had not been for Heryion then he would have been burnt.

"Thank you, it seems as though I underestimated you," Alaric apologised.

"Don't think anything of it. I would have done exactly the same thing in your situation."

"What I don't understand is where the food came from?"

"I can't be completely sure, but I would be assuming that it was a trap by Dhlark. Now I think it's time we were moving again."

Alaric looked around the room. The only sign that there had ever been a table was a small char mark on the floor. There were three doors leading out from the room and Alaric wasn't sure what to do.

"Which door should we take?" Alaric asked with absolute confidence in Heryion.

Heryion walked to the centre of the chamber and closed his eyes. Lines appeared on his face as he concentrated on his surroundings. He looked back at Alaric and shook his head.

"I'm sorry, Alaric. Dhlark must be masking his position. I can't tell where he is. You are going to have to make the decision."

Alaric scratched his head thoughtfully. Something that Heryion had said didn't make sense; it also confirmed his suspicions about his magical abilities. "I thought that we were looking for the others. Why would it matter if Dhlark is hiding his location?"

Heryion looked a little sheepish, as though he had been caught out in a lie. "Well, there are two reasons why Dhlark is masking his location. The first is that he knows you have escaped. The second is that if he doesn't have the stone, then I'm a black cat. We need to get the stone before we rescue your friends."

His words made sense, although Alaric was still not totally convinced. He did need to get the stone back and Dhlark's residence would be the obvious place to start looking.

There were no markings on the doors to help him with his decision. "Okay, here goes nothing." Alaric spoke to steel his nerves as he opened the door to his right.

Jumping back in shock Alaric gasped as he saw a group of bones tumble to the ground. The door didn't lead to another tunnel, but instead a small cupboard. The only thing in the cupboard was the bones, which were thick with dust.

Once the initial shock was over, Alaric dismissed the bones and walked towards another door.

"I don't like this." Heryion's eyes stared at the bones.

Alaric's hand rested on the hilt of his sword when he heard Heryion's words. "What's wrong? It's only a pile of old bones."

Alaric was about to start again, but was silenced by a noise coming from behind him. He spun around quickly and stared as the bones started to rattle. One by one the bones started to join themselves until they had formed a perfect skeleton, holding a sword and shield. Alaric took a tentative step back, his hand tensing on the hilt of his weapon.

The skeleton stared at Alaric. Even though it didn't have any eyes, Alaric knew it could see him. He could feel the hatred emanating from it. The creature was pure evil and with one thought in its head. Kill Alaric!

"What do we do know?" Alaric had to choke down his fear, which was steadily rising.

"I think that it wants you to fight it."

The skeleton advanced on Alaric. Its bones creaked as it moved on steady legs. It was clear by the way that it moved that it was a skilled swordsman. Its movements were almost hypnotic.

Sweat started to appear on Alaric's brow in anticipation of the attack. Almost forgetting himself, Alaric drew his sword at the last minute and blocked the first of the skeleton's attacks. When it came, the attack was hard and fast. The skeleton was a fierce warrior.

The skeleton's sword strokes were quick, powerful and precise. Each swing was clearly calculated. Alaric's training came back to him. He used all his skill to defend the barrage. It was untiring in its attacks and soon it had Alaric backed up against the wall, his muscles aching.

"I don't know how long I can hold him. You have to help me Heryion," Alaric puffed between words.

"I am helping you. There is more to this battle than what your eyes can see. You need to concentrate. You have the skill and the ability to defeat it. You must attack. If you keep defending, it will just wear you down until you no longer have the strength to fight. It will never tire and never stop," Heryion tried to reaffirm Alaric's confidence.

Alaric knew that he was right. He had to find the opportunity to attack, but the skeleton was too quick. Each time Alaric tried to make an offensive, the evil creature moved to block. From against the wall, there was little opportunity.

As Alaric made one final move to get away from the skeleton, it pushed out with its shield. It caught Alaric on the side of his head and sent him flying across the room. The blow knocked him to the ground, but it also gave him space.

Staggering to his feet, he felt a trickle of blood run down the side of his face. The skeleton was not going to give him time to recover. With a flash, it had returned to his attack with a renewed ferocity. The blow to Alaric's head was its first sign of victory and it was not going to give up the advantage.

"Don't give up. You have to attack!" strain had entered Heryion's voice. Whatever it was he was doing was starting to take its toll.

Alaric knew that Heryion was right. If he kept going the way he was, then he was going to die. A fire burned within him which gave him renewed strength. He moved into an attack position and struck out. The first attack took the skeleton by surprise. It was so used attacking that it was confused at having to defend. This gave Alaric a sense of hope.

The attacks were measured and pushed the skeleton back across the cavern. He concentrated his attacks, but forgot the skeleton's shield. After it had blocked a succession of blows, it hit out with its shield and struck Alaric in the ribs sending him across the room again. The collision knocked the wind out of his lungs and forced him to his knees. He tried to stand but his legs would not carry his weight and he returned to his knees.

Knowing that Alaric could no longer attack, the skeleton physically relaxed. Slowly it walked triumphantly over to where Alaric knelt. Alaric looked up as the skeleton stood over him. A smile crossed his face as the skeleton lowered its guard to make to its final blow.

Seizing all his remaining energy, Alaric grasped the hilt of his sword and swung it upward. The blade sliced through the skeleton's right humerus before it had a chance to defend. The skeleton retreated as its sword crashed to the ground, all its confidence gone. With its remaining arm, it dragged itself closer to where Alaric was standing. With one final downward thrust, Alaric skewered the skeleton's skull. The creature shuddered for a second and then the bones collapsed to the floor.

With the skeleton lifeless, Alaric stumbled backwards until he hit the wall and sunk to the ground. The battle had exhausted him and his body ached, a mixture of blood and sweat trickled down the side of his face.

Heryion also took the opportunity to rest. His part in the fight was just as draining. If it wasn't for his aid, then the skeleton would have easily overcome Alaric. He knew that they could not rest for long. It was obvious that Dhlark knew where they were and it would only be a matter of time before he would send something else to attack them.

After a few minutes Heryion returned to his feet. He looked as though he had not suffered at all by the experience. Alaric, on the other hand, had laboured breathing. Heryion couldn't risk giving him any more time to recover.

"We need to keep moving. The way is clear to me now," Heryion spoke softly, but left no doubt to his command.

Alaric brushed off a helping hand and slowly returned to his feet. Breathing deeply, he regained he composure and followed Heryion through the only door that remained. The other door had vanished. The short rest was not enough for his muscles to regain their strength. He trudged along behind Heryion struggling to keep pace

"You need to rest." Heryion almost sounded surprised. "We are close to Dhlark and you need to regain your strength."

Alaric was about to argue, but as soon as Heryion had finished speaking his muscles gave way under the weight of his body. It was as if half the mountain had just collapsed on his shoulders. There was something strange happening. He did not know what it was, but he was sure that Heryion was somehow manipulating him. He could barely move a muscle. Heryion simply rolled him over and placed something soft under his head. Alaric was thankful for the support.

"Sleep now, Alaric. We don't have a lot of time and you need to get your energy back, rest easily knowing that nothing will happen to you."

Those were the last words Alaric heard before he drifted off into sleep. Something called out to him in his dreams, something far off in the distance. The voice was too soft for him to hear. The words were too far away for him to understand. Without knowing how, he started to move closer towards the sound. He did not know why, but he knew that he had to hear what the voice was saying.

Just before he came close enough to hear, he was woken. He slowly lifted his head to look at his surroundings. His muscles still ached, but his mobility had returned.

"What's happening?" he asked slowly as he senses returned.

"We don't have any more time. Dhlark is almost ready to fulfil his part in the prophecy and we need to be present if you are going to have any chance in defeating him," Heryion spoke quicker than usual.

"What are you talking about?" Alaric seemed even more confused than normal as he slowly got to his feet.

"There is no time to explain, we need to hurry."

There was no opportunity for Alaric to question him as he hurried along the passageway. He knew that something had happened that he was not supposed to know. He was about to walk into a situation in which he had to trust someone he had only just met. Something in the back of his mind said that he was crazy, but on the other hand he still had no other option.

The further they walked the more that Alaric believed they were travelling in the right direction. Wherever they were going, they were heading straight for the Ruby Stone. Regardless of whether they were going to confront Dhlark he knew that fact was true and that was enough to keep him going.

They rounded the corner and Alaric stopped in his tracks. It was as if something had slapped him in the face. There was no doubt in his mind that they were close.

"What are you doing? We don't have time for this," Heryion sounded rushed.

Alaric didn't reply, he just stared off past Heryion. He looked over his shoulder to see Alaric looking at a dreary stone wall. Whatever Alaric was concentrating on, it was something Heryion couldn't see.

A voice in Alaric's mind warned. "Be careful Alaric. Dhlark is not someone to underestimate. You are strong, but you are not strong enough to defeat Dhlark without my help."

"What do you want me to do?" Alaric became transfixed.

"Do what Dhlark asks of you. Do this and everything will be alright."

That was all the voice was willing to say. As soon as it stopped speaking, Alaric returned to normal and his eyes refocused on Heryion. "What are you waiting for?"

"It was…" Heryion was about to interject, but realised that it would be no good. "Nothing. We should keep going."

With each step they took, Alaric could feel they were getting closer. Alaric knew that Dhlark had possession of the stone. There was no doubt in his mind. His first priority had to be to recovering it, nothing else mattered.

"The room is just ahead," Heryion spoke softly. "You must not listen to Dhlark's words. He will try and trick you. His magic is strong and it will overwhelm you. I will try to protect you as much as I can, but it's your responsibility."

Alaric only just heard what he was saying. The words from the unknown source still echoed inside his head. He didn't know who to believe. Both suggestions seemed honest enough, but only one of them could be correct. If he made the wrong decision, then he knew he would die and the world would be lost.

"Come on. We don't have any time to lose." Heryion had spoken again, but Alaric wasn't listening. He already knew all that he needed to be victorious.

"Feel free to come out of hiding at any time. I have been waiting for you." The voice boomed from somewhere in front them.

Heryion waited for Alaric to make the first move. He had led him so far, but it was Alaric who needed to take the final steps. He had hoped they would have the element of surprise. The fact that Dhlark knew where they were, was disturbing.

Alaric didn't seem to mind. If anything, he was happy that Dhlark was expecting them. Normally he would have preferred to sneak in and sneak out with him not even knowing he was there, but for some reason he felt different.

With some confidence Alaric started forward. He walked past Heryion without concern. He knew that the stone waited for him and that filled his heart with joy. With the stone back in his possession, there was no chance of Dhlark defeating him.

Heryion watched him with concern. Something had clearly changed. Something had affected him and he knew it wasn't his speech. Shaking his head, he started after Alaric.

Alaric turned a corner and walked into a large cavern. The light was much brighter than that of the tunnels. Then his eyes fell on the man he had been looking for and his heart filled with terror. This was not going to be as easy as he had expected.

Chapter 17: Crystal Waters

The terror left Alaric almost as quickly as it had come. There was nothing rational to cause the fear and it was clear that it was Dhlark who had caused it.

The rogue wizard stood almost in the centre of the large cavern. He was nothing like Alaric had expected. Dhlark looked more like Eldred and not the disfigured monster he had envisaged. He stood a good foot taller than Alaric and retained much the same features as the old wizard.

Beside the wizard, directly in the middle of the cavern, was a small well. It was a pace in diameter and a pace high. It seemed to be a natural fissure rather than a man-made feature. It was clearly the focal point.

There were many shelves around the walls that contained many vials of potions and books. Alaric noticed none of them. The only thing in the room that he could see was the small ruby stone lying just out of reach of Dhlark on a stone table. With Alaric in the cavern, it started to pulsate.

"Look in the well," Dhlark's voice boomed throughout the cavern.

"Don't listen to him Alaric. It is a trick," Heryion spoke softly.

"I thought that I'd gotten rid of you," Dhlark's sounded both shocked and confused. His confidence had clearly waned.

"I think that you have worse things to worry about than me. I'm just here to make sure that things are even." Heryion was stalwart in his answer, if somewhat cryptic.

Alaric ignored the exchange. He had something more pressing on his mind. It was time to make his decision. He could listen to the voice in his head or the stranger he had just met. Either option seemed as pointless as the other.

"Do what I tell you," the voice inside his head commanded more than it coerced. "You have no other option. Do as Dhlark tells you and I will make sure that he pays."

The other two had continued their conversation forgetting about Alaric who had slowly started to move towards the well. He had made his decision, or it had been made for him. Either way, he was going to do as Dhlark instructed.

Alaric took another step forward and peered over the side. The water was clear and looked very refreshing. For some reason, he took a handful and drank it down. As soon as the water passed his lips all the fatigue left his body. The water completely rejuvenated him.

As Alaric withdrew his head, he caught something out of the corner of his eyes. There was something moving in the water. When he returned his gaze, the clearness of the water had changed. A faded image of his friends appeared and slowly became clearer. They were standing at the base of a large single mountain. They were talking amongst themselves with worried expressions on their faces. Then the image suddenly changed and Alaric fell back violently to the floor. The image kept repeating itself through his mind as a voice started to laugh loudly. He thought that the laughter was coming from Dhlark, but he couldn't be sure. The image was of a grotesque face which had two gnarled horns protruding from its oversized head. The rest of the face was dark purple and looked as though it had been severely burnt. Alaric screamed out in anguish.

"That is the future that you see in the well and there is nothing you can do about it. All your friends will die and you will become a slave. Relinquish yourself now and save everyone the pain." This time there was no doubt that the chilling voice had come from Dhlark.

"Where are my friends?" Alaric had a glazed look on his face, like he was not all together there.

"They are safe for the time being. Whether they stay that way all depends on you. All you have to do is a small task and I will set them free and that image you saw in the well will not come true." Dhlark was a lot sweeter this time.

"What is the task?" the question was slow to come from his mouth.

"A simple task that will ensure the safety of your friends. All that you have to do is take the stone and place it in the well. Nothing more than that." Dhlark was almost giddy with anticipation.

"That image he showed you is fake. He conjured it up to trick you. It's a simple trick that was magnified by the power of the well," Heryion pleaded with Alaric.

"Shut up you impudent fool. I should have killed you when I had the chance. I won't make the same mistake twice. Can't you see that he is already under my power? He will do whatever I want him to do and there is nothing you can do about it." Dhlark almost spat the words. "When I have finished with him, I will finish with you."

"You must trust me." The voice in his head was very convincing.

Alaric walked towards the stone table and took the Ruby Stone in his right hand. As soon as he touched it great warmth filled his body. A rightness returned to him that he had not felt since he had woken in the mountain range. He now knew what he had to do, what he was destined to do.

Without thought he returned to the well and dropped the stone into the crystal-clear water. The stone instantly turned the water a soft red. After a couple of seconds, the water started to bubble and steam. Beams of light flashed from the well around the cavern. Dhlark made sure than none of the beams touched him. Both Alaric and Heryion didn't have to move to avoid the beams.

A comforting feeling settled over Alaric, like a weight had been lifted from his shoulders. He didn't know what was happening, but he knew it was the right thing. A smile spread across his face as the water started to settle.

"Step away from the well. Step away now!" Dhlark slavered at the mouth.

Without really hearing the words, Alaric obeyed his command. Everything in his body told him not the let Dhlark near the stone, but he could not ignore the voice in his head. It screamed to him to obey Dhlark. Alaric didn't need to see inside the well to know what had happened. He knew the Ruby Stone would be free of its crystal prison. The power of the stone would be truly unlocked. The voice inside his head went silent. Even though there was no noise, he knew the voice was still there, waiting.

A wind blew through the cavern almost extinguishing the torches on the walls. It blew through the pages of the many books and rattled the many vials. Dhlark started to laugh uncontrollably. He had not truly believed that he would succeed so easily. He ambled to the well once he had finished laughing. The stone sat in the water waiting to take its rightful place in the world.

"You can feel the power I possess and you fear me." Dhlark reached into the well and plucked the stone from the water.

Alaric stood and watched. Now he couldn't move. He had listened to the voice in his mind and now they were all doomed. Dhlark would surely destroy them all.

"Trust me." The voice whispered.

Dhlark raised his left hand above his head with the stone still in his right. Suddenly a small bolt of lightning appeared from nowhere and came to rest on his palm. It gently flickered and glowed.

"Where are my friends?" Alaric broke the uncomfortable silence.

Dhlark turned his attention away from the stone as he heard Alaric's voice. The lightning bolt suddenly blinked out of existence. He seemed perturbed at the interruption. He was enjoying his new-found power.

"Did you really think that I would let you go? I only needed you to remove the crystal from the stone. I probably could have done it myself, but I didn't want to risk being disintegrated by one of those beams. Now you are no use to me all. I think that I will dispose of you now, but don't worry, I will dispose the rest of your friends in due course."

Alaric thought about drawing his sword, but he knew there was no point. A sword was not going to win the battle. Unless Heryion had a new trick up his sleeve, they were both trapped. "Trust," was all the reassurance the voice would give him.

The stone started to glow as Dhlark again forced his will. This time Alaric could feel the power surging from the stone. Instead of fear, which he should have felt, he felt calm. The word trust kept repeating itself in the back of his mind as he watched the stone grow brighter and brighter.

The smile that had been on Dhlark's face ever since he had collected the stone suddenly disappeared. A look of horror quickly replaced the evil grin. Whatever spell he had been conjuring had obviously not worked. He snatched at the stone with his free hand and tried to wrench it free. No matter how hard he tried Dhlark could not relinquish his grip.

A great roaring filled Alaric's head and a sense of joy past over him. He felt as though the world was at peace. He should have felt shocked at what was happening in front of him, but all he felt was calm.

The confusing situation continued, and to make things worse Heryion had started laughing at the top of his voice. Dhlark dropped to his knees, still clutching at the stone. A look of pain crossed his face and a cry echoed through the cavern.

A small wisp of smoke appeared from under the stone. Alaric could feel the heat emanating from it as it bit into Dhlark's skin. There was a great sense of hatred coming from the stone. A yellow flame sprouted with a soft crackle. As the flame touched Dhlark's skin brightly coloured sparks flew in all directions. He screamed again.

"Make it stop! Please! Make it stop!" Dhlark begged Alaric for mercy.

"Don't listen to him Alaric. He can't be trusted." Heryion stopped laughing and tried to reassure him. "Remember that he trapped you, you must finish him."

Little did they both know that Alaric did not hear a word that they said, nor could he do anything if he had. What the stone was doing was of its own volition.

"Stay out of it," a voice whispered behind the screaming in his head.

The flame started to dance up Dhlark's arm. Heryion could only imagine the agony the wizard was feeling and almost felt sorry for him. Alaric remained in his trance like state. The sound inside his head consumed him and he felt like there was nothing else in the world.

The fire leapt up Dhlark's arm and then down his body until all but his head was engulfed in flame. Although the fire was hot enough, it had not marked his skin or burnt his clothes. The fire was waiting for something, a signal to finish the job.

"Finish!" Alaric wasn't sure if it was his thought or the voice inside his head, or if there was any real difference.

The word was all that was needed. Dhlark's clothes and skin joined the rest of him in flame. His screaming intensified as he was consumed by the fire. With the last of his power, he regained control of his body and threw himself into the well.

The water did not refresh his body like he had hoped. The fire did not extinguish, but increased in intensity as Dhlark splashed frantically in water. The last sound he made was a gurgled scream before he was silenced forever.

With Dhlark's silence also came peace in Alaric's mind. The deafening noise was instantly cut off and Alaric slumped to the ground.

"Are you okay?" asked Heryion as he moved to Alaric's side.

"I can't move," Alaric gasped.

"You don't have to move far, just enough to drink from the well."

Alaric looked at the stone for the first time and realised the crystal encasement had completely disappeared. His heart fluttered as he saw the pure red stone finally released from its prison. He thought it was the most beautiful thing he had seen in his life.

"You must first drink from the well. It will restore your energy." Heryion put a hand under his arm and tried to help him to his feet.

Alaric didn't hear a single word. The only thing that he could do was focus on the stone. There was nothing else in the world that he wanted more than to snatch it up and hold it again. Once he possessed it, everything would be back to normal. Nothing could hurt him.

Without really feeling it, Alaric pushed Heryion aside. Although he thought he was walking, he was in fact crawling towards the stone. Heryion could only watch. He knew there was nothing he could do to convince Alaric otherwise. His mind was set on one goal.

When he was within reach of the stone, he reached out a tentative hand. Once he touched it, all doubts left him. With his feelings of doubt also went all his fatigue. Within a second, he was on his feet and feeling as well as he ever had.

"Kill him. He will try and take the stone. Trust me. I am the only one who is trying to help you." The voice returned calm and convincing.

"You must put the stone back in its chest." Heryion arrived at Alaric's side holding the chest. Alaric didn't know where he had found it, but was sure that his motives were not honest. "Can you hear me?" Heryion put a gentle hand on his shoulders, which was promptly shrugged away.

"You want the stone for yourself. I will never put the stone in the chest again." Alaric snapped without thinking.

Heryion took a step back and watched him intently. There was something different about him. It was only subtle but his façade had changed somehow. He seemed more cold and calculating. If Heryion didn't know better, he would have been afraid.

"You must fight it Alaric. You have to overcome your desire to succumb. You have the strength. The stone wouldn't have chosen you if you were weak. I will do all that I can to help you."

The words caressed Alaric, making him feel safe and warm. The voice in his head quietened, but still urged him to kill. There was still sense in the words, but not as much as there had been. With each second that passed, the words seemed less convincing.

"Give me the chest." Alaric forced the words from his mouth.

"Don't do it. You need me as much as I need you. Without me you will die." The voice pleaded.

Once he had the chest he held it as far away from the stone as he could. His mind knew what he had to do, but relaying it to his body was harder than ever. It was a struggle for him to retract his arm and imprison the stone.

"It's okay Alaric, you have the strength." Heryion returned his comforting hand.

Slowly his arms started to relax. As the stone came closer to its prison the voice intensified. As soon as it increased in pitch, it was suddenly dampened. A battle of wills was happening inside him.

Sweat broke out on his face as he strained with the effort. He paused for a second as his hand hovered over the chest. All he had to do was tip the stone into the chest, but he was not sure it was the right thing to do. Closing his eyes, he made his decision. There was a slight cry of anguish in his mind as the stone landed in the chest and he shut the lid.

With the stone safely in the chest, Alaric's body shut down. Every muscle in his body started to spasm before he collapsed to the ground. At the same time, the voice inside his head completely disappeared. For a moment Alaric thought he could hear an echo, but even that was gone.

"Are you alright?" asked Heryion as he knelt over Alaric.

"What do you think?" Alaric's voice was weak, but did not lose its sarcasm.

"Rest for a while. The others can wait for you to recover," although it was offered by Heryion there was really no other choice. Even if Alaric wanted to continue his body would not comply. "The water from the well will revive you, once you can stand again."

Alaric fell asleep as soon as Heryion stopped talking. He was completely exhausted. He lay on the cavern floor without a care; his sleep was deep and restful, but ended all too quickly.

"It's time to go Alaric. Can you stand up?" Heryion asked as he shook Alaric awake.

Lifting his head Alaric placed his hands on the floor. Gathering all his remaining strength he pushed down and lifted himself from the floor.

His muscles ached. Standing was a great effort and he wobbled on unsteady legs.

"What now?" Alaric's voice sounded weak, clearly not knowing where he was.

"Go to the well and drink the water."

Alaric did as he was told without question. He stumbled towards the well and as soon as his hand touched the water he started to feel better. Cupping his hands, he scooped the water into his mouth. It was cool and refreshing and as it filled his stomach the tension and pain washed away. His muscles relaxed and his head cleared. He breathed a sigh of relief.

"Won't this just work as the stone did? It's only a false sense of rejuvenation and once its effect wears off, I will break down again. I could feel it before I touched the water, my body is dying. I need to rest before we continue on."

Heryion started to laugh. "It's okay Alaric. The water is completely different to the effect the stone has on you. It has the power to heal all illnesses. It has been lost in the mountains for a long time. Now that Dhlark is dead, there is a chance that people will be able to find it again."

Alaric looked at all the bottles and vials on the wall. "We should bottle some of the water and take it with us?"

"That is the curse of the well. If you take water away, then it will only last for two days. That's enough time to exit the mountain range if you know where you're going. After that time, it becomes ordinary water." Heryion explained.

"Then we should at least take enough if the others are injured." Alaric had already started to collect some empty bottles.

Once he had them filled he turned his attention to Heryion. With the stone safely in his possession, he was going to get some answers. He was sure Heryion wouldn't kill him, but his motivation for helping was still suspect and worrying.

"What were you doing in that chest?" Alaric eyed him carefully, watching for any response that might indicate a lie.

"I told you. I was waiting for you to arrive. I have been waiting for a very long time," he replied without really answering the question. "Now we need to find your friends."

"Do you know where they are?" The distraction worked.

There were many exits from the cavern. All of them looked pretty much the same. There was nothing to indicate where they should go. "Concentrate. You will know how to find them."

"What are you talking about?" Alaric was more confused than before.

"Just do it!" Heryion was starting to lose his patience.

Alaric closed his eyes. He didn't know if it would make any difference, but he had to make a show that he was trying. He didn't know what Heryion wanted him to do. There was no way he would be able to find the others.

Taking a deep breath Alaric realised that he could feel something. There was a tingling in the back of his neck. He had felt it before, only this time it was very faint. As he concentrated on that feeling, he knew which way he had to go.

"Straight ahead. If we follow that corridor, then we will find the others. I think that Dhlark would have wanted to keep them close." Alaric pointed at the doorway directly in front of him.

"Very good," Heryion muttered under his breath as he followed Alaric.

They walked through the doorway and into another tunnel. The walls were cut smoothly into the black rock. Many torches lit the wall and Alaric wondered how they remained lit.

After they had walked for an hour, a dull rumble sounded in the tunnel. Heryion stopped and concentrated on their surroundings. The sudden noise came as a shock to him. Alaric, on the other hand, looked slightly embarrassed.

"What was that?" Heryion looked confused at Alaric's reaction to the noise.

"That was my stomach. I haven't eaten in a long time."

The water from the well had returned his strength, but it did not make up for the lack of food. His stomach growled again, he didn't think he could take another step without eating.

"That's easy to remedy," a broad grin crossed Heryion's face.

Alaric closed his eyes and sighed. Everything seemed to be a joke to Heryion. He wondered if he was sent to help him or just mock him. If they went back to the cavern, they might be able to find food there. He wasn't going to die of hunger in the mountains.

Whilst Alaric tried not to think about food, Heryion made good his word. Soon the aroma of hot meat and steaming vegetables filled Alaric's nose. Opening his eyes, he saw a plate of hot food in front of him. Alaric looked around trying to find the place where Heryion had found it, but there was nothing.

"Where did this come from?"

"Don't worry about that now. The food is good and it will fill your hunger. That's all that matters." It was clear that Heryion was not going to give anything away.

Alaric was still suspicious of the food, but his hunger was overpowering and it smelt so appetising. He knew that he was not going to get any answers. He gave Heryion one last questioning look before eating. Stuffing food in his mouth, he hardly chewed before swallowing. When the plate was empty, Alaric's hunger had been completely sated.

"Now we should keep moving. The others shouldn't be too far away," Heryion urged Alaric to his feet.

It was not long before they rounded a corner and came upon a large wooden door. A steel padlock hung from the handle. There was no key in sight and nothing to break it with. There was no doubt in Alaric's mind that all his friends were on the other side.

"How are we going to open the door?" Alaric sounded crestfallen. "I am certain they are there."

"There is something magical about this door. There is more than just a steel lock barring entrance. Dhlark has sealed it. I just need to find the key."

Alaric caught his words and wondered what he was talking about. It was clear that there was no key. Instead of standing there wondering, Alaric thought he would help look for it. Heryion had a slight chuckle to himself when he realised what Alaric was doing.

An audible click returned Alaric's attention. To his surprise, the padlock remained firmly in place

"The lock should be easy to open now."

He looked surprised, but knew better than to ask any questions. He ran his fingers over the lock. It remained firmly in place. Alaric grabbed it and pulled it hard. The lock simply opened and dropped to the ground.

"Do you think they're inside or is this another of Dhlark's tricks?" Alaric asked, nervously.

"There is only one way to find out."

Alaric closed his eyes and reached for the handle. He turned it slowly with a feeling that something bad awaited him on the other side.

Taking a deep breath Alaric pushed the door open. As he did a tingling sensation started at the back of his neck and then ran down his spine like a bolt of lightning. As he took a step into the room the trap was tripped and there was a sudden blinding flash. Alaric didn't know what hit him as he dropped to the ground, unconscious.

"Stop!" Heryion called from the passageway. "We are here to help you," but it was too late.

Alena quickly dropped to Alaric's aid as Eldred stepped over his limp body to see who had called out. A look of confusion crossed his face when he saw Heryion standing in the tunnel. "I thought it was Dhlark coming back to torment us. I should have known better when the enchantments were lifted." Eldred scolded himself.

"No harm done; He will regain consciousness soon. Whilst we wait we should get ready to move. Time is running short and we need to be out of the mountains. There is more evil here and the more we linger than greater the danger."

After short introductions, the group prepared to leave. They accepted Heryion without question; they we all too preoccupied with the fact they were free. All, but the dwarves who enjoyed being in the mountains, longed for the open skies and a fresh breeze.

Slowly, with a little help from Alena, Alaric regained his consciousness. Even with Alena's calming touch, he woke with a start. He was about to strike out when he saw her face. He relaxed back into her arms with relief. His heart raced with joy that he had found his friends, but it did not last long.

"We need to keep moving. We are not out of danger yet." Eldred had resumed control of the situation and had made his plan.

Alaric came to his feet with the aid of Alena, his head still ringing from the blast. He took a long draught from one of his bottles and the ringing disappeared. Eldred led the way from their prison cell with Heryion at his side. The mystery of the strange man continued.

Alena left Alaric to walk with Bern, as the tunnel was only wide enough for them walk two abreast. As much as she wanted to talk to him she knew he needed to be with his old friend.

Bern listened, as did the others who were within earshot, as Alaric recalled the story of his meeting with Heryion and the battle with Dhlark. They all seemed happy enough without the need to go into much detail.

The further they walked the fresher the air became. The tunnel steadily sloped downwards giving everyone a new spring in their steps. Even the dwarves seemed happy to be on the way out of the mountain range.

Soon enough they rounded a corner and rushed out into the forest. The moon was high and the forest was dark. The crisp night air rose over a fog that had rolled in on the forest floor.

"I don't like it Eldred. The forest is too still." Palentonal could sense there was something wrong.

"I don't think it's anything too major. It's possible that it's the remnants of one of Dhlark's spells. Either way, I don't think we have much choice. We all need a good night's sleep. Under the cover of the trees we should be able get that," Eldred's words brought some relief.

They settled down in a small grove of pine trees. No one had rested since they had been captured and they were all tired.

Eldred and Heryion shared the watch throughout the night and into the morning. It was decided that the more sleep they had, the more ground they could cover until they acquired more horses. When everyone was awake, they tried to gain their bearings. They had not left   the mountain in the planned location and decided the best course was to head due east until they came upon a familiar trail.

Everyone ate a substantial meal even though their food supplies where dwindling. There was little talk around the campfire. They all wanted to forget what had happened inside.

Once they started off, a strange feeling came over Alaric. It was nothing dangerous, more familiar than anything, like an old friend had returned. He couldn't pin point the exact direction, but he did know the general area. Without thinking he started to stray off course. It was as if someone was talking to him, telling him which way to go. The pull was so compelling there was nothing he could do.

"Where are you going?" Hawthorne barked.

Alaric didn't answer, but quickened his pace. He knew he was close. Whatever it was that was out there was urging him closer.

Hawthorne informed the others, but they could do nothing except follow behind. No one tried to speak to him after their initial contact was rebuked.

Alaric's heart leapt with joy when he saw splashes of white amongst the trees ahead. He had no idea how they had managed to get there, or how they had passed through the mountains. He didn't care. He was just happy to see the brilliant white horses again.

As he approached, Adelanta walked over to him. He nuzzled his head against Alaric's shoulder. The white stallion seemed just as pleased to see him as Alaric was. The others were also amazed when they saw where Alaric had led them.

"How did you know where to find them?" asked Bern in disbelief.

"I think some questions cannot be answered," Heryion spoke before Alaric had a chance to answer.

"We are near the town of Bordertown," Hawthorne said.

"How do you know that?" Hulkan asked.

"I have been here before and I recognise those markings." He pointed to some scratches on a nearby tree. "The hunters use it so they can find their way home."

"Very well then. We should be in a nice warm inn by nightfall." Eldred already felt as though they had stayed too long.

Alaric never thought he would be so grateful to be back in the saddle. Once he was on Adelanta's back, he felt at peace. As much as he had never enjoyed horse riding, walking with a pack on his back was a lot worse.

"This place looks deserted," Bern commented when they reached Bordertown.

"Bordertown was founded as a trading town. King Kjeld IV realised that there was more profit if they could buy the dwarves' goods straight out of the mountain. Without the added transport costs, the King was able to bargain for better prices. When the mines were still operational, Bordertown was one of the most profitable towns in the kingdom. After the mines were shut down, so did most of the trade. Now it is more of an outpost than a town," Hawthorne explained.

"All being well there is someone that I need to meet here," Eldred added mysteriously.

"Who is that?" asked Alaric.

"An old friend of mine. He is the Duke of this land, although you wouldn't know it by looking at him. He looks more like a farmer than a Duke. He will be able to replenish our supplies. I will also need to speak to him about supporting our cause. King Lisle XII has shown interest, but we will need some help to get him to commit soldiers."

Out of the forest the feeling of unrest suddenly left them. The dim lit streets were more depressing than the forest, but they felt safer. The outer walls were abandoned and falling apart. They looked as though they had not been maintained in years. They also looked as though they had been attacked recently.

The outer buildings were all abandoned. Very few remained intact. Like the wall, the buildings had been left to decay. Rubble filled the streets and made the ride more difficult than it should have been.

"I don't recall Bordertown being this debilitated," commented Hawthorne. "I haven't been here for a long time."

"I don't think this is normal. There is something very wrong." Eldred was about to continue his speech when they heard the sound of many chinking armours and hooves on the cobbled streets. Soon a group of soldiers blocked the street in front of them. The soldiers did not look happy to see them. Their armour was dirty and dinted, as if they had just been in battle.

"Halt and state your business," called their Captain.

Eldred motioned for the others to comply with the command before riding to meet him. A lieutenant aimed a crossbow at Eldred's head.

"That is far enough. State your business or spend the night in the stocks."

"My name is Eldred. I'm an associate of Duke Hadar. I believe he is in town awaiting my arrival." Eldred had hoped to keep their arrival a secret, but could ill afford to get held up by an overzealous Captain.

"There is no record of you or your party on our register and every visitor is registered. These are dangerous times and we cannot bend the rules for anyone."

The sun had all but set as did everyone's hopes. They had all been looking forward to spending a night at an inn and some entertainment at a tavern or two. Now it seemed as though they would be spending another cold night in the wilderness.

"There is an inn on this side of the town. You will be confined there until I can confirm your story. The Duke is in his country villa and not expected until tomorrow morning."

At a wave from the Captain, the crossbow was lowered and Eldred knew he had a won a small victory. Any further conversation was only going to work against him, so he accepted the Captain's order.

Once it was clear that there was going to be no more conversation, they were promptly escorted to the inn. The accommodation was not at all what they had been expecting. It was obvious that it was one of the stingiest inns in town. Only two people sat in the common room, each nursing a grimy mug of ale. There was a rotten smell that could not be identified.

The lobby wasn't any better. The smell was only slightly different and an old reception desk and a couple of dirty chairs barely filled the room. Asleep, with his head resting on the desk, was a fat old man who smelt revolting. He didn't wake up until Eldred nudged him with his staff.

"Huh, who's there?" the man woke with a start and reached for something under his desk. He blinked his eyes.

"I need rooms for this evening. Do you have anything available?" Eldred suppressed the urge to gag.

The man laughed hoarsely before answering. "I've got nothing but vacancies, hasn't been a guest here for nearly a year now. As you can imagine, they ain't going cheap, one guest a year hardly pays the bills. I can see that you have been put under house arrest for the night, so I don't see that you have any choice." He grinned widely.

Hawthorne was about to interject, but Eldred silenced him before he could speak. "You will get one silver half-crown per person and be grateful for that," Eldred replied with a defiant tone.

The innkeeper was about to argue, but Eldred had already placed the coins on the counter. His other hand rested on the hilt of his sword. The man took a quick glance around the group and realised that he was badly outmatched. He was already receiving over twice the rate for any other inn in town.

"Does Penley still run the tavern on the North Side?" Eldred asked as he picked up the keys to their rooms.

"No. His son runs it now with his wife, Penleyson and Engrace. Prices there aren't cheap either, much better here. Don't think you have any option," the innkeeper sniffed loudly after he had finished speaking.

Eldred had already turned back to the others before the innkeeper stopped speaking. He assigned Palentonal the job of stabling the horses whilst the others made for their rooms.

"You aren't serious about going out?" Hawthorne asked.

"Don't worry about me. I'll be alright," Eldred's words gave no one a good feeling.

Chapter 18: Kidnapping

Eldred crept away once the others had settled themselves in the common room. Despite the repulsive smell, they were all grateful for being indoors, anything was better than spending the night outside.

Donning a dark robe Eldred crept through the dark streets of Bordertown. There was clearly something wrong. The last time he had been there, even though it was well past its prime, there were more people about. The streets were dead. The only ones out where the night watch, which made it all the easier to avoid them.

The tavern Eldred was looking for, named the Wandering Dwarf, was brightly lit. By the sound of the noise coming from inside, a night of frivolities was well on its way. He hoped that he would be able to remain anonymous.

The main bar was filled with people. The Wandering Dwarf was clearly a much classier establishment than the one where they were staying. The building was clean and the patrons well dressed.

It didn't take Eldred long to find the person he was looking for. He was sitting by himself in the corner at a small table. He nursed a mug of ale and he wore a brown robe with the hood almost completely covering his face. No one seemed to take any notice of him. He blended into the room as if he was part of the furniture.

Eldred ordered himself an ale before making his way to the table. He wanted to remain inconspicuous, even though it was almost impossible. Ever since he entered the tavern, the other patrons had been watching him suspiciously.

"I'm glad you're here," Eldred spoke as he sat in the empty chair opposite him.

The man looked up briefly from his mug. "I wasn't sure if you were going to make it. You're very late. I didn't know how long I was going to be able to remain unnoticed."

"I know. I would have sent word, but you know how it is. There was nothing I could do. Freshen your mug and I'll tell you what happened." Eldred kept his voice low so no one else could hear. The din of the room almost lost his words completely.

"No thank you. I never drink the local ale. It's usually watered down and not the best. I know it's not very patriotic of me, but I do like my little comforts," the man spoke with a warm voice.

As Eldred started his tale, the room seemed to fade away. All the noise disappeared into the background. There were only two people in room.

***

Bern and Alaric were the first two to come down to the common room. They had managed to find a couple of baths upstairs, but there was no one to heat the water for them. Despite the cold water they felt refreshed for being clean.

They might have felt more at home if they had not bathed. Another dozen people had entered the common room and looked just as grimy as the room. No one had bathed or changed out of the clothes they had clearly been working in all day. The smell, if anything, had only become worse.

"I don't think this is going to be the best of evenings," Alaric commented jovially as they sat at a table against one of the walls.

"I don't really care. It has been that long since I've had an ale, I could drink it out of a trough," Bern joked, not realising how close to the truth he was.

Shortly after they were both seated, a short serving woman walked past the table. It was clear that she was not interested in serving them as she made a point not to make eye contact.

"Excuse me," Alaric spoke.

"What can I do for ya, darling?" she asked, looking closely at Alaric. There was something about her accent that seemed fake.

"I was wondering if you have any red from Zenza?"

"Sorry, only got the local brew." Bern was happy to hear those words.

"We'll take two mugs thank you." Bern cut in before Alaric could complain and flipped a small copper coin towards her.

"Not from round 'ere are ya?" she asked when she returned with their drinks.

"No. We're just passing through," replied Alaric, not wanting to give too much away.

"Where ya off to. Not a popular travellin' route this place."

Two streaks of dirt smeared her face and her long blonde hair was ratty. Her clothes were torn and dirty, she fitted her surroundings perfectly. However, there was something that was not right with her appearance. It was as if her dishevelled look was deliberate. Alaric was suddenly suspicious of her motives.

"On our way through to the capital. Thought we'd see the world before we get too old." Bern spoke with a smile on his face and a glint in his eye. "Didn't think we'd end up here, but things look good at the moment."

The serving woman giggled slightly and then walked to another table. Bern's words had lightened her standoffish mood. Alaric glared at him, although he was grateful for the lie, albeit a thin one.

"I didn't realise how much I missed a warm tavern, even if it is a rat hole." Bern smiled at Alaric.

In truth, the common room was not that warm. A small fire crackled in the far corner, but was only adequate if standing directly in front of it. It was more of a token effort than any great use.

"I know what you mean. I think this is as friendly a welcome as I ever received in Arsiliac," sarcasm was thick on Alaric's voice.

Taking a large drink from his mug, Alaric let himself sink back into his chair. The ale was bitter and the chair was uncomfortable, yet he was still at ease. Spending weeks on the road made the small creature comforts seem like luxuries.

"What really happened to you in the mountain?" Bern asked after he had taken a large mouthful of his ale.

"I... I don't remember. I remember waking up in the prison room and meeting Heryion. I remember confronting Dhlark and the water in the well. The next thing that I can recall is riding on the back of Adelanta coming into town." Alaric seemed a little sheepish about admitting the truth. "Enough about me, what about you? Are you regretting your decision to leave Arsiliac?"

"Not really. I admit that I do miss my family, but I couldn't stay in Arsiliac knowing what you were doing. From what I understand, this prophecy wouldn't have let me stay anyway," with that Bern drained the last of his ale and walked to the bar.

Alaric watched the exchange carefully as he finished his ale. Bern seemed to be getting on famously with the serving women. Even when they had been younger, Bern had always been better at talking to girls. There was something natural about him that meant he didn't have to try. Alaric was always jealous.

Bern and the serving woman shared a laugh before he returned with two fresh mugs. The woman watched Bern walk back to the table. Alaric saw something in her face that he didn't like.

"When do you think the others will get here?" Bern asked as he looked around the common room.

"I'm sure they'll be here soon," replied Alaric quietly. "I don't think they would pass up a night out."

Well if they don't get here soon I'll have to order dinner without them. I'm starving. I don't think I can wait much longer."

Alaric nodded his agreement before he spoke. "If the ale is anything to go by, I don't think the food is going to be anything special.

Why wait? I think we should eat now and get it over and done with. I'm sure the others can look after themselves."

Bern agreed quickly and waved the serving woman over. She came over with a smile on her face, which seemed to irritate the other patrons, some of which were trying to catch her attention.

"What can I get yer lads?" she drawled.

"I was wondering if we could trouble you for some food. We haven't eaten in a long time and we are deathly hungry," Bern made a puppy dog face.

"I'll see what we've got out the back. I think there might be some left-over stew," she smiled sweetly.

"Bern! You're the worst flirt in the world. I don't know how Mary puts up with you," a hint of jealousy touched his words. Under her grimy appearance, Alaric could see that there was an attractive young woman.

"I don't know what you're talking about," replied Bern, an honest look of surprise on his face.

Alaric just shook his head without answering. He tried to conceal the broad grin on his face by taking another drink.

The serving woman returned shortly with two steaming bowls of stew and two, not so fresh looking, bread rolls. After another short interlude between Bern and the barmaid, she returned to the bar. Alaric didn't wait for her to leave before he started to eat. The bread was stale and the stew was bland, but he didn't care. He ate it quickly.

"That must be the worst meal I have ever eaten," laughed Alaric after he had scraped his bowl clean.

"I know what you mean, but I still wouldn't have passed on it for the world."

Before they said anything else, two burly men entered the common room. By their rowdy attitude, it was clear that they were locals. They took one look at the two strangers and sauntered over to them.

"Well, well, Griffy. What have we here?" The closer of the two men sneered. He had a head of thick red hair and two days' growth on his face. His teeth were stained yellow and his breath reeked like he had been drinking for the last week nonstop.

"It looks like someone forgot to take the worms out. I hate it when they do that." Griffy was only slightly shorter than his friend, but was just as stocky. His short cut hair was a light brown. His teeth and breath were just as bad.

"I think you could be correct. I suppose it will be our job to clean up again."

"Hey fellas, we don't want any trouble," commented Bern as he tried to get the serving woman's attention.

"Of course you don't want any trouble," Griffy scoffed.

"You boys better run along before you get hurt. These are our regular seats and you're not invited," the other man continued.

Alaric felt for his sword. His heart sank as he realised that he had left it in his room. There was not much chance that they were going to leave without a fight. Even if they left the table, he knew that would not be the end of it.

"Liron, Griffy, we don't want any trouble tonight. Please sit down and I will get you both a drink," the serving woman called from behind the bar.

"Stay out Leane or *you* will be next."

"You don't talk to a lady like that." Bern bit down on his rage as he stood from his chair only to be shoved by Liron.

"Not so fast my young friend."

"I really think you should leave now." Alaric had pure confidence in his voice. He knew his training by the elves would be enough to defeat a couple of bar thugs. "You're getting in deeper than you know."

"It seems that we have philosopher amongst us Griffy," the jest didn't make any sense. It was obvious that neither of the two had their wits about them.

Alaric knew that words were not going to do any good. He stood up quickly and kicked his chair out of the way. Being so close to the wall he felt uncomfortable. It gave him no opportunity to retreat. He would have to go on the offensive from the start. Both men went on the attack without thinking about the consequences. Alaric easily ducked out of the way of Liron's drunken punch. Without much effort, he used Liron's force to switch places and take the advantage.

Taking a step back, Alaric prepared for another attack. He knew that he could easily defeat his opponent, but he didn't want to become over confident. He knew that would be the only way he could lose.

"Think you can run away from me?" Liron slurred his words.

Without waiting for a reply, Liron charged towards him. If he had not got out of the way, the man would have surely bowled him over. Alaric was too quick and this time prepared to attack. As he side-stepped, Alaric struck out with his left fist and hit Liron across the chest. The blow was powerful enough to knock Liron off his feet.

Bern was having just as much ease with Griffy. If anything, the man was drunker than his friend. Bern simply blocked a number of attacks and waited patiently for his own chance. His moment came quicker than he expected, a quick up thrust smashed Griffy and he sunk to the ground. The fight would have been over quickly if they had been aware of their surroundings. Neither of them had noticed some of the other patrons taking an interest.

A chair came crashing down on the back of Alaric's head, knocking him to the ground. Bern was also dealt with in a similar fashion. Looking up Alaric could see two men standing over the top of him. His head ached and his vision blurred in and out.

"What's going on here?" Alaric recognised the gruff voice of Hulkan and breathed a sigh of relief.

"Stay back. This doesn't have anything to do with you. This isn't your fight," the voice came from one of the men standing over Alaric.

"It doesn't look like it's your fight either," Dorn's voice was clearly fierce.

There was movement around them, but it was clear that they were not leaving. It had been a long time since a dwarf had visited the town and the residence had obviously forgotten how fiercely they fought.

As soon as he had the chance, Alaric returned to his feet and surveyed the scene. Five more men had joined the fray. Liron had returned to his feet, whilst Griffy remained on the ground nursing a broken nose. Bern lay on the floor unconscious, as everyone else kept their distance.

Alaric waited for his opportunity to fight, but it seemed as though the two dwarves had everything under control. He helped Bern to his feet as he regained consciousness. When he looked around, the fight was over. There were many bodies either lying still on the ground or crawling towards the door.

"I think you should all leave." Leane's voice didn't drawl like it had when they had arrived. "I'm sure someone would have alerted the night watch and they won't take too kindly to strangers starting fights."

"But we didn't start the fight," Alaric protested.

"It doesn't matter. The night watch will believe the locals over outsiders."

"Thank you," Bern murmured, as he rested on Alaric's shoulder.

The four of them made for their bedrooms. They were sharing two to a room. The dwarves, who were still reminiscing about the fight, left Alaric and Bern at their room and continued to their own.

Bern didn't last long before he was sound asleep. He was still suffering from the blow to the back of his head. Alaric was just happy to lie down. He wanted nothing more than to forget all about it.

The mattress was lumpy and smelt just as bad as the rest of the inn. Alaric didn't mind, anything was better than the thin bedroll that he had been sleeping on.

Alaric was awoken in the morning by an impatient knock on the door. He lifted his head from the pillow and looked over at Bern who was no longer there. Before he had a chance to comprehend the situation another knock came.

After yawning and stretching Alaric rose, his body ached from the fight and the uncomfortable night's sleep. His shoulders dropped even lower when he saw who had come.

"Sorry to disturb you," Eldred greeted him with a hint of sarcasm.

"Good morning Eldred. I didn't realise we had a deadline today," Alaric turned as if to go back to bed.

Eldred's tone turned serious. "We always have a deadline and if we don't meet it then we are all dead."

Alaric knew that he was right and there was no point in arguing. He had hoped that he was going to be able sleep for the rest of the day. He doubted if there was ever going to be an opportunity for him to rest.

"We are going to visit Hadar today with Alena and Hawthorne. The others will stay in town and try and get some information. Something strange is happening here and I want to know what it is."

The other two met them out in front of the inn with their horses. Alaric thought Alena looked beautiful in the morning sun. "Good morning," she smiled. He replied quickly, but had to stop himself before his staring became inappropriate.

They left the town through the north gate. No one challenged them as they rode through the village although they received some strange looks from the locals.

The forest was sparse and the conifers let plenty of sunlight through; the road was well maintained and easy to ride. After they had ridden for almost two hours the forest suddenly stopped and before them was a broad, open plain. In the centre stood a small castle surrounded by small stone wall. Livestock roamed around freely whilst herdsman lazed around in the sun.

They rode through the pastures without being confronted, but once they arrived at the main gate a group of six guards quickly stood to attention. Their armour gleamed in the sun light and it was obvious that they all took their position very seriously.

"I am Eldred. Duke Hadar is expecting me and the others," Eldred's voice was relaxed.

"Of course, we have been expecting you." The Captain spoke cordially.

A clear tension left the group at the Captain's words; things were finally running smoothly. It had been too long since things had gone their way. Eldred wasn't completely sure it was a good sign

Three of the guards led the group through the outer courtyard. On each side, there were many barracks where the Duke's soldiers resided. The rest of the square was used for practise and training. They passed a small group in sword training and Alaric watched them closely as Adelanta followed behind Eldred.

At the stairs leading to the castle, they all dismounted. From a small hut came two groomsmen to take the horses. Alaric watched them closely as they led Adelanta and the other horses away.

"Come on Alaric, we don't want to keep the Duke waiting," Eldred called down from the top of the stairs. "He'll be alright; they'll take good care of him."

The large double doors leading into the castle were mainly unadorned. Made from solid oak they were strapped with thick bands of iron.

They were met inside by two youthful pages, by Alaric's guess they were no older than fifteen. They were dressed in the Duke's purple livery, the ducal crest emblazoned on the chest.

Inside, large marble and granite pillars lined the great entrance foyer. Rooms spread off to either side. The pages brought them to a black stone stairway leading to the Duke's conference room.

The doors to the conference room had a roughly carved map of the Seven Kingdoms on them. Words were written underneath in a language that Alaric didn't recognise.

"Your guests are here, my lord," called one of the pages.

"Well, bring them in." His voice was gruffer than Alaric had expected. There was something commanding and angry about it. He hoped it was going to be a good meeting.

The room inside was relatively plain. A large mahogany table sat in the centre with twelve matching high backed chairs. Seated at the head of the table was a large man. He looked up when the door was opened, but did not rise. His dark hair was neatly cut as was his dark beard. It was obvious to all that this was Duke Hadar. Two other men were only slightly smaller than the duke. The both shared his features with only subtle differences.

"Please, sit down," Hadar offered with a wave of his hand.

"Thank you Hadar." Hawthorne had to stifle a scoff at Eldred's familiarity. "This is Hawthorne, Alena and Alaric." This time Hawthorne physically choked at the lack of his title.

"Very good. These are my sons. Hagar, my heir and Garag, my youngest." Hadar introduced his two sons before anyone sat. "Let's get this meeting started. I believe that you came here for a reason."

"As you know we are building an army to the east. I will not bore you with the details as you already know them. What we need is your full support. If we don't defeat Nyrra's army, then the world is doomed."

"Unfortunately I don't think that is going to be possible. As you know we are the first line of defence from attack from the Cloumid Mountains." Hadar spoke rationally. There was something about the exchange that didn't seem right to Alaric.

"But there hasn't been an attack from the mountain in over a hundred years," Hawthorne blurted out.

"What would you know?" Hagar snapped.

"Calm down Hagar," Hadar waved a hand at his son. "There have been a number of attacks on Bordertown over the past years. Goblins have come out of the mountains and raided the town, killing indiscriminately. The attacks are random and seem to serve no purpose."

A look of shock crossed Eldred's face. "They're a smoke screen, a diversion to keep your soldiers from the real battle."

"That may be correct, but even so, I cannot leave my people defenseless. If I take all my soldiers out of the land, then the next time the goblins attack they will kill everyone. What is point of winning the war if no one is left to enjoy it?" Hadar kept his mind rigid.

"The point is if we lose this war than everyone dies. What does it matter if these people live for an extra two or three years? After that they will either be killed or enslaved. No, there is no other way." Eldred kept his reasoning calm. "There is something more, more than the goblins. There was something wrong about the forest when we arrived."

"I see that nothing gets past you. You are absolutely correct. The last time the goblins raided, which was a little over a week ago, there was a sighting of a dark man on horseback. The townsfolk who saw him said the man sent shivers down their spines. More than that there was a great sense of terror that didn't leave them for two days. No one could make out any of his features. Some doubt they even saw the man. Some of the stories have been so outrageous that it is hard to say if he actually exists. From what we can gather, he is somewhere between six and seven feet tall, clad completely in black armour. Some say he wore a black helmet with the visor down, others say his face itself was as black as night." There almost seemed to be a touch of fear in Hadar's voice as he recalled what he heard.

Eldred remained quiet.

"We need to go." Eldred came to his feet in such a hurry that both Hawthorne and Hagar jumped in their seats.

"What's wrong?" Alaric asked Eldred as they raced down the stairs.

"A lot and I have a bad feeling that once we get back to town we will know more about it." Eldred stared ahead giving Alaric no real answer.

Back on the plain, Eldred spurred his stallion to a gallop. The other elvish horses followed after their leader and Alaric grasped the reins tightly as he was nearly jolted from Adelanta.

As soon as they returned to the inn it was clear that things were not as they should be. The door leading inside was hanging from its top hinge and inside the inn keeper had been murdered. His lifeless body lay on the floor in a pool of blood, a single sword cut across his neck. There was a look of stunned surprise on his face, his eyes still opened wide. Nothing else in the lobby had been touched.

"Goblins?" asked Alaric, repressing the urge to vomit.

"Not very likely. If this was a goblin attack, then the entire town would be in an uproar. This was a localised attack and by the look of the sword stroke, it was done by an experienced soldier." Hawthorne stared at the inn keeper.

"What about the others?"

It was as they all feared. All the rooms were in disarray. It was clear that there had been fighting, and they must have been taken by surprise. All their weapons remained safely stored away. In the final room, they found Heryion searching for something.

"What happened here?" asked Eldred.

"I was out around the town when it happened. I saw soldiers in town, but I didn't put two and two together until I returned. They wore red armour with a black dragon on their breast plates. I didn't recognise the crest of any of the local nobles."

"They are Count Kerwin's elite knights." Everyone spun around at the sound of a new voice.

"What are you doing here?" Eldred asked quickly when he saw Hadar.

"As soon as you left, I had a messenger arrive. People saw the remainder of your group be carried through the forest by Kerwin's soldiers; it wasn't like they were trying to be secretive. Now I think that we should keep moving. I will explain the rest on the way back to my castle. Bring only your weapons. I will have my pages bring the remainder of your possessions."

"Who is this Count Kerwin? I thought I knew all the family coat-of-arms in this land, but I have never seen a black dragon on red backing before." Heryion rode at the front of the line with Eldred and Hadar.

"Kerwin is the son of Count Rork, whose coat of arms was the golden eagle on a field of green. Kerwin was never much of a man no matter how much his father tried to train him. Last year somehow he raised a revolt and assassinated his father. There was no way to prove that it was him, but we all knew. It is believed that he is a follower of Nyrra." Hadar explained as they rode at a walking pace.

"Then why didn't you kill him?" Alaric called angrily from behind them.

Hadar ignored the attack and continued to speak. "If we could be totally sure then we would have had him arrested, but there was no solid proof. Now that he has kidnapped your companions, I have all the proof that I need."

"Remember that our companions are being held prisoner. I think that if you storm the keep, then they will be killed and if that happens I don't think it would matter whether you join us or not."

"Regardless, there is nothing we can do about it today. I will have my army mobilised by morning. By then, I'm sure we will be able to work out the best course of action."

The sun was wavering when they rode through the southern gate. The courtyard was a hive of activity. Soldiers and groomsman were racing around preparing for the inevitable campaign. No one paid them any attention, although they made a point not to get in their way.

Hadar had ordered rooms to be prepared for them before he left. No one was invited to his council and Eldred's objections fell on deaf ears. Hadar wanted revenge. Count Rork was a good friend and he would not rest until his murderer was brought to justice. He knew that Eldred would tell him to wait and he didn't need to hear it again.

After eating a light meal, Alaric retired to his room. The shock of the entire situation had finally set in. His best friend had been kidnapped by a rogue count. His life hung in the balance and if it tipped the wrong way it would be over.

He didn't notice the door open or the person walk into the room. He sat on the bed within the dull candlelight. His head was bowed as he watched his hand shaking involuntarily. He nearly jumped to his feet when he felt a gentle hand rest on his shoulders.

"Don't worry Alaric, we'll get them back," Alena offered as she sat next to him.

"How do we know if they're still alive?" Alaric's voice was broken.

"I think that we would know if they were dead. I don't fully understand how it works, but I think that somehow we are all connected." Alena spoke softly and reassuring.

"I will not rest until we have rescued them." Alaric's resolve had returned.

"I think that you should get some sleep. Rest will help you tomorrow. I have a feeling it's going to be a very trying day for all of us." Alena stood when she spoke.

"Yes, you are right." Alaric said no more as Alena left the room.

With Alena gone Alaric slid the small chest out from under the bed. He picked it up and let it rest on his lap. There was something very relieving about it. Even with the stone safely guarded inside, he thought he could still feel its warmth. If he had to, he would use the stone to destroy Count Kerwin and anyone who followed him. With that thought in mind, he let himself drift off, to sleep.

Chapter 19: Count Kerwin

Alaric was woken before the sun had risen. Eldred had walked into the room without knocking and shook him awake.

"What's happening?" Alaric asked sleepily.

"Hadar has his mind set on moving his army against Kerwin. I think that stealth is better than a full-frontal attack if we are going to save the others. If Kerwin is painted into a corner, then I believe he will kill the others out of spite if nothing else." Eldred words brought Alaric's attention back to their current predicament.

They all met in the courtyard. Eldred had managed to arrange for the groomsmen to ready their horses without Hadar being made aware of their plan. Secrecy was the key. If Hadar knew what they were planning, then there would be no doubt he would try and stop them.

It wasn't until they were back in the forest that they all relaxed. Alaric wasn't the only one who took the kidnapping to heart. The attack was personal and all of them wanted their revenge.

"Do you know where we are going?" Hawthorne asked.

"That is one piece of information that I did receive last night. It is a full day's ride to the east and then another half day's ride to the north. It will take Hadar at least three times that to move his army. He will push them hard, but there will be foot soldiers as well as cavalry. He will also need to transport siege weapons to take the castle. With any luck, we should have two to three days to rescues the others. After they are safe, Hadar can destroy them, the castle for all I care," Eldred's words were promising.

The day passed without incident. Every one kept to their own thoughts. There was no discussion until they stopped for the night. The air was cool and Eldred afforded them a small fire. There was a chance that Kerwin would have soldiers in the forest, but if they froze to death they would be no good to anyone.

"We attack tomorrow." Alaric watched the flames dance in the fire.

"We assess tomorrow." Eldred watched him carefully. "The last thing we want to do is underestimate this man. Make no mistake the others would not have been taken without a fight. We need to be very careful. We don't know what agenda this Count has, but be sure that he knows that we are coming."

"How do you know that?" asked Alena.

"If they didn't want us to follow, then there would be no point in taking prisoners. You can be assured that the others are only still alive because this Kerwin wants us to come to him. He is yet to reveal his plan, but I guarantee that he will be prepared."

"So what *is* the plan?" Hawthorne was just as keen as Alaric for revenge.

"We shall just have to wait until tomorrow. There is nothing we can do until we know what we're up against."

The rest of the night passed much the same as the day. No one felt the need to talk. If they couldn't think of a plan, then there was no point speaking at all. After they had eaten, they were all keen to sleep. Their bedrolls had not been delivered to the castle by the time they had to leave, so they had to make do with the bare ground. No one got much sleep.

In the morning, they were on the move as the sun crested the horizon. No one cared that they had not eaten. They all wanted to be away from the campsite and closer to achieving their goal.

By mid-morning, a horse could be seen cresting a small hill, galloping straight for them. The rider atop looked to be swaying in the saddle, as if he was asleep. They all drew their weapons.

As the horse came closer, they could see that it was Palentonal in the saddle. His arms were tied behind his back and his feet strapped to the stirrups. There was no way for him to control the horse as it continued towards them at breakneck speed.

Hawthorne prepared himself to grab the reins as the horse drew near. He was about to jump when the horse stopped of its own accord. Blood stained the mares grey coat; she was clearly distressed and seemed somewhat comforted at finishing her mission.

A large gash ran across the top of Palentonal's left eye. His white linen shirt was soaked with blood; his eyes were glazed and he was struggling to remain conscious.

Alena quickly raced to his side and cut him free. Hawthorne helped to lower him to the ground. His breathing was laboured and there was not much life left in his body.

"Get him some water," cried Alena.

Alaric reached for one of the vials he had brought from the mountain. Before he pulled it out, he remembered what Heryion had told him. The water would only survive two days out of the well and that had passed.

Eldred quickly handed her his pouch and she tried to pour the water into his mouth but he brushed it aside.

"No, I will be alright," Palentonal coughed up a small amount of blood. "They told me that if we ever want to see the others again then Alaric has to come to castle alone. Count Kerwin assured his safe passage and the return of the others. He said he just wants to speak to him."

"And you believed him?" asked Eldred, a little surprised.

"Not for a moment, but as you can see I was in no position to argue." After he finished speaking, Palentonal grabbed the pouch and poured the water into his mouth.

"Alena," Eldred spoke with command in his voice. "You take Palentonal back to Hadar's castle. He will have physicians there."

"But I want to help save the others," disappointment rose in her voice.

"Please, he has lost a lot of blood. He needs serious attention and we need to keep moving. You can tend to his wounds before you take him back." Eldred was clearly upset at being questioned.

Alena couldn't argue. As soon as Palentonal arrived, she knew that he was going to be left in her care. She didn't want to leave the others, but his life was just as important. She simply nodded her head in agreement and retuned her attention to her fellow elf.

They continued their journey and Alaric hoped that his friend had not been treated the same way as Palentonal. The thought of Bern being beaten and tortured made his stomach churn. He steeled his emotions and focused his anger on the Count. He would need to stay focused if he was going to rescue his friends.

Shortly after midday a fog rolled in from the north. The familiar tingling sensation returned to the back of Alaric's neck. It was so subtle that he wasn't even sure it was there. He scratched thoughtfully and then thought nothing of it.

"This fog is not natural," Eldred spoke as he stopped the group the edge of a small grove. "It seems that the Count is expecting us."

"What does that mean?"

"If we ride up to the castle now, we will be seen for sure," Eldred mused.

"No one can see through this fog. If anything, it will work to our advantage," retorted Hawthorne.

"This fog is a spell. What is hidden to us is clear as day to them. They will see us before we get within a hundred feet." Eldred was impatient.

"Then I will go alone. The others will be freed if I meet the Count." Alaric's voice was steeled, although it was clear he was nervous.

"Don't be so quick to martyr yourself," said Heryion. "If there is one thing you will learn, it is never trust anything that Nyrra or any of his agents say. They will lie to your face and you will never know it. I would bet my life that once you are in the castle, Kerwin will kill the others. Once he has you there is no reason for him to keep them alive. He will revel in their death and then not think another thing about. No. We cannot do what he asks."

"Then we are all lost," Alaric's voice broke with his realisation.

"Now that is not completely true," a wry smile crossed Eldred's face. "We must leave the horses and continue on foot. Hawthorne... You must look after the horses, when night falls lead them towards the main gate. Be careful, even in the dark you can be seen. Remember that evil gains strength in the darkness; make your camp in whatever cover you can once you are within sight of the gate. Wait for us until morning. If we have not returned by then find Hadar's army and tell him what has happened."

Hawthorne nodded his agreement, although unhappy he knew better than to argue. When there was magic involved, he knew his place and he didn't want anything to do with it.

"But what will happen when they see us approaching?" Alaric asked slowly, confused at Eldred's confidence. "The message was for me to come alone."

"Let's make for the castle. I'll explain on the way."

As they walked past the tree line Eldred made a flourish with his hands. Alaric had a strange feeling that something had happened. The light tingling sensation, which had been at the back of his neck, had disappeared.

The trees suddenly thinned out until they were out in the open. The ground underneath became hard rubble and dry dust. It was as if the land had become diseased. Without the cover of the trees, Alaric felt naked. He felt as though there were a thousand pairs of eyes watching him.

"Kerwin has sucked this land dry," Eldred almost spat the words as he looked at the desolation around him.

"How can he survive in this? There are no crops or livestock." Alaric was in disbelief of their surroundings.

"Nyrra's evil thrives on this kind of destruction. If we fail, then this is what the rest of the world will become. There will not be a blade of grass left untouched."

"What do they eat?"

"I don't think that you really want to know." Heryion answered.

Alaric's stomach churned and then he thought again of his friends. He didn't want to think about what would happen to them if he failed. He would not fail. Their lives depended on him being strong and that was exactly what he was going to be.

The sun had almost set when Eldred signaled for them to stop. There was still no sign of the castle although Alaric had a feeling they were close. He had a bad feeling that Kerwin knew they were coming.

"We need to wait until nightfall," Heryion spoke softly, as if he thought someone was within earshot.

"But won't they be more powerful at night?" Alaric followed Heryion's lead and kept his voice quiet, although he didn't understand the reason. "Didn't you say that Nyrra and his followers gained power from the darkness?"

"Be that as it may, to not wait until night will be fatal." Heryion's words were very mysterious and Alaric gave him a confused look.

The fog suddenly dissipated once the sun had set and the sky became black with storm clouds. There was something very unnatural about them. It was as if there was a secret horror lurking inside. As soon as the fog lifted Alaric felt an itching on the back of his neck. This time is was a lot more prominent. There could be no doubt that it was there and he scratched it subconsciously until he realised the other two were watching him.

"Are you alright?" asked Eldred.

"Ah, yes," Alaric forced his hand away from his neck.

"Good. Then we should make for the castle."

"How do we get inside?" Alaric asked.

"With a little magic," Eldred looked at Heryion who promptly shook his head. "And with a lot of luck we will prevail."

Eldred closed his eyes and muttered a couple of words under his breath. After a few seconds, the sensation that had been a mild itch nearly knocked Alaric from his feet. A roaring sound, like a gale force wind, filled his ears.

"As I suspected," Eldred commented as he watched Alaric's reaction.

"Someone is searching for us. You were lax with your spell, you may as well of sent them a written warning that we were coming," scolded Heryion.

His cutting remarks only brought a smile to Eldred's face. The change in his façade brought a questioning look to Heryion. "They always knew that we were coming. That was never a doubt. Since we can't hide our arrival, I thought that I should give them something else to chase. My little decoy should give us enough time to enter the castle unnoticed."

The rushing sound stopped as abruptly as it had begun. Alaric thought he could see it pass to the north, but brushed the feeling off as idiotic. He needed to direct all his focus on the job at hand. Now that Kerwin knew they were coming, their lives were at greater risk.

"By the time they realise my ruse, we will be deep inside the castle," Eldred's voice wasn't as confident as his words indicated.

As they neared the castle, they could see movement on the battlements. Large torches were aflame. The light seemed to fade away from the figures keeping guard. There was something very discerning about the situation. The land surrounding the wall was pitch black. This should have aided their plight, but Alaric knew that it was not the case.

Kerwin's guards would be able to see into the gloom. He was sure the evil of Nyrra would aid them.

"How are we going to get inside?" Alaric whispered.

"Magic." Eldred replied mysteriously.

"It's risky." Heryion added. "They are looking for us and one wrong move they will know exactly where we are."

"They are using a large amount of magic to try and locate us. I don't think they will notice a little more." Eldred spat. "If there was anyone with any great talent, they would have already found us. I am beginning to doubt the worth of this Kerwin. I don't think that Nyrra has bestowed much power upon him."

"Regardless, we shouldn't make the mistake of underestimating our enemy. One wrong move could see us all dead. Let's assume that Kerwin is as powerful as Nyrra himself and that way, we won't fall into an easy trap," Heryion's words were like a lecture to a school boy.

Eldred ignored the scolding words and continued on. They travelled slowly and cautiously. Although they were covered in darkness, they knew they could still be identified. The night was still and every sound travelled.

When they reached the wall, Eldred motioned for them to stop. He moved his hand against the cold stone wall sending a shiver down his spine. He pulled his hand back sharply.

"What was that?" asked Heryion.

"This is going to be harder than I thought. There is a magical reinforcement on the wall. The risk just doubled." Eldred had to force himself to keep his voice at a whisper.

"Can you break it?"

"We'll find out soon enough," there was little confidence in his voice. "You better close your eyes Alaric. This can be disturbing at the best of times," Eldred was about to start when a thought occurred to him. "And when you open your eyes again, refrain from calling out."

Alaric was unsure what Eldred meant, but he nodded his head in reply. He slowly closed his eyes, although in the darkness he wondered if there was any point.

Eldred started a low chant that was only just audible. The words were indiscernible, but it was clear that they were having an effect. The now familiar tingling sensation returned, however this time it was not on the back of his neck. It started on his front and then slowly passed through his body until it left from his back. When the feeling left him, a shiver ran through his body.

"You can open your eyes now, and please remember not to scream," Eldred spoke casually.

Although Eldred had tried to prepare him, the surprise nearly made him cry out. It took all his self-control to keep his mouth shut. They were no longer standing on the outside of the castle. They were now standing in a small room. Eldred had created a small ball of light so they could see. By the smell and the look of the room, it was a rarely used store room. Cobwebs lined the walls and shelves.

"Where are we?" asked Alaric, his heart-beat slowly returning to normal.

"It seems that we are in some outer store room. This couldn't have worked out better if I tried. We have passed through the outer wall. Everything being well, this storeroom will be connected to the castle," Eldred's voice was relaxed.

"I don't think that we are going to be that lucky." Heryion spoke from the other end of the room with the door open.

On the other side of the door was a large courtyard leading to the castle. The courtyard was not well lit, but there was enough light to see. Eldred let his little ball of light extinguish itself. There was no one in sight, but anyone on the battlements would easily see them.

"How are we going to get across the courtyard?" Heryion asked.

"I don't think that we have much other choice. I was able to mask the spell so no one will be coming for us, but we can't stay here forever. We have to make for the castle and hope that no one recognises us," Eldred sounded resigned.

Eldred led the way from the storeroom with Alaric in the middle and Heryion at the rear. It was hard for Alaric to remain calm as they made their way to a side door used by the servants.

The courtyard was completely empty except for the three of them. Alaric had to suppress the urge to look around. The feeling returned that there were thousands of eyes watching him. Little did he know that it was the exact opposite. All the guards on the battlements were focused on the outside. No one even glanced back at the three lone figures as they slowly made their way towards the castle.

Once they were safely inside they all relaxed, but for only a moment. The servants' entrance had brought them to a small dimly lit hallway. There were two doors along the walls and one at the far end.

"Where do we go from here?" Alaric asked.

"This is where it starts to get tricky." Eldred gave Heryion a questioning look who in turn replied with a nod of his head. "We need to separate if we are to rescue the others."

It was obvious that there was something Eldred wasn't saying. The look that Eldred had given Heryion was enough to prove that something was up and he knew that he was not going to like the explanation.

"We will find the others whilst you will have to confront Count Kerwin." Eldred looked at Alaric.

"What?" Alaric raised his voice without a thought for their current location. "I thought the idea of us all coming here together was to avoid a meeting with Kerwin."

"Please calm down Alaric. Getting caught now will do none of us any good." Eldred tried to soothe Alaric, but knew only answers would appease him. "The idea of all of us coming was to rescue the others and this is the way we are going to do it. Kerwin will be expecting you, but not Heryion and myself. You need to keep Kerwin distracted whilst we rescue the others."

"But then I'm trapped. How is that going to help the situation?"

"We will come and find you. Don't worry. You are much stronger than Kerwin. I have the utmost confidence that you can defeat him." Heryion cut in before Eldred could answer. "Now we can stand here talking all night or we can help."

"But how will I find Kerwin? He could be anywhere in the castle." Alaric was trying to find a fault in their plan.

"Don't worry. It won't take long for someone to find you. I will make sure that you will be easy to find, once we are out of sight. Go through the door at the end of the hall, I am sure that will lead you in the right direction."

Before Alaric could voice his protest, Eldred and Heryion left through one of the side doors. His initial reaction was to follow, but he knew that would do him no good. The hallway seemed to loom in front of him. He had never felt so alone. He couldn't shake the feeling that somehow he had been betrayed.

Taking one step forward he made for the door. The small chest, which was strapped to his belt, felt suddenly heavy. He thought about taking the stone out and leaving the chest behind. For some reason, he wanted the comfort of the stone. Taking a deep breath, he pushed the feeling aside and made for the door.

Alaric hesitated as his hand closed on the handle. Whatever was on the other side was going to terrify him. If nothing else, he was sure of that. Taking another deep breath, he pulled the door open. On the other side, a large entrance foyer greeted him warmly. The room was brightly lit with many torches on the wall and a great chandelier handing from the ceiling. A long red carpet led from the main entrance to a door at the far end.

A large robed man stood in front of the door. The hood covered his face; he looked as though he was waiting for Alaric. Whatever Eldred had done had sure worked. There was no doubt that this man would lead him to Kerwin. Alaric stood completely calm, he knew he should be scared out of his mind, but he felt no fear.

"Come with me." The voice seemed to come from much deeper in the hood than it should have. There was also a slight hiss to his voice that Alaric thought was very strange. Alaric touched the hilt of his sword as a precaution.

The robed man led Alaric down a long corridor. They took a left at an intersection and then down a small flight of stairs. The man did not speak at all, but simply assumed that Alaric was following him. At the bottom of the stairs the man led Alaric to a small room.

With Alaric safely in the room the man left. When the door closed there was an audible click indicating the door had been locked. His heart sank. Up to that point he thought there was a chance that their plan might have succeeded. Now he was trapped and all was lost.

The room was not the cell that he had been expecting. There was a couch, lounge chair and low table. A small candle on the table was all that lit the room and cast many shadows.

Not knowing how long he was going to be prisoner Alaric decided to make the most of his surroundings. The chair was as comfortable as it looked. His legs ached as he sat and he let out a sigh as he relaxed.

About half an hour later a feeling of evil passed over him, as it did another click came from the door. Slowly it was opened and the cloaked man entered. His hood still covered his face. Alaric peered to see inside but to no avail.

"You will come with me!" he hissed.

Alaric nodded and returned to his feet. A sudden wave of terror passed over him. Until that moment he had remained calm. Even when he had felt that all was lost he still remained hopeful. He was going to meet the man who had captured his friends and he knew he was going to die.

The hooded man waited until he saw Alaric's reaction before he turned and led him away. The feeling of hopelessness had come so suddenly that Alaric wasn't sure if it was his true feelings. The further they walked the more he thought that someone was trying to alter the way he felt. He didn't think that he was going to die. He had the protection of the stone and he could easily defeat one of Nyrra's henchmen. He had defeated Dhlark and he had captured all of them.

The thoughts raced through his mind and his confidence returned. Wherever the thoughts of doubt had come from they slowly disappeared. By the time they reached the large double doors to the throne room he had as much faith as he was going to have.

The room was surprisingly lit by hundreds of candles and chandeliers. The room was painted completely black, as if it had been freshly and badly painted. The original colours showed through in patches. Large portraits lined the walls. They were all of grotesque and disfigured creatures. Some were maiming or eating humans. In each of the paintings, there seemed to be something in the background. It was if there was a face watching over them. Whenever Alaric tried to focus, it seemed to disappear. The images made Alaric feel sick. He wondered what man could decorate in such a fashion.

At the far end of the throne room, there were four high backed thrones. The two in the middle had higher backs and were more ornately decorated. The thrones, like the rest of the room, had been painted black. Spots of gold peered through the paint work and Alaric could imagine what they would have looked like before Kerwin had usurped power.

Sitting on the middle left throne was a large man. He was dressed completely in black and almost faded into the background. A slender rapier leaned against the side of the throne and he stroked the hilt as they approached.

When they were within half a dozen paces, the hooded man bowed and then left the room. Neither of them spoke until the doors were closed and they were alone. A large grin crossed Kerwin's face as he looked up.

"Well Alaric, we meet at last!"

Chapter 20: A Rescue Attempt

The voice was sickly sweet, even odd. Kerwin's face was deathly pale and looked as though he had not seen the sun in decades. His hair was dark black which made his face look comical. His body was large and muscular, although it did not look natural.

"I must admit that you are not at all what I thought you'd be. I thought that you might have put up more of a fight." Kerwin paused shortly before he continued. "My name is Count Kerwin, the owner of this castle and the surrounding lands. I presume that you know why I have gathered you here?"

Alaric nodded. His hand drifted to the hilt of his sword. The feel of it gave him renewed confidence.

"Very good. That will make this go a lot quicker." Kerwin smiled, showing he was missing almost half of his teeth. "Now we should get down to business. My lord will be pleased when I offer you to him as a servant. I don't know why he thought you would be such an adversary. You know, I think that he was actually worried that you might be victorious. Now give me the Ruby Stone and I will set your friends free."

Alaric knew that it was a lie. Once Kerwin had the stone, he would kill all of them, however, there was something inside telling him to do what Kerwin said. His hand left the hilt of his sword and went to the chest, which he held firmly in his left hand.

"I would rather die than give you the stone." Alaric drew his sword as he spoke and instantly wished he had not used those words. Now that he had started he could not stop. "Don't overestimate your abilities. You still have a lot to learn. Release the others and I might spare you your life." The words poured out of his mouth.

"I see that you have a little fire after all. Well I guess we are going to have to do this the hard way." Kerwin stood and picked up his rapier. "It looks like you've just signed the death warrant on your friends. You know I was actually considering letting them go."

Although Alaric's sword was larger and heavier, the rapier was still a formidable weapon. Alaric had never trained against a rapier and Kerwin looked very proficient. He knew that he could not be over confident in his abilities.

Alaric waited. He was in no hurry to engage Kerwin. The longer he could stall the more chance there was of rescuing the others. There was no doubt that this was not going to be any ordinary sword fight. To make matters worse, he had to keep the chest in his left hand.

Kerwin sniggered at Alaric's hesitation. He took Alaric's caution as a sign of weakness. His confidence was brimming and a broad smile crossed his face. He waved his rapier in front of his face, mocking him.

Alaric stayed his ground, waiting as Kerwin approached. The Count made one more flourish with his blade before he readied himself for the fight. As much as he knew he was going to win, he knew better than to be over confident. There was something disturbing about Alaric's stance. He stood completely unguarded. He was either completely useless or completely confident. Even the worst swordsman would have taken some kind of defensive stance.

Kerwin made his first attack. A combination of blows that even a novice could have defended. He wanted to feel Alaric out before he judged the best offence. There was still something nagging him. Alaric didn't feign anything in his defence. He pushed all the sword strokes aside without trying to make a counter attack. He too wanted to feel Kerwin out, to see what sort of swordsman he was.

Once he had finished his initial attack, Kerwin walked backwards until he was out of lunging distance. Another taunt was in order. He was confident he could talk Alaric off his game.

"I would have thought we would have heard the screams of your friends from here. You know I ordered them tortured before they are to be killed? In fact, I think that it's about time for them to die. I'm sure if you listen hard enough, you will be able to hear them," Kerwin sniggered as he spoke.

Alaric tried to ignore his words, but the thought of his friends being tortured was disturbing. His mind started to wander and Kerwin knew that his words had taken effect. He didn't wait to launch his next attack. This time he didn't hold anything back.

Only at the last minute did Alaric remember to keep his guard up and nearly dropped the chest in the process. The attack came fierce and fast. If Kerwin had continued the verbal barrage, he may have been able to finish the fight, but Alaric was quick to regain his composure. Alaric quickly took up his defence.

The rapier was a fast weapon, but so was the elven blade, the extra weight giving Alaric a slight advantage. Kerwin's attacks were by the book and easy for Alaric to read. Before the count changed his forms, Alaric knew what he was going to do. Alaric did his best not the let Kerwin realise that he knew everything the Count was doing and his plan was working perfectly. Kerwin actually believed that he was winning. Finally, Kerwin changed his current form and Alaric struck.

As much as Kerwin seemed blinded by his own attack, he still remained ready to defend. A quick slash across the chest was all that Kerwin received before he jumped back. A streak of blood appeared on his shirt, but beside a little annoyance there was no real damage, however Alaric was quick to go on the offensive.

"You have already failed. If I don't kill you today, your master will when he finds out. You made the wrong move," Alaric smirked as he spoke.

"It is not over yet," Kerwin's voice still held its confidence.

He knew there was not much chance of beating Alaric in a sword fight. He had been using all of his best moves and all that he accomplished was a slash across his own chest. It was now clear to him that Alaric was the better swordsman; however, he had still had another trick up his sleeve.

Kerwin backtracked towards the thrones and Alaric lowered his sword and relaxed. Even if Kerwin charged, he would have enough time to prepare his defence. Kerwin had no intention of starting another sword attack. What he had in mind would be much more potent.

"Things are about to get very messy. I believe that your friends are now dead and you are about to join them." The words didn't have the venom as before. It was as if he didn't fully believe in them.

Alaric watched him closely. Something had changed about his demeanour. His body was now more rigid and there was a glazed look on his face. Suddenly the familiar tickle on the back of his neck returned. By the time he realised what Kerwin was doing it was too late. Even if he knew what to do he would have no time to react.

Slowly Alaric was lifted off the ground and then propelled across the room. He picked up momentum until he crashed into the far wall. He hung there for a brief moment before collapsing to the ground, his sword clanked as it fell. Despite his effort he could no longer hold onto chest.

The spell also took effect on Kerwin. His breathing had become laboured and he stumbled back onto one of the thrones. Alaric had noticed some labouring when Eldred had cast spells, but nothing like what was happening to the Count. Kerwin was physically drained. Alaric struggled to return to his feet. The blow had knocked the wind out of him. The only thing that had kept him alive was the fact that Kerwin didn't have the strength to finish him off. He slowly collected his sword leaving the chest where it lay and made his way towards him.

Before Alaric came within striking distance, he was again repelled to the back wall. His sword again was dislodged from his hand as he slunk to the ground and the air was knocked from his lungs. This time he was not so quick to return to his feet.

"You see Alaric. There is no way for you to defeat me. Give up now and I will spare your friends," Kerwin's words were laboured. "Save yourself the pain and give me the stone. There is no way out for you."

"I thought you said they were already dead?" Alaric struggled to speak as look at the small chest. The stone was the only way he could defeat Kerwin, but he had not used it since the Cloumid Mountains. He knew that it would be a test, but he couldn't see any other choice. He couldn't use magic without the stone and there was no other way to defeat the Count.

As Alaric fingered the latch there came a loud noise from the direction of the thrones. Alaric looked up slowly to see them in flames with Kerwin standing gingerly by. He could only think that one of Kerwin's spells had backfired until he saw the little man standing in the doorway.

"Well, my good Count, we meet at last," Heryion spoke with deference in his voice.

"You must forgive me, but I have no idea who you are or what you are doing here, but if you wait a moment I will get to you in due course. Unfortunately, I have more pressing matters to attend to." Kerwin did his best to hide his annoyance.

"No, I think that you will have to deal with me now."

"Are the others safe?" Alaric's voice was weak.

Heryion seemed to ignore the question; he didn't want to let his attention drift. He knew that the Count was no match for him, but could easily defeat him if he became distracted.

"So you are the one that was sneaking around. I must admit you are exactly what I thought. Only a fool would have tried what you did." The Count had now become extremely confident.

Heryion smiled. Things were working out better than he thought. Eldred's spells, the ones that were easily identifiable, had been attributed to him. Kerwin was going to get a rude shock when he realised the calibre of his opponent.

"It's your lucky day. I have no business with you, so if you leave now I will spare your life. If you stay, then you will suffer the same fate as the others." Kerwin was clearly becoming impatient.

"I'm not going to make things that easy for you," Heryion kept his voice calm.

The irritation was clearly getting the better of Kerwin. Raising his arms above his head he started waving them madly. Heryion snorted at Kerwin's obvious lack of imagination. Someone who had no idea of magic would be destroyed by the attack, but even the lowliest of apprentices would be able to avoid it.

Heryion took two steps to the left, unnoticed by Kerwin. When he had finished with his incantation he lowered his arms. Two bolts of black light shot out of his fingers and passed through where Heryion had been standing and engulfed the wall. The light fizzled out taking part of the wall with it.

Heryion stood and smiled without retaliating. His passive, smug posture did more to rile Kerwin than any retaliation. A purple vein bulged from his forehead.

Alaric had watched the attack as he rested. Initially he had felt helpless, but now with Kerwin distracted he saw his opportunity. If Heryion could keep Kerwin's attention, then he might be able to make a counter attack.

"You think that you're funny, little man?" Saliva flew from the sides of his mouth. "Well you should know that the angrier you make me the worse it will be. My rage will consume you?"

"I haven't seen anything too impressive yet. In fact, I've seen better from small children."

"This time you will not be so lucky."

It was clear to Alaric that Kerwin's attention was completely on destroying Heryion. He had already started waving his arms in the air again and screaming out an incantation. He didn't care who heard his words. All he could think about was crushing Heryion. With a clap of his hands, he cast the spell.

Nothing seemed to have happened, although the smile, which could be called a grimace, which crossed Kerwin's face, showed that he had completed the spell. Heryion remained perfectly still, the smile never leaving his face.

"It seems that you are out of time," Kerwin puffed heavily, but couldn't pass up the opportunity to gloat. "You were all that I expected you to be."

Suddenly the room started to shake. It was as if the castle had been hit by an earthquake. Large cracks opened up in the roof above Heryion's head. Within a moment, large blocks of stone started to fall. Just as they were about to be struck Heryion disappeared.

All Kerwin could do was look on in horror as his second spell failed. The falling stones subsided and the room was still, except for Alaric who was stalking Kerwin, making sure his movements went unnoticed. Kerwin kept his attention on the pile of rubble that he knew was empty.

Kerwin couldn't believe that his spell had failed and now he was too weak to launch another attack. They were the two most powerful spells he knew and his adversary evaded them without strain. His fury and terror all but consumed him. If it wasn't for the small pot on a pedestal, Kerwin would never have seen Alaric coming.

Alaric almost cursed loudly when the pot rocked on its pedestal before crashing to the floor. The sudden noise snapped Kerwin out of his intense reverie. His face turned from shock to pure hatred.

"You will pay for the insolence. Your partner in crime has just confirmed your death."

Alaric chose not to become involved in the sledging. His confidence had returned. By the sound in his voice, Alaric knew that Kerwin had lost his control. He would make rash decisions looking for a quick victory.

"Nothing to say? Well then let's finish this. I want to find your little friend and destroy him." Kerwin advanced upon Alaric.

He swung his sword wildly with no real pattern. The ferocity of the attack took Alaric by surprise. He knew that Kerwin would go on the attack, but he assumed he would have kept to his training. All he did was try and batter Alaric into submission.

The tactic might have worked had Kerwin had a heavier weapon. The weight of the rapier was not enough to cause any great effect. Once Alaric regained his composure, it was his turn to go on the attack.

Letting Kerwin continue, Alaric waited for the right moment. With the wild barrage, it wasn't easy. If he moved at the wrong moment, then Kerwin would certainly slash him. The only advantage was that Kerwin wasn't defending, just swinging wildly. Alaric simply side-stepped and the speed of his attack and the sudden movement sent Kerwin off balance. Alaric kicked out with his right foot and struck Kerwin across the backside. Taking two stumbled steps Kerwin hit the ground and slid for a couple of feet.

Even though the attack came as a shock, Kerwin was quick to recover. He jumped to his feet before Alaric had a chance to finish him. Kerwin's rage was now beyond control. Lowering his sword, he charged toward Alaric with no thought to his attack.

If it wasn't for his training, Kerwin would have skewered Alaric with his rushed attack but Alaric was just as quick to react. At the last possible second, Alaric sidestepped and stabbed with his sword. The blade caught Kerwin on the chest and sunk in. The pace of his charge brought the blade through him until he hit the hilt. Kerwin cried out in pain and anguish and Alaric relinquished his sword. He had scored a vital blow!

Despite the obvious pain Kerwin quickly jumped back to his feet. His shirt was becoming stained as the blood trickled from his wound. Sweat had already appeared on his brow and the little colour had all but faded from his face. With his left hand, he pulled the blade free from his body. A gush of blood spurted from the wound. He took a stumbled step forward before he let his sword drop to the ground. His right arm hung limply by his side. The only sign of movement was a slight twitch in his hand. In his left hand, he held onto Alaric's sword with all his remaining strength.

"You think you could kill me that easily?" his voice was hoarse, but even in dying he had delusions of victory. "Now it is your time to die. I will deliver your dead body to my master myself." He stifled a laugh. He took another laboured step forward, his eyes sunken and any remaining colour drained from his face.

Alaric walked backwards until he was happy that he was out of reach. He almost felt sorry for Kerwin. His worshipping of Nyrra had made him crazy. Now he was going to pay the ultimate sacrifice. All Alaric had to do was to wait.

"Don't think that this waning body will stop me. Death is but a trifle. It will not stop…" A gurgle rose from his throat and a trickle of blood appeared on the corner of his mouth. He no longer had the strength to stand. His legs wobbled and then he collapsed to his knees. Alaric's sword remained firmly in his grip. There was no chance of him letting it go. Alaric would have to pry it from his dead hand.

The Count's eyes glazed and then closed. The sight of the man dying did not fill Alaric with a sense of peace, but instead filled him with regret. It was a waste of a life, no one deserved to die.

"Drop the sword and I will help you," the words came out of his mouth involuntarily. He didn't want to help the man who had tried to kill him, but he could just watch him die.

Slowly Kerwin opened his eyes and looked up towards Alaric. A small smirk crossed his face before he breathed his last breath. Even in death his evil remained.

Alaric was loathed to touch the dead man. It was as if he touched Kerwin then the evil would consume him. Slowly he bent over the dead body and tried to pull the sword free without having to touch him. The blade was slippery with blood and no matter how hard he tried, he couldn't get enough grip to release the sword. There was no other option. He would have to peel the fingers back himself if he wanted to regain his sword. Kerwin's fingers had already turned cold; it was as if all of his life was suddenly sucked from his body. His fingers remained tight. Alaric used all of his remaining strength to try and pry open Kerwin's fingers. There was nothing that he could do.

Not more than a few paces away, lay Kerwin's rapier and he quickly scooped up the sword. The blade felt strange in his hand. He wanted nothing more than to drop it, but he had to finish the job. Kerwin's fingers were not as easy to remove as Alaric had expected. He felt repulsed at his actions. There was something strange about the way the Count's body was degenerating so quickly. Slicing the fingers didn't work so he was forced to hack instead. He had to repress the urge to retch as the fingers slowly came apart. After, what seemed like hours, his elven sword dropped to the ground.

A wave of relief past through his body and even though his sword was now free, he was loathed to pick it up. He had killed before, but that had been in the heat of battle. This was more personal and it upset him.

"Kerwin had made his choice to worship Nyrra. His end was of his own doing and now his torture is only just beginning." Heryion's words were not comforting.

Alaric was relieved when he spun around and saw Heryion's smiling face. The man always reminded Alaric of a naughty child who had just been up to mischief. His body physically relaxed when he recognised his friend, although he wondered at his words.

"You should clean your blade. The blood will rot the steel if you let it dry."

Alaric couldn't bring himself to clean his sword on his slain enemy's clothes. Instead he walked to the far wall and wiped the blade on an ancient tapestry. He would sooner ruin a work of art than touch the Count again. When his sword was safely sheathed he returned his attention to Heryion.

"We must go now. I don't think it will be long before someone checks to see the outcome of your fight." Heryion's attention had quickly diverted to their surroundings.

"Are the others safe?" the question remained unanswered.

"I don't know. When I left Eldred, he seemed to have everything under control. Now if we don't get moving we will end up a permanent resident of this place."

It was clear that Heryion was not going to give him a straight answer and he did make sense. There was no point in them standing around talking. There would surely be someone coming to wait on Kerwin shortly and when they saw the dead body there would be chaos. Alaric quickly took up the chest when he suddenly realized it was still on the floor. He felt much better with the stone back in his possession.

After carefully checking the corridor, they left the throne room. Heryion led the way with Alaric nervously following behind. Alaric had a bad feeling that every step they took brought them closer to danger. Even though Kerwin was dead, he felt as though a greater evil still resided in the keep.

They walked through the extensive hallway system. Alaric always remained two steps behind, making sure they were not being followed.

Heryion was the first one to hear the footsteps. He reacted before Alaric even knew what was happening. "Quick! In here!" Heryion opened the nearest door and ushered Alaric inside.

As soon as Alaric entered the dimly lit room, he knew that something wasn't right. It was clear to him now that the feeling of evil had originated from the room. He wondered if Heryion had made the move deliberately.

When Heryion closed the door behind him, he too realised his mistake. Whether or not they had been in danger before, there was no doubt that they were in grave danger now. He wondered if what he had heard was indeed footsteps or in fact an elaborate trap.

With the door shut, the occupants opened the shutter on their lantern bathing the room in light. A small table stood at the far end and sitting behind it was the hooded man who had escorted Alaric to the throne room. His hood was still drawn and although there was plenty of light in the room his face was still completely hidden. Standing on either side of the table was a soldier dressed in black livery. The blood red crest was not that of the Count. It was a crest that Alaric had never seen before. The crest was that of two winged serpents wrapped around each other with their heads ready to strike. They each held a long sword in their hands.

Alaric was quick to react and drew his own sword. Although he was weary from battling Kerwin, he was prepared to fight for his life again. A new burst of adrenalin rushed through his body and gave him the strength to continue. The two soldiers remained motionless, even though they had the perfect opportunity to attack. It was as if they were waiting for an invitation.

"Kill him!" the voice hissed from beneath the hood. The words sent a chill down Alaric's spine.

The soldiers approached slowly. It was clear that they did not want to fight Alaric. They had heard of the chosen one and did not feel like confronting him. It was obvious that they were more frightened of the robed figure.

Alaric's strength seemed renewed. Heryion had seemed to remain unnoticed whilst Alaric prepared for the attack.

The soldiers were clearly shaking as they approached, they were hoping if they would wait long enough something would happen to save them. Their hopes would remain unanswered.

Alaric's sword was as quick as lightening. Even if the soldiers were at their peak performance they would not have been able to defeat him. Within a matter of minutes both soldiers lay on the floor, their eyes staring blankly at the ceiling.

With the soldiers out of the way, Alaric levelled his sword at the hooded figure. There was still a sense of wrongness emanating from him. He wanted to run away, but he knew that was not an option.

"Here's a message from my master."

Whilst Alaric had been fighting he hadn't noticed the annoying tickle in the back of his neck had returned. He knew now that the soldiers had just been a diversion for some new evil. It was lucky for Alaric that Heryion had remained unnoticed and had been watching the man intently.

The hooded man raised his arms and pointed at Alaric. Instantly a bolt of purple light shot from his hands. It all happened so quickly that all

Alaric could do was to raise his sword. Just as the light was about to strike it fizzled out. Although neither of them could see into the hood, they knew there was a look of surprise on the man's face. Heryion stepped into the light and made his presence known.

The man on the other side of the room snatched something small and round from the table and threw it towards Heryion. Heryion dodged it and let it bounce off the floor and into the corner. With the distraction, the hooded figured took his opportunity to exit via a door at the back of the room. Alaric's initial reaction was to pursue, but he thought better of it.

Before either of them could say a word, there was a loud bang and the entire room started to shake. Dust filled the room before everything started to settle. Alaric looked around wildly trying to figure out what had just happened, but when the dust settled nothing had changed. Only a few seconds passed before there was another great bang.

"What was that?" asked Alaric.

"I think that we might have misjudged how long it would take Hadar to arrive," Heryion looked around the room.

Alaric physically relaxed at Heryion's words even though the tension seemed to remain. There was something not right about his attitude. They were about to be rescued and Heryion still remained on edge.

"What are you still worried about?"

"I doubt very much that Hadar's soldiers will know that we are here. If we are not very careful, we could end up dead. We have to get out of here now!"

"But we have to find the others and make sure that they are safe."

"We are going to be no use to them now. If Eldred hasn't already freed them, then they will be rescued when Hadar's army storms the castle. The prison is probably the safest place for them. Since Kerwin is dead, there is no one to give the order to execute them." Heryion's words made perfect sense. There was no way Alaric could argue with him.

The castle was now a hive of activity. Soldiers and servants alike were cluttering the hallways. The soldiers swore at pages and maids calling for them to move out of the way. No one took any notice of the two men heading for the exit. The timing of the arrival of Hadar's army couldn't have been any better. In the chaos, they would be able to remain unnoticed.

They joined the mayhem and hoped that someone would lead them out of the castle. They wandered around for about ten minutes, trying to look as frantic as possible, before they were finally led out into the main courtyard.

They were not prepared for the chaos they found outside. Large holes marked the main wall. Boulders and rubble were strewn across the courtyard. Armed men ran frantically around trying to make sense of it all. The main gate had been secured and had received no major damage.

"How are we going to get out of here now?" Alaric looked around for a means of escape. "All the holes are too high."

As Alaric spoke there came a sudden change in the madness. The soldiers stopped their panicking and became suddenly calm. It was as if whatever had been driving them had come to a sudden halt.

"What are we doing?" they heard one soldier cry out. "Hadar's army is outside these walls. If we stay and fight, we'll all be destroyed!"

"What should we do?" another cried out.

"Throw down your weapons."

"Surrender!"

The sounds of chinking metal rang out throughout the courtyard as the soldiers dropped their weapons. The boulders kept crashing into the wall intermittently, the sound sent a new wave of terror.

"What's happening? Why are all the soldiers suddenly defeated?" Alaric couldn't make sense of what he was seeing.

"We need to get to the other side. If we don't tell Hadar what is happening, then they will rush the castle and many people will die needlessly."

"Why should we worry about them? They made their decision to follow Kerwin and now they will pay for it. This is a war and they have decided whose side they are on. Death will be too good for…" Alaric's sudden hostility shocked Heryion. He raised a questioning eyebrow before he answered.

"I have a theory on that, but now is not the time or the place. Just don't be too hasty to deal out death. Remember this: today's enemies are tomorrow's allies."

Heryion didn't wait to see if Alaric understood what he said. He made his way towards the main wall. All Alaric could do was to follow behind and wonder yet again at what the strange man was talking about. It was becoming slightly more than annoying, but there was nothing he could do about it. He knew well enough now that when Heryion didn't want to explain something, then it would remain unknown.

A large hole had appeared in the wall about a span higher than Alaric's reach. There was plenty of rubble around, but it would take them too long to pile it up high enough for them to escape.

"What are we going to do now?" asked Alaric, worried that another bombardment might be the end of them.

"Just wait," Heryion took a few steps backwards and motioned for Alaric to do the same.

Before long came a high-pitched whistle. It was clear that the sound was getting closer. With a gasp, Alaric suddenly realised there was another boulder flying through the air and it was heading directly for them. Alaric started to backtrack, but Heryion steadied him with a surprisingly strong hand. Alaric tried to struggle free as the projectile came closer, but Heryion would not relinquish his grip.

The large stone came crashing down into the wall. Debris sprayed out all around them. One of the only places that didn't get hit with shrapnel was where they were standing. Alaric's heart had been racing and he only realised when the dust settled and they were still standing. The hole in the wall was now low enough for the both of them to climb through. As they stepped over the wall, they could see the grey of dawn off to the east. They would now have to be especially careful. Hadar's men would be on patrol and they would not be expecting two people to be wandering around outside the castle.

Seeing the light of dawn only made Alaric realise how tired he was. It had been a long night and he was now exhausted. His eyes drooped and his body sagged.

"Come on Alaric. It's not far now. You can rest once we reach the encampment."

Alaric steeled himself and followed Heryion. The lights from the campsite didn't seem that far away. Another boulder flew overhead and came crashing into the wall. That was all the encouragement he needed to keep going.

Again, Heryion kept the lead. He made sure that Alaric stayed close behind. The last thing he wanted was to lose Alaric. In the dull light of dawn, he could easily be mistaken as a spy.

They had only made it half way towards the campsite when they were stopped by a group of soldiers. Alaric had no idea until the soldiers were upon them, Heryion did not seem surprised. Four of the soldiers were armed with crossbows, two aimed at Alaric and two at him.

"Put your hands in the air. You are now our prisoners," the commanding officer spoke gruffly.

"We are not...!" Alaric started to plead their case, but Heryion quickly silenced him.

"We demand to see whoever is in command of this army. We have vital information and need to speak to him now." There was nothing but confidence in his voice.

"I don't think so. All prisoners are to be taken to the corral," the officer had a no-nonsense tone in his voice.

"We are not prisoners. This is Alaric and the Duke will be looking for him."

The soldiers looked at each other. They had obviously heard something of Alaric or else they would have completely ignored them.

"I think we should listen to them chief. If they were from inside the castle, how do we they know who we are looking for?" the soldier sounded somewhat concerned.

"Come with me. Everyone else return to your patrol."

Even though they seemed to trust what Heryion had said, they still walked them in front as though they were prisoners. Alaric was relieved they were finally safe. He almost collapsed as the tension left his body. Everyone noticed him stumble, but no one offered him assistance. Until there was confirmation from Hadar of who they were, the soldiers would not completely trust them.

"Wait here and I will see if Hadar wishes to speak to you."

The campsite was a hive of activity. The siege was almost complete and as soon as the sun had completely risen, the foot soldiers would storm the castle. The soldiers were all preparing themselves for battle.

"He will see you now," the officer returned with a worried look on his face. "Come on now lieutenant, we have work to do."

"I was wondering how long it would take for you to get here," Hadar barked when they arrived at his command tent. "I was a little surprised when Eldred turned up with the others, but he said that you two were still inside. I didn't give you much chance of success. It looks like I've misjudged you."

"So Eldred has made it back with the others?" Alaric's heart jumped at the news.

"Yes. They came back about an hour ago and are now resting." Hadar was about to say something else when there came a loud cheer from outside.

A moment later Hagar entered the tent. There was a broad smile on his face, which showed that his news was going to be good. "We have breached the outer wall. The soldiers are preparing for the attack. All we need is your word and the final stage will start."

"Very good. Give the word. I want the castle secured and Kerwin's head on a plate by mid-morning." Hadar barked the order without any emotion in his voice.

"I don't think that will be necessary," Heryion spoke before Hagar could leave the tent. "The soldiers will offer you no resistance and Kerwin is already dead. All you will have to do is walk up to the castle and they will all surrender."

Hagar waited at the tent flap for his father's instructions. "How can you be so sure that they will not fight to the death?" Hadar didn't completely believe Heryion.

"I don't know what happened, but I saw it myself. None of the soldiers have the will to fight." Alaric added.

"Tell the men to be careful when they take the castle. Make sure that no one attacks unless they are being threatened. That last order is not to be broken, by punishment of death," Hadar left no room for discussion. His order was final and would be obeyed. "You look like you could use something to eat and some sleep. It will be a while before we completely secure the castle so you may as well get some rest."

Alaric didn't argue and Heryion had already disappeared, all Alaric could think was how hungry and tired he was.

"Ah, Alaric! It's good to see that you made it out okay." Alaric was greeted by Eldred as he arrived in the food tent. "I'm glad to see that you were able to confront and defeat Kerwin." Eldred kept his voice low.

"I don't think that Kerwin was behind this," Alaric's voice was pensive. "I think there was another involved. I think that Kerwin was just a pawn." Although Alaric was dead tired there had been something on his mind ever since he left the castle.

"What are you talking about?" Eldred seemed confused.

"There was someone else in the castle. I thought that he was human, but now I'm not so sure. He had a full length robe on with the hood drawn, so I didn't get a good look at him, but when he attacked me, I saw his hands and they looked as though they were green and scaled. I was tired and exhausted so it might very well have been a hallucination, but I can't get the image out of my head. The creature radiated pure evil. It was a feeling that I didn't get from Kerwin. Kerwin just seemed a fanatical fool who believed that he would one day lead the Seven Kingdoms. I don't think that he could arrange a full-on rebellion." As soon as he finished speaking he continued to eat hungrily.

"Was there anything else about this man that you noticed? Anything strange I mean?" Eldred's voice remained low, but seemed extremely concerned.

Alaric tried to think about anything else that could help with the creature's appearance, but nothing came to mind. He was sure that there was something he was forgetting, but all he could think about was sleep.

"Nothing comes to mind, but I'm sure if I get some sleep then I will be able to remember more," Alaric's voice was only just audible.

"I think you're right. You look as though you are ready to drop," Eldred watched Alaric carefully. His face was pale and he looked like he had aged a few years since he had entered the castle. "I will help you to your tent. We'll talk after you have had some rest."

Eldred helped Alaric to his feet once he had finished eating. He was shaky and looked as though he could collapse at any minute. By the time they reached Alaric's tent, Eldred was practically carrying him.

Before his head even touched the hard pillow, Alaric was fast asleep. The ordeal of the previous day and night didn't fade from his mind so easily. His dreams were riddled with past events. His mind twisted things until he wasn't sure what was real and what was fantasy. All the time he thought there was someone in the background watching him. Whenever he tried to see the person there was no one there.

When he awoke, it was late in the day. His mind was still weary although his body felt better. The sun was low in the sky when he surfaced from the tent. The campsite was a buzz. The soldiers were busying themselves with dismantling their tents and moving towards the castle. There had been little time to set up camp, so pulling it down wouldn't take long.

Alaric walked towards the command tent, which had already started to be dismantled. He looked around to find Hadar, but he was nowhere to be seen. Eventually he asked one of the soldiers.

"Excuse me, do you know where the Duke is?" Alaric asked the nearest soldier.

"He has already left for the castle. I wouldn't be surprised if he was already in the Count's room preparing his next move." The solider spat when he mentioned the Count.

Alaric was about to ask after his friends, but the soldier had already gone back to work. There was nothing left for him to do than return to castle. He looked towards the carnage and sighed. It had taken all his energy to escape and now he was going to casually walk back in. He knew that there was no danger there anymore, but he still cringed. The only advantage was another night indoors before they started off again.

Chapter 21: The Orb

Eldred, Heryion, Hawthorne and Alena sat with Hadar and his eldest son in the council room. The taking of the castle had been just as easy as Alaric had explained. Once Hadar's soldiers had breached the walls, they had been met with no resistance. By lunchtime all the opposing soldiers had been locked up and Hadar had moved into the castle. It was late in the day when he had called Eldred and the members of his group to a meeting.

"When Alena and Palentonal arrived at the castle, I knew we had to be on the move quickly if we were going catch you. We pushed hard, but it still seems as though we were a little late."

"I would say that you made good time. I wasn't expecting you for a least another day," Eldred remarked.

When the dwarves and Bern were allowed back into the castle, they made their way to the tavern. The owners had been spared, more because the soldiers wanted somewhere to drink than their implied innocence. They had not been ill-treated since they had been captured, but it was still traumatic, at least that was their excuse for missing the meeting.

After Hadar had finished speaking, Eldred gave them an account of what had happened. When he was finished, he looked towards Heryion for a further account. It was clear that he was not going to speak and Eldred did his best to recall Alaric's account.

"I don't think there can be any doubt, it was definitely a serpentant."

"I'm sorry. You are going to have to back up a moment." Hagar looked puzzled. "I'm sure it was just his imagination. There is no such thing as a serpentant. They are just a myth, a story to tell troublesome children to stop them from misbehaving."

"There are a lot of things in this world that are not easily explained. I think that you'll find that for every old wives' tale there is some amount of truth. The serpentants are a race that have been all but forgotten in the sands of time. It has been many a century since anyone has seen a serpentant, but that is not to say that they don't exist." Eldred crossed his arms.

Before Hagar had a chance to rebuke, there was a knock on the door and a young page entered the room dressed in the Duke's livery. Hadar was not going to take any chances until he was sure that he could trust the Count's people again.

"There's someone here to see you," the page's voice was soft and Hadar could hardly hear him.

Hadar snorted in disgust at the lack of information given. "Well, are you going to tell me who it is?"

"Ah, yes, sorry your grace. He says his name is Alaric." The page's voice only slightly louder.

It was all Hadar could do to remain in his chair. He wanted nothing more than to walk across the room and belt the page across the back of his head; instead he had to bite his tongue and wait for a more appropriate time to scold the page. "Well, let him in!"

"Yes, your grace," the page made an awkward effort to bow before he left.

Alaric was glad to see that most of his friends were there. He looked at Alena and couldn't help himself but smile. Even after all that had happened, she still looked beautiful.

"I'm glad you could join us," Hadar said "You are just in time for Eldred to give us a lesson in mythology." Hadar held the same opinion as his son.

"Thank you." He looked questioningly at Eldred who motioned for him to relax.

"I was explaining that we believe the hooded creature that you saw was a serpentant." Eldred explained.

"A what?" Alaric looked at the others in confusion.

"It seems that there is a lot be learnt here today. This may be a blessing in disguise. A long time ago, the Goddess of Serpents, Serpentine, wanted to create creatures she could use as concubines. She created the serpentants, a half man-half snake like creature. She created seven of these creatures with the hope to breed many more. When the God Kings found out what she had done, they placed a curse on her never to be able to bear children. They also stripped her of the ability to create any more. The seven serpentants were imbued with her powers when she created them and they became very powerful sorcerers. Nyrra promised to help Serpentine to get her revenge on the God Kings. She listened to every word he told her. All Nyrra wanted to do was to steal her power and take control of her followers. Serpentine was betrayed to her death by Nyrra. It seems now that her serpentants have arisen and are working for Nyrra. This is something that I had not been expecting." The words didn't seem real. It was as if he was repeating a story he had heard when he had been a child.

"If they are such powerful magicians, then why did it let Alaric leave? Why didn't it stay to destroy him?" Hadar asked the question that they were all thinking.

"I don't know. All I can do is try and surmise. Nyrra took control of the serpentants by force, which would have hurt their pride. I don't think that they would be joining the fight, but it seems that Nyrra's control is more powerful than I had thought. Whatever the reason, it doesn't bode well for us." Eldred explained.

"Then we should chase down this creature and destroy it!" barked Hawthorne.

"Even if we knew where the serpentant was going, it wouldn't make any sense for us to chase it. This is something that we weren't expecting and I need some time to think it over."

"So what do we do now?" asked Alena.

"We wait here until Palentonal gets better. The physicians say he should be ready to be on the move again by lunchtime tomorrow. All the wounds were superficial and there will be no lasting damage. Now I think the best thing is for us to do is relax until then."

"I think that is a marvelous idea. I think that we could all do with a good rest." Although it was Eldred who suggested it, it was Hadar that brought the meeting to an end.

After they left the room Eldred pulled Alaric off to the side. "We need to have a talk. Heryion told me what happened." The words weren't coming easy for Eldred. "I need to have a talk with you about magic."

They continued in silence until they came to a vacant room. Eldred opened the door and walked inside. There was a small table and four chairs in the centre of the room. A small lamp sat in the middle of the table, which Eldred lit before they sat.

"I had hoped that we would have had a chance to talk at Elhjem, but unfortunately we ran out of time. I should have started your training sooner. If it wasn't for Heryion, I don't know what would have happened."

"What are you talking about?"

"I'm sorry. This was never going to be an easy conversation. I suppose the best way to explain is to tell you the different forms of magic. This might get a little confusing so if there is something that you don't understand please stop me." Eldred paused before he continued.

"Now there are a number of different factions of magic, but there are two major divisions. There is incantation and gesture magic, and there is thought magic. Now to get your terminology right from the beginning, those who practice incantation magic are called magicians. Those who practice thought magic are called sorcerers. Those who can do both are called wizards. Anyone can become a magician; all it takes is many years of study. Most kings and some high nobles will have a magician in their court. Most of them are harmless enough, only those who constantly study come into any great power. A lot of magicians are nothing more than glorified court jesters and are happy just to get a few laughs and cheers. Most of the ancient texts which contain the most powerful spells are stored on the Isle of Wizards. Sorcerers, on the other hand, can be very dangerous. The ability to practise magic purely by thought is a hereditary trait. All sorcerers must have a direct blood relative who has the skill. Whether or not they receive training, they will practice magic. Sometimes it is nothing more than causing rain when they ask for it or receiving a nice gift on Harvest Day, but it will happen. However, some people are more dangerous than that and can even cause the death of others or themselves. It takes a lot of will power and strength to control the type of magic required to be a great sorcerer. A wizard, who can practice both types of magic, is very rare to this world."

"Kerwin practised magic. His spell was very powerful; does that mean that he was a sorcerer?" Alaric asked.

"No, but that was a very good question. There are a number of magical artefacts that can increase someone's ability to create magic. He would have had to know some incantations already. The artefacts are very rare and vary in power." Eldred explained.

"Like the Ruby Stone?" Alaric added.

"Yes. The seven stones are the most powerful of magical talismen. I doubt very much that the artefact Kerwin possessed would have been anything like the stone, but from what Heryion has told me, it contains a considerable amount of power."

"So is that why I can create some magic, because of the stone?"

"Yes and no," Eldred said rather slyly. "The stone contains a great deal of power, most likely the most powerful of the seven. That is not where you gain your power from." Eldred walked around the table.

"What are you saying?"

"You are a sorcerer Alaric." Eldred blurted the answer out knowing that Alaric already truly knew the truth. "It is the only way you can use the Ruby Stone. If you didn't already have the power in you, then the stone would consume you." Eldred tried to add in some extra information ease the burden.

"Why didn't I know until now? Why didn't you tell me?" Alaric sounded shocked.

"I knew that this wasn't going to be easy for you to handle and I had already dumped enough information on you when we met. I thought that I would wait until we reached Elhjem before I spoke to you, but then we ran out of time.

"So you're saying that my parents were also *sorcerers*?"

"Yes, but not in the way that you think…"

"You would have thought that I would have noticed my parents using magic when I was growing up." Alaric didn't seem to hear what Eldred had said.

"You have the power in you and it was passed down from at least one of your parents, more than likely both. The only thing is that the parents you knew when you were growing up weren't your birth parents." Eldred paused and waited for Alaric to respond.

Alaric felt foolish for the question. He knew that his parents weren't his own. Now there was a chance he could find out who they really were. "Then who are my real parents?"

"That is the problem. We don't know who your birth parents are. That was one of the things with being the Chosen One. Your life must be shrouded in mystery and not knowing your parents was one of the conditions of the prophecy." It seemed to be the easiest way for Eldred to qualify the situation.

Alaric didn't respond. The look on his face was enough answer for Eldred. It was obvious that the revelation had come as a shock. Eldred had always known it was going to be hard telling Alaric the truth, but he had hoped his response would have been different. He hoped that he had not waited too long to tell him.

"I think that I would like to be left alone now," Alaric's voice was deflated.

Eldred wanted to say something, but knew that it would be better to let Alaric have time to think about what he had just been told. The conversation was never going to go well, but he had hoped it would have gone better. They had only a day or two before they had to continue and they needed Alaric at full strength.

Leaving Alaric in peace,, Eldred wandered the halls of the castle. There was still a lot on his mind. The appearance of the serpentant worried him. He knew more about the creatures than he told the council. More to the fact he wanted to know *which* of the serpentants they were up against.

Without paying much attention Eldred found his way to his room. He was sure he was going to find something in the prophecy to explain their situation. The only problem was that he didn't know where he would find it. With their new revelations, the information could be anywhere amongst the thousands of pages. In his room, he was greeted by someone sitting on his bed.

"What are you doing here?" Eldred seemed a little put out.

"I thought that we should have a chat. I figured after that meeting you would be having a little talk with Alaric." Heryion didn't seem to notice the irritation in Eldred's voice.

"You saw the serpentant. Do you know who it is?" Eldred walked further into the room and sat at the small table against the opposite wall.

"I have my suspicions, but I don't know for sure. That is neither here nor there. The question you should be asking is, what the creature was doing here. Kerwin was not exactly one of his elite knights. I would have guessed he was more of an annoyance to Nyrra than a devoted follower. Why would Nyrra send a serpentant? And if I'm right, Kerwin was looking after the serpentant and not the other way around. The serpentants have never liked the yoke that Nyrra placed on them. I don't think they would be helping him keep check on a minor noble, with no great army to speak of. These are some very disturbing questions." Heryion was being as mysterious as ever.

"There is no need to take that tone with me. I know the questions as well as you do, what I need are the answers," Eldred barked without really thinking what he was saying.

"If I had answers, be sure that I would be sharing it with you."

"I'm sorry. There have been a lot of things that aren't making sense. On a side issue, I would really like to know who you are and what part you are to play?"

"I think that you will find some more answers in the morning." Heryion dodged the question. "This entire situation might make more sense then, although I have a feeling that it will give us more questions than answers." Heryion stood.

"What are you talking about? Is this going to be another game of cryptic clues? I am too tired to play." Eldred's shoulders had physically slumped.

"There is something here, something magical. Unfortunately, I don't know where it is. I am sure that if you relax, you will know what I am talking about." With that Heryion promptly left the room.

Eldred sighed deeply once the door was closed. He knew the little man had an important role to play, but he didn't have to be so annoying. Heryion knew more than he was telling and that was very frustrating. There had been a gentle tug ever since they had returned to the castle. He had just put it down to some left-over traces of Kerwin's magic and blocked it out of his mind. Lying down on his bed, Eldred let his senses roam. What Heryion had said was true, there was a powerful artefact somewhere and he couldn't leave it behind.

Before Eldred could find what he was looking for, he fell asleep. The strain of the previous night had taken its toll. He had not slept in two days and couldn't keep his eyes open.

Eldred was woken with a huge roar in his ears. What had just been a gentle pull at the back of his mind, was now deafening. Eldred put his hands up to his ears, but even as he did, he knew that it was not going to stop the sound. Nothing was going to stop the roaring until he discovered where it was directing him. His senses had continued to work even though he had been sleeping.

Eldred walked as if he was still asleep, in a trance. The sound inside his mind was directing him to what the probe had found. Whatever it was Eldred knew it was not good. Kerwin had found or been given something very powerful.

The path led him towards the Count's bedroom. Eldred should have known that was where it would end up. Kerwin would not have left anything so important lying around where anyone could get it. The closer he came to the room, the stronger the feeling became. Whatever it was, it was giving off a huge amount of magical energy. There was also something else, a feeling of dread, a feeling that made Eldred very uncomfortable.

As soon as Eldred touched the door handle, the screaming inside his head was suddenly silenced. All that remained was the feeling of dread and the clear feeling of magic. He hesitated before opening the door. He wasn't sure that he wanted to find out what was inside. Whatever it was, it was pure evil and contained a huge amount of magic.

"I thought that I would find you here sooner or later." The sudden voice made Eldred jump.

"I really wish you wouldn't do that." Eldred felt like he was a child breaking into his brother's room. "What's inside?"

"That is what we are about to find out." Heryion's attention was diverted. "I have never felt anything like this before."

"I know. There is something extremely evil in there." Eldred breathed once, before opening the door.

A great wave of evil struck Eldred across the face as he entered the room. He staggered backwards until he was out in the corridor and suppressed the urge to vomit. The evil seemed to have no effect on Heryion. He wandered into the room without a worry and busied himself lighting the wall lamps whilst Eldred composed himself and re-entered the room. The pure evil still radiated, but Eldred was able to block out the dread that he had been feeling. He still looked unsteady on his feet as he scanned the room.

With the room sufficiently lit, Heryion went straight to the desk at the far end of the room. Although his senses were not in tune with the radiating evil, he knew exactly where to look. A small chest sat in the middle of the desk. It was clearly the focal point even though it looked completely out of place. It was obvious it was what they were looking for.

"What do you think is inside?" Heryion asked as he ran his hand over the chest.

Eldred shook his head. "Whatever it is, I don't think that you are giving it the respect that it deserves. I have never felt this way before. Whatever is in there, it is very evil and very powerful. I think that we might have found the source of Kerwin's power and the reason why the serpentant was here."

Returning Eldred's look with a frown, Heryion slowly opened the chest. When he saw what was inside he whistled loudly. Whatever it was had impressed him, which made Eldred even more irritated.

"I never thought I would live to see the day." A large smile appeared on Heryion's face. The feeling that Eldred was getting from the chest brought a grimace to his face. "It is truly spectacular."

"What is it?" the irritation thick in his voice.

"It's the Orb of Hazyra," the words made Eldred flinch back against the far wall.

"What in the names of the God Kings is the Orb of Hazyra doing here?" There was horror in his voice. "I thought the orb had been lost many centuries ago. If Nyrra had found the orb, it doesn't make any sense for it to be given to such a lowly servant. With the orb in his possession, he would have been able to break the seal on his prison."

"It seems as though it has been found."

"I wished it had remained lost. The Orb is pure evil. Its power has corrupted absolutely everything in the past and it seems as though it is doing so again. Things are starting to make sense. If Kerwin had stumbled across the orb, then he would have been able to communicate with Nyrra. Nyrra must have sent the serpentant to keep an eye on Kerwin until he was able to send someone he could trust to regain it." Eldred added.

"Does that mean we can use the orb against Nyrra?" The question came from the doorway.

"What are you doing here, Alaric?"

"All of a sudden I felt a sudden urge to come here," Alaric seemed confused.

Suddenly a shadow passed over the room; even though the lamps had not dimmed, it seemed as though the light had been sucked out. The orb started to glow a deep purple and the feeling of horror increased. As it did, Heryion quickly shut the lid.

"And not a moment too soon," Heryion almost chuckled as he spoke. Even with the lid closed, the evil still radiated from the orb.

"To answer your question, no. There is no way we could use the orb against Nyrra. The orb itself is pure evil. There is every chance that Kerwin was a good man before he found it. As soon as he touched the orb, Nyrra would have trapped his soul," Eldred explained.

"You know the Orb wasn't always evil?" Heryion sounded somewhat surprised. "It was once a symbol for peace before it was corrupted by Nyrra's evil. It looks as though I've forgotten how powerful that evil is."

"Then we leave it here and move on," Alaric looked as though he was suffering the evil effects.

"I think you should go back to your room and get some rest," Eldred interrupted before Heryion had a chance to answer. "There will be time in the morning to discuss everything. I think for now we all need our sleep."

Eldred gave Heryion a knowing look before he placed a reassuring hand on Alaric's shoulder.

Once Alaric was safely back in bed, Eldred returned to the Count's room. He knew that Heryion would be waiting. The orb presented more than one problem. They could not take the orb with them, nor could they leave it behind. They couldn't risk someone else falling under its spell.

When he returned to the room he found Heryion sitting at the desk. The lid was open and he was staring at the orb inside. The room was still normal even though the orb was glowing a gentle purple. There was a strange look on his face. Eldred couldn't describe it, but it filled his mind with concern.

"What are you doing? Shut the lid!" Eldred almost lurched towards the desk. The only thing that stopped him was Heryion's raised arm.

"Relax, Eldred, the orb has no effect on me." As if to qualify his remark, he negligently picked up the orb and tossed it from one hand to another.

"Okay, okay, I get your point. There is no need to show off. There are plenty of things that I can do that you cannot." There was a slight twitch above Eldred's left eye before Heryion replaced the orb and shut the lid.

"I'm sorry. I guess sometimes I'm still a child at heart." Heryion looked past Eldred, as if there was someone behind him, before he returned his attention. "But that isn't important. I think I know what to do with it."

Eldred wasn't sure if he trusted him. There was something about him that didn't fill Eldred with confidence. He knew that the orb didn't have any effect on Heryion, but he wasn't sure that was a good thing. If the orb got into the wrong hands, then they would be in a lot of trouble.

"I don't see how you could have found a solution so quickly. There is no apparent answer to the riddle. We can't take it with us and we can't leave it behind."

"I thought that there might be a chance to reverse whatever it was that Nyrra did to the orb, but it seems as though that's not an option. It is a shame really; it was once a wondrous talisman. Anyway, I will destroy the orb," Heryion spoke with a touch of sorrow in his voice.

A look of pure horror came over Eldred's face. "I don't think you have really thought this out. We don't know for sure that the orb can be destroyed. If it can, I'm pretty sure that will mean certain death for whoever does it and whoever is within a twenty-league radius. This thing is so closely tied to Nyrra that I doubt he would let it be destroyed. I think this is an unnecessary risk. There has to be another solution."

"There is no other. If we take the orb with us, it is only a matter of time before it corrupts one of us. At the very worst it will corrupt either yourself or Alaric. I think you can vouch for it yourself, the feelings you have been getting from the orb, even when it's protected in the chest. It seems whoever made the prison didn't make it good enough. I don't doubt the serpentant, whatever its motives, knows that the orb exists. After we leave, I'm sure the creature will come back in search of it, if it hasn't already left. I know the risks involved in destroying the orb and I know how to destroy it. I think that you are being a little melodramatic with your forecast," there was nothing but confidence in Heryion's voice. "The risk of someone getting their hands on the orb is worse than the risk of destroying it."

Eldred knew he was right. There was no other option. They couldn't leave the orb behind; it would certainly end up in Nyrra's hands if they did. If they took it with them then at least one of them would be corrupted by its power. Eldred could mask the power of the orb for a short period, but eventually the evil would return. Destroying it was the only option. It was another turn that he had not expected. The prophecy was continually changing and it was impossible for Eldred to keep up. He was sure that Heryion was going to be at Alaric's side at the end, but now that was going to be impossible.

"You're right. There is no other option. It's too much of a liability to leave around. Are you sure that you can destroy it? There is a great amount of power in the orb. It will take a lot of power to destroy it." Eldred conceded to Heryion's point. "When will you leave?"

"I will leave right away. The fact that Alaric was drawn here tonight means I must leave. There is no telling who else the orb will try and reach out to. We were just lucky that we made it here first." Heryion thought for a moment after watching the reaction on Eldred's face. "You don't need me to continue. Don't worry about me. I will find you again." Heryion picked up the chest and walked towards the door without waiting for Eldred to respond.

"Good luck!" Eldred spoke to the empty desk as Heryion walked out of the room.

The further Heryion walked away the more evil feeling lessened. There was nothing more that Eldred wanted to do than go back to sleep, but he knew there was no time. It would be morning soon and there was a lot that he needed to do before everyone woke. In the morning, he would have to move quickly to allow them to leave.

Chapter 22: Leave the Past Behind

Eldred found Hadar in what he had made his military study. After taking the castle there was a lot of planning to do. Hadar would have to reassign the hierarchy and place new people in charge until a new Count could be found. The first task, however, was to rebuild the walls.

"Now is not really a good time. I have a parade of meetings this morning. There are so many people I have to see and they all have appointments." Hadar didn't seem interested in speaking with Eldred.

"We go back a long time Hadar. I have helped you through many tough situations, both you and your father, and I think I have earned the respect to gain your ear." Eldred was angry.

Hadar sighed loudly, his shoulders slumped. "Of course, I'm sorry. Ever since we took the castle, I have been swamped by potential Counts, pages, accountants and other minor positions. It seems no one was happy with their last. It will take me all week to sift through the paperwork and see all the people who want to see me. This is truly the ugly side of warfare." The joke wasn't lost on Eldred and he shared a brief laugh with his old friend. "Now what is it that I can do for you?"

"We have to leave this afternoon. Palentonal is fit to ride and we need to replenish our supplies. We need enough to reach the capital."

"You are going to see the King?"

"I need to get King Lisle XII to pledge his support. Time grows short and we need all the help we can get."

"Well, I have instructed Hagar to put together two battalions and send them east. I will need to keep the rest to keep the order here, with my son to take control. There is no telling how many other followers are in my province." It was not much, but it was better than nothing.

"I thank you for your support. Every man will count." Eldred had not come to discuss further aid from Hadar, but was glad that he offered it freely.

"Your next problem is convincing Lisle that he needs to support the Alliance. He will be as stubborn as ever, especially if there is no gain in it for him," Hadar added.

"I know, but I must try. We need to pass through Lel Dinion anyway, so I may as well try my luck."

"I can tell you what else I can do for you. I'll come with you to the capital. I will need to send him a report of what happened here anyway and the knowledge that Nyrra has agents in his land might sway his decision. I also need to ask him for some financial assistance. Besides, I think that my sons can deal with the boring details of this place." The offer suited Hadar more than Eldred, but any assistance was welcome.

"I thought that you had one of the richest Duchies in the Kingdom. Why do you need to ask Lisle for money?"

"Unfortunately, I don't have a bottomless treasury. It will take a small fortune to repair the damage that Kerwin has done to the land. All the fields have been destroyed, not to mention the damage we did breeching the walls. It seems that Kerwin wasn't the most frugal of Counts. There is not a cent left in the coffers. All the money to get things back up and running will have to come from my own treasury. Lisle has a special wartime fund for his nobles. If a castle has been taken, then he will pay for some of the repairs and re-staffing bills. I still think he wonders why there are so many battles between the minor nobles." Hadar shook his head at the thought. "I will have everything ready for our departure after lunch."

The brusque knock on the door brought their meeting to an abrupt end. Eldred was more than happy with the result. He had only been hoping for some supplies, but had received so much more. As he left, he cursed the prophecy for again being so obscure.

Eldred had already visited everyone else and explained everything. The only person he still had to see was Alaric. He was hoping that Alaric might have come to terms with his situation.

Alaric was not in his room when Eldred came to see him. To his surprise, he found Alaric training in the exercise yard with some of Hadar's soldiers. By the sweat on his face, it was clear that he had been working for some time. Eldred waited for him to finish sparring before he approached.

"I'm glad that I've found you," Eldred started when Alaric acknowledged him. "We need to talk."

"I've had enough talking. It seems that all I do is talk. It's time for action," Alaric spoke between puffs of breath. "Who wants another round?" Alaric turned his back on Eldred and called out to the soldiers.

There were a few murmured responses before someone volunteered. It was clear that Alaric had yet to be bested and no one wanted to be embarrassed for a second time. Eldred watched the fight until Alaric had successfully defeated another man.

"We're leaving this afternoon. I would take your chance to rest. It will be a long journey to the capital."

"I'll be ready." Alaric didn't even face Eldred when he spoke to him. He kept his watch on the soldiers waiting for someone else to volunteer to fight him.

Eldred spent the rest of his time pouring through the prophecy. He was sure he was going to find some more information that would help them on their journey, but when the time came to leave he had not found anything useful. He rubbed his eyes before he looked at the pageboy who had come to collect him.

"The horses are all saddled and ready, my Lord. All the others are in the courtyard waiting for you," There was a quiver in the page's voice, as if he was afraid.

Eldred didn't respond. The prophecy was the only thing remaining of his. His packs had been taken earlier, but he refused to be separated from the large tome. He felt comfort when he was near it.

The group had assembled in the courtyard by the main gate. Alaric remained on the outer, it was clear that he didn't want to socialise with the others. Eldred watched him closely as he joined the rest of them. There was something disturbing about his demeanour.

"Are we ready?" Eldred spoke as he had mounted Tormenta, his white stallion. Everyone murmured their response.

They rode out of the castle with Hadar at the lead. In the light of day, it was more apparent the devastation that Kerwin had caused to the land. The fields remained bare and the land looked diseased. The only trees that remained were old and leafless. Hadar's face was stony hard as they rode past the desolation.

"How long will it take us to get to Lel Dinion?" asked Hawthorne as he rode at the head of the line with Hadar.

"If we ride hard, then only two days, but I don't think we will be able to ride that hard with Palentonal. Hopefully, it won't take us more than four. The highway runs straight towards Lel Dinion. It should be a pleasant enough journey."

Alaric rode for the morning by himself. They all tried in turns, except for the two leaders, to speak to him. He muttered a brief response, but it was obvious that he wanted to be alone, his mood only decreased as they continued.

The land around them had the opposite effect to Alaric's mood. The desolated landscape quickly changed to lush farm-land and then to sparse forest. The highway remained and shortened only slightly as they entered the forest. The road was one of the major trade routes in Hondin Lel and was always maintained by the King, making it a lot easier for them to travel.

They stopped for lunch by a small brook. The sweat dripping off Palentonal showed he was desperate for rest. As much as he had not said anything, it was clear that he was struggling. Alaric took his lunch alone.

"What are we going to do about him?" asked Alena.

"I don't know. The news of his heritage must have been hard. I hope that he just needs time to come to terms with it. I'm sure he will be fine in time." Eldred was trying to reassure himself as much as anyone else.

"I think that I won't try and speak with him until we are ready to go again, it will be at least another half an hour before Palentonal is fit." They wanted to make it to Lel Caminon before nightfall and would have to ride hard to make it. An extra half hour's rest should give them an extra two or three hours in the saddle.

Alena sat down next to Alaric and put a comforting hand on his shoulder. He thought about brushing it off, but decided he liked it. There was something very comforting about Alena. Alaric felt an affinity with her and couldn't think of anyone he would rather be with.

"Are you okay?" she had thought to comfort him with much more eloquent words, but when she sat down they were all she could think of.

Alaric thought for a moment, still staring across the stream, and then turned his head to hers, the expression on his face was unusual. The wry grin almost turned into laughter when he saw her reaction. "I am sorry," Alaric smiled. "I'm fine."

The revelation shocked Alena more than the expression on his face. "What do you mean? We have all been so worried about you and you tell me you're fine."

"Please let me explain before you get upset. I didn't mean to make you worry. The news about my parents was disturbing to start with, but after I had a moment to think about it, it all made perfect sense. I knew in my heart that there was something different about me and it wasn't just that I was from out of town. I realised that this was something that I had come to terms with a long time ago." The smile remained on Alaric's face. He started to reach out and stroke Alena's cheek, but withdrew at the last moment.

"Why have you not been speaking to anyone? Eldred is worried that he has broken something inside of you."

"Good, that was the idea. He should have been honest with me from the start. How am I supposed to trust him if I know he's keeping secrets? I think this has more of an impact than just telling him. He needs to know that he can't manipulate me anymore. I've accepted who I am and what I must do," the words cut from Alaric's mouth and Alena knew he spoke the truth. "I think that we should head back to the others and please don't give away our little secret. I will speak with Eldred in due course."

They returned to the group and Alena remained quiet as promised. She hinted, if she didn't outright lie, that she had talked things through with Alaric and he was now alright. The lie wasn't far from the truth, but it still didn't sit right and made her uncomfortable, however, everyone seemed happy, which did settle her conscience.

It wasn't until they were on the road again that Alaric realised that Heryion was missing. He had been so wrapped up in his own thoughts. "Where's Heryion?"

"We found something that was very evil and Heryion has gone to take care of it," Eldred's answer didn't give any information and this irked Alaric.

"If we are going to continue together, then you must trust me. I need information if I am to defeat Nyrra."

"I know Alaric, and I am sorry. I don't mean to be so obtuse; it's just when you have led my life, it is hard to let go of your secrets." Eldred paused and Alaric thought he was going to leave it at that. "We found the Orb of Hazyra," Eldred sighed. "Besides the seven stones, it is one of the most powerful magical artefacts still remaining from the ancient world. The orb itself is imbued with evil and Heryion has gone to destroy it."

Eldred continued to explain in more detail the power of the orb and why they could not take it with them. As they spoke, some dark clouds loomed in the sky ahead of them. The more he spoke the darker and closer they came. It wasn't until he had finished did the skies open up. At first the rain was only a light drizzle and a mild inconvenience, but as the afternoon wore on the rain increased in both size and intensity.

The wind whipped as the rain beat down. An occasional bolt of lightning lit up the sky and the inevitable peal of thunder made the horses whinny and jump. Even the well trained elvish horses seemed afraid of the weather. There was something very unsettling about their circumstance. The once dry, hard packed road was now muddy and slippery. The ride was becoming all but impossible.

"This is getting ridiculous. We should take shelter and wait for the rain to pass," Hawthorne called to Hadar.

"The trees will not give us much cover and besides, we are not far from town. It will be nightfall in less than an hour. There is no point staying outside when we can be sitting inside by a nice warm fire," Hadar called back over the storm.

"I don't think that this is a natural storm." Eldred had done his best to ride to the front. "At first I wasn't sure, but now I'm positive. Someone is controlling this storm and directing it towards us. Our only salvation will be reaching Lel Caminon," Eldred's words, only heard by the two in the lead, brought no reassurance.

They should have reached Lel Caminon well before nightfall, but the extreme conditions made it impossible. The night was well upon them before the lights of the town were in view. The weather belted down on them and with each passing, miserable, minute the storm increased. With the light completely gone, the road became more treacherous.

"We need light!" Hadar called into the darkness, hoping Eldred was within earshot. "There is no chance of lighting any of the torches in this storm."

"This is a good chance for you to learn some magic." Eldred spoke to Alaric who was riding next to him.

"What did you say?" asked Alaric, whose attention had been elsewhere. He had felt the abnormality when the storm had begun. Since then, he had been trying to focus on the source. Just when he thought he had found it, something had distracted him.

Eldred repeated himself and waited for Alaric's response. He also included what they would be doing. "Wouldn't it better for us to try and find the source of the storm?" Alaric called out.

"I have been trying to. No matter how hard I search, I can't find their exact location. Whoever created the spell is very powerful. They are blocking their location and there's nothing I can do can break it." As Eldred finished his statement there was a cry from the leaders.

"The lights of the town! It can be no more than half a league away," Hadar's voice boomed into the storm.

It was an hour past dusk when they arrived at the gates Lel Caminon. A small spiked wooden fence circled the town. The posts stood three paces high and would stop attack from bandits only. A besieging army would have no problems breaching the wall. Despite the terrible conditions, a pair of sentries guarded the southern gate. The two looked drenched and not pleased to be out of the warmth of the guardhouse.

"Halt, and state your business!" One of the sentries boomed towards the travelers, not sure which one was the leader.

"It's raining quite heavily out here friend. We're looking for shelter and some hot food. If you let us in, we will make for the Laughing Donkey. That was the best inn when I was last here." Hadar was trying to familiarise himself with the guards. If they seemed like locals, it would be easier for them to gain entrance.

"I'm sorry *friend*, but after dark there is no admittance into the town without written notice. These are troubling days and we cannot be too careful. You'll have to turn around and go back the way you came. If you are lucky, you might come across a friendly farmer who will let you sleep in his barn." The guard couldn't hide his displeasure.

"I am Duke Hadar and this is Prince Hawthorne of Remidia. You have one last chance to admit us or you'll spend a week in the stocks. Do you think the Mayor will be pleased if you left royalty standing out in the rain?" Hadar's tone was filled with confidence and more than a hint of irritation.

The sentry now seemed less sure of himself. They had received no word that the Duke and a Prince would be arriving late, but they were not always privy to such information. The weather could easily have delayed their arrival to past nightfall. He wanted nothing more than return to the warmth of the guard house, but he would not be bullied into opening the gate, no matter how much he wanted to be out of the rain.

"Okay. If you are who you say you are, then you will have the required documents to prove who you are. If you show me your papers, I will let you pass." The sentry would not be bluffed.

"Of course I have the papers, but I will not bring them out in this weather. Now I will not ask you again to open these gates!" It was at the point that Hadar realised that he had left the appropriate documentation behind. In the rush of battle, he had not thought to take them with him. It was clear that he was losing his temper as the storm still raged around them.

"I'm sorry then, my instructions are clear. No one can enter after dark." The guard had a smug smile on his face.

The sentry dropped his guard for a second, but that was all the time Hadar needed. With a move, quicker than his build would have suggested, Hadar kicked out and struck the guard across the side of his helmet. The blow was enough to knock the sentry off his feet. Hawthorne was just as quick to act. He had drawn his sword and levelled it at the advancing sentry.

"I'm sorry that it had to come to this, but I really must insist that you admit us now." Hadar had also drawn his sword. "If you really want to, you can alert the night watchman after we have passed through the gates."

The sentry knew when he had been beaten. There was no doubt that they would kill both if they were not allowed into the city. He would alert the night watch as soon as they were out of sight. There was no way he was going to let them get away with the insult. The only problem was if they were who they said they were, chances were good that he would lose his job. The thoughts passed through his mind as he opened the gate.

Hadar led the way into the city. Hawthorne waited until everyone had passed through before letting the other sentry go. The sound of their horse's hooves, sloshing on the cobblestones could just be heard over the rain. The buildings of Lel Caminon gave them some shelter, but it was still a miserable night. Soon enough they saw the lights of the Laughing Donkey and by the sounds of things that the inn was full of life.

"Wait here," Hadar said as they reached the front door. "I will send someone out for the horses and our bags. After they take the horses, come inside and meet me in the back room. They don't like people from out of town and things can get rough. I will speak to the owner and he will have a room prepared for us."

As much as no one wanted to remain out in the weather, they didn't want to get involved in a bar fight. They waited out in the rain as they were told until a number of groomsmen came for the horses and bags. When the last of their pack donkeys were taken away, Eldred led the way into the backroom, ignoring the onlookers. Hadar was waiting for them as he had promised and on one table there were a number of towels. On another, there were places set for them to eat. A roaring fire crackled in a fireplace on the far wall.

"The rooms are being made ready and baths are being drawn. Dry yourselves in here and the evening meal will be brought in shortly," Hadar explained as he dried himself. He had already removed his shirt and was working his towel furiously. His muscles rippled and Alaric couldn't help but be impressed with his physique.

"I might go and have a bath. I will eat when I get back." Alena was never shy, but she felt as though she should leave.

No one spoke as she left. There was a clear tension in the room that dissipated when she was gone. The fire did an excellent job in drying out their clothes. The owner of the inn had left them all dry robes in which to change into and as soon as they were changed their meals were brought in. Alena returned and a smell of rose water followed her, which caught Alaric's attention. The scent was only there for a second before it was smothered by the smell of wet clothes.

Their meal was interrupted by the owner of the inn. There was a concerned look on his face and he motioned for Hadar to speak with him in private.

"Keshet, I have no secrets. You can speak freely in front of the others," Hadar spoke will a half mouth full of food.

"Yes, my lord. It seems that the sentries have gone to the Night Marshal and told them of your entry. There is a group of the night watch on their way here," Keshet spoke nervously.

"Who is the Night Marshal? Is it still Salem?" Hadar asked after he had swallowed another mouthful.

"No! Salem was killed over a month ago in a hunting accident. There is a new Night Marshall. His name is Benoni and he is a tough man. They say he came from the capital with a grudge on his shoulder. Rumour has it that he was part of the King's own guard, but was disgraced for his methods of interrogation. He hasn't been here long, but I have not heard a soft word spoken about him. Please Hadar, I don't want any trouble," Keshet sounded truly worried.

"At peace Keshet. There will be no trouble tonight," Hadar spoke calmly as he pushed his empty plate away.

"You know that you are out of favour with the King. Benoni will know this. He will not give you any special treatment because you are a Duke."

"It will be fine. You can leave us now." It was clear that Hadar did not want to discuss the matter further. He also seemed annoyed with what Keshet had said.

Keshet did as he was told. There was nothing more that he could say and he knew better than to argue with Hadar. The man was overpowering not only in stature but in spirit as well.

Looking around the room Alaric realised that all their weapons had been taken by the groomsmen. They were completely unarmed. The only weapon they had was the Ruby Stone, which was safely tucked away in the chest hanging by his belt. He was still loathed to use it; he still didn't know if he controlled it or it controlled him. He would need a lot of training before he was comfortable using it again. The new revelations had made him more curious at his talent.

"Don't worry. Everything is going to be alright." Hadar looked around the room at the concerned faces. It was obvious that Alaric was not the only one to realise that they were unarmed.

It was not long before they heard the sound of many footsteps outside their door. There could be no doubt who was on the other side. There was a short pause before the door was pushed open. Everyone in the room remained calm as Hadar instructed. Most of them ignored their sudden intrusion and continued eating. Hadar casually looked up from his tankard at their visitors.

"Ah, you must be Benoni. How can we help you this evening?" Hadar stayed seated as he spoke.

"That would be Marshall to you!" Benoni's voice didn't have a hint of humour. His demeanour was sour, as if he had been interrupted from doing something much more important. "My guards have told me that you and your companions have broken the law. I would appreciate it if you came along peacefully. I would hate for someone to lose their life." Benoni looked around the room, sizing up his opposition as he spoke. When he saw that they were all unarmed, his confidence grew. "A night in the cells and then we shall deal with you in the morning."

"I don't think that will be necessary. My name is Duke Hadar and this is the personal entourage of Prince Hawthorne. You would be ill advised to detain his highness. He is to be in Lel Dinion by tomorrow night and I would not be the one to make him late." The soldiers standing behind Benoni shifted uncomfortably at the mention of Hawthorne. Benoni on the other hand, did not miss a beat.

"If this is who you say it is, I would have been informed of your arrival. If this is the Prince of Remidia, then he is travelling in this land unannounced and therefore does not have any diplomatic rights. Now if you please, I have some more pressing matters to take care of." Benoni's arrogance was infuriating.

Hadar's anger was only dwarfed by Hawthorne's. The Prince's face had turned red and it looked as though he was about to tear the arms off his chair. Benoni's words were enough to start an incident between the two Kingdoms. Hadar spoke before Hawthorne had a chance to retaliate.

"I would think very carefully about your next move, it could be the last you ever make," Hadar's tone had changed from friendly chatter to stone cold.

"I know who you are, Duke Hadar," he almost spat the words. "You would be the last person the King would trust with such a mission. Unless you can produce the appropriate papers, I will be forced to place you under arrest."

It was clear the Benoni was not going to back down unless he had hard proof. The proof that he required was proof that they could not provide. Hawthorne no longer had the documents he needed to prove his lineage. When there was no movement from the table, Benoni walked into the room allowing his soldiers to follow. There was only room for half of them; the others had to wait outside.

It was now clear that there would be no easy resolution to their argument. Benoni would not back down and they could not spend the night in prison. Eventually they would be freed, but that would waste too much time. The soldiers had already drawn their swords and were preparing for the inevitable.

"Eldred, if you would do the honours." Hadar didn't take his gaze off Benoni.

"I really wish that it didn't have to come to this." Eldred grumbled as he rose from his seat. He knew from the start what Hadar was doing and that he would be the only one who could save them. Hadar's rhetoric had given him enough time to draw the energy he needed to create his spell.

"Dyelichna!" The word had absolutely no relevance to the spell, but Eldred felt that he needed some theatrics to get his point across.

The spell took effect immediately. The soldier to Benoni's left went suddenly rigid. His sword dropped from his hand as his arms were pinned by his side.

"What's happening?" the soldier could only mumble his words before his lips froze.

The other soldiers stopped their advance when they saw what had happened. Hawthorne was also quick to react and snatched up the fallen sword. He kept it level as he stepped back. His movements were met with no response. Benoni was the only one who didn't seem scared by what had happened, but he was smart enough not to lower his guard.

"What is this devilry?" Benoni's voice had not lost any of its command. "Call off your witch, Hadar. You can't defeat all of us."

"On the contrary," Eldred was the one who replied. There was not a hint of stress in his voice. "I can do this all night," that was a lie, but a convincing one. He would be able to entrap half the soldiers and keep them trapped, but that would be all. "I think that you're defeated."

Benoni was now not so sure of himself, there was something wrong with the situation, but he wasn't sure whether it was to his favour or not. He watched Eldred carefully for signs of weakness. There was a slight twitch in Eldred left eye, but that was only for a second and was not conclusive enough for Benoni. He had to resign himself to the fact that he had been beaten.

"Fine. We will leave, but believe me when I say that you have not seen the last of me." His words sounded more menacing than they should, there was something deeply threatening about him.

Eldred released the spell when they marched away and Hawthorne returned the soldier's sword. The man raced out of the room as fast as his legs would carry him. The look on his face was a mixture of relief and terror.

With the room cleared of soldiers, everyone relaxed. The tension had been thick and was quick to wash away. Eldred was the only one who didn't seem pleased with the result. He didn't like Hadar playing on his abilities, but there were very little other options for them.

"There is something not right about that man." Eldred was the first to speak.

"I know what you mean. I think that I might try and get some information on him." Hadar drained his tankard and promptly left the room.

"I think that we should all have an early night. It's been a troubling day and we'll need to be gone early in the morning." Eldred made the suggestion.

Only the two dwarves disagreed with him. They never gave up an opportunity to drink themselves silly. Eldred gave them one warning to behave before letting them leave. They made sure they took their weapons before leaving the inn.

Alaric was glad to be out of the common room. His bedroom, which he was sharing with Bern, was on the second floor. It overlooked the mountains to the west, which were only a tip on the horizon, but could not be seen in the dark. He stood and stared out the window at the storm still raging outside as Bern prepared himself for bed.

Suddenly, as Alaric stared blankly out the window, trying again to sense the source of the storm, there was a great flash in the sky. A ripple of magical energy flowed through the room and passed to the east. The power was something that Alaric had never felt before. He knew instantly what it was.

"Wow, that lightening must have been close," Bern commented from the other side of the room.

Alaric thought about telling him what had happened, but decided to let it go. There was something wrong. It was as if the dispersal of such great power had created gaps in the world. Alaric was sure that something very bad had happened, but he didn't want to think what that might have been. He just hoped that Heryion had survived whatever it was that he had done. As much as he hoped, he doubted that the little man, being so close to the energy, would have survived.

To block the thought out of his mind he returned his attention to the storm. To his surprise, he noticed that the rain had settled and the wind was calming. The feeling that there was someone out there had also disappeared. With nothing else to worry about, Alaric decided that it would be best to get some sleep.

Chapter 23: Poison Arrow

When the morning came, the storm had completely passed and the sun was shining. The only remnants of the storm were the many puddles on the ground. The wind had died to a light breeze and the morning could be called nothing but pleasant.

The horses were all saddled before the sun had risen and the group ate a quick breakfast before they were on the road again. The night's sleep had done Palentonal a world of good. His recuperation was better than they had expected and with a little luck they would make it to Lel Dinion by nightfall.

They left Lel Caminon without seeing Benoni or any of his solders. There was a feeling of unrest about the town and it was not just from their presence. Hadar and the dwarves had found some interesting information about the men.

The group rode hard for most of the morning. They only rested for a moment for Palentonal to catch his breath. He claimed that he was still fit to ride, but Eldred insisted they stop. He was not going to take any risks. An unnecessary death could be fatal for their entire mission.

They ate lunch on the banks of the Hondin River, the major artery of Hondin Lel. The river supplied over half the water demands of the Kingdom and was one of the pivotal reasons for the economic and population growth. The river was wide enough for trading boats to travel up and down.

"What did you find out about Benoni last night?" The question was directed at Hadar, but Eldred put it out to anyone.

"He is as bad as Keshet said. He was one of Lisle's best soldiers until his tactics got out of hand. It is said that he laughed in the face of the King when Lisle handed out his sentence. If it wasn't for his years of service, he would have been sent to the stocks. From what I've heard, he rules the town with an iron fist. Even the mayor is afraid of him. I think that we were very lucky to leave unharmed," Hadar explained.

"I don't think that you know the half of it." Hulkan was the next to speak. "We heard some very disturbing news. It seems that our good Night Marshall has a thing for torture. I think that if we had gone along with him last night, we would have had a taste of his handy work. I don't think there is one citizen of Lel Caminon who isn't afraid of him. Rumour has it that he tortures and sacrifices small animals, when he doesn't have a person to harm. I would take his threat seriously when he says we haven't seen the last of him." His words didn't bring any comfort.

The initial reaction of everyone was to look back down the road. They expected at any minute to see a group of horsemen riding up on them. There was a very uncomfortable feeling about them as they rode.

No one complained when Hadar suggested they should keep moving. They were still a hard afternoon's ride to the capital and they would need to rest the pack animals. The morning had left them panting and looking haggard. The elvish steeds could keep charging for the rest of the day.

As the afternoon wore on, the road continued to rise towards the north. The river remained in sight on the left and the Great Hondin Forest began to loom to their right. By mid-afternoon, the forest started to close in on them. At times the road brought them within paces of the tree line and the group became very nervous. The further they travelled the more enemies they had accumulated.

They rounded a corner where the river took a sharp dog leg to the east. Standing in the road, blocking their path, was a group of burly looking men. From their dress and their crude weapons, it was obvious that they were bandits. Even without looking, they knew that there was another group of men closing in behind them.

No one drew their weapons, although this was clearly another situation where talking was not going to help. If there was any chance of passing without a fight, it was worth a shot. Their weapons were in clear view of the bandits just to show that they weren't an easy target.

"There are archers with arrows aimed at each of you. Hand over your valuables and we will let you pass by," barked the head bandit as he slapped his left hand with the end of a mean looking cudgel.

Palentonal, with his elven eyes, scowled the forest for the archers. Eldred waited to see his reaction before speaking. Hadar was about to take the lead, but Eldred signaled for him to wait. Palentonal signaled that he could see two archers hidden in the forest.

"If your archers were that good, then we would already be dead. Why don't we just call this a misunderstanding and leave it at that. You go your way and we will go ours," Eldred's voice was filled with its usual confidence.

"We don't like to kill needlessly. We are robbers not murderers, but if you don't surrender then our archers will be forced to fire. They will cut your numbers in half before you can take a step." The lead bandit didn't seem impressed by Eldred's speech.

"Can you take out their two archers?" Eldred spoke slowly out of the corner of his mouth.

Palentonal nodded with only the slightest of movements. His bow was strapped to his saddle and well within reach. His hand slowly reached down and touched the string.

Eldred cast a small spell so Palentonal could hear the words that Eldred never spoke. "I don't think that I'm going to be able to talk them down. When you feel confident take the shot. Warn the others that there will be fighting soon. I will do all that I can to distract them."

"As you can see," Eldred spoke confidently. "We are not merchants. We are simple travelers and have nothing of value. We do not want a confrontation, but be assured that you will come off second best."

"It's you who should be careful. Our numbers are more than three times yours and our archers are the best in the land. We do not ask for much, but we will take a lot more."

As the bandit finished talking Palentonal let loose his first arrow. The motion was so fast that no one had time to react. Before the first arrow had struck its target, Palentonal already had his second nocked and ready to fire. A cry of pain from the forest indicated the first arrow had hit its mark. A second cry confirmed that both archers were now dead. The seven bandits all stared at the group in horror. They had not been expecting such an attack. This gave Palentonal the chance to nock another arrow. Before he had a chance to fire, the group had burst into action. Hadar, Alena, Eldred and Alaric attacked those in the front whilst Dorn, Hulkan, Hawthorne and Bern concentrated on the rear.

In all the commotion, Palentonal didn't see the third archer hiding in the forest. The arrow missed its intended target of Eldred and struck Alena above her right breast as she moved to swing her sword.

"No!" cried Alaric.

Within a flash, he was by her side. She wavered in her saddle, but still remained upright. Alaric arrived just in time to block a sword swing that would have slashed across her stomach. In return, he caught the bandit across the chest with a glancing blow.

Ignoring the bandit who was now retreating with blood oozing into his shirt, Alaric caught Alena as she was about to fall. Even though she had just been struck, a great sweat already soaked her body. Her face looked deathly pale and her eyes were glazed.

Palentonal desperately scanned the forest for the third archer. Before the man could shoot again, Palentonal located him and let loose with his own arrow. The bandit sunk to the ground before he could draw his bow again. With the forest cleared, Palentonal replaced his bow and drew his sword.

The battle was never going to last long. With the bandits on foot, they didn't stand much chance against the mounted. The dwarves were the only ones who jumped from their horses. Before long the bandits realised their plight was useless and retreated into the forest. Only a harsh word from Eldred stopped them from following.

"Let them be. We will shed no unnecessary blood. There will be enough of that to come," Eldred spoke with an authority that could not be broken.

Alaric had helped Alena to the ground. Her condition had not worsened, yet it was far from good. The impact of the arrow should   not have caused Alena to deteriorate so quickly. It was obvious that there was something else in play.

Palentonal gently moved Alaric out of the way so he could assess the situation. Firstly, he snapped the arrow and pulled it through. Alena, in her delirious state, didn't even cry out. A yellow liquid oozed out with the blood. Palentonal quickly applied some herbs from his pouch and then bandaged the wound.

"There was poison on the arrow. I tried to bandage the wound as quickly as possible, but I'm afraid I was too late," he explained, a worried look on his face. "The poison is like nothing I've ever seen before."

"Those damn apothecaries in Lel Dinion. They're always trying to outdo themselves. They don't care who buys their drugs," Eldred swore.

"It's the way in Hondin Lel. Murder and intrigue is one of the top ten pastimes amongst the nobles. Lisle's magician usually keeps it in check. All potions, poisons, drugs and antidotes are required to be registered before they are sold," Hadar explained. "There has to be a record of this poison somewhere. If we take the arrow head to the palace, I'm sure there will be a cure."

"Are any of those bandits that you shot still alive? They should be able to tell us what the poison is, or at least who they bought it from," Eldred asked Palentonal.

"I wouldn't think so. When I shoot to kill, they don't survive." Palentonal was simply stating facts. "We could chase after them."

"That would waste too much time. We need to make for Lel Dinion. We need to get her to Lorio." Eldred looked extremely concerned. "Find some unused arrows as well as the one that hit Alena. Also, strap one of those bodies onto one of the pack animals."

"What are you getting at?" asked Hulkan, shocked at what Eldred was suggesting.

"If Lorio doesn't know what the poison is, then we may need to look at other means."

"We need to get moving quickly," Hadar urged. "There is not a lot of time left and we are still a good way away from the city."

With the help of Hawthorne and Palentonal, Alena was returned to her saddle. She was barely conscious yet she managed to remain upright. After they started to move out, Palentonal went into the forest to retrieve his arrows.

They moved as fast as they could without unsettling Alena, but it wasn't long before she started to sway. It was slow at first, but soon enough it became more noticeable. Alaric, who had not left her side since they had started, caught her as she was about to fall.

"This is ridiculous. She won't make it another mile, let alone to the city," Alaric said as he passed her limp body down to Hawthorne.

She had lost consciousness and her breathing was laboured. It was clear she did not have long left.

"Isn't there something you can do?" Alaric pleaded with Eldred.

"There is one thing. I had hoped I wouldn't need to use it, but I don't think we have any choice." Eldred paused and looked at Alena. "Everyone get back on your horses and continue. We'll be along shortly."

The rest of the group did as they were directed and rode off. The day had turned out to be quite pleasant after the previous day's storm. The sun was shining and a cool breeze blew off the river, but no one was enjoying the ride. They kept a slow pace so it would be easy for the other two to catch them. They hadn't ridden long before Alaric felt the now familiar tingle in the back of his neck. He knew that whatever Eldred had planned was done. It would only be a matter of time to see if it had worked.

It didn't take long for Eldred and Alena to catch up with them. Eldred led the way with Alena sitting upright in her saddle half a length behind. The sight of her was uplifting yet strangely disturbing.

"What are you doing?' asked Hawthorne, shocked. "How can you leave her by herself?"

Hawthorne was about to rein his horse next to Alena, but Eldred quickly stopped him. "Let her be Hawthorne. You cannot touch her. She will make the ride to Lel Dinion, which is all you need to know."

Alaric watched the encounter with Hawthorne and then turned his attention to Alena. From up close, he could see that there was a blank look on her face. Her face was still deathly pale, but now her eyes were wide open. They stared blankly out in front of her and to Alaric's horror he realised that she was not blinking.

"We can ride harder now. She will hold up to the pace." Eldred's words left doubts in their minds, but they knew that they had to make the capital before nightfall.

"What did you do to her?" Alaric asked when they were well on their way again.

"I don't think that you really want to know." Eldred kept his face cold and stared out in front of him.

"I need to know. I felt what you did and there was something wrong with it."

"It seems that you are coming into your power quicker than I expected." Eldred seemed pleased with what Alaric had said. "I suppose that I need to start your training very soon. I will tell you what I have done, but you must promise to remain calm."

Alaric nodded his head.

"In short I have captured Alena's soul, or her life essence if you prefer," Eldred kept his voice low.

It was all Alaric could do to hold himself back from yelling out. He took another look at Alena and knew that Eldred was telling the truth. She was obviously still alive, but there was no life to her.

"How long will she stay like that?" Alaric asked when he managed to calm himself.

"She could stay like that for an eternity. The only problem is that the poison will still be coursing through her veins and doing great damage. I have slowed everything within her body. It won't last forever, but it has given us some more time."

As the day wore on and the afternoon slipped away, the terrain didn't change much. Alena continued to ride at the back of the group as Eldred had instructed. They all tried hard not to look back at the lifeless body riding behind them. Eldred didn't tell anyone else what he had done, even though they all asked at least a dozen times. Each time he was asked, he simply told them she would be alright. They had to take his word for it no matter how unnerving.

The sun was wavering in the sky when the road turned sharply to the north. As it did the forest suddenly dropped away to the south and the river followed the road. A hooded figure stood in the road no more than a hundred feet in front of them. The creature radiated evil and there could be no doubt who it was.

"I was afraid this was going to happen," Eldred cursed as he called the group to a halt. Alena's horse followed the command.

"What do you mean?" asked Hawthorne who had a confused look on his face.

"The serpentant was able to follow the spell that I created to keep Alena alive. I'm afraid that I won't have the strength to counter any attacks, I only hope that he doesn't realise it," Eldred explained to everyone, although he directed his speech at Alaric. "I'm going to need you to help me try and bluff the creature. If he thinks that we are at full strength, he may be loathed to act. The fact that he has come here by himself is very curious. We will ride out and speak to it. I want everyone to remain here; your weapons will be of no use, only attack if I give the signal. If anything else happens, you need to ride off and try to find another way into the city."

Eldred gave Alaric a grave look and then urged Tormenta to a slow trot towards the creature. Alaric breathed deeply before letting Adelanta follow. He could feel the evil radiating from the creature in front of them. His heart beat faster, more in anticipation than fear.

"Hello there Great One." The serpentant didn't wait for Alaric to arrive before he started. "I just want the girl. The others are of no concern to me," the creature hissed. He created a spell allowing the words to drift over the rest of the group.

Hawthorne drew his sword as he heard the words and the dwarves fingered their axe blades. The words were an obvious ploy and Eldred signaled for them to relax, although he didn't let his focus drift from the serpentant. The demand took Eldred by surprise. Of all the things that the creature could have asked for, a dying she-elf was the last on his list.

"You will not speak to me Great One? Is it that you are afraid of me? Have your powers waned that much?" The creature's voice held a hint of mockery.

"What do you want with her?"

"Ah, we meet again Chosen One. My name is Viper. I do not have a grudge against you. You may go free once I have the girl."

The words sounded so sweet in Alaric's head that he was tempted to hand Alena over right then. There was something hypnotic about the way Viper spoke and how he moved. The tingle in the back of Alaric's neck, which had been there since Eldred had cast the spell on Alena, changed slightly.

"Why should I trust you? If you let us go, I will destroy your master." Eldred let Alaric speak. The more Viper spoke the better understanding he would get on situation. The fact that they were still talking was a surprise.

"My mistress has nothing to do with this. I care nothing for what happens to the Evil One. He is not my master and never will be," Viper hissed the words in disgust.

"Be that as it may, I will still not give up one of my friends for any reason."

"My reasons are my own. This is your last warning. Give her to me or I will destroy you all!" Although they could not see inside the hood Alaric knew that Viper's façade had changed.

A broad smile crossed Eldred's face and the sudden change made Alaric falter.

"I don't think we will be doing that," Eldred's smirk never left his face as he spoke. "You will leave here empty handed and there is nothing you can do about it."

Viper was silent for almost a minute. Alaric wondered what the creature was thinking. He was also surprised at Eldred's comments. The words he spoke could have easily sparked retaliation, but instead he just stood there in silence.

"You're right. This is not the time or the place for an attack. There are more important things that we have to get done. For one thing, the longer we stand here the more chance she has of dying. If you give her to me, I can cure her. There will be no risk to her life." The words were spoken as if the information had just come to Viper.

"I'm sure that you can. I know that venom is your specialty, but there will still be no deal." Eldred knew that Viper would be able to cure Alena, but how long she would remain that way was another question.

"Okay then, I can trade you for some valuable information. There is something waiting for you at Lel Dinion and it will not be pleasant. I can tell you when, where and what is going happen. I can even tell you who is going to do it." Viper was obviously grasping at straws, but the news wasn't promising.

"I think that we will take our chances, thank you. Now if you have nothing better to say, I think that we will be on our way."

"I see that you have made your choice. Know that I will have her and you will all die." As Viper finished talking, he disappeared.

Eldred motioned for the others to join them. The smile on his face showed that he had called Viper's bluff. Alaric was not as convinced that Viper was lying. There was something menacing in his final words.

"What's going on?" boomed Hadar once they were within earshot.

"We have to get moving again. How long do you think it will take for us to get to Lel Dinion?" Eldred asked.

"It shouldn't be much more than an hour. We should be able to see the city once we crest that hill."

"I thought you said it was going to take us four days to reach Lel Dinion, this doesn't make any sense. Are you sure you are right?" Eldred sounded confused.

"I know my home land. I can't explain it, but we are only an hour or so away."

True to his word, the city came into view when they reached the top of the hill. The great city of Lel Dinion spread out below them. Small houses and farms scattered the land around the city. The sight of the city brought little comfort to their minds. With the sun low in the sky, it would be almost impossible for them to arrive by nightfall.

Alaric watched in awe at the city as they rode down the other side of the hill. He had been to Zenza City many times, but it paled in comparison to the capital of Hondin Lel. The city stretched for miles with the spirals of the mighty palace of King Lisle XI reaching up towards the clouds. With the city in sight, their travelling seemed to be painfully slow. The minutes past and they seemed like hours.

It was now a race against time. They were still bound by the speed that Alena could travel. Although she was still upright in the saddle, if she travelled any quicker than a walk she would be thrown off. No matter how quickly the sun was setting, there was nothing they could do to hasten the pace.

Soon they started to pass the small farmhouses that dotted the land. Smoke came from their chimneys as the wives prepared for them husbands to return from the fields. The smell of food filled the chilled evening air. Most of the houses were of the same design. They were small timber cottages with thatched rooves. Although there was obviously life inside the houses there was no one to be seen.

The closer they came to the city walls, the farms became smaller and the solitary houses became busy streets. The sun had almost completely set when they finally reached the main gate. The gate remained open although the guards were preparing to shut it for the night. The walls loomed over them as they approached the sentry.

"Getting late to be wandering around these parts." The greeting was not friendly as the guard was eager to be on his way home. "Where are you destined tonight?"

"We are here to see King Lisle," replied Hadar in his most commanding voice.

The sentry took a quick look at the group, scowling as he did so. Seeing the dead body, he was about object, but he suddenly changed his mind. If he started questioning, then he would be there half the night. The thought of going home was overpowering and it was clear that the other guards felt the same way. One of them would tell the night watch of their entrance and then it would be their concern. "You better hurry then, the gate to the palace closes at night and no one is allowed entrance without a royal directive."

"Thank you," replied Hadar, surprised that their entry was so easy.

Once they were all through, the sound of cogs grinding and timber creaking could be heard as the gate was slowly lowered. There was a secondary wall thirty feet from the first. The gate was unguarded and they passed through without hassle. The city inside the walls was alive with people moving around. The markets had just closed and businesses had been shut for the night. People were on their way home or on their way to the many taverns through the city. No one seemed to take any notice of the strange travelling group, even with the dead body and statuesque appearance of Alena.

Suddenly a bell tolled, signaling that the sun had set and no further business was to be conducted that day, except the night businesses of the taverns, inns and brothels.

With the sound of the bell, their hopes of gaining entrance into the palace faded. They were not expected and it would take a lot of persuasion to gain them entrance. Hadar's apparent falling out with the royal family would also play against them.

"I don't think it's a good idea to arrive at the palace with a dead body," Eldred called the group to halt. "Hadar, do you know of an inn nearby here?" Eldred was also thinking about Hadar's disfavour.

"Yes, there is a nice little place close by. I know the owner so he won't ask any questions about the body." Hadar didn't need time to think.

"Good. I think we will have more chance gaining entrance if there are only a few of us. Hadar, take Dorn, Hulkan, Bern and Palentonal to the inn. Hawthorn and Alaric will come with me and Alena."

They all moved into action without question. Eldred was hoping with Prince Hawthorne at their lead, they would be able to bluff their way in to see the King. Without the right documents, they would have to rely on his royal ring to pass. Hopefully the guardsman knew the many royal insignias.

Night had well and truly fallen when they reached the main gate to the palace. The walls were very ornate, although they were still very defendable. The large wooden gates, strapped with half foot-wide iron belts, were closed. A bell hung at the side of the gate and the gatehouse was built into the wall. A steel plate covered the only window facing the street. Eldred dismounted and rang the bell twice. Acting as the Prince's assistant was their best bet to gain entrance. There was a moment of silence before the steel plate swung back and a head poked out.

"No one is allowed admittance after nightfall. Go away and come back in the morning." The guard didn't wait for an answer before shutting the steel plate.

Eldred quickly rang the bell again. He had expected such a response and knew that he needed to be persistent. The plate was opened again and the guard's head poked out again. This time there was a less than pleased look on his face.

"If you don't leave now, I'll have you arrested and you can speak to the local magistrate in the morning."

"I am the advisor to the Prince of Remidia," Eldred indicated Hawthorne who was sitting regally on his horse. "We have ridden all day. His fiancé has fallen ill and we need to see the King's healers." Eldred hoped the lie would gain them entrance. If the guard let a future Queen die, then his life would be worthless.

It was clear that his words were having an effect. The guard looked from Eldred to Hawthorne to Alena and back to Eldred. There was a chance that Eldred was not telling the truth, but the guard was not willing to bet his life on it. Shaking his head the guard shut the plate.

Within moments the sound of cogs grinding could be heard and the gate slowly opened. Everything had not gone to plan. On the other side of the gate stood a dozen armed men.

"I told you. No one gets through these gates after nightfall," scoffed the guard.

The men on the other side of the gate looked as though they were seasoned soldiers. They were dressed in the livery of the royal family.

Each wore shining breastplates and their swords were already drawn. They looked ready for trouble.

"I am Prince Hawthorne of Remidia. I demand to be treated with respect!" Hawthorne boomed.

"If there was going to be a royal visitor, then we would have been informed. I think you are lying to try and sneak your way into the palace to assassinate the King. We will escort you to the dungeons and in the morning, you can plead your case to the magistrate. Unless, of course, you have the appropriate documents?" The guard was not budging.

"I have no papers, but I wear the royal ring of Remidia." Hawthorne made a motion to show the guard his ring, but was dismissed with a wave of his hand. He wished he had not forgotten the documents in Elhjem.

"I care not for rings. I need papers to allow entrance."

Hawthorne could only shake his head as the guard waited. The fury was rising in his body, yet he would expect nothing less from his own guards.

"I didn't think so. I think that we should introduce you to the dungeon." The guard signaled the advance.

Both Hawthorne and Eldred drew their swords. With the exertion of maintaining Alena's spirit, Eldred could not create any spells. Their only chance of surviving would be to fight.

Alaric watched as the soldiers slowly advanced, throughout the argument a rage had been building inside him. Every moment they wasted, the chance of Alena dying increased. If they were sent to the dungeons, there would be no chance. By the time Eldred revived Alena's spirit, her body would be well and truly dead.

"Enough!" boomed Alaric. "We do not have time for this."

"Oh no," Eldred could only whisper, he knew that he was too late for anything else.

Whether it was Alaric's words or his posture on his horse, the soldiers stood still. The wind started to swirl around the horses and the soldiers. Eldred wasn't the only one who could feel the electricity in the air and the hairs on the back of his neck stood up. The ground started to tremble and the gate started to shake. The torch light seemed to shrink back as if it was afraid.

Alaric could feel the power building inside. His anger had taken control of his body and there was nothing he could do to stop what he had started. Raising his hands in front of him, although only for show, he released the spell.

Chapter 24: Lel Dinion.

A ripple passed through the air as if the fabric of the world was being stretched. No one could move. All they could do was wait for whatever Alaric had in store for them. First a huge rush of air blew over them and then all the soldiers were suddenly knocked to the ground. Eldred was also knocked over and Hawthorne was thrown from his horse. The gate splintered with a loud crack. Shards of wood and straps of iron flew backwards. Chunks of stone smashed from the wall as if it had been hit by a boulder.

The soldiers lay unconscious as Eldred and Hawthorne picked themselves up. The gate and surrounding wall were partly destroyed. Inside the debris scattered the ground as far as twenty paces. With the spell complete Alaric collapsed on Adelanta's neck.

"What in the God King's name just happened?" Hawthorne cursed as he lifted himself back into the saddle.

"Something that shouldn't have! Something that should have been impossible," was all Eldred would say as he mounted Tormenta.

Eldred looked back at Alaric. He was still slumped over Adelanta and his breathing was strained. He was still conscious but only just. There was nothing Eldred could do for him except to urge him forward.

"Do you know where to find Lorio?" Hawthorne asked as they picked their way around the soldiers. "It will only be a matter of time before someone comes to see what the explosion was. I don't think this was the best of ideas."

"At this time of day, I would be assuming that Lorio will be with Lisle in the main hall. Once we get inside the palace, we should be alright. The main door will be guarded by two soldiers. There is a stable off to the left. I used to know one of the groomsmen. If he is working tonight, he should be able to sneak us in."

Everyone followed Eldred towards the stable. Once they left their horses, it would be more difficult for them to move. Alaric was barely conscious and Alena was a statue. They would be very conspicuous when they entered the palace.

It was quiet in the grounds, a few servants and pages wandered around, but there were no soldiers. They found the stable, but the man that Eldred was looking for was not there. In fact, the stables were completely empty.

"This is strange," commented Eldred as they stabled the horses.

"I wouldn't complain. This give us free access into the palace," Hawthorne almost joked.

Hawthorne helped Alaric from his horse then turned. "Don't touch Alena," Eldred warned before mumbling a few words. Alena dismounted herself; although there was little life in her she managed it without falling. Alaric wasn't so delicate. Without the aid of Hawthorne, he would not have been able to walk.

Their luck continued as the door leading from the stables to the palace was open. The first corridor they entered was completely empty. The closer they came to the main hall the more people they saw moving about. Everyone seemed too concerned with their own business to worry about the four strangers wandering the corridors.

The door to the main hall was guarded by two pages. Before they approached the door, Eldred handed Alaric a small vile of the rejuvenation potion. Alaric didn't hesitate in drinking. The liquid warmed his entire body and the fatigue washed away as his strength returned.

The pages were there to attend to the guests needs. They ignored the four until they reached the door. They took a quick look at them, but didn't move to help. It was as if they knew they were not invited guests.

The boys didn't try and stop Eldred as he pushed the door open. The room was abuzz with people and entertainment. The hall contained a large u-shaped banquet table filled with people, with only one or two seats vacant. King Lisle sat at the head table with his wife Queen Mara to his left sat their two sons and daughter. On his right sat a man who was no doubt Lorio, along with some minor nobles. At each side of the table stood two soldiers, it would be harder than they thought to gain access to the magician.

In the large space in the centre of the room between the two arms of the tables, a group of entertainers entertained the King and his guests. A young looking male was juggling knives, a young woman was stretching herself in a number of impossible positions, whilst another three were tumbling and tossing and generally making fools of themselves.

Only Lorio looked up when they entered. He peered at them for a moment, as if trying to work out who they were. He spoke briefly with the King before returning his attention to his food. Lisle glanced up briefly to inspect his new visitors.

"This is not going to be easy," Eldred whispered.

"I don't care if I have to tear this place apart if I have to," Alaric spoke through clenched teeth.

"Calm down Alaric. Now is the time for diplomacy. Keep your anger in check; a repeat of what happened at the gate would be disastrous. Remember that there is more than Alena's life at stake here."

Eldred led the group towards the table until they were stopped by the pair of guards. Both guards stared straight ahead as if there was no one there. There was not enough room to pass without shoving one of the guards out of the way.

"We need to speak to the King urgently," Eldred spoke softly so as to not make a scene.

The two guards continued to stare past the group and ignore the words that were spoken. Eldred could feel the anger building in Alaric again. This time he was prepared and motioned for him to calm down.

"Is this the way you treat guests these days," Eldred spoke in his normal voice, but the small spell he cast let his voice travel throughout the hall.

"What is the meaning of this?" Lisle boomed from his chair, slamming down his cutlery.

If the room wasn't completely silent after Eldred's comments, it was now. The entertainers stopped and one of the knives dropped and sunk into the floor. Everyone's attention was now locked on the new arrivals.

"With deference, your majesty. I am Prince Hawthorne of Remidia." Hawthorne hadn't seen Lisle since he was six, when his father took him on a diplomatic tour of the capitals. He was sure that Lisle wouldn't remember him. "One of my companions was struck by a poison arrow on our journey here and she is in desperate need of medical advice. I understand that your magician is the foremost expert in the field. I would speak to him immediately."

Lisle squinted in an effort to recognise the prince. "Hawthorne… hmmm." He scratched his chin. "Very well, take him. Just don't disturb my meal any further."

Lorio did not look impressed at having his meal cut short. He looked as though he was about to protest, but thought better of it. He slowly stood and walked over to the door. He used a large staff to help him walk. Eldred had to suppress a sneer at the man's obvious penchant for the theatrical. He'd had problems with Lorio in the past and did not want to do anything to upset him.

"This better be good." Lorio deliberately ignored Hawthorne and spoke to Eldred.

"I think we should go somewhere private." Eldred indicated Alena standing dead straight and looking like death itself.

"It looks like your friend doesn't have long left to live. There is nothing I can do for her," Lorio dismissed the situation and turned to leave.

"You were always a perfunctory student. She will live and you will help us find the cure."

Lorio stopped; there was something about Eldred's words that piqued his interest. Alaric watched him carefully. There was definitely something more between the two than Eldred had let on.

"Okay, we will go to my office," Lorio sighed. "So what is it that is so deadly that the great Eldred couldn't devise a cure," Lorio sneered once they were out of the hall. "It seems that you are not the be all and end all."

Eldred bit down the urge to retaliate. Lorio would be happy to think he had one up and he needed the court magician in a pliable mood.

No one spoke again until they reached Lorio's office. The room was large enough to fit a full council. The walls were lined with books and scrolls in no particular order. A great rectangular table sat in the middle of the room. At the far end was a smaller desk with a solitary chair. Behind the desk sat a chest containing many vials, both large and small, with a myriad of coloured liquids.

"Have her seated." Lorio went to his desk and took something from one of the drawers.

Eldred had Alena sit and Lorio returned with a strange looking device. It had a container at one end and a long, thin needle at the other. Without warning, Lorio plunged the needle into her arm. Alaric cried out and was about to pounce on the magician until Eldred restrained him.

Once Lorio had filled the chamber with blood he returned to his desk. He injected the blood into five small test tubes and then added a number of different coloured liquids. One mixture bubbled, another smoked, another changed into a dark green colour and the last two didn't react at all. Watching the test tubes intently Lorio shook his head.

"I have not seen anything like this before. Do you have a sample of the poison?" Lorio did not seem happy.

Hawthorne passed the arrows, including the one that had pierced Alena, to Lorio. The magician looked at the tips closely before doing another series of tests. Eldred had to admit that the magician had come a long way since they had last met.

"This is very disturbing. There are compounds that are common amongst the poisons I have on record. This is something that I have never seen before." Lorio spoke to the chemistry set sitting on his desk.

"Is there nothing you can do?" asked Alaric who had moved to be by Alena's side

"I'm afraid there is nothing. There are a few things I could try, but with this strange compound, there is a greater chance I would kill her. I could give her something for the pain, but it looks as though Eldred has already covered that." His failure to diagnose made him more placid. "I will have a room prepared for her, but I think that it will be a short stay." With that Lorio stood and left the room.

Alaric let his head slip into his hands. He didn't want anyone else to see the tears welling in his eyes.

"What do we do now?" Hawthorne asked, not willing to give up.

"That's where Plan B comes into fruition. There is a reason why I brought that dead body along with us." Eldred wasn't defeated.

"What are you talking about?" asked Alaric as he realised there may still be hope.

"We must get the body to a necromancer. It's our only chance."

"Bah," scoffed Hawthorne. "Necromancy has been outlawed for centuries."

"Everywhere except for Lel Dinion. There are a lot of things you can only do in Lel Dinion and luckily for us, practicing necromancy is one of them. Hopefully the bandit we have will know what the poison is. Alaric and I will go and find a necromancer; you take Alena to her room and make sure she is not disturbed."

Hawthorne was about to protest, but he knew he would be no use in a search for magic. When he thought about it, he preferred to be by Alena's side.

They all followed the pageboy to the room that had been prepared and Eldred made sure that Alena was safely tucked into bed before leading Alaric away. Alaric looked back at Hawthorne who seemed pleased to be able to stay.

"What *is* a necromancer?" asked Alaric, trying to put the thoughts out of his mind.

"A very good question. Necromancy was all but banned many years ago. The art of dealing with the dead can be linked to Nyrra. His necromancers delve a lot deeper into the arts than those who work in this city. Many centuries ago it was a common trade, but now it is more of a calling. Like sorcery, necromancy is genetic, only necromancy can skip generations. In the past those who practiced the art were killed as Nyrra worshippers, so there are very few left with the talent. For the most part, they can speak to the dead, raise spirits, that sort of thing. Nothing that can really be called dangerous, although delving into the dead is never a safe occupation."

The stable hands had returned from wherever it was they had been. They were looking at the white stallions, wondering where they had come from. They all got a shock when Alaric and Eldred turned up in the stables looking for their horses.

As soon as they mounted, they made for the main gate. A group of soldiers were walking around trying to make sense of the mess. All the soldiers who had been on duty had been taken back to the barracks to recover.

"How are we going to get passed them?" asked Alaric as they neared the gate.

"We'll think of something, we have to."

As they made their way to the gate they were stopped by one of the soldiers. "Where do you think you're going?"

"We need to go out into the city," Eldred didn't rein Tormenta, but slowed his walk.

"I don't think anyone is leaving until we get to the bottom of this mess." The soldier looked bewildered.

"We really need to get into the city. I don't think that the two of us are anything to worry about."

"Fine, leave, but I wouldn't be expecting to get back into the palace tonight." The soldier didn't wait for any response.

Out of the palace, they made for the nearest inn. It wasn't until they were out of the grounds did they realise they didn't know which inn the others had gone to.

"Is it going to be easier to find the necromancer directly? Can you even find a necromancer at this hour?" asked Alaric after they left the second inn.

Eldred couldn't help himself but laugh. "At this hour? I don't think you fully understand the nature necromancy. You can only bring the spirits back after dark. The spirits don't like coming out during the day and it causes too much strain on the necromancer to try. We need to find Hadar. Necromancers don't exactly advertise their wares. It's very hard to find one if you don't know where to look." Eldred finished talking when they came to the door of another inn.

Alaric waited out the front while Eldred went to see if the others were inside. For some reason Alaric thought that this was the place. True to his feelings a few minutes later, Eldred walked out with Hadar.

"What did you do with the body?" Alaric asked Hadar.

"It's on a wagon. The stable boy is getting the horses ready now. They won't be long."

True to his word, the stable boy appeared leading the horse and cart. Hadar slipped him a small copper coin before the boy returned to the stables as Hadar climbed onto the wagon and started down the road.

"Do you know where you're going?" Alaric asked as he rode beside the wagon.

"We are heading into the dirty underbelly of Lel Dinion. Many years ago, King Masos VI decided to push all the unsavoury types to one area of the city. It houses the poor, the destitute and most of the brothels in the city. It's where the thieves and cutthroats fraternise. During the day, it's safe enough, but at night it's a place best left alone. I know of one who practices the dark craft. Keep your eyes open and stay aware," Hadar warned.

The well-lit streets quickly turned into dimly lit alleys. The buildings were run down and the streets were dirty. A few mangy dogs and a couple of dirty whores were the only ones on the street. The group ignored both as they rode past.

"Here we are," Hadar said after he led them down a narrow alley to a dead end. A set of stairs led down to a basement. "Wait here for a moment."

Hadar jumped from the wagon and ran down the stairs. There was something very unnerving about his movements. He paused at the door before pushing it open. A few minutes passed, then there was an ear-piercing scream from somewhere in the distance, and then Hadar returned.

"Grab the body and follow me," Hadar spoke quickly and quietly. "And make sure you keep your swords on you."

Alaric and Eldred were quick to comply. The dead body was cold and clammy and the touch of dead skin made Alaric shiver. There was something very wrong with the situation. Not in his wildest dreams, a few months ago, would Alaric have believed he would be carrying a dead body in the stinking back streets of a capital city.

"The necromancer's name is Jazelle. Let me do the talking when we get inside. She's a little nervous about strangers, so don't do anything to upset her."

Hadar opened the door and waited for them to walk inside. Eldred and Alaric stopped in a small archway leading into a large room. Many candles scattered the walls giving an eerie ambiance. Sitting at a small table was a beautiful woman. Alaric would have thought the necromancer would have been an old hag. He was very surprised to see that Jazelle was an attractive, young woman. In the centre of the room, there was a large stone altar, big enough to fit two bodies. Surrounding the altar and included within its lines was a pentagram drawn in some phosphorescent paint.

"Enter into the House of Death. Place the body on the altar. Do not make yourself comfortable for you will find no relief here," her voice was sickly sweet. There was something not quite right about it, as if it belonged to another person.

Eldred and Alaric did as they were told. Once they were inside the pentagram, there was a strange feeling that there was someone else in the room. It was as if there was someone looking over their shoulders, just out of their peripheral vision. Once they stepped back from the altar and out of the pentagram the feeling disappeared.

"What is it that you seek from the spirits?" asked Jazelle standing up from her table and walking slowly around the altar.

"This is a bandit. His gang shot one of our friends with a poison arrow. We need to find out what the drug is and where he bought it," explained Hadar.

"How is your wife?" asked Jazelle, the question seeming completely inappropriate. Alaric raised a questioning eyebrow at Eldred who in turn shrugged his shoulders.

"She died over five years ago," Hadar replied, somewhat sadly.

Jazelle watched him carefully. There was something in her eye, a flicker. Alaric was sure that something had passed between the two of them. "Shackle him to the table. I will do what I can to help?"

Alaric and Eldred moved to go back to the altar when Jazelle stopped them with a wave of her hand. "Not you two. He must do it."

Hadar hesitated before he moved to the altar. Once inside the pentagram, the feeling that someone was watching him came. The feeling made him shiver. Quickly he grabbed the chains and shackled both the bandit's wrists and ankles before moving back outside the pentagram.

With the body safely chained to the altar, Jazelle placed a number of multicoloured bowls at the points of the pentagram. Inside each of the bowls she sprinkled a white powder. When the powder touched whatever was in the bowl, a puff of white smoke rose. She crossed her arms across her chest and gripped each of her shoulders. Taking two deep breaths Jazelle closed her eyes and started to chant.

For a minute, nothing happened. The body remained limp and nothing changed in the room. All of a sudden there came a great wail from the body. The noise made the three men jump. A gust of wind blew through the room nearly blowing out the candles. The room went almost completely black and when the light returned, the body had suddenly sprung to life. It writhed on the altar, the temperature in the room had dropped considerably and condensation could be seen on everyone's breath.

"Ask your questions quickly. I cannot contain this spirit for long," Jazelle cried, her voice strained. "Only Hadar ask the questions."

"What is the name of the poison that you dipped your arrows in?" asked Hadar, his voice still filled with surprise.

"Why should I tell you?" wailed a voice from somewhere inside the writhing body.

"Our friend might die. We need to know what the drug is," Hadar barked, his anger rising at the spirits answer.

"Your friend is already dead. No one could have survived this long." There was a hint of laughter in the wail.

"No, our friend is still live and needs the antidote," Hadar urged.

"I care not for the mortal world anymore. Your friend can die for all I care."

Hadar sighed in despair. He did not know how to make a spirit do what he wanted. The man was already dead and there was nothing else to threaten him with. If he knew the man had family, that would be a different story, but they had no background on him, not even a name.

Alaric was not going to be dissuaded so easily. His mind reached out until it came in contact with the spirit. "I am Alaric, the Chosen One. I carry the Ruby Stone of Power. Answer our questions quickly and I will let you go. If you do not help us, I will trap your spirit in a place between worlds. You will suffer a pain unimaginable for the rest of existence if you let my friend die." There was nothing but confidence in his mind's voice.

"I swear I do not know what the drug was," the voice trembled. The other two were surprised at the sudden confession. "We didn't ask the name when we bought it."

"Then tell us from whom you purchased the drug," Hadar continued.

"We got it from a shop in Lel Dinion," the voice spoke quickly.

"What shop? Where is it?" yelled Hadar.

"It's close by. It's owned by a man named Yoseph. That is all I can tell you. Now please, let me go."

"I must let him go," cried Jazelle, her voice weak.

The body went limp. The temperature returned to normal and Alaric felt his body relax. It was only at that moment did he realise how tense he was.

"You will go now. Take this man with you," she sighed.

She tossed some keys onto the altar. Hadar returned inside the pentagram, however, this time there was no feeling of someone watching. He quickly used the key to unlock the chains and release the body.

"I will come back and see you," Hadar offered before he removed the body.

"No my love. Our life together is in the past. I am tied to the dead now. There is nothing that can change that," Jazelle sounded sad, but he knew that she would not change her mind.

Hefting the body over his shoulder, Hadar followed the other two out of the room. Alaric wasn't sure in the dim light, but he thought he saw a tear in the large man's eyes. Hadar threw the body onto the back of the cart, not worrying about it. It had served its purpose and could now rot in the gutter for all he cared.

"Do you know where we have to go?" asked Alaric as they rode out of the alley.

"Yes, unfortunately. He is one of the most dishonorable drug merchants in town. I should have known when Lorio didn't know what the poison was where to look. Yoseph will be easy to crack. When it is said and done, he's a coward," Hadar explained.

Hadar led the way through the dimly lit streets. There was no one out although there seemed to be people lurking in the many shadows.

Whoever it was, they were well trained in remaining invisible. It was more of a feeling that people where there than actually seeing them. Hadar looked around nervously, which in turn made Alaric nervous. He fingered the hilt of his sword, a nervous reaction and a warning to those who could see him.

Hadar stopped the cart outside a shabby looking house at the mouth of a small alley. The house was boarded up and it looked abandoned. If something dodgy was happening, then Alaric thought that it was a perfect place for it.

"Is this the place?" asked Alaric as he dismounted.

"No. It's down that narrow alley," Hadar indicated. "It's too narrow to get a horse and cart down. I think that's the reason why Yoseph took the shop. There is only a small amount of people who can fit down there at one time. It gives him ample time to slip out the back door if ever the city guard comes looking." Hadar looked around. "I don't think that we should leave the horses unattended."

"Don't worry about the horses," offered Eldred.

Before they started down the alley, Eldred whispered something to Tormenta. Once finished, both the white horses trotted off back the way they had come. Alaric was about to protest, but Eldred silenced him.

"They will find their way back to the inn. No one will harm them," Eldred explained.

Hadar and Alaric only just fitted walking side by side with Eldred following behind. The alley itself was not lit. The only light came from the lantern from the street behind and the dim light of the moon. The sound of someone moving around could be heard just ahead of them.

"Let me do all the talking," Hadar whispered. "I am here to see Yoseph," Hadar called to the man at the end of the alley.

"There is no one here by that name," a voice croaked from the dark.

"I have business with him. It's Jadar. I have something that he might like to purchase," Hadar called back.

There was a pause as the man thought about what he had just been told. It was clear that he was now unsure of himself.

"I don't have all night. If Yoseph doesn't want to do business, then I will go and see Yahin. I'm sure that he will do business with me."

"Okay. I will let you in," the man from the end of the alley didn't sound happy about it.

The three of them approached the end of the alley cautiously. They could only see the outline of the man waiting for them. The man pushed a door open and motioned for them to enter. He then stepped out of their way, making sure they couldn't see his face. Hadar led the way. Inside the light wasn't much better than the alley outside. They walked down a corridor with four doors on either side. At the end was an open doorway was covered with thick curtains.

"Is that you, Maslin? I told you I didn't want to see anyone tonight," Yoseph had his back turned to the group as they walked into the room.

"We need to have a word," Hadar's voice was harsh.

Yoseph spun around in his chair at the sound of Hadar's voice. He didn't look happy to see him. "What are you doing here, Jadar? I thought I made it quite clear that I didn't want to have any dealings with you again." Yoseph was trying to reach for something under his desk. As he did, he looked at his other guests. When he saw Alaric, he stopped what he was doing. "What are you doing bringing him here?"

"What are you talking about?" Hadar asked, confused with his reaction to Alaric.

"There are people looking for him. His likeness has been shown around this area. Anyone caught aiding him will be dealt with." Yoseph actually looked scared.

"Who's been asking about him?" Eldred spoke before Hadar could say anything.

"I don't know you," Yoseph turned his attention to Eldred. "I think that it's time you all leave."

"Okay, we will leave as soon as you answer my questions," Hadar stepped closer. "Tell us who has been asking after my friend."

"Fine! There has been a man, dressed totally in black. He wore black chain mail over his chest and he looked as though he knew how to use the sword that hung by his side. I didn't get his name, but I can tell you one thing. I have never felt so afraid for my life. If I never see him again in my life I will be more than happy."

Both Hadar and Alaric looked at Eldred. He thought for a moment, but he couldn't answer their unasked question. There was something very disturbing about the man's description.

Shaking his head Hadar decided to get to the point. "One of my friends was hit by a poison arrow. The poison was bought from this shop and there is a component that cannot be identified."

"I don't see what that has to do with me. I sell a lot of things to a lot of people," Yoseph eyed his exit as he spoke.

"I'll tell you what it has to do with you." Hadar advanced on Yoseph. Before he came within striking distance Yoseph grabbed the sword he had hidden under his desk. Hadar stopped just before he impaled himself.

"If it's an antidote you're after, I can't help you with that. Go and see the court magician. For a fee, he has all the antidotes that you need."

"Well that's the problem. We don't know what this mystery drug is, so we can't use any of his antidotes. Now if I told him who sold the poison, it wouldn't be long before you would be hanging in the palace courtyard. I know that you wouldn't make a new poison without creating an antidote. There is more money to be had if you sell both ways." Hadar didn't seem to be perturbed by the sword point that was only inches away from his stomach.

"Okay, okay. There is no need for threats. Tell me, where you're staying and I will get some of the antidote over to you." Yoseph now looked extremely distraught. Sweat had appeared on his forehead and his sword was starting to shake.

"I don't think so. Not that I don't trust you, well it is that I don't trust you. You give me the antidote now and then you are going to come with us to the palace to make sure that my friend survives."

"I don't think that you're in a position to make threats like that. Remember I am the one with the sword," as he spoke, Yoseph started to rise from his chair.

Quick as a flash Hadar took a step back and drew his rapier. Two quick flicks with his sword and Hadar had disarmed Yoseph. The alchemist retreated, whilst Hadar blocked off any chance of him sneaking out the back.

"Now I wouldn't try anything stupid. My patience is well and truly used up." Hadar threatened with his sword.

"Okay, please don't hurt me," Yoseph was all but crying. "I will give the antidote, but please don't take me to the palace."

Returning to the other side of his desk, Yoseph pulled out one of the drawers. After a moment of rifling and chinking glass he produced a small vile of purple liquid. He swirled it once, had a close look and then handed it to Hadar.

"This is the remedy that you need. Give her half now and half in another twelve hours. Now get out of here," Yoseph was a little too keen the get rid of them.

"I don't think so. You are still coming to the palace," Hadar spoke forcefully.

"I only have one unregistered poison now; hence there is only one cure. You have what you need, now leave before you get me killed." Yoseph's entire body was shaking.

"Something's not right here," Eldred commented.

A terrified scream came from somewhere outside. The sudden noise diverted their attention. Yoseph took the opportunity to push Hadar back before making his escape out the back door. The sound of a bolt being slid into place indicated that he had locked it.

"It looks like we're expecting trouble," said Eldred.

"I think an escape out the back might be in order," suggested Hadar. "If they induced that much fear in Yoseph, I don't think that we want to wait around to find out who they are."

"But the little rat has locked us in," Alaric spat the words.

"Don't worry. I can take care of that," Eldred smiled.

"Well, I think we should move," said Hadar as a crashing sound of splintering wood came from the front door.

There was a light brush against the back of Alaric's neck and the sound of the bolt sliding out could be clearly heard. Hadar didn't waste any time in pouncing on the door and flinging it open. After passing through, he waited for the others. Just as Alaric was about to walk through, he heard the sound of the curtain being parted.

"I've found you," the voice sounded familiar, but Alaric wasn't waiting to see who it was.

When they were all through, Hadar shut the door and slid the bolt back into place. Eldred looked shaky on his feet. The small spell that he had cast had taken a great toll on him.

"Quickly, we must leave!"

They were in small room behind Yoseph's house with two torches hanging on the wall and an empty sconce. A narrow flight of stairs led downward and Hadar snatched a torch off the wall as he descended. Alaric followed next and then Eldred took the last torch.

As they descended beneath the streets of Lel Dinion the air started to turn musty. There was a rank smell coming from below. When they reached the bottom, Alaric realised they had come out into the city's sewer system. They stopped at the bottom of the stairs to get their bearings. The rancid smell made Alaric's head swim.

Suddenly he felt a tingling sensation on the back of his neck. There was something not right about it. He knew instantly that it was not Eldred who had cast the spell. Whoever it was had unlocked the door the same way they had.

"We need to move," Alaric had to control himself to keep his voice low.

The sewers were set like canals running under the city. The paths ran on either side allowing free passage without having to step into the grime. The only light came from the torches they carried.

"These sewers are like a maze. We need to be careful or else we could spend a lifetime racing around," Hadar's voice was too calm. He obviously didn't know that the man had already passed through the door.

The sudden sound of footsteps on the stairs brought him round. Without a second thought Hadar decided to go right.

They rushed through the sewers as if it were Nyrra himself on their tail. Hadar took the many intersections without thinking where they were going. After a while he stopped.

"What are you doing?" asked Alaric as he just stopped before barreling into Hadar.

"Something is not right here. Look," Hadar waved the torch at the floor. The ground in front of them was completely clean of dust. It was as if someone had just recently swept the floor. "This passage has been used recently."

Alaric ducked suddenly for no apparent reason. "What was that?" asked Eldred, his voice frail.

"I don't know. I just felt like something was flying towards me," Alaric seemed confused.

"Whoever is chasing us is scrying for our location. I can only hope that means that he's not on our trail," explained Eldred.

"Do you know how to get out of here?" asked Alaric as he slowly relaxed.

"Not exactly. There are manholes in the roads that lead down here. All we have to do is find a way up. There has to be ladder or stairs. It is either that or we can keep wandering until we find an exit drain," offered Hadar.

"We are running out of time. We need to find a way out of the sewers now," Alaric was again starting to worry about Alena. They had the cure, but it would be no good if Alena was already dead.

"There has to be a way out around here. I can't see someone just randomly sweeping out a sewer," Hadar offered.

Alaric wasn't as confident as Hadar. They had been wandering through the sewer for over an hour and there still was no sign of an exit. Alaric placed his head in his hands and leaned back against the sewer wall. There was a soft click and the wall suddenly swung open and Alaric went crashing to the ground.

When he looked up he came face to point with half a dozen swords. The men on the other end didn't look friendly. They wore rough leather jerkins and dirty pants. Their appearance showed that they were not part of the affluent class. Alaric surmised that they were thieves hiding from the night watch. He knew that if he made the wrong move he would be skewered.

"Well, well, well. What have we here? What are the three of you doing down here at this time of night?" One of the men spoke in a rough voice.

The six men slowly let Alaric get to his feet. They also motioned Hadar and Eldred to step inside the small room out of the sewer. With them all in place, the wall swung closed and the man in charge told the others to lower their swords.

"We are being chased. Our only chance was to come into the sewers," explained Hadar quickly.

"What are your names?"

"My name is Jadar, the merchant. This is my apprentice and this is my father," Hadar indicated Alaric and Eldred respectively. Eldred had to suppress a groan at being called Hadar's father.

"Apprentice? He looks a little old to be an apprentice," scoffed the man.

Hadar motioned for the man to come closer, indicating that he didn't want Alaric to hear what he was saying. "This is my wife's brother. He's a little slow. I'm only doing this as a favour for her, if you know what I mean. She was quite adamant on the situation," Hadar whispered.

The man laughed out loud. "Very good Jadar. Let's say for now that I believe your story. There are very few people who know the entrances to these parts of the sewers and none of them are what you would call savoury characters. How is it that you came by one of them?"

"I was trading with," Hadar paused as if he was thinking of what to say next. "I was trading with Yoseph when we were set upon."

Hadar was about to continue when the man interrupted. "Very good, that is a story I can believe and you need not explain what you were doing at Yoseph's. The next problem I have is what am I going to do with you? No one can know of my little operation here, which means that I can't let you go."

"But we need to get home. My wife will kill me if I'm late. I told her that I was coming in just after midnight." Hadar's lie almost had Alaric believe him.

"I'm truly sorry, but that is not my concern. My name is Tildon and these men will keep you company until I decide what to do with you."

Alaric moved for the hilt of his sword. As the men saw him move, they raised their own. Hadar shook his head and Alaric relaxed his hand. He thought that they could take the six men, but he trusted Hadar's judgment.

"I will leave you now," Tildon spoke.

The room could barely contain the nine men. The walls were made out of grey stone. A table and half a dozen chairs in the centre were the only other things in there. On the table was a map of the city and the building blueprints to the palace. Hadar only had a quick glance before Tildon swept up the documents and left the room up a flight of stairs.

The men watched Hadar closely as he moved to sit at the table. The name Tildon was familiar to him, but he just couldn't place it. There was something wrong about the situation. The men held their weapons with the confidence of trained soldiers, not career criminals. Their appearance was also wrong. It was almost as if they were deliberately scruffy, not from years of living in the dust and grim.

"So what is it you're doing down here?" Hadar thought if he could get the men talking, he might found out some important information.

"I don't think that you should be talking. Tildon is a fair man, but you don't want to give him a reason not to like you. He'll have your head rolling along the sewer floor if he thinks it'll be profitable," one of the men warned.

Alaric, who had also sat, looked across at Hadar. His eyes pleaded with him to find a solution to their latest dilemma. There was no telling how long Tildon would hold them and there was still the man who was chasing them. If he came across the secret room, there was no telling what would happen.

"How long do you think Tildon will be before he lets us go?" Hadar asked.

"It's hard to say. It all depends on whether your story checks out or not. He has ways of finding things out about people." A wry smile appeared on the man's face.

"That's it!" Hadar exclaimed suddenly as he jumped up from his chair.

The five men all looked nervous at his sudden movement. One of them almost ran him through, but just stopped in time.

"Sit down Jadar. This is not the time for sudden movements," barked the man who nearly killed him.

"Oh, relax the lot of you," the large grin was brimming on his face. "I knew that I had heard of Tildon before. You're all part of the Royal Secret Service. Tildon was in the army when I knew him. It's been a few years, but he is still the same man," Hadar was doing his best to explain, but was only making the men more nervous.

After a few moments of looking at each other, one of the men decided to get Tildon. It was clear that none of them was comfortable with Hadar's words. None of them wanted to say anything in case Hadar was bluffing.

Tildon returned with the other man shortly after he had disappeared at the top of the stairs. He had a concerned look on his face. He looked at Hadar carefully when he returned to the room.

"So, you say you know who I am. I can't recall ever meeting a merchant by the name of Jadar," Tildon challenged. He knew that Hadar wasn't who he said he was.

"That's because my name is not Jadar. I am Duke Hadar. I knew you when you served in the King's army, by reputation only," offered Hadar.

"Well, I knew that your story was a lie. A merchant does not hold himself in quite the same manner as a Duke. I have seen you before, when you were visiting the King. So why were you really running through my sewers?" Tildon visibly relaxed.

"As I said, we were doing a deal with Yoseph when we were interrupted. We all had to bail at the last minute. It was our only means of escape."

"They are Nyrra's soldiers. I saw one of them briefly,' added Alaric. Tildon seemed shocked to hear Alaric speak, but then he remembered that Hadar's story was a lie. "Damn it. That's just what we were worried about. There have been rumors that Nyrra has sent spies to infiltrate the city, that's why we're down here. Now that confirms it."
Tildon swore.

"We need to get to the palace; it's the greatest of urgencies. Can you help us?"

Tildon watched Hadar carefully. "I suppose I can help you. There is a way into the palace via the sewers. It is the only way I will be able to get you inside. Since I joined the R.S.S., I can't come and go as I please. None of my men can be seen waltzing past the palace gates. All of you must be blindfolded. No one can know the entrance to the palace."

"I wouldn't worry too much about that. We have been wandering around the sewers for an hour and have no idea where we are," returned Hadar, who knew if they would be blindfolded, it would take twice as long for them to reach the palace.

"All the same, it's not a risk that I'm willing to take," Tildon would not be persuaded.

Hadar was about to protest again when Alaric spoke. "We will do whatever it takes to get us back inside," Alaric's voice was rock hard and took everyone by surprise. As soon as he finished speaking his entire demeanour changed. "We have been found. They know where we are."

"What are you talking about?" asked Tildon.

"The soldiers have found us and will be here in a few minutes. If we don't move quickly they will be upon us." Hadar motioned for Tildon not to press Alaric further, but accept what he was saying.

Tildon rushed them back into the sewers. He wasn't sure what had transpired, but he wanted them out of his way. If the soldiers knew where their hideout was, then their entire operation would be compromised. He would prefer to give away his secret passage into the palace than what they had been working on for the last six months.

Tildon raced through the sewer tunnels like he was racing through the streets above. Two of the other men followed behind to make sure no one got lost. It didn't take long for Tildon to find the alcove he had been looking for. A small, rickety looking ladder led upwards.

They came up in the palace stables. There was no one around to watch their entrance and Tildon left them to return to the sewers. As much as he wanted to confirm their story, he had more important business to take care of. If all went well, he could uncover Nyrra's agents and finish his work in one night.

Hadar took the lead once they were inside the palace. It didn't take long to find a pageboy who knew where Alena was resting. They rushed to the room in the hope they weren't too late. Hawthorne jumped up from his chair when he heard the door burst open. He relaxed as soon as he saw who it was.

"Thank the Gods you're back. Did you get what we need?" the remaining sleep quickly leaving him as he spoke.

"Yes we did, but we are going to need Lorio to administer it," Hadar answered.

"He dropped in after he had eaten and said to ring that bell if you came back with the antidote. I spoke to him for a while after you left and made him realise how important she is."

Shortly after he stopped ringing, a young man appeared at the door. Hawthorne quickly explained the situation and the man was off again. Alena did not look like she had long left. Alaric hoped that Lorio returned quickly.

It did not take long for Lorio to return with the page. He had a sleepy look on his face and a small case in his left hand. He was still dressed in his nightgown and he didn't look impressed to be awake.

"I take it you found the missing ingredient?" Lorio asked Eldred.

"Even better! We managed to get the antidote," Hadar replied.

Lorio didn't look impressed. "I hate to break it to you, but I doubt very much that you would have been able to get the real antidote. As you know, not registering a drug is a hangable offence. They would be a fool to admit to manufacturing the poison. I'm afraid that what you have there will be useless."

"That's okay. I know whom it was who made the poison. He is a shifty character, but I don't think he would have given us the wrong cure. When he gave it to us, he was under the impression that he was coming with us," Hadar reaffirmed.

"Well I hope you're right," Lorio placed his case on the side table and opened it up. He moved a few things around inside before pulling out a needle.

Hadar handed Lorio the small vile with the antidote. He filled the chamber and then poked Alena in the arm. Once the chamber was empty again he withdrew the needle and replaced it in the case. Everyone stood in silence and waited for Lorio to comment.

"Well I guess we will know more in the morning. I would advise you all to get some rest. I will have my page show you to the guest rooms," Lorio didn't wait for anyone to speak before he left.

"I will stay with her," offered Alaric as he watched her closely for any hint of a change in her condition.

"That's okay. I am happy to stay," replied Hawthorne. "I have already settled in for the night and you should get some sleep."

Alaric was about to protest, but Eldred silenced him by placing a hand on his shoulder. It was late in the night and the last thing they needed was an argument.

"Nothing will happen tonight. I will return in the morning and release the spell," Eldred spoke before Alaric had a chance to say anything.

There was no arguing with him. There was no point staying in the room if there was going to be no change in her condition. Alaric still wanted to be by her side, but he also needed a good night's sleep. He was exhausted and it was going to be another long day. He didn't complain when he was showed to his room. Things would be different in the morning.

Chapter 25: King Lisle IV

In the morning, Alaric was woken by the sun shining on his face. His body ached, but he couldn't remain in bed. He was sure that Alena was going to be up and about and he wanted to visit her. He put off his morning exercises and raced to her. He paused outside the door, his heart racing. Slowly he pushed it open and peered inside. Hawthorne was still asleep in the chair beside her bed and there seemed to be no change in Alena's appearance.

Hawthorne slowly woke with Alaric in the room. He looked around slowly. "Is she better?" he asked groggily.

"I don't know; I just got here. Have you seen Eldred?" Alaric asked.

Eldred appeared in the doorway. He looked as though he had not slept at all. In truth, he had managed to get two hours sleep in between his studying. Again, he had spent the rest of the night reading through the prophecy and again he had found no answers.

"I think it's time to restore her health." Eldred seemed strangely perky.

No one spoke. The tension in the room had already started to build. Eldred walked to the window and pulled the curtains wide open and a blast of sunlight engulfed the room. He then returned his attention to the she-elf on the bed. Her breathing didn't seem as laboured as it had been and some colour had returned to her face.

Eldred sat on the bed. "You two should leave now. You can't be here for this."

"What are you talking about, Eldred? I want to be here when she wakes up," Alaric spoke before Hawthorne had the chance.

"Returning her from the spell will not be pleasant. I wish to do it in privacy. The slightest disturbance and we risk killing her."

There was no arguing with Eldred. Both men grumbled, but didn't waste any time. As soon as the door was shut, Alaric felt the familiar tickle return to the back of his neck. A faint glow could be seen from under the door and Alaric wondered what it was that Eldred was doing. Now that he knew his potential, he wanted to learn.

It wasn't long before the feeling went away and the light dimmed. Alaric was confident that whatever it was that Eldred was doing, he had finished. There was nothing more that he wanted to do than open the door, but he would wait for Eldred to let them back in.

Alaric and Hawthorne moved tentatively towards the bed. Slowly, as they approached, Alena opened her eyes. She still looked frail, but the colour had returned to her face and she looked alive for the first time. She smiled as she saw the concerned looks on their faces.

"Where am I?" her voice cracked.

"Don't worry about that now. Get some sleep and I will come and see you at midday," Eldred returned her smile. "Now we shall leave you in peace," the last comment was more directed at the other two.

Once they were all out of the room, Eldred spoke. "It seems that Lisle wants our company this morning. I don't think that he was too impressed with what happened last night."

Eldred led the way to the King's meeting room where they would have breakfast prepared. It was an informal meeting, but if they said the wrong word they could end up in the stocks.

Inside the room King Lisle IV sat at the head of the table with Queen Mara sitting on his left. On his right sat his two sons, Prince Lisle and Prince Rives. On his left sat his daughter, Princess Romana and Hadar.

"I thank you for joining us," Lisle didn't sound impressed as they sat down.

Alaric watched the royal family closely as Eldred made their introductions. Prince Lisle was the spitting image of his father. They both had dark shoulder length hair, hazel eyes and a slightly upturned nose. A powerful upper body with broad shoulders indicated that they had both done hard labour in their lives. Rives and Romana shared their mother's fair hair and slender features. They too wore the same unimpressed look on their faces.

"So what is it that is so important that you interrupt my evening meal?"

"Alena, one of our companions, was struck by a poisoned arrow. We had to see Lorio to find a cure. I'm sorry for any intrusion, but it was a matter of urgency," Hadar spoke quickly, recognising Lisle's short temper.

"I wasn't talking to you, Duke! Be sure that I know the story behind your arrival, but I also know with whom you companion yourself. I address the wizard. What brings you here?" Lisle only glanced at Hadar once before continuing his glare at Eldred.

"As Duke Hadar explained, our friend was hit…" Eldred started but was cut short.

"And as I told you, I know of your woman or whatever she is. It is not her I am interested in. I know you never travel anywhere without a purpose and I want to know what it is." Lisle's temper was growing short. Eldred sighed. "As you know, we fight the forces of the Evil One. We are building an army and we seek your aid." Eldred knew there was no point dancing around the subject.

"At last the truth!" Lisle picked up a piece of fruit and ate it thoughtfully. "It seems that my kingdom is awash with this filth. I heard about your little run in with Kerwin. I never liked him when he was a boy and even less when he was a man. I should have done away with him years ago. Nyrra's reach is very long indeed, now why do you think he had chosen my Kingdom to invade?"

"As you well know, Nyrra has been building an army in an attempt to break free of his prison. Over the past year, he has been coming closer and closer to breaking through. His agents have been casting dispersions around the many kingdoms in a hope that we don't unite against him. The only way he can defeat us is if we do not unite. If you believe that your Kingdom will be the one attacked, then you will not commit the necessary forces to destroy his army on the fields of Avalon," Eldred had been prepared to make his speech for a long time and did not falter.

"It is all lies," Lorio started. "He has never told anything but lies."

"Be still Lorio," Lisle barked.

"Are you still bitter that you did not have enough power to be trained as a wizard?" Eldred's words cut into Lorio

"That's enough," boomed Lisle before Lorio had a chance to retaliate. "Petty bickering will get us nowhere. Tell me why I should believe you. The threat to my Kingdom is real, but there is no proof that he will bring his army to the fields of Avalon."

"The threat to Hondin Lel is a ruse. The only way Nyrra can regain his true former strength is to reach his fortress and regain his lost power. The shortest route is through the fields of Avalon. That is where the battle with his army will take place."

"I see. As you may know, I have had my own men investigating the situation. I am the closest Kingdom to Nyrra's and the supposed battle zone. If the Alliance fails, then I am the next logical target." The words didn't sound promising. "With that in mind, I have already started to move my army to the east. I will lend six of my battalions to the Alliance. I have also sent word to my nobility stating the support that I require from them."

"I have received no such letter!" Hadar looked at Lisle as though he had just told the biggest lie in his life.

"That is quite strange. I sent the messengers over a month ago. You should have received it before you left to come here." The surprise on Lisle's face was genuine. "In fact, I would have thought you would have brought your army with you."

"I think that I may know what has happened to your messengers." It was clear that at least one of the messengers had been waylaid by Nyrra's agents.

Even without the King's demand, Hadar was planning on pledging his full support, but things had changed. With Kerwin's betrayal, he really didn't have any troops to lend. He needed all of his soldiers to keep the balance in his own lands.

"I do not think that is a wise decision." It was clear that Lorio did not agree with Lisle decision. "We cannot leave ourselves so utterly defenseless. Without the army to maintain order, there will be complete anarchy."

"You know I always appreciate your council Lorio, but my mind is made up. The remainder of my army will stay behind and the city will be under martial law. Things will be tough for a while, but the alternative is much worse." Lisle spoke.

"Then we shall go to war," Prince Lisle banged his fist on the table.

"You will not be fighting this war. There are more important things for you and your brother to do. Your Kingdom needs you and you will stay," Lisle spoke with the command of a King, not that of a father.

Prince Lisle was about to speak, but his father silenced him with a wave of his hand. "You and your friends are more than welcome to stay here at the palace until you are ready to leave. The remainder of my army will be ready to move by the end of the week. If you wish to travel with them, then you are more than welcome." King Lisle stood when he finished speaking.

"Thank you. We will be leaving as soon as Alena is fit to ride." Eldred also stood and motioned for the others to do the same.

King Lisle gestured for the others to leave the room. He was done talking to them and wanted time to speak with his family and Lorio. Eldred knew that there was no point in staying. They had been given more than what he had been expecting and it had been so easy.

They walked out of the room and headed down the corridor. There was a new sense of hope as if everything was going to be alright.

"I'm surprised Lisle didn't mention the huge hole in his main gate," Eldred said jovially.

"I would make the summation that he hasn't been told yet," commented Hadar. "I don't think he's going to let that one slide. I should probably go back and explain."

Hadar left the three of them and returned to see the King. Alaric was glad that Hadar was going to explain. He wasn't sure exactly what had happened.

They checked on Alena who was still sleeping soundly. Her breathing had returned to normal and the colour had completely returned to her face. There was nothing they could do for her. Her recovery was coming along as best it could. Hawthorne remained by her side whilst Eldred led Alaric away from the room.

"We need to start your training," Eldred said when they reached his room. "I have been very remiss."

They sat at different sides of the small table. Alaric was a little nervous, but more excited. Something had changed in him and he wanted answers. He could feel the power inside, but he had no idea how to use it.

"As I explained to you before, you have the power within you   but you need more than that to use it successfully. What happened at the gate is what happens to those who do not receive the proper training. Most will go through their lives without really harming anyone, but those with a temper can cause great pain to those around them and to themselves. The first key lesson is understanding where we get the power to cast spells." Alaric watched Eldred intently. "We draw on the energy of the world around us. Everything in the word creates energy. The trees, the people, the animals and even the rocks and stones; they all have an energy that we draw upon to increase our own. What I want you to do is close your eyes and concentrate on your breathing." Alaric did as he was told. "Now reach out with your feelings."

Alaric took another deep breath and then he forced his mind to focus on the room around him. There was nothing more he wanted in the world than to feel the energy around him. No matter how hard he tried, he could not feel anything. Eventually he stopped searching and opened his eyes.

"It's useless. I can't feel anything," Alaric sighed.

"That is because you tried to force it. You must open yourself up to the power around you. You must be at one with your surroundings and not try to control them. To force the energy away from its owner is to crack the very fabric of reality. Now try it again and this time relax," Eldred spoke softly, like he had done with too many apprentices before.

Slowing his breathing again, Alaric attempted to feel the energy. Even though he couldn't feel anything he remained calm and gently pushed out with his mind. After a few minutes the strange tingling sensation returned. This time the feeling wasn't on the back of his neck; it was in the room all around him. It was the strangest sensation that he had ever felt.

"Very good," Eldred's sudden words brought Alaric out of his reverie.

At first Alaric wondered how Eldred knew that he had felt the energy in the room and then realised that he had a large smile on his face. The look on Eldred's face was somewhat surprised.

"What is it?" asked Alaric.

"Usually it would take up to a day of training for an apprentice to feel the energy around them. Sometimes it can take up to a week." Eldred tried his best to hide his excitement. "The key now is to be able to feel the energy by will. When the time comes for you to use your power, you will only have a split second to call on the energy of the world."

Alaric was indeed a quick learner, but this training required patience. It took time for anyone to master the art of controlling the world's energy. Each time Alaric felt the energy around him, Eldred made him let it go and start again. Each time the feeling came quicker and quicker. It may have only been a second or two each time, but sure enough it was becoming easier. It was late in the day when Eldred finally let him rest.

"That was very good. You can now sense the power around you almost instantly." Before Eldred could say any more there came a knock on the door. "Enter!"

The door swung inwards and Hadar entered. "I have smoothed things over with Lisle. He wasn't happy when I told him what had happened, but I managed to convince him that it had to be done." He shot Alaric a questioning look, but continued before anyone had the chance to speak. "It's getting late and I am going to get the others. I think it would be best if we were all together."

"Very good. I think that you should go with him," Eldred spoke. "It has been a long day in here and I think some fresh air will do you some good."

"I would rather check on Alena." Alaric hadn't realised how late it was. "I'm sure that she would be awake by now."

"I will check in on her. You should get some fresh air. You will feel better for it in the morning." Something was underlying in his words. Alaric wasn't sure what it was, but he knew there would be no arguing.

Hadar led Alaric through the corridors. Alaric kept a step behind. Every so often Alaric would reach out and sense the energy surrounding him. He was surprised at how each time there were subtle differences. He tried to remember each feeling, to recognise the differences between stone and wood. Once they were outside, the sensation changed so abruptly that Alaric was nearly knocked from his feet. The feeling wasn't unpleasant and brought him joy rather than pain.

The sun was starting to set and the night was nearly upon them. The sky shone a blazing red as the sun came down. Alaric let the feeling go and looked back over his shoulder. His jaw dropped open as he saw the palace walls reflecting the brilliant colour.

"Oh, I forgot to tell you about that," said Hadar casually as they walked towards the stables. "It is one of the most defining features of the palace. On a night like this, there is no better view in the world."

"It's truly magnificent," Alaric's voice was filled with awe.

Hadar just laughed. He would feel better once they had found the others and brought them back to the palace. He had received some disturbing information when he returned to speak with Lisle and the last thing he wanted to do was to be outside the palace walls.

To Alaric's surprise, a makeshift gate had been erected and the damaged section of the wall had been patched. None of the debris that had been strewn across the ground remained. The soldiers at the gate were different to those from the night before. Hadar made sure he had all the appropriate paperwork to get them readmitted when they returned.

The sun set quickly leaving the streets dark. The street lighters were furiously trying to get all the lanterns lit before the sun disappeared altogether. The streets had an eerie feel in the perpetual twilight. To add to the macabre feeling, a strange mist started to sweep across the city.

"Something's not right," commented Hadar as they rode towards the inn. "Something doesn't feel right about this fog."

Alaric felt the same. It became very thick very quickly and soon enough they could only see three feet in front of them.

Slowly a chinking sound could be heard through the fog. It was impossible to tell where it was coming from. It was almost like the sound of coins jingling in someone's pocket. They both stopped and tried to pin point where it's location. One thing was definite; it was coming closer. Hadar clearly relaxed in his saddle when he recognised it.

"It's okay. It's just the city guard," Hadar let out a deep breath.

"No!" Alaric exclaimed. "It's coming from all around us. This isn't right at all. Ride!"

Adelanta sensed Alaric's urgency and jumped into action before he had a chance to settle himself. It was all he could do to stay in the saddle. Hadar wasn't as quick to react, but when he realised what Alaric was doing, he followed suit. A man suddenly came out of the fog in front of Alaric. With the fog obscuring Alaric's view, there was not time for him to maneuver Adelanta. The man took a glancing blow which knocked him to the ground, the man tried to roll out of the way as Hadar followed behind, but was not quick enough. Hadar's horse's left hoof landed directly on the man's breastplate. The man cried out in pain as the hoof dented his armour. Hadar also cried out as he felt his horse slip on the polished steel. Anticipating the horse's fall, Hadar jumped from the saddle. He hit the ground on his feet, but the speed sent his body tumbling forward.

On the ground, Hadar could see under the fog. He quickly counted twenty pairs of legs standing around him. He could also see Adelanta disappearing in the distance. The fog was the only chance for him to escape. He could see his horse was only a couple of paces away, but there was a set of legs blocking his path.

Taking a deep breath, Hadar jumped to his feet and made a dash for his horse, adrenalin pumped through his body as his footsteps alerted his pursuers to his location. The deep fog was unnerving and he hoped that his horse wasn't startled by the sudden movement.

With one swift movement, Hadar was back in the saddle. He knew that it was only a matter of seconds before they would be on top of him. Kicking his heals he galloped away.

After what seemed like hours, but in fact were only a couple of minutes, Hadar stopped to check where he was. The fog had made it impossible for him to see any of the usual landmarks. He looked from building to building for one that he recognised. To his horror he realised the he had no idea where he was. Normally the sight of the palace would point him in the right direction, but now it was nowhere to be seen. Slowly he moved his horse forward. The only thing that would be more dangerous than riding straight towards his attackers would be to remain stationary.

***

After a mad dash through the streets, Alaric reined in Adelanta outside the inn. It was more due to Adelanta's skill that they reached the inn in one piece. Once he had stopped, he looked behind him to see if Hadar was far behind. The fog was a little lighter, but he still could only see for a few paces. He could hear the sound of rowdy voices from inside the inn's bar and presumed that Hadar must have taken a quicker route and already be inside. After dismounting and handing Adelanta's reins to the groomsman, Alaric walked in.

As he knew he would, he found the two dwarves drinking. Both had large mugs of ale and were having a loud discussion with a group of locals. It looked harmless enough, but Alaric wasn't sure it was going to stay that way.

"Ah, my young friend," Hulkan barked when he saw Alaric. "What brings you to this part of town? The palace not good enough for you?" Hadar and Dorn both roared with laughter. Their new friends didn't seem to understand the joke.

"Has Hadar arrived yet?" asked Alaric, trying to ignore the bait.

"Not unless he's hiding at the bottom of this mug. I'll just check for you," Dorn said, quickly draining his mug before continuing to laugh.

"This is serious," Alaric was quickly becoming frustrated. "We ran into some trouble on our way from the palace. There is something strange happening tonight. If Hadar hasn't arrived yet, I fear that he is in danger," Alaric spoke quietly so no one else could hear.

"We better get going then," Hulkan's voice turned deadly serious. "You get the others, whilst I get the horses ready," Hulkan said to Dorn.

Dorn quickly moved into action. Hulkan and Alaric both walked towards the stable door. Before they could leave, a voice called out to them from the bar.

"Hey you! Where's my cart? I needed it today," the innkeeper called.

"I'm sorry, Hadar still has it. He will bring it back in the morning." Alaric blatantly lied, but he didn't have time to waste explaining the situation.

Without waiting for a response, the two of them left the room and made their way to the stables. Hulkan looked at the fog with surprise, but didn't think much of it. The groomsman didn't seem too happy with having to prepare so many horses so late in the day, especially as he had just taken the saddle and bridle off Adelanta.

Then horses and pack animals were all ready when the others arrived. The fog, if anything, had become thicker. It was almost impossible for anyone to see anyone else. It would be difficult for them not to get separated on their way to the palace. Only Alaric knew the way and he would have to rely on Adelanta's sense of direction.

Although Alaric was in a hurry to get back to the safety of the palace, he kept Adelanta to a walk. If he lost one of the others, then it would be almost impossible to find them. The lights from the town only made the fog seem more eerie.

"I don't like this at all," commented Palentonal. He was only just within view of Alaric. "I've seen some thick fog in my time, but nothing that compares to this. It's almost as if it isn't natural."

Alaric didn't want to let his suspicions out. The others seemed worried enough without anything adding to their concerns.

As they rounded a corner, the sound of chinking armour and horse hooves returned. Alaric whispered for the others to stop, his heart racing. It was impossible for them to figure out where the sound was coming from. It sounded as though it was all around him. All Alaric could do was to draw his sword and wait for the inevitable. Hearing the sound of Alaric's sword coming out of its hilt prompted the others to draw their weapons.

"What's going on Alaric?" asked Dorn from somewhere in the fog, his voice filled with frustration.

Alaric didn't answer. He stared out, waiting to see who was approaching. Suddenly, as the tension was almost unbearable, a horse appeared.

"Thank the gods I found you. This fog is really starting to play on my nerves," Tildon breathed a sigh of relief.

"You're a sight for sore eyes. I know what you mean. We really need to get out of this fog. There is evil about tonight."

"Is Hadar nearby?" asked Tildon.

"We were ambushed on our way to the inn. I lost him from there. I thought that he was behind me. In this fog, it was impossible to tell. He never made it to the inn and we didn't have time to wait for him. Hopefully he will make his own way back to the palace," Alaric explained. "What are you doing out here?"

"The King sent us to find you. Apparently when the fog rolled in, Eldred urged the King to send someone. It seems it was important enough for the King to send me," Tildon answered.

No one understood the exchange, except for Alaric, but they were grateful they had someone to lead them towards the palace. Alaric seemed to know the stranger and that was good enough for them.

It was an uneventful ride; the fog remained just as thick throughout the trip. With Tildon and his men for guides, Alaric's nerves had settled. He didn't completely relax until they had passed the guardhouse. The fog blanketed the entire palace grounds.

Tildon took them directly to Lisle's office. Inside Eldred, Lisle and Lorio were waiting; they all looked concerned. A letter sat in the middle of the table. It was clear that they had all been staring at it.

Eldred made a quick introduction. It was clear that Lisle didn't want to wait. There was something on his mind and he wasn't interested in a formal meeting. He let out a deep sigh as Tildon continued the introductions. "That's enough Tildon. You can leave us now."

"Very good, your majesty," Tildon bowed once before leaving the room.

Eldred picked up the letter before he realised that Hadar was not with them. "Where's Hadar?" There was a hint of concern in his voice.

Alaric explained what had happened. Their expressions turned even graver. The news was never good, but he didn't think he would get the response that he did. "Tildon has sent some men to look for him. I'm sure he will be alright." Alaric added to try and lift their spirits.

"That is neither here nor there," Eldred's words were not what he was expecting. "Before we left Kerwin's castle, I sent a letter to Orric explaining what had happened. We received a reply from him today. It was not the news we had been hoping for." He motioned for the others to sit before he started the letter.

Eldred,

I hope that this reaches you before you leave Lel Dinion.

The news of the Serpentant is most disturbing. I had hoped that we had seen the last of their kind. Our list of enemies is growing, whilst our list of allies is reducing quickly. I had no luck in convincing the High Chancellor to join our plight. There was something not quite right in his manner. This is something I will need to look into further, but now I do not have time

Two nights ago, there was a bright flash in the sky. I'm still trying to figure out what it was. All I know is that it was not natural. As a result, Nyrra is now free. The blast, or whatever it was, caused a great crack to appear in the force field. Obviously, it didn't take long for him to take advantage of it. We couldn't repair the crack before Nyrra broke through. There are too many things happening for it all to be a coincidence.

Now that Nyrra is free we must double our efforts to get to Avalon before him. His agents will be out in force now, with renewed strength. Nyrra's evil will radiate through the Seven Kingdoms. His agents will be stronger than ever. I wish I had more time to realise these new riddles, but time is not something we have to spare.

Your quest now becomes even more perilous. Leave the Serpentant alone, it will reveal its own agenda when the time is right. I do not believe it is in league with Nyrra. You must leave at once for the Cauldron Mountain. You must reach it before Nyrra or all is lost.

Orric

The room was silent as everyone let the information sink in. Even those who had already heard the letter didn't want to speak. It was a good a minute before Alaric broke the silence.

"What are we going do? We can't leave until Alena is fit enough to ride." Alaric's words did nothing to lighten the mood.

"We must leave in the morning. Hopefully by then she will be able to handle the ride," Eldred's words were not comforting. "We will have to keep a slow pace for a while, but we have to leave as soon as possible. I have no doubt that Nyrra knows where we are and it won't take long for him send more of his agents our way. The road will be even more dangerous from here on."

"I will send my best soldiers with you," offered Lisle. "They will give you some protection."

"No, but thank you Lisle. What you need to do is start sending your army east to Avalon. You need to get the first battalion moving as soon as the sun rises. We will leave via the north of the city. I'm sure that Nyrra's agents will believe that we will try and leave with your army. Tomorrow should give us enough time to make our escape. We all have our part to play and no one's is more dangerous than anyone else's." His last statement was a lie. "Now I don't think there is much more we can do here tonight. I think it would be a good idea if we all had something to eat and then retire for the night."

There would have been some arguments from the two dwarves, but they didn't have the courage to speak. They had all known that eventually Nyrra would break free, that was the entire reason for their mission, but they had always thought they would have been further on before it happened. Now it was a true race to see who would win.

Eldred pulled Alaric back as they all left Lisle's office. He waited until everyone else was out of earshot before he spoke. "I have arranged for some food to be sent to your room. You should sleep once you have eaten." Eldred words were very matter of fact.

Once he was back in his room, the guilt of losing Hadar returned. The last thing he wanted to do was to fall asleep. The words in the letter echoed in his mind. The pure evil of Nyrra had finally been released.

Although he wanted to join the search for Hadar, he did what Eldred told him. His sleep that night was very disturbed. His dreams were filled with strange, evil creatures. There was something different with the dreams than the previous nightmares he had. It was as if they were more potent. In the morning, Alaric felt as though he had not slept at all. His body ached as though the blows he had suffered in his dreams had been real.

They all met in Lisle's smaller entertaining hall for breakfast. Alena still remained absent. Lisle's physicians were preparing her for the day's ride. Until she was fit enough, she would ride in a carriage. Lisle donated his most luxurious carriage to ease the burden.

Lisle joined them at the stables where the horses had been prepared for their departure. He had given strict instructions for their horses to be treated with great care. They looked refreshed for their rest in the royal stables.

"I'm just sorry that I won't be coming with you. I think that it's a momentous task that you have set and I would have loved to be a part of it," Lisle spoke sincerely.

"One day we shall return when times are better and sit in your great hall and celebrate our victory. I cannot thank you enough for your hospitality and supplies." Eldred shook the King's hand.

Lisle left them as they rode towards the northern gate. Earlier in the day he had sent his first battalion off to the east. Hopefully if there was anyone watching, they would assume that they had left with the army.

The carriage that Alena travelled in served two purposes. With Alena safely inside and hidden from prying eyes, the rest were dressed in the armour of the royal guard. Without looking too closely, the royal carriage and entourage would look plausible.

As they approached the northern gate, a solitary figure could be seen riding towards them. The rider seemed to tremble in his saddle. As he approached, to their relief, they recognised it was Hadar. Their relief only lasted for a moment before they realised that something wasn't right. He stared towards them with a blank look on his face, as though he didn't even see them. As he rode closer, they could see his face and clothes were drenched with blood. Ropes were tied to his body to stop him from falling. His eyes were open, but there was no comprehension. His breathing was laboured as they helped him from his horse.

"Get some water from the supplies," ordered Eldred as he pulled his helmet off. He was sure that their ruse had been discovered.

"I'll get help," Palentonal called.

Eldred poured the water over Hadar's face. Slowly, as he washed away the blood, Hadar regained his senses. His eyes focused on Eldred and relaxed when he realised who it was.

"Thank the Gods that I made it. Hadar coughed as he spoke and blood appeared on the corner of his mouth.

"Don't talk, just relax. Palentonal has gone to get help. It shouldn't be too far away."

"No," Hadar coughed again. "I must talk to you now." Before he could continue he lost consciousness.

Eldred quickly checked his pulse and breathing. Both were weak, but he was still alive. Eldred did a few more rudimentary tests before he stood. He looked at the others with a worried expression on his face. They knew that the news was not going to be good.

"Is he going to be alright?" asked Alaric, still feeling guilty about leaving him.

"He has lost a lot of blood, but I think he'll survive. As long as help gets here soon," Eldred paused as he looked towards the gate. "This is most disturbing. There was something he was trying to tell us before he lost consciousness. I have a feeling it was something very important. I don't think that we should leave until we know what it is."

"So we're just going to wait. The entire reason why we moved Alena is because we don't have time to wait," barked Hawthorne, surprising the others with the harshness of his words.

"Things have changed Hawthorne. There is obviously more to this than I had originally thought. I need to speak to Hadar before we leave. There is no telling who is waiting for us out there and I for one do not like riding blind." As Eldred finished speaking, the sound of horses could be heard charging behind them.

Palentonal had returned from the palace with three physicians and a dozen guards.

"There is a carriage on the way. I thought that I should bring back some soldiers, just in case. How is he?" asked Palentonal.

"Not the best, but he should be alright now." Eldred watched the physicians closely as they tended to Hadar.

They looked at each other and shook their heads. Before they could give their diagnosis, the carriage arrived. They kept to themselves as Hadar was slowly lifted in. With the carriage on the way back to the palace, the physicians finally turned to Eldred.

"It doesn't look good I'm afraid," the man spoke with a huge degree of pomposity. "I don't know if there is going to be anything we can do." He looked at the others who nodded their agreement.

Eldred did not look convinced with their diagnosis. "I know his condition and it is not that bad. If you are looking to fleece someone out of their gold, you've come across the wrong people. We are in a hurry and I'm in no mood. If you want extra compensation, I suggest you speak to the King. Now if you don't mind, I think that we should get moving," Eldred's tone didn't break the physicians' spirit.

"Well I'm glad you think you know so much about medicine, but we have studied the science for all our lives. We know when we see a lost cause. I think you should prepare the mortuary for a new customer." There was not a hint of pity in the man's voice. "Now I'm sorry, but there is nothing we can do."

The physician was about to mount his horse when Eldred grabbed the man's arm and pulled him away. He was not going to let the scholar get away with his rude attitude. Without waiting for a response, Eldred quickly drew his sword and moved the blade to the physician's throat.

"Now I was wondering if you would like to reassess your status report on my friend?" Eldred smirked.

"Yes, yes. I'm sure he will be alright," piped one of the physicians.

"I think I have something that will help him regain his consciousness," cried the other one.

"I can get him back on his feet in a couple of days," pleaded the one in Eldred's clutches.

Strengthening his grip, Eldred made his intentions clear before releasing the physician.

They passed the carriage before it reached the palace gates. The ride was nervous with the physicians looking to bolt if they were given the chance. Hawthorne remained with Alena; they had decided there was no point in moving her further away.

In turn, each of the physicians spent time with Hadar in the back of his carriage. After Eldred's forceful speech, the physicians' attitudes had certainly changed. Each time they left the carriage, they looked as though they had just saved Hadar's life. Each time Eldred thought of punching their smug faces.

When the last physician exited the carriage, he turned to Eldred and spoke. "He is awake now. Make it quick. If he doesn't get bed rest soon there is a good chance he will die, his wound's need to be cleaned before they turn septic." The smugness had returned

Slowly Eldred stepped into the carriage. Hadar's face was deathly pale, but his eyes were open and there was a smile on his face. The look of his old friend lying, almost on his deathbed, was disturbing, but Eldred had a job to do and nothing could get in his way.

"How are you feeling?" Eldred asked.

"We have no time for pleasantries. There is a great evil out there and it is waiting for you," Hadar paused as his words of doom sank in. "After Alaric escaped, I got waylaid by a group of thugs. They were not much to contend with, but they kept coming from the fog. I took down as many as I could, but in the end there was nothing I could do. They struck me and cut me, but they would not finish me off. When I thought I was going to die, a man stepped out of the fog. Instantly, I knew there was something not right about him. He loomed and the fog seemed to shrink back from his dark armour. I thought he was going to kill me, but instead he tied me to my horse and led me away," Hadar paused and took two deep breaths, slowly his eyes started to roll back into his head.

"Stay with me, Hadar," Eldred urged.

Shaking his head, Hadar looked back towards the wizard. "I'm okay. It's just a little hard to talk. He let me go. Before he sent me on my way he spoke. There was no tone in his voice. His words left a chill in my bones. He said that he was waiting for us. That whoever tries to leave the city will die. There was something very compelling about the way he spoke. I had to believe what he said," Hadar coughed as he finished speaking.

"Was there anything else? Is there anything else about him you can tell me? Did he say anything? Could you see what he looked like?" Eldred pushed.

"I don't know. I know that I saw his face, but now I can't remember what he looked like. I can't remember anything about his physical appearance. It's like I never saw him, isn't that funny, there was something strange about the way he was behaving."

"That's okay, my old friend. Rest now, we will meet again." As Eldred finished talking Hadar lost consciousness. "Get him to the palace," Eldred called to the driver.

"What happened?" asked Alaric quickly, still concerned that it was his fault.

"We have to leave now. The situation is far worse than we thought."

They all moved into action as Eldred had commanded. No one knew what had been spoken, but they knew it wasn't good. They had all begun to feel nervous about leaving Alena and Hawthorne by themselves.

If the threat was as bad as they thought, then they all needed to be together.

Once they had joined the other two, they continued on towards the northern gate. At the rate they were travelling, they would never leave the city. The morning was wearing and before they reached the city wall, Eldred called them for another stop.

"There is something I need to tell you all." Eldred had been deliberating whether to tell everyone what Hadar had told him. In the end, he realised that he could not keep it a secret. No matter how scary the news, not knowing would be more disastrous. "There is something waiting for us beyond the wall. I couldn't find out exactly who it is from Hadar, but I know that at least one of them is extremely powerful. I don't know what they want, but be assured that it's nothing good. Everyone be on their guard. The last thing that we want is to be caught unawares. If we do meet them, follow my lead and no one attack without my say. Things will not be as it seems, but I don't think that they want to kill us," Eldred spoke to the gate and didn't look at anyone.

"What are we likely to encounter?" asked Hawthorne, fingering the hilt of his sword.

"It's hard to say. I would imagine there are going to be a lot of soldiers. If there is, then there will be one amongst them who will be different. No matter what happens, no one is to attack him." This time Eldred looked directly at Hawthorne and then the two dwarves.

"What happens with Alena if it comes to battle?" asked Palentonal before the others had a chance to protest.

"I will try my best to protect her. We can't let anyone pass us. If they do, then I don't think there will be any way to defend the carriage."

Before anyone could ask any more questions, Eldred geed Tormenta to a walk. They rode in silence until they reached the gatehouse. The ride was tense, with everyone on edge. Every movement, every person that they passed, was a would-be threat. The tension was only relieved as they arrived at the safety of the gatehouse.

The King had made the guards aware of their departure and had instructed them to assist anyway they could. The two guards informed them that there had been no unusual movements outside the walls. The day had been progressing much as usual. The news didn't seem to lighten Eldred's sombre mood. He would have preferred news of their enemy. At least that way he would have known what they were doing.

Outside the walls there were a few people milling around. The buildings and streets were relatively quiet. Eldred looked around suspiciously. Nothing seemed out of the ordinary. With a shrug of his shoulders, he led them out of the city.

The outer town was relatively quiet. There was not a lot of movement around them as they rode along the highway. No one, except for Eldred, seemed to notice. They were all concentrating on the people that were in the streets. Any one of them could have been their attackers

"Does something seem strange to you?" Eldred threw the question out to anyone who was listening.

There was a short silence before Alaric spoke. "Now that you mention it Eldred, ever since we left the physicians, the city has seemed rather, sluggish," he paused for a moment to think about what he had said. "Maybe not sluggish, maybe blurred. I don't know exactly what I mean. I guess that's what the problem is. Nothing seems to be working right."

"Of course," called Eldred suddenly. "I don't know why I didn't think of it myself." His sudden good mood quickly changed. "I think that we should prepare ourselves for trouble. I'm afraid to say that we've been duped."

The group looked at each other with confused expressions on their faces. They knew what Eldred had said, but it didn't seem to make any sense. The only thing that sunk in was the tone in his voice. They knew that something very bad was about to happen.

Chapter 26: A Clever Deception

The air in front of them seemed to shimmer. It was slow at first, but soon enough great changes could be seen in their surroundings. The entire landscape changed. Buildings made way for scattered trees. Where there had been nothing, there was suddenly a group of armed men. Front and centre on the highway, sitting on the back of a horse, was a man robed in black. The hood covered the man's face in much the same way as the serpentant, but it was apparent that he was not Viper.

The land was quiet, for a second everything was still. The shock of the sudden change stunned them. Suddenly the man started laughing. Alaric thought that he recognised the voice.

"I can't believe you made my life so easy, Eldred. You should have listened to my warning. If you had stayed inside, then I would have left you alone. It seems that you are not as wise as everyone says you are," he paused as something caught his eye. For the first time, he saw the carriage. "And it seems that you brought me a second gift as well."

"Myria, you will have to get past me if you think you are going to get to Alena," yelled Alaric, grasping the hilt of his sword.

"Easy Alaric. Things are not what they seem. Let me do the talking," Eldred kept his voice low.

"Yes, I think you should take the advice of your wizard, Cursed One," Myria spat the last words.

"You know that nothing will happen here today. You do not have enough men to make a serious attack. Twenty by my count and probably all substandard by my reckoning," Eldred spoke confidently.

"Quite true, but don't worry. There are more on the way," Myria pointed to his left and right and suddenly another fifty men appeared on either side. "I have an entire army hiding within the city. I have spies throughout the palace, or else how do you think I knew of your plan. They will be here shortly. You have no choice but to surrender to me."

"You know I will not do this. You don't honestly believe that I didn't know what you were planning?" Eldred smiled.

What Eldred said registered with many armour-clad men approaching from the south. Myria shifted uncomfortably in his saddle as he realised that the approaching soldiers were not his men. He didn't know how the wizard had pulled off such a feat, but he was not about to hang around to find out. Knowing he was beaten, Myria screamed and kicked his horse into action, riding directly at Eldred. Drawing his sword as he rode he swatted it madly above his head. Eldred motioned for everyone to remain calm as Myria approached. Just before he was about to strike, his horse leapt into the air and the both horse and rider disappeared. Along with Myria, the extra men also vanished. The remaining twenty looked unsure of themselves. With their leader gone and the approaching soldiers, their chance of survival had rapidly declined.

Alaric caught a glimpse of his old employee's face before he disappeared into thin air. There was something different about him. There was no doubt it was the same man who had worked for him, but his face had changed. Alaric tried to focus on what he had seen, but he couldn't. He had not seen his face for long enough to be able to discern the difference.

With the disappearance of Myria, so did the sound of the approaching army. "Myria is not the only one who can play tricks," Eldred winked at Alaric.

The remaining soldiers didn't know what to do. The situation was changing so rapidly they couldn't think. At last one of them had the sense to turn tail and run. Like dominos, the rest of the soldiers started to flee and within a matter of minutes the road was quiet again.

"I think we should keep moving," Eldred's words echoed their own thoughts.

They left quickly keeping a keen eye for any more soldiers. The situation had confused everyone. The sun was lower in the sky than it should have been and when they reached the top of a small hill they could see the city in the distance. The feeling of displacement was almost overwhelming. A small township lay at the bottom of the hill about half a league away. Although there was at least two hours of daylight left, no one wanted to travel past the town.

They quickly rode to the town and found the only inn. "This will have to do," Eldred commented. It was not very suitable and they went to the local tavern to eat. No one, including the two dwarves, stayed long. Once they had eaten, everyone was keen to return to the relative safety of their rooms. The day had been disturbing enough without waiting to see what the night might bring.

Alaric made his way to Eldred's room as soon as they returned. The meeting with Myria was plaguing his mind. There was something very disturbing about it.

"What was Myria doing here?" It was not the question he had wanted to ask, but it seemed like an appropriate way to start. "Has he tracked us all the way here?"

"I don't know. I think that he was the one who attacked us when we left Orric's village. I wouldn't be surprised if he had a hand in Count Kerwin's attack. What is more disturbing is how he was able to infiltrate the city so easily. There is something else that is even more disturbing," Eldred paused as he looked for the words. "I don't think this will be easy for you to hear. The man you knew as Myria has changed, if he ever truly was that man in the first place. What you saw today is pure evil."

Alaric didn't understand what Eldred had just told him. He knew there was something different about Myria, but another person? All he could do was give Eldred a confused look.

"This is very hard to explain and if I didn't see it with my own eyes, I wouldn't have believed it to be true. The man you saw today is Morgoz, one of Nyrra's seven Dark Knights. We believed that all of them were killed when we imprisoned him. It seems that is not the case. If one is here, then there is no telling how many others might be about. They are all as bloodthirsty as Nyrra and will stop at nothing to deliver his will."

"How is this possible?" Alaric seemed in shock.

"I don't know. There is little written on the Dark Knights, but it seems as though they can shape-shift," Eldred paused and looked across at Alaric who still didn't seem to know what was happening. "Now I have yet another piece in this ever growing puzzle. I have a lot to contemplate and will need more than this night. I think that you would do well to get a good night's sleep." Eldred was already deep in thought before Alaric had even left the room.

Alaric's sleep was again riddled with evil creatures. The pain and anguish seemed so real that when morning came around Alaric felt as though he had not slept a wink. Large bags appeared under his eyes and his head felt as though it was filled with sand. He quickly dressed and met the others for breakfast.

The meal was eaten quickly and soon they were on the road again. Alena was again absent during breakfast. Palentonal had made sure she had eaten before helping her into the carriage. She looked better than she had the previous day, but she still looked weak.

They followed the Northern Highway for the rest of the day. The northern region of Hondin Lel was more densely populated than the eastern. They passed many small towns and villages along the highway. The group passed through seemingly unnoticed by the townsfolk. The towns seemed untouched by what was happening around them. Although every now and again Alaric thought he saw people shrink away into the shadows as they passed.

"How can they carry on as if nothing is happening?" asked Bern.

They stopped at a small farming village just before dusk. The ride had been slow again with Alena remaining in the carriage.

"They're simple farming folk around here; don't get me wrong, I'm sure that there are rumours of what is happening in the outside world. If they knew the severity of the situation, their lives would crumble around them. There is nothing they can do, but continue their lives. They wouldn't know one end of a sword from another," explained Hawthorne gravely.

The evening meal was sombre with very little conversation. Alena joined them briefly and ate lightly. Her appearance at the table lifted their spirits and everyone doted on her. They were all happy to see her recovering. It would not be long before she was fit enough to ride.

"How long do you think it will take for us to reach Avalon?" asked Bern as they sat and talked in the tavern.

"We'll ride north until we reach Lel Cornion. That will take us the good part of tomorrow. From there we will take the Darshival Highway southeast for another day and a half. Then we cut due east through the Great Eastern Forest," said Eldred. "A week's journey should bring us right in the middle of our army. All being well, we should get there before Nyrra. When I say, "all being well," I mean that we have to get there before Nyrra"

"When do you expect him to arrive at the battlefield?" Palentonal asked.

"It's impossible to tell. I suspect that he will move his army magically, which means it will depend on how many sorcerers and magicians he has at his call. Not only will he have to use them, but he will need to make sure that they are rested enough to fight. At best, I would imagine it would take him at least a month, but that is a very rough estimation."

"Will Lisle's army make it by then?" asked Bern.

"I honestly don't know. I think some of his battalions will. I doubt his regional armies will make the start of the battle, but I hope they will make the finish. I doubt that this will be a long campaign. Nyrra will be quick and brutal," Eldred realised that the other people in the tavern were starting to look at him. "I think that we should retire. Nyrra has spies everywhere and we can ill afford to get caught in a trap now."

To accentuate the point, Eldred stood from the table. When he was sure that the others were going to do the same, he returned to his room. He had poured through the prophecy at every chance he had and yet he had found no new information. There had been nothing that indicated the appearance of Morgoz and that was most disturbing. It was an event that was in itself worthy of mention. He would not get much sleep again.

Again, Alaric's sleep was disturbed. His dreams were getting more vivid and more painful. By the time morning came around, Alaric could hardly move. His eyes were bloodshot and some bruises had appeared on his arms and legs. There was no chance of his normal morning routine training. When Eldred came to raise him, he could instantly see something wasn't right.

"What in the Gods' names were you doing last night? Did you go back to the tavern and start a fight?" Eldred asked the questions seriously, without a hint of jest.

"Not that I know of," Alaric replied wearily as he crawled out of bed.

"Then what happened?"

Alaric tried to shake the cobwebs out of his mind, but they still remained. He knew that he should have told Eldred about his dreams as soon as he started having them. "Over the last few nights, I've been having these strange dreams. It's hard to explain, but when I wake up my body feels like it has experienced everything from them. It wasn't too bad at first, but it's been getting worse. Last night was obviously the worst it had been."

"Damn it! I should have seen this coming," Eldred cursed to himself.

"What do you mean?"

"These dreams started ever since Nyrra escaped and Morgoz found us?"

"Yes they did. What are you trying to say?" Alaric was starting to become disturbed.

"Nyrra knows where we are. More importantly, he knows where you are. He is casting a spell on you. He's got inside your head and is controlling your dreams. I wish you had said something earlier. It's going to be more difficult to get him out, this will take some time to prepare," explained Eldred.

"Does that mean we stay here?" asked Alaric, hoping for some rest.

"No. I can do this whilst we ride. If Nyrra knows where we are, he will know our movements. That gives him a huge advantage. I don't think that you would gain any rest if we stayed here anyway. Whilst Nyrra is in your head, he won't give you any peace. It's just one of the ways he will try and stop you. At least if we are on the move, his hold on you won't be as strong. He won't have an impact on you during the day and by tonight, we will get him out." Eldred placed a comforting hand on Alaric's shoulder to reassure him. Alaric flinched away in pain. "Get dressed. We need to get moving. We have to be in Lel Cornion before nightfall."

It was another uneventful day on the road. The town became further and further apart and the farms became larger and were separated by small woodlands. Alaric was amazed at the contrast between Hondin Lel and Remidia. He also struggled to remain awake in the saddle. At one stage, he drifted off to sleep. His nightmare continued, although it didn't have the potency of the previous night. He woke with a start and looked around nervously, but no one had seemed to notice.

They reached Lel Cornion just before dusk. The ride had remained at a slow, gentle pace. Alena rode on horseback for a brief period before returning to her carriage. The next day, they would have to leave the carriage behind. The use of it had already cost them half a day of travel and they couldn't spare anymore time.

Lel Cornion was not a farming town like the others they had passed through; it was a small city. Although it was not as impressive as the capital, it was still very beautiful. A small external wall, more for presentation than protection, surrounded it. Many small spires could be seen above the rooflines. It was a very religious city and many people came from the farming towns to pay homage to the various Gods.

It did not take long for them to find an inn. There were nearly more inn's than houses. There was accommodation for everyone, from the poorest of paupers to the richest of merchants. All the reputable inns' prices were over-inflated, but after some quick haggling, Eldred was able to get a sizeable discount. The letter of introduction he had been given by King Lisle helped immensely.

Once everyone was settled, Eldred took Alaric aside. It had taken him all day to work on the spell to exercise Nyrra from Alaric's mind. He knew that the evil wizard would not give up his hold on Alaric easily. Nyrra would be expecting Eldred to try and counter his magic.

"This is not going to be easy," started Eldred when they were alone. He wanted to make sure that no one else was around when he performed his spell. There was a chance if someone was close by that Nyrra's spell could jump to them. "Nyrra has been inside your head for a while now. He knows his way around and will try and hide. Therefore, I'm going to need your help."

"What can I do?" Alaric tried to ignore the fatigue, but it was evident in his voice.

"I need you to open your mind to me. All you have to do is relax. If you try and fight me, then it will give Nyrra a chance to hide. If your mind is open, then there will be no where for him to hide."

Alaric sat on his bed and closed his eyes. His head was rushing with thoughts on what was about to happen.

"Relax Alaric," Eldred's voice held no affliction.

Slowly Alaric emptied his head. The air in the room started to sizzle. Alaric could feel the power growing. Carefully Eldred released his spell. Alaric felt a sharp pain in the back of his head that nearly knocked him over. He could feel a presence inside his mind. His first reaction was to push it out, but he suppressed it. The feeling was not unpleasant so Alaric tried to ignore it. The presence seemed to be searching for something, then he felt a sudden rush of energy pass through his body and he was no longer in the room.

Everything was dark. His eyes were open, but he still couldn't see anything. There was someone close by, but he could not see who it was. Slowly Alaric started to move. For some reason, he knew that the person close to him was friendly. Alaric thought about light and suddenly a bright light appeared. He recognised the man instantly. It was Eldred. In the distance there was another figure, a man whom Alaric could not recognise. His presence was not friendly. Besides the two other men, there was nothing else around him.

"What are you doing here?" asked Eldred, his voice seemed distanced.

"I don't know. I felt a strange sensation and then all of a sudden I was here," replied Alaric.

"This is not a place you should be. Just don't get involved," Eldred barked.

"What's going on?"

"Just stay where you are."

The man in the distance didn't seem to be taking any notice of them. Alaric couldn't be sure, but it looked like the other man was playing with something. When he did, he instantly disappeared.

"I really wish you hadn't put the lights on like that," Eldred seemed upset.

"What are you talking about? Where are we?" Alaric was really confused.

For the first time, Eldred realised that Alaric didn't consciously enter his mind. He didn't know where he was. He hoped that the realisation wouldn't destroy him. "We are inside your mind. I don't know how you got here, but it's not safe. No one should know what goes on inside one's own head," Eldred explained.

"Why is it so plain?" Alaric was very curious now.

"Because I told you to empty your mind. This was the last thing you were thinking of before you entered," Eldred paused. "Well the last thing you thought was blackness. Since you came here, you created the light. It also seems that there is more to your mind than meets the eye, so to speak. Nyrra shouldn't have been able to disappear like that."

"If it's my mind, then I should be able to help with Nyrra. If it's my head, then I make the rules," Alaric was starting to get excited.

"I'm afraid it doesn't quite work that way. Nyrra is very skilled. It makes things even more dangerous for you to be here. You could quite easily get trapped. If that happens, I don't like our chances of getting you out. There is too much risk involved."

"Well what do you want me to do?" Alaric's sounded deflated, even though his words were monotone. There was something very disturbing about their environment.

"You have to translocate. Close your eyes and think about being back in your room. It shouldn't be hard for you to do," Eldred explained quickly.

Alaric did as he was told. Closing his eyes was a lot harder than he thought. Since he was only a projection inside his head his body didn't work like it did outside. After taking a moment to compose himself, Alaric started to imagine his room. At first it was hard, as he had only spent a few minutes there, but eventually his memories came back to him. He felt a small rush in the air around him. To his surprise, he found that he had not translocated, but was still in the same space less environment. The only difference was that Eldred was no longer there.

"I hope you can hear me Alaric," Eldred's voice echoed through the air. I don't know exactly what happened, but it seems that you translocated me back to your room. I expended a lot of energy casting the original spell to get inside your head. To do it again, I'll be too weak to expel Nyrra. You must do it now. What you have to do…" the voice was suddenly cut off.

Alaric stared at the space around him. Even below there was nothing substantial. The thought started to make Alaric panic. Then he thought. 'This is my reality. I can make it whatever I like.' With a single thought, grass and dirt was created under his feet. The suddenness of his creation made him dizzy. Within an instant, he had created the town of Arsiliac, to his best recollection. Even people started to walk the streets, much as they had done when he lived there. A sense of contentment came over him. He was home again,

The streets were so familiar. It was as if his life had not changed. His entire journey had been a long, bad dream. Old acquaintances waved to him as he walked home. The smells of the spring flowers were in the air. The sun was starting to set, marking the end of another peaceful day. Alaric was pleased with what he had done that day. He had secured himself a large client from the capital. It wouldn't be long before he was going to need to expand. It had always been his dream to open an office in Zenza City. It looked like he was one step closer. He started to whistle as he walked home.

Something nagged at the back of Alaric's mind. There was something he had forgotten, something important. The evening was too nice and the day had been too much of a success for Alaric to worry about inconsequential matters. He was going to cook himself a special meal in recognition of his triumph.

The front door was open when he arrived home. Alaric tried to remember back to the morning when he left. He was sure he had locked the door, but could not quite remember. The thought was fleeting. He knew almost everyone in town and no one would break into his house. He must have left it open when he had left for work.

Familiar smells filled his nostrils as he walked through his front door. He wasn't sure, but it felt like there was someone else in his house.

Alaric's heart started to race at the thought of an intruder. He felt like running, but there was something holding him back. Something was telling him that he had to confront them. He looked around his lounge room for a suitable weapon. The only thing he could find was a small statue on his mantle-piece. Alaric thought that something wasn't right. Something was missing. He could swear that there was something that hung on the wall over his fireplace, but he could not remember what it was.

Slowly Alaric started going from room to room. With each room, he thought he was going to find his intruder. There was still something not right. When he had completed the search and found nothing, he decided he was just being paranoid. His motivation to cook had gone now and he wasn't even hungry. He would just go to bed and get a good night's sleep. He had a big day ahead of him finalising his big deal.

Waiting for him in his bed was Alena. She was lying in a seductive manner. There was something nagging him that the situation was not right, but he couldn't figure out what it was. He had been married to Alena since he could remember. Alena and his bed looked so inviting that he didn't take any notice of his worries.

"Come to bed sweetheart," Alena cooed to him.

"Yes dear," Alaric could think of no better place he would rather be.

Just as Alaric was starting to undress there was a loud knock on the door. Alaric sighed and moved to answer.

"Leave it Alaric. Come to bed. I'll make it worth your while," she winked.

Alaric thought about it. He took his shirt off and the knock came again. It was more persistent this time. Alaric looked at Alena and shrugged his shoulders.

"I'll be quick. It sounds important," offered Alaric.

"No!" Alena almost spat the words at him. "Stay here with me. It can be no good, someone knocking at this time of night. It is well past midnight."

The comment seemed strange. He was sure he had just returned home and the sun was still outside, but when he looked to the window it was pitch black. The knocking came again, louder and longer. Alaric was getting a strong sense that something was wrong. He had never known Alena to take that tone with him. Then it struck him. He had not known Alena until he had left Arsiliac. Someone was playing a trick on him. He knew that he had to answer the door.

"Damn it," cried Alena in a strange voice as Alaric left the room.

Alaric ran down the hall to get to the door. When he pushed it open, he knew who was on the other side. Looking somewhat bedraggled was his old friend, Eldred. The old wizard had a concerned look on his face.

"Thank the Gods you are here Eldred. Something is happening and I don't know what it is," there was a touch of terror in Alaric's voice.

"I must not stay long Alaric. It nearly drained all my energy to return," Eldred puffed as he spoke.

"What are you talking about? I don't understand," Alaric whimpered.

"Think back to earlier. After you translocated me, you were left alone in your own mind. It seems that you made some adjustments. This is why you were not supposed to come here. I think that Nyrra may have added his own special touch. You created Arsiliac. The problem was you forgot that this is not real. Nyrra has no doubt tampered with things to make you more comfortable. He's been inside your mind for a while now and will know a few things about you. You have been unconscious for half the night now. That is why I came back in to see what was happening. If you're not careful, you could get trapped here," Eldred warned.

"Half the night, but I've only been here for a few minutes, an hour tops." Alaric really had no idea how much time had passed.

"Time has no meaning here. What seems like a minute here could possibly be an entire year in the real world. Nyrra is going to try and keep you here now. Unfortunately, Nyrra can be in two places at once. He's vulnerable in the real world, but he's still mobile. We can't move you, the result would be disastrous. Your body is undergoing a great deal of stress at the moment." Sweat was pouring from Eldred's face.

"What can I do?" Alaric was terrified.

"Relax. Your mental state is a direct result of what you are going through. It's hard to explain, so just trust me when I say you have to remain composed. I don't think that Nyrra is going to try and hide now. I think he will try and coax you into staying. If he can trick you into thinking this is the outside world and make you content, then he will win. You must remain focused. It will be easy to get carried away again. Try and focus on something from the real world that is different from here. I must go now. Find him and get rid of him, soon." With that Eldred vanished.

"Something that is out of place," Alaric said to himself as he walked back to his bedroom to join Alena. Already he was slipping back into the illusion. "Maybe Alena will be able to help me. She'll know what to do."

As Alaric turned the doorknob to his bedroom, a thought struck him. Alena was still sick. She had not yet recovered from the poison arrow she was struck with outside of Lel Dinion. Alena was really Nyrra, that's what was out of place. Alaric steeled himself as he pushed the door open. To his disbelief the room was empty. It wasn't just that Alena wasn't there, but the entire room was empty.

"This is my mind. I make the rules, not you," Alaric spoke aloud to the empty room.

Alaric decided to make some radical changes to the scenery. The house slowly started to melt away and in its place was a lush field of grass. Apart from Alaric, there was only one other object in the field. A man stood no more than fifty feet away. Alaric wasn't sure, but he thought he recognised him; as he moved closer he realised it was Hadar. He stood with his cuts and bruises gone.

"It's good to see you again, Alaric. I had to ride hard to catch up with you. There is something I have to tell you. Come with me," offered Hadar, although he was still way out of earshot Alaric could hear him clearly.

"I know who you are and I want you out," ordered Alaric confidently.

"Really? Well I think that you might want to rethink that. I have been nice up until now. You don't want me to get angry," Hadar's voice had completely changed.

Alaric had no idea how to get rid of Nyrra. He had expelled Eldred without knowing what he had done. If he tried translocating again, he might actually get it right, then he would be stuck with Nyrra inside his head. The only thing that came to mind was a physical battle. With a slight gesture, a sword appeared in his hand.

"So it's going to be like that then? I think that you are getting in over your head, so to speak," the image of Hadar grinned as he spoke. "I think that I better change into something a little more formidable."

The man he knew changed before his eyes. Soon enough before him stood an evil looking beast. Alaric recognised the creature instantly and recoiled in fear. Standing before him, no more than twenty feet away, was the creature from his nightmares. It stood over seven feet in height. Its head was awfully deformed with a pair of horns protruding from the front. Its skin was a horrible deep purple colour. With a fierce snarl, the creature showed its razor sharp teeth. Alaric recoiled in terror.

"Now you are not so smug," the creature spoke with a rough drawl. "I'll give you one last chance to change your mind. Remember how nice it was back in your own house. It can be like that forever. All you have to do is submit," the voice now was very soothing.

Alaric's head felt heavy and all of a sudden he felt very tired. The thought of sinking into his own bed was very tempting. Shaking his head Alaric regained his current train of thought. He knew that he could not stay. He had too much to do in the real world. He would not succumb to Nyrra's trickery.

"This is my mind. I make the rules and I say that you are not welcome," Alaric tried his best to sound commanding. He could still remember all the painful things the creature had done to him in his dreams.

"Very well then. Let's see how strong you really are," The voice changed again, this time it boomed and echoed.

Alaric readied himself and Nyrra did the same. In his right hand, a huge sword appeared. The blade had large, jagged edges and was stained with blood. Alaric thought it looked very intimidating, but not very efficient. Unfortunately for Alaric, it was quite the contrary. Nyrra attacked with a flurry of sword strokes. It was all Alaric could do to keep from losing his head.

Nyrra was relentless with his attacks. The extra weight of his sword knocked Alaric from side to side. Alaric knew that he was not going to win the fight. He needed to shift the advantage, Alaric fended off the blows, more by luck than any real skill. Just when Nyrra looked like he was going to make the final blow, Alaric managed to defend his attack. Suddenly an idea came to him. They were in his reality and Nyrra had to play by his rules.

A broad smile appeared on Alaric's face as Nyrra continued his attack. Nyrra retracted his sword in preparation for another advance. When he brought the sword back, it was no longer there. In its place was a large fish, which didn't last too long against Alaric's blade. Nyrra took a couple of steps backward and returned to his previous form.

"You can't win, Nyrra. This is my reality and you're not welcome," Alaric laughed.

Nyrra also started laughing. "I don't have to win here. You still don't understand, do you?"

Suddenly Alaric was not so sure of himself. There was something about Nyrra's attitude that just didn't feel right. He was destined to lose, yet he was still smiling. Alaric had a bad feeling that things were not as good as he thought. He had to find a way to expel him.

"I think that I will be leaving now. You can try and find me if you like, but I have been here for a while now and know where all the good hiding places are," Nyrra smirked.

There was a short pause. Alaric just stood and watched. He knew something that Nyrra didn't. Alaric almost started to laugh when he saw the look on Nyrra's face when he remained.

"I think that you have overestimated your own strength. Remember that you are in my world now. I make the rules and right n o w

I don't think that I want you here anymore." Alaric was now brimming with confidence.

"Don't worry. I think that I will leave anyway. My job here is done. You will see me again soon enough and the next time we meet you won't have the upper hand." Nyrra promptly disappeared.

Alaric suddenly felt very relaxed. His head went dizzy and slowly he collapsed to the ground. It was not a bad feeling; it was almost euphoric. His head swam and everything started to go black. The air around him started to waver. When he opened his eyes, he was back in his inn room. Standing over him was Eldred and Palentonal. The two looked concerned, which changed to relief when they saw Alaric open his eyes.

"Thank the Gods that you're back. I wasn't sure if we were going to see you again," Palentonal laughed when he finished speaking.

"How long was I out?" Alaric spoke with a hoarse, dry voice.

"You were unconscious for about two days. It will be another day before you will be out of bed. You'll want to get some sleep now. Although you've been unconscious you have been very active, not only your mind, but your body as well." Eldred explained.

Trying to lift his head, Alaric realised what Eldred was saying. His body felt like it had been working for the last week without a break. His muscles ached and he could hardly move. A wave of exhaustion rippled through his body.

"How are we doing for time now?" asked Alaric slowly.

"It's going to be a lot closer now. We just have to hope our forces can delay Nyrra enough and we don't have any more interruptions," explained Eldred gravely.

"Is there anything to eat?" The only thing that was overpowering his fatigue was his hunger.

"Certainly. I will have something sent in," replied Eldred.

Shortly after they left the room, someone returned with a large tray filled with food. Alaric only briefly thanked the serving girl before he started to eat. He stuffed the food into his mouth as fast as he could. With the plate empty, Alaric's hunger had been satisfied.

It was not long after he had finished eating before Alaric was fast asleep. His dreams were peaceful. Eldred had cast a silent spell before he left the room to make sure that Nyrra could not return and he slept for a full day without waking.

When he finally woke, he saw that the room was completely dark. He had no idea what time it was, but he assumed it was early in the morning. There was no noise coming from the rest of the inn. Shutting his eyes, Alaric tried to return to sleep. After fifteen minutes, he knew it was an impossible task. He had slept for over twenty-four hours and could not sleep any more.

As he lay in his bed, he thought he could hear someone moving around outside. Just when he thought he heard a noise, it would stop. It was the most infuriating thing he had experienced. Quietly, not wanting to alert whoever was outside, he felt for the lantern beside his bed. Nearly knocking over the bedside table Alaric found it. Drawing back the shutter only slightly, Alaric allowed a sliver of light into the room. It was not long before Alaric found what he wanted, folded neatly on a chair in a corner of the room. He quickly dressed before he found his sword.

Again, Alaric heard the noise and it was clearly the sound of someone rustling around outside of his window. His heart started to race as he went to see, shuttering the lantern as he came closer. Peering through the glass, he could definitely saw a shadow moving around in the dim moonlight.

The sound of a dry twig snapping came suddenly and the closeness of the noise startled Alaric, making him fall backwards. He hit the floor with an audible thud. He held his breath as he waited for a response from outside.

"There's someone up," came a muffled voice.

"Let's get this job done and get out of here," another voice spoke, not too far away from the first.

"But we don't know which room it is." Alaric sat, frozen, listening to the conversation.

"Just pick a room. Let's go!"

A bright light suddenly appeared outside the window. With a low gasp, Alaric realised what was happening. Pushing with his feet Alaric scooted across the floor. As he did, the torch came crashing through his window before a second one followed.

Instantly the floor caught on fire as well as the curtains. The bright flash of light caused by the exploding torch blinded him. Even with his eyes closed, he could only see a brilliant white light. To make matters worse, the room was starting to fill with smoke. On his hands and knees, Alaric tried to make his way the door. The sudden commotion had left him disorientated and Alaric didn't know which way to go. Smoke filled his lungs and he coughed and spluttered. If he chose the wrong way, he would end up crawling straight into the fire.

The smoke grew thick and Alaric's head started to swim. He kept low and groped his way along, hoping he was heading in the right direction. The flames flicked at his body as he managed to reach the door. Alaric fumbled with the handle as he struggled for breath. Just when he thought all was lost, he finally managed to turn the knob and pull the door open. Taking in a deep breath Alaric collapsed on the floor.

The rest of the inn was beginning to come to life as the smell of smoke alerted the other guests. Alaric felt his way along the wall. A loud crash behind him indicated that part of the ceiling collapsed in his room.

"Alaric! Are you okay?" came a voice from the end of the corridor. Alaric recognised it as Palentonal.

"I can't see. The stone is still in the room, you have to get the chest," Alaric sounded panicked.

"Relax, Eldred removed the chest when he started the spell. All your things are in another room. Now stay low. The smoke is starting to fill the hallway," Palentonal spoke quickly.

Soon Alaric felt a reassuring hand on his left arm. Palentonal promptly led Alaric from the inn. The rest of the group had assembled outside. Slowly his eye-sight started to return.

"What happened?" asked Alaric.

"It seems that we picked the wrong inn. The attack was completely unrelated. We were fortunate enough to escape without any losses," as he spoke the two dwarves appeared with their horses and pack animals.

"There was a hooded figure loitering around the stables when we took the horses. I think that he might have had something to do with the fire. When he saw us coming, he left in a hurry," explained Hulkan.

"I don't think so and that brings us to our next problem. I believe that Viper has found us again. I thought I caught a glimpse of him last night, but I wasn't sure until now. He must have followed the strong smell of magic that has been radiating from Alaric for the last few days," Eldred explained.

"Then it would make sense for Viper to start the fire," added Palentonal. "The creature is pure evil. Why wouldn't he want to destroy us? Burning down the inn with us inside sounds exactly what he would do."

"No Palentonal, Viper does not have the same agenda as Nyrra. I don't believe that Viper wants Nyrra to win. If you destroyed Nyrra, then he would be free. That's why I need to speak to him and find out what he wants. We don't want to be fighting Viper as soon as Nyrra is destroyed. We can't leave until I've found him." Eldred sounded distant as he spoke. "You take the horses and find a more suitable inn. Alaric and Alena will come with me."

It was the first time that Alaric had seen Alena since he had woken. She looked like Alaric had remembered before she had been poisoned. Alaric marvelled at her beauty.

"How are we going to find Viper?" asked Alaric as the others walked away. The streets were starting to become crowded with onlookers as well as helpers.

"I will find him. I believe that he wants to speak to me as much as I want to speak to him," Eldred spoke as he led the others away from the burning inn.

***

It didn't take them long to find a new inn. Lel Cornion was the city that never slept. It was common for visitors to arrive at all hours. Along with the inns, the taverns were also open late. The art of finding a place to drink was not as hard as it could have been. Finding drinking partners, however, was a different story.

"There is no point going back to sleep," Hulkan urged his companions.

Dorn, of course, was the first to accept his offer and did not need any convincing. Palentonal and Hawthorne were quick to decline. Bern knew that he should try and get whatever sleep remained that night, but the two dwarves would not leave him alone. Before he had made his decision, they were ushering him towards the tavern.

They made their way to the tavern named the Builder's Arms. The raucous noise coming from inside indicated that the tavern was in full swing.

"If we have any luck, there'll be some young ladies in the bar. What do you think Bern?" laughed Dorn, giving him a dig in the ribs.

"I'm married, remember?" he laughed, returning Dorn's dig. Despite Bern's massive bulk, Dorn didn't take a backward step.

The two dwarves roared with laughter as they entered the tavern. Bern and the two dwarves had become quite close over the past few weeks. Hulkan and Dorn had taken Bern under their wing since Alaric didn't have much time to spend with his old friend. They had been continuing his training with the war axe.

Inside the tavern was crowded. Most of the patrons were male, although there were a few older ladies walking around. Hulkan and Dorn had them pegged as whores from the start. This did not dampen their enthusiasm. A haze of smoke filled the room and the smell was not pleasant. Stale beer and pipe tobacco were the major aromas, with a hint of rotting food and body odour. Dorn took a deep breath through his nose and then exhaled contently from his mouth.

"It has been a long time since I've been in such an establishment. This brings back memories," Dorn spoke with genuine fondness.

Bern, on the other hand, did not share his friend's enthusiasm. He liked a drink as much as the next guy, but his stomach churned with every breath. Just before they reached the bar, Bern excused himself and raced outside. The two dwarves laughed again as they purchased some dark ales.

No one seemed to take much notice of the foreigners. The two sat on some timber stools at the bar and sipped their ales, which were of a surprisingly good standard.

"That's what I love about these places. They're smelly, smoky and full of whores, but the ale is always the very best of quality," explained Dorn as he took a large draught from his mug.

"At these prices, it would have to be. I've never paid this much for a mug of ale in my life," scoffed Hulkan.

"Supply and demand," offered the proprietor from behind the bar, who was fat, unshaven and unwashed. "There are many taverns in the city, but only a few who stay open as late as we do. We have the best ales and the best wines and we charge accordingly. If you want a cheap drink, go to the Miller's Inn, that's if they are still open," his tone sounded cocky. He didn't wait for a reply before he went to serve another customer.

"Pompous ass!" snapped Hulkan.

"He's right though. He might be an unkempt rogue, but he has a great little business here. I think that before he started drinking his stock in excess, he was a brilliant business man," returned Dorn.

"I think that he inherited this bar and doesn't have a clue what he's doing. He just has great support from his staff," Hulkan pointed at the two waitresses and the bar tender who looked tired from a long night's work.

"Either way, it's not going to stop me drinking my fill tonight." Both the dwarves raised their mugs to Dorn's comment before draining them.

"What do you say my old friend? We'll put down another couple of these and then get some entertainment to pass the time?" Dorn asked after he ordered more ale.

Before the ales were brought out for them, Bern returned to the tavern and joined them at the bar. Hulkan quickly passed him the ale they had ordered for him. Bern declined the drink.

"What's the problem with ya? Don't have the stomach for it anymore?" Dorn dug an elbow into Bern's side.

"There are two men who just walked into the tavern," Bern tried to find to them, but had lost them in the crowd.

"There's nothing strange about that. What are you so worried about?" Hulkan laughed.

"It was dark outside, but I could see that they had charred stains on their faces and clothes. They looked shaken. I figured they had been fighting the fire. Then I heard one of them speak. He said something like, 'I don't think we should have done it. I don't think we're going to get paid. I don't trust that man.' There was something strange about him.

Then the other one told him to shut up when he saw me standing next to the tavern. I'm pretty sure they are the ones who torched the inn."

"Where are they?" asked Dorn between his teeth.

Bern peered through the smoky bar. He looked around the room, but could not see where they had gone. He was sure that they had come inside. When he returned his attention to the bar he saw the men standing no more than three paces from where he sat.

"There they are. At the end of the bar," Bern pointed to the two men as they ordered their drinks.

One of them looked over and saw them looking and pointing. He whispered something to his friend and they started moving towards the door. Hulkan quickly moved to intercept them whilst Dorn and Bern exited via the second door by the bar.

Just before the two men reached the exit, Hulkan was upon them. The first man slipped past before Hulkan could stop him. The second was not as lucky and Hulkan shouldered his attack and struck the man in the stomach. The blow sent him flying and he hit the floor two feet away. Suddenly the other man came crashing back through. Dorn had run around the outside of the tavern and hit the man as soon as he stepped outside.

The commotion had aroused the attention of the other patrons. A crowd had started to appear around the group. Bern quickly noticed that they were getting some dangerous looks from the other men around them.

"I think that we are in trouble," offered Bern as the two men were returning to their feet.

"I've had worse odds," laughed Dorn,

"We just want to talk to you about what happened earlier. If you want to do it the hard way, you're more than welcome," offered Hulkan.

The crowd and the two men stood still. The confidence of the two dwarves had them intimidated. They were clearly outnumbered, but they had not wavered. Even without their weapons, they were confident they would win. Either that or they were not afraid of losing.

"There will be no fighting in here," boomed the owner of the tavern as he came crashing through the crowd. With a quick swing of his arm, he hit an onlooker in the back of the head with a thick wooden club. The man promptly sunk to the floor, unconscious. "Now if anyone else wants some this then keep up the shenanigans."

Before anyone could make a decision, two more large men appeared at his side. Both were holding a club of their own. With the additional muscle and the sight of the man lying on the floor, the crowd quickly dispersed, leaving the eight of them standing alone. Suddenly the two men made a break for the door. Dorn and Hulkan quickly blocked their paths and knocked them to the ground.

Instantly they recovered and prepared themselves for an attack. As they expected, the bouncers were just a couple of large brutes, with no real fighting abilities. With a couple of quick movements, both men were disarmed and sprawled out on the ground.

"Now I told you we don't want any trouble. If anyone else wants to argue, we'll be more than happy to accommodate," Hulkan threatened.

Silence responded to his statement as the brutes returned to their feet. Neither of them, to the disgust of the owner, looked like they wanted to try again. Finally, the owner had to concede.

"Very well. Take those two and get out." He didn't wait to see if they were going to comply. He had already lost enough face and he was not going to be openly refuted again.

"Good, then I think we should get moving to somewhere a little quieter," ended Hulkan.

The two brutes clearly relaxed when they were sure the dwarves were going to leave. The two ashen faced arsonists slowly returned to their feet. They knew now that there was no escape and moved towards the door quietly. Bern smiled at his two friends. They had a strange way of doing things, but the result was always a success.

"What do you want from us?" asked one of the men after they had left the tavern.

"Are you going to kill us?" asked the other.

"For starters, why don't you tell us your names, then we will decide whether you live or die."

"I'm Joab and this is my brother, Peretz," Joab introduced.

"That's a good start. Why don't you take us somewhere where we can talk," Hulkan always found that if someone he was interrogating instantly told him their names, then they would be open about other questions.

There were wild looks on the two men's faces. The dwarves had obviously rattled them. Bern raised his hand to silence them. He didn't want to risk the two trying to make another run for freedom.

"Don't worry about them. As long as you tell us the truth, I will make sure no harm will come." The men physically relaxed.

"We can go back to my house. It is not too far away from here," offered Peretz.

"Very good. Lead the way," Hulkan's voice had softened.

"And get something to eat," Dorn added.

Peretz nodded his agreement without speaking. He was visibly shaking as he walked. Both men had blood trickling from cuts on their heads. Bern seemed somewhat sympathetic to them.

Peretz lived in one of the poorer parts of the city. His house was a small single room dwelling. It was dark and dirty inside. The two dwarves complained about the lack of food in the cupboards. Peretz was surprisingly apologetic about the state of his abode.

"Let's get down to business. Hulkan! Get out of the cupboard. We have work to do!" Bern's voice was harsh and that set Hulkan to attention and he quickly did as he was told. "Why did you torch the inn?" asked Bern

Peretz looked as his brother, eminent fear in his eyes. Joab also looked scared. There was obviously something they did not want to talk about. Slowly Joab nodded before resting his face in his hands. Peretz's face went pale. Bern thought he was going to pass out.

"I never saw the man before. Joab and I were walking home after work. I didn't even notice him approach. He started talking to us. It was like he had known us all his life. I can't remember what he was saying. There was something strange about his voice. I couldn't pick it at the time, but now that I think about it sounded as if he was hissing. All I could think about was fire. I could see the inn burning. I could see the torch in my hand. The fire burning, it was unnatural." Bern tried to piece together what Peretz was saying. Peretz had a distant look on his face as he spoke. "He talked to us for hours. He seemed like a nice man. Then the next thing I knew, is we were standing outside the burning inn. I thought I had just finished talking to him. I still don't know how we ended up there. I didn't even know it existed."

"Did the man say anything else to you? Did he tell you why he wanted you to burn the inn?" pushed Bern.

"He didn't tell us to burn the inn. It was just meaningless small talk," Perez sighed

"He's going to kills us, isn't he?" asked Joab, finally adding to the conversation.

"We'll do our best to stop him from doing that," comforted Bern. "I think we should get back to the others now. The sun is starting to rise and Eldred is going to be very angry if we're not back before him."

Chapter 27: Viper

They had been walking for about five minutes when Alaric started to feel something tugging on his right side. When he looked down, there was nothing there. Suddenly he felt another tug and yet again, there was nothing there.

"I think we should turn right," suggested Alaric after more tugging.

"Why do you say that?" said Eldred with a knowing look in his eye.

"I don't know. It's just a feeling I have," Alaric replied.

"Ha!" laughed Eldred. "It seems that you power is growing."

Alaric looked at Eldred closely, but when it was clear that he wasn't going to say anything else, they started in the direction of Alaric's tugging. They were now moving towards the poorest sectors of the city. Slowly a foul stench drifted in on the night's breeze. As they continued the smell became stronger. It was like a cross between sewage and rotten rubbish. Alaric could feel his stomach churn with each breath.

"What is making that smell?" asked Alena.

"I'm not sure, but I think it might have something to do with Viper. Like all snakes, they shed their skin to make way for their new one. When this happens, they emit a terrible stench. I have never witnessed it myself, but I am almost positive that is what is making that dreadful odour," explained Eldred.

The streets they passed through were dark and dreary. Lanterns were at a bare minimum and produced very little light. The buildings were very drab and run down. With the added bleakness of the stench, Alaric thought this was the most depressing place he had ever been to.

"I think we are close now. There has been no change to the smell for the last few minutes," Eldred's words only added to the depressing situation.

With a slight gust of wind the horrible smell suddenly disappeared. The tugging sensations Alaric was feeling had also stopped. There was no doubt that their searching was about to come to an end.

"Now I know I was right." Eldred stopped to think.

"What's happened?" asked Alaric.

"Viper has finished malting his skin. His power will be weak for the next couple of days. It takes all their energy for Serpentants to regenerate their skin. After those days, they become more powerful than before. It's a never-ending circle. At the start, they are strong, but as the days and years go by their power diminishes. We need to find him tonight and then leave town immediately. It will be at least a day before he will be able to chase after us."

"How do we find him now?" asked Alena.

"He won't be able to move for the next hour or so. We know he's around here somewhere. We can only hope that we find him before he starts moving again. I think that he wants us to find him. He has something he wants to say to us."

"So if he can't move then we can kill him," suggested Alaric.

"That is an option, but something tells me it is not a good one. There is more to Viper's appearance than meets the eye. I do not believe that he is the enemy that we perceive him to be. I am sure he has another motive and I want to know what it is before I condemn him to death," Eldred started moving again when he finished speaking.

The three of them searched the streets around the area where they had lost the scent. Nothing seemed out of the ordinary. There were no signs of disturbance. After a while, they returned to the place where they had started.

"This is hopeless," Eldred sighed. "I thought that I might have been able to sense him. His power is so weak that even I can't even find him. When his power returns, he will be on the move again and we don't have the time."

Alaric lowered his head in defeat. As he did, something reflected the light of a nearby lantern. Bending down Alaric picked up a small, translucent object, no bigger than a finger nail. Looking at it he suddenly realised what it was. He looked on the ground until he found another and another. There was a trail of scales leading to a small run down house.

"He's in there," Alaric pointed.

The back door to the house was open ajar. A similar, but less potent smell was coming from inside.

"Be careful. He may be weak when we first see him, but he will gradually be regaining his strength. There is no telling how powerful he will become whilst we are in there. We must be quick and not get sucked into long conversations," Eldred warned them.

Carefully Eldred led the way into the house. The only light inside came from the open doorway. All the windows had been boarded shut. Eldred mumbled a couple of words under his breath and a light appeared on the end of his staff. The room they were in was littered with rubbish and old furniture. It had clearly been abandoned for a long time.

"We know you're in here. Show yourself!" ordered Eldred.

"So you have come," hissed a voice.

Viper was dressed in his usual black robe. In the dirty room, he had just looked like a dirty pile of rags in the corner. The light from Eldred's staff seemed to shy away from Viper. His face was covered, but Alaric could still sense the change in him. He could feel the frailty of the creature and Alaric almost felt sorry for him.

"What do you want?" asked Alaric in a harsh tone.

"I've come to help you. To give you some advice," answered Viper.

"Why should I trust anything you say? You have been trying to hinder us ever since you came upon us," retorted Eldred.

"I have done nothing to hinder you." Viper almost sounded hurt by the accusation. Before Eldred could say anything else, Viper turned his attention to Alena. "You mustn't go to Avalon. If you do, the Evil One will take you. You will only be safe if you come with me. I can protect you from him." Viper reached out a reptilian hand towards her.

Hearing his words, Alaric drew his sword and advanced on the weakened creature. Remembering what Eldred had said he stopped just out of striking distance. Hearing the creature speaking about Alena made him angry, but he knew that it could also be a trap. He couldn't let his emotions make him do something foolish.

"I don't think we shall do that. Speak quickly if you don't want me to end your life here and now." Alaric tried his best to sound menacing.

"My life means nothing, Chosen One. If you don't listen to me, then your enemy will defeat you. My real master has told me this. We move towards the same ending Chosen One. You must listen to me." Alaric noticed that there was a new edge to Viper's voice.

"I think that we've seen enough here," stated Eldred. "Unless you have some useful information for us,"

"I think that you're right. There is nothing we need to know," replied Alaric.

"Very well. I will give you one piece of advice. Do not go into the forest. There is death waiting for you there," Viper's voice again sounded stronger.

"You know very well if we do not cut through the forest we will not beat Nyrra to Avalon. You have no information for us and you are not here to help us," Eldred sneered.

"Don't be a fool," cried Viper as he suddenly came to life.

The Serpentant sprung at Alaric with his hands outstretched aimed at his throat. Alaric was ready for the attack and merely side-stepped the advance. Viper went crashing to the floor. Alaric readied himself for another attack. Viper, on the other hand, did not attempt another one. Instead he sprung to his feet and pushed his way past Eldred. He didn't look back as he rushed through the door.

"Should we chase after him?" asked Alena, making her way to the door.

"No. We better get back to the others. I think that we should get back on the road. The sun will be coming up soon and it will not be long before he can start following us."

They started to make their way to find the others. There was no sign of Viper. The streets of Lel Cornion were still empty. Before they had gone too far they ran into Bern and the two dwarves. Eldred did not seem happy to see the three of them still out. Once Hulkan had explained what had happened Eldred relaxed.

"It seems that I have misjudged Viper. This is quite disturbing," Eldred mused.

Eldred wondered if he knew anything. At every turn, there was a new surprise and each time it was something that he thought he knew was definite. Now he didn't even know if they were heading in the right direction. He hadn't found anything new in the prophecy and he could only hope that soon he would find something that would help him. Viper's advice kept running through his mind. If he had been wrong about the things he was sure of, then who was to say that Viper wasn't right.

They walked the rest of the way in silence. Alaric wasn't sure why, but he was inclined to believe what he was saying. The thought of leaving Alena with Viper was enough make him disbelieve his words. There was one thing he did know, he felt better when Alena was around. If he was going to defeat Nyrra, then she would have to be there for support.

Back at the inn Hawthorne and Palentonal were waiting for them. They had busied themselves readying the horses. They were relieved to see everyone was in one piece. After they had all eaten a small meal, they were on the road again.

The streets were starting to fill as they rode by. It did nothing for Eldred's nerves to have so many people see them leave. It was no big secret where they were headed, but the least number of people who saw them the better. Eldred's mood passed on to the others. They could sense something was wrong with him and that made them all nervous.

The morning sun was high in the sky as they reached the eastern gate. There was no guard on watch and the gate was wide open. The road swung around to the south east to join the highway and was the major trade route between Hondin Lel and Darshival. Lel Cornion was the last city along the highway. There where regular caravans and merchants passing them towards their final destination. It was not a widely-used road as the major trade went directly to Lel Dinion before being dispersed amongst the many towns and cities.

"Is this safe for us to travel along the highway?" asked Hawthorne. "All these merchants love to talk in the local taverns. If anyone is looking for us, it won't be hard for them to work out where we are."

"I think that everyone who is looking for us knows where we are at the moment. The key for us is that no one sees us leave the highway and enter the forest," Eldred explained, making sure no one was passing when he spoke.

They rode for the rest of the day, stopping only for lunch. By nightfall, they had reached a small village. Eldred stopped the group before they reached the local inn.

"I think we should stay here tonight," Eldred suggested.

"Wouldn't it be best if we kept riding and camp outside of town? That way we could start in the morning and no one would know where we were," Hawthorne spoke firmly.

"This is the last town before we head into the forest. I think that it would be a good idea for us to sleep in a bed tonight and get a nice cooked dinner. It's going to be a long time now before we will have the opportunity again."

Hawthorne was about to protest, but the unanimous response from the others silenced him. The inn was small, but it was clean and dry. There were plenty of rooms available and at a cheap price.

After they had eaten a substantial dinner, they all retired for the evening, even the dwarves forwent a night of drinking for a night of rest. They all knew that their journey was coming to an end. Things were going to get a lot more difficult and for some it may be the last time they ever slept in a bed. Eldred resisted the urge to pour over the prophecy. He needed a good night's sleep just as much as everyone else.

In the morning, they all woke with renewed spirits, bathed and ate a hearty breakfast. The weather, however, did not reflect their mood. As soon as they left the village, the dark clouds started to roll in. By mid-morning, rain was imminent. When the sky finally broke, it did so with a vengeance. With the rain came hail, thunder and lightning. It came so quickly and powerfully they had no chance to hide. Although the rain beat down on them they continued their journey.

The Great Eastern Forest loomed up on their left, steadily growing nearer as the morning wore on. The mere expanse of the forest was awe-inspiring. Great elm, oak and ash trees grew side by side and from a distance it almost looked like they were on top of each other.

"Can't you do anything about this rain?" yelled Hawthorne to Eldred.

"No. It's natural rain. To upset it would cause a terrible ripple effect. We will just have to endure it," Eldred yelled back over the tempest.

By lunchtime the forest was no more than a hundred paces from the road. They stopped for a brief, soggy lunch. The rain was still relentless and their bright spirits from the morning had been dampened. There was no hiding from the terrible conditions.

It was only a short stop before they were on the move again. No one complained about the time. Although it was not pleasant riding in the rain it was better than sitting in it. Eldred took the lead, searching for a small road that supposedly led off into the forest.

"I must admit I have never heard of a track that leads through the forest to Avalon. The only way I know is to go through Darshival," argued Hawthorne as Eldred called them to a stop.

"That's because there is no trail that leads to Avalon," Palentonal defended the wizard.

"Then what are you looking for?" asked Hulkan.

"There is a small road that leads into the forest. It continues for about two or three leagues before it disappears. The trail itself points directly to Avalon. All we have to do is continue on the same course," explained Eldred.

"That's easy for you to say." Hulkan boomed. "That forest looks pretty dense to me. It's not going to be easy to keep track of which direction we are travelling."

"That's because you are no elf," Palentonal laughed loudly.

Hulkan seemed to take the supposed insult with good humour. He wasn't sure if Palentonal was being sarcastic or insulting. Dorn gave him a stern look.

It was not long before Eldred found the road he had been looking for. There was a small caravan of merchants passing by to the North West just as they were about to turn off. Eldred quickly motioned for the others to continue along the road. They waited until the caravan was out of sight before they returned to the track.

"Palentonal, you cover our tracks for about half a mile. I don't want anyone to know that we have come this way. All being well, anyone following us will think that we have gone the long way around," ordered Eldred.

As soon as they reached the forest the already dim light had almost completely disappeared. The rain, on the other hand, did not lighten. The trees did give some protection, but the rain still made its way through. The cold wind, which had plagued them for the last few leagues, had almost completely dissipated.

They reached the edge of the trail and waited for Palentonal to catch them. He finally reached them just before dusk. He had a worried look on his face.

"What's the matter?" asked Eldred.

"The rain and mud didn't make it easy to cover our tracks. The horses made large prints in the mud. I did the best as I could, but there were a number of caravans passing whilst I was still out in the open. I don't think they saw me, but I couldn't be sure," Palentonal explained.

"Okay then. We better continue on into the forest before we camp for the night. If anyone is following us, they're going to find it harder to find us the deeper into the forest we are," said Eldred.

"I don't think we should travel after dark," suggested Palentonal. There was a nervousness in his voice that made the others uncomfortable.

Eldred simply nodded his head and then started into the forest. They only rode for half an hour before the sun had completely disappeared. The moon was late rising leaving a deep blackness. Eldred seemed intent on travelling further, but after a quiet conversation with Palentonal he called for a stop. Thankfully the rain had stopped, although it looked as though it could break again at any minute. Palentonal quickly lit a fire as the others prepared the campsite.

"What do you think that was all about?" Bern asked Alaric as they ate dinner. It was the first time they had spoken in a long time.

"About what?" asked Alaric, not really paying him much attention.

"What do you think those two were talking about? They seem to be very secretive all of a sudden. I don't know that I trust them," replied Bern.

Alaric was surprised at what his old friend was insinuating. It was very out of character. "I think you've been spending too much time with the dwarves. Palentonal and Eldred have both saved my life on a number of occasions. If they are being secretive, there is nothing sinister about it. I'm sure there is a simple answer and we'll find out in good time," Alaric didn't really have any respect for the two dwarves. They were solid in battle, but that was about their only good trait. He didn't like their attitudes rubbing off on Bern.

He didn't truly believe what he was saying. Palentonal was in tune with the forest and Alaric could feel that something wasn't right. Alaric didn't want to start anything without knowing what was out there waiting for them.

"I will keep the first watch tonight. Palentonal will take the second. No one walk outside of the fire light during the night. We will try and keep it burning as bright as possible," explained Eldred.

"What's going on?" snapped Dorn. "Why shouldn't we go outside the light? What if I need to do my business!"

"Hold it," offered Hawthorne coolly.

"Okay. It has been a miserable day. I think we should all get some sleep. Everything will look better in the morning. You will just have to trust me." Eldred's tone of voice left no room for discussion.

The fire did not seem to take any of the dampness out of the air. Even though Alaric had changed his clothes for the night he still felt the chill of the day's rain. Palentonal and Eldred's warnings plagued his mind.

He could sense something was wrong with the forest. It was almost as if there was evil in the air.

It was well past midnight when Alaric woke. He didn't know what had woken him. He had been having quite a peaceful night when a sudden feeling of dread passed through him. Something was definitely wrong; he could feel it.

"Alaric." Although the call was no louder than a whisper Alaric heard it clearly.

Slowly he peered into the forest. It was too dark to see anything. The light of the fire made it all but impossible. Slowly, as he peered, he thought he saw a wisp of white light out of the corner of his eye. When he turned to look, it was gone. Alaric thought he must have imagined it when suddenly it returned. It was there only for a brief second and only on the edge of his vision.

Alaric sat, staring into the blackness, for twenty minutes waiting for the light to return. He sat transfixed. When the light did not come again, Alaric lay back down. He fell asleep shortly after and there were no more disturbances.

In the morning, he woke feeling unusually refreshed. The others were also very relaxed. It was as if they had spent the night in a luxury inn. Alaric sat by the fire and ate his breakfast. He listened intently to the other conversations, trying to hear if anyone else had heard the strange voice or seen the white light. If they had, they didn't mention it.

After they had all eaten, they started off again. Palentonal led the way and for the most part, there was enough room through the trees for them to ride comfortably. The rain, from the day before, had completely cleared. The sun shone through the trees giving some light, but the heat created steam from the forest floor and increased the humidity to an uncomfortable level.

When the small trail finally ended, the undergrowth became thick. Vines and shrubs tangled around the horse's legs making riding almost impossible. At times the undergrowth was so thick that had to dismount and lead the horses through. Even the magnificent elvish horses could not traverse the terrain. Each time they had to walk, Eldred looked frustrated.

When they stopped for lunch the conversation became heated.

"I thought that you knew your way through the forest," argued Palentonal.

"I do, or that is I did. It has been a long time since I rode through to Avalon. The trees have grown and changed. We are still heading in the right direction, it's just taking longer than I thought," Eldred explained defensively.

"I thought it was you who knew their way around the forest," Dorn accused Palentonal.

Palentonal set Dorn an icy glare before returning his irritation to Eldred. "You of all people should know what could happen if we stray off course. Not even an elf would risk getting lost in this forest."

"I know. We are still on course," assured Eldred.

"I've had enough of this innuendo," barked Hulkan. "What is going on here? You two have been acting very suspiciously ever since we left the highway yesterday. Ever since we entered this forest, I have been getting a bad feeling and I want to know why. I know that the two of you know something and it is time you share it with the rest of us."

"For that matter, so do I," added Dorn.

"I too would like to know what is out there," Alaric's voice was calm as he looked at the dwarves.

"Very well then," conceded Eldred. "We didn't want to tell you because we didn't want to worry you. Palentonal, why don't you do the honours?"

Palentonal looked at Eldred gravely. When it was clear that Eldred wasn't going to say anything further Palentonal started his theory. "The Great Eastern Forest has been cursed for almost a thousand years. Elves used to live here, but that was a long time ago. No one really knows what happened, but the result was catastrophic. All the life was sucked from the forest. Of the Elven clans who stayed, nothing was ever heard from them again. Those who left were too distraught to comprehend. They say there was an Elven clan that started to practise evil arts. They transformed themselves into mystics. Now they roam the forest at night, taking all who stray out of the light. The only way to survive is to keep a constant light going. The mystic will not travel into light. That is why we have to keep the fire burning. No one knows what the mystics want, but we know enough to stay away from them."

"So why did you lead us here if it was so dangerous." Bern's voice was riddled with concern.

"Because we have no other choice. We must get to Avalon and this it's the fastest route. Not to mention the safest."

"The safest!" Dorn almost spat the words. "How can you tell us that it is the safest route with what the elf just told us?"

"The closer we get to our goal, the more Nyrra's agents will be searching for us. On the open road, we will be sitting ducks. As far as we know, the mystics have no allegiance to Nyrra, so they won't be drawn to us. None of our routes from here will be safe. It is just a matter of which one is the least deadly."

Suddenly the events of the previous night made sense. It must have been a mystic that Alaric had seen in the dark. He wondered how they knew his name and what they wanted with him. It was clear that evil was being drawn to him. He thought about telling the others, but decided against it. Everyone was on edge already without Alaric adding to their stress.

They moved off without another word spoken. The news of the mystics did nothing to lighten their spirits. The rain, which had dogged them the previous day, had returned. It took the heat out of the forest, but made things even more miserable. The rain filtered down between the trees and dripped on their heads. Alaric wasn't sure which was worse, the driving rain or the dripping rain. They spent most of the afternoon leading the horses through the thick undergrowth. For the first, time Alaric noticed that there was no sign of life in the forest. Besides the sounds coming from the group and the rain, there were no other noises.

The rain persisted into the evening and Palentonal and Eldred tried to start a fire as the sun started to set. Darkness quickly crept into the forest. The damp wood would not light and the rain kept extinguishing any fire they managed to ignite.

"It's no good," started Palentonal. "The wood is too wet. We need to find something dry."

"There is no dry wood. We looked everywhere," complained Hulkan.

Eldred looked at the sky and then back towards their makeshift fireplace. "I had hoped it wouldn't come to this. Now every mystic in the forest will know where we are."

Eldred held his hand over the top of the fire. Alaric felt the slight tickle in the back of his neck and everyone could feel a heat coming from the wood. All of a sudden, a small flame ignited from inside the pile and in seconds there was a blazing fire burning in the centre of their campsite. The light came just in time as the sun had completely set, leaving the rest of the forest in complete darkness.

No one stayed up late that night. After they had eaten, all but Eldred, who was again taking the first watch, went to sleep.

It was late when Alaric woke to the sound of someone calling his name. This time he wasn't sure if he had dreamt the sound or whether it was real. When the voice didn't come again, he assumed that he must have been asleep and started to drift off again.

"Alaric," the call came again, no louder than a whisper.

There was no doubting it this time. He sat up and stared into the forest. The darkness again was impenetrable and Alaric couldn't see anything. The only sound was the crackling of their fire and the soft breathing of the sleeping group. He was about to lie down again when he saw the same white wisp. The same feeling of dread returned to him and he had a compulsion the leave the campsite and enter the forest. Slowly, all these emotions subsided and Alaric returned to sleep.

In the morning, Alaric again woke refreshed. Even the sound of rain splashing the leaves could not dampen his spirits. The rest of the group also seemed to be in the same mood. They all seemed happy and ready for the day's journey.

Like the previous day, they spent most of the morning leading their horses through the thick undergrowth. Their previously high spirits were again soon diminished. The entire purpose of them entering the forest was for them to gain time. Now it seemed like they were going to lose it. To make matters worse the rain stopped mid-morning and the sun came out. The forest returned to the steam room it had been the day before, making everything uncomfortable.

"This is getting ridiculous. We are losing more and more time. At this rate, it is going to take us another month before we reach the border of Avalon," Palentonal complained when they stopped for lunch.

"I know, but there is nothing we can do about. This is the only path we can take through the forest. We have no choice but to press on," conceded Eldred.

"We go back," stated Hulkan. "We go back and take the highway to Tyborn. From there we will ride to Avalon.

"That is no longer an option," replied Eldred.

"What do you mean? So, we've lost two and a half days. We could lose over a month if we continue along this trail. I can feel evil magic in my bones. The entire forest reeks of it," argued Hulkan. "I'm not as ignorant as some might believe.

Eldred laughed out loudly. "No you are not, Master Dwarf," Eldred laughed again. "It is that very magic that will not let us turn around and go back. There is something they want to say to us, but they will not do it until their time is right. Not even I could guess what their agenda is."

Hulkan didn't seem to accept what Eldred had said, but he did not push the point. Things were starting to make sense to Alaric now. He knew there had been magic at work.

They moved off again, leading their horses. If anything, the undergrowth had become thicker as they continued. It was as if they were being herded to a specific place. As if confirming Alaric's suspicions, just before nightfall they reached a small clearing. Eldred looked at the clearing with doubt. As he did, the rain started to fall again.

"What do you think?" asked Palentonal.

"I don't think that we have a choice. If we stay outside the clearing, the mystics are going to make it as uncomfortable as possible. I don't like it, but we have little choice," explained Eldred.

Slowly Eldred led the group into the clearing. As he did, the rain disappeared and the sun returned. Eldred looked up towards the sky as if he was expecting something to happen.

"We make camp here tonight. There will be no fire," ordered Eldred.

"What are you talking about?" asked Palentonal in shock. "You know what will happen if we don't have light."

"Calm down, Palentonal. Relax for a minute and feel the forest. We were brought here for a reason and we should not be afraid. There will be no fire. I doubt very much if we could light one anyway. We shall eat a cold meal this evening."

Palentonal did as he was told and very soon he understood what Eldred had meant. The very trees themselves were issuing a message of peace. He knew that they were going to be safe. Whoever it was that was tampering with their reality was not hostile.

As instructed, there was no fire that night and it became extremely dark very quickly. Eldred produced a small amount of light, which radiated from the end of his staff as they ate and when they were done, they all went to sleep. Eldred didn't sit watch that night. He could already feel the enchantment floating down around him and knew that he would be happily sleeping in a few minutes.

It was dead on midnight when Alaric was woken. It was not by any sound, but a feeling. The feeling of dread, which had plagued him the past two nights, was now a feeling of contentment. He slowly dressed, without knowing why and got to his feet.

"Alaric!" came the same soft whispering voice.

The white wisp was now clear to him. On the edge of the clearing was a white silhouette, which looked to be of a man. The glowing creature stretched out an arm and beckoned him to follow. He started to walk although he made no conscious decision to move. Everyone else in the camp was fast asleep; no one heard Alaric's footsteps as the enchantment still lay thick on the clearing.

As he walked following the white figure, he felt as though he was in the middle of a dream. His head felt light and his vision blurred. The light coming from the figure was dim, but it was enough to let him find his way.

Suddenly Alaric snapped out of his daze. He was in a clearing, like the one where they had made camp. He was now surrounded by more glowing figures. Alaric was suddenly gripped with fear. The feeling only lasted a couple of seconds and as soon as it came it disappeared. He was left feeling very curious.

"Who are you? What do you want from me?" asked Alaric.

"We are the keepers of the forest. We have brought you here to give you a message." As the figure spoke, the light they were all emitting started to fade, all except for one.

The creature standing before Alaric looked like the other elves he had seen, but there was something different about them. They had darker skin and hair. Their faces did not have the same beauty to it as was common with elves.

"Why should I believe what you say?"

"Before we can tell you what you need to know, we have to explain where our race originated. Maybe then you will be able to listen to us with an open mind. My name Xynate and I am the Queen of the Dryads." Xynate was the only dryad still glowing. "We were once elves, like those who travel in your group. Many cycles ago, our ancestors knew that they were different. They had a greater connection with the trees than their brothers. It was so much so that they started to change. At the same time, there was another tribe of elves who started to practise evil rituals. We named them the Morel; in the old language it means the diseased. The Morel drove the other elves from these lands. At that time the elves had no weapons of their own. Their perverse weapons were too much for the peaceful elves. They chose to run instead of staying and fighting. When they could not kill the elves, the Morel started to cut down the trees and befoul the forest. They sacrificed the innocent animals and then the forest decided to fight back. It would no longer sit idly by and watch itself be destroyed. The change to my people, who had slowly been evolving, increased. All the trees pushed their life force into our ancestors. A great war broke out between the Morel and the Dryads. Our numbers were not great and their magic was strong, but the spirit of the forest was with us. We fought the Morel to the death. Only at the very end did the Morel retreat deep into the forest. Unfortunately, part of the forest is also evil and we could not chase. Without the aid of the forest, we could not win against the Morel. When their numbers grow strong they attack us. Now our numbers are dying out. We are not long left for this world and then Morel will have complete control."

"So you want me and my friends to destroy the Morel for you? Well, unfortunately we do not have time. We have our own wars to fight," interrupted Alaric.

"I know of your war. That is why I have brought you here. The safe trail that has been granted to the Council of Wizards now runs through part of the forest that is held by the Morel. Their evil is spreading throughout the forest like a plague. Your coming has been foretold since the beginning of our existence. Our destinies have been intertwined since the start of time. If the Dryads die out, then the Morel will control the forest and eventually it will die. We will grant you safe passage, there is nothing you can do to help at this time, but I ask you to take a message to the Council of Wizards. In this forest is the Spring of the Trees. If the Morel capture it, they will become more powerful than you can imagine.

We are the Guardians of the Spring. Will you help us?" Xynate asked, her voice sweet with the sounds of the forest.

"That seems simple enough, although I don't know how much influence I will have, but I will tell one of my travelling companions, he is one of the council. I will tell him what you have told me," replied Alaric, now feeling for their plight.

Xynate seemed pleased with the result. "One more thing before you go. When you reach Nyrra's stronghold, you will be faced with a number of challenges. Go with your heart Alaric, the obvious answer is not always the right one. Remember these words Alaric..." the last words trailed away.

The next thing Alaric knew was morning had broken and he was back in his tent. Had he dreamt the entire night? It couldn't have been real. Something was different though. Alaric looked around. Nothing had changed since he had fallen asleep. Then it struck him. Around his neck was a necklace, something that wasn't there when he went to sleep. On the end of the necklace was a small wooden figure. The more Alaric looked at it the more it resembled Xynate.

At breakfast Alaric decided to tell the entire group of the previous night's events. Originally he was only going to tell Eldred, but he knew that there had already been too many secrets and he was not going to divide them any further.

Alaric sat and explained the history of the Dryads. Palentonal, Alena and Eldred watched with understanding on their faces. The others looked at Alaric in amazement. Almost as if they didn't believe him.

"Well, I thought the Dryads were all but extinct," Palentonal commented when Alaric had finished.

"They were, but it seems the forest wasn't ready to let them be forgotten. We had always believed that there was good in this forest as well as evil. Now we know for sure," returned Eldred.

"What about these Morel?" asked Dorn.

"Xynate granted us safe passage away from the Morel," repeated Alaric.

"How do we know that we can trust the Dryads? They might just be leading us into a trap so they can kill us," argued Hulkan.

"If they wanted to kill us then they would have done it by now. They are one with the forest. No one can enter without their knowledge and consent. They need our help for survival. There can be no doubt that what they said was true," rebutted Eldred.

"What about the Spring of the Trees?" asked Alaric.

"It is one of the seven locations where the God Kings left the world. The Spring of the Trees is the exiting place of Emerald. Just the same way, the Well of Cleansing Power was the exit of Topaz and the

Cauldron Flame, in the Cauldron Mountain, was the exit of Ruby. We had guessed that the Spring was in the forest, but we could never find it. We knew that Nyrra's coming would have a ripple effect throughout the world. All evil is coming into power," explained Eldred. "There's nothing for it now. We must keep moving towards Avalon. We have no choice but to trust the Dryads will protect us and hope that they can last until our return."

No more conversation was had on the matter. Since they had long finished breakfast, they quickly packed and started off again. The undergrowth was now not as it had been. At some parts, they could even travel at a slow trot. Alaric wondered to himself if it had been the Dryads that had slowed their travel from the beginning. The day passed without any incident, the weather stayed fine throughout the day and they were all in high spirits when they made camp. The majority decided that it would be best if they did not break the old rules and travel after dark. They had made some good distance during the day so no one complained.

The night also passed without incident. Alaric slept the entire night without stirring and the next day they were all keen to make up ground.

As the day wore on, the feeling of dread returned to Alaric. Now he was unsure whether it was because the Dryads were near or the Morel. Just before twilight, the path they were following swung sharply to the left. Alaric knew that they were nearing Morel controlled territory. There was no definite trail they were following and when they strayed the undergrowth became too thick for them to pass.

"We need to be careful tonight," commented Alaric as they ate their evening meal.

"We need to be careful every night Alaric," replied Eldred, dismissing Alaric's comment.

"I know that Eldred," sarcasm dripping from Alaric's comment. "We need to be extra careful tonight. We're very close to Morel country. I've been having a bad feeling for most of the afternoon."

Eldred nodded his apology. They had all been having feelings of dread throughout the afternoon. Now they knew why, or could at least justify their feelings. They knew that sooner or later they would encounter the Morel.

It was the worst night sleep Alaric had experienced since they had entered the forest. Although there were no incidents, Alaric woke many times. The feeling that something bad was going to happen stayed with him and if anything strengthened.

In the morning, no one felt as though they had slept at all. The sombre mood stayed with them over breakfast. There was little conversation until Alaric spoke.

"Do you think that it is Nyrra who is causing this feeling that we're all having?"

"No, I don't think so, he doesn't know we're here. For him to cast a spell on us, he needs to know our location or at least the general direction. Even if he knew we were here, it would be pure luck for him to cast a spell that would affect us. I don't think he would waste the time and it would take too much of his energy." Eldred paused as he finished his last mouthful. "I do think that you are right though. I think that there is magic at work here. Whether it is specifically aimed at us or at the forest in general, I'm not sure. If I had to make a guess, I would say it was at the forest. I have a feeling this is the way the Morel decay the land."

They moved off at a cautious pace after breakfast. The fear of attack was deep within them. They could feel eyes watching them as they rode. The entire experience was extremely uncomfortable.

A small group of Morel were waiting to ambush, early in the afternoon. There were only a dozen of them and they were poorly armed. It did not take long before they were disposed of. As Eldred had expected, there was no sign of the Dryads to help them.

After the second attack came, it was obvious that the first had been to test their skill. A number of Morel came flying out of the trees, knocking them off their horses. When they were all on the ground, another fifty Morel came from behind. The only weapons they had were crude spears. Instead of attacking they, tried to herd the group into the forest. Even though the weapons were rudimentary, they still had a pointy end and with sheer numbers the group had to follow their lead and back into the thicker undergrowth.

"What are they doing?" asked Dorn.

The ground beneath them suddenly came to life.

"Help!" cried Hawthorne as thick rope net scooped them up and carried them into the air.

"Whoa!" cried Bern as the net closed around them it knocked their weapons from their hands. The net bounced a few times and then came to rest about ten feet in the air. They were so tightly packed together that no one could move their arms to reach any concealed weapons they still had.

"What do we do now?" asked Palentonal.

"What can we do? I don't know about you, but I can't move an inch," replied Eldred. Whatever you do Alaric, don't use the stone. We don't want Nyrra knowing where we are."

After the Morel had cleared away their weapons, they lowered the group to the ground. To show they meant business, they kept their spears aimed at the group. They stayed there for a moment while they decided what they were going to do with Alaric and the group. They spoke a foreign language that even Eldred couldn't interpret.

"What are they saying?" asked Dorn quietly.

"I don't know," replied Eldred.

"It's a very perverted version of ancient Elvish. I almost understand what they are saying, but it's hard to be sure," added Palentonal.

"I can tell you one thing. They aren't planning on letting us go. I'm sure they are deciding to kill us here or somewhere else," added Hulkan sarcastically.

One of the Morel grunted and waved his spear in front of them. They all guessed that it meant for them to be quiet. Slowly the Morel started to disperse. They left a space in front of the group and Dorn, who was standing at the back, received a firm poke in the back. He was about to say something, but remembered that he didn't have his axe.

"I think that they want us to move in that direction," commented Dorn as he rubbed his back.

Slowly they started to move, the Morel surrounded them and kept their spears close.

"No one do anything rash. Let's see where they are taking us," whispered Eldred.

They all resigned themselves to the fact that they had no choice.

Chapter 28: The Morel

The Morel outpost was crude, yet beautiful. Small timber huts hung mysteriously in the trees. There seemed to be no supports to keep them from toppling over. They did, however, stand up to the worst of weather conditions. Most of them were high in the forest canopies, but there were also larger dwellings wrapped around the base of the trees.

From the ground, there seemed to be no way to reach the upper levels. There were, however, many Morel racing around the rope bridges that joined the high huts.

The scenery should have been spectacular and the architecture magnificent, but the huts seemed to reflect the dreariness of the forest, or vice-versa. The trees seemed to lack life itself. Both the trunks and leaves looked diseased. The boles were a sick grey, instead of the rich browns in the rest of the forest. The leaves were covered with black spots and were a dull, lifeless green.

The group were suspended individually in cages which were hung from a long length of rope suspended between two large trees. The cages hung more than ten paces from the ground; the thought of trying to break out was unthinkable. None of them would survive the fall.

"What are we going to do?" Bern whispered from his cage, trying his best to keep his voice low.

"I don't think there is anything we can do at the moment. We have to wait and see what the Morel want. I don't think they will keep us here long. We just need to keep our wits and wait for our opportunity to escape," replied Eldred calmly.

The melancholy that had struck them earlier was now at its peak. A deep depression had set in and Palentonal and Alena seemed to be suffering the most. The disease that had attacked the forest was having a similar effect of them.

They remained in the cages for the rest of the afternoon. Occasionally a Morel would check on them, but that was the only movement they saw. Once the sun had disappeared, a number of torches were lit.

It was not long after sundown when a Morel addressed them from a nearby platform. He seemed different to the others, his skin was not as pale and he looked more like an Elf than a Morel. When he spoke, they could understand him.

"You are not of the Dryad, why are you here? Are you here to help them destroy us?" his harsh accent was almost comical, but no one laughed.

"We are just travelling through," Eldred spoke slowly. "We have no business with you or the Dryads."

The Morel closed his eyes and did not reply. Suddenly Alaric felt a sharp pain in the back of his head. Without thinking, Alaric instantly blocked the spell. The Morel cringed. Alaric suddenly regretted his decision to tell the others what Xynate had told him.

"There is more to this small group than meets the eye," commented the Morel as he opened his eyes. "I know that you are lying to me. There is something not right."

"Could you at least give us the courtesy of a name?' asked Eldred, realising a slight advantage.

When the Morel had cast the spell, Eldred had done his best to blanket everyone's thoughts. It was obvious that he had managed to gain some incite, but the majority still remained a secret.

"My name is Erelious and that is all you need to know about me at the moment, Master Wizard," Erelious didn't seem happy. "I will be back presently. I would advise not making too much noise either. It took a lot of persuading for my brethren not to kill you. I don't think they're going to need much of an excuse to drag you down and slaughter you."

Erelious smiled as he walked away, something didn't seem natural. No one knew what to make of him.

"What do you make of that?" Hawthorne asked once he was sure Erelious had left.

"I don't know. There is something different about him. I think that he may have a secret agenda. As he said, the others wanted to kill us immediately," explained Eldred.

An angry looking Morel came to the platform and grunted at the prisoners. He waved his spear at them, demanding silence. When all was quiet, the Morel returned to his hut. When he stared at them, there was a look in his eyes that repulsed Alaric. Suddenly the Morel licked his lips and started to pull in Alena's cage. A rage started to build inside Alaric and he could feel himself drawing in the energy around him. As he did, he felt his head swim and his stomach churn.

Just before the cage reached the platform, Erelious reappeared. He took one look at the other Morel and then cracked him across the back of his head with the blunt end of his spear. The Morel's eyes rolled back into his head and slowly he toppled off the side of the platform to his death. Fear remained on Alena's face, she didn't know what the first Morel had in mind for her.

"This is the deal," started Erelious. "I can help you escape, but you must do something for me in return."

"What might that be?" asked Eldred, truly interested.

"I want you to take me with you," he asked sincerely.

The response from the group was not what he was looking for. All but Eldred burst out laughing. The thought of taking the Morel with them was ridiculous. Eldred, however, did not find the offer completely out of the question, though he did want to find out more before he made a decision.

"I must admit that I was not expecting that. I think that you're going to have to explain yourself a little better if you want us to bring you along." The others were just as surprised to hear Eldred not dismiss the proposal as they were when Erelious asked it.

Before Erelious had a chance to answer, there was a loud cry from somewhere in the forest. The next thing they saw were the glowing figures of the Dryads and more Morel were coming out of their huts to defend their outpost. Another came out onto the platform to check on the prisoners. Erelious quickly disposed of the new Morel like had done the last, he wasn't going to let the prisoners die. They were his only chance to fulfil his destiny.

"Damn it," cursed Erelious. "I don't think we have time for explanations. In a matter of seconds, more of my brethren will come out here to kill you. The choice is yours. I know where they have your weapons and I know where your animals are."

They all knew he was right. The Dryads wouldn't enter the light and the Morel knew it. The commotion they were causing was their only chance to escape.

Erelious fended off another Morel before they finally made their decision.

"Fine, we will go with you." Eldred yelled.

One after the other Erelious brought in the cages and set them free. The platform was just large enough for them all to stand and Erelious quickly led the way down to the forest floor where chaos was ensuing.

The Dryads sent a volley of arrows into the outpost, but their numbers were not a match for the Morel. Their only advantage was that the Morel were too afraid to leave the safety of the light.

Erelious quickly led them to their weapons, through the chaos. "We cannot enter the forest without torches," cried Erelious   as they reached the edge of the light.

"It's okay, the Dryads will give us free passage. There is nothing to fear." Alaric tried to calm the Morel.

"For you maybe, but I will be dead before I take two steps," Erelious was visibly shaking.

"No harm will come to you whilst you travel with us," Alaric's words seemed to calm Erelious.

"I see," Erelious smiled, "I think that we should get out of here."

He wouldn't enter the forest first. He waited at the edge of the light for the others to move into the darkness. Eldred led the way, followed by Hawthorne. No one was confident about stepping into the dark, but the other option was certain death.

Once they were in the darkness, Erelious took the lead. The horses had followed the group to the outpost and it didn't take long for Erelious to locate them.

"Now that I have shown you that I can be trusted, I hope that we can travel together in peace," Erelious' voice was filled with hope.

"Do we make camp for the night or do we keep travelling in the darkness?" asked Hulkan before they started again.

"I think we should keep going. We need to get as much distance as we can before the sun comes up. Once the Morel can roam the forest again they will come looking," said Eldred.

"I think we should light a fire and make camp," suggested Erelious, who was obviously not keen to spend any more time in the dark.

"If the Dryads wanted to attack us, they would have done so by now. I agree with Eldred. We need to make as much ground as we can," Alaric's voice sounded strangely commanding.

As much as Alaric wanted to rest, he knew his words were the only way they would survive. More than that he wanted to know what Erelious' agenda was. He didn't think he would be taking on a Morel as one of his companions. The prophecy was certainly working in mysterious ways.

"Very well, we shall ride until dawn," Eldred didn't sound confident.

They travelled in complete darkness. Erelious continued to lead the way to make sure they didn't pass too close to any more outposts. The journey was slow; the undergrowth was thick and without vision it was almost impossible to traverse. By the time the sun was starting to rise, they were questioning if they had made any progress at all.

"I think we should keep moving," suggested Erelious. With the new light, his nerves seemed to worsen.

"No. We will rest for a short period." Again, it was Alaric who decided. Something had changed in him. Eldred watched him closely, but was happy to defer command for the moment.

"What is your design here?" Hulkan put the question to Erelious as soon as they had made camp.

"Let's get some sleep. We can discuss matters later," Eldred cut in before Erelious had a chance to answer. It was more of an order than a suggestion. He could easily sense the rage growing amongst the group and wanted to avoid any confrontation. He knew there was a reason for Erelious to join them and he needed some time to consult the prophecy before he could answer them.

Erelious deferred to Eldred. There was no apparent reason for his sudden attack. It was his brethren who had captured them and it was Erelious who had rescued them at great risk to his own life.

It was just before midday when Eldred woke the group. Again, he had found nothing in the prophecy to give him any clues on their current situation. The sun was shining high and there was not a hint of rain.

"You haven't told us why you wanted to come with us. To me it doesn't make any sense," Bern asked.

"That's a very good question. I still don't understand it myself," started Erelious, glad for the chance to be heard.

"Why don't you start from the start and go from there? There are a number of things that need clearing up," interrupted Eldred.

"Very good then," Erelious paused "It happened a long time ago, when I was barely of age. We had captured a man from a nearby town who had strayed too far into the forest. It was my first assignment from my clan. The man pleaded every day to let him go. At first I couldn't understand a word he was saying. But after a while, I started to pick up his language. My kin do not keep prisoners for long though and soon he was executed, but my fascination had been piqued. Whenever we captured a man, I made sure I was in a position to be close to him. One day a young man came to be captured. He begged to me to let him go. He said he had a young wife and child. He looked so innocent. He told me that if I helped him escape, he would take me with him and show me how good life could be outside the forest. I thought about it for a while before I agreed to his terms. I had always wanted to see what it was like outside the forest, so I got myself on night watch and together we snuck away." Erelious seemed to be rambling, not making a lot of sense. "I lived in a small village not far from the forest; it was a completely different world. I thought that we were advanced, but there was no comparison. Man was open to learning new experiences, the Morel are set in their ways. They are too cut off from the rest of the world to ever change. I finally felt alive. I had always known there was something missing, but until then, I didn't know what it was. The townsfolk thought that I was an elf. They didn't really know the difference, so when the man told them I was an elf they believed him. He told them how I risked my life to rescue him. He didn't even tell his wife the true story. I was happy and had no intention to return to my clan," Erelious paused and looked off into the woods, as if something had caught his attention. His expression was that of sorrow.

"So why then did you return to the forest?" asked Palentonal, a little suspicious. "My life was going along nicely. I had a nice job as a hunter. Being a Morel, it was the perfect job for me. I could track the animals like no one else in town. I had left the man's house and moved into a house of my own. The town had accepted me. Then one night that all changed. I don't know even if it happened or whether it was dream. A man came to me. He looked similar to Eldred, dressed in a robe with a long grey beard. Even straight after he left, I couldn't recall any other features. The only other thing I could remember is what he told me. The man said 'Return to your people. A strange group will be passing through the forest. Your clan will capture them. If you ever want to be happy outside of the forest, you must help them escape and travel with them.' I protested against the man. The last thing I wanted to do was to leave my new life. I was happy. Then he told me that bad things would start to happen if I did not leave. I woke the next day and didn't know what to think. I had made myself a life, a life like none of my kind would ever know. He was right though. Bad things had started to happen. It was slow and subtle at first, a fire here and a disease there. Then the drought came and then the famine. Everyone I had grown to love was suffering and it was all my fault. One day, I returned to the forest. I didn't want to, but I knew it was the only way for things to return to normal. It was the worst day of my life. I walked through the forest until I came across a clan of Morel. It took me long time before I could convince them I was one of them. They imprisoned me for a year, beating me every day. When they finally agreed that I was Morel, my spirit had been broken. I returned to my normal life with no real will to live. The only thing that kept me going were the words from the strange man. As the years went by, I eventually gave up waiting for you and returned to my old way of life. I joined in on the raids and helped with the contamination of the forest. I thought that I was a fool for believing in fantasies. My life was over. There was no way I was ever going to leave the forest again. I wanted to destroy my entire race. They think that they are the greatest species of all time. Their methods are so archaic that if it wasn't for the Dryads protecting the forest, they would have been wiped out years ago. Kill them all, I say, they are a joke on evolution." On that note Erelious stopped talking.

"Don't forget that you are part of that perversion. You can't change your heritage," Palentonal almost spat the last word.

"I am no more a Morel than you, anymore," replied Erelious, a touch of anger in his voice.

"We should keep moving. We're still a good three days' ride from the edge of the forest," explained Eldred, stopping the conversation before things got out of control.

Since Erelious didn't have a horse, he had to travel on one of the pack animals. Their supplies had diminished quite considerably since they had started and they could easily spare one of the donkeys. Now that they had Erelious to guide them, the travelling was a lot quicker. He knew where to go to avoid not only the Morel, but also the thick undergrowth.

There was very little talk when they stopped. Eldred made sure that the situation didn't get out of hand. Besides himself and Alaric, Hawthorne was the only other one who didn't seem to mind the Morel's appearance. The others tolerated him only because of his ability to navigate the forest.

Just before dusk on the third day, they reached the edge of the forest. The sight on the other side was breathtaking. There were leagues upon leagues of sweeping plains. Fields and fields of untouched grasslands. It was completely perfect. The only thing that broke up the plains was the horizon. They rode to the top of the closest hill and stopped there for the night.

The feeling wasn't as high as it should have been. The journey through the forest had brought them too far to the south. They were supposed to exit the forest and arrive at the army, but now they were at least another day's ride away.

"Isn't this a rather open place to set up camp? Anyone within twenty miles will be able to see us," commented Hawthorne as he surveyed their surroundings.

"There is no cover in Avalon. It doesn't matter where we camp. Anyone who wants to find us will be able to. We need to be up high, because there is someone who I need to signal," explained Eldred, somewhat impatiently.

They all sat on top of the hill and ate a nervous dinner. Erelious was the only one who didn't look nervous. He stared around the countryside with a look of wonder as Eldred went off to make his signal. Alaric concentrated on feeling Eldred's magic, but nothing happened.

It was a strange feeling being out of the forest. Alaric lay back and watched the night sky. The stars seemed so different in Avalon. There were no clouds and the moon was full. Alaric had never appreciated the night sky before. It was so peaceful it was hard for Alaric to think that in a few days' time, there would be a great battle that could tear the land apart.

The sun shone brightly the next day. There was a real feeling of anticipation amongst the group. They were close to the end of their journey and time was of the essence. Now that they were out in the open, Erelious on donkey-back was starting to slow them down. To everyone's surprise, he who suggested he should dismount and run. Even more surprising was that he could keep pace with the horses without tiring.

"All being well, we'll will join the army by lunch time tomorrow," commented Eldred. The news was what everyone was hoping to hear as they sat around the campfire.

In the morning, Eldred gave them some more good news. "I am reasonably confident that Nyrra's army has still not reached the battlefield. I'm not sure where they are, but it looks as though we have beaten him."

"How do you know this?" asked Erelious, watching Eldred with a questioning look on his face.

"I am sure that I would know if the battle had started. I doubt that Nyrra will wait to attack." explained Eldred.

There was a short silence before Hulkan let out a loud hoot. It was a mixture of joy and relief. His cries were joined by the others. The news that they were ahead of the enemy was the best news they had heard in a long time. For the last month, they had felt like they were just wasting their time trying to defeat Nyrra. Now they had confirmation that it was not all for nothing.

The mood was a lot brighter as they started out for the morning. Before midday, they crested a small hill and were hit by a sight that dumbfounded them all. The long, sweeping plain before them was filled with men, tents, siege engines as well as many other tools of war.

"How many people are there?" asked Alaric in awe.

"I would estimate about ten thousand men, two thousand elves and about the same in dwarves. It is one of the biggest armies that has ever been mobilised," Eldred explained.

"What is the biggest?" asked Bern.

"That is something we will find out soon enough. We've estimated that Nyrra's army is around fifty thousand."

Alaric felt his heart sink. Just when he thought they had won, he realised they were further away than ever. There was no chance they could defeat an army that was over two times its size.

"Don't worry. Lisle's army is another three or four thousand and should start arriving any day now. Faxon also has troops on the way. I know, all we need to do is stall them for a while and the numbers will soon even out. Anyway, the sooner we get down there, the sooner we can work out what is happening."

"I wouldn't be surprised if they are already there. I know that General Jarwe was pushing them hard." Hawthorne added.

They rode down towards the camp in silence. No one could see the positive in Eldred's words. It now seemed as though it didn't matter what they did, there was no hope. Nyrra would be upon them any day now and then it would soon be over.

No one stopped them as they rode through the camp. Many soldiers rushed around them, seemingly taking no notice. The camp was a hive of activity and tension was thick in the air. They could all feel it. Eldred led the way as if he had been there before.

"How do you know where you're going?" asked Bern.

Eldred didn't seem to hear the question. Before Bern could ask the question again, Hawthorne rode up beside him.

"All alliance war camps are built the same, or at least with the same principle in mind. The highest-ranking officials are based at the centre and then they fan out in order of rank. The infantry and archers are housed around the perimeter."

The ground was no longer the sweeping, untouched grass that they had been riding thought for the past few days. The area had been trampled down into dust. There was nothing beautiful about it. Alaric thought it was a shame that such a beautiful place was going to be turned into a wasteland. He doubted if it would ever look the same again.

It was not hard for them to pick the command tent. It was the largest. Two armoured guards stood at the entrance, each holding a menacing looking pikes. They eyed the group carefully as they dismounted.

"State your business," commanded one of the guards.

"Let General Jarwe know that we are here," commanded Eldred.

"And who are you?" asked the guard as a matter of fact.

"Let him know that Eldred and his company have arrived," Eldred kept his tone cool.

The guard disappeared into the tent. Soft voices could be heard inside and then he returned. His façade had not changed. There was no telling what was going through the man's head.

"The General will see you immediately," boomed the guard, in his most official voice.

Eldred scoffed slightly before leading the group into the command tent. Inside the tent was walled off into several sections. There were quarters for the commanders to sleep, as well as meeting and eating areas. Eldred found his way to the meeting room without any difficulties.

General Jarwe was sitting at a large table with some of the commanders of the other armies which made up the alliance. Jarwe took the head of the table as the leading commander of the Remidian Royal army, the largest army in the alliance. Next to him was Captain Derwin from the Zenzarian Ducal army, part of the Remidian army. Pernian was commanding Orric's forces as well as the small number of elves who belonged to no army. The only other at the table was Gilgi of the Dwarf guild.

As soon as Gilgi saw Hulkan, he stood and spoke brashly. "What is the meaning of this? What is he doing here?"

Gilgi was the son of the new guild leader and Hulkan's nephew. There was a strong dislike between the two families. Hulkan's appearance jeopardised the guild's position. Gilgi reached for his sword.

"There will be no fighting now," boomed Eldred. "Sit down Gilgi. Remember that your father pledged his army to the alliance and agreed to relinquish command to General Jarwe once you arrived."

"I will not sit at the same table with that dwarf. He is a traitor to his kind. The guild has a price on his head and I'm here to claim it." Gilgi didn't like what Eldred had implied and pointed his sword as he spoke.

As soon as Gilgi had drawn his sword the entire group, except for Eldred, drew their own weapons. For the first time since their arrival, the General saw his prince. Seeing that Gilgi was not about to stand down, both Jarwe and Derwin stood between the dwarf and Hawthorne.

"Eldred is correct. Your father deferred command to me and I say he stays," General Jarwe would not back down.

"I know we have had our differences in the past, but things are different now. When this is all over, I will be more than happy to give you a chance for satisfaction," offered Hulkan.

Realising that there would be no chance for reprisal, Gilgi sheathed his sword. "I don't think so. The guild will have no further part in this. We will no longer fight with you."

"You do not have the authority to withdraw your army. Your father has pledged the army to our service. If you try and lead your army away from this battle field, you will leave in disgrace and disgrace your entire family," returned Eldred, keeping his voice even.

"Well I don't think my father will see it that way. I'm taking my army and leaving," Gilgi wasn't waiting for a reply as he stormed out of the tent.

Everyone found a seat sat after Gilgi had left. With the dwarf gone, everyone took a deep breath. The situation could have blown right out of control, although the dwarf couldn't have caused too much trouble by himself.

"This is not a good sign," started General Jarwe. "We need the dwarves. Nyrra's army will be here any day now and we can ill afford to lose anyone."

"Glogin has pledged his services to us. Gilgi knows that he cannot return without written authorisation from his father and a peace treaty signed by both sides. His commander will know this. It will take a lot of convincing to remove the army and he doesn't have time to get word to his father," explained Eldred. "I think that we should get down to business. How are we positioned?"

"Better than we first expected. I have mobilised most of King Faxon's army. As you already know, Glogin has given us a dozen small garrisons more than we initially thought. Pernian arrived last week with two thousand elves. A month ago, we received one thousand men from Tyborn. The commanding officer said that King Unwin had commissioned more men from Darshival, but none have arrived yet," explained Jarwe.

"Have you heard any word from Lisle's army?" asked Eldred.

"None! We have not heard anything."

"That's not a good sign. I would have expected them to be close by now," Eldred's voice was thick with concern. "What about the High Chancellor? Have we managed to convince him to join us?"

"The last word from the High Chancellor is that he is still refusing his support. The largest army of the Alliance and he will not lend us any troops. There is something seriously not right there. I know he is the furthest away from the battle zone, but he can't honestly think that distance will keep Nyrra away forever," Jarwe seemed as worried as Eldred. "I fear the Nyrra has agents in the city,"

"I too fear that you are correct. Thirty thousand in his regular army, Five thousand specially trained knights and one thousand of his elite guard. Half of his army would be enough to sway the tide, none of which will be joining us. There is evil at play here, it only goes towards helping Nyrra's cause," Eldred paused for a moment. "What about Nyrra? Do we know how far away he is?"

"By all accounts, he is no more than two days from reaching the battlefield. Our spies tell us the he is bringing his entire army this way. It seems he has brought enough supplies for a long campaign. I don't think he's planning on throwing everything at us on the first day as we had anticipated."

"There is something not right," Eldred mused to himself. "Has anyone arrived from the council?"

"No, there has been no word for the Council of Wizards."

Eldred swore. "I was afraid this was going to happen." He paused for a moment before addressing the group. "Okay, you all have a decision to make now. Nyrra is closer than we had hoped. At this stage, we had planned to be at the mountain. However, that is not the case. You can decide to stay here and fight or to continue with Alaric. Either way, there is great danger and honour. We will meet back here for breakfast. You will need to have made your decision by then. We shall leave after we have eaten," explained Eldred.

Chapter 29: Nostiria

Alaric woke in the morning more nervous than expected. He would find out at breakfast who was going with him to the mountain. He had become accustomed to his companions and considered them all friends, but he thought that he would miss Bern the most. He couldn't stop thinking about what would happen if Alena didn't come with him. He shook the thoughts from his head as he entered the tent for breakfast. Everyone was already waiting for his arrival.

"Now that we are all here, I don't think there is any reason to wait. I hope that you have all made your decisions," Eldred started as Alaric sat down.

"We certainly have." Hulkan was the first one to speak. "Dorn and I will stay and fight. It has been a pleasure to travel with you, Chosen One, but our path remains here." Dorn nodded his agreement.

"I will be staying as well." Hawthorne didn't wait long after Hulkan had finished. "I will stay to command my father's army. Hulkan and Dorn can fight with me. I don't think that it would be a good idea for you to join with the other dwarves, all things considered. I would like to continue, but I don't think it would be good for morale if their prince abandoned them on the eve of battle."

Eldred nodded gravely, understanding Hawthorne's decision. He suppressed the urge to smile.

"I will go with Alaric. It was not perchance that brought us together and I will not leave now. My destiny lies with yours." Everyone was surprised to hear Erelious, the Morel seemed somewhat serene now. Not the evil creature they had first thought him to be.

"I will also continue on with Alaric," Palentonal watched the Morel closely.

"I will stay and fight," Alaric's heart sank when he heard Bern's decision. He had thought that his friend would be staying with him. Bern didn't make eye contact with Alaric when he spoke.

"I will also go with Alaric. There is more to come and I need to be there," Alaric's heart lifted when he heard Alena. There was something mysterious about her words, as if she knew something that the others did not.

"Very good, then it is all settled. We should eat a hearty meal before we leave."

The conversation during the meal was surprisingly light. They all spoke about what had happened over the past few months. They remembered all the good times and some of the bad. Alaric was glad that he got to spend one last meal with his friends. He knew that it would be the last time he saw some of them.

It wasn't until after breakfast and they had left the tent did Alaric speak to Bern. He was going to miss him, but knew that it could not have been an easy decision for him to make.

"This has been one of the hardest decisions of my life. At first I thought that I would be going with you to the end. Then when I thought about it, it wasn't so clear. There was something that made me think that I should stay, a feeling that if I left then I would be jeopardising your mission." Alaric could tell that Bern's words were genuine.

"I must admit I thought that is what you were going to do. If I had the choice, I think that I would stay and fight," replied Alaric.

"No you wouldn't. Admit it Alaric, you like to play the hero," laughed his old friend. "I don't think that there is much hope for us. From what I can understand, we are only here to give you more time."

"I don't know about that. I still think there is a good chance we can win. There are more men on the way and there are some good tacticians in charge.

"We must go now Alaric, everything is ready." Eldred poked his head inside the tent, but didn't wait for a reply.

"I'm going to miss you," Alaric spoke softly as he stood.

"Don't go soft on me. We will meet again, when the war is over and we have won." The two men embraced briefly before Alaric walked away.

It didn't take long for Alaric to find the others. Their horses were saddled and they had been given a wagon for their possessions. Erelious was asked to ride in the wagon, as he didn't have a horse. They were all wearing dark robes, one of which Eldred handed to Alaric.

"What is this?" asked Alaric, looking at the robe distastefully. Taking a sniff of the robe he scrunched up his face in disgust.

"Although the country is mostly uninhabited, there are a few nomad tribes. Wearing these robes will help us blend in. The nomads can be quite aggressive when they think someone is trying to invade. They will also give us some shade from the intense sun."

Alaric shrugged and draped the robe over his shoulders, keeping the hood down. Eldred tapped his head indicating that Alaric should cover his head. Reluctantly he pulled the hood up, the smell was not pleasant and made him gag.

They rode out of the camp in silence. There was something very ominous about their situation and no one felt like speaking. They rode in a south-easterly direction away from the battlefield. There was nothing they could do to help now. Whatever was going to happen would happen.

Around lunchtime Alaric started to get a bad feeling; they stopped by a small grove of willows. The sun was high and not a cloud could be seen. A small stream trickled passed and a cool breeze rustled the leaves keeping the sun from having too much effect. The grass was still lush and green with colourful flowers dotted around the trees.

"Something is coming," Alaric spoke with a far-away look on his face.

Suddenly Eldred felt what Alaric had felt. He stood quickly and reached out with his feeling. The look on Eldred's face didn't fill anyone with confidence.

"Nyrra is here. I would estimate that he is about a day behind us. We must keep moving." There was a fear in Eldred's voice that had never been there before.

Even though no one had finished lunch no one complained about moving. They had always known that Nyrra was after them, now it was more apparent. The reality of their situation was finally hitting home. If they were held up for any reason, Nyrra would be upon them.

Throughout the afternoon's ride, they kept looking over their shoulders for any sign of their pursuers. None came. As they day wore on the terrain slowly started to change. The lush green grass, which was synonymous with Avalon, slowly started to thin out and he green had now taken on a brown tinge. Small stones and rocks started to appear on the ground where they had only been rich, dark dirt before. The cool breeze from the grove had disappeared and the sun was starting to become extreme. The dark robes they wore did nothing to help and by the end of the day they were all sweating.

As night fell, the grass had completely disappeared. The ground was a dry, dusty earth. The horses' hooves stirred up the dust making it more uncomfortable. Alaric was now glad for the heavy robes, keeping the dirt off his skin. With the sun setting, the temperature started to drop considerably and it wasn't long before Eldred called the group to a stop.

"Damn it," he cursed as he reined Tormenta to a halt.

"What's wrong?" Alena asked.

"I had hoped we would have been through the pass of Androniclus before nightfall. We can only be a couple of hundred paces from the precipice. If only we hadn't stopped for lunch. All we can do now is hope that Nyrra is still far enough behind," Eldred explained.

"Why don't we continue through the night?" Alaric asked. "I know I would prefer to sleep, but if it is that important I'm sure we'll all survive.

Eldred laughed at Alaric's suggestion. "Oh no, my friend. We are very close to the border of these two lands. If we stray off course, even by a couple of feet, and we could all end up falling off the cliff. Even if we do find the trail leading down, it is a narrow treacherous journey. Even during the day it will be dangerous. To do it at night would be suicide." Eldred stared at the night sky as he spoke. It was as if he was trying to read something in the stars. "I think that we should be safe enough tonight. Once we have travelled through the pass, we will be able to make up time."

Eldred instructed them that there would be no fire that night. In the dark, it would be harder for Nyrra to follow their trail. He did not want to light a beacon for him. The temperature kept dropping and it was not long before they were all shivering.

No one enjoyed the night's sleep. Everyone remained cold no matter how many clothes they piled on. Just before dawn, Eldred woke them. He allowed them a small fire over breakfast to warm themselves, but as the sun started to share its light they could see they were at the bottom of a small hill. The base was more of a crater with the hill bending around them with the crest of the hill only half a mile from where they camped.

They all stared up at the crest waiting for sight of their pursuers. It made them all very nervous as they ate a small breakfast. The coldness added to their discomfort. The small fire gave off little heat and they all wanted to keep moving.

In the cold greyness, they started off again. It was not long before the horizon started to become closer and closer, indicating the ridge that they were looking for. Soon Eldred led them to the edge, showing them what lay before them.

The expanse of Nostiria was breathtaking. The dry, red earth spread for miles. There was not one single tree in sight. There seemed to be no life at all. The land was broken up by many mesas, mountains and plateaus, as well as craters, fissures and canyons. The absolute wasteland was quite beautiful. In the distance, Alaric saw something that made his blood freeze. It was only a small dot on the horizon, even so he knew exactly what it was, the peak of the Cauldron Mountain, the highest peak in the world. Alaric pulled his eyes away from the mountain. The mere sight of it sent a feeling of dread throughout his body. The longer he looked at it, the more he wanted to ride as fast as his could in the opposite direction.

Eldred continued along the ridgeline, making sure to keep a safe distance.

"Keep your eyes open for anything unusual. The trail leading down isn't as obvious as you would think," Eldred explained as the morning wore on.

"There was something I noticed about half a mile back. I didn't think anything about it at the time, but now that you mention it..." Erelious pointed.

"Just spit it out, we don't have all day," Eldred's words were harsher than he intended.

"I was watching the ridge line when I thought I saw a stone that was out of place. Not only was it out of place, but it was incomplete. As I said, I didn't think anything of it at the time. I just figured that I had been staring at the rocks for too long and was starting to see things," Erelious explained.

"Damn it," cursed Eldred as he turned Tormenta around and kicked him into a gallop.

The others looked at each other with dumb expressions on their faces. The sudden reaction of Eldred surprised them all. Alena was the first one to recover her senses. By the time they all started after him he had already slowed Tormenta to a walk and was carefully studying the ridgeline. The intense look on his face showed that he did not want to speak with anyone.

After they had been travelling for another mile Eldred stopped the group again. The expression on his face was not friendly. He glared at Erelious as he spoke between clenched teeth.

"Are you sure that it was along here?"

"I don't know what I saw, but I do know that it was not this far back," Erelious replied defensively.

"Okay then, back we go," Eldred almost seemed as though he was giving up.

It was Alena who called the group to a halt shortly after they started back in their original direction. Eldred gave her a stern look, but stopped and waited to hear what she had to say.

"I think that we should stop and have some lunch," she said, challenging Eldred to refute her.

Eldred had no problem in taking the bait. "Do you think that we have time to sit around and eat?" The fury that crossed Eldred's face had them all scared. "I don't know if you realise this but we are being pursued and they are very close. We need to find the trail and get through the pass of Androniclus before they reach us."

"Racing up and down the ridge isn't exactly getting us anywhere either. In my experience, sometimes it's better to stop and forget about what you're doing. Then when you take it up again, the solution will hit you in the face." Alena's tone was just as icy as Eldred's was hot. "Everyone is nervous enough without making it worse."

To everyone's surprise Eldred conceded. "You're right, I'm sorry. We should stop."

Eldred sat by himself while they ate. There was something very disturbing about his mood that made everyone uncomfortable. Under Alena's instruction, they all faced away from the ridge, everyone except for Eldred who studied it intently. Even with the ridge behind them, it was still foremost in their minds. What Eldred had said was all too true. Nyrra was hot on their trail and it would only be a matter of time before he was upon them.

They didn't wait long after they had eaten before they were up again. Alena's idea was good, but no one could stand sitting around. Alaric looked towards the ridge before he mounted Adelanta. To his dismay, he found that there was nothing remarkable about it. As he turned towards his horse, he thought he saw something shimmer. He was about to shrug it off as an illusion when he remembered what Erelious had said. The others had already started riding, but Alaric wanted to alleviate his suspicion.

Slowly he led Adelanta to the edge of the cliff. He tested the ground to make sure it was solid and the closer he came to the edge the stronger the feeling that something wasn't right. The terrain he focused on seemed normal enough, but something in his peripheral vision seemed to change slightly. When he tried to focus on the changes, nothing seemed to happen. Alaric was sure that this was what they had been so desperately looking for. He laughed when he remembered the conversation Alena and Eldred had before lunch. She had been right. The answer had been under their noses the entire time.

The others were almost out of earshot when Alaric called out to them. The noise coming from far behind them set them on edge. As soon as they saw who it was their fear turned to excitement. Eldred was the first to reach Alaric and dismounted instantly. After a couple of minutes Eldred turned to address the group. A broad smile had appeared on his face as he started to talk. "It looks like Alaric has found what we've been looking for," his tone suddenly changed. "And it looks like not a moment too soon." He pointed behind them at the horizon.

Their worst fear had finally come true. A group of riders could be seen in the distance. They had a maximum of an hour before the riders would be on top of them.

"Where is this trail of yours, Eldred?" asked Alena, a slight quiver in her voice.

"Quiet," Eldred barked.

Eldred raised his hand and felt the air around him. He moved from left to right for a couple of seconds before he found what he was looking for. Suddenly he called out two words that no one understood. Alaric felt a rush through his body, like a sudden gust of wind. When it was gone the air shimmered around them. Suddenly the land changed. Where the ridge had been the land now stretched out for half a mile. Right where Eldred stood a narrow trail led downward.

"You weren't wrong when you said the trail was treacherous," commented Palentonal as he led his horse.

The trail itself was only just wide enough to fit the wagon. The cliff wall was to their left leaving a sheer drop to their right. To make matters worse the trail had a steep incline. The hard clay surface made it hard to keep their footing. They were forced to lead their horses in single file. It was going to be a long, slow journey, but at least their pursuers would not be able to travel any faster.

The trail took a couple of twists and turns, but always the cliff remained on the left and the ravine on the right. They could neither see what was chasing them from behind nor what was waiting for them at the bottom.

It took them over an hour to reach the base of the cliff and were now at the beginning of a huge canyon. They were all glad to be at the bottom. On more than one occasion someone had lost their footing and come within inches of losing their life.

As they were about to leave, an ear-piercing scream could be heard from somewhere behind them. The noise indicated two things. The first was the Nyrra and his followers had made it to the trail. The second was that he was pushing everyone hard to make up time. One of his followers had lost his footing and fallen off the side of the ravine.

"The pass of Androniclus." Eldred raised his hand in front to emphasize his statement.

The pass was fifty feet wide and continued for a mile dead straight in front of them. The cliff walls loomed above them on either side. The red clay reflected the sunlight, creating a beautiful red gloss throughout the pass. It was completely awe-inspiring. Eldred didn't give them a chance to take in the wonder as he pushed Tormenta to a canter.

"Be on your wits. This can be a dangerous place!" Eldred warned. They moved cautiously once the walls loomed on either side as Eldred slowed them to a walk. There was no doubt now that they were trapped. If anyone was to come at them, there would be no where for them to hide. Their nerves were all on edge, and their hearts pumped faster.

When they were clear of the pass they all relaxed. They could now see why there was a red tinge to their surroundings. The sky had changed from a bright blue to a reddish purple. The sun was now a ball of blood red. The atmosphere was eerie and sent shivers down their spines. Alaric had never seen anything like it before. It reeked of magic, an evil magic. That thought made the sky seem even more ominous. They all stopped and stared at the phenomenon.

As they were about to continue, they were surprised to see Eldred dismount. He walked back towards the mouth of the pass before he stopped, his staff firmly gripped in his right hand. Raising his staff above his head he called out to the sky. Again no one could understand what he was saying. Alaric suddenly felt very cold and Eldred slammed the butt of his staff on to the ground so suddenly that the horses jumped. Then there was silence.

"We have to get out of here," called Palentonal, fear in his voice. "They will be here soon."

Eldred remained stationary, he gaze never leaving the pass. Slowly the ground started to rumble and vibrate and the cliffs started to tremble. A solitary rock fell from the top of the pass, slowly at first, but soon there was a steady downpour of rocks and boulders. The ground shook as the first of the boulders crashed into the ground. Before long, the pass was completely blocked by the rubble.

Once the dust had settled, Eldred returned to the rest of the group. The pile of rocks and boulders stood almost half way up the cliff face. Even though the pass was completely covered, it seemed as though the cliff was still the same height. The feeling was overwhelming.

"That should keep him busy for a while. It will take them a long time to clear the pass and there is no other way around," Eldred looked most impressed with himself as they started off again. "Now we should try and get some miles behind us before dark. Be very wary!" Eldred warned, the joy completely gone from his voice.

"What is the story with the sky?" asked Palentonal as they started off again. "It can't be natural. It is as if the sun is bleeding."

Eldred chuckled at Palentonal's analogy. "Yes, I suppose it is. It is one of the marks of the evil one. This is his land. He scarred the sky many years ago turning it the purple colour that you see today. It is a strange rotting of the cloud, a way he putrefied the sky. Occasionally on a clear day, the sky appears as normal, but most of the time it remains as you see it now." Eldred didn't seem to give the sky much notice. It didn't hold the same dread as it did with the others.

The terrain did not change as they continued. They travelled inside a small ravine. The walls stood only a half a dozen paces high on either side and the ravine floor was about the same in width and it allowed them to travel unnoticed. Even though the land around them was seemingly uninhabited, Eldred insisted that they should not travel in the open. The ravine kept in the heat of the sun and stopped any breeze from having an effect. It was not long before they were all sweating again. Even the horses were sweating and they were only travelling at a slow walk.

Just before nightfall the ravine ended abruptly. Off to the right was a small trail leading out and they were all glad that they would be leaving the ravine. Although it was nice to be able to ride without being watched, there was something unnerving about it. If there was an attack, there would be no escape. Palentonal was the first to start up the small trail.

"No!" called Eldred from the base of the ravine. "We will camp here the night. There is no need to leave our cover just yet. We will not travel at night whilst we are here. There is a small cave where we can spend the night. We will be able to light a fire and trust me when I say we are going to need all the heat we can get."

They all looked at him strangely. No one believed that they would have to camp inside with a fire. The temperature was the hottest they had experienced in a long time. With the constant cloud cover and the ravine, there was no way they were going to need heat. As they set up camp for the night, Alaric couldn't help himself. He had to leave the safety of the cave and stare at the top of the ravine. Claustrophobia was getting the better of him and there was something very unnerving about the land. He couldn't help feeling that someone was watching him.

Alaric was the only one outside the cave when the sun finally set. The temperature dropped as if the darkness was sucking the heat out of the air and it wasn't long before he returned to the others, visibly shivering. He was glad to see that Eldred had already lit a fire.

Surprisingly the cave was large enough to fit the group plus their animals.

"This is one of many caves scattered throughout the land. The tribes travel from cave to cave and share the resources of the land. Each night we must find another cave or else we will freeze to death," explained Eldred. Alaric confirmed that there would be no chance of surviving outside.

The fire warmed the cave sufficiently. They had brought stores of firewood in the wagon along with the food they would need. There was also wood in the back of the cave, but they wouldn't use it until their own stores were depleted.

Once they had finished eating, they spoke for a short while, but it wasn't long before they were all ready for sleep. There was no need to post a watch as anyone who was left outside would be dead.

When the sun had risen, they started again and it didn't take long for the temperature to become uncomfortable. When they exited the ravine, they found themselves at a crossroads leading down into another network of canyons. Eldred led them down the southern path.

"Why are we heading away from our destination?" Alaric questioned Eldred as they started down into the canyon.

"There is a well near here. They are sparse and hard to find. If we are going to survive this land, we must find water. It is the most important and the most dangerous thing we must do between here and the fortress."

"Why is it dangerous?"

"The nomad tribes survive only by knowing where they can find water. Wherever there is a well or an oasis, you can be sure that there will be nomads nearby. If they feel threatened by our appearance, then they will attack. That is why we wear these robes, even though the temperature would call for something lighter. If we can pass for a small group of nomads, then maybe we can pass without notice. Remember that this is Nyrra's homeland. Although they may not follow him, his taint is surely upon them, as much as it is on this land. Would you believe that before Nyrra, this was all lush grassland? It was only broken up by vast and beautiful forests. That has all but been forgotten. Nyrra's disease has destroyed the land and all that abides in it. I'm sure you can all feel it around you. That feeling is not natural. A lot of the water is also poisoned." Eldred explained as he continued to search.

Alaric nodded; he knew that the feeling of unrest was coming from the landscape. He could feel the sickness as they rode. It was somewhat comforting to know the reason for his feelings, even though they were not pleasant, he could handle them.

Suddenly Eldred stopped the group. They could all clearly see a look of concern on his face. The canyon they had entered had large buttresses and mesas protruding from the earth, cutting up the ground. The canyon walls were a lot higher than the small ravine and the floor of the canyon was also a lot wider giving a greater sense of safety. There were also a lot more paths leading through the canyon, which gave them more options to escape.

"There is something coming. We need to hide," Eldred called.

He led the group to a small cave cut into the canyon wall. It was too small for them to ride into, but when they dismounted they could lead their horses. With the horses safely inside, they all returned to the mouth to see who was approaching.

Slowly a group of nomads came into view. Alaric counted forty of them in total, all wearing dark robes, like the ones they were wearing. It was difficult to distinguish between the males and the females. They looked peaceful enough as they travelled on foot, leading their pack animals. There seemed to be no good reason to be hiding from them. Alaric thought that it was too hot for fighting and was sure that the nomads would feel the same. They continued past the cave without noticing them. Alaric did not realise it at the time, but he had held his breath as the nomads passed. When they were gone, he exhaled. Hearing the others do the same, he had to suppress a laugh. He found comfort that he wasn't then only one on edge.

When Eldred was sure that they were safe, he led the group out of the cave. When he did, there was no sign of the nomads. Eldred seemed rather pleased with himself as he started off again.

"Why are you looking so pleased with yourself?" Alaric asked suspiciously.

"Nomads never travel far from water. That means that we are close to a water supply. Also, tribes very rarely meet at the same supply, so with any luck we shall have this one to ourselves. It seems that luck is on our side. At least for now." Eldred's comments lifted the group's spirits. They knew that Eldred would not offer them false hope. It was good to finally have things going their way.

They stopped at another small cave for lunch. The caves were the only cool places and they were all glad to be out of the sun and the intense heat. With the increased heat, their water intake had also increased. During lunch,, they had all but finished their supply. The search was now more desperate, a matter of survival. Their break was all too short and soon they were back out in the heat. No one complained. The sooner they found water the sooner they could relax.

The look of intense concentration returned to Eldred's face as he scanned his surroundings for a clue to where the water was located. The others started to become worried as the day wore on. Their mouths became dry as the sun took its toll. Eldred also seemed concerned for the first time today.

The terrain seemed to be all the same. One mesa looked much the same as another. For every path they took, it all looked the same. Caves were cut into the canyon walls much the same no matter which path Eldred chose. There was no certainty that they were not travelling in circles. Eldred pressed on and did not falter when they came to a crossroad. He chose path after path with the utmost of confidence.

As the day waned the horses started to falter. The riders swayed in their saddles and it was becoming increasingly more difficult to stay conscious. The slowly setting sun only seemed to gain potency. The sun beat down on them without prejudice.

"It's not far now, but I think we should lead the horses. I don't think they will be able to carry us much further," Eldred commented as he dismounted. Tormenta seemed glad to have his burden eased.

All the horses seemed happier without their riders on their backs. There was a renewed spring in their steps, but it didn't last long. The horses and their leaders struggled along. With every step, Alaric thought it was going to be his last.

"Water, I see water." Erelious jumped from the wagon and raced to a spot on the canyon floor.

No one else could see what had made him cry out so. He was pawing at a dry, dusty ground. It looked as though he was trying to pool something in his hand and pour it on his face. It was Eldred who was the first to realise what was happening.

"He's hallucinating."

Palentonal passed the reins to Alena and moved to Erelious' side. It wasn't until Palentonal touched his shoulder that he realised what he was doing.

"What? Oh!" was all the response he could muster.

He was more concerned about trekking back to the wagon still dying of thirst, than the embarrassment of what had just occurred. He didn't know how long he could keep going. When he left the safety of the forest, he knew things were going to be tough, but he had no idea what that meant. They all waited for Erelious to return to the wagon before they started again. They were all secretly jealous that he was still about to ride while they all had to walk, but someone did have to steer.

After rounding another bend, Eldred cried out in elation; with what had just happened, no one became excited. Even though they knew why Eldred was calling out, they could not see why. There was nothing in front of them that looked like it could contain water. They instantly assumed that he was also hallucinating.

Eldred continued like nothing had happened and suddenly their hopes started to dwindle. Eldred, on the other hand, had a renewed spring in his step. He knew that he had found what they had been looking for. As they came closer, they could see a small crack in the ground. Eldred snatched his water pouch from his horse and dove towards the crack. Soon they could all see the splashes of water as Eldred pulled his pouch out.

The crack, which was a small well, was no more than three feet in length and one foot wide. Eldred passed his pouch to Alena before grabbing another. As soon as the others realised what he was doing, they rushed over. Alaric quickly started scooping water in his hand and throwing it into his mouth. Even in the intense heat of the day, the water was still cold and crisp. It was the freshest water Alaric had drunk in a long time. After they had all filled their pouches and drunk their fill, they allowed the horses to drink.

At first they led the horses to the crack until Eldred stopped them. "We can't let the horse's drink directly from the well. We can't chance letting any diseases into the water. If we infect it, then we could inadvertently kill every nomad tribe in this land," Eldred warned.

They slowly watered their horses from their pouches and then filled them again as the sun started to set. The failing light cast shadows across the canyon floor. Eldred led the group away from the crack and as they rode away they all looked back, longingly. Alaric was surprised that the water was so pure in a land so evil.

Just before the sun had completely set, Eldred led them into another small cave. The cave was large enough to house them for the night and there was a secondary cave inside that would act as a stable. It was as if the cave was made exactly for that reason.

"Are we going to be safe here tonight?" Erelious asked. "Not that I doubt you, but it just seems as though this cave was designed for just this purpose. What I mean is the walls look polished. It's as if the cave was man made."

"It was man made," Eldred said as he lit one of the kerosene lanterns they had brought with them. "It was made for exactly this purpose. Small groups caught outside of their tribe would have somewhere to stay. If they were collecting water and ran out of light."

"Then what if a group comes here for the night?" Alena asked.

"No one moves around at night. It gets dangerously cold. If you get caught out in the open, then more often than not it will be your last. That's why there are so many caves around. If a cave is empty at nightfall, then it will remain that way for the rest of the night."

"Why was the water so clean?" Alaric asked, trying to change the subject.

"That is simple. When the rain comes, and believe me when I say it is very rare, but when it does come there is nothing like it in the world. Imagine the most powerful storm you have ever experienced and the times it by ten. The rain gets filtered through the tightly packed clay before it comes to rest in the natural reservoirs below the ground. The filtered water is the purest water in the world. There is nothing like it anywhere," Eldred sounded jovial as he spoke.

As they sat around their small fire and ate dinner Eldred explained how the caves were perfectly insulated. They were cool havens in the extreme heat as well as warm areas in the cold of night. It was a way the land adapted for the survival of her creatures. Without the sanctity of the caves, the nomad tribes would have no chance.

In the morning, they ate a small breakfast. Their food supplies were starting to run short and they were still a good week's ride before they reached their destination, not to mention the trip back. The situation seemed perplexing, but Eldred didn't seem concerned so no one else worried.

Before they continued, they stopped at the crack and filled their water pouches. Eldred took the lead, no one knew how he knew where he was taking them. Alaric wasn't sure that Eldred did know where he was going, but he kept a calm demeanour as he rode and he never faltered when they came to yet another crossroad.

Every now and then Eldred would call them into a cave as he sensed another nomad tribe approaching. The further they rode the more frequently the nomad tribes would pass by. On one occasion, Eldred nearly allowed them to ride straight into one. Just before they rounded   a corner, Eldred commanded them to turn face and gallop to the nearest cave. Just as they entered the cave, the nomads came into view. Each tribe that passed all looked the same: all wore dark robes with the hoods on. No one could ever see their faces. The only skin that showed was on their hands, which poked out of their sleeves. They all moved at a gentle pace, conserving their energy in the intense heat of the day. They all seemed so placid.

The constant stopping and waiting meant that they did not travel far that day. When the sun started to set, they were still in the canyon. Eldred stopped the group suddenly before they reached the next cave. A worried expression filled his face. Alaric knew instantly what was wrong. He was beginning to sense approaching nomads.

"This is the moment I have been dreading. We are too far away from another cave. I can only hope that they are friendly. Be prepared for anything. A meeting between tribes is not often, but when it comes at night, more often than not, it will be a battle to the death. Just follow my lead and keep your heads down. I will talk with the tribal leader. No one else can speak until we have finished," Eldred explained.

With the warning out of the way, they continued towards the cave. Alaric fingered the hilt of his sword under his robe. A touch of anticipation surged through his body. He could feel the tension building inside him. Something had changed, he was looking forward to a confrontation.

They reached the mouth of the cave as the nomad tribe came into view. Although no one could see any facial expressions, they could tell that they were not pleased to see them. There was rigidness to their posture that showed their feelings. It was a tense wait at the mouth of the cave as the nomad tribe approached. There was something about this tribe that was different than the others. Alaric could feel it.

"Hark et mi, Sha'an," Eldred greeted in the general nomadic language.

Eldred pulled his hood back as he spoke. It was customary that when two Sha'ans addressed each other that they reveal their faces whilst the others in the tribe remained covered. The facial expressions were thought to show the true feelings of a person and should not be hidden when talking with other tribes. The Sha'an also removed his hood.

"Easy outlander. I know your tongue," the Sha'an replied very roughly.

Eldred was taken aback. He was not expecting such a response. The surprise clearly showed on his face. The Sha'an seemed to ignore his reaction.

"My name is Sha'tian. We have been travelling all day and need rest. We offer you food and water in return for letting us share this haven. As you can see, it is big enough to house both our tribes." It seemed clear that Sha'tian meant no harm to them.

"It would be an honour to share this haven with your tribe. I do not ask for anything in return," Eldred replied cautiously, speaking slowly so there could be no confusion with what he was saying.

"You would do me and my tribe a great dishonour if you did not let us share our food," Sha'tian's tone became suspicious.

"Certainly, I would never bring dishonour upon you. I give many thanks for your generous offering," Eldred paused and looked towards the sky. "Let us get inside as it is already getting late and the sun is almost spent."

Eldred motioned for the others to enter the cave first. According to tribal law, the first to reach the cave owned that cave for the night. There were two ways of entering the cave. One with the permission of the owner and the other was to fight for it. Eldred was relieved that they took the first option. There was something different about this tribe. Eldred watched Sha'tian carefully as he led his tribe behind them.

"You can remove the hood now," Eldred whispered so only they could hear.

Eldred lit a lantern so they could see. Like the cave they had stayed in the night before, this one also had a separate chamber for the horses. This cave, however, could house twice as many. When the horses were all seen to, the tribe joined them in the main cave.

Sha'tian brought wood from his supplies to light a fire. Alaric was surprised to see the timber. They had not seen a single tree since they had entered Nostiria. There had been no sign of life, beside the other tribes. Sha'tian did not use the wood sparingly and soon there was a roaring blaze in the centre of the cave. The added warmth was welcome as the cool night air blew in. With the added light, they could see the rest of Sha'tian's tribe. It consisted of five men and ten women. This was generally considered small. Most tribes usually consisted of at least twice as many with some numbers as high as fifty. The most unusual thing about the tribe was the complete lack of children. It was common for there to be more women than men, but all tribes had at least a couple of children running around.

"Forgive me for asking," Eldred started as the women prepared meat over the fire. Alaric could not begin to guess what animal the meat may have come from. "Your tribe is a fine one, but it seems to be very small," Eldred tried not to sound offensive. "And your use of our language is something that has me baffled."

"They are very fair questions, Great One. There will be time for talking once the food is ready, but now we must pray." Sha'tian did not sound offended that Eldred did not remember one of their most sacred customs.

Eldred scolded himself for forgetting. Whilst the women prepared the evening meal, the men would pray to their god. They would thank him for surviving the day and pray for the strength to survive the next. It was the only custom that was concurrent throughout the tribes. The prayer would take place within an hour of dusk. Even if a fight for a cave was in progress, they would all stop and pray once the sun had set. For an outsider to watch it would seem quite comical, but for the tribes it was worse than death to miss the prayers.

If there was any doubt in the tribe's mind that they were not tribal, it was obvious when the men in their group did not start the prayers. Eldred knew that he should have been prepared for a friendly meeting. It seemed that they already knew that they were outsiders. There was something that didn't add up. Eldred knew that something was wrong. The problem was there and there was nothing he could do about it. He couldn't lead them out of the cave and he couldn't get any answers until the prayers were over. He could lead an attack whilst the tribe was in prayer, but it would be against everything he believed in. All he could do was to wait and see wait Sha'tian had to say.

The cave was silent, except for the crackle of the fire and the roasting of the meat. The prayer lasted for about ten minutes. When it was finished, the men sprung into life. Sha'tian moved into a position where he could speak with Eldred whilst the other men helped the women. Eldred had told the others not to help. He didn't want to risk offending them.

"I know you must have many questions for me. There is no doubting that it has been a strange day for you. I will try to explain to you my side of things first. Then you can ask me what ever questions you have." Sha'tian spoke well, albeit with a strange accent. "It was over thirty years ago. I was just a boy, ten years old, when we came across a man in this canyon. He was dehydrated and out in the midday sun. He had no horse and no means of transportation. Normally tribes would just leave a man like that to die. My father, the Sha'an, wouldn't leave him there. We carried him to the nearest haven. We stayed there for two days whilst the man recovered, even though our own supplies were wearing thin. Many of the men argued with my father. None of them wanted the man to stay, it was unnatural. My father would not be deterred. He knew that there was a reason that we came across this man when we did. When the man recovered enough to be able to speak, he told us that he had been searching the land for us. He learned our language and he taught us his.

After two years of travelling with us, he told my father why he had been looking for us. He said that at this exact point in time, a small group would be staying at this exact haven. The rest of the tribe laughed at this, but my father believed him. There was something strange about the man's words. There was something about them that had my father transfixed. He said that we were to find a group and help them to the Mountain. My father agreed to do what the man asked. The other men in the tribe did not agree. They had plotted for the past two years. The next day the man had gone and the men in our tribe took their vengeance on my father. He knew what was going to happen. He told me what the man had said and that it was up to me to fulfill his wishes. I left the tribe with all the children so I could rally to my cause. They are the fifteen that you see before you. We kept using his language so that when we found you we would be able to understand each other. As the years rolled on we started to doubt, but as you know, you are here and we are here. One might say it is destiny. At least my father did not die in vain. We are here to aid you to the mountain," as Sha'tian finished a plate of food was put in front of him.

Eldred had an even greater look of surprise. "And I thought I knew all of the prophecies. It seems that I am still but a bumbling student. I would dearly love to know who it was who you met those many years ago." Eldred's voice sounded somewhat sad.

"I fear that I will never see the man again. I knew that is was my destiny to meet you here tonight, even before my father had finished telling his story. What lies ahead for me now is unknown." There was something in Sha'tian's tone that made them think that he didn't truly believe what he said.

"This is a very strange turn of events," Eldred paused and thought. "I thank you for your offer Sha'an, but I do not think we can accept. There are still many great dangers that lie ahead of us. We are also riding against the clock and since you are travelling on foot, you would only slow us down. I'm sorry Sha'tian." Eldred didn't sound like he truly believed what he was saying.

"Great wizard, we have gone through uncountable hardships to get to this place. We know what danger lies ahead as well as what has been laid before you. We have travelled many thousands of leagues to be at this place at this time. It is destiny for us to meet. You cannot complete your mission if you do not come with us. Times have changed since you were last here. Only we can lead you safely to the mountain." Sha'tian did not sound as sure of himself as he had previously. His voice had a slight waver to it.

Eldred looked around at the faces of Sha'tian's tribe, who had all stopped what they were doing when Eldred said they could not travel with them. There was a mixture of disappointment and anger. It was clear that they all felt as strong as their Sha'an. There was something very disturbing about the situation, but he knew that Sha'tian was right. He knew he would eventually find his way to the Cauldron Mountain, but he didn't know if he could get there before Nyrra. Travelling with the tribe would more than likely be quicker than stumbling around.

"I guess that you are right. We will accept with great gratitude any help you can give us," Eldred offered his hand Sha'tian.

Sha'tian looked at Eldred suspiciously before taking his hand in a fierce handshake. A broad grin spread across his face. He knew that Eldred had been testing him and that he had passed.

Chapter 30: Sha'en Tre'tien

The tribe had breakfast prepared when they woke. The breakfast comprised of the remainder of the previous night's stew and some dried damper. Alaric wondered where they got the ingredients for the damper, but ate it hungrily all the same. When the sun had risen and it was time to go, Alaric's stomach was full. He had not eaten so well since they had left the war camp.

"I noticed last night that your food supplies were running low," commented Eldred as they rode out of the cave.

Alaric, who was listening to conversation, felt guilty for eating so much. Not once did he think that the tribe's food supply might be as low as theirs. No one stopped him when he went back for seconds. They seemed happy to feed him.

"I know. We are only a day's ride from the Sha'en Tre'tien Oasis. We have enough to last us until then. From there, we can replenish our supplies," explained Sha'tian.

When everyone pulled their hoods over their heads, there was no way to tell the difference between the two groups. The tribe only had three horses; each pulled a small cart which carried their supplies. There was no room for any luxuries.

Alaric dismounted and walked over to what he thought was a male tribal member. With the heavy robes, they wore it was impossible to tell the difference between the men and the women. To his surprise, it was a woman.

"Can I help you master?" asked the woman, keeping her head down not looking at him.

"My name is Alaric, you can call me that."

"Thank you. My name is Yesh'tien," Yesh'tien replied as she lifted her head.

The hood still shadowed her face, but now Alaric could make out her features. Alaric was surprised to see that she was quite attractive. She had green eyes and brown hair, wisps of which brushed across her face. Her skin was pale like the rest of her tribe. Alaric realised they did not go outside without their heavy robes. There was not chance for the sun to have any effect on their skin.

"Why do you stay in this desolate land?" asked Alaric. "Why do you not leave?"

Yesh'tien didn't seem to understand the question. "What do you mean? Where else would I go? My place is here, with my tribe. No one can survive outside of their tribe."

Alaric realised that she didn't know any different. She didn't know what life was like outside Nostiria. Slowly Alaric started to explain what it was like in the rest of the world. As he started, she looked at him in disbelief. She asked many questions, some of which confused him. They spoke throughout the morning.

"I would like to visit your world, but unfortunately I don't think I will be able to." There was a sadness in Yesh'tien's face that made Alaric think there was more to her words than she said.

Alaric thought about asking what she meant, but she turned away from him. He worried that he had said something to upset her and she would tell the rest of the tribe, but she just continued on with her head down.

During lunch the two groups sat separately. Sha'tian spoke harshly to his tribe, especially Yesh'tien. Instead of getting upset, the tribe seemed to take the berating with good grace. Alaric was the only one who seemed to notice. He was sure it was his fault.

"Why is Sha'tian speaking like that to the rest of the group?" Alaric was greatly concerned.

"It is hard to say. It is not often that two tribes will travel together, when it does, only the two Sha'ans, or leaders, can talk to each other during the heat of the day. I guess that he thinks she has crossed that boundary. Since we are not a nomadic tribe, I didn't think that he would care. I think that it would be best if we give them some space. You can talk all you like when we camp for the night." Eldred also seemed concerned. "I will speak to Sha'tian when the time is right, but for now I think we should respect his wishes. As much as I didn't want to admit it, I think that we will not survive without his help."

The midday meal was short. Alaric only ate a small portion of what was allocated to him. He knew that they were running short on food and he didn't want to be the cause of them starving to death. The nomad women seemed offended with him not eating any more, but he would not indulge them.

The afternoon passed without incident. There was no sign of any other tribes and Sha'tian led them to another, larger cave. Normally it was lucky to have two caves within a mile of each other, but in the canyon, there were at least a dozen, some small, some large. Sha'tian looked around the canyon floor before he entered the cave. When he sat down, he seemed to be in a better mood.

"It looks as though there are no other tribes in the area. We might be lucky," Sha'tian explained.

"If there are no tribes in the area, why are there so many caves?" Alaric asked.

"The oasis is only an hour's walk from here. The reason why there are so many caves is that oasis is where we get our food. All the tribes need them to survive and travel to them frequently. It is very rare for a group of caves like these to be empty. Meeting another tribe at an oasis leads to a fight more often than not. Since these caves are vacant, it means that we are unlikely to meet another tribe when we travel to the oasis in the morning." Hearing this made everyone relax.

Eldred took Sha'tian aside once the prayers had finished; no one seemed to take any notice of them.

"The sky brings grave news I'm afraid. I could feel it in the sun. There was no heat in it today," started Sha'tian.

"Yes, I did notice that, but that could mean nothing. There are plenty of days that are colder than others, right across the entire world," Eldred hoped.

"I think you know as well as I do that there is only one reason why the temperature drops so considerably in this land. A storm is coming and it is coming soon. We can only hope that is does not come tomorrow," Sha'tian sighed.

"We cannot get stuck outside in a storm. It would be suicide," Eldred replied.

"I know, but we have no choice. To be stuck without food in a cave is just as bad. There is no telling when a storm will strike or how long it will last. We can only read the signs and hope that we interpret them correctly." Sha'tian shrugged his shoulders as if he didn't truly believe it.

"How long will it take to gather enough supplies at the oasis?" Eldred asked.

"It's a three-day journey to the Mountain, so we will need to gather enough to last us eight days. That is if we do not get delayed. I have to make allowances for the storm, which could last up to seven. With that in mind, it will take the good part of the day. We will have to spend another night in the cave. We leave a lot to chance, but food and water is not one of them."

"We can only do what we can. If we die before we reach the mountain, then it is all lost. At least with the storm we won't lose any time. Our pursuers won't be able to ride in it either. Now, I think we should eat."

Over dinner Eldred spoke to him about the tribe being treated as equals to their group. At first Sha'tian did not agree, but Eldred finally convinced him that things wouldn't work otherwise. When he finally agreed, it seemed as though a great weight had been lifted off his shoulders. Sha'tian did not agree with all the old ways of tribal law, but for appearance sake he had to uphold them.

When Sha'tian and Eldred explained their agreement, the tension between the two groups melted away. Each group had many questions for the other and there was soon much talking and laughing in the cave. Eldred and Sha'tian both looked on like two proud parents. They   would have talked long into the night if Sha'tian hadn't suggested they sleep. It was going to be a long, hard day and they all needed their rest.

In the morning, the men left at first light towards the oasis. Only the men were ever allowed to enter the oasis. Even Alena had to stay behind. They emptied the wagons before they left so they could maximise their load. As much as Sha'tian had said they only needed food for eight days, they really needed enough for two weeks, taking up all of the room on their wagons.

It was only an hour since they had left the cave when they rounded a corner and was met with a sight Alaric thought he could never see again. Before them was the Oasis of Sha'en Tre'tien. Tall palm trees and lush grasses filled a small cove in the canyon. Alaric stared at it in awe. He had seen palm trees before, but only in books. The ground underfoot was no longer the hard-packed clay, but instead it was soft white sand. The sand was also something new to Alaric. The sickly purple haze, which infected the rest of the land, had no effect on the oasis. Alaric had to rub his eyes as the sudden change took effect. He had become used to the purple and was glad to have his normal sight back. There was a general feeling of calm, which had replaced the constant feeling of dread which had plagued him ever since he entered Nostiria.

"How can this place exist?" Alaric asked as he picked up a handful of sand.

"There are several these oases throughout the land. These areas have not been affected by the disease. Without them, we would all die. They are our only source of food, all but a few are shared by all tribes. Only a few are controlled by a single tribe and are constant battle grounds. We must move quickly, we do not want to risk meeting an unfriendly tribe here," Sha'tian explained.

Atop the palm trees grew bananas and coconuts. Two of the tribal men quickly shimmied up the trees and started tossing down the fruit. Alaric motioned to Palentonal that they should do the same. Alaric was the first to attempt climbing the palms. He had seen the others and thought that it looked easy enough. The palm bark was ridged for easy foot and hand holds. He only managed a couple of feet before he lost his grip and tumbled to the ground.

"You better let me do that," laughed Palentonal after Alaric's third attempt.

With his Elvish climbing skills, Palentonal was confident he could manage the palm. He managed a little further up the tree than Alaric, but was still not able to reach the fruit at the top. Alaric laughed as Palentonal slid down the trunk.

"You two better stay on the ground. Climbing isn't easy as it looks and we don't have all day to train you," a nomad by the name of Ha'listan explained.

"Why don't you show me how it is done?" Palentonal didn't sound happy.

"I am a hunter, not a forager. You will see my skills later," with that Ha'listan continued on his way.

Bushes and small trees were scattered around and each plant contained fruit. Alaric was surprised to see fruit he recognised. Apples, pears, oranges and cherries, to name a few. He knew that they could not grow in such soil, but there they were. Eldred and Erelious had already started foraging.

"I know it might seem impossible, but these oases were created for a purpose. Things grow here that otherwise would normally die," Sha'tian explained to Alaric. "No one knows why, but we are not really in a position to question."

He led them towards the centre of the oasis where there was a brilliant blue lake. The water was clear and calm and Alaric stared at the water, it looked so inviting. He felt like nothing more than stripping off his clothes and jumping in. He could feel the past days sweat and grime all over his skin. He couldn't remember the last time he had bathed. Without thinking, Alaric started to take off his robe.

"I wouldn't do that if I was you!" Sha'tian called from over his shoulder.

Alaric suddenly realised what he was doing and stopped, pulled the hood back over his head and started to blush. He hoped that the hood hid his face from the embarrassment.

"The water is deathly cold. You wouldn't be able to take a dozen steps before your body would go into convulsions. They say that the water comes from the very heart of the world. That is why it is so cold. It is the purest of all waters," Sha'tian laughed as he explained. "It is mesmerising though. Stare at too long and it will swallow you whole."

Slowly Alaric and Palentonal returned to the others. When they were back in the orchard, Sha'tian threw an armful of foraging bags at them. Slowly Alaric picked up one of the bags and studied it.

"That food isn't going to jump into that bag by itself. If we're going to get out of here before dark, we must work together. Don't take too much from one plant. There is a delicate balance here." Sha'tian spoke from behind a bush.

Alaric started plucking fruit from the trees. It wasn't long before he was covered with a deep sweat. Even though the sun did not have as much heat as it had the previous day, the manual labour made it feel twice as hot. Alaric thought the riding had been hard, but this was much worse.

When they stopped for lunch Alaric and Palentonal had managed to fill all their bags and return them to the wagons.

They sat by the lake and ate the fruit they had collected. A refreshingly cool breeze blew in off the lake. Alaric thought that it was the first time that he had felt the wind since they had arrived in Nostiria.

Suddenly, as Alaric stared at the lake, he thought he saw a slight movement on the other side. When he looked harder, he realised that there was an animal drinking. Alaric stared it and no matter how hard he looked the animal did not look right. It looked as though it had the body of a cow, but the size and head of a sheep. Alaric shook his head and put the thought down to the distance.

The arrival of the animal seemed to get Sha'tian and the other tribe members excited. The other tribal members also perked up when Sha'tian pointed it out.

"It seems that luck is on our side again today. The yetsan usually don't come out until the end of the day. With a little more luck, we could be eating roast meat tonight," Sha'tian kept his voice at a whisper. "We have enough fruit. We wait for more of the yetsan to come to the water and then we go hunting."

A number of the nomadic men returned to the wagons as they waited by the lake. When they returned, they carried a number of large hides. Carefully they placed them on the ground before they slowly unwrapped them. Inside were a number of short bows and quivers full of arrows. Palentonal's eyes lit up.

"It has been too long since I have hunted," Palentonal mused to himself.

"Yetsan are crafty prey," Sha'tian spoke. "They have lived here long enough to know danger when they see it. We attack in two groups of five, two from each group will try and push the herd towards the shooter. If the herd scatters, which they will more than likely do, try and keep the main part moving in the direction we want. The yetsan have good ears, so we must sneak around the outside. Remember, they can hear everything, so be careful not to make a sound." Sha'tian tried to explain to the outsiders as best he could, but he had his doubts whether this was going to be a successful hunt.

Both Palentonal and Erelious were quick to grab a bow and quiver. Palentonal eyed Erelious suspiciously, but did not comment. Erelious seemed too focused on the yetsan to worry about Palentonal. The tension seemed to be only coming from the Elf. The Morel didn't harbour any ill will.

Sha'tian selected the groups, quietly, as the rest of the herd came down to the edge of the lake. Alaric, Palentonal and three of   the tribesman started off around to the eastern side while Eldred, Erelious, Sha'tian and the two-remaining tribesman took the west.

"You two will circle around the back of the yetsan," one of the tribesman pointed at Alaric and Palentonal.

"I think that I should stay and shoot. Not to sound conceited but I am one of the best shots in my land, only rivalled by the Elven Lords themselves." Palentonal already had a bow in his hand and wasn't about to relinquish it.

"Okay then," he eyed Palentonal suspiciously, but did not want to offend him. "The three of you will sit off to the side of the lake at distances of at least twenty paces. Remember, we only take six carcasses with us so that's three for us and three for them. We only get one chance at this so let's make it count," he looked at Palentonal.

As they came closer, they started creeping between the bushes and the trees. If even the slightest of movement caught the eye of the yetsan, then they would flee. They were still a long way away when the three of them stopped and took up position. Alaric followed closely behind the nomad, making sure not to make a sound. He could feel his heart beating. He knew that their survival counted on killing the yetsan. One wrong foot and they would all scatter. Occasionally the nomad would stop them suddenly when he felt that they were making too much noise. They kept a constant eye on the yetsan as they came into view. Every time one of the yetsan lifted its head from the lake, Alaric would freeze on the spot. He wouldn't even breathe until it lowered its head again.

Slowly they rounded the lake and came up behind the animals. The nomad spoke softly to Alaric. "We wait until we get the signal from Sha'tian. When it comes, we charge at the yetsan."

"What is the sign?" Alaric asked, but the nomad ignored him, more intent on waiting for the signal.

It was a nervous wait. With every noise, Alaric's heart raced. He had not been this nervous in a long time. He looked across at the nomad. With his hood up, it was impossible to see his face. He squatted like he was ready to pounce on an unsuspecting prey, not a muscle moved. He looked so calm and relaxed. Alaric wondered how he did it.

Suddenly a piercing whistle filled the air. As soon as it sounded, the nomad started charging towards the herd. Alaric was startled by the sudden movement, but soon realised what was happening. With the sudden noise, the yetsan started to bolt in every direction. Soon Alaric saw a pair charging towards him. Alaric skidded to a stop, surprised that the animals were coming towards him. The closest yetsan lowered its head as it charged forward. Alaric realised what it was doing and dove out of the way. The yetsan's head just missed Alaric's right knee. The second yetsan nearly trampled Alaric as it ran over the top of him. The first yetsan slowed to a stop before turning around to face Alaric who was just starting to rise to his feet. Before he drew his sword, Alaric looked the yetsan in the eye.

The yetsan scraped the ground with its front hoof and snorted. There was no doubt in Alaric's mind that the animal meant to attack. Alaric reached for his sword, but realised that he had left it with the wagons. As the yetsan started its charge, Alaric started his retreat. He knew his only chance was to reach the waiting archers.

As he ran he came across other yetsan, also fleeing for their lives. None of these animals thought twice about joining in the chase for Alaric. He could hear the hooves trampling on the ground behind him. With every step, the sound came closer and closer. The heavy robe made running more difficult and just when Alaric thought the creature was about to run him down he heard a sharp twang. Alaric dived out of the way just in time to see an arrow shoot past. The yetsan was also quick to move and narrowly avoided being skewered.

Alaric rolled onto his side. The animal looked at him in the eye with an expression of hatred, not fear as Alaric was expecting. The other animals were more sensible and stopped their charge. The one remaining yetsan hissed at Alaric before leaping out of the way as another arrow shot into the ground. The animal did not wait for another shot to be fired before it disappeared into the bushes. Alaric rolled onto his back and breathed a sigh of relief when he knew that he was safe.

Ha'listan came crashing through the bushes to Alaric's side.

"Are you alright Alaric?" he asked in a controlled voice.

"Yes, thank you Ha'listan. The animal didn't touch me. I'm fine," Ha'listan helped Alaric to his feet. "I wish someone would have told me that they were so aggressive. I might have been prepared for an attack," he said with a touch of venom.

"I have never seen them do anything like this before. They are usually placid and timid. That's why we have to corner them like we did. Whenever you get close to them, they run like the wind. This is quite strange. Anyway, we better take our catch back to the wagons," Ha'listan insisted.

The two of them hurried back to the others where there were three dead yetsan lying on the ground. Two of the yetsan only had one arrow through their necks whilst the other had four protruding from its body. Palentonal was standing over them with a large smile on his face. The other nomads seemed to be sulking.

"Ah, Alaric you missed out on all the fun," Palentonal laughed loudly.

The nomads had doubted his ability and Palentonal had more than proven them wrong. He stood over his kill like he was the new saviour of the world.

They picked up one of the yetsan and started back to the wagons. The beasts were heavier than they looked and Alaric strained under the weight of his. Once they reached the wagon, they met the other group, who had already returned with their three carcasses. Sha'tian seemed quite pleased with himself.

"This has been quite a productive day," Sha'tian laughed.

"I have some disturbing news." Ha'listan's face was grave when he spoke. Ha'listan continued to tell the story of what had happened with the yetsan and Alaric.

"Was there anything unusual about the yetsan? Anything at all, no matter how insignificant it might seem," Eldred cut in before Sha'tian had a chance to speak.

Alaric thought about the animal that attacked him. He had never seen a creature like it before. He didn't know what was normal and what was strange. Everyone looked at him expectantly. Slowly Alaric started to speak, saying the only thing he could think of that might have been uncharacteristic of the yetsan.

"There was one thing, but I don't really know," Alaric paused in mid- sentence, trying to think if it was the right thing to say.

"Just spit it out Alaric," Eldred barked, sick of the suspense.

"After Ha'listan's first arrow missed, the yetsan hissed me. Now that I think about it, there might have been a slight green tinge, but only for a second. It might have been a trick of the light though, with all the greenery around us." Alaric looked down at one of the dead yetsan. "There is one other thing. The yetsan opened its mouth when it hissed at me. It looked as though it had fangs, as well as its normal teeth. Here and here." Alaric pointed to the two top eye teeth.

Eldred looked even more concerned. "What is it?" asked Sha'tian. "If something evil has invaded the oasis, we could all be in danger. Life as we know it in this land could cease to exist."

"I wouldn't worry about the oasis. If it is what I think it is, then it will leave when we do. What I am worried about is how it managed to gain entrance. My understanding was a being of great evil could not enter the oasis. Is that true?" Eldred asked the question without giving away any answers.

"That has always been our understanding. Though I don't know if anyone has ever tested the theory," Sha'tian answered.

"What do you think it was?" Alaric asked, though he already had an idea.

"I have an idea, but nothing I wouldn't like to guess at now. I will speak to you later."

Alaric knew that whatever it was, Eldred did not what Sha'tian to know about it. This doubled his suspicions. There was something in Eldred's tone that told him things were not as simple as he thought.

Soon the others returned with the final carcass and they were all loaded onto the wagons with the fruit. When they started back towards the cave, the horses struggled with the load they were carrying. Once they left the oasis, the feeling of dread washed over them again. Alaric shuddered when the feeling came. The rest of the group reacted in the same manner. The nomads didn't seem to notice the difference. They trundled along slowly, much slower than when they had travelled to the oasis. Alaric looked worriedly towards the sky. The sun was already half way down and Alaric could only hope that the horses would make it back to the cave before nightfall. Sha'tian's expression had not changed since they left the oasis. This lifted his spirits slightly.

They made it back to the cave an hour before sunset. Long before they reached the cave, Alaric knew that something was wrong. He could feel the nomads ahead of them and he knew that it was not their women. There were too many and he could sense males. The feeling he was receiving was hostile. When they reached the cave, they met by a frightening sight.

While they were gone, another tribe had approached the cave. Their numbers were much more than theirs. There were fifty in total with an even number of men and women. They stood in front of the cave with a variety of weapons in their hands. Most of the weapons were long spears and cudgels. Only the Sha'an and half a dozen others had swords. No one else carried bows or any other weapons.

Behind them, just in front of the mouth of the cave, was a pair of wagons. Each wagon had a large cage on the back. Split between both cages were the women from the tribe as well as Alena. Their hoods had been removed as a sign of submission. A cut above Alena's eye showed that she had a least put up a fight before they had been taken. Two dead bodies on the ground showed that she had given better than she had received.

"Who are they?" asked Eldred as they came within earshot keeping his voice low.

"They are my old tribe. It seems that they believed in the prophecy after all." There was no humour in Sha'tian's voice.

"Whether or not they believed the prophecy, they knew that you would be here. It seems that they have been planning this attack for a long time," Eldred replied.

"We didn't leave on good terms. It seems that Sha'grian has kept a grudge. This is not going to end well. They have already made the first move and it was not peaceful," Sha'tian also kept his voice low.

As they came closer, Alaric could see Alena in the cage. She had cuts and bruises on her face. She looked like she had taken a number of blows. A rage started to build inside him as he watched her. He could feel a power growing inside as he started to pull in the energy from around him.

"Alaric, stop that!" Eldred shouted when he realised what he was doing.

The sudden noise set everyone on edge. Alaric let the power flow out of him. As he did, his stomach started to churn and he thought he was going to vomit. The other tribe started edging forward, brandishing their weapons. It was all Sha'grian could do to stop them from attacking. Sha'tian's tribe had also looked as though they were ready to attack. Sha'tian calmed them with a wave of his hand. They had now moved close enough for the two Sha'ans to speak without raising their voices. They both, however, chose to speak in a loud and commanding manner.

"How dare you take my women prisoners? I demand you release them immediately." Sha'tian spoke in the communal language of the nomads. Ha'listan translated for the others.

As if reading his thoughts, Sha'grian started laughing. "That will never happen. The day you left, you declared war on my tribe. Now is the day when we can settle the score. Your father should have never let that man join our tribe," he snarled.

"Prepare yourself for battle. This is not going to end well," Sha'tian whispered to Alaric. "Open your eyes. The prophecy has come true. Let us be on our way. We don't want any trouble with you."

"The prophecy will never be fulfilled as long as I am alive. You still need to get to the mountain for the prophecy to be finalised. You will not leave here alive," Sha'grian almost spat as he spoke.

"Their women will fight as well as the men." Sha'tian warned.

"I was on your trail five years ago when again it led to nothing. Then it finally struck me," Sha'grian continued. "On this day you would be here, whether or not these men showed up, you would be here and here you are, ready to die."

"What happened to you? We used to be friends."

"That is in the past. Now you will die. The time for talking is over Sha'tian. Surrender and I will spare the lives of your tribe," Sha'grian smiled wickedly.

Sha'tian looked at the others around him. He knew that it would come to this. He didn't want to condemn his tribe to death, but all that they had fought for would be a waste if he lay down now. It was obvious to him that the rest of his tribe felt the same.

"I think that you have underestimated us. Only one of us will be walking away today and I don't think that it will be you." When he finished speaking Sha'tian flung open his robe revealing a polished steel mail shirt and a sword at his waist. The gasps from the other tribe showed that armour was never worn by nomads. It was also uncommon for nomads to open their robes outside, even in battle. As if on cue, the other five tribesmen also opened their robes. It was as if they had known this was going to happen. "You see that the man also told my father that you would betray us. 'On the second day after meeting the Chosen One, an old enemy will return. Only in preparing can thee overcome all adversity,'" Sha'tian quoted directly from his father. His face was still set as he spoke, but he knew he had won a small battle. Sha'grian was now uncertain.

"This makes no difference. You will die now and everyone with you." It was clear that he was not expecting Sha'tian to be ready for his ambush. A sudden thought crossed his mind and he spun around to look at the cages. To his chagrin both cages were empty. Sha'tian's women have been set free. Only then did he realise that it was him who had been set up.

The ambush? The struggle? Two men died taking them. It had all been a trap. The thoughts poured into Sha'grian's head. It was too late for him to back down now. There were murmurs within his tribe. He had to make a strong front.

"So this is how it ends, brother?" Sha'tian's voice did not waver with the revelation.

Alaric was now completely taken off guard. The look on Eldred's face showed that he too was surprised. Erelious was the only one who seemed to take little notice of what was being said. He fingered the hilt of his sword. There was a look in his eyes that said he was looking forward to the fight. Palentonal still held the bow that he had used the hunt the yetsan. With the fighting eminent, he wanted to strike the first blow.

A sharp twang broke the silence. The arrow flew true and struck a tribesman in the chest. The man died instantly. Palentonal didn't waste any time in knocking another arrow and firing. The second arrow hit its target as true as the first. A second tribesman sunk to the ground. No one could tell if it was a man or a woman. That was the last arrow Palentonal had and without wasting anytime he drew his sword and waited for a reaction.

Sha'grian's tribe did not advance with the same confidence as they arrived. The women had joined Sha'tian's ranks. Alaric was relieved to see Alena amongst them. Sha'tian had his tribe stand in a single line, waiting for the advance.

"Leave Sha'grian," boomed Sha'tian.

On Sha'tian's word, his tribe started to charge. They spread out around them, leaving a direct corridor to Sha'grian. There was no doubt in either man's eyes that this would be their final battle. Sha'grian drew his sword as he came closer. He watched his brother suspiciously. He had lost all of his confidence, but none of his anger. Sha'grian stopped just outside of striking distance. Sha'tian remained steadfast, his face frozen. With a scream of terror and rage, Sha'grian made a lunge at Sha'tian. The sound of steel on steel was smothered by the sound of fighting all around them.

Neither of the two were very good swordsman. Nomads very rarely fought with the sword. Those who carried them generally used them as a form of intimidation. Sha'tian had practiced with his tribe, but without any formal training, their skills were substandard. They were evenly matched and although their skills were lacking, they were both ferocious. Each one had a life time of adversity and was destined to fight their final battle here.

The sheer weight of numbers did not seem to hold much of an advantage to Sha'grian's tribe. Alaric was amazed, with all the stories Eldred had told them of how hostile the nomads were; they couldn't fight as a unit. It would have been harder for them to fight a single man then it was for them to fight three at a time. Each time one of Sha'grian's tribesmen gained the advantage, another would get in the way and ultimately one of them would die.

Sha'grian's tribe did not think that the outlanders were any threat and did not attack with any enthusiasm. Their halfhearted attacks were met with extreme prejudice. After Palentonal had dispatched the first man a slight grin appeared on his face, it was only there for a second before he engaged another. His sword whistled through the air as he deftly defended the wild blows. Before long, there was a pile of five bodies around his feet. Even though their brethren were dropping like flies, no one would go to their aid.

Eldred was also having an easy time, although he was not enjoying himself as much as Palentonal. There was a certain amount of worry on his face as he fought back the nomads. The concern was not for his attackers, but for the other situation. It had come as a shock to him, which was happening all too often for his liking. For this reason, he did not want to kill any of Sha'grian's tribe. There was something not quite right, but each time his hand was forced, it was a matter of kill or be killed.

Erelious received even less attention than the other three. His sword work, although not as skillful as the others, was far superior to the nomads. His first kill was by stabbing a man in the back who was attacking another tribal member. Erelious felt guilty afterwards. There was no glory in killing someone whilst their back was turned, but it was the only way he could enter the fray.

Alaric's confidence was growing with every attack. Technically he was by far the best swordsman on the battlefield, but his experience left him lacking. A single nomad came at Alaric from the start. From the back of Adelanta, who also had great skill as a war horse, but not much practice, there was no competition. The long spear the nomad fought with looked extremely sharp and the man looked like he knew how to use it. The nomad seemed to ignore the sword in his hand and made a stab at Alaric's chest. Without thinking, Alaric defended the jab and then struck out. The hood of the man's robe flew backwards as Alaric slashed across the man's face. The look of surprise showed that the man had no thought that he was going to lose.

With every nomad that came to attack, the situation remained the same. They had no thought that Alaric would have the skill to fight back and each time they fell under his sword. When he had disposed of the fourth nomad, he had a chance to survey the fighting field. The fight was still hanging in the balance. Two of Sha'tian's men and three of his women had been killed. Sha'grian had lost many more, mostly to that of the outlanders. The battle between Sha'tian and Sha'grian still raged on in the middle of the battle field. Alaric almost laughed at how badly they were fighting.

"That is enough!" Eldred boomed suddenly. His voice echoed throughout the canyon. His voice was so commanding that everyone stopped what they were doing and took a step back. "This will end now," he spoke directly to Sha'tian and Sha'grian.

"We must end this," Sha'tian puffed after the strain fighting, he did not realise that he had already lost over half of his tribe.

"You have to take us to the mountain. You cannot do that if you are dead!" Eldred shouted.

"Only one of us will leave here today. It is destiny," Sha'tian spoke with his own superiority.

"Very well," Eldred conceded. "But we will take no more part in this madness."

Sha'tian had a stunned look on his face. He had faith in his own tribe, but knew that there was no way he could win without their help. A smile appeared on Sha'grian's face as he could see a certain loss change to certain victory.

"Now you can continue to kill each other, if that is what you want," as soon as Eldred finished speaking the two tribes started fighting again.

"You cannot be serious," argued Alaric as tried to wipe a smear of blood from his face. "If we don't help they will all be slaughtered."

"Just wait and see," Eldred's words were as mysterious as ever.

The short break seemed to work in the favour of Sha'tian. He started back with a new passion. He knew that killing Sha'grian was the only way to save the rest of his tribe. With the little skill he had, he went of the attack. Randomly swinging his sword was the only form of attack he knew. Luckily for him, Sha'grian's only form of defence was doing all he could to put his sword between himself and Sha'tian.

Sha'tian kept at him with a barrage of attacks. Sweat poured down the side of his face. His muscles ached with every swing of his sword. The effort was taking effect as Sha'grian started to weaken. With every blow, Sha'grian's strength started to falter. Each attack came closer and closer to killing him.

With one final effort Sha'grian made a lunge at Sha'tian's body. Sha'tian moved, but was too late to avoid the blow. Sha'grian's blade sliced through Sha'tian's side, but it was not fatal. This was the opportunity Sha'tian needed to kill his brother. With the force of his attack, Sha'grian continued with his sword past Sha'tian. With a wild swing of his sword Sha'tian slashed across Sha'grian's back. His sword wound was deep. Sha'grian dropped his sword and sunk to his knees in pain.

Sha'tian slowly walked around to face his brother. With the end near, the fighting had come to a halt. Everyone wanted to see the result of the battle between the two Sha'ans. Sha'grian looked up at his brother, a sneer on his face. His breathing had become laboured as he struggled to remain as upright as possible.

"You murdered our father. Now I will take my revenge." Sha'tian's words were icy.

"You will never have your revenge." With his last ounce of strength Sha'grian picked up his sword and pushed it through his own heart. A trickle of blood appeared in the corner of the smile that looked out of place on his face.

The death of their Sha'an brought his clan to their knees. They let their weapons fall to the ground as they dropped. Twenty-five men and women surrendered against the two remaining men and five remaining women. They would all pledge allegiance to Sha'tian and he would accept.

"Ha'grian, take your father's disgrace and leave this place. You will never be welcome to return to this haven."

Alaric was about to interject when Eldred cautioned him to be quiet. "This has nothing to do with us. Just sit there and wait."

Ha'grian picked up his weapon and returned to his feet. He didn't look at his uncle as he lowered his head and started walking away. One by one, the remainder of his father's tribe started after him. They would be forced to spend the night outside as punishment for losing. Only if they survived would they be worthy to travel the land again.

Sha'tian gathered his tribe to him. He looked at the bloodied faces with a smile of recognition on his face. The sun had almost set and the canyon was suddenly very quiet. Ha'listan suddenly let out an ear-piercing war cry. The other remaining nomads joined in the cry. They had won and now it was time to celebrate their victory.

"Let's get these bodies together and give them a proper send off. Even Sha'grian deserves an honourable death."

It was nomad custom to give honour to those who died in battle, even those from the opposing side. It was said when the body burned it sends the spirit to heaven. If the body was left, then the spirit would rot with the body for eternity.

The sun had disappeared when they lit the pyre. It was not long before there was a huge blaze on the canyon floor. Eldred kept the others away. Sha'tian stood with his tribe and said a few words to remember the fallen. When he was finished, he turned and led everyone towards the cave. The smell of burning flesh filled the air. Alaric gagged at the stench. He had never smelt anything so bad. It wasn't until they entered the cave did the smell disappear.

"We have enough water for baths tonight. I had a feeling that if the prophecy came true that there would be a need for a bath," Sha'tian laughed as he spoke.

Ha'listan and Ha'roan, the two remaining men, brought in two large, wooden tubs from the wagons. Both tubs were placed out the back with the horses. At the same time, water was brought in and heated over the fire. It was going to take a while to heat up enough water for a warm bath, but they were willing to wait.

Once they had all bathed and washed the sweat, grim and blood away from their bodies, they all returned to the main cave. The women had prepared one of the yetsan and it was now roasting over a large fire. It would be a hearty meal and a reward for their victory.

"What was that thing today?" Alaric asked Eldred when they finally had a chance to speak.

"Not now Alaric. It has been a long day and I need to think. It is quite disturbing and I need to try and work out what it means. Try and relax. Things are only going to get harder from here." It was a common response for Eldred, but Alaric knew when he should leave well alone.

Chapter 31: Storms

They left at first light, the sky had become a dark purple and the red ball of fire that was the sun was nowhere to be seen. Sha'tian kept looking at the sky nervously throughout the morning. Eldred picked up on it and also looked towards the sky. Without the sun, the temperature did not increase much. Normally the cool conditions would make the morning more pleasant, however the depression was even greater now and it attacked them like a virus.

The group rode slumped over their saddles whilst the nomads walked, their heads lower. There was something unnatural about the way they were feeling. The entire land seemed to be depressed.

They stopped for lunch at a small well and refilled their water supplies. No one spoke. Alaric just looked at Eldred. He wanted to complete the conversation they had started the day before, but Eldred kept his head down as he ate, ignoring Alaric's gaze. Alaric was about to say something, but decided against it. The melancholy that had plagued them all morning had Alaric worried.

As they continued after lunch, Alaric thought he saw a flicker of movement on top of the cliff. When he looked closer, there was nothing there. He looked around at the others to see if anyone else had seen it. No one seemed to be taking any notice though, so Alaric put it down to his imagination. The last thing he wanted to do was go crazy.

By mid-afternoon, Alaric was beginning to become frustrated with the slow pace. With the nomads on foot, there was nothing they could do. Adelanta could sense his feeling and jumped around as she walked.

The feeling was mutual throughout the group. Nyrra and his men were all on horseback and would be travelling twice as fast. If they did not get to the mountain soon, then Nyrra would beat them. As Alaric thought about how they could get away from Sha'tian, he saw the same flicker of movement. Again when he turned to look, but there was nothing there and again no one else seemed to notice.

Throughout the afternoon Alaric had three more unsubstantiated sightings. With every sighting, Alaric thought that he was finally going crazy, yet each time he could swear that someone was there. Alaric was grateful when they came to the cave. The afternoon had become quite cold to add to his misery and as he rode towards entrance a droplet of rain brushed his cheek.

Soon a fire was burning and Alaric was starting to forget about the day's events. There was something comforting about being inside. He could understand why the nomads called them havens. With the withering weather, his spirits were also dwindling.

"The storm will be here tonight. There is nothing we can do about it."

"We don't have time to be stuck. We have to get to the mountain before Nyrra. If we get held up here, we will never make it," argued Eldred.

"Nyrra will not be able to travel in the storm. We will not lose any time," Sha'tian urged.

"But we are only two days from the mountain. We have to be able to make it before the storm hits," Eldred almost pleaded.

"All we can do is wait until the morning. You can have a look at the weather yourself and see what I mean," Sha'tian was sick of arguing.

Eldred still didn't like what Sha'tian said. He was looking for someone to support his cause, but knew that what Sha'tian said was true. He had a bad feeling that the storm was not natural. If Nyrra did conjure up the storm, then they would be the only ones trapped inside and there would be no doubt that Nyrra would make it to his fortress before they would.

Alaric looked at Eldred. Even though he didn't look like he was up for conversation, Alaric had to tell him. "I saw something moving at the top of the ridge today. It was only out of the corner of my eye and when I went to look it was gone, but I swear that there is someone following us."

"Yes I saw it as well," Eldred paused to think. "I'll discuss it with you tomorrow. Right now, I need to concentrate. If it is Nyrra causing this storm, then maybe I can counter him enough for us to travel." Eldred sat staring into the fire as if waiting for an answer.

Alaric looked at the others. He wanted to talk to someone. The silence was oppressive, but no one looked as though they wanted to speak. He was sure Nyrra was involved. He was sure that the evil he felt when they had entered the land had steadily grown. It was as if the land itself was trying to stop them from reaching their destination.

He lay awake for a long time, pondering the events of the past week. The land had taken over their lives. The oasis had been the only time that the fear had disappeared. Alaric wished that he was back there. He hated feeling the evil around him. Eventually he fell into a restless sleep where his dreams were full of evil creatures and monsters. No matter how many different places and situations Alaric dreamt about, there was always one certainty: somewhere in the background someone was watching him.

Alaric awoke in the morning with a short sharp scream. He was glad to be awake. Looking around quickly, Alaric wanted to see if anyone had noticed. Luckily his scream was stifled by a booming peal of thunder. Alaric noticed that the cave was a hive of activity.

"What's going on?" Alaric asked Alena as he stood up.

"The storm is here."

Alaric slowly walked to the mouth of the cave. Another peal of thunder came, but the rain had yet to fall. As he stepped outside, he was nearly knocked from his feet as a roaring wind struck his body. The air around him swirled with colour: reds, purples, oranges and blues mixed together in an unstoppable rage. The surrounding land seemed different from the previous days. The evil that had lain dormant was now in full rage. Alaric shuddered at the thought.

"Don't stand out there," Eldred called from the mouth of the cave. "It's not safe!"

Alaric turned to go back inside, but there was something holding him back. It was as if his boots were anchored to the ground. Alaric was being drawn to the sky as if the swirling colours were calling to him.

"Come on Alaric. This is no time for playing games," Eldred called out again when Alaric hadn't returned.

Closing his eyes Alaric tried to block out the evil surrounding him. The presence of it roared inside his head. Eldred's words were but a shadow in his mind. The more he tried to force the evil from his mind, the stronger the feeling came. Just when he thought he was going to be overwhelmed, he felt a strong pair of hands grip his shoulders. He was nearly lifted off the ground as he was dragged back inside the cave. Once he was inside, the evil dissipated. Although the feeling had not completely disappeared, it was now sitting in the back of his mind.

Opening his eyes, he saw a concerned look on Eldred's face. Alaric wondered what had happened.

"You can feel something, can't you?" Eldred asked softly.

"I don't know what it is. As soon as I was outside the cave, I could feel an intense evil, more so than usual. I just couldn't move," Alaric whimpered.

"It's Nyrra. I thought it was him, but I couldn't be one hundred per cent sure. You're more in tune with his magic than I am. I don't know why I didn't ask you before," Eldred pondered.

"What do you mean? How can I be in tune with Nyrra? I can't stand this place."

"You have the Ruby stone and have been in contact with it for a long, long time. Remember that the Ruby stone is a part of Nyrra and vice-versa. Ever since we came to Nyrra's land, you have been having feelings of dread, feelings that there is constant evil, muffled only in these caves and completely gone only at the oasis. How am I doing?" Eldred mused.

"That's about right, but hasn't everyone been feeling the evil?" Alaric returned

"I can feel it and I'm sure the others in our group can feel it, though not as strongly as you. The nomads on the other hand, can you imagine what it would be like living here if you had that dreadful feeling all the time? You would go mad with it in the first six months. No, there is nothing normal about what you are feeling. I should have realised earlier, but I had my mind on other things. I had to make sure it was Nyrra and not Viper." With his last comment, Alaric gave him a knowing look.

"The yetsan? That was Viper, wasn't it? That's who has been following us, but why?" Alaric asked.

"Yes, at least that is my theory, unless there is another serpentant running around. I could feel him before we entered the oasis. I just don't know what his agenda is. I have a bad feeling that Nyrra has gained control over him again. Things are just getting worse and worse. Things don't make a lot of sense though; I wouldn't think that Nyrra would have trusted Viper to roam around alone. This leads me to think that he is still working on his own plan. Either way, he is something that I didn't plan on and that makes things even more dangerous."

"You aren't making a lot of sense Eldred," Alaric replied, frustrated.

"That's because I don't fully understand what is happening. Everything up until we entered this land has gone to plan, but since we did, nothing makes sense. There are always going to be some inconsistencies, but nothing like this. I just don't know what to think," Eldred started to raise his voice as the storm strengthened "I do know that it is not a natural storm outside. If Nyrra created it, and I don't think there is much doubt that he did, then he will still be able to move. The only plus to the situation is that this will drain his energy and he won't be able to move very fast."

"What can we do?" Alaric was unsure if there was anything they could do.

"We must try and shift the storm around so that is covers a greater distance. If we can trap Nyrra out in the rain, then we might yet defeat him. At least he will have to stop the storm if he wants to continue," Eldred paused and thought for a moment. "This will not be easy. Nyrra's power will have increased considerably since entering his land and there is something else."

Alaric sat and waited for Eldred to continue. He seemed lost in thought. With a quick snap of his head, Eldred returned his gaze towards Alaric.

"What is it Eldred?"

"This land is tainted with evil, not so bad in these caves though. When you try and draw in the power from around you, you will also draw in the evil. You must be very careful or it will cause you to go mad and become a minion of evil," Eldred explained slowly trying to emphasis the danger. "I'm sure you would have felt it when you started to draw on the power near the oasis."

Alaric thought for a moment. He did remember nearly losing his lunch when he released the power. There was something very disturbing about the revelation. Evil was creeping into his life and there was nothing he could do about it.

"So that is the reason you told me to stop?" Alaric realised that Eldred was waiting for him to speak.

"That is one of the reasons, yes. The other was you were drawing in too much energy. You would have killed everyone, including yourself. You must never use rage as a conduit for magic. Anger is a tool of the Evil One. He will use it against you and force you to bow before him. Remember these words for they may save your life one day. I wish I had time to train you better, but I do not. You can only learn what we must use to survive," again Eldred seemed to drift off into his own conversation. "This is what I need for you to do. You must channel as much power as you can from within the cave. Whatever you do, you must not try to draw any power from outside the cave. The storm is wreaked with Nyrra's evil and will double the effect. You must not take any power from the living creatures. Once you can no longer draw any more power, you must open yourself up to me so I can use your energy. It is very important that you don't release the power. If you do, you will risk bringing the cave down on top of us, not to mention the fact that you will burn yourself to crisp. I will use your energy and mine to move the storm back towards its beginning. Hopefully it will not take too long before Nyrra stops it and we can keep moving. If this fails we might have to try something more drastic."

Suddenly a plate of food was dropped on Alaric's lap. He had been so engrossed in his conversation that he didn't notice the smells of cooking meat. He ate hungrily, knowing that he was going to need all his energy to survive what they were going to attempt. Eldred had moved away to give Alaric some space. He moved to speak with Sha'tian. He wanted to get them prepared for what they were going to do. He needed them all to stay out of the main cavern until they had finished.

"The others are all in the back and are going to stay there until everything is over. Now this is not going to be easy. You must be strong Alaric, and remember what we are fighting for. This may very well be the most important thing you ever do."

Alaric had been practising drawing in the energy from around him since Eldred had shown him how. A lot of the time he did it unknowingly when he was afraid or angry. He had worked on controlling the flow of energy, but had not had a lot of practice converting it into magic. Slowly Alaric stood and stretched, he found that it was easier to channel if his body was loose. When he was comfortable, he returned to the floor and crossed his legs.

Alaric felt a sudden rush of air as he opened himself to the energy surrounding him. He knew that Eldred could also feel it. Normally when he tried to channel, he would try and stem the initial rush, but now he didn't care. Anyone who was close enough to feel him channel had nothing to fear and Nyrra already knew where they were, at least close enough to aim the storm at them.

"Don't be so sure Alaric." Eldred spoke with a strain in his voice, indicating that he had also started drawing energy from the cave. Alaric had not felt a thing, not even the usual tingle in the back of his neck. "This is his land. There is no telling how far his reach goes. Remember what I taught you and suppress the noise. We can't give him any warning of what we are doing or else he will have a chance to stop us."

Alaric tried to concentrate. It was the initial rush that made most of the noise, but now that Alaric had started he found it hard to stifle the rest. He needed all his concentration not to let the energy he had collected to disperse, yet he knew he had to. As he muffled the sound, he could feel little wisps of energy filtering away.

"Concentrate Alaric," Eldred's voice sounded even more laboured.

Alaric stole a quick glance at Eldred. Beads of sweat had formed on his forehead and were on the brink of running down his face. His face grew red under the strain. Alaric wondered if he looked the same or whether Eldred was just further advanced than he was. The thought did not stay long in his head as Alaric closed his eyes in an effort to contain the energy. He was sure he had completely muffled the noise now and concentrated of gathering more. The new power flowed into him and he gasped for breath. The sudden surge was more than he had expected and it knocked the breath out of him. Sweat now drenched his entire body. No matter how hard Alaric tried, he could not stop the flow of energy now rushing.

The cave was suddenly void of energy, but the rush did not stop. It was all Alaric could do not to drain the energy from the other living creatures in the cave. The only option he had was to pull in energy from outside. The difference in the energy from within the cave was remarkable. There was something putrid about it and his stomach started to churn as if he was going to be sick, but he couldn't stop.

"Stop it Alaric. Resist the urge or it will kill you," Eldred's voice was back to normal.

The voice rang inside Alaric's head as something tried to push it aside. It was as if two forces were fighting inside him and he had no control over it. The words from Eldred came again and Alaric furrowed his brow in concentration. He searched inside himself for the force that was drawing in the energy from outside of the cave. Just when he felt he found it, another retching urge forced him to lose his concentration. With a final effort, Alaric pushed deep within himself and stopped the flow of energy. As soon as it stopped the strain on his body lessened. The sick feeling from the tainted energy did not leave him and he could not separate it from the other.

"There is nothing we can do about it now," Eldred answered, as if reading Alaric's mind. "I don't think that there is enough taint to harm us, but I will need to be careful anyway. When you feel the energy pass out of your body, try to hold onto the tainted energy. It will not be pleasant, but we have more chance of succeeding if I don't use any of it."

Alaric knew that Eldred was right, but the thought of holding onto the tainted energy was not pleasant. All Alaric wanted to do was to expel it from his body. If he tried to let some of it go, he knew that it all would leave and he didn't want to go through the whole process again. Without warning, Alaric felt a scratching at the back of his head.

Slowly Alaric opened his mind and body to Eldred. At first he had no control over which of the energy Eldred took. He could feel the tainted energy flowing out with the rest. Each time he thought he could stop it as it flowed from another place. Frantically, as more and more of the taint escaped, he continued to search. When he found, it stopping it was easier than he thought. Each time it tried to release itself, Alaric pushed it aside leaving room for the clean energy to pass.

His stomach churned, a pain started deep inside his stomach and grew with each passing minute. Soon it was all Alaric could manage to sit upright and not double over.

Suddenly a great emptiness started to fill Alaric as the last of the energy started to drain from his body. Besides the pain, it was the only other sensation he could feel. A thought crept into his mind. To rid himself of the emptiness, he wanted to release the remaining energy. Eldred made a deep grunt as he tried to figure out what Alaric was thinking. The urge came a lot stronger as time passed and the emptiness consumed him.

The next thing Alaric knew he was face down on the cave floor. Surprisingly to Alaric, his body did not feel like he had just survived a grueling battle; it felt relaxed. When Alaric went to lift himself from the ground, he found that he couldn't move. His arms and legs were completely weak. All he could do was to listen to the storm still raging outside. Alaric tried to call out for help but all that came out was stifled gasp.

Panic came over him, he was still feeling empty from the loss of energy and now depression was creeping in. The fact that he couldn't move and was completely helpless only added to his misery. The only thing Alaric could do was gather in more energy. The cave had been completely sucked dry and would not replenish itself for at least another two hours. Alaric drew the energy from outside the cave. The nausea came quickly, but Alaric started to feel better immediately. The emptiness was being consumed and the depression was disappearing. Alaric could feel the strength returning to his body.

Just before Alaric felt strong enough to lift himself off the ground there was a thunderous boom which shook the cave. As it happened, Alaric lost his concentration and let the tainted energy race out of his body.

"What... do... you... think... you're... doing?" Eldred puffed.

Alaric could still feel the dark sickness inside him. The one plus was that a lot of the strength remained and he was able to roll onto his back and then push himself into a sitting position. He looked up towards Eldred. The others had come in from the back cavern to see what was happening. Alaric's eyes were shrunken and his face was deathly pale. He looked as though he was at Death's door. Alena quickly came to his side when she saw him. She caught him just in time as he collapsed in her arms.

The others went to Eldred's side. He was shaking on his feet. The extra age on Eldred's face made him look worse than Alaric. The strength, which never seemed to have left him, still remained. He looked as though he could lose consciousness at any time. Palentonal helped Eldred to sit against the cave wall. Eldred tried to shake him off, but he was exhausted.

Once seated, Eldred seemed to regain some of his strength; he looked across to Alaric who was barely conscious in Alena's arms. Eldred waited to catch his breath before he spoke.

"Can you hear me Alaric?" there was no pity or gratitude in his voice.

"I don't think now is the time for that Eldred. He needs to rest," Alena barked. "And by the looks of it you need to rest too."

"Don't be overdramatic Alena, he'll be fine in a few minutes and I need to get some answers," Eldred did not lose his edge.

"Well, you can give Alaric a couple of minutes and tell us what that boom was that shook the cave?" Alena received muffled agreements from the others.

Eldred shook his head. "Just as I was finishing, Alaric started to gather energy from outside. I couldn't stop him and continue the spell at the same time, so I had to release the spell prematurely. The result was that loud boom." Eldred's voice was gaining strength.

"So did the spell work?" Sha'tian's voice sounded small and quiet, he was obviously unsure whether he should speak or not.

"It's hard to say. I had to stop what I was doing to stop Alaric from bringing the canyon down on top of our heads. I couldn't finish the spell, so there's no telling what could happen. At best, it will have the desired effect. At worst, I could have made the storm a lot stronger than it is." Eldred gazed at the entrance to the cave as he spoke, but the noise proved that nothing had changed.

Alaric had still not moved. His breathing was laboured and his face was still pale. The sweat had not ceased from pouring down the side of his face. His eyes stared blankly at the roof of the cave. Alena slowly passed a hand over his face. There was no recognition. Alena let out an audible gasp.

"I think that you should have a look at this," Alena choked on the words.

There was something very disturbing about Alaric's appearance. It was as if there was no life in him at all. The only movement was his chest slowly rising and falling as he struggled for breath. Alena strengthened her hold on him, fearful of death.

Slowly Eldred came to his feet. The spell was obviously having a greater effect on his body than his temperament. The look on his face was not of concern as he looked towards Alaric. He still kept the same angry look as when he finished the spell. He walked over to Alaric's side and looked down at him.

"Let him go Alena," Eldred's voice left no room for argument.

Alena looked up at him, confusion written all over her face. The stern look on Eldred's face showed her that she had heard him correctly. She was about to protest, but Eldred waved an impatient hand at her. Slowly she let Alaric come to rest on the cave floor.

Eldred simply stood over the top of him and looked down, clearly unsympathetic. Without changing his demeanour, Eldred lowered himself to his knees. Besides the noise of the storm outside, the cave was completely silent, everyone was waiting breathlessly, to see what Eldred would do.

Suddenly Alena screamed. Eldred retracted his arm and then slapped Alaric across his face. Alena was about to strike Eldred when Palentonal grabbed her by the wrist.

The first sign of colour returned to Alaric's face. Unfortunately, it was a large hand print. Eldred seemed unconcerned. There was a kind of malice in the way Eldred looked at Alaric. Alena could swear that Eldred was not trying to help at all. "What are you doing?" she shouted and twisted her arm free of Palentonal's grasp.

A couple of minutes passed without any movement from either Eldred or Alaric. The tension was starting to grow in the room and no one made a sound as they waited for either to make a move. It was almost like Eldred was now in the same state as Alaric. Just as the red mark was starting to disappear from Alaric's face Eldred moved to strike again. This time Alena was quicker than Palentonal. Before Eldred could strike, Alena dropped her shoulder into his side and knocked him flat onto the ground. Quick to recover Alena raised her fist to Eldred. The look on Eldred's face was completely different to what she had expected. Instead of the rock-solid glare, there was now a look of surprise. He was so surprised that he didn't even raise and arm to defend himself. Her fist stopped only a couple of inches from his face.

Regaining his composure Eldred boomed at the top of his voice as Alena retracted. "What's going on?"

Everyone looked at each other, unsure of what to say.

"Don't just stand there looking like a group of fools. Tell me what happened? And why is Alaric lying on the floor?" he added.

"You told Alena to put him there. Then you started to hit him," Erelious still sounded confused.

"What are you talking about, oh…?" Eldred let his thoughts drift off as a look of knowing crossed his face.

"What happened? You know something?" Palentonal pushed.

"Later, now make Alaric comfortable. Get him off the stone floor," Eldred barked his orders and everyone quickly moved into action.

When Alaric had been placed on a bedroll with a number of blankets over him, Eldred returned to his side. Slowly Eldred tried to gather in energy from within the cave. The only energy he could find came from his companions and he did not want to resort to that.

"Go to my bag. There are some herbs there in a number of pouches. Get them for me. Boil some water as well," Eldred spoke at Alaric, not directing his orders at any one in particular.

Alena and Palentonal both rushed to the back of the cave. Soon they returned, each with a dozen small pouches. Eldred motioned for them to lay the pouches on the ground next to him. Sha'tian had instructed the rest of his tribe to build up the fire and boil two pots of water.

Eldred quickly found the two pouches he was looking for. The first contained a dark green herb, which was extremely pungent. The smell quickly escaped in the cave and it filled the nostrils of everyone and made their stomachs churn. They all made an effort to cover the smell. Eldred, to the disgust of the others, took a deep breath, inhaling the aroma, before retying the pouch.

The second pouch contained a small, dry, shrivelled, red herb. Unlike the last, this one had no smell at all. Eldred sprinkled two pinches of the herb into one of the pots. A small puff of purple smoke blew up and when the smoked disappeared Eldred carefully pulled the pot away from the fire and placed it on the floor. Throughout doing this, he did not look up once at the people staring at him.

When the liquid had cooled sufficiently, Eldred scooped up two handfuls and drank them down. Instantly Eldred collapsed to the floor and started to convulse. Alena moved forward, this time to his aid. Yet again Palentonal grabbed her arm to stop her from interfering.

"He knows what he is doing," Palentonal said it as much for Alena's benefit as it was for his own.

After a few seconds Eldred's body went limp. His eye lids were open, but his eyes were rolled up into his head. Alena started to shake. Palentonal released his grip and placed a comforting arm around her.

It was not long before Eldred started to move again. Slowly at first, but as the time passed he became more mobile. He pulled himself up onto his knees. Leaning over Alaric he started a low chant. A faint glow appeared around Alaric. It was only visible if they did not look directly at him. If they did, the glow would disappear.

When Eldred was done, he stood. For a moment, there was complete silence in the cave. Even the noise from the storm outside seemed to be dampened. The first sound was a slight groan coming from Alaric. The next was everyone exhaling in unison. With the exhaling, the noise from the raging storm returned to the cave and slowly Alaric opened his eyes.

"What happened? Where am I?" his voice was quiet.

"Rest now Alaric. There will be time for questions later," Eldred answered just as quietly, even with his rejuvenating potion, he still looked very frail.

Alaric slowly lifted himself to rest on his hands with his arms stretched out behind him. At first his arms started to shake under the pressure, but after a few moments his strength slowly returned. Colour started to return to his face and the sweat had completely disappeared.

"Did the spell work?"

"It's hard to say. I couldn't finish the spell. Hopefully what I sent out there was enough to turn the storm around. I must admit that there was more than enough energy to dump the entire storm on Nyrra's head. If only we had more time."

Alaric remembered the feeling of the tainted energy and his stomach started to churn. The feeling was sickening, he still felt as though he could feel the remnants of the taint, even though he was sure he had released all that he had channeled. His head felt very light and he was sure he was going to be sick.

"Try not to think about it Alaric," Eldred spoke softly. "Every time you channel part of that energy will stay with you for a long time, some will even stay for the rest of your life. It's what makes it easier for you to channel each time. You can build on the energy that is already contained in your body. Most of the time you don't notice the energy. It's only when you gain energy from an unusual source that you will feel the after effects, but in time you will learn to recognise that energy and block out those feelings. It's just unfortunate that one of your first experiences involved Nyrra's taint, although it may not be such a bad thing. I don't think that you will be trying to draw power from outside any time soon."

Alaric tried to put the thought out of his head. Instantly he started to feel better. The taint was still there, but now it was only a background itch. He knew that eventually he would not even notice the energy.

"What do we do now?" asked Palentonal, when he realised that the other two had stopped their conversation.

"We wait," Eldred paused for effect. "There is nothing we can do until we know if the spell worked."

"How will we know that?" asked Alena.

"When the rain stops falling!" Eldred's response didn't answer the question.

His sarcastic answer was not well appreciated and Sha'tian was the first to speak up. "You mean we just sit and wait for the rain to stop? What happens if the spell hasn't worked? Do we just wait here until the end of time?"

"Calm down Sha'an. I will know by morning if the spell has worked or not, although I don't know if that is going to do us much good. If the spell hasn't worked, then I'm not sure we have any other option than to risk the weather."

The expressions around the cave showed they were not happy. Eldred's words did not reassure anyone. Alaric was the only one who didn't seem to take any notice. A grim look was on his face. He didn't want to contemplate what he was thinking, but he wanted to reassure the others that if Eldred's spell didn't work, then they still had a chance to leave.

"There is a way!"

"How?" the question was in stereo around the cave.

Eldred looked at him and spoke quickly before Alaric had a chance to explain. "There will be enough time for answers tomorrow. Right now, you need to get some rest. If the rain lessens, then we have to be ready to leave immediately. You should all get some rest as we may have to leave during the night.”

If his previous comment had lowered their spirits, then his last destroyed them. Alaric noticed Sha'tian had a look of concern on his face. He knew that Eldred was not joking. Travelling at night was almost as dangerous as travelling in a storm.

Alaric was not about to argue with him. He was deathly tired and knew that he could sleep for the next week. There was no reason for him to stay awake if all he was going to do was wait the rain out. The sick feeling had also returned unbidden. Without saying anything, Alaric returned to his bedding and lay down. The others, except for Alena who watched him intently, seemed not to notice his movements at all.

As Alaric lay, he could hear nothing over the sound of the raging storm. If anything, Alaric felt as though the storm had increased in its intensity. The thought made his stomach churn even more. Alaric did all he could to stop himself from vomiting as he tried his best to fall asleep.

***

“Do you understand what is happening?” Erelious asked Palentonal.

The elf had taken an opportunity for some solitude at the mouth of the cave. He was so concerned with the maelstrom in front of him that he hadn't noticed the Morel standing next to him. It wasn't until he spoke did Palentonal realised he was there.

“I don't understand much these days. It seems the further we travel the less sure of myself I am.” Palentonal didn't take his gaze from the storm.

Erelious wanted to push the elf for more information, but decided that it was better if he left Palentonal to his thoughts. As he returned to the cave, he wondered if he had made the right decision. Life was not great inside the forest with his brethren, but it had to better than the conditions he was currently forced to endure. Either way, nothing was going to change. He had made his decision and now he had to live with it, no matter how short a time that may be.

Chapter 32: Threats and Promises

A cool breeze blew against the back of Alaric's neck. The sensation was pleasant and it felt neither hot nor cold. His surroundings seemed somewhat unnatural, yet still perfectly normal. He had no idea how he got there, he could have sworn the last thing he did was lie down to sleep. That was just a distant memory in the back of his mind that didn't make any sense.

There was something familiar about his surroundings, though he was sure that he had never been there before, like déjà vu. He was alone on top of a precipice overlooking a desolate land. In the distance, he could see the peak of an ominous mountain. Alaric said to himself that he should know the significance of that mountain, but the answer was just out of reach. The sky was a rich purple colour, another thing that seemed unnatural, yet completely normal.

As Alaric stared at the mountain he suddenly realised that he was not alone. There was someone else, standing somewhere behind. Something inside him told him to run, told him to run as far and as fast as he could. It didn't register though and Alaric kept staring at the mountain. "So you finally decided to come," came a voice soft and sweet to Alaric's ear.

The sudden noise startled him. He hoped that whoever it was behind him didn't notice, but he knew they would. Alaric didn't turn around.

"You wanted this."

"So is this where it is to happen?" The question was asked with a certain amount of surprise. "Or are we to reach a compromise?"

A voice inside Alaric's head screamed at him, but Alaric ignored it. He was enthralled with the conversation. He couldn't leave without the answers he was searching for.

"How could we compromise? Our paths set us on different courses, there can be no compromise."

When there was no immediate response, Alaric slowly started to turn around. He felt somewhat sorrowful at leaving the view of the mountain, but he knew that he was going to have to face the man eventually.

Standing before him not more than ten yards away was a tall figure dressed in a black robe, the hood completely shading the face. The first thing that Alaric noticed was that the breeze had no effect on the robe. There was no movement at all, even as Alaric's own robe swirled around. "Something's not right!" called the voice inside his head, but again he couldn't seem to understand the words. Alaric shook his head violently, but it didn't help.

"You already know the answer. You wouldn't be here if you didn't know," the figure mocked as the voice inside Alaric's head grew louder.

Alaric shook his head again, this time in refusal to believe what the man was telling him. There had to be another answer, he knew there was another answer. A smile crossed his face.

"You have nothing you can offer me. There is nothing you have that I want," Alaric laughed as he spoke.

The man in front of him pulled the hood back, revealing his face. Before him was the most handsome man Alaric had ever seen. Shoulder length blonde hair framed his strong facial features, his deep blue eyes were the most resounding feature. As Alaric stared into them he almost lost himself.

"Think about what I can offer you before you so openly reject it. We are not so much different, you and I, Alaric. I've just been around for a lot longer." The expression on the man's face did not change. Alaric thought he could put a name to the face.

"Stop Alaric!" the voice inside his head screamed.

"What are you talking about?" Alaric asked, now more confused than ever.

"I've seen the world move and change over the years. People come and people go, but I'm still here. Together Alaric! We can rule this world together, for this life time and all to come. Think about all the good we could do to. Ultimate power, Alaric? Think of everything you could have." His voice was as sweet as honey and it dripped from his mouth.

Alaric was taken aback. It was the last thing he had expected. The words echoed in his head. Maybe there was another choice. Maybe he didn't have to go to war with an unbeatable force. What was he doing? This was madness? He was in the middle of nowhere for no reason?

"Stay here with me Alaric and we can rule together. That is how it was ordained."

The words were enticing, yet they seemed wrong. The voice screamed again inside his head, "Wake… up… Alaric…" The words repeated in his head, but he did not know what it meant. Wake up from what?

"No," Alaric barked.

The man laughed loudly. "Do you think that you have any choice? You are mine now and forever more."

Alaric reached for his sword and drew it with one swift motion. There seemed to be no weight to the blade. Alaric took a stance which he had practiced many times.

Again, there was the sound of laughter. When all was quiet, the air next to the man seemed to shiver and suddenly a figure appeared who Alaric recognised immediately.

"No, this cannot be real," Alaric grabbed at his head as a sudden pain shot through it.

Alena was now standing with him. Her face was completely devoid of emotion. Her dead eyes stared at Alaric and filled him with dread. He stared into them and pleaded that it was not true.

"You knew from the start that she was always mine. Join us Alaric." When he finished speaking, Alena outstretched her arm towards Alaric, beckoning him.

"No!" Alaric screamed into the sky, it was as if his entire world was falling apart.

Suddenly Alena changed. Her soft skin cracked and peeled. In its place were now dark green scales, which seemed to sparkle. His yellow eyes stared at Alaric, and evil grin cemented on his face. He felt as though he should know who this creature was, but he couldn't remember. Alaric knew that he was in trouble now, there was no way he could fight these two and win.

"You see Alaric. Whichever way you turn, there is only one answer."

"No!" Alaric screamed again, this time dropping to his knees and burying his head in his hands.

"What are you doing here?" his voice dripped with pure evil.

Alaric kept his head down. Whatever new horror was upon him he did not want to know.

"You can't have him. Not like this. You know that, now let him go," Alaric thought he recognised the voice, but he refused to look up.

Suddenly the ground started to convulse and the air around him started to reverberate. Then sound came. An ear-shattering yell of despair filled the air. Alaric knew exactly where it was coming from. Even with his hand over his ears, the sound penetrated, blocking out any chance of thought. Alaric thought his head was going to explode, he couldn't breathe.

***

Suddenly Alaric woke, gasping for breath the only thing stopping him from screaming. The cave was a dark grey. Small embers from the fire were the only light. Alaric looked around quickly and saw his companions, fast asleep, lying next to him.

It had all been a dream, but it seemed so real. Alaric shook his head. Sweat flew from his forehead. At that moment, he realised that he was drenched in sweat. He tried to remember what he had dreamt about to make him feel so unsettled. He knew that it was important, but he could not settle his head to think.

Slowly things started to filter back, but only fragments. A man, a woman, a voice, another voice, many voices, nothing specific, nothing that could unlock the riddle, if there was one. He was sure that there was one. After another short struggle, Alaric figured that it would be stupid to stay awake.

Returning his head to his pillow he closed his eyes.

***

Alaric walked through his garden. It was a beautiful autumn day in Arsiliac. The golden leaves on his trees were just starting to fall. Life was too perfect.

The back door to his house opened and a woman walked outside. She was the most beautiful woman he had ever seen; he never stopped believing that, from the first moment they met until that very moment. Their wedding day was the happiest day of his life. There was nothing that he wouldn't do for her.

"Good morning my love. You slept in late today. Are you still feeling sick?" Alaric spoke with pure love in his voice.

"I think I have figured out why I've been feeling so nauseous these past few weeks."

"Are you saying what I think you are saying?" Alaric's heart started to race.

The broad smile of Alena's face was all the answer he needed. They had been trying to have a baby for the last year without luck. Alaric was sure that it was never going to happen. Now his life would be complete.

Quickly he ran to her and embraced her in a monstrous hug. Alena returned the hug just as fiercely. He laughed loudly, it was all he could do to burst from excitement. He thought that he could never be this happy again.

"Are we still on for dinner tonight?" Alena asked.

"Yes!" Alaric exclaimed, surprised at the sudden change of subject as he released his wife. "And now we have something to celebrate. I can't wait."

Alaric knew he should know who was coming. He did in a way, but he just couldn't name him. Something as simple as knowing which guest was coming for dinner should have come naturally. A voice inside his head screamed out. Shaking his head Alaric put it down to the excitement of Alena's pregnancy.

The day blurred past.

Alaric wasn't sure what he did with the rest of the day. All he knew was he was sitting in his dining room, waiting for his guests. Alena was preparing the meal. The smells coming from the kitchen made his mouth water. He couldn't remember when he had been happier.

A knock on the door made Alaric jump. He scolded himself for being a fool. There was no reason to be jumpy, but he couldn't for the life of him remember the name of his guest. Another knock came.

"Are you going to get the door, sweetie?" Alena called from the kitchen.

It seemed so natural, yet something was horribly wrong. Alaric shook his head. He was fast becoming a very rude host. He placed his hand on the door knob about to turn it, but he couldn't bring himself to open it.

A fourth knock came. Twisting the knob Alaric paused, but only enough time to scold himself again. This time he pulled the door open.

The man standing on the other side was someone so familiar that he was surprised that he didn't know his name. The shoulder length blonde hair and strong facial features seemed unforgettable. His deep blue eyes stared at him, as if knowing his deepest, darkest secrets.

"Alaric, how are you?" his voice had a jovial tone and sounded very sweet.

"Ah… Come in. Dinner is almost ready." Alaric stumbled over his words. To his relief, the man didn't seem to take any

notice. "Mmm, something smells really good."

A voice screamed out inside his head.

"Thank you," Alena called from the kitchen as she overheard the compliment. "Please have a seat in the dining room. I'll be there in a minute."

The man smiled at Alaric as they walked into the dining room. There was something about the man that wasn't quite right. Alaric shook his head. His was being rude again. He shouldn't think such things about his guest. He laughed to himself has he sat, not realising that he laughed out loud.

"Is something funny?" the question seemed innocent enough.

"No, sorry."

Alena seemed to like him and they didn't have too many friends. People in Arsiliac resented their marriage. He didn't know why. It was not like she was from… Alaric let the thought drift away. Where was she from? Arsiliac? No! He couldn't remember. At that moment, he realised that his guest was staring at him. Staring at him with his deep blue eyes.

"Sorry, what did you say?" Alaric assumed that he was waiting for a response.

The man just sat and smiled. There was something very eerie about his posture. It was relaxed, yet very threatening. Just before Alaric was going to re-ask his question, Alena drifted into the room.

"That smells delicious," the man soothed.

"Thank you, and how are you today?" Alena smiled deeply as she spoke. Alaric could only think of how beautiful she was.

Dinner passed without any conversation. When he finished, Alaric felt full, though he could not remember exactly what they ate. It seemed strange to him that he could not remember. A voice cried out inside his head.

"Are you okay Alaric?" asked Alena as she started to clear to table.

Alaric instantly blocked the voice out. "Yes dear. I think we will retire to the sitting room."

Slowly Alaric stood and led his guest into the sitting room. It was strange that he couldn't seem to remember anything... he couldn't even remember what his friend did for a living. He couldn't think of anything to start a conversation.

The voice screamed inside his head.

"So you have a good life here, Alaric?" the man spoke when they were both seated.

"Yes, I do. I don't think I could be happier anywhere else."

"Then you'll be staying here?"

"Yes. Where else would I go?" Alaric answered, a little confused at his question.

"That's good!"

Before Alaric could say anything, Alena returned to the room. The sight of her made him completely forget what he was about to say.

"Well, it seems that everything is in order here. I'll see myself out. I will bid you both a very good night," he spoke directly to Alena.

As soon as the door closed, Alaric relaxed. He had not realised he was so tense. There was something about the man. The way he spoke and the way he acted made Alaric shiver.

"Are you sure you are alright, my dear?" Alaric shrugged, still thinking about their guest. "Why don't you go bed? I'll be in shortly," Alena was about to stand when Alaric grabbed her arm. "Alaric!" Alena cried out.

Slowly Alaric lessened his grip, not realising he had grabbed her so hard. He could not go to bed without knowing.

"Sorry," Alaric started slowly. "Who was that man?"

"What are you talking about? You know who he is."

Alaric stood up quickly. Nothing was real. This was not real. "Who are you? Where did you come from?" Alaric was starting to yell as the voice inside his head reached full pitch.

"You know who I am. Do you want me to get the doctor? You don't look well," Alaric knew the worry on her face was not for his well-being.

Suddenly Alaric had a sword in his hand. He couldn't remember drawing it, or even wearing it. He levelled at Alena's head.

"Very well, Alaric. If this is the way you want it," Alena's voice had changed, she now hissed.

Slowly she stood and as she did her form started to change. Alaric knew that this should have shocked him, but for some reason he expected it. Before his eyes, she changed. Her soft, white skin started to peel and flake. Soon her body was entirely covered with green scales. The smooth white dress she had been wearing was now a dark black robe covering all but her hands and face. Alaric knew that he should recognise it, but he couldn't.

"So this is what it comes down to? You could have been happy here." A sword magically appeared in the creature's hands.

Suddenly the room wavered. The voice inside Alaric's head started to cry out again and Alaric dropped to the ground. His head ached.

"What?" the reptilian creature cried out in surprise.

"This is not the way." The voice sounded familiar to Alaric, although he could only just hear it over the sound inside his head.

Suddenly the ground started to convulse. The air around him started to reverberate. Then sound came. An ear-shattering yell of despair filled the air. Alaric knew exactly where it was coming from. The sound penetrated his head, blocking out any chance of thought. Alaric thought his head was going to explode, he couldn't breathe.

***

Suddenly Alaric woke, again gasping for breath. The cave was again pitch black. The fire had long burnt itself out. Alaric could hear his companions, fast asleep, next to him.

It had all been a dream, but it seemed so real. Alaric shook his head. Sweat flew from his forehead. At that moment, he realised that he was drenched in sweat. He tried to remember what he had dreamt about to make him feel so unsettled. He knew that it was important, but he could not settle his head to think.

Slowly things started to filter back into his head, but only fragments. A man, a woman, a voice, another voice, many voices. Nothing specific. Nothing that could unlock the riddle, if there was one. He was sure that there was one. After another short struggle, Alaric figured that it would be stupid to stay awake for no real reason and he still felt very tired.

Something seemed very familiar, but Alaric couldn't figure out what. He put it down to déjà vu and exhaustion. Returning his head to his pillow Alaric closed his eyes.

Alaric let his head rest against the cold stone walls. The room seemed somewhat unreal. From the dull grey stone wall to the rusted iron bars in front of him. He had no idea how he got there or what he did to be jailed. There was a voice in the back of his mind telling him that things were not right and he was inclined to agree. He had always been a good person. He couldn't believe that he would ever do something to warrant this sort of treatment.

Bruises on his arms and legs showed that he had been reprimanded recently. He felt pain all over his body

His mouth was dry, as if he had not drunk anything in a week. He wondered if that was part of his punishment. Although his mouth was dry, he did not feel thirsty. He was confused.

"So have you made your decision yet?" Alaric looked up with a start. He did not realise someone was standing on the other side of the bars.

The man wore a dark robe with the hood pulled up covering his face. There was something very familiar about him. Alaric could swear he had seen him before. He laughed to himself.

"Is something funny?" the man barked at Alaric, his voice cutting like a knife.

Alaric had not even realised that he had laughed out loud and was a little embarrassed. For some reason, Alaric felt as though the man outside was not the one who had put him inside. He did not trust him though, but didn't know why.

"Sorry. What is it that you want from me?" Alaric became suddenly defensive.

"Is your answer yes or no? This is the last time that I'm going to ask you." The voice boomed, dripping with malice.

Alaric thought really hard. The question seemed to be on the edge of his mind. The answer was just as vague. He did know that the wrong answer would have catastrophic results on his life.

Suddenly the voice in Alaric's head spoke at a clear and calm level for the first time. "This is not real. Do not be afraid." Then the voice disappeared.

Without the constant screaming inside his head, Alaric was able to think rationally. He still couldn't figure out exactly what was wrong, but he knew he had to do something.

"What is my crime?" Alaric tried to steel his voice.

"You know your crime. Only I can help you now," the voice became friendly.

"What are you offering?"

"Freedom, Alaric. Freedom."

"I do not want your freedom." Alaric wasn't sure what he was saying, but it sounded right. "There are too many catches with your freedom."

"Then your answer is no?" The man didn't seem to care now.

"My answer is no and it always will be no."

"Don't you realise what I can do for you? What we can do forever? I can give you the world. I can give you everything you ever wanted. All you have to do is say yes."

"You cannot give me anything I want. Your words are riddled with lies," Alaric spoke with confidence.

"Oh, can't I?" the man sniggered.

Another person came into view. Alaric knew who she was instantly. He also knew that it was false. Even so, he could not stop the feeling of wanting. He had wanted Alena ever since he met her.

"No, it is not real," Alaric yelled, trying to reassure himself more than anything else.

"I am real, Alaric. Please. Let me help you," she spoke so sweetly that Alaric could feel himself falling under her spell.

Alena pressed herself against the bars. Her arms reached through towards him. Her face pleaded with him to come to her.

Slowly Alaric got to his feet and took a tentative step forward. He was drawn to her. Those arms were so inviting. He wanted nothing more than to lose himself in them.

Just before Alaric was close enough for her to touch him he lunged forward. The sword plunged deep into Alena's stomach, he didn't even realise it was in his hands, yet he knew exactly what he was doing. As he drew closer, her hands brushed against his face the soft green flesh felt horrible against his skin.

A chill started to fill his body, as if someone had poured ice into his blood. His chest compressed making it hard for him to breathe. The hands gripped onto his face, struggling to stay alive. With every second that passed, Alaric thought he was going to collapse. When he felt he couldn't hold on any longer, the hand released his face and the limp body slowly slid off his sword.

As soon as Alaric was freed of the death grip, his body returned to normal. Taking a deep breath, he backed away from the bar. He knew that it would take more than a surprise move to beat his other adversary.

"That was a very silly move Alaric. You could have been happy here. All you had to do was submit to me and I would have given you the world. Now you will suffer like no one has every suffered before." The man spat the words at Alaric.

"This world is not real. You are not real." Alaric wanted to sound confident, but now he did not know if the voice inside his head was right.

The man laughed out loudly. "You don't know how real this world is. I'm here and you are here. Now you are mine and I am not about to let you go."

Alaric raised his hand, only to realise that he was no longer holding his sword. Now there was nothing there and no matter hard he tried he could not bring it back.

"See? I control this world." The words sent shivers down Alaric's spine. "There is no help for you anymore."

Suddenly an earpiercing scream filled Alaric's head. The pain knocked Alaric from his feet. His head hit the ground hard and bounced. When it came to rest, the sound was gone, the voice was gone. For an instant, nothing but silence filled his head.

When his thoughts came back to him, he knew that he was in trouble. Slowly he returned to his feet to try and assess the situation. He knew that somehow he had to get out of the cell.

"You see what thought of power I have now. The power that I can offer you. I can make you the strongest wizard the Continents have ever seen. All you have to do is say yes. Bow down before me." The voice was harsh, but calm.

"I will never serve you. It is all lies. This is my world, not yours," Alaric steeled his voice.

"We'll see about that. Let's see how long you can stay in this cell before you crack. Believe me when I say that eternity is a very long time." With that, the man turned his back on Alaric and walked away.

Throughout their entire conversation the man's facial expressions and his body language did not change. Alaric thought this was odd. He was not sure whether he would be able to use it or not, but it was something to think about.

There were no sounds in the cell. Even Alaric's normal body sounds were absent, his heart beat and his breathing. Even when he moved, there were no sounds. No matter what he did, there was no sound. He was afraid to try, but he had to. Opening his mouth Alaric tried to speak, but no words came out. There was complete silence.

Alaric slumped to the ground and covered his ears. The deathly, unnatural silence ate at him. He knew the man was right. He was trapped. The voice inside his head was gone and with it, all of his hope. Even time seemed to stand still. Nothing else moved, not even dust.

Slowly Alaric returned to his feet. There was nothing he could do, but surrender. He stared at the bars of cell. They looked so strong.

"Okay you win," Alaric yelled out towards the bars.

The instant Alaric finished, the man reappeared. A broad smile crossed his face.

"I just have one question for you," Alaric spoke very softly.

"What is that?" The man was almost drooling with anticipation.

"What would you do if I escaped from this cell?" As Alaric raised his head to look the man in the eye, a smirk appeared on his face.

Suddenly look on the man's face turned to horror as the bars slowly melted away. Alaric took a step forward, his sword appearing in his hands.

"This cannot be!"

"I told you. This is my world, not yours." Alaric's smile broadened as he advanced.

"We will meet again, soon!" the pure evil returned to the man's voice.

After he had spoken, the man quickly retreated down the corridor. Alaric knew there was no point in going after him as he would already be gone. Slowly Alaric walked towards the door of his cell. There was something holding him back from stepping outside. He didn't know what it was, but he did not want to leave.

Taking a deep breath Alaric closed his eyes and walked through the opening. As he did, he suddenly woke up. Light had returned to the cave and he could see Eldred standing over him. The sound of the storm had completely disappeared.

"Quick Alaric! The storm broke not five minutes ago. We must be leaving."

Chapter 33: A Meeting with Evil

Considering the intensity of the storm, there was very little water on the ground as they left the cave. It was an hour before noon and the sky had returned to normal, or at least as normal as the land permitted. The temperature had returned to the blistering heat before the storm.

Alaric sagged in his saddle. Although he had slept for almost a full day and night, he felt as though he had not slept for days His body was sore and weary as if he had been in battle all night. It took all his energy to remain upright in the saddle. His arms and legs ached and his head throbbed.

Only a faint memory of his dreams remained. The last one he could remember the best, although only fragments. He knew that the dream was somehow very important in what was happening to them. The faces seemed familiar, but just when he thought he could name them, their images disappeared.

There had not been time for Alaric to eat before they left. The storm broke so suddenly that no one had been able to plan for it. Eldred pushed them to continue to make up for lost time and did not let them stop for lunch.

It was not until the sun had completely set, that Eldred finally let them stop. He pushed them until the sun disappeared and then found a small cave, barely large enough for them to fit with all their horses and supplies.

They had made good ground that day, although Eldred still muttered to himself about the slow pace. It was all Alaric could do to keep himself awake. His stomach growled. He had not eaten all day and was starving.

Soon the smell of roasting meat filled the cave. Alaric's mouth started to water. He felt as though he had not eaten in days. No sleep, no food, Alaric wondered how much longer he could survive until his body gave up. He was a lot stronger than when he had left Arsiliac, but no one could take the constant punishment he had endured for so long. His resolve was finally starting to weaken.

"You look weary Alaric. You slept for such a long time, I would have thought you could have kept going for longer than any of us," Eldred looked concerned as he sat next to him. "Are you alright?"

"I don't know how much rest I got from all that sleep. My dreams, they were strange. I woke up this morning like I had been in battle all night. I can only remember vague pieces; I can't even put a name to the people I saw."

"Tell me everything you can remember. I think I have a fair idea who the people in your dreams are," Eldred looked even more concerned.

Slowly Alaric tried to recall his dreams. At first he tried to explain what the people looked like, but he couldn't even remember if they had been male or female. Eldred nodded his head, as if in agreement, with every possibility Alaric explained. Next he tried to recall that in his last dream, he had been held prisoner. He couldn't remember why he was there, who had imprisoned him or how he escaped.

Eldred kept nodding his head, even when Alaric had finished. Alaric was even more confused now than when he had started. Eldred seemed to know what it all meant.

"Here, have something to eat," Alena handed Alaric a plate of hot food.

Alaric ate hungrily as Eldred watched him.

"What do you think they mean?" Alaric mumbled with half a mouthful of food.

"I think it means that you were very lucky last night. I think it means we were all very lucky," Eldred spoke half to himself as if he was still trying to decipher what Alaric had told him.

"What are you talking about?" asked Alena who had sat next to Alaric. Her being there felt familiar to Alaric, as if it was the missing link he was looking for. But just as he thought he had the answer, it escaped him. Her presence was comforting nevertheless.

"It seems that Nyrra knows, or at least he knew yesterday, exactly where we were. He invaded your dreams, apparently with the help of Viper. He is closer than I thought to be able to break through the wall I put up. It's not quite as dangerous as before, but dangerous enough," Alaric shivered at the thought of Nyrra being inside of his head. "These are most disturbing facts. One thing that doesn't make any sense though, is why the storm stopped when it did. If Nyrra knew where we were, he didn't have to keep the storm so wide spread. He could have isolated it to a couple of leagues around us and it would have kept us pinned down until he reached his stronghold. My spell would only have worked if he didn't know where we were. At least we know that Viper is working with him." Eldred didn't really sound confident with the last.

"I don't think that is a good thing," Alena said.

"It's better than not knowing," Eldred replied ruefully.

"So can you stop them from haunting Alaric's dreams?" Alena asked slowly.

"I don't know. If Nyrra and Viper are combining their powers, then I don't think that I will have the strength to defeat them." Eldred sighed.

"I don't think that they will be back," Alaric looked up from his empty plate as he spoke. He wondered if there was anything more to eat.

"Why do you say that?" Eldred asked suspiciously.

"I just have this feeling that the only reason why I was able to wake up this morning is because I beat them. I think there was someone helping me, but I can't be sure," his last statement had Eldred baffled.

"Well, that is a comforting thought," Alena said.

After another full plate of food, Alaric retired for the evening. Although the food made him feel better, he was still sore and tired. Only moments after Alaric's head came to rest on his pillow, he was fast asleep. His dreams during the night were pleasant and in the morning, he woke refreshed.

He sat around the small fire with Eldred. Eldred was glad to see that he had woken on his own volition. He looked a lot less drawn than the previous day, but his body still ached. His spirits, however, were a lot brighter.

"Did you have a good sleep last night," Eldred asked.

"Yes I did, thank you," Alaric was in a jovial mood. "Not a hint of Nyrra or Viper. It was the best sleep that I have had in a long time."

After a quick breakfast, they were on the road again. The sun had only just crept over the horizon when they left the cave. Eldred was already starting them on a brisk pace. It was not easy with the wagons and the nomads on foot. On more than one occasion, Eldred thought about leaving the nomads and continuing on at a gallop. Each time he thought about it, he remembered that they didn't have any food and not a great deal of water on them. There was no other option but to continue on at the same pace.

They stopped briefly for lunch, at Alaric's insistence. Since the day before, Alaric had decided he was not going to miss an opportunity to eat. He needed all his strength for when he would finally meet Nyrra and missing too many meals was not going to help. He was also tired of riding on an empty stomach.

Towards the end of the day, the ground slowly started to rise. With the rising ground, their spirits were also lifting. Sha'tian explained to them that they were now only two more days from reaching the stronghold and by lunchtime on the next day, they would be out of the canyon.

Alaric didn't sound too enthusiastic about being out in the open, especially with Nyrra so close.

"It will be easier to ambush us in the canyon once we are out." Sha'tian told Alaric. This eased his mind, but only slightly.

Again, Eldred pushed them until the sun had set. The temperature had dropped considerably once the sun had disappeared and it was close to freezing when Sha'tian was able to find a cave suitable for them to spend the night. A fire was lit quickly and soon they were warming themselves.

"That was very close, Eldred. Another hour or two and we would all be dead," Sha'tian tried to hide the anger in his voice, but failed.

"And if Nyrra makes it to his stronghold before us, then we are all dead. It's a fine line we tread, but if we are going to survive, we have to push our luck," Eldred did not sound offended, but he was not going to admit he was wrong.

There was not a lot of talking over dinner. The tension was thick between the two group leaders. Sha'tian insisted that they should not ride after dark, whilst Eldred urged that they needed to make time.

In the morning, they seemed to have forgotten their argument and they continue on as if nothing had happened. The thick tension that had been there the night before had completely disappeared.

As Sha'tian had explained the day before, they exited the canyon about an hour before noon. Cauldron Mountain suddenly appeared rising out of the horizon. The black mountain sent a shiver down Alaric's spine. He had seen the mountain before, but there was something unnerving about being so close.

The ground around them was completely flat as far as Alaric could see. He wondered at where they would spend the night, since he couldn't see any caves. He was heartened, however, that he couldn't see anyone else worrying.

"Be careful where you walk. There are cracks and fissures all over this land. You can be on top of one without ever realising it. Most drops are a least a quarter of a league deep. Some are so deep that no one knows if they have a bottom," Sha'tian explained, deadly serious.

They started off at a gentle pace. Even Eldred heeded Sha'tian's warning. He had travelled these lands before and knew of the dangers. No matter how much time he wanted to make up, he could not risk losing someone down a hole.

They picked their way along the ground as the sun beat down on them. Without the canyon walls to give some shade, the riding was unbearably hot. Their thick cloaks, which protected them from the searing sun, made it even hotter. They all wanted to take their robes off, but they knew the sun would roast them.

They only stopped for enough time to make lunch, which they ate on the road. They kept moving until an hour before sunset. Sha'tian insisted that they find a cave for the night. Eldred was about to protest, but he knew Sha'tian was right. It was more difficult to find a cave in open land.

After about half an hour of searching, Sha'tian led them into a small canyon, which no one else had seen before they were a couple of feet away from it. Alaric thought he could have wandered the land for a year and he still would never have found the cave Sha'tian was leading them to. He knew that he would never be able to find it again.

Once inside the cave the group sat close together.

"It's hard to believe that tomorrow we are going to be at the stronghold," commented Alena.

"It'll all be over soon," no one was sure if Palentonal sounded happy or sad.

"Be on guard tomorrow," Eldred warned. "We're close, but so is Nyrra. I have a feeling that there are going to be a number of surprises waiting for us."

"What happens when it's done," Alaric asked, joining in the sombre mood.

"Let's concentrate on the job at hand. If we don't get it done, there will be no tomorrow," Eldred's tone left no room for questions.

It wasn't long after they had eaten that they all went to sleep. It was going to be a long hard day and they all wanted to be rested for it. Even Eldred went to sleep early. He left Sha'tian to arrange a watch for the night.

In the morning, they were all up before dawn. No one could sleep in with the anticipation of the impending day. As soon as the sun peaked over the horizon, they started again. They were all keen to get moving. By the end of the day they would be in the mountain and their journey would be over.

After an hour of riding, they came to a ridge, where Eldred stopped and dismounted. He led the group towards the edge to survey the land before them. The mountain loomed out of the ground directly to the east, its peak lost in the morning clouds. Around the base was Nyrra's stronghold. A black stone building, which would have been massive in any other setting, was dwarfed by the immensity of the mountain. The sight of the stronghold sent a shiver down Alaric's spine. He could sense the evil.

Surrounding the fortress was the city Nyrra built for his followers. Brown and red brick houses filled the land for about a mile. The city was just as spectacular as the mountain and fortress. Alaric marvelled at the sight. He was amazed that something so evil could look so magnificent.

Finally surrounding the city was an immense grey stone wall. From the distance, Alaric estimated the wall at fifty feet high. He could see now what Eldred had explained to him. Once an army was inside those walls, it would take an army twice as large just to break the outer defences. Alaric couldn't imagine how many men would be needed to take the fortress.

"The foremost defensive position in the world. None have been built before and none since. Many have tried to copy the design, but have all fallen short," Eldred explained as they all marvelled at the sight before them. "Even Castalia, a city that has never had its wall breeched, pales in comparison.

"How did we ever get Nyrra out of there?" Alaric asked, still in awe.

"He left. He brought his entire army out of the city to wage war on the rest of the world. We were able to split his armies and drive him to the north. His thirst for domination was too much. The remaining residents of the city were forced to leave. Those that survived became nomads." Before anyone could condemn Sha'tian's tribe, Eldred continued. "Many of the nomads still follow Nyrra, but not all of them," Sha'tian nodded his thanks. "I believe that they are waiting for his return so they can return to their city."

"I have only seen the fabled city of night once before in my life. We do not like to come to this place. It is a constant reminder of the life that we should have had if this land had not been corrupted." Sha'tian spoke as if lost in thought.

"We need to keep going," Eldred urged Sha'tian. "The way down is only a short ride to the south."

"We will leave you here Wise One. We cannot pass this ridge, we dare not," Sha'tian spoke very solemnly. "We have done what was prophesized and brought you safely to this place. The rest is up to you."

As Sha'tian finished speaking, there came a shrill scream from behind them. The noise almost sounded like it came from a horse, yet there was something not right about it. The sound made Alaric shiver. No one had to turn around to know who was behind them.

"You must ride Alaric. We will try and give you as much time as possible. It is solely up to you now to take the stone to mountain top and destroy it," Eldred spoke quickly.

Alaric almost laughed to himself. It had always been solely up to him. "How will I find my way?" Alaric's voice was shaky.

Quickly the nomads loaded Adelanta with two saddle bags, one with food and one with water. He would need both if he was going to survive the final journey.

"The pass down is easy to find. We will stay here and try and stop Nyrra from getting passed. If we succeed, then we will meet you at the stronghold," Eldred spoke quickly, not wasting any time.

"But..." that was all Alaric was able to get out. With a word from Eldred, Adelanta sprung into action.

"Ride Alaric," Palentonal called after him.

They all watched Alaric, but only for a moment before they turned to see what was approaching. In the distance, there appeared to be a group of about a dozen riders. There was something strange about them. It was almost like they were surrounded by a black fog. When anyone tried to focus on the haze, it would disappear.

"This isn't good," Eldred spoke so quietly that only Alena and Palentonal could hear.

"What is it?" Alena asked, just as quietly.

"If I'm not mistaken, Viper is in that group, with at least one of Nyrra's Dark Knights," Eldred let out a gasp of surprise as he surveyed the group. A small spell increasing his sight made him the only one able to see them. "Nyrra is not with them. I don't know whether this is a good thing or a bad thing."

They all drew their weapons, their horses moved around nervously. There was a feeling of approaching dread. With every passing minute, the feeling became stronger and stronger. The nomads, more so than the others, were showing signs of fear. The look on Eldred's face didn't inspire confidence in anyone. By the way they were moving, it would only be a matter of minutes before the approaching group would be upon them.

"You all must leave Viper for me," Eldred said suddenly. Palentonal and Alena, you must take the Dark Knight. The rest of you, do your best. There is evil magic at work here. Try not to let them get too close to you. We must give Alaric enough time to reach the mountain. Nothing else matters." They all nodded their confirmation. They knew that this would be their last battle. "You take the lead Alena. I will try and counter their spell."

The minutes past slowly and felt as though they were hours. Soon enough, twelve dark riders approached them. They rode animals that looked like horses, yet were not. They had the same body and head, but instead of flat teeth, they had jagged fangs. Claws adorned their front and rear hooves. Their eyes were a bright red and looked as mean as the rest of the creature.

"What in the Gods name are those?" asked Erelious as he stared at the creatures.

"They are the horselings, Nyrra's horse atrocity. An experiment of his," Palentonal explained in disgust.

Leading was a man who they had seen before, dressed in black. His black main shirt seemed to darken the area around him. Morgoz did not have a smile on his face, though it was obvious that he was pleased with himself.

"Let us pass and you will be given a quick death," Morgoz spoke as though he didn't expect a negative response.

Alena laughed at the request before she spoke. "You will not pass this ridge. We should have finished you at Lel Dinion," Alena almost spat the words at Morgoz, although her gaze was fixed on the creature behind him.

Viper returned her gaze, watching her intently. She wasn't sure but there seemed to be a smirk on his face, as if he knew something that no one else did. His reptile-like yellow eyes had her transfixed. She couldn't take her eyes off him. She could only barely remember where she was.

"Then you choose death," Morgoz snarled at her.

When Alena didn't answer, Palentonal rode up to her side. "We will fight you until the end. There is nothing you can say that could convince us otherwise.

"When my master gets here, he might convince you otherwise. If you live long enough to meet him."

"We don't fear you," Palentonal hoped he could buy some more time if he kept talking.

"What is the matter, Mangy One? Are you afraid to face me yourself? Will you only send your whore and pet elf to face me?" Morgoz ignored Palentonal and tried to get Eldred's attention.

"Enough," Eldred cried when he realised what was happening. "Attack!"

Palentonal kicked his horse into action with a loud war cry and rode towards Morgoz. As he did he brushed past Alena. Viper cried out in anguish as his spell was broken. Eldred didn't give him a chance to recover and was quickly upon him.

Viper's black sword flicked towards Eldred. A blackness surrounded Viper's cloak and Eldred knew that if he came into contact with it then he would die. He did not have time to break the spell that Viper had created so he had to be careful. Along with the fighting on horse-back, there was a battle on the ground. Tormenta and the horseling bit, kicked and screamed at each other, both looking for an opportunity to kill.

Eldred did not give a quarter. He pressed Viper as much as Viper pressed him. At each stage of the physical attack, Eldred had to concentrate on Viper casting a spell. He needed to make sure that the serpentant didn't gain any advantage. Eldred would have to counter any attack Viper made, which meant he couldn't attack himself. The pace of the battle would not last long. Soon enough one of the competitors would burn out and defending was much easier than attacking. At that moment, the other would succeed.

Palentonal and Alena both took the attack to Morgoz. Mystically and singularly, neither of them were a match for him, but together they had a chance. Being elves they could command some spells, but nothing that would be able to kill. All they could do is counter his spells which allowed them time to defeat him physically. Not only was Morgoz a skilled

Magician, he was also a supreme warrior. He defended and attacked with the skill of a swordmaster. No matter how hard they tried, the elves couldn't break his defences.

Erelious led the nomads in the attack against the regular soldiers. The nomads on foot did not have much of a chance against the mounted soldiers. Erelious did his best to coordinate, but infantry against cavalry is tough at the best of times and without extra numbers, it was almost impossible. Morgoz's soldiers were well trained and knew how to fight.

Their fight removed them from the others. Erelious deliberately led his battle away, knowing that there was no chance he could win; he had to play for time. Duck and run was the tactic he used. The tactics only worked for a short time before the soldiers realised. A change in tactics quickly reduced the nomads' numbers considerably. Within five minutes, there was only Erelious and Sha'tian left alive and only two of the soldiers had been killed.

"Well it has been fun," Sha'tian didn't sound convincing as there was a break in the fighting. "At least I got to live to prove my father right."

"Two against eight! I still think we have a chance," Erelious gave Sha'tian a rueful smile, not really believing his own words.

Erelious tried to keep his horse between the soldiers and Sha'tian. The soldiers all moved in together, taking their time so they didn't make any mistakes. Erelious kept his sword level. He mainly wanted to gain time. He knew that he was going to die and when the attack came, Erelious knew where it was coming from. Defending the first blow, Erelious had decided the he would take at least one of the soldiers with him. Instead of trying to defend another attack, Erelious made a fatal blow to the next soldier who had moved in to attack. As his blade slashed across the soldier's face, the man's blade stuck him through the stomach. As he rolled off his horse, he saw the other soldier slide limply from his horseling.

Erelious could feel the blood gushing from his wound, the sword still embedded in his stomach. He knew that the stab wound was fatal and he only had a few moments to live. Before he could try and stand, a sword pierced his back. The last thing he heard was a war cry coming from Sha'tian. A smile crossed his face as he remembered the soldier he had managed to kill before everything went black.

Sha'tian leapt at the soldier who had killed Erelious. Unfortunately, he did not see the other soldiers waiting for him to move. Before could come within striking distance, seven other blades sliced into his body. He died   before   he   could   drop   to   the   ground.

Eldred and Viper were locked in battle. The two were evenly matched with neither giving an inch. With every strong attack, either physically or magically, saw an even stronger defence. Sweat poured from Eldred's face under the strain, Viper on the other hand only seemed to become stronger. It seemed that it would only be a matter of time before Eldred would falter. Suddenly there was a loud war cry from one of the other battles. The sound was cut short and Eldred knew that it was not good.

Eldred kept his attack up, but he could hear the sound of horselings approaching from behind.

"I want him alive," Viper called as he looked over Eldred's shoulder at the approaching soldiers.

Knowing the end was near, Eldred swung Tormenta around to face them. The first soldier to approach, fell under Eldred's sword. That was all Eldred could do before he felt his arms snap to his side and his sword dropped to the ground. His body was completely immobile. The only thing he could move was his head. He turned to face Viper just in time to see the flat of Viper's sword strike the side of his face. Not completely unconscious, Eldred fell to the ground.

"Tie him up and make sure he can't move," commanded Viper.

Even though Eldred could not feel the ropes, he knew that they were being tied tight. The ground felt hot under Eldred's face and he savoured it, being the only thing he could feel. It was the only way he knew he was still alive. Viper wanted him for something and he knew he would find out soon enough.

***

Palentonal and Alena's tactics had Morgoz in trouble. His strong chain mail shirt was the only thing stopping him from being sliced open. The dual attacks started to wear him down. A lesser man would already be dead, but Morgoz was a formidable opponent.

The mixture of physical and magical attacks was wearing down both attacker and defender. Alena and Palentonal's only advantage was that Morgoz didn't have time to launch an attack. Neither one of them would have been able to have defended a powerful attack.

Suddenly Sha'tian's cry diverted Palentonal's attention enough to give Morgoz the advantage and he attacked. Palentonal moved just in time to deflect the sword away from his heart. The sword sunk deep into his chest. He cried out in pain and fell from his horse, the blade this protruding from his chest.

Alena swung her sword with all her strength. She knew she only had one chance to kill Morgoz. Just before she struck, her arms froze. There was nothing she could do to get the blade any closer. She was completely stuck.

The sound of horses could be heard coming from behind. Alena hoped that it was Eldred and Erelious, but she knew that is was not. She knew that it was all hopeless now. Alena tried to move, to defend herself, but there was nothing she could do. She couldn't even attempt to break the spell. The next thing she knew was a heavy knock on the back of her head. Her eyes rolled into her head as she fell from her horse. Next she heard a scream coming from somewhere over the top of her. The sound was horrible.

Morgoz stared at the soldier who had knocked Alena from her horse. The soldier gripped his head in pain. Morgoz smiled at the contorted face. Slowly he increased his grip on the spell and the soldiers cry was suddenly cut short as the man slipped from his saddle, dead.

"If anyone else wants to disobey orders, please, feel free?" Morgoz addressed the remaining six soldiers, puffing as he spoke. "When I said she is not to be harmed that means…" Morgoz let the last comment trail off as Viper rode towards them.

Viper dismounted and knelt beside Palentonal. The elf's breathing was weak and his chest was only just rising and falling. His face was pale and sweaty. It was obvious that he was going to die. Viper lifted Palentonal's head so it was close to his. Palentonal cried out in pain.

"You will not die today elf, as much as it pains me to do so," Viper hissed the words at him. "You will stay alive until Alaric returns to this place and you will tell him where we have taken the other two.

Palentonal laughed softly, followed by a bout of coughing. A small trickle of blood ran down from the corner of his mouth. "Alaric will be in the mountain soon and it will be all over. You have already lost."

Viper hissed a laugh at him. A smile crossed his reptilian face. "How little you know. It is a very long way from being over. Unfortunately for you, though, you will not be around to see us win. Everything is falling into place."

Viper let Palentonal's head drop to the ground. Standing over him he pulled the sword from his chest. Palentonal opened his mouth to scream, but no sound came out. Palentonal knew that he only had a few minutes to live.

The next thing Viper did surprised everyone. A dull yellow glow appeared around his hands. Shortly after a similar glow appeared on Palentonal's wound. The wound closed over, leaving only a small scar.

Palentonal sat up, a new pain filled his body. He felt as though he had been tainted with an evil spirit. Whatever Viper had done had left him polluted. Viper grabbed the back of his head and pulled him close. Palentonal's face changed to anger as Viper whispered his instructions to him.

Returning to his feet, Viper returned his gaze to Morgoz. "What are you waiting for? Go to the mountain. You know what you have to do." Viper's words were cold and sent a shiver down Morgoz's spine.

Morgoz spat at Viper's feet. "I don't take orders from you, snake! There is plenty of time." The worst thing was that Morgoz knew that Viper was right. He should already be on his way to the Mighty City.

Turning his horseling, he didn't wait for Viper to respond. He started towards the mountain, leaving the others behind. He didn't know why Nyrra didn't dispose of the creature.

Viper ordered his prisoners to be strapped to the rider less horselings. Once they were ready to go, Viper turned to Palentonal. "Remember what I told you, elf."

Slowly, before Palentonal could think of something to say, they started to waver. Soon enough they had completely disappeared. Palentonal slowly came to his feet and looked towards the mountain. He could only hope that Alaric was able to succeed.

Chapter 34: Evil All Around

Alaric nearly fell off the back of Adelanta as he suddenly jumped into action. His hands instinctively firmed their grip on the reins and he steadied himself in the saddle. He wanted to look back over his shoulder towards his friends, but Adelanta was now at a gallop.

With Adelanta charging, Alaric nearly missed the pass leading down the cliff face. With all his strength, he pulled on the reins, even with all the pressure Adelanta didn't want to stop. Alaric dug his heels into his flank, pulled even harder and Adelanta skidded to a stop.

As they returned to the pass, Alaric could see back towards his friends. The fight hadn't started and he could see a great deal of distance between the two parties. Something tugged at him, urging him to go back to help. He was about to put his boots into Adelanta's flanks when he heard a faint cry. The sound sent a chill down his spine. In that instant, Alaric knew what he had to do. Pulling himself away from his friends, he made his way down the gentle slope.

Alaric struggled to keep Adelanta at a walk. Although the slope was gentle, the drop was still a long way down and Alaric didn't want to risk Adelanta losing his footing

It was a nervous ride, but soon he was at the base of the cliff. The land was flat and straight towards the city wall. The only other sight was the mountain and the fortress. None of the other buildings could be seen over the walls. Staring at them, he had a sudden urge to ride at full pace, straight towards the city. It was strange. If anything, he thought he would want to ride in the opposite direction.

He hoped that his friends were winning. Taking a last look up the pass towards the top of the cliff, Alaric checked to make sure that he wasn't being followed. As he took a firm grip on the reins, he didn't realise that the land around him was full of cracks and fissures. The holes were disguised and impossible to see. At the pace he was travelling, it would be too late to see one, luckily Adelanta was able to work his way around.

Alaric's heart raced and sweat poured down his face as they came closer to the city. A glistening stream of sweat also lathered Adelanta. The midday sun beat down on them, making the ride more uncomfortable. With every league they gained, the mountain grew in front of them. The sight was ominous and Alaric was starting to have second thoughts. The wall around the city and the fortress, which poked its head up, was enough to place fear his heart. Gritting his teeth, he continued.

It was just after midday when Alaric arrived at the city gates. The wall seemed over fifty feet high and the main gate on the eastern side of the city was closed and the gatehouse stood more than half way up the wall. A black iron portcullis barred the large double wooden doors, which were also shut.

Slowly Alaric walked to the gate. Before he tried the portcullis, he knew it would be hopeless. Putting all his energy into it Alaric tried to lift it.

Taking a step back, Alaric looked towards the guard house. His heart sank when he saw the windows boarded up. Even if they were open, there was no way for him to reach it. He had come this far only to be stuck outside of the wall without any way in. The comforting thought was that anyone following him wouldn't be able to get in either.

There was one way that might work, but it was not something he wanted to try. He would have to try to draw energy from the land around him and the thought made him shiver and feel sick in his stomach. He didn't even know if the gate was locked magically. If it was, then it may all be for nothing. It would have to be his last resort. He decided that he would have something to eat and then ride around the wall in hope of finding another door. He wished for the others to be with him. He knew that Eldred would know what to do.

Alaric unloaded the food and water pouches from Adelanta. After giving him a drink of water, Alaric sat down with his back against the wall and ate. The sun beat down on him and made any rest he was hoping for utterly impossible.

Once he was finished eating, he was back on his feet again. As much as he had faith in his friends, he knew that they were fighting a hopeless battle. It wouldn't be much longer before Nyrra and his soldiers would be upon him.

Taking one last look at the gate and portcullis, Alaric remounted his horse. He wanted to be able to enter and be done with his mission. He knew things were not going to be easy, but he didn't think that they would be impossible. Laughing at the thought, he slowly started Adelanta moving towards the northern side of the city.

Before he had gone more than twenty feet, Alaric reined Adelanta to a halt. Slowly, without making any sudden movements, he drew his sword. He had a sudden feeling that someone was behind him. Looking around, he gasped in surprise. Without releasing his grip, Alaric started to laugh,

"Well! Of all people I thought that I would see out here, you would have been last on the list. How is it possible?" Alaric's voice was dry and cracked.

"I said that if I survived, I would find you and it looks like I have arrived just in time," Heryion had a broad smile on his face.

"But how? We all thought you were dead," Alaric was still shocked at seeing his old friend.

"Let's keep moving. I know a way into the city without using any of the main gates. I'll explain as we go."

Heryion was travelling on foot, yet he had no problems in keeping pace with Adelanta. He was also dressed in his usual clothes and Alaric wondered how he survived without the thick robe to protect him from the sun. There were still a lot of things that surprised him about Heryion. He truly wondered if he knew anything about the man he had met in the Cloumid Mountains.

"Once I left you, I took the orb to the summit of the Scorpion Mountain. That is where I needed the help of a dragon to destroy it," Heryion started to explain, but Alaric cut him short.

"A what?"

"That's right Alaric, a dragon. I thought with all that you've seen, that dragons would be run of the mill for you. I suppose they are few and far between these days. They are very dangerous, but I needed the fire from a dragon's breath to destroy the orb," Heryion continued.

"You're starting to lose me. You said that they are very dangerous," Heryion nodded his agreement. "Then how were you able to get its help?" Alaric sounded even more confused.

"I couldn't just walk into his lair and ask if I could borrow his breath. Kahn, his name, is one of the deadliest dragons still alive. Back before the great dragon wars, Kahn was the King of the Black Dragon Clan. Now he is the only black dragon left alive. As I was saying, I needed the fire from Kahn and I couldn't ask him. So, to cut a long story short, I woke Kahn. It seems that he wasn't too happy about being woken up from a hundred year slumber. I raced to the summit of the mountain and waited for the mighty creature. After making two passes over my head and nearly frying me three times, I had him just where I wanted him. As he flew towards me, I threw the orb towards him. Before he realised what it was, it was too late. Kahn blew a fireball towards me and the orb. The orb was quickly consumed, but unfortunately, I hadn't thought about the consequences. The destruction of the orb set off a mighty explosion. The blast sent me flying half way around the world. I didn't get to see what happened to Kahn, but since he's a dragon, I'm assuming that the blast didn't have a great deal of effect on him." Heryion ended his story with a smile on his face.

"So if it blasted you half way across the world, how did you get back here?" Alaric was wondering if should have dared ask the question.

"That's an entirely different story, and it looks like one that might have to wait. Here is where we enter."

Alaric reined Adelanta to a stop without even noticing that he was a foot away from riding into a large chasm. The rip in the ground ran straight up to the wall. The other end disappeared into the distance. Alaric looked at the wall, searching for signs of an entrance; when he found none, he looked questioningly towards Heryion.

"You didn't think it was going to be that easy, did you?' Heryion laughed.

"What are you talking about, Heryion?" Alaric was starting to get frustrated; it seemed everything was a joke with him.

"At the bottom of that chasm is where all the waste is flushed out of the city, at least it was when the city was inhabited. It's only a small drain and it's a perilous journey down, but it is the only way into the city, unless you can climb walls, that is." The broad grin had not left his face since he started telling his story.

"What about my horse?" Alaric had formed a bond with Adelanta and didn't want to let him go. The thought of leaving him alone in the land was not pleasant. There was no chance he would survive.

"Unless he can make his own way down into the chasm, I think you are going to have the leave him here. I think that he will be alright on his own. This horse has a special power and I don't think that it is his time to die." Heryion's words gave Alaric some comfort.

As if understanding the situation, Adelanta let out whinny and shook his head, indicating that Alaric should dismount. A tear almost brimmed in Alaric's eye. The animal was so brave to willingly let Alaric go. He patted the stallion's neck affectionately before he dismounted. Alaric took one last look at Adelanta before walking to the top of the chasm. Taking the food and water pouches, he wondered how he was going to return from the mountain without his horse. Then he realised that he was more than likely to never leave.

Alaric removed the chest from the front of Adelanta's saddle. The chest, even though it was small, would be too bulky for him to carry it down the cliff face.

"Here. I think this will help," Heryion handed Alaric a small cotton pouch. "It won't work as well as the chest, but it will dampen the stone's power."

Slowly Alaric opened the chest. He was expecting something, but instead nothing happened. The stone lay lifeless, as if dead, or at least not interested. Alaric wasn't sure if he was relieved or disappointed. Stuffing the stone into the pouch, he tied it to his belt and then walked to the edge of the cliff.

The chasm wall was a straight drop to the bottom, which Alaric guessed at about two hundred feet. He looked left and right, but there didn't seem to be any way to climb down. He took another look and then returned his gaze towards Heryion.

"There is no way down. The walls are too sheer and there aren't any handholds," Alaric sounded defeated.

"At first glance yes, but if it was easy to find, then it wouldn't be a secret and I'm sure Nyrra would have blocked it off many years ago. I don't know if anyone else knows this way into the city. I found it many years ago, escaping, not trying to get in mind you, but it works both ways." The grin on his face returned.

Alaric was lost in thought as Heryion approached the chasm. 'How old was Heryion? If he used this route to escape from the city, then he had to of been there when it was populated. Alaric wasn't exactly sure, but he thought it would have been at least a thousand years since the city had been occupied. Alaric thought as he looked directly towards Heryion. His doubts returned and he was starting to wonder about his motives and if he was truly on his side.

Alaric walked over and Adelanta waited behind. Alaric stood at the edge of the chasm and looked down. At first he didn't see anything, but the more looked, he could see small bumps and cracks in the wall.

"Do you think that you can climb down there?" Heryion asked, concerned with his abilities.

"Well, I've never descended a cliff face before, or climbed one for that matter, but as you said, I don't have a choice. There is no other way."

"Just be careful. It's not as easy as it seems," Heryion warned. "Leave those with me. I'll take them down," he added, pointing at the pouches.

Alaric felt even less confident. He expected it to be hard, but now he wasn't sure if he was going to be able to do it. Slowly Alaric lowered himself and found his first foot and handhold without any problems. From there it became much harder. All the training he had done and his general lifestyle had increased his strength, and he had no problems in lifting his own weight. He was about half way down when he could no longer feel another foothold. As he looked down, the cliff face looked smooth. His arms started to burn and he started to panic. He thought about pulling himself back up, but he knew that he would never make it. Just as he was about to give up, he caught a glimpse of a new way down. Slowly he started to lower himself again.

Once Alaric had settled himself on his new perch, he looked for his next foothold. Again, he couldn't see anything. He was sure that before he had moved, there was a clear path. It took a while, but he finally found another bump that would be suitable. With each new foothold, it was taking longer to find the next. With each delay, Alaric's muscles burned.

After an hour, he looked back up the chasm face. He was shocked when he realised Heryion wasn't following. He was very quickly running out of daylight. If he had to wait for Heryion to reach the bottom, he would still be out of the city when night fell. He thought about calling out, but he didn't want to attempt anything that might put him off balance.

After another long stretch of climbing, Alaric found himself on a small ledge. The ledge itself was no more than half a foot in width. Although it did give Alaric some rest, it was not as good as solid ground. When Alaric was ready to move again, he notice that the ledge he was standing on sloped gently downwards. The gradient was very small, but Alaric thought that it would save him some time.

Alaric started off casually and after his first step, nearly overbalanced. After a tense few seconds, Alaric regained his balance and hugged the chasm wall. When his heart rate slowed, he started again. Inch by inch Alaric worked his way down the wall. He didn't know what was worse: what he was going to do or what he had just done.

With each step, Alaric thought they were going to be his last. Now there were definitely no more footholds or handholds in the chasm wall. The ledge slowly started to become steeper the further he travelled. Although he was making better distance with each step, each step was becoming gradually slower. The greater the slope, the greater the difficulty and there was still no sign of Heryion. Alaric wondered if his so-called friend had led him into a trap.

Alaric continued on without looking down. The travelling was slow and frustrating. Every time he tried to speed things along, he nearly lost his footing and fell. Each time his heart raced and his breath was short and sharp. After a short break, he continued along more carefully, until his need for speed pushed him forward.

Losing his balance again, Alaric slammed his left foot down on the ledge. The weight of his foot crumbled the ledge giving him no support. Desperately reaching for a handhold, Alaric found one, but that too crumbled to dust. With one last effort, Alaric scratched the chasm wall, but to no avail. Falling away from the cliff, he thought that it had all been for nothing.

Alaric felt like a lifetime had passed as he fell. In reality, it was only a couple of seconds. Alaric had not realised it, but he was only ten feet from the ground. He hit the ground feet first and as he did his left leg twanged on impact. A loud snap echoed through the chasm as his leg broke.

The pain shot through his body as he thudded to the chasm floor. Hoping that the sound he had heard was not his leg, he tried to stand. He cried out in agony as his leg gave way underneath his weight. The frustration outweighed the pain. It seemed as though he was going to die on the canyon floor just outside of his final destination.

"So close," he yelled at the sky.

With an effort, Alaric dragged himself along the chasm floor until he was able to rest his back against the cliff wall. The ledge had carried him away from the city. As he looked down the chasm, he could not see the entrance Heryion had spoken about.

As he looked back up the chasm, Alaric noticed that he walls looked completely smooth and he wondered how Heryion had ever found the ledge in the first place. He knew that it was directly above him, but no matter how hard he looked, he could not see it.

The chasm floor was shaded from the sun, but as Alaric looked towards the sky he realised that it was steadily growing darker. For the first time, Alaric noticed that the temperature was dropping and Heryion was still missing.

"I thought I told you to be careful," the sudden voice would have normally surprised Alaric, but his utter despair robbed him of all other emotions.

"Why did you send me down here? No one could have survived that descent unharmed." Alaric did not look at Heryion as he spoke.

"You're probably right, but you made it without dying. I think that proves a lot," Heryion didn't even seem to notice that Alaric's leg was bent the wrong way.

"What does it matter now anyway? If you haven't noticed, I've broken my leg and can't walk. You could drag me to the city, but by the look of the sky, we don't have more than hour before the sun sets." Alaric sounded completely defeated.

"Oh that! That's nothing." The constant light heartedness of Heryion was starting to annoy him.

"Nothing for you," Alaric boomed, his pain replaced by anger. "It feels like more than nothing to me."

Heryion did not reply as he slowly moved towards Alaric, the grin still strong on his face. Kneeling next to him, Heryion placed his left hand on the break and his right hand on Alaric's foot.

"Now this is going to hurt, a lot. It won't last long though, if that is any comfort," Heryion explained brightly.

Alaric wasn't sure what he was talking about, but the pain had returned and he wasn't in the mood to ask questions. Heryion wasn't waiting for questions. Before Alaric could prepare himself, Heryion put all his weight on his left hand. As he did he pulled on Alaric's foot. The pain shot through Alaric's body and he thought his head was going to explode. As Heryion had said, the pain only lasted a moment. When it was gone, Alaric felt an intense heat in his leg. There was no pain, just heat.

"There we go. Good as new!" Heryion jumped back to his feet. "Give it a couple of minutes and you won't even know it was broken."

After a few minutes, Heryion helped Alaric to his feet. To his surprise, Heryion was right. There was absolutely no pain at all. To emphasise the point, Alaric jumped up and down.

"Easy Alaric! It will take a little while for your leg to repair properly. It will be alright to walk on, but don't put too much pressure on it," Heryion warned quickly. "Now, I don't want to be wandering around the city after nightfall."

"How did you do that? It is wonderful, thank you." Alaric was amazed.

"It is a simple process of transferring energies, but there is no time for explanations, we must be on the move again."

Alaric spoke as they started walking towards the city walls. "The city has been abandoned for a long time. Why would we be worried about moving around at night?"

"There's a very simple fact. Although Nyrra has not been here for many, many years, his evil still lingers. Night is when his evil comes to life. Spirits and the likes roam the streets, dangerous for anyone who doesn't follow Nyrra. In fact, it is still dangerous for most who do follow him. These spirits have been left unchecked for a long time. Only the return of their master could control them."

Alaric looked shocked. He thought he was coming to an undefended stronghold. He knew it wasn't going to be easy, but he didn't expect to have to fight anyone once he was inside. Heryion saw the expression on his face.

"Don't worry too much about it. These spirits are few and far between. I just don't want to take any chances and I'm sure you don't either."

It wasn't long before they came to a small tunnel, leading into the city wall. Alaric estimated the drain was no more than a pace in diameter. As Alaric came closer, his heart sank. Just inside the opening were a number of iron bars covered in a thick coat of rust.

"It seems that you are not the only one who knew about this exit," Alaric gave Heryion a sharp look.

"You should know by now to trust me." Heryion still had the grin on his face, which was starting to make Alaric angry.

Heryion walked to the opening of the drain and raised his hand until they were level with his chest. Slowly he started to chant an incantation in a language Alaric couldn't understand. Alaric suddenly realised what he was doing and called for him to stop.

"Wait Heryion! You can't use magic out here. You will be consumed by Nyrra's evil."

Heryion's shoulders dropped as his concentration was broken. "I see that Eldred has not taught you very much at all," Heryion then said something under his breath, which Alaric could only assume was derogatory. "Incantations don't use as much energy as spells. In fact, some, like the one I was going to use, doesn't need any at all. You have a lot to learn, Alaric. Hopefully you'll get a chance before it is too late."

Alaric wasn't sure what Heryion's last comment was supposed to mean, but it was comforting.

Heryion resumed his former pose and restarted the incantation. Slowly, as Heryion chanted, the bars started to waver. They seemed to be losing their solidity. Alaric reached into the drain and touched one of the bars. It felt like clay, soft and malleable. Without thinking, Alaric started to bend the bars until there was enough room for him crawl through.

"Maybe I was mistaken," Heryion spoke when he finished and saw what Alaric had done.

"Let's get going," Alaric said as he slid through the bars.

Alaric kept to his hands and knees after two minutes of crouching. As much as he didn't want to crawl through a sewer, his back wouldn't let him continue. With the city vacant for so long, the drain was completely dry. There was a slight aroma of human waste, but it was nothing like Alaric had expected.

Before long, the light had completely disappeared. Alaric thought about using a spell, but he could feel the evil growing around him. The closer he came to the city, the more he could feel Nyrra's evil. The feeling weighed him down. The complete darkness did nothing to raise his spirits.

"I think we need some light," suggested Heryion after they had been crawling in darkness for about fifteen minutes.

"What about the evil?"

"You let me worry about that. I still have a few tricks up my sleeve." The tone in his voice showed he meant business.

Alaric felt a small rush, like a brief gust of wind against the back of his neck. The next instant there was a small globe of light about a pace in front of them. Alaric closed his eyes as the sudden light took effect.

The light remained exactly a pace in front of Alaric. At first he was surprised to see the small orb glide through the air away from him. For the first five minutes, Alaric tried to catch it. Each time he thought he could fool it, but each time he didn't gain an inch. He knew it was silly, but at least it kept his mind off the ever-growing sense of evil.

"How far have we got to go?" Alaric asked after another thirty minutes had past. "It has to be getting close to nightfall outside."

"Not long now Alaric. Soon on your left, you will see small grooves cut into the wall leading up to the surface. This is where we will make our exit," Heryion explained.

As Heryion had said, Alaric soon found the small grooves in the wall. They looked no more than a passing cut from a blunt blade, but Alaric was sure he could use them to climb. If he could make it down the chasm face, then this would be a walk in the park. The grooves led up into a vertical shaft the same diameter as the one they were in. Alaric was glad to finally be able to stand up and stretch.

Looking up, Alaric couldn't see what was at the top. The light didn't travel far up the vertical walls. Carefully Alaric started to climb. Before he could lift both feet off the floor, Heryion put a restraining hand on his left arm.

"I think you should let me go first."

Alaric gave no argument. He didn't want to have to face whatever was waiting for them at the top. If it was night, as Alaric suspected it was, then there was no telling what was out there.

To Alaric's surprise, Heryion scampered up the tunnel. Before Alaric had started, Heryion was out of sight. He didn't think the little man was quite that nimble. He knew that there was no way he could climb that quickly.

"Come on, Alaric. We don't have all day. We have to be out of here before nightfall," Heryion called down.

Alaric slowly started to climb. It was not as hard as the descent, but still difficult enough. The muscles in his arms and legs burned with the strain. They had not yet recovered from the descent and once he had made it a pace up the shaft, the orb arrived at the base. The light shone straight up to the top. Taking a glance, Alaric was glad to see that the climb was not as far as he had thought. Although he had not noticed, the drain had gradually sloped upwards. He could see that Heryion was almost to the top, which was blocked by a stone plate.

At the sight of the stone, Alaric initially thought of returning to the drain. Before he moved, he remembered that Heryion had not let him down since they met. He had to have faith. Continuing his ascent, Alaric thought that his arms and legs were going to drop off.

No more than half way up, Alaric heard a grinding sound coming from above him. Slowly the stone plate was sliding and he could see clearly that Heryion was using magic again. Alaric wondered how Heryion could stand using magic. He had only briefly drawn in the evil and the thought of it still made him nauseous. His head started to spin as the thought stayed in his mind. He wavered for a moment before he regained his composure.

A dull red light crept into the shaft. As it did, the orb suddenly blinked out. Alaric was relieved that there was still light outside. At least he would not have to contend with evil spirits.

"Come on Alaric. There's only about fifteen minutes of light left and we still have further to go." The urgency in Heryion's voice pushed Alaric into action

Sweat poured from Alaric's face as he continued to climb. With each new step and handhold, Alaric's muscles burned. He tried to hurry, but he could only go as fast as his arms and legs would allow.

When Alaric finally made it to the top, the sun had all but set. Only a very dim light remained, just enough for Alaric to see the worry on Heryion's face.

"We must move quickly now. I know of a safe place for us to spend the night, but it is about half an hour's walk from here and we don't have that much light left."

All Alaric wanted to do was collapse on the ground, but necessity moved him to a slow run. The dark stone buildings blurred passed him. It took all of Alaric's concentration to stay on his feet. He took no notice of the city around him.

The sun finally disappeared before they reached the safe house; as soon as it had set, Heryion called Alaric to stop. The building completely shadowed the soft light from the rising moon and the air was becoming cold. Although he could not see Heryion's face, he knew he was worried.

"We must be very careful now. The evil will start to stir. We are only five minutes from the house we are looking for. If you hear or see anything, prepare yourself for an attack. Your sword will give you some protection, but more than likely you will have to use magic. I know that it is not the ideal situation, but it is better than dying."

Alaric nodded his reply. A shiver suddenly ran down his spine as a gust of cool air blew against him. There was a distinct evil feeling to it. He had a terrible feeling that someone or something was watching them. Looking around quickly, to his relief, he couldn't see anything.

Heryion continued on at a walk. Alaric followed quickly at his heels. The further they walked, the stronger the feeling of being watched became. The hairs on the back of his neck prickled; he knew that he was not being paranoid, there was something outside watching him.

Just before they reached their destination, there came a wailing cry on the night air. Both Heryion and Alaric froze where they stood. They were in a small alley, just large enough for them to walk side by side. Double and triple storey buildings loomed on either side. The cry came from somewhere in front of them. They stayed still for a full minute. When nothing happened Heryion started them moving again.

As soon as they moved, another cry came from behind them. "Run!" Heryion screamed at the top of his voice.

A white apparition filled the space where Alaric had been only a moment before. A second apparition dropped down at the exit in front of them. Alaric and Heryion both skidded to a stop. Alaric's heart was racing as panic filled his body.

The ghostly white figure in front of them seemed to be a woman dressed in tattered rags. The face would have been considered somewhat beautiful except for the look of pure evil. It floated about a foot from the ground blocking their exit. The first apparition blocked any chance of retreat. Neither of them made any move towards them. Their gazes were fixed on the sword hanging from Alaric's waist.

"What do we do now?" Alaric asked, his voice dripping with fear.

"Well this definitely could be worse, I'll say that much." His confidence reassured Alaric a little. "They are dai-mari, which means bride of evil. Whatever you do, don't let them touch you. Their touch is death. On the bright side, they hate steel. They will avoid it like the plague. So, I think that you should draw your sword."

Alaric immediately drew his sword. As he did, both dai-mari let out another fear inspiring wail. The sound was enough to make him want to drop his sword and run for his life. He steeled himself and slowly started to walk towards the dai-mari. At first the creature looked puzzled, but when it realised what Alaric was doing, it started to withdraw.

Heryion kept a close watch on the dai-mari behind them. The creature was cautiously advancing on them. He was sure that it would not attack as long as he kept close watch on it.

A gap had opened at the end of the alley as the dai-mari retreated. Alaric kept his sword level with the spectre. Its retreat slowed and Alaric slowed his advance. The creature had a look on its face that made him nervous.

"I think that it is up to something," suggested Alaric.

"I think that you're right. It is giving in too easily. I think that there might be a surprise waiting for us once we reach the end of this alley. We don't have any choice, but to continue. Just be ready," Heryion agreed.

Alaric inched his way along. He had a feeling that the longer he took, the more the advantage was changing.

They were within two paces of the opening when a large animal jumped out at them. The creature looked like a cross between a wolf and a dog, only twice as big. Its sharp teeth were bared as it snarled at them. Drool dripped from the animal's mouth.

"A dragwor!" was all that Heryion could say.

Increasing his grip on his sword, Alaric swung around, slashing as he did. As he made it one hundred and eighty degrees, the sword struck the dai-mari, which had used the advantage of the distraction to attack. Surprisingly the sword did not penetrate what looked like an insubstantial body. Instead, the sword knocked the creature half way back down the alley. Smoke appeared and the dai-mari wailed in pain as it retreated.

The dragwor didn't wait for Alaric to recover. As soon as his back was to the creature, it leapt at him. Just before it sunk its teeth into Alaric's neck, it hung in thin air. Heryion had released the spell he was conjuring just in time. The remaining dai-mari wailed again, obviously calling for more support.

Without waiting for Heryion to make suggestions, Alaric spun around and stuck the dragwor in the neck with his sword. This time his sword passed through the creature as if it was thin air. It was all Alaric could do to keep his balance.

"Your sword will do no good. Things here are not what they seem," Heryion explained, his voice sounded strained. "Let's go before reinforcements get here."

Alaric didn't need to be told twice. Keeping his sword level at the dai-mari, Alaric advanced to the end of the alley, carefully avoiding the dragwor which had a confused look on its face.

The street they walked out onto was completely empty, aside from themselves and the dai-mari. Noises coming from both the left and the right indicated that it would not remain that way for long. Heryion led the way, being careful whenever they came to an intersection. There was a tension in the air that followed them.

It wasn't long before Heryion stopped at the door of a building that looked no different to any of the other buildings. Carefully he put an ear to the door and listened.

"We're here" he paused and looked back down the street past Alaric. "And it seems not a moment too soon,"

Alaric spun around to see a procession of terror coming towards them with the dai-mari at the head. Flanking the leader were two more dragwors. Behind them were a number of creatures; Alaric couldn't imagine what they were. Hearing the click of a door opening, Alaric returned his attention to Heryion who was entering the building.

"We have to get out of here," Alaric spoke in a hoarse whisper. With the fear racing through his body, it was all that he could muster. "Those things will be upon us any minute. What is here that it going to stop them?"

"You'll find out once you get inside. Now unless you want to wait around and see what they want, I suggest you hurry."

Alaric took on quick look back down the street and then rushed inside the building. Heryion closed the door behind him.

Chapter 35: Inside the Mountain

The door closed with a sharp click and Alaric felt secure. He could hear the wailing and screaming coming from outside and he waited for the door to come crashing down, but it didn't. Alaric let out a sigh of relief. It seemed as though for the moment, they were safe. It didn't seem possible, but Alaric wasn't about to complain.

Looking around the room Alaric was surprised to see that it was quite delicately furnished. Heryion had quickly lit the many candles that adorned the room. The walls were painted white with many brightly coloured tables and chairs scattered around. It had a very friendly feel about it. It was the last place Alaric thought he would be.

"So what is this place?" Alaric's voice was laden with wonder.

"This is a little haven I found quite a while ago. There is always a bright light. Even in a place like this. None of the creatures out there will pass through that door. If they did, they would cease to exist. There is a ward surrounding the building. I doubt even Nyrra himself would try and enter." Heryion sounded very pleased with himself. "I think that you should try and get some sleep. It's going to be the hardest day of your life tomorrow."

Alaric knew that he was right. At the mention of sleep, Alaric dropped to the floor. His body gave way to the strain of the day. "I think that I might need a hand." Alaric's voice was weak as he tried to lift himself off the floor.

Heryion went to his side and helped him up. He half carried Alaric down the hallway to a room with a number of beds covered in brightly coloured blankets. Alaric looked as though he was in heaven and as soon as his head hit the pillow he fell fast asleep.

Heryion stood over Alaric for a couple of minutes before returning to the front room. He knew that the following day was going to be hard; he also knew that Nyrra would be waiting for them at the summit.

Heryion woke Alaric just before dawn and although he had slept all night, his body felt as though he had no rest at all. He looked at Heryion, moaned and rolled over.

"It's not even light yet."

"It'll be light soon and you need to get something eat. As soon as the sun breaks the horizon, we have to be on the move again. I have a bad feeling that Nyrra or some of his agents are already in the city. We have to get an early start if we are going to beat them."

Heryion had prepared a light breakfast from the food in Alaric's pack. There was enough to last another day, two at the most. The wailing and screaming from outside was just as prominent during breakfast as   it had been the night before. Alaric wondered if the creatures would in fact leave once the sun rose. He trusted Heryion, but they had lost none of the persistence. He wouldn't have been surprised if they were still waiting for them when they left.

Suddenly the noise stopped and the room was completely silent. It was only quiet for a moment before Heryion got Alaric to his feet and got them on the move. Outside the streets were now completely empty. The sun had only just risen and all the evil creatures had disappeared. There was no sign of the madness that had pursued them the previous night. Regardless of the apparent safety, Alaric still looked up and down the streets for any sign of movement. When he was confident there was nothing, he followed Heryion towards the stronghold.

"The only way into the mountain is via the citadel," explained Heryion as they walked through the empty streets.

The city looked less ominous during the day. The buildings still stood as though they were made yesterday. The houses were all at least two storeys and Alaric wondered at how many people had lived in the city when it was populated.

Nothing moved as they passed through. There was no wind and the only sound was their footsteps on the street. The feeling was eerie. There was still the ever-growing evil presence. Alaric knew that the citadel was the heart of that evil.

They walked in silence. Heryion seemed to be concentrating on his surroundings. Alaric kept straining his ears to try and hear something other than their footsteps.

Just before midday they came to a large square out in front of the doors to the fortress. The large black structure looked a lot larger up close, but still tiny compared the giant mountain behind it. The fortress was completely black and ominous in design. One tall tower poked up through the middle of the building. Alaric couldn't hazard a guess at how tall it was. A number of turrets surround the tower, but no flags flew or had flown for many centuries. Large steps started at the far end of the square and led to large double doors, and in front of the steps, stood four crucifixes. Alaric shuddered at the thought of what they were used for. The rest of the square was completely empty. He gave Heryion a questioning look. In reply, Heryion shook his head, indicating that Alaric really didn't want to know what happened those long years ago. Alaric could feel the hatred radiating from the square. He knew that there had been many atrocities, too horrible even to talk about.

Slowly they crossed the square and started up the steps. With each step, the urge to turn and run became harder and harder to suppress. The only thing that kept him going was Heryion leading the way. He didn't know what would have happened if Heryion hadn't met him outside the wall.

They both paused at the top of the stairs. The huge double doors loomed in front of them. Slowly Alaric placed both his hands on the right-hand door. The door itself radiated pure evil. Alaric felt a shock ripple through his body and he pulled his hand away. As much as the feeling sickened him, it was also exhilarating.

"You have to be strong Alaric. You can't stop now," Heryion urged.

Taking a deep breath, Alaric placed his hands back on the door. Again the surge of evil rushed through his body. After the initial rush, the feeling relaxed to a gentle pulse. Tensing himself Alaric pushed hard on the door. Nothing! Not even a creak. After trying the left hand side, he returned his attention to the first one, putting all his weight against the door. Still it did not move. Taking a step back Alaric charged at the door. A dull thud was the only proof that Alaric had made contact.

"This is hopeless," Alaric sounded defeated.

"All is not lost. You better take a few steps back," Heryion suggested.

Alaric did as he was instructed and took five steps back down the stairs. Heryion moved his right leg back to brace himself and Alaric could feel a surge of energy. He knew that whatever Heryion was doing, it was not simple. Next thing Alaric saw was Heryion flying backwards away from the door, so far that he landed in the square below. Rushing down the stairs, Alaric went down to help.

"Heryion, are you okay?" Alaric's heart sank, but as he started to stand Heryion groaned and opened his eyes. He had a knowing look on his face, as if he should have known what was going to happen.

"You'll never get in that way." Alaric jumped in surprise as a voice boomed from the far-right hand side of the square, Heryion also seemed unsettled.

Alaric spun around quickly to see the most unusual creature he had ever seen. A snake like head, with a slight beak on the upper lip, a long neck ran to a body that was as big as three horses. Trailing behind was a thick tail with a small triangular point at the end, which looked sharp enough to slice through steel as if it was butter. The entire creature, from head to tail, was covered in bright green scales. The scales looked as though they were as strong as armour plating. Sharp teeth filled its mouth and a forked tongue flicked at them as if it was waiting for a response.

To Alaric's relief, the creature was trapped in a cage, with thick bars. The large door was locked with the biggest padlock Alaric had ever seen, even though it only slightly eased his fear.

"What in the Gods names is that," Alaric whispered, more than a hint of fear in his voice.

"That is a dragon, Alaric," Heryion moaned as he remained where he had fallen.

"Are you just going to stand there staring or are you going to help me?" The deep dragon's voice had a rasp to it.

Alaric was in shock. He had not believed the dragon had really spoken. Not only that, but was asking him for help. He remembered what Heryion had told him the day before. Some were good and some were evil. He had no idea which this one was, but he guessed since it was in the city that it was evil. Nyrra's pet that he had forgotten to let out before he left.

"What should we do?" Alaric asked, his voice like a mouse's squeak.

"Simple. You decide whether to trust the dragon or not," Heryion said.

"But is he good or evil?" Alaric pleaded.

"I have no idea. This is a test for you to complete. I cannot help you."

"You'll never get in there without my help. There is a ward on the door. Your friend should be more careful than to use magic hastily in this place." The dragon sounded impatient. "Now that you've woken me up, you can at least let me out."

"How are you going to help us get in?" Alaric asked, trying to sound confident. "I tried to push the door open and it didn't budge and magic obviously doesn't work." Heryion shook his head at Alaric's comment.

The look on the dragon's face could only be called confusion. It was as if he was trying to figure Alaric out. "I thought you were a powerful wizard." The dragon shot Heryion a quick questioning look before returning his gaze on Alaric. "I can sense an aura around you of great power, yet you know nothing. I didn't say you could not open the door with magic, or I should say unlock the door."

Alaric was now completely confused. He wished that Heryion would speak to the dragon, but he didn't look like he had any intention of helping him. Slowly Alaric thought about what he was going to say next. He had to work out if the dragon was going to help him or kill him.

"How… then… can you help?" He spoke slowly at first, trying to think as the words came out.

"I was trapped here when Nyrra put the lock on the door. I saw the spell he used and know how to unlock it. Now, you don't look like you have all day and since no one has lived here in over a thousand years, I assume that you have not come for a visit. If you let me out, I can help you and then be on my way."

Alaric thought for a moment. He knew that the dragon was right. He really had no choice. If Heryion knew how to unlock the door, then he would have done it but now and he knew that he had no hope of unlocking it. Since Heryion was not going to offer any assistance, he knew what his choice had to be. If the dragon was evil, then he would be dead either way. His only chance was to take a risk.

"How do you suggest I let you out? I'm not good at picking locks and I'm sure if that padlock was easy to break you would have escaped by now." Heryion groaned again as Alaric spoke.

The dragon also had a look on his face as if he was speaking to a child. "I cannot use magic inside this cage and that is what is required to break the lock," he snorted when he finished talking.

Moving close to the cage, but still outside of striking distance, Alaric closed his eyes. This was the last thing he wanted to do, but he had no choice. As Eldred had instructed him, Alaric started to gather in energy from around him. Instantly the evil filled his body making his stomach churn. Alaric wanted nothing more than to release his hold on the energy, but he knew he had to concentrate. He gathered in the least amount of energy he could. Once he was done, he felt for the lock and could instantly see the pattern of the spell used to secure it. The spell was surprisingly weak and Alaric had no problem in breaking it. When he opened his eyes, the padlock still remained on the door.

Both the dragon and Heryion looked disappointed. Quickly drawing his sword, Alaric swung it over his head. Taking a deep breath, he brought his sword down on the padlock with all his strength and the padlock clattered to his feet.

Hearing the cage door swing open, Alaric jumped and took three large steps backwards. He stared towards the cage, keeping his sword in hand, as the dragon slowly lumbered out the cage door. The creature didn't look as though it was very dangerous. As the creature entered the square, Alaric gasped as it flexed its previously hidden wings. The wings spanned out for at least fifteen paces.

The dragon moved closer to Alaric. His next movement was so quick that it caught Alaric by surprise. The dragon lowered his head and pushed it towards Alaric until they were face to face. Carefully the dragon moved his head closer until he was nuzzling Alaric.

Returning to his previous stance, the dragon now had a broad smile on his face. He looked down at Alaric before he spoke. "Thank you my new friend. My name is Cain, Lord of the Green Dragons. I can't tell you how long I've been waiting for you to arrive. I can't even remember how long it had been since I have been able to stretch."

"Nyrra imprisoned me a long time ago when I refused to help him. I would not lead my dragons to evil. I was a fool for even coming here to see what he had to offer and…"

"I hate to stop your reminiscing, but you did say you would help us." Alaric was over his initial shock and was now full of confidence since he was sure that Cain meant him no harm.

"Yes, sorry. It's just been so long since I've had someone to talk to that I ramble on a little," Alaric shot Cain an evil look as he was about to get side tracked again.

Without saying another word, Cain lumbered towards the stairs. Slowly he moved until he was half way up. The dragon rotated ninety degrees until he was square with the door. Alaric watched him carefully and waited for the inevitable rush when Cain cast his spell.

Suddenly there was a loud click. Alaric stared at the dragon. He knew that the spell must have been complex, especially since Heryion could not break the lock.

With one quick motion, Cain whipped his tail into the door. To Alaric's surprise, the blow did not break the door. Nor did it even rattle the hinges. The door simply swung open as if it had been pushed by a gentle breeze.

Looking rather pleased with himself, Cain returned to the bottom of the stairs. "There you go. Nothing to it. Now I think that I will go and find the rest of my kind. I have been away too long." Cain sounded excited.

"I hate to give you the bad news, but I think that they are all dead. I don't think that any green dragons survived the dragon wars," Heryion explained sadly.

"The what!" Cain sounded shocked. "Dragons fighting dragons? So that is why Nyrra lured me here," Cain paused, looking off into the distance. "No! I can feel them. It is only faint, but there is at least one other. If it is female, then we still have hope. I will find them." There was a new hope in his voice. Looking down at Alaric, Cain spoke again. "I owe you my life. In exchange, I will give you the Ring of Dragons." As he spoke, a small golden ring appeared in the palm of Alaric's right hand. "Wear this ring. When you need my aid, twist the ring one full revolution and I'll be there. But do not use it foolishly, as you can only use the ring three times; until then I am bound to you." Without waiting for response, Cain beat his huge wings and lifted himself into the air. The huge gust of wind knocked Alaric from his feet and when he stood again Cain was just a dot in the sky and then he was gone.

Alaric looked at Heryion. "Well that was something I didn't expect."

Suddenly he realised he was still holding the ring. The ring itself looked too big to fit on his finger. In fact, he thought he would be able to slide it on two fingers. It seemed to have no weight at all, although it did look heavy. Slowly Alaric slid the ring onto his middle finger. As soon as it was in place, the ring shrunk until it was a snug fit. Giving it a little tug Alaric affirmed the fit. As he tried a little harder, he realised that the ring would not come off. A worried look crossed his face.

"The ring will come off when you use it three times. Until then, it will remain on your finger. Now I think that we should get moving. We don't want to lose the small advantage that we have." Heryion started back up the stairs. He seemed to have recovered completely from his blow.

Alaric followed behind him. Heryion moved quickly through the now open double doors. Alaric, on the other hand, paused just before he reached the door frame. He knew that there was an unimaginable evil waiting for him on the other side. For a moment, he thought about turning back.

"Come on Alaric, there is no time to waste," Heryion urged from two steps inside the fortress.

Gritting his teeth, Alaric stepped through the door. The pure evil struck him as if someone had punched his face. The blow was enough to send him to his knees. Looking up at Heryion, he wondered why the evil presence didn't seem to have any effect on him. The sickening feeling only lasted a few seconds before it subsided enough to allow him to continue.

The large hall they were in was completely dark, except for the small amount of light coming through the doorway. As he took a couple of steps past Heryion, the many torches suddenly came to life. Alaric gasped as he could now see the immensity of the room. Large black granite pillars supported the ceiling which stood more than thirty feet above their heads. Each pillar had a sconce with a torch attached to it. As he looked around the room, he realised that the floor, walls and ceiling was also made of black granite.

"Where do we go from here?" Alaric asked as they reached the middle of the entrance hall.

"There is only one way into the mountain and that is at the back of the throne room. The throne room is at the back of the fortress. We need to go through the door at the back of this room. Be very careful now. No one had entered the fortress since Nyrra left, so there is no telling what will be waiting for us," Heryion warned as he continued walking.

At the back of the hall, the door was shut. Alaric was about to turn the knob when he suddenly pulled his hand away. He remembered what happened to Heryion at the entrance doors and didn't want to rush into anything.

"It's good to see that you are learning. If you jump into anything here, you could end up dead before you realise what happened," Heryion smiled.

Carefully Heryion studied the door. There didn't seem to be any ward protecting it. Heryion wanted to cover all angles before they tried to open it. When he was comfortable that there was no danger, Heryion slowly turned the knob.

The door came open without any extra effort. Alaric breathed sigh of relief when Heryion walked through the door without anything happening. Alaric followed quickly after. As he shut the door, he had a feeling someone had just entered the hall behind them. He wanted to open the door and check, but at the same time he wanted to keep moving. They were now in a narrow hallway. Again, as they entered, many torches suddenly came alight. In between the torches hung many paintings. Some of them Alaric could recognise as men, or men-like, but the others he had no idea what creatures they were.

"It's best you don't look at the paintings. Sometimes, just by looking at something, you can set the spell off. I can feel a strong presence. Let's hurry along." Heryion quickened his step.

Alaric tried to concentrate on the energy around him, but he couldn't feel anything that would indicate the use of magic. He knew that Heryion was more in tune than he was, but he thought he would have been able to sense something. There was still the hint of evil, but nothing to say where any traps might be hidden. Alaric did as Heryion had suggested and kept his eyes on the ground. Every now and then Alaric had strong feeling to look up at one of the paintings.

Again, Heryion studied the door in front of him carefully before slowly opening it. Alaric kept his head down until he passed through the door. They were now in a small square room. The black granite had been replaced by cream plaster. Except for the torches on each of the walls, there was nothing else in the room. Four doors led out, including the one they had entered through.

The evil feeling that Alaric had felt since he entered the fortress suddenly disappeared as Heryion closed the door. Normally Alaric would have been grateful, but he now had a bad feeling that things were about to get much worse. The look on Heryion's face showed that he felt the same. "I have a bad feeling about this?" Heryion looked around the room nervously. "You need to pick one door. One will lead us to where we need to go and the other two will lead us to trouble."

"Which one should I pick?" Alaric asked quickly.

"I don't know. This room is new since I was last here. I don't think this room is or ever was part of the fortress," Heryion replied mysteriously.

"What are you talking about?" Alaric spoke frantically, expecting to see something come crashing through one of the doors at any moment.

"I think that by passing through that door we've been transported to this room, which could be anywhere, or nowhere. More than likely, it would be the latter. One of the doors will lead back to the fortress, the other three will lead to the Gods only know where. The door we came in will lead to somewhere completely different now. It could send us to the other side of the world. Damn he's good." Heryion slammed his fist into the palm of his hand. "I thought that the paintings were the trap, but again it was in the door. I need to be more careful, that's twice I've walked straight into his trouble."

Slowly Alaric walked around the room, trying to get some feeling. There was nothing, not even a hint of magic. He knew that now they had set off the trap that whoever was following would be able to pass straight through. He did not have time to waste.

Opening the first door Alaric looked through. There was a hallway on the other side, much the same as the one they had entered from, except there were no paintings on the walls. There was a subtle feeling that this wasn't the right way. Alaric lifted his leg and was about to step through when he stopped.

Alaric spun around and then moved to the next door, leaving the one behind him open. He didn't hesitate to open the door. The hallway in front of him was exactly the same as the last. The same feeling came over him that this was not the right path. The feeling almost pushed him through the doorway. Again, Alaric lifted his leg about to walk through when he stopped.

Slamming the door shut Alaric went to the next door. Opening it Alaric saw what he had expected to see, the same hallway as the last two. This time there was no urge. If anything there was a feeling telling him not to choose this one. Before he knew what he was doing, he had already closed the door and moved on to the last one.

He didn't need to open the door to know what was on the other side. The same hallway and the same urge he felt on the first two doors, except it was stronger this time. It took all of Alaric's willpower to pull himself away from the door. After a short struggle, Alaric managed to close the door and drag himself to the middle of the room.

"We have to be quick and strong. There is something drawing me away from that door. If we wait too long after opening, we won't go through. As soon as I open the door, we must enter," Alaric explained.

Heryion nodded his as if he had expected as much.

Alaric steadied himself when he came to the door. Taking a deep breath, Alaric reefed the door open. Instantly the urge to walk away from the door came, stronger than before. Alaric closed his eyes and walked through the door. A rush of air passed his face and stumbled as the floor was closer than he had expected.

When he opened his eyes, he was in the fortress' throne room. Heryion followed close behind, seemingly not having any problems. Looking back at Heryion, Alaric noticed that the doorway was further back than it should have been. Instead of being near the entrance, they were in the middle of the room.

"You have chosen well. It had ended up being a short cut," Heryion let out a short laugh, Alaric also joined in.

Looking around the room made Alaric stop laughing. Like the original hall they had entered, the throne room had large granite pillars supporting the high ceilings. On the walls were the remnants of bodies that had clearly been sacrificed many years ago. The sight made Alaric feel sick. As he stared at the bones, it was almost like he could see the sacrifice taking place. The more he looked the clearer the images were becoming.

"Alaric!" Heryion called from behind the throne. Alaric hadn't even noticed Heryion had moved. "Come on Alaric," Heryion looked around the throne when Alaric had not replied. "Don't stare at the wall. This room is full of evil and atrocities that are too horrible to speak of. It will transfix you," Heryion urged Alaric.

Slowly he started to move towards the throne, still watching the wall as if waiting for something to happen. When nothing did, Alaric turned his attention to the throne. The throne stood more than ten feet tall and was about the same wide and was again made out of granite. There was no padding on the seat and the only decoration was what Alaric could only describe as a ram's head, although it was quite a bit different, which stood at the top.

It was what was behind the throne that held Heryion's attention. A crude cut in the wall was all there was to the entrance into the mountain, no door or archway. A number of lit torches lined the wall to either side of the cut. When Alaric came into view, Heryion grabbed one of the torches and made his way into the mountain.

Alaric took one last look at the throne room before taking a torch. He shivered at the thought of all the horror that he occurred in the room thousands of years ago. Shaking his head, Alaric moved into the mountain.

After the first couple of steps the floor sloped upwards. At first it was a gentle slope, but as they continued it became quite steep. Soon the muscles in Alaric's legs started to burn under the strain. He pushed on for as long as he could, but soon enough he had to stop.

"I have to rest. This slope is too much for me. If we don't then I think that I'm, going to collapse," Alaric gasped for breath.

Heryion made no complaint. Although he did not show any sign of fatigue, he looked happy enough to have a rest. As soon as Alaric sat down, he knew that he was not going to recuperate much. It took a lot of effort to stop himself from sliding down the corridor.

"How much further do we have to go? Alaric asked as he finally gave up on sitting down.

"Not very far now. This slope will start to level out after about ten more minutes. Then we will reach the first chamber. We will have two more chambers to get to before we reach the final chamber at the top of the mountain. It will take us most of the day to reach the top, but this is definitely the hardest part of the climb," Heryion explained.

Heryion led the way up to the first chamber. When he reached it, Heryion paused just inside the door trying to peer into the blackness.

By the time Alaric reached it, he was panting heavily. His legs ached from the steep ascent. The dull light from the two torches was not enough to light the cavern. Alaric tried to stare into the darkness but outside of the torch light, it was completely black. Alaric walked past Heryion to try and get a better view of the cavern. Before Heryion could say anything, Alaric felt a stone sink under his foot. It sunk only a quarter of an inch, but it made an audible click, which echoed throughout the cavern. Alaric froze where he stood, his heart started to pound in his chest.

"What was that?" Alaric asked, when nothing happened, straining his neck to look back at Heryion.

"We'll find out soon enough. When you lift your foot, I think that the trap will release," Heryion sounded concerned. "That is why I don't go racing into places without a thought," Heryion sighed.

"What should I do?" Alaric asked, not wanting to lift his foot, although he had an overwhelming urge to.

"There is only one thing you can do," Heryion paused, waiting for a response from Alaric. When none came, he continued. "Lift your foot and prepare for anything."

Alaric held his breath and slowly lifted his foot. As he did, he could feel the stone rising under it. When his foot had completely left the floor, the trigger clicked again. Suddenly a hundred torches were lit along the cavern wall. The sudden light made Alaric close his eyes and lower his head.

There was a moment of silence before Heryion started to move again. Realising that he could now see what was around him, Alaric opened his eyes and gasped at the size of the cavern; it was immense. The floor was worn smooth, but the rest of the cavern was rough, as though no one had taken any care when it was made. The path they were on led up around the outside of the cavern. It made three circuits before it disappeared into the far cavern, near the roof.

"The entire contents of this cavern were used to build Nyrra's fortress, the Tower of Isna'hel, a name that is all but forgotten," Heryion explained as he started up the path.

As Alaric walked, he looked down. He knew that no one had set foot in these caverns for hundreds, possibly even thousands of years, yet the floor was completely void of dust. There was not even a hint of it. If anyone had been here before him, there was no sign of it.

"Why is there no dust?" Alaric asked as they rounded the second corner.

"That even I cannot explain. There seems to be no logical reason for it. There are a lot of things in this land that cannot be explained. Maybe only Nyrra himself knows the answers. Sometimes evil cannot be explained," Heryion seemed a little unnerved at not knowing the answer.

The ascent around the outside of the cavern was not as steep as the path leading to it and Alaric was glad, although he was a little concerned at the amount of time it took. Heryion walked a little too slowly for his liking. He knew that they had to be careful, but he was so close now and he wanted it just to be over with. The longer they took, the more chance he had of having to face Nyrra.

Once they had left the first chamber, the torches behind them suddenly blinked out. Alaric jumped as the sudden darkness came over him. The light from the two torches were no comparison, but they were adequate for the narrow passageway they were now in.

When they reached the second chamber, they found it in the same condition as the first. The light from their torches was only enough to light a few feet in front of them.

"Don't walk into the chamber this time," Heryion warned as Alaric came up from behind him. "You were very lucky the first time. This time you may not be as lucky."

Alaric stood off to the side, against the wall next to the entrance. He could see Heryion was concentrating on the darkness in front of him. When he made no indication that he was going to move in a hurry, Alaric decided that he was going to relax. As he did, he felt as small stone sink into the wall. As it did, there was another audible click, the same as the first cavern. Alaric let out a moan.

"What did I just tell you?" Heryion asked as he spun around to look at Alaric.

"I didn't move into the cavern. All I did was sit down for a break. This isn't my fault."

"Well come on then. Let's see if you found the torch switch," Heryion sounded resigned.

Alaric slowly returned to his feet, letting the stone return to its place. Another click was heard and again torches along the walls were suddenly lit. The cavern they were in was much the same as the first, except quite a good deal smaller. As Alaric spread his gaze across the cavern, to his shock he found that they were not alone. Alaric recognised who it was immediately.

"Myr... Morgoz!" Alaric corrected himself.

Chapter 36: The Final Meeting

Slowly Alaric drew his sword. Morgoz did not make a move. Before Alaric could walk into the cavern, Heryion put a restraining arm on his shoulder.

"Be careful Alaric. Remember he is a dark knight now. His magic will be increased tenfold in this place."

As if his words prompted Morgoz, a bolt of bright white light shot passed Alaric's head, missing him by half an inch. Heryion pulled him to the ground as another blast came past. The light exploded into the wall behind them, creating a multitude of coloured sparkles.

"Come on Alaric. I expected a lot better from you," Morgoz's voice was rough, as if he really didn't believe his taunt.

Alaric quickly returned to his feet. He was about to start into the cavern when Heryion grabbed him again. Before Alaric could place a foot on the floor, Heryion pulled him back.

"What are you doing? I need to fight him," Alaric shrugged Heryion's hands from his shoulder.

Before Alaric took another step, he looked to where Heryion was pointing. On the floor was a bright red stone. The stone was dropped in a roughly cut hole. Alaric shook his head. The stone didn't even look as though it belonged there. His rage had gotten the better of him and he nearly walked straight into Morgoz's trap.

Alaric reached out with his sword until its point touched the stone. With very little pressure, Alaric depressed the stone and it sunk about an inch into the cavern floor before it stopped, there was a soft twang and a short spear flew through the air at Alaric's head height. If he had of been standing on the stone, the spear would have pierced his head.

"You'll have to do better than that, Morgoz." Alaric wasn't confident, he knew that the odds were stacked against him now. If he had made it without having to face any of Nyrra's henchmen, he would have completed his task. Now he was not so sure.

"Come and get it Alaric. If you think you are a match for me. I'll even let you come to me unhindered."

Alaric kept a close watch on Morgoz as he sidestepped the coloured stone. He could not let Morgoz have a slight advantage. He knew that Heryion would be able to warn him if there were any other traps.

The brightly coloured stones were visible from the corner of Alaric's eyes. Each time he saw one, the urge to look became stronger, but he could not take his eyes from his opponent. The further he walked into the cavern the closer together the stones became.

As Alaric reached the centre of the cavern, there was only a small path of uncoloured stones for him to follow. A wrong foot now would surely mean the end of his life. As if reading Alaric's thoughts, Morgoz hurled another bolt of light towards him.

Without thinking, Alaric drew some energy from around him. Before he had a chance to stop the light it was gone. As it disappeared, Alaric dropped to one knee. A stabbing pain wrenched at his stomach. Realising what had caused it, Alaric slowly released the energy he had gathered. The pure evil still raced through his body, even though he had relinquished it. His breath was short and sharp and he felt as though he was going to be sick. Heryion's voice was all that kept him from fainting.

"Treachery will not win you this battle, Morgoz. You will face Alaric and he will destroy you," Heryion's voice echoed throughout the cavern.

The effect was clear on Morgoz's face. Turning he tried to flee, but Heryion held him in a spell. The look on his face was pure horror. The spell would only hold him for as long as it took Alaric to cross the cavern.

"Destroy him, Heryion," Alaric puffed, still on one knee.

"I cannot change your destiny, Alaric. I can only help you mold it. Some things you have to do yourself."

Slowly rising to his feet, Alaric continued to walk. This time he was able to concentrate all his focus on the stones. The next blank stone was four feet in front of him, and was only a foot square. Sheathing his sword Alaric jumped, his left foot landing squarely on the stone. Waving his hand in the air, Alaric slowly gained his balance. The ever-familiar sweat poured down his face.

He was now only two more leaps from the other side, where Morgoz was waiting for him. They were similar jumps as the last, but now the stones were more than six feet away. Alaric marvelled at how Morgoz had managed to cross without being skewered alive.

Holding his breath, Alaric prepared himself for the jump. Lifting off with his left foot Alaric leapt toward the vacant block. As his right foot touched the stone, he pushed off again. Not a second had past when a spear passed through the air where he had just stood. Again, not waiting to see if he had hit the spot Alaric made the final lunge towards the safety of the other side. He fell as he passed the final coloured stone and as soon as he hit the ground Morgoz sprung to life.

Luckily for Alaric, Morgoz's last movement was to flee, so his first movement was in the same direction. Alaric quickly rolled to his feet and drew his sword as Morgoz spun around to attack. Alaric instinctively brushed the attack away and started one of his own.

The two swords flashed in the torch light. Morgoz had clearly more training, but Alaric had learned quickly. With every attack, there was a defence and counterattack. The fight went backwards and forwards. Neither opponent gave an inch. After another attack, Morgoz withdrew a couple of steps and lowered his sword, yet ready if Alaric advanced. Alaric waited to see what Morgoz had to say.

"I see that you are stronger than I gave you credit for." The grin on his face showed that it was not a full compliment. "I think you will find that I am more powerful than you; I am not the same man you thought you knew in Arsiliac. The Great Lord has made me so much more. I am the Great Knight Morgoz and your superior in every way. Surrender to me now. Serve the Great Lord and I will not have to kill you. He can offer you more than you could ever know." Morgoz's smile made Alaric start to doubt. There was definitely no shortage of confidence.

"I do not want to grovel at Nyrra's feet for what ever scraps he wants to throw. I am no one's lap dog. I will destroy you and then him. I too have grown powerful since I left Arsiliac. I think you will be surprised."

Alaric suddenly realised that Morgoz was just wasting time. He knew that Nyrra was close. Without another word, Alaric advanced. Easily defending the attacks, Morgoz retreated further. Alaric did not give him a chance to rest. He kept the attack until Morgoz was pinned against the wall. At that moment, the look on Morgoz's face turned to horror. In his retreat, he had trapped himself. Alaric sent a fierce attack which Morgoz could only just defend. The advantage was all Alaric's. The reign of blows continued until one finally passed Morgoz's guard. Alaric's sword sliced through his shoulder severing his arm completely from his body.

Dropping his sword, Morgoz sunk to his knees. Defeat was eminent now and all he could do was beg for his life. "Please don't kill me Alaric," his voice hoarse as the blood flowed from his wound.

Alaric knew that without immediate treatment, the wound would be fatal. He would not have to spare his life. He stared at Morgoz before he slowly turned his back on the groveling man and started towards the passage leading out of the cavern. Before he sheathed his sword, Alaric heard a slight movement from behind and a flash of light in the corner of his eye. Spinning around Alaric only just managed to deflect Morgoz's final attack. Morgoz had poured his last ounce of strength into it and when it was blocked, he fell to the ground. With one last attack, Alaric brought his sword down on Morgoz's neck severing his head completely. A couple of short convulsions and then the body became still.

Alaric stood over the body of his old friend. He was amazed that he had known the man for so long, yet not really known him at all. He shook his head in disgust. It was a fitting end.

Placing a comforting hand on his shoulder, Heryion spoke. "He stopped being Myria a long time ago. The person you knew has been dead a long time." Giving Alaric a soft pat, he turned and started towards the door leading to the final chamber.

Taking one last look at Morgoz, Alaric sheathed his sword and followed after Heryion. He stopped briefly to wonder how the little man had managed to make his way across the floor so quickly. Every moment that passed, there seemed to be something new about Heryion that surprised Alaric.

Suddenly his heart started to pound as he neared the door. This was his final test, to destroy the stone and finish his journey. It sounded so easy. He held his breath as he walked through the doorway. The floor sloped gently upwards as they continued further into the mountain. Heryion kept the light aglow ahead of them. The passage was much the same as the others. As they rounded one bend, the temperature suddenly increased dramatically. As soon as the heat hit his face, Heryion paused.

"The final chamber is just around the corner. The heat is coming from the molten lava in the heart of the mountain. That is where you must go. Whatever happens you must be strong. I cannot help you anymore."

Again, Heryion was being cryptic. The heat penetrated Alaric and his sweat drenched clothes were now completely saturated. His head became light and he thought he was going to faint. Slowly he rubbed his temples and then followed after Heryion.

As they rounded another corner, the floor started to level out. As he took his first step past the entrance, he felt a warmth against the side of his leg. The heat felt... angry. Suddenly all the pain he was feeling disappeared, even the heat didn't seem to have any effect. As soon as the feeling came, he knew the stone had finally come to life. He didn't mind the extra energy, but was afraid at what cost.

The chamber was near the peak of the mountain. Of all the chambers, this one was the original. It was created by the God King Ruby himself and had remained unchanged for thousands of years. In the centre of the chamber was the cauldron. Although the volcano contained a high level of magma, it had never erupted, also adding to the mountain's name. The light from the centre made the entire chamber glow a bright red. A dim light came from the many open windows cut into the walls. The roof of the chamber, which Alaric assumed reached to the top of the mountain, was shrouded in darkness. Tall pillars reached up towards the ceiling, although Alaric wondered if they held any structural significance. The chamber itself spanned for over three hundred feet, the cauldron taking up about a quarter of that space.

The cauldron was an overstatement. It was nothing more than a crack in the floor. At some point in time, after the cavern had been made, the lava had risen and pierced the floor. Over the years, the lava had increased the size of the hole and in time the floor would be completely consumed by the fire.

Since Nyrra had made his home by the mountain, he had created an altar in the chamber. Alaric could only imagine at the horrors that had been performed on it. The dark stone still had the stains of dried blood from the thousands of sacrifices.

Alaric's attention was focused on the gaping hole in the floor in front of him. This was the moment he had been waiting for. He had beaten Nyrra to the mountain and now he would be able to destroy the stone.

As soon as the thought entered his mind, all the extra energy that the stone had given him was suddenly sucked from his body. He knew that the task was not going to be easy, but now it would be all but impossible. He sunk to his knees and the exhaustion caught up with him.

"This is not the way," the voice roared inside his head. "All the things I have done for you and this is how you want to repay me."

"Who are you? What do you want from me?" Alaric screamed out.

"Alaric!" Heryion called out when he realised Alaric was slumped over the floor.

Alaric didn't respond to Heryion's cry. The voice still spoke to him inside his head. "I am the only one who can help you now. You must listen to me. You have to defeat Nyrra. Destroying the stone will do nothing."

For the first time, the words made sense. He didn't know why but he knew that the voice inside his head was telling the truth. For the first time, things were starting to make sense and as the thoughts passed through his head, Alaric's strength started to return. Only then did he notice Heryion was trying to help him to his feet. With a wave of his arm, Alaric brushed aside Heryion's aid and returned to his feet.

"Good Alaric, please understand that you had to come to the realisation on your own. It was the only way this could happen." Heryion's words were cold.

Alaric returned his attention to the gaping hole in the floor in front of him. He could feel the heat emanating from deep below. Slowly he took a step forward and then another. There was something compelling him towards the cauldron. He held the stone out in front of him and it glowed a soft red. He wasn't going to destroy the stone anymore; the voice had convinced him that wasn't the right thing to do. He knew that it wasn't his true mission. There was something else drawing him towards the cauldron, something he couldn't resist.

"You cannot destroy it, can you?' The voice sounded familiar. Turning around Alaric faced the man he wished he would never see. Standing no more than ten paces away was a familiar looking face, though he could not place where he had seen it. He knew he had never met Nyrra; if he had he would surely have been dead by now. He had expected to see the most terrifying face he had ever seen, but this face was pure beauty. Shoulder length blonde hair framed the strong facial features. The deep blue eyes stared at him, waiting for a response. Nyrra stood tall, at least a foot taller than Alaric, and loomed over him. Alaric could feel the evil radiating, no matter how hard Nyrra was trying to hide it. In this place, there was no denying what he really was.

The voice inside Alaric's head was suddenly silenced. Until that moment, Alaric didn't realise that there had been a constant ranting inside his mind. The silence was somewhat disturbing. The Ruby stone had stopped glowing and was now cool to the touch. Alaric wasn't sure what had happened, but he knew that it was Nyrra's appearance that had caused it.

"So the prophecy is true. 'The Chosen One will come to the brink and he will falter,'" Nyrra quoted. "It is your destiny to die. The prophecy has foretold it."

Sensing the drop in Alaric's spirit, Heryion spoke for the first time since Nyrra had entered the chamber. "Then you also know that it not the only line that matters. 'At the final moment, he shall learn the truth. The lies will fade away and the battle will ensue.' The truth had been revealed and you will not win."

Suddenly Nyrra boomed out laughing. The sound resonated throughout the cavern. Alaric put one hand up to his left ear to block the sound. The other hand retained its firm grip on the Ruby stone.

Nyrra looked at the little man carefully with a confused look on his face, as if he was trying to place where he had seen Heryion before. After a few seconds had passed, a knowing look came across his face and then a look of concern. "What are you doing here? This is not the way it was supposed to happen. You are not supposed to be here."

A broad smile crossed Heryion's face. "The prophecy has brought us here, but it has not written the result. Only time will tell."

Nyrra laughed again before he spoke. "Two true prophecies have been written. The Prophecy of the Stone and The Crenallous. One was given to both sides. Each prophecy containing its own version of events. Each giving tips and reasoning for each side. Now I shall read you the passage that has been ingrained in my mind for over a thousand years.

The Chosen One will come to the brink
and he will falter,
Deception revealed,
an option before.

The impossible choice
only he can make,
On the edge of destruction
he shall meet the saviour of evil,
At the last moment
The Chosen One shall make his choice,
To live or die
the world shall suffer,
On the peak of Crenallous
shall the battle take place,
The wills of two
but not the end…

"Don't quote the scripture as though I don't know," interrupted Heryion. Alaric had a feeling that there was something important that Nyrra was about to reveal. He wondered why Heryion had stopped him. "Quickly Alaric, use the stone and destroy Nyrra."

A surprised look crossed Nyrra's face at Heryion's words. Alaric watched the exchange and wished he knew what was happening. There was a passing of knowledge between the two that made him very nervous. He now wondered if Heryion was truly on his side at all.

"I think that it is time that you disappeared," Nyrra looked at Heryion.

Alaric wanted to do something, but he was not sure what. He knew that he had to wait until Nyrra and Heryion had finished their exchange before he could act. A strange sensation suddenly coursed through his body. He knew instantly what it was. The feeling made him feel like emptying his stomach all over the cavern floor. He knew what it was and there was nothing he could do to stop it.

Suddenly a burst of flame engulfed Heryion. The little man did nothing to try and counteract the spell. He stood still as the fire consumed him. There was something strange about his posture. He showed no visible pain. After a couple of seconds, Heryion disappeared in a puff of smoke. The flames died down leaving only a small pile of ash. There was no doubt in Alaric's mind of the little man's loyalties.

"Now that is finished with, we can get down to business," Nyrra's voice was dripping with venom.

The sickly feeling did not leave Alaric's body when Nyrra had released his spell. He knew that there was another attack coming and this one was coming his way. Fear raced through his body and his heart pounded. He didn't know what was coming but he knew that there was nothing he could do to counter it. He hadn't received enough training and he would die.

Without warning, the feeling suddenly left his body. He looked up at Nyrra who had a confused look on his face. The gently glowing stone in Alaric's left hand was all the answer that he needed.

"So it seems that magic will not work." Nyrra sounded angry, though his composure didn't change.

Alaric hadn't realised that he had already drawn his sword. He tried to draw energy from around him to counter with his own spell. He didn't know what he was going to do, but if he could use the stone he was sure he would be able to defeat Nyrra. To his surprise, there was nothing for him to use. He knew there was energy in the room, more than enough for what he wanted to do, but it was just out of reach. He felt as though he was on the end of a leash and whenever he came close, someone yanked him backwards. Then he realised the stone was blocking both their abilities.

Taking a fighting stance, a sword of fire appeared in Nyrra's right hand. It seemed that the wizard was still able to use the energy and the sword itself looked as though it would pass right through Alaric's sword of steel. This was what all his training would come down to. He knew that this would be the hardest battle of his life.

Slowly Alaric advanced. His legs felt as though they were weighed down with stones. He watched the eyes of his opponent carefully. Small flames flickered in Nyrra's eyes. There was only one way he could win the fight and that was for him to go on the offensive.

As the two opponents neared each other, there came a great rumble from the depth of the mountain. Nyrra kept his composure as Alaric stared frantically around him. Although it threatened to erupt, the magma remained in place. Nyrra was not one to waste the advantage and went on the attack. Alaric only just recovered in time to block a barrage of attacks.

Nyrra gave his opponent little credit.

The fire blade flashed through the air, sparks flew from Alaric's blade as the two swords came into contact. Given the chance, Alaric retreated a couple of steps to catch his breath. Nyrra didn't seem to mind. He stood back and watched his quarry pant for breath.

"Give up Alaric. I have an offer for you." There was no strain in his voice. He sounded as relaxed as if he had just risen from bed.

"I don't want anything from you, Lord of Lies."

"Wait and hear what I have to offer before you reject it. I have no need to rule this world alone. If you submit to me, you can rule which ever land takes your fancy." The words sounded sweet. "There is no need for you to die here today. Lower your sword, give me the stone and we can both walk out of here winners."

Alaric thought about it for a moment. He looked at the stone, still sitting dormant in his left hand. Suddenly Alaric felt something on the back of his neck. It was nothing like anything he had felt before, but he knew that Nyrra was only biding his time. Alaric couldn't believe he had walked straight into Nyrra's trap. Pure terror ran through his body as he watched the stone slowly disappear from his hand.

As he looked up, he thought he would see Nyrra holding the stone in triumph. Instead he saw Nyrra, again looking confused, holding his sword casually in front of him. There was something rewarding about the look on his face. Alaric didn't know what had happened to the stone, but knew that Nyrra did not possess it.

"Never mind." Nyrra was speaking to himself before he returned his attention to Alaric. "I will kill you one way or another.'

Nyrra reached out and clenched his fist. Alaric felt his throat go tight as if Nyrra was actually strangling him. He grabbed at his throat as if there was a chance he could pull Nyrra's magical grip away. There was nothing he could do.

Slowly Alaric was lifted off the ground. His legs flailed below him as he gasped for breath. He could only just breathe under Nyrra's grip, but that would not last for long if Alaric couldn't get free.

"Do your worst," Alaric gasped.

"It's over Alaric. In moments, you will be dead. Eventually I will find the Ruby stone and when I do the world will be mine. No one will be able to stop me."

With a flick of his wrist, Nyrra threw Alaric towards the nearest wall. His rage caused him to lose concentration and Alaric was sent flying through one of the windows. Alaric gasped for air as Nyrra released his grip. One freedom led to the loss of another as he plummeted towards the razor-sharp rocks below.

Nyrra didn't bother to wait to see the result. Slowly his body started to shimmer, before his image disappeared. There was the sound of soft laughter as the cavern was suddenly empty.

The wind whirled around Alaric as he fell from the top of the mountain. His mind became clear as if a veil had been lifted. As his death was imminent, he suddenly remembered the dragon. The ring suddenly felt very heavy on his finger and he slowly gave it a twist. At first there was nothing and Alaric's heart sank. Deep down he knew that his life was over.

Just as he was less than twenty feet from the jagged rocks waiting for him, he heard the sound of great wings beating somewhere above him. Just before he struck the ground he felt a strong talon grip around his waist and lift him into the air.

"Well, Alaric. I see that it did not take long for you to need my help," Cain's voice sounded friendly.

Alaric said nothing. He looked back over his shoulder towards the Cauldron Mountain, Crenallous. He knew that as long as the Ruby stone was in the open, the world would never be safe. He had to find his friends, if they were still alive and then find the stone. If he was going to face Nyrra again, then he would need all the help he could get.

Epilogue: Endings

Nyrra collapsed on the floor of the cave, gasping for breath. Things had not worked out exactly how he had planned them, but they were still much better than they could have been. As much as he had always known Alaric wasn't going to destroy the stone, there was still a chance he could have been wrong.

Now it was time to start again. It was but the first chapter of his plan over with, but it would take him a little time to regain his energy. The stress of the spells he had been using had finally taken its toll, none the least the spell to cast his image into the mountain to fight Alaric.

Although he had remained in the cave in Remidia, his image was more than just a corporeal form. It was easy to shoot an image across the world, but a completely different story making it solid. He wasn't sure how long he would have been able to keep attacking Alaric and was glad when things came to an end.

It would be a good number of days before Nyrra would be able to move again. He had prepared for such an event. He had sealed the mouth of the cave and had eaten a large meal. He wouldn't be able to eat again until he had regained enough strength to move.

There was a new mission for him now. He had to find the Ruby stone. If he was able to locate it before Alaric, then there would be no one to stop him. His followers would be able to keep Alaric busy.

He forced a smile on his face. Things were finally going his way. He had been imprisoned for so long and now it was time for the world to suffer.